Ironw

Tales Of Blood, Steel And Vengeance

PUBLISHED BY DEORADHAN PUBLISHING 2016

COPYRIGHT 2016 BY JASON L. STONE

Copyright Registration # TXu-1-622-655 * <u>January 2008</u>

Work completion date 2007

COPYRIGHT 2016 (ALL ILLUSTRATED WORKS WITHIN)

ISBN 978-0-9974395-2-6

PRINTED IN THE USA

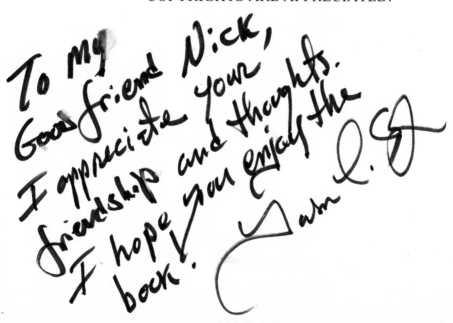

To my Good friend Nick, I appreciate your friendship and thoughts. I hope you enjoy the book! Jason L.S.

Acknowledgments

To God! (For obvious reasons)

To my amazing wife, Sandy, for her encouragement and for holding my feet to the fire with an unwavering deadline. Without you, this book would never have been published. Thank you for everything!

To my great friend and editor, Doug Kruse, for the countless hours he spent combing through my pages, making painstaking corrections, listening to my endless tirade of ideas and for the great advice he gave me. Thank you!

To my kids, Connar and Rachael, thanks for being my biggest fans. Hearing your excitement as you read my stories supercharged my motivation for writing. Thank you both!

For others who read my manuscripts and gave me encouragement and advice, (Jesse and Mechell, Jennifer, Eric, Morgan, Mike and any others I may have forgotten) your excitement has been positively invigorating. Thank you!

TABLE OF CONTENTS

THE ART

The artwork in this book is a mixture of approaches, styles and medium. My work accounts for the bulk of the illustrations and Michael Mino's works is nearly the entire first story, "A Thorn for a Rose". I really enjoy the mixture of style that **Mike Mino** demonstrated from stylized pen and ink to traditional charcoal (the charcoal really works well for the creepy scenes). I also want to acknowledge Nicole Boggs for her illustration of horses in "Raging Sands". She has a real talent.

TABLE OF ILLUTRATIONS:

Author's Notes

Don't worry reader; I don't plan on boring you with an endless montage of my life and motivations. I simply wish to thank you for reading my book and express the hope that you will enjoy it.

Illustrating this work has been an enormous undertaking. Thank goodness for the talented **Michael Mino** or I would not have been able to finish it.

I wrote this book because I have always been a fan of Robert E. Howard, Karl Wagner, Edgar Rice Burroughs, Norvell W. Page and the like, and for a while it seemed that their kind had vanished from the shelves. No matter how hard I looked, there were none who came close to matching their style, though there are some new authors that are doing a good job of reviving the true form of Sword Fiction, Sword and Sandal, and Sword and Sorcery. It's interesting to see how some people define the differences in genre between "Fantasy" and the fiction of Howard and Wagner. I have always felt that the pulp writers incorporated an element of horror and some semblance of historical backdrop. Conan's world was based on a time pre-dating our own ancient history and Wagner's Kane was the same. I have taken the opposite approach when it comes to the backdrop of these stories. Rather than going with the antediluvian world, I chose to go forward…way forward; as if we have been pummeled back to the Stone Age by our technology (nuclear weapons, dependence on tech, screwing around with viruses). As if the planet has lost all knowledge of us and the things we built. For the purpose of this story I would say fifty thousand years ought to do it. In this world, man has barely worked his way out of the Stone Age and is at it again.

Sword Fiction heroes are forces of nature and I have conjured Shasp Ironwrought to create the same "feel" if you will. He is a character with more than enough personal baggage to make him realistic and is supported by other personalities that you just might find in any back alley today. He is not the hulking barbarian with a fifty pound axe, but rather a lean wolf that uses a katana the way a neurosurgeon uses a scalpel. He survives by his wits, not by divine intervention (although there is some of that) and taking a beating just inflames his sense of vengeance. Like Conan or Kane, when someone crosses him…look out!

Like the stories of the pulp writers, there are no fairies or unicorns; no flying dragons breathing fire or elves or dwarves. Nevertheless, there is the horror of dark and mysterious forces, dabblers of shadowy magic, slithering, shambling lurkers of ancient tombs and some of the nastiest villains ever belched forth from dark places and don't forget the gritty realism of armies smashing together and the seething hatreds of opposing powers.

So enjoy a thundering ride with Shasp through time distant North America or "Nomerika", and I hope I have achieved my goal of writing stories that are as exciting as the pulps of yesterday. Only you can say.

IRONWROUGHT

TALES OF BLOOD, STEEL
AND VENGEANCE
BY J. L. STONE

DEORADHAN
PUBLISHING

1

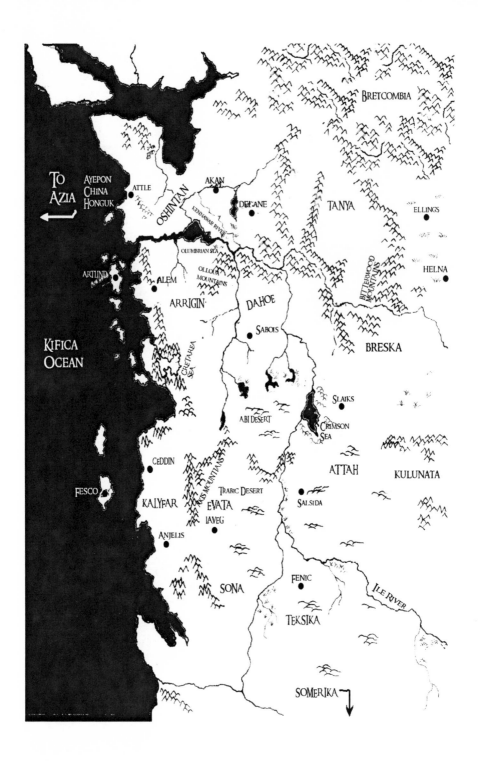

To
Azia

Ayepon
China
Honguk

Attle

Oshintan

Akan

Decane

Bretcombia

Tanya

Ellings

Kennawar River

Olumbrian Sea

Artlind

Alem

Ollora
Mountains

Arrigin

Dahoe

Sabois

Helna

Bittermood
Mountains

Breska

Kifica
Ocean

Cretarea
Sea

Slaiks

Abi Desert

Crimson
Sea

Ceddin

Ras Mountains

Trabic Desert

Evata

Laveg

Salsida

Attah

Kulunata

Fesco

Kalyfar

Anjelis

Sona

Fenic

Ile River

Teksika

Somerika

2

Book I
A Thorn for
A Rose

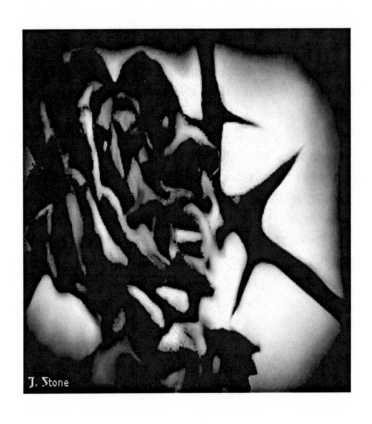

J. Stone

Prologue

The cloying stench of death permeated the massive cavern, intensifying its already sinister ambiance. Dripping stalactites and stalagmites sprang forth like the teeth of some ancient leviathan, poised to gnash and grind away flesh and bone.

Rose whimpered as she stumbled through the murky shadows, groping desperately toward the only perceptible light; a seductive glow that drew her inexorably, without will, as all living things are drawn to light when in darkness. She stumbled through the slimy cave until she was close enough to recognize the source of the glow; a trio of bulky copper braziers heaped with fiery coals and clustered together in a loose triangle. Orange flames scurried along the surface and the light flickered over the greasy limestone floor. As she advanced, Rose felt something crunch beneath her slipper and looked down only to see many slimy skulls gaping back. She stifled a scream, stumbling out among the braziers and into the center of the eerie light. On the polished obsidian floor within the circle, chalked outlines of bizarre runes were scribbled to the furthest reaches of the dim firelight. She twisted around, peering into the forbidden depths, expecting some nameless horror to slither forth.

A low odious voice hissed within her head, "Oh yes, ssssoooo young, ssssoooo much life."

Terror poured through her like ice water, freezing her blood. She stood paralyzed by a violent tremor of fear that made her teeth rattle and bile surge up in her throat.

"Sssssoooo much to feast on!"

Rose snapped and shrieked long and high as she plunged blindly into the blackness, frantically searching for a way out. In the distance came a low howling, slowly gaining volume until it burst suddenly from the cavernous depths in a bone chilling cyclone of rank wind, blasting her with hoarfrost. Insidious laughter thundered as her scream froze into a clog of ice.

Rose bolted upright, shaking uncontrollably with spirit crushing fear. Cold sweat plastered her dark hair against her forehead and her nightgown to her pale flesh. Wide-eyed she searched the room, confused, and then, with a new realization of her surroundings, she drew a deep shuddering breath and then sobbed with great abandon. The bed chamber had become abnormally cold again just like every other time she woke from this nightmare and her breath became a frozen vapor in spite of the pile of smoldering coals in the hearth beside her bed.

She shook her head crying, "Not again. Not again. No more can I live with these dreams. No more I say." She screamed into the night, "No More!!"

Chapter 1

The sun was burning its way into the horizon as Bric sat on a large moss covered rock next to a ring of stones that contained a meager fire. He grumbled to himself as he turned his boot over in his hands and considered the hole in the bottom. It didn't seem that long ago since he'd jerked them from the cooling feet of an unwary traveler whom he'd murdered. He was particularly annoyed because he rather liked this pair. They were unique, with silver caps on the toes and heels and he felt they gave his otherwise drab apparel a touch of flare. Well, he'd better find another hapless victim soon or he would be barefoot again. His bandits chaffed and grumbled much over the lack of spoils and he worried that he would have to kill one of them to maintain order again. Too many brigands had poured into the mountains after the territory wars. The struggle for survival was growing fierce between bands. As it was, they were ambushing every gang of thieves they found, only to find them as impoverished as his own sad-assed lot. He stuffed a ragged piece of leather into his boot and crammed his calloused foot in. It had been months since they had a good robbery and actually came away with any decent loot. Some of his men had gone to scrounge for food while others languished about the camp, seven in all; perhaps soon to be six.

Bric heard the snap of twigs and thresh of grass as some of his thugs approached from the tree line, though he smelled them long before he heard them. As the bulbous head of Harn became visible over the arc of high ground where the camp was, he called out to his chief.

"Bric!! Take a look at what we found!"

Bric really didn't give a shit what Harn had found as much as his constant racket.

"Hey Harn, why don't you climb that tall rock over there and scream at the top of your lungs for every cutthroat bastard in these woods to come to our camp tonight and kill us in our sleep? You may as well, the way you crash through the fucking woods and bellow like a cow in heat all the time."

Now that he thought about it, maybe it would be Harn he would kill for his example. Bric stood up and drew his filthy fingers through his oily black hair. Harn stopped and glowered at Bric, flexing his maul-sized fist. More of his men appeared shoving and pulling a young woman with their fists twisted into the shoulders of her fine wool jacket. She was beautiful and slender with shining, curling hair of jet.

Harn motioned toward her as they brought her toward Bric, "Me'n Rudd found her down on the river bank. Snuck up on her when she's get'n a drink."

Bric took a quick stride toward the girl, who shrank from the stare in his vicious black eyes. He reached up and clamped her face between his dirty thumb and fingers, and turned her head slightly. "What's your name girl?"

Rose was terrified, eyes wide and darting, body trembling, "Rose." She said, barely audible.

"Is that right?" He leaned into her and took a wolfish sniff of her hair, held it in for a moment, then exhaled slowly. He let go of her face and stepped back, appraising her, "Those are decent clothes and boots. He snatched at her hands and looked at her fingers and palms, "No callouses and no dirt in your nails. Where did you come from my young Rose?"

Rose glanced over her shoulder and her spirit sank even further as she realized she was ringed in all the way around with nowhere to run, "Kulan," she managed to say. She was scared before, but now, looking at all the hungry, leering faces surrounding her caused her stomach to wrench and her knees to quiver.

Bric gave Harn a withering stare, "Are you sure she wasn't with a bigger party? Makes no sense, a woman like this traveling alone through here, or any woman for that matter. There must be others and the way you blunder around they're probably sniffing your trail already."

Rudd interjected, "No way Bric. I checked her back trail for a half a mile. I only just saw her tracks, twern't no others."

Bric regarded Rose with saturnine consideration before he spoke again, "You're worth some weighty coin to someone; I'd wager it."

Rose flooded with hope, "Yes! Yes, my father raises beef in Anatone," she blurted, "not too far from here. He'd pay handsomely for my safe return! I'm certain of it!"

Her statement evoked a rash of snickers and laughs from the gang of dirty brigands and an evil grin split Bric's cracked lips. "No,

I'm afraid that isn't what I meant. We do business sometimes with some not-so-respectable merchants from Dahoe, if you get my meaning. I'm sure they would pay much more than a farmer from Anatone. By the way, the cut of your clothes appear a bit better than I'd expect from a farmer's daughter. Looks like you have been keeping high company. Am I right?"

Rose did not reply right away, weighing the horrors of her nightmares with those of her current situation. Would the Lady of Kulan even pay for her return since she fled without warning three nights gone? Rose had no other bargaining leverage. "Yes. I am a ward of the Lady Blaquet of Kulan, recently of the king's court. And, yes, she would pay much to see me safely returned."

Bric nodded thoughtfully, "I know of Kulan, an ancient and haunted place or so I'm told. But, it's been abandoned for a century, so why should I believe there is some courtesan there now?"

"We only came there a year ago. She is there."

"Hhmmm…with men no doubt; perhaps the kind of men that would take you without paying and then stretch our necks from their walls for our trouble."

"She is honorable! She will pay."

Again Bric paused, weighing the risk and return of ransom or slavery. "Very well, ransom it is, but I'm still wondering why you risked these woods alone."

Rose's mind raced for a contrived response, caught off guard by the question and unprepared with a ready lie. "I…I wanted to see my parents…and she couldn't spare a man for an escort…there was too much to be done with the keep."

Bric could smell a lie like a buzzard could smell carrion, but the truth mattered little to him. "I see. Well, if she doesn't pay what I ask, you you'll be headed to the slaver's block and a little worse for wear at that."

Harn stepped cautiously toward his rangy boss, "Bric." His eyes tore at Rose like claws, "Bric, you know we've been outa coin for a long time now…and none'uv us been hav'n a woman for…"

Bric stepped back and read the starving countenances of his raggedly armored men. If their eyes had been tongues, they would have been licking the girl's skin.

"If she is spoiled it could affect her value," he said to the men. At heart, his crew were more beasts than men. Bric's ability to think as well as kill was the only reason he remained the leader. The grubby robbers grumbled and shuffled a step forward.

"Promise we won't hurt her…much," someone said.

The other reason Bric remained a leader to this band of killers was because he knew exactly where the very thin line of his control ended. "I see." Bric huffed, "Well, if that's the way it's going to be, then as chief, I will be the first to taste the pleasures of this little vixen and I'll kill anyone who challenges me. After that, the rest of you can have a turn, but only once, and not you Dulen," he pointed to a weasel of a man, "you have the pox." Dulen's face dropped.

Bric turned to Rose, "So, are you going to be a good girl so we can go easy on you or are you going to fight us?"

Rose's eyes became huge, her mouth dropped open and she began to back away, "No! No! I said she would pay, you can't do this!" Two men grabbed her arms from behind and she instinctively lashed out, striking one in the ear with her elbow. The brute growled and gave her a wicked blow to the ribs with his fist. Rose crumpled, breathless as white hot pain shot through her body.

"No more of that you fucking idiot!" barked Bric, "I said you could have a turn! I did not say you could damage her! The next sorry scab who strikes her, I'll gut you like a fish! Or are you worthless shits not man enough to take a woman without fucking breaking her?! Now pick her up and take her to that downed tree and draped her over it."

They dragged Rose by her upper arms with her toes trailing through the dirt, and forced her down over the tree. Bric motioned for Harn and Rudd, "Get her boots and britches off boys." The two jerked and tugged at her clothing until she was naked from the waist down.

"And her jacket," said Bric.

As they were pulling the jacket over Rose's head she managed to catch her breath enough to rise up and jerk one arm free, shrieking her defiance with all of her strength. Her screams echoed off the surrounding hills until Harn caught her by the hair and brutally jerked her head back. Rose shrieked again.

Bric spat, "By the blood of the giants, someone stuff something in her mouth before she calls down every bastard in these hills."

Rose was still screaming when Rudd shoved a dirty piece of leather in her mouth. Tears streamed down her face and someone had a hold of her arm, forcing her down again, but now wearing only her

9

silken red undershirt. She tried to scream again, but the leather in her mouth muffled her rage and practically suffocated her.

Bric stood behind her, "Finally," he snapped and started to unlace the front of his leather breaches as the others tensed with anticipation, grinning and drooling like hyenas.

The pack of bandits had been so distracted that no one noticed the heavy clomp of a horse's hooves until the sound reached the perimeter of their camp and they turned as one toward it.

A massive black charger plodded toward them, huffing and snorting; its rider covered in a dark gray cloak with the hood pulled up. The light of day had mostly faded and the lengthening shadows revealed little detail to the villains caught in the act of rape.

The rider paused a moment a few yards away and dismounted casually with a gentle slap to his horse's flank. The beast moved off a few feet and the intruder took a few strides closer. Within the flickering firelight Bric could see the stranger was wearing expensive riding boots, black, heavy and knee high. It wasn't every day that someone just ambled into the camp of a bunch of bloodthirsty bastards like Bric's crew, in the middle of a rape no less, and then stood about like he was ready for a drink and a meal. As such, the crew was caught off guard and more than a little stunned with disbelief.

Bric shook his head as if to clear it from a momentary trick of the eye. "Humph." His hand slid down to the bone hilt of his saber, "Who the fuck are you?"

"Who am I? Wanderer maybe…, angel of death, maybe," replied the rider with a dangerous growl.

Then Bric remembered the girl, her clothes, and where she said she came from. Perhaps this unlucky fool had something to do with her, but either way, he couldn't believe his luck. Weeks of nothing in the way of booty and now they had a fine woman, and soon a fine horse, and some fine riding boots, not to mention whatever other loot this suicidal mad man may have, which stood to be plenty by what little he could already tell. Bric relaxed a little as his men poured around him, thinking the same thing as their ringleader. "Well, if you've come for the girl, it's going to cost you some fat coins." Bric had no intention of settling. Why trade for what can be taken by force?

The stranger glanced over the shoulders of the greasy brigands to where Rose was being held down. "No, I'm not here for her."

10

"Then what?" asked Bric. "You must be some kind of idiot coming into this camp." He was giving his men time to slowly fan out.

"Actually I'm looking for some 'thing' and I believe I've found it."

Bric's men finally surrounded the man but he acted indifferent, "Really," Bric laughed, "and what would that be?"

Unbeknownst to Bric, beneath the cloak, mailed hands played over plated armor, checking straps and buckles with familiar skill before one slid from the folds and pointed at Bric's worn out boots. "Your boots; there's a man in Agrand willing to pay a hundred silver dragos for them."

Bric scoffed, "Bullshit. Who wants a pair of worn out boots bad enough to pay that kind of money."

"Well, you might say the boots are more of a token. What he really wants is the man wearing them. If I find the boots; I find the man who killed his brother."

Bric's mind shot to the traveler he had waylaid to get the boots, "How about that; well, you can't have them. In fact I'm due for a new pair." He motioned to his men, "Kill this cocky bastard already."

Bric's saber had barely cleared its scabbard when a naked sword shot from the cloak, knocked his saber half out of his hand and then sliced cleanly through the back of his thigh. Brick howled and crashed to the ground, astonished by the celerity of the attack.

His crew were lunging and slashing viciously, only to find the intruder moving and twisting at impossible angles. One of them finally connected with a sword cut to the hood of the cloak, only to have his blade shatter against the steel of a concealed helmet. Harn and Rudd were still holding Rose down and Harn yelled to Dulin, "Hold her!" Dulin grabbed Rose's arm and twisted it behind her back. "I got her."

The rider's blade darted like a viper, and all the while he slipped between thrusts and slashes. Within a few breathes two more bandits lay dead in spreading pools of dark crimson.

Harn and Rudd plunged into the fray, roaring battle cries. The cloaked man ducked, leaving Rudd's blade to taste only air, then spun and took off his head. The corpse stumbled from the momentum of the rush and collapsed into the fire with a shower of embers. Only Harn and one other bandit faced him now. Harn screamed at Dulin, "Get

11

over here and fight you fuck!"

As soon as Dulin let go of Rose, she shoved him and fled toward the woods, tearing the rag from her mouth. Dulin snatched up a spear and leapt past Bric, where he lay trying to close the gaping wound in his thigh. Dulin leapt around, trying to position himself for a thrust or a throw. The stranger stepped back, reached up with his off hand and pulled back the hood revealing a closed-faced helmet. A long eye slit gashed the visor and two black onyx horns protruded from each side of the helmet's forehead. A black plume cascaded from its glinting golden crown. The scant firelight lent to its already fierce aspect, but they knew it was not gold that shattered a blade.

The strange slender blade rolled in the man's right hand while his left reached under the cloak and came away with a heavy knife. He flipped the knife and reversed his grip. "Well, are you worm-ridden curs going to bite or run with you tails between your legs?"

Harn and the other brigand moved, hoping to get their enemy to expose his back to Dulin. Astonishingly, the stranger did just that. Harn smiled as he saw Dulin heave back the spear for a deadly throw, but the smile quickly vanished when the huge black charger suddenly reared and crushed Dulin's head to a pulp. The stranger struck with the swiftness of a lion. Harn went to parry but found his arm was suddenly missing along with his sword. He staggered sideways, dumb with shock, and glanced around for his limb. The warrior dispatched the last brigand with a thrust of the big knife through his heart. Harn collapsed on his ass in the dirt just before the stranger walked up and, with a flick, slashed him across the neck.

Bric was losing a lot of blood and when he realized his gang was being slaughtered he tried to crawl away into the underbrush but he didn't get very far. The sound of the cloaked man coming up behind him caused Bric to resign from his wasted effort and he rolled over gasping. The man kneeled next to him, resting his arm on one knee, narrow sword still dripping in his bloody mailed fist. He glanced at Bric's boots again. "You know, where I come from, there is a saying. 'If a panther is fierce enough, it will resist a pack of wolves.' And I don't suffer wolves." With that, he stood, and whipped the blade in an arc, disemboweling Bric. Entrails spilled onto the forest litter and Bric looked down with the disbelief that always accompanies the sudden realization of death. The stranger pulled off Bric's boots, collected the girl's clothes and mounted the charger

12

before he ambled back toward Bric. He leaned over in his saddle, "Those wounds won't kill you right away. It should be some time before you get around to dying." With that, he turned the horse and cantered away.

Beneath the staring eye of an early moon, the slender pines creaked against the autumn wind as it whispered through their boughs and cast jagged shadows over the mountain trail.

Rose's bleeding feet pounded out a staccato against the rocky ground, and she let out a cry as she stumbled over a treacherous limb and sprawled on the scattered tamarack needles. Forest dust and dead vegetation filled her nose and mouth, but she gathered herself and, sobbing, lurched forward again. The pain of her smarting face was only overshadowed by the ache in her lungs, filled to the point of bursting. Her black curls lay tangled against her neck and face, sticky with sweat and the remnants of her red silk shift clung to her young body in tattered ribbons. Beneath it deep scratches throbbed and stung.

She whimpered a prayer to the One God and glanced wide-eyed over her shoulder for any pursuers. She veered off the trail and pushed through the raking underbrush until she came out onto an adjoining path then turned downhill once more, but tripped on a jutting rock and collapsed again. She lay stunned and breathless as her pulse pounded in her head, her body starved for air. Slowly, she stood on quivering legs, but the forest spun about her, leaving her disoriented and causing anguish to well up in her soul until she thought she would drown in it. It didn't matter that she did not know where to go, Rose only knew she needed to keep moving and was about to stagger on when she heard the slow methodical clomp of a horse's hooves. Her mind shot back to the dark rider that faced her tormenters only hours before and shuddered.

A massive shadow moved out from the night shaded evergreens and filled the trail, the black charger, snorting and stamping the ground as his rider pulled on the reins. Rose stood frozen as the cloaked rider leaned forward against the creaking pommel of his saddle.

He had tracked her through the early moonlight and cut off her escape. She had gone from victim of the band of murderers and into the hands of… someone much colder, and much more deadly. Horror stricken and exhausted she fought to keep her feet. She saw the strange boots the brigand leader had been wearing now hanging from the stallions flank.

"Please…" she sobbed, "please don't hurt me, please, my father will pay…Please just…don't…"

The rider tilted his head and regarded her from the depths of the hooded cloak then slid from his saddle and stalked toward her.

Rose's lips parted to beg even more but before she could, the sum of her exhaustion and trauma fell on her with the weight of a great stone and the world around her shrank into darkness.

Chapter 2

Rose sensed the sickly light from an overcast sky seeping through her eyelids and blinked them open to gaze up into low leaden clouds. The distant roaring of a river reached her ears as she rose up on slender arms to glance around. She found herself at the edge of a meadow beneath a heavy green blanket, draped over her to fend off the morning chill. The lazy smoke from a smoldering campfire shifted against the morning breeze. She fanned weakly at the acrid plumes, and confused, tried to remember the events of the previous evening. When the jumbled images of her overwrought mind finally fell into order, she nervously scanned the glade for the man who now held her captive.

As if prompted by her thoughts, he suddenly emerged through the trees, returning from the river. Naked from the waist up, he was dripping wet and shaking water from his hair, spray flying from his nape-length dark brown hair.

It occurred to her that this was the first time she had seen his face. Water ran down his athletic frame as Rose regarded the corded muscles of his shoulders, chest and arms. Long leg muscles flexed under black leather pants, radiating tiger-like strength and his lean waist rippled. He was tall, though not unusually so, and his physique appeared to be one born from years of hard training. He dragged his wet locks out of his eyes and then dashed the water from his face, revealing high cheekbones and a square jaw. The handsome, cleanly shaven face was crisscrossed with a variety of scars as were his torso and arms, testament to many savage struggles. His almond-shaped eyes focused on her reclining figure and he smiled with one side of his mouth. She had never before seen eyes that shape or thier icy gray color. They locked on her for a moment before she realized he was only returning her stare and she quickly averted her gaze as sudden fear flooded through her.

"You hungry?" he asked as he stepped over her to lift a wooden plate from a rock at the edge of the fire. He handed it to her, "Fresh fish and hard tack. Probably not the sort of fare a woman like you is used to."

She accepted the plate and ate eagerly, stuffing the food into her mouth while watching him with fear filled eyes. "Why do you

15

say that?" she asked between bites.

He pointed to the britches and boots next to her, "And your silk bed shirt, or what's left of it. I picked up your clothes before I set out to look for you. Who are you?"

Mino

She froze for a moment holding a piece of dense bread before her parted lips, uncertain of her reply. "Rose," she said quietly, "and I'm not wealthy, just the ward of a courtesan."

"The same person you're running from?"

"I'm not running from her."

"If not her, then who? Because only a woman who is running would dare these hills alone. You don't look mistreated, and I see no whip marks on you, only a lot of scratches."

Rose looked up, her eyes probing deeply, searching for his intentions, but his cold grey stare revealed nothing. "You will think I'm a fool," she said softly, "I'm sure of it."

He gave her a hard look, "You might be amazed by what I think. Not much surprises me anymore."

Her bottom lip trembled with her reply, "I suppose if you were like those other men, my virginity would have been forfeit by now, but you still haven't said if you intend to…make a profit from me."

"No doubt, so, let's hear it, and I'll decide whether you need to

16

go home or to the slaver's block." The smirk afterward told Rose that maybe he wasn't serious.

Slowly, she set down her plate and faced the dripping man whose deeply-tanned skin remained absent any goose bumps in spite of the chill fall breeze.

"As you wish; I came from a small village called Athora, about forty leagues west of here. My father is a rancher. It's a simple place that relies mostly on farming and cattle with some local trade. We were fortunate enough to be near a major trade route and my father did well enough."

He nodded, "I know the place."

"My mother insisted that I have a proper education, so I could wed well. Father agreed, and when I turned seventeen, last year, he took me to Anatone to sell some cattle and look for future prospects."

"You mean husbands."

"Yes, husbands. While we were there we met this incredibly charming woman named Blaquet. She was a dignitary from Alem, wanting to settle in the Eastern Arrigin. We talked for a while and she seemed much taken with me. She told my father not to rush me into a marriage and claimed she could educate me in grace and knowledge beyond his wildest hopes. Of course then the consideration for a wedding dowry would be much greater. It took little to convince him, and in only a day, I was on my way with her. My head was spinning from all the possibilities that I never before imagined. Blaquet's family owned a keep in the Olloua Mountains not ten leagues from here, though no one had lived there for decades. She has a huge entourage of trained fighting men for her protection and a score of ladies to attend to her needs; she is quite wealthy and eccentric. My life has been pleasant enough for the last year. I learned things, enjoyed life and wanted for nothing." Rose paused and her expression fell.

"Go on."

Her voice tightened, "About three months ago, just after my eighteenth birthday, I began to have these horrible nightmares. They are always the same. I am in a cavern; I'm not sure where or how deep but the feeling of isolation is beyond description. I am stumbling through stalagmites in the dark when I see a light. I head toward it and I find three copper braziers burning and in their midst is a chalked circle filled with curious runes. I look around and see the floor is covered with bones. Something whispers in my ear, or maybe the voice is in my head. I turn but see only darkness. Whatever spoke to me is hidden, but," Rose's voice pitched higher, "it tells me it intends to devour me, but I know this is not meant in the sense of a cat devouring a mouse but something much worse, much more terrifying. It's my soul! I turn and flee but I am suddenly caught in a freezing wind. I am being drawn down into a horrifying darkness like nothing anyone ever dared to imagine." Rose began to shake but the man still said nothing, so she continued, "I wake covered in sweat…and my room is always ice cold afterward, like something evil has just left. At first the dreams came to me only off and on, then more frequently, and now I have them every night. I thought I was going mad, but I knew it was not just an ordinary nightmare. There is something ancient and sinister there, in the keep, perhaps in the mountain. Then, a few days ago, I was out gathering in the woods that surround Kulan and the mountain it perches on. I was working my way toward the backside of the mountain when I chanced to look up toward the cliffs there, and I saw a cave, high up. I was immediately overcome with terror so powerful that I could not stop shaking and I ran as fast as I could until I reached the keep. But even when I did, the fear would not subside. I gathered a few things and fled from Kulan like a rabbit flees from a wolf; the rabbit does not think, it just runs until it no longer feels the wolf behind it. I have not dreamed that dream since I left three days ago.

The man had listened carefully and said nothing for several seconds, causing Rose to wring her hands in worry while she waited for his response.

"One could say that, perhaps, you suffer from some sort of malady of the mind, and that may very well be the case, but I've been around enough to experience things...unexplainable things...that there are no explanations for. I'm also wise enough not to believe everything I hear. Your story is intriguing but..." he shrugged, "people who are crazy usually don't know it. I'm not saying you are, just that there is no way for me to know one way or the other."

He retrieved a wine skin from his pack and offered it to her, "Clearly *you* believe it, and you seem sincere enough."

She took the proffered skin and sipped on it gingerly. "What will you do with me?"

He stood and shrugged, "Do with you? Nothing; go where you want."

Rose let out a deep sigh of relief until she thought of traveling the mountain trails alone again and her anxiety came rushing back. "Where are you going? Anatone is a long way from here and...well, I don't..." she looked around like she was expecting a ravaging storm of bloodthirsty assassins to break from the tree line and rush her.

The stranger seemed to know exactly what was going through her mind, "I'm going back to Agrand to deliver these boots and get paid. You can travel with me for a while but I'm nobody's servant. You take care of the gear and I'll make sure there's food."

Rose exhaled her second sigh of relief, "Thank you. Can I ask your name sir?"

He stood and stretched, then snatched a dark green wool shirt from a drying line, "Shasp...Ironwrought."

She stood and began rolling the blanket, "I won't be any trouble."

Shasp's eyes lingered on her bare legs for a moment before he picked up her britches and jacket and tossed them to her. "Probably should get dressed, before I forget my better self." He smiled at his remark.

Rose caught the clothes and nodded her thanks. "Don't you think we should go soon? I'm worried there may be more…of them."

He draped his sword and harness over his shoulder and turned away, "There always is. Once you're ready to travel, we can leave."

Shasp broke camp with an efficiency born of endless repetition and soon had his mount packed and ready to ride. Stroking the flanks of the stallion, he whispered a few soothing words before swinging onto the saddle.

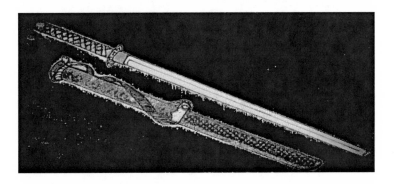

"What's your horse's name," asked Rose as he pulled her up behind him.

Shasp slapped the massive charger's neck, "Grimm, like his personality."

Darkening clouds threatened rain, but Shasp secretly hoped for a downpour to wash away any signs of their trail. Mountain brigands were like hunting dogs; their noses were always to the ground sniffing for a scent. For that reason Shasp traveled in his full armor and Rose mused at how different it was from any other she had seen before.

He wore a cuirass of black metal over a black steel-shod jacket with rounded pauldrons of a light gold color. A skirt of black chainmail, split up each side for riding, protected him below his waist. Black thigh plates and greaves covered him from that point down. His forearms displayed bracers of gold steel and the full-faced helmet hung by the chin strap from his pommel like the head of some mythological cyclops. All of the strange metal plate armor was covered in foreign markings and runes; black and gold from head to toe. The unusual sword that he called a 'Katana' was strapped to his

20

At that remark Balam and the others forgot about Goshun's fresh corpse in the grass and hands moved cautiously toward sword hilts again, but this time the looks on their faces were less haughty and much grimmer.

Rose felt the sudden tightening of nerves on the air and swept between Shasp and the men. "No! I will go back! Please, no more killing. I will go." Her sudden declaration was like the deflation of a breath held too long, and the men eased out of their coiled pre-fighting tension and regained their relaxed composure. She turned to Balam, "But Shasp must come with me. He has protected me from evil out here, perhaps he can protect me from what I fear so much in Kulan."

Balam folded his arms, "Very well, but ultimately the decision to whether he stays or not belongs to Blaquet. Now...what is this terrible fear that makes you brave a mountain range full of robbers?"

Rose looked to her feet, embarrassed to tell the men that they were forced to track her for days and that Goshun was slain because she had nightmares. "I alone will explain my reasons to the Lady Blaquet when we return."

Balam nodded, "Very well." He turned to Shasp, "Your camp is already made but I do not wish to stay in these woods any longer than I must. I will leave Etgur to guide you to the keep. He is wearing on my nerves anyway."

Shasp tilted his head toward where Goshun lay, "And him?"

Balam raised a brow, "You killed him. You can bring him back."

Shasp smirked, "I'm not dragging his corpse through these woods. The vultures and wolves can have him for all I care, but I'll wait for your boy there to put him in the ground if he doesn't take too long."

"Shasp is it? The Lady will want to know your name."

Shasp nodded, "Yes...Ironwrought."

Balam turned away and headed for his horse, "I'm sure you are."

After the riders collected Rose and rode out, he turned and frowned at Etgur, "Well, get digging." Shasp would have to wait a little longer for the bounty on the silver toed boots.

Chapter 3

Etgur was an amiable and lanky young man of about eighteen winters who prattled incessantly about his recent appointment to the ranks of the warrior class protecting the keep. He boisterously proclaimed his aspirations of glory as they rode through the woods and Shasp listened with faltering tolerance to the tawny-haired youth. In spite of Etgur's incessant chatter, he was unable to shake the nagging image of a forlorn Rose looking over her shoulder at him as she rode away on Goshun's horse.

Slowly, the trail wore on with the dissipation of the day until the shadows grew long, overtaking them and causing them to stumble in the growing darkness. Even Etgur stopped his annoying rhetoric to concentrate on the path.

"I think we should camp soon," Etgur muttered, "the trail will rise and become narrow. I don't think we should risk it in the dark."

Shasp was reluctant to accept Etgur's advice. He knew the others were less than a half-hour up the trail, and he may have even overtaken them except that Goshun's corpse had slowed them down at a couple of river crossings. Nevertheless, he conceded to Etgur's suggestion. "Is there a clearing soon?"

"Yes, maybe another two or three miles."

Ironwrought dismounted and dug in his saddlebag, found an old copper lantern and lit it. "We should lead the horses from here."

Etgur trailed behind while Shasp shouldered his way through the clutching fir branches always searching the farthest edge of the lantern's light. As he strained his eyes in the darkness, Shasp suddenly noticed a dim glow in the distance. "Does the trail turn here?' he asked Etgur who had stumbled on a rock.

Etgur hopped on one foot, hissing at the pain in his stubbed toe, "No, it should continue straight for several miles."

"Do you see that?"

Etgur peered toward the light, "Yes, I wonder what it is?"

Shasp turned the wick of the lantern to its lowest point, leaving just enough flame so see by. "Keep damn quiet boy," he hissed, "could be another pack of bandits. It would explain why the light is so far off the trail; I almost missed it. Now follow on carefully, you hear me?"

Limbs from the pines scratched and plucked at cloak and pants as they pushed off the trail and into the denser growth. They drew nearer to the light and finally came to a small stone and log hut hedged in closely by thick evergreens. The roof dripped with thick moss and Shasp now realized that the glow which beckoned them had emanated from a dusty window, not a campfire.

They wrapped the tethers of their weary horses around a twisted pine and Shasp called out to the house.

"Hello! Is anyone there?"

Tense moments ebbed away before Etgur raised a dubious brow, "Either no one is home or they don't want to talk to us."

Shasp eased up to the cottage and began to reach for the door latch when the portal was forced suddenly outward, and he had to leap back to avoid being struck.

A stooped silhouette appeared in the doorway, "Who's there!" challenged a deep gravelly voice.

"Just two tired riders. We saw the light from your cottage," Shasp answered, peering at the man through the dark.

The figure hovered in silence, and then limped into the lantern light. The figure shuffled forward, inspecting each of them with cautious interest. The grizzled man was large with a shaggy beard and tangled hair the color of dark clouds before a storm, matting his head and face. Old leather and fur trappings, stained by countless rains, draped his barrel-shaped body. "Brigands I'd say by the looks of ya, but don't think for a moment that the likes of you frightens me. I've dealt with bloodletters before and as you can see . . . I'm still here."

Shasp gave him a hard look, "So you are old man, but I'm no brigand, nor do I keep company with such filth. We were looking for a place to rest when we stumbled on your cottage. I have money and things for trade if you would be willing to give us shelter for the evening."

The hermit stared at Shasp with his one good eye, "May as well. If you *are* brigands there is nothing here to steal anyway," he grumbled as he turned and shuffled back inside.

Etgur shrugged and started to follow him, but Shasp dropped his hand on the boy's shoulder and jerked his head toward the horses. "Unpack the horses and give them water. I'll find some food for when you're finished." Etgur sighed and turned to his tasks with resignation, while Shasp followed the old hermit inside.

29

The interior of the tiny cottage was clean if nothing else. A cheerful fire crackled in the hearth and he could smell the aroma of rabbit stew wafting from a black pot simmering above the flames.

The hermit plopped onto a sturdy log stool and clasped his hands together on top of the rough-cut table before him. "Where are you from," he asked with a rumbling voice?

Shasp, unaffected, unbuckled his sword belt and leaned his weapon against the wall before easing himself onto a stool facing his host. "Everywhere and nowhere. I've traveled most of the last fifteen years." He extended his hand toward the old man, "Shasp."

The hermit paused, eyeing him, then took his hand in a surprisingly firm grip, "Ormund. Who is that stripling with you?"

"Etgur, he's my guide to a keep less than a half-day's ride from here. I only met him this morning."

Ormund carefully poured some mead into a wooden cup and pushed it toward Shasp. "You would mean to say Kulan Keep, Yes?"

Shasp frowned, "Yes. What do you know of the place?"

Ormund was pensive for a moment and leaned his back against the wall, resting his folded hands on his chest. "All sorts of things. The savages that live in these mountains, and no; I don't refer to the cutthroats and thieves, I mean the tribes; they say that Kulan was there since just after the time of the ancient ones, after the cataclysms ripped mankind from the sky and the stars. It is said by some that the giants built Kulan and ruled from there. Others say it appeared overnight, the product of sorcery. One thing is for certain, it's very, very old and most of the stories around it are not happy ones."

"I see," said Shasp, "I'm going to meet the current owner; a woman named Blaquet, some lower aristocracy from the court of the Arrigin in Alem. I came across one of her ladies in the forest who had a run in with some of the locals, and no I don't mean the tribes. Some of Blaquet's men came to get her. They're on the trail ahead of me. We should make it there by tomorrow."

Ormund barked out a brief laugh that almost made Shasp jump, "Ha! Ladies in distress! How often does a man find himself in the right place at the right time to affect such a recue! Lucky man you are. I guess the others were…not so lucky, huh?"

Shasp smiled, "Not so lucky. Not that I have a lot of faith in luck. I'll trust to my own arm to keep my hide in one piece, not luck."

"Well," replied Ormund with his growling tone, "Lucky or not, you better keep your wits about you if you're going to Kulan. I would not venture there for all the ladies in the land. There is some evil soaked into the brick and mortar of that place, though what it is, I cannot say."

Shasp was chewing on Ormund's last ominous words when Etgur returned from his duties looking vexed.

"Your horse isn't very friendly, in fact, I'm not sure he's even tame."

Shasp smiled apologetically, "He bit you. I forgot to mention he has a mean streak. You can't turn your back on that one."

Etgur rubbed a sore spot on his shoulder. "Thanks but your advice comes too late. I'm guessing he's done the same to you."

"Only once shortly after we first met, but we came to an…agreement."

Ormund hefted himself off the stool, took down some wooden bowls, and ladled out the simmering stew. Etgur settled himself near the fire and ate like a starved dog, burning his mouth on the still steaming bits.

After dinner Ormund poured them some more mead, but the hermit spoke scarcely a word to Etgur, and the youth fell asleep shortly after his meal, annoyed by the lack of attention.

As Shasp and Ormund conversed late into the evening, Shasp perceived the old man was some sort of druid, speaking of the forest and mountains with great fondness, his speech inferring the mystical. Shasp found he was refreshed and captivated by the old man's talk of rivers, streams, mountains and trees as if they were old friends. It was late when fatigue finally quelled their talk and Shasp bedded down on the floor.

Morning came earlier than he would have liked, and his head throbbed from Ormund's mead like hammers banging against an anvil. Gathering himself on unsteady legs, he gazed about the hut and was surprised how the place took on an ethereal quality as morning rays splashed through the broad windows causing even mundane items to glow with sunlight. Occasionally, a curious sparrow flitted in then out again, startled by Etgur who still snored under his horse blanket. Ormund, however, was gone. No sooner had Shasp thought of him than the hermit bustled through the door, his arms loaded down with firewood and fish, still dripping, and hanging from a string on his belt.

"You should have wakened me," Said Shasp as he stepped forward and took the bundle of wood, "Let me help you with that."

Ormund waved him off shaking his head, "It's part of my morning ritual, but if you build the fire, I'll clean the fish."

Shasp nodded, "Of course."

Soon, the hearth was blazing and fried trout popped and sizzled on a skillet. Shasp reached into his saddle bag, retrieved two corked wooden vials, and proffered them to Ormund, who gave him a blank look. "Salt and crushed cloves," said Shasp.

Ormund's eyes widened as he accepted the spices. "It's hard to find these up here. I don't generally like people enough to seek them out for trade," he chuckled as he spiced the fish.

Shasp settled down on the log stool and pulled on his boots. "Keep them and this," he said, placing a gold coin on the table.

Ormund looked at the coin with much less interest than the wooden vials. "Keep your money, Shasp. I have no use for it but thank you for the spices."

After a leisurely repast, the two travelers saddled their horses, but Shasp lingered with Ormund as Etgur mounted, anxious to leave.

Ormund clasped his hand warmly, and Shasp felt an object pressed into his palm. Shasp held the item up and marveled at the strange stone which dangled from a leather thong. It was unique in appearance, if not beautiful, with a mottled color of reddish hues and strange symbols carved on its face.

Ormund leaned close to him and whispered, "Kulan is an evil place and no one should ever live there. But, people will do what they desire to do. Listen to me, wear that and *don't* take it off. It should protect you when your sword can't. It is said that the stone contains a single drop of blood from the One God; the wellspring of all that is good."

Shasp lowered the amulet over his head, happy to humor the old man. He had seen more than a few things in his life to know that there were forces in the world that men did not understand, nor control, "I'll see you on my way back Ormund."

Ormund nodded gravely and stepped out of his way. "Stay on your guard, warrior."

Shasp swung onto his saddle, "And you, keep your eyes open for bandits."

32

"Don't worry about me, my friend, the tribes watch my back."
Shasp waved goodbye to Ormund as they trotted down the trail into the warm morning sun.

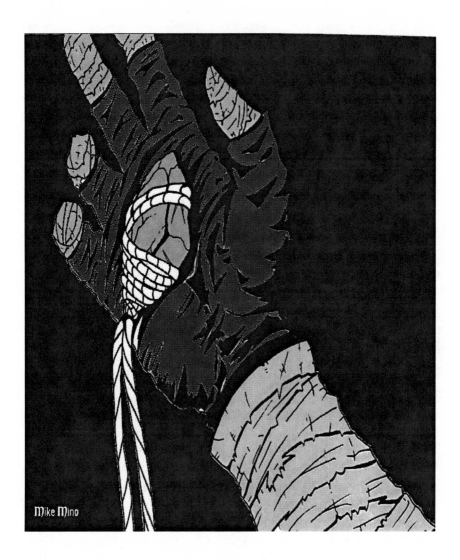

Mike Mino

Chapter 4

The forest trail snaked into the mountains, constantly rising toward the distant snow-capped peaks of mottled gray and white. The sky seemed to narrow as the slopes crowded in, leaving long shadows stretched across the path. The horses clambered uphill, snorting and heaving until the men were forced to dismount and lead them. Trees became stunted and sparse as soil surrendered to rock and thinning forest gave way to sloping fields littered with boulders. As the morning ebbed, they worked their way along precipitous and narrowing trails until midday, when a monolithic granite crag rose up to greet them. Its slopes and peaks were jagged with chaotic edges, scoured clean from eons of wind and rain, and long cracks raked the rock liked a scratched face.

Kulan fortress hugged the rugged peak like a child clinging to its mother's waist. Its massive stone walls reached out like arms, embracing the rock, while the child's back took the form of the forward battlements. Flanked by two towers, ten times the height of a man; the front wall spanned nearly a hundred yards by Shasp's estimate. The walls terminating against the rock face were slightly longer than the front, and all bore the tell-tale castellation of a fortified stronghold. The entire structure, like a true child, was made from the speckled granite of its mother.

They trotted up to the main gate and Shasp hailed the guard as the portcullis heaved upward with a clatter of gears and counterweights. He gazed up at the tower, the sun glaring in his eyes, and saw Rose waving enthusiastically. Shasp held up his hand to acknowledge her as his black charger clomped forward through the yawning gate. Beyond the brooding walls of Kulan an ancient courtyard greeted them; brimming with the same mountain flowers he had seen growing along the trail. Even though the blossoms were withering in the coming cold of late fall, their pleasant fragrance persisted in the crisp mountain air. The courtyard had been laid with flag-stones, mortared together with clay. Rows of rock and timber barracks were constructed against the inner walls. Most were single story domiciles but more than a few had an upper floor. Before him the keep rose like a great block of carved granite, dotted with windows and verandas, its roof, crowned with battlements for secondary defense. It was easy to see where newer architecture met the ancient.

Shasp handed his reins to Etgur, who gave him a vexed look, and walked toward the wide steps leading to the looming oak doors of the entrance. Shasp raised a steel-cased fist to bang a staccato on the carved surface, but the door swung open before his hand fell and Rose, startled by his raised fist, smiled and swept out to meet him. She was accompanied by a burly guard, and Shasp gave the man a withering glare, eyes narrowing with accusation.

"My lady's orders sir," he stuttered defensively.

Shasp turned and grinned at Rose, "How was your ride home?"

Rose took a quick peek over her shoulder at the guard. "I was hoping we would stop so you could catch up, but Balam refused to stay the night in the forest, and one of the horses stumbled and is lame for it."

Shasp brushed a capricious strand of raven hair from her eyes as it danced in the wind. "We were lodged by an old hermit."

Rose became perplexed, "We didn't see any homes along the way."

Shasp nodded, "I wouldn't have found it either, being off the trail as far as it was, but we saw his light through the trees after dark."

Rose grabbed his steel-shod hand, "Come inside. I'll get you something to eat and then you can rest."

Inside Kulan, it was cool and dry, and gentle light poured in through generous windows, lending the interior a warm, welcome glow. Apartments had been constructed adjacent to the main hall, while above, a balcony encircled the interior with even more adjoining rooms. Great redwood columns, so large two men could not clasp hands around them, held up a high, pitched roof. Each was carved with sanded reliefs depicting hunting and warfare. At the apex of the roof was a capped hole that allowed smoke to escape but would not let rain or snow in. At the center of the hall, and in the midst of the Olympian pillars, was a raised hearth crackling with fire and large enough to burn a wagon. Encircling it were long benches and tables of rough cut pine, and as he walked through them with Rose, he enjoyed the mingling scents of pine, smoke and cooking food. He paused to examine the murals and tapestries which covered much of the walls and mused at the simple, yet brilliant, architecture which created a very communal and warm atmosphere. It was much different than he had imagined after listening to Rose and Ormund.

Rose led him to a modest, rudimentary apartment on the ground floor containing a bed and table. A stingy, shuttered window on the back wall allowed only meager light to illuminate the cramped space within.

"Meet me in the hall when you are settled," she said then scurried off to find food while the burly man hustled after her, complaining bitterly. "I wish you would stay still for one damn moment!"

After Rose left, Shasp returned to the stables and collected his gear from Etgur with thanks that seemed to stall the youth's growing resentment, then returned to his quarters. Once he un-packed he went back to the hall where he dropped onto a bench near the flaming hearth. He tugged one of his boots off and was shaking out a nagging pebble when a woman's voice startled him.

"You must be Shasp Ironwrought. "Welcome to Kulan Keep. I hope your journey was no great trial." Shasp looked up to see a woman that could only be the Lady Blaquet descending the staircase, accompanied by an enormous bald, black warrior, wearing a black leather cuirass and heavy, curved sword.

Shasp stood with his boot in his hand, "And you must be the Lady Blaquet from the court in Alem. There was no trouble nor am I a stranger to trials."

Blaquet took a seat in a padded chair on the corner of the table next to Shasp and appraised him with a broad smile. Her teeth were large and white, and her deeply red hair cascaded down milky shoulders in soft waves. A red velvet dress squeezed her waist, accentuating curvy hips and large breasts. Her face was just beginning to show the first signs of middle age in the form of small cracks around her eyes and mouth, but she was nonetheless quite attractive. In fact, Shasp could almost feel her sensuality on his skin, like tangible and expanding warmth. "Sit with me awhile." She turned to her guard, "Natu, bring us some wine."

Hesitating, Natu glowered at Shasp then spun on his heel.

Shasp sat and pulled his riding boot on, "So, I guess you have had time to talk to Rose. I hope you are not too angry with her. She has already been through a great deal."

Blaquet waved her hand dismissively, "Oh no, not at all. The poor child has been beset by terrible nightmares and knows not what to make of them. I wish she would have talked to me about them before running away." She dropped her hand to her chest, "And when I think of what almost happened to her, if not for your intervention. I am grateful to you Sir."

37

Shasp winced, "Probably not so grateful on the account of your man, Goshun, I imagine."

She raised a perfectly tweezed brow, "Balam said Goshun attacked you unprovoked and you slew him. Of course, it's no secret that Balam and Goshun hated each other. I do, however, hope you are willing to replace him for the winter, my being a man short now and all."

"I'll be glad to earn my keep until the spring if that is acceptable."

"It pleases me greatly Sir," she said with a beaming smile.

"Your guard is enormous," Shasp changed the subject, "I haven't seen many men that large."

"Oh, Natu? Once, I watched him clear out an entire tavern singlehandedly. I found him slaving away in a silver mine in the southern Kalyfar territory a few years ago. It seemed a waste for a physique like his to be used for hacking out silver when there are much nobler uses, so I purchased him and had a weapons expert train him for over a year. Without a doubt, he is one of the most deadly men I know."

Shasp was wondering what a lady of Blaquet's standing was doing in a tavern. "You must keep hard company. You said 'one of the most deadly men you know'. Who are the others?"

Blaquet smiled and looked away in feigned shyness, "You would certainly rank among that number."

"Me? We've only just met."

"Balam told me he found that camp of ruffians that tried to rape Rose. He said you killed seven men by yourself, though he doubted it until he saw how effortlessly you slew Goshun. He said you moved like a master. However, from your accent and your armor, I gather you leaned your skills somewhere else, beyond the western sea, perhaps; Aypon maybe? You have some of the look of an Ayponese man. They came often to trade when I was in Alem. I've even met some dignitaries from that island."

Shasp was about to reply when Rose appeared with a steaming elk steak, bread and wine. Behind her the guard puffed, red-faced, with Natu at his shoulder. Natu sat a brass goblet in front of Blaquet then stood behind her like a loyal hound.

Rose glanced uncomfortably before turning to Shasp, "I will see you this evening."

He watched her for a moment then turned to his meal but caught himself before he broke etiquette, "With your permission, I'm famished."

"Of course," Said Blaquet smiling, "I love to watch a man eat."

Hoping to deter an uncomfortable silence while he ate and avoid questions concerning his origins, he spurred the conversation in a different direction, "Tell me about your keep."

Blaquet scanned the room with a warm expression of fondness, "The name, 'Kulan,' comes from the locals. They claim it was built even before their ancestors came here, probably just after the cataclysms. All of them shy away from the valley, fearful of the many myths and legends surrounding the keep. Stories of giants, ghosts, and ancient kings . . . but no one really knows who built it, when or why. One of my distant family members willed it to me long ago, though none of them has lived here until now. I believe it was given to them by the minister of the Arrigin territories for some noble service of some kind. I was looking for an isolated place and forgot it was even among my holdings. For me, it's perfect. I need to be…away from court for a while."

"It's truly amazing, but you impress me as a cultured woman, so why do you want to live so far from civilization?"

Blaquet leaned back in her chair in a fashion more reminiscent of a bar maid than a lady. "Impressions can be misleading Shasp, but if you must know, I ran afoul of the queen. It seems she was angry about all the attention I was giving to her husband. The next thing you know, hired assassins were dogging my every step and if not for Natu's vigilance and sword arm, I would be but a memory. So, I have come to this place until the damage at court can be repaired. In fact, envoys should be arriving in a few days, sent secretly by the king to assist in my return."

Shasp sensed wistfulness in her tone and was beginning to understand Blaquet's aspirations of power; aspirations which had backfired. Blaquet continued to entertain him with stories of the keep while he finished his food and wine.

Shasp stood up, "Thank you for the meal, but I've rested enough and I think it's time Natu explained my duties. I look forward to speaking with you more this evening."

"Of course, but Natu is not the captain. I need his complete attention on my protection. You will find Captain Navun in the courtyard or on the walls and he will explain your duties."

Shasp nodded, buckled on his sword belt, slung his crossbow then started toward the courtyard, but sensed Natu's eyes burning into his back as he left the room.

Atop the wind-blown battlements he approached a group of woodsy looking men, laughing and sharing a wineskin.

"Where do I find your captain? I need to report."

His only answer was a few cold stares before they turned their backs and swaggered off, muttering to one another. Shasp turned and leaned on the granite lip of the battlement, then gazed out over the seemingly endless expanse of mountains. He discovered that the vista generated an unwelcome feeling of insignificance. Suddenly, a hand fell on his shoulder and he spun knocking it free. A large man with wooly red hair, and an even shaggier beard, stood grinning at him, his large white teeth gleaming through a crooked smile.

"Easy there, new man! I don't need you skewering me like you did old Goshun, not that he was worth a rat turd anyway. I'm Navun, the captain of these louts who call themselves soldiers, and you must be that Ironwrought fellow everyone is a buzz about."

Shasp nodded and jerked his thumb toward the gang of hostile guards, "I guess I'm not too popular around here."

"Faahh...Goshun had friends but he had enemies too. If he was worth a damn, you'd be dead and he'd still be here. I imagine his mates will be happy to steer clear of you."

"Blaquet invited me to winter here and I told her I would earn my keep."

"Good," said the captain as he clapped his hand on Shasp's shoulder, "we rotate guard duty and hunting parties. You can imagine which one is more popular. Combat exercises are in the courtyard everyday rain or shine. If the weather is too stormy then it's held in the hall."

"How many men do you have here? A garrison?"

"Hah! Used to be seventy, but now, with you, there's sixty eight. Hardly enough to hold down a large fort like this, though I don't expect any sieges, but my lady high and mighty seems fearful enough after the last few attempts on her life. You can stand post on this section. Duty is a four hour rotation."

Shasp nodded and thanked Navun before beginning his

tedious pace along the wall.

Evening had fallen over the Olloua Mountains before Shasp found himself at Blaquet's table again. The mountain queen questioned him endlessly, as he suffered quiet scrutiny from Natu. The night wore on but the wine never ceased to flow. The men at arms and ever present ladies of Blaquet's entourage soon grew wild and the hall became as raucous as any Tanyan tavern. Blaquet was obviously enjoying herself as she called out jesting insults and flirtatious remarks, one after another. The roar of merriment and general drunkenness increased within the keep, but Shasp grew weary of the noise and excused himself to seek a quieter corner.

He wandered through the keep away from the clamor until he found his way to the roof where he gazed into a clear, star-speckled sky. His experiences had taught him that it would be foolish to drink too much with so many potential enemies nearby. As he wandered along the edge of the empty parapet he could not help but wonder why he was there, why he had not just continued on, but something about Rose had nagged at him, something he did not completely understand.

No sooner had she crossed his mind, than she suddenly appeared behind him. "I saw you leave the hall," she said timidly as she eased up next to him and looked out at the silhouettes of the distance ridges.

The sad look in her eyes pricked him, "I haven't made up my mind about you." He looked away so she wouldn't see the sudden flush of his face.

"I'm telling the truth. There is something terrible here and if you are the man I think you are, you will see that too."

Shasp cleared his throat, "Where's this cave you mentioned; the one that leads into the mountain?"

She pointed up, "It's on the other side of this peak."

Shasp looked over her shoulder, "Where is your guard?"

"He's below at the bottom of the stairs," she shrugged, "he knows I can't go anywhere from here."

Shasp leaned back against the battlement and to his surprise, Rose pressed her warm body gently against his, tears of anxiety welling in her eyes. Shasp inhaled the intoxicating perfume of her soft hair but Rose sensed the rigidity of his arms and lowered her face.

"Please help me, I cannot stay here," she said barely audible

41

but then louder, "I *cannot*! They all think I'm mad, but they are the ones who are insane, just listen to them, carousing while something wicked haunts these halls."

"There is nothing insane about people having a good time, Rose. The world can be a harsh place and people need their pleasures."

"You don't understand it never ends; every night it's like this."

Shasp lifted her chin until their eyes met again, "I'll look for this cavern from your dreams.   If it's real, I'll find it."

Rose sniffed and nodded, "I trust you."

"Are you sure that's a good idea, trusting someone you just met?"

Rose made a serious face and for a moment he regretted his words, but then she pressed her soft pouting lips against his. They lingered for a moment in the embrace and his hands slid down to her slender waist, but Rose suddenly broke away and ran down the stairs. Shasp watched her until she disappeared, then closed his eyes and concentrated on the taste of the girl which lingered on his lips. "Tastes like trouble," he muttered to himself and turned back to the landscape. "I sure hope she's not crazy."

Shasp returned to Blaquet's table shortly after his rendezvous with Rose, trying to appear festive and occasionally searched for the girl in the crowd, but she was nowhere to be seen.

Blaquet, face flushed from wine, stood unsteadily and calmed the rambunctious crowd. She lifted her arms, "I want to see some combat. Who will wrestle for my pleasure?"

"I'll wrestle you Blaquet!" came a drunken man's reply.

"Not me, you dolt!" she laughed, "Who will wrestle Natu?"

"We have all taken a beating from Natu," came another.

"I'll sweeten the pot," she yelled over the din, "I'll give ten gold coins to the man who beats him!"

The offer was received with a blend of gasping, cheers, and disbelief, but when it seemed there would be no takers, Captain Navun stepped forward.

"For that kind of money I'll test the brute!" he roared through his fiery beard.

The crowd screamed their approval and bets changed hands while others pushed back the tables to make room.   Odds *only* on

Navun.

Blaquet yelled over the crowd again, "No striking, gouging or crushing the other's manhood. It ends when one man yields or becomes unconscious!"

Navun stripped off his brown wool shirt revealing his hairy and scarred barrel chest. He was a thick, muscular man, and his physique denoted a life dedicated to war. The spectators knew that not all of his confidence was from the wine.

Natu swaggered leisurely to the center of the floor, unbuckled his armor and stood in his loin cloth. Women squealed in delight over the spectacle of Natu's body while the men bugged their eyes in amazement. His chest hung like a ceiling over bulging stomach muscles and his arms were larger than most men's thighs.

Even Navun was beginning to doubt the wisdom of his decision, but he was in the middle of it now, and his pride would not allow him to retreat.

Blaquet clapped her hands to signal the beginning of the contest and they circled slowly, assessing one another, but when Natu stepped forward, Navun lunged for his legs. He managed to clasp his hands behind the giant's knee, but Natu dropped his body weight, breaking Navun's grip. Navun, sensing the danger of being underneath so massive a man, rolled to his side and came away smoothly. Natu frowned over the escape and closed again, but this time Navun decided to attempt a throw and locked his right hand in a clench behind Natu's neck while reaching under the opposite arm. Using the bodyguard's weight and forward momentum to his advantage, he slipped his hands together behind Natu's back and twisted his hips underneath. Natu came off his feet with ease and arced overhead as Navun rotated underneath. It was a perfectly executed throw, and Natu landed with a thud on the flagstone floor with Navun on top. Navun squeezed his arms against Natu's head with as much force as he could muster. The pressing spectators became hysterical with excitement but, suddenly, Natu reached around Navun, locked his own hands together, arched his back and rolled. Once Natu had pulled Navun over to the other side, he turned his hips around and reversed Navun's hold. Now it was Navun feeling the pressure of Natu's mighty arms around his own head and neck. He clawed at Natu's fingers in a desperate attempt to break the brute's hold, but they were like forged steel. Navun's body soon relaxed as

43

the flow of blood was squeezed off from his brain and consciousness faded. Natu let go then stood over Navun, but not to accept praise. Instead, he straddled the defeated captain, placed a large hand on each side of his neck and rubbed vigorously. Immediately, Navun came around, slow and bewildered.

Most cheered and some bemoaned the loss of money, but all agreed Navun had been the first to even come close to defeating the juggernaut. Natu quietly returned to his place beside Blaquet.

Blaquet beamed as she leaned toward Shasp, "Do you wish to try your luck?"

Shasp shook his head slowly then chuckled, "I don't think so. Gold isn't always a fair trade for broken bones."

Her voice became suspicious, "Somehow, I don't think it is fear that holds you in your seat."

He quaffed the last of his wine, "Natu is clearly experienced. Perhaps I would fair no worse than Navun, nevertheless, some other evening when I'm more in the spirit." He excused himself and retired to his room but did not sleep.

In the quiet hours of pre-dawn, when the revelers had staggered off to their rooms, some alone and many coupled, Shasp wandered to the battlements to clear his head and ponder the secrets of Kulan.

Chapter 5

That morning Shasp stumbled out early to the sound of Navun, yelling and cursing. It was the way the old captain liked to greet his men at dawns first light and most hated him for it. Shasp buckled on his mail shirt and greaves, slung his scabbard over his shoulder, and then headed toward the courtyard for practice, anxious for a good workout. Outside, Navun was barking orders for the men to form up on the broken flagstones. After an hour of exercises, they broke into groups of four and Navun handed out wooden practice blades, each dipped in black tar so contact could be easily seen. The guardsmen partnered with Shasp were eager to test the mettle of the man who had killed seven brigands and one of their peers. At first, Shasp held back just enough for them to be emboldened, enjoying the game, and even allowed one or two glancing blows. However, by the end of practice, when his sparring partners limped away covered with black marks, there was no question of his deadly superiority.

As the men passed around oil-soaked rags to wipe off the tar, Navun barked out the days guard roster, but when Balam discovered he was assigned to the night watch he complained bitterly. Navun quickly came toe to toe with Balam, fuming over his insolence.

45

Balam's nature was becoming clear to Shasp as he listened to the argument intensify, and when Navun raised his fist to strike the belligerent subordinate, Shasp yelled over the file of men.

"Captain Navun!"

Navun's fist stopped short, "What is it newcomer!" he answered, still standing face to face with Balam?

"I'll take the night patrol if it will calm the quarrel. I wouldn't mind a few hours more sleep."

Navun spat on Balam' boot then shoved his way through the ranks to Shasp. "Oh, You will, will you? You and Balam will both work the day *and* the night watch! You, Balam, for your grumbling and you, Shasp, for speaking in ranks!" Navun walked back along the file, returning to the front of the formation. "Ironwrought and Balam will make selections for both watches. As for anyone else who thinks this is their mother's hut, the next time I make assignments, I had better only hear 'Yes Sir!' Do ya understand?"

The men acknowledged him with a muttered, "Aye," and Navun stormed away leaving the men to their selections.

Balam swaggered out of the formation and selected ten men for the day watch.

"You can pick the night shift," he sneered.

Shasp gave Balam a wry smile and shrugged; it was what he was hoping for anyway. He took his time choosing the men who appeared the most hung over, concluding they were the ones most in need of rest, then dismissed them and took his place on the roof. Shasp looked across the courtyard to the opposite battlement where Balam secluded himself on the north wall, surrounded by his cronies.

He waited patiently throughout the morning, hoping Rose would come and she did, but this time with a guard who was not content to sit at the bottom of the stairs. It was Etgur. Navun must have realized it would take a more energetic guardian to keep up with the busy girl. Rose greeted him and held out a warm jack of broth. Shasp liked Etgur well enough but also noticed Etgur's eyes roaming over Rose. When she looked in Etgur's direction, his eyes darted away like fleeing sparrows. He found the boy's infatuation amusing, and chuckled to himself. A pallid sun melted on the horizon as the early moon usurped its throne, bathing the mountain peaks in blue light. The wind, aroused by the fall in temperature, bit through wool and leather, leaving most of the guards huddled next to the glowing braziers with their backs to the cold.

It was late when Shasp paused near the top of the stairs which led down to the hall, no longer hearing the revelry that had floated up hours before. Near the end of the watch, he had dismissed his men early and lingered on the roof, awaiting the change in guard. He had only minutes to speak with Rose *privately* and had spent the day conceiving the plan which he now put into action. Snatching up a spear he had secured from the armory, he jabbed its point deep into the crack where the battlement met the floor of the roof. When he was sure it was firmly lodged in place, he put his helmet on top of the haft and whipped his black cloak over the construction, pulling the neck string tight. He stepped back, examining his work, and hoped that, in the struggling firelight, his makeshift dummy would have the appearance of a vigilant watchman.

Silently, he uncoiled a length of rope and looped one end over the crenelated wall, then lowered himself to Rose's window directly below, where he tapped on the shutters. Long moments passed before they opened, revealing a sleepy, and shivering Rose in flimsy bed clothes, her eyes wide with surprise. Like an adept thief, he eased through the window and gently closed the shutters. The daring rendezvous was mostly unnecessary as Shasp could have discussed most of his thoughts with Rose openly, but some of them may have made her uncomfortable in mixed company. Besides, the thought of being alone with her, even if it was only for a few short minutes, had plagued him all day.

With a finger to his lips he whispered, "I wanted to talk to you about that cave entrance that frightened you so badly."

Rose's eyes widened slightly at the very mention of it. "Yes? What of it?"

"What do you think the connection is with your dreams? Do you think the cavern you see in them is there, beyond that opening?"

Rose shrugged, "I don't know, perhaps."

He persisted, "Was the chamber natural or hewn out by human hands?"

"Natural, full of mineral and lime."

"If the place you dream of is real, and as you described, it must be here someplace." He had trouble keeping his eyes from her pert breasts where they strove against the paltry thinness of her gown, "I can't wait too long to look for it; winter is here and the snows might bury the entrance. I'll see if I can find it tomorrow. If it's there, that will give credence to your fear and Blaquet will have to listen to you."

Rose's eyes shifted and tears welled.

"What's wrong," he asked?

She wiped at her cheeks with a pale sleeve. "You have no idea what this means to me. I was completely without hope before you found me and later, I was afraid everyone would think I was losing my mind. But you...you're willing to believe me. And, I'm afraid. What if you go to look for this place and it *is* real? What will happen to you then if this...*thing* catches you?"

Shasp laid a hand on her shoulder, "Rose, I'll find out the truth; if it's there or not; if you're mad or not. And I'll be careful, I promise."

He turned to go but Rose suddenly threw her arms around him, "Wait! Don't go . . . .not yet!"

"I have to, my dummy won't last long in this wind, and I don't think I need to tell you what might happen if someone finds me here."

She clung to him insistently and Shasp eased his arms around her trembling back. He'd been imagining the curve of her soft form all day and now he was suddenly filled with her warmth. Gently, he placed a finger under her chin and lifted it until she met his icy grey eyes. They lingered in silence, neither sure of what to say next, but then, without warning, Rose thrust her lips yearningly against his, and Shasp's blood surged as he gave back and savored the wine of her mouth. As they kissed passionately, an instinctive warning scratched and kicked at the walls of his mind, telling him it was time to go. However, the soft warmth of Rose's full pouting lips had purveyed his thoughts from the moment he met her, and now that her body was pressed firmly against his, he was in no hurry to leave, even if all the armies of the Arrigin were on their way to her small chamber. In the end, Shasp was a disciplined man, not the sort to let his body dictate to his wits, and he pushed her away with great mental effort.

"I have to go," he said reluctantly, "but come find me tomorrow." With a single fluid motion, he leapt through the window, snatched the rope, and clambered out of sight.

Rose leaned on the window sill, shivering from the frigid wind as it quelled the flame of her passion, and considered the cold planks beneath her delicate feet. Snow began to fall outside her window, as she silently wondered what her future might hold, or if she even had one, but regardless, she hoped the mysterious Shasp was part of it.

Shasp slumbered through part of the following day, after he
finished the obligatory morning drill.   Navun must have felt pity for
those who kept the night watch and exempted them from duty.
Besides, the old captain knew there would be enough trouble makers
to fill any gaps in the watch schedule.

Once Shasp was rested, he donned his gear then made an
excuse to leave the keep, telling Navun he was going hunting. The
salty old captain was impressed, assuming Shasp would rather lounge
about the keep, the same as the others, given the cold weather.

As the wind calmed, snowflakes the size of a wolf's eye fell,
blanketing the woods in a sheet of virgin white. Shasp trudged down
the slope of primordial rocks which led away from the keep and
melted into the woods at the far end. He slogged through tall pine
trees, laden with wet snow until he was certain to be out of sight, then
skulked along the shadowy tree line, rounding the southern base of the
peak, and came to the backside of the mountain. With grave analysis,
he surveyed the rocky heights, and the heights glowered back at the
impudent mortal who skulked below. He surveyed the cracks and
crevices of the mountain's sheer face. Several dark shadows among
the high cracks and shelves of the cliffs inspired his imagination as he
tried to make a sober assessment of the direction he would need to
climb.   He stretched his fingers and arms before beginning the slow
assent of the jagged monolith, but within the first few feet of his
ascension, he found the granite to be wet and slippery from new fallen
snow. As he continued up the granite wall, he caught himself more
than once, nearly plummeting to his death. Like a spider on a wall, he
clung to tiny protrusions and cracks, inspecting every shadowed
cavity and shelf. When he found nothing but recesses and deep
gouges, he continued upward then back across the rock, ever mindful
of death's nerve-wracking presence.   By the time he reached the
middle of the peak, his fingers were bleeding and his cloak was
drenched. Shasp paused to catch his breath on a narrow ledge,
tottering precariously, when he saw a dark depression in the rock
above him, deep enough to hide an opening. Rose must have been
standing in just the right place to have seen it from below. With his
back to the wall and toes hanging over the ledge, he warmed his
frozen fingers in his armpits. Once the circulation returned to his

tortured digits, he carefully turned around and jabbed his right hand into a crack overhead, and pulled himself up, then did the same with his left hand. Shoulders and biceps contracted as he dragged his feet up high enough to gain a toe-hold, then he started the process all over again.

With only the vertical crack to cling to, he inched along the fracture, grunting with effort as loose rock chips broke off and fell away out of sight. When he thought his arms would fail him, he finally reached the rock ledge and heaved himself over. As he lay on his back, gasping for breath and shivering from the cold, he yearned for the warmth of even a simple candle. Lifting his body onto his elbows he stared at the cave entrance, its yawning mouth swallowing the winter light. He massaged the feeling back into his fingers as he studied it, and reasoned that the cave was far too high to be a predator's den, but the hair on his neck still prickled from an instinct which warned him of unseen danger.

With a rasp of steel, he slid the Katana from its sheath and started into the mouth, but as he progressed, the walls gradually closed in, eventually forcing him to his hands and knees. It did not take long before absolute darkness engulfed him, and with aching fingers he fumbled through the folds of his damp cloak. Shasp rolled onto his side and managed to find his flint, then worked up a spark strong enough to start the wick of a small candle he had brought with him. To his surprise, the flickering candlelight illuminated drawings of beasts, the likes of which he had never seen, sketched in charcoal and other stains on the cave's ancient wall. Farther on, the tunnel choked down again until he was worming along on his stomach. With the dust of eons invading his nose and throat, he wriggled through a stretch nearly twenty yards long and squirmed free into a dank cavern. Shasp stretched, shook off the claustrophobia, and then wrinkled his nose at the rank, stale cavern air. It was the nauseating odor of old death, a stench he knew well.

The puny candlelight revealed only his immediate surroundings. Colorful stalagmites, shiny with moisture, sprouted from the floor like dragon teeth while the constant dripping of water echoed from deep within the cavern.

Shasp had been in his share of caves and had known more than one man who had never found his way out again. Before doing any exploration he would take precautions. He uncoiled a length of hemp rope and draped a loop over a stalagmite closest to the tiny mouse hole he had squeezed in through, and as he slowly picked his way through the mountain's teeth, he let it out. After walking the length of a market square, the floor sloped upward to a natural dais, free of mineral deposits. When a glint from the edge of the candlelight caught his attention, he stepped out to his last length of rope and let it fall. In the dim half-light, three large copper braziers glimmered, standing upon tripods of brass, their legs carved with hideous reliefs. As he approached the dais, something crunched under his boots. Shasp looked down at his feet and discovered heaps of bones laying in various stages of decay, some covered with lime deposits and others black with mold. A shiver wormed through his flesh as his feet clattered against the bones on his way toward the dais and he thought again of Rose's account. Kneeling down to inspect the raised floor of shining obsidian, he ran his hand over its polished surface and quickly realized there was nothing natural about its surface. The empty eye sockets of a hundred pleading skulls regarded him as he inspected some chalked markings upon the surface, and discovered odd shapes and runes just as Rose had said. He was so engrossed in his discovery that his heart nearly stopped when a jet of cold and putrid air suddenly snuffed out his candle.

Shasp knew immediately that it was no draft, for the air in the cave was stale and ancient. Rather, it was as if someone had appeared next to him and extinguished the small flame with their rank breath. The paranormal occurrence sent a rush of adrenalin surging through his veins, and he dropped into a fighting crouch, senses straining, his cold steel licking the darkness. "Who's there! Show yourself!"

Then, without warning, an invading presence burst forth in his mind like an infected boil. *"Who are you?"* demanded a low resonating voice, clawing at the inside of Shasp's skull. Shasp sensed an ancient evil with an insatiable hunger like a bottomless pit and resisted the intrusion. The presence withdrew from his mind; its hollow laughter rolled through the cavern, echoing against the distant walls and growing with intensity. Thoughts of the shadow entity Rose described caused him to break out in a cold sweat and his pulse hammered in his ears. Shasp knew instantly he was about to become prey . . . food for a malevolent demon. Slowly he retreated toward the fallen rope, feeling with his feet as he went. Suddenly, a screaming wave of arctic air gushed over him. Immediately, his arms and legs became as lead, and his breath caught from a cold more intense than any on earth; a cold straight from the underworld. Stiffly, he turned aside, stumbling in the dark, gasping for air and, in his haste, stumbled over a stalagmite and fell headlong against the floor. Fighting fear with every ounce of courage he could muster, he shoved himself to his knees while his very core was freezing solid. Again, the rushing wind thundered across the cavern through the inky blackness. Shasp lashed out with his weapon at the first sensation of touch and slashed into the ethereal gust, but a shock of cold electricity coursed along his arm, causing the sword to fall from his paralyzed fingers. Curling up on the cave floor, he cried out in pain and cradled his unfeeling arm against his chest. With his left hand, he groped for his frosted sword until he found it, then crawled across the cavern floor on all fours like an arthritic dog. Evil laughter echoed from the cavern's unknown depths as despair and futility ripped at his courage. Searing cold infused his body, slowing his heart and shattering his concentration, but as he dragged himself through the jutting stalagmites, Ormund's amulet dropped out of his shirt. The talisman dangled by a leather thong from his neck and he unconsciously brushed his hand against it. Warmth instantly surged back into the worthless limb with a sensation so profound that he stopped crawling and paused, incredulous. Hope had valiantly appeared in his severe crisis, and Shasp quickly seized the stone in his hand, squeezing it within his frozen knuckles. This time, warmth flooded through his entire body, and his limbs loosened. He slammed his sword back into the scabbard then began feeling for the rope trail. Within moments, he felt the rough weave of hemp under his fingers and started back toward the entrance, listening for the next volley of ghostly wind. Again, the howling wind surged toward him with the deafening clamor of an avalanche, and he braced himself as the gelid gale slammed against him. The demon's icy vortex enveloped him, seeking to push its tendrils deep into his flesh for the coup de grace but as the cold intensified, the stone in his hand seemed to grow even warmer, driving the entity back and restoring warmth. Shasp stumbled toward the opening until he came to the end of the rope then groped against the rock for the tunnel. Like a desperate mouse fleeing a hungry cat, Shasp dove into the cramped entrance and quickly wormed down its length until he emerged into the wider stretch of tunnel. Hair bristled on his neck as he sensed the specter's pursuit, and he staggered along painfully until, finally, he broke into the welcome light of day, and stood upon the lofty shelf. Standing with his back to the cloudy winter sky, he stared back down the passageway, wide-eyed, and listened as the wind howled down the shaft. At the edge of the opening, an awful, twisting black cloud burst forth from the tunnel. Shasp's heart hammered in his chest as the roiling blackness collided with the light, and shrieked in a clamor that was a vial mixture of beast and wind. The convulsing darkness took on the shape of a sinister face, its mouth twisting in a snarl, and then suddenly, it disappeared as if sucked backward into the mountain. Shasp collapsed to his knees, whispering a prayer of thanks to the One God, then, exhausted, fell over, clutching the amulet. Muscles aching, he slowly regained his strength. "By the eyes of my ancestors," he muttered to himself, "What the hell was that?" Eventually, he struggled to his feet and took in the sprawling view of mountain peaks, unable to recall the last time he was so overjoyed to see daylight and breathe fresh air. Getting off the peak without his rope would be difficult, but in light of his recent trial it seemed a minor challenge.

Shasp managed the descent and trudged back to the keep, arriving just after nightfall with a doe over his shoulders. He wondered at his luck, coming across the animal inside the tree line and finished cleaning it out near dusk. Then, he relied on the fires from atop of the keep's battlements to guide him home. He and Rose would have a lot to talk about.

Chapter 6

From Kulan's wall, Rose searched the darkening landscape and was relieved to see Shasp tramp through the gates, greeting Navun just after nightfall. Etgur peered over her shoulder, pressing uncomfortably close, and looked down at the two men.

"Why do you gawk over him all the time? He's much older than you."

Rose shot him an angry look, crossed her arms defensively and turned her back. "What would you know, Etgur? You're only a boy."

Etgur flushed in the torchlight, clenching his fist at his sides. "I'm as good as any. As good a hunter and as good a warrior! You're just too infatuated to see it!" He stalked away, brooding as he looked down into the bustling courtyard. Watching the men congratulate Shasp only further inflamed his jealousy.

"Humph," said Rose, "What do you care about a madwoman anyway? I'm crazy, remember? I might chew your nose off as look at you."

Shasp scanned the wall, caught her eye, and waved.

Etgur fumed, "I don't trust him. Nobody knows who he is or where he's from, and he's not telling either. A man that can kill like him; there has to be trouble behind him somewhere."

Rose sensed the jealousy behind Etgur's words and softened. "I'm sorry Etgur; I know that you're not a boy anymore. Why else would they trust you to guard me?"

He forced a grudging smile then looked away, "We should come down. They'll be serving dinner pretty soon."

At the evening festivities, Shasp sat apart from the others in a remote corner wiping the water from his sword and applying oil to its narrow blade. Rose sat next to him, having sent Etgur for some wine. Shasp stopped his cleaning for a moment to meet Rose's searching eyes. He drew a deep breath and exhaled, "It's there Rose. And so is that...*thing* that you feared."

Rose looked as if she would faint for a moment and Shasp began to reach for her but she held up her arm, "I'm okay." She shook her head as she struggled to accept what he was telling her, "What do I do now?"

"We get the hell out of here as fast as we can."

Rose's eyes narrowed with thought, "Wouldn't Blaquet just send men after us again?"

Shasp shrugged, "Maybe after I tell her what I've discovered we will *all* leave."

"It's a risk. You are new among the men and many of them grumble that they don't trust you, Balam more than most and he has Blaquet's ear. He will say that you are plotting somehow."

Shasp went back to wiping oil on his sword, "I guess I could take someone to the cavern to confirm my words, but they probably wouldn't live to tell of it and again it would look suspicious, someone going in and only me coming out."

They sat together quietly for a while trying to think of a way to make the facts known to the Lady of Kulan in a way that was direct and indisputable but neither of them could think of anything.

Shasp sat back and let out a sigh, "I guess I will need some time to think on it Rose. Something will come to mind, and if nothing does, then we'll run like hell."

Etgur returned with wine for Rose and she took a sip before noticing that Navun was coming toward them, "Come on Etgur. It looks like Captain Navun wants to talk to Shasp." The two stood and worked their way through the crowd as Shasp looked toward the advancing captain.

Navun staggered over to the small table and dropped onto the stool next to him. He ran his thick fingers through his shaggy red mane, took a pull on the sloshing tankard, and dragged a sleeve across his glistening beard. "That's the oddest sword I've ever seen. Where'd ya get it?"

Shasp grinned, happy to see Navun looking relaxed, even if he was drunk. "It's an Ayponese katana," he said, looking down its straight single edge. "The point is designed with only one taper to make it stronger and it can punch through harder armor than that long sword of yours....here," he flipped it over and laid the blade across his forearm, offering it to Navun for his inspection.

The captain took it, examined the blade with watery eyes, and then stood up on unsteady legs, swishing it back and forth.

Again, Shasp smiled, shook his head and laughed, "That's not the way one handles this kind of blade, Captain."

Navun handed it back, and pretended to be offended. "Oh

really? Pray tell, mighty swordsman," he said sarcastically.

Shasp gripped the long pommel gently, and began weaving the sword in a smooth forehand to backhand motion then rotated the blade from back cut to forward cut and in the middle of the weave changed hands, continuing the pattern without altering the rhythm. Slowly, he went through a series of sword katas, and Navun watched in bleary amazement as the blade moved in a geometric dance of defense and attack. Then, as a final display of mastery, Shasp rolled the blade once and sheathed it in a single fluid movement, smoothly, without looking or hesitating.

Navun raised an eyebrow, "Well...aren't you the little dancer," he slurred. "What the hell were you doing in Aypon anyway? You a sailor too?" he said with a crooked smile.

Shasp made to answer but was interrupted by a sudden loud chant. It was his name. Men began working their way toward his table where they urged the bewildered Ironwrought to his feet.

"What the hell is going on, Navun?"

Navun grinned and raised his tankard, "Time for your initiation into our little band!" he yelled over the din.

"What are you talking about?" Shasp called over his shoulder as the mob pushed him toward the center of the hall where benches and tables had been moved back to create an empty space on the floor.

"Oh shit," breathed Shasp as realization dawned.

Navun appeared at his side, "You're the only man among us who hasn't had his ass handed to him by Natu, but don't worry. It won't hurt as much tonight as it will tomorrow. Probably ought to lose that shirt though....if you don't want it torn up."

Natu stood ready on the other side of the floor, naked from the waist up, sweating from the heat of the crowd. Shasp stripped off his shirt revealing his lean frame. Where Natu was the embodiment of the bull, Shasp was the panther.

"Can't I just forfeit?"

His answer was a stiff shove from behind which sent him reeling into the middle of the circle. Natu strode confidently toward him, stopping only a few feet away before dropping into a crouch. Ironwrought did the same, but led with a foot forward. Like a dart the giant dove for his opponent's legs but Shasp sprang upward and let him pass beneath. Natu spun around, face to face again and opened his arms wide; backing the other to the edge of the crowd, but Shasp felt a multitude of hands pressing against his back, forcing him forward. When Natu closed, the panther shot forward and wrapped his arms around the bull's head, rolled his hips underneath and jerked. However, Natu's weight was too great, leaving Shasp with only a head lock, and unable to move the behemoth off balance. The black warrior reached behind Shasp's thigh and lifted the lighter man off his feet, tossing him bodily to the wine stained floor with a thud. Shasp lay stunned, trying to catch his breath, but was quickly dragged to his feet by screaming spectators.

Wine soaked breath invaded Shasp's nostrils as Navun yelled over his shoulder, only inches from his ear, "I got money on you, so you better not go down for at least another two minutes!" then Navun shoved him back into the contest.

Natu was waiting and doggedly attacked Shasp's legs. Again Shasp leapt into the air, but this time Natu caught his heel in one huge hand, and Shasp toppled backward. In an instant he was laying on his back underneath a mass of angry muscle. Natu wrapped one arm around the back of Shasp's head, the other across his throat in a scissor, and began to squeeze off his airway. Panicking from a lack of oxygen, Shasp struggled to tip the monster and immediately realized it was futile. Forcing himself to be calm, he made his middle and index fingers ridged then sharply jabbed them into a pocket of nerves alongside Natu's windpipe. Natu released Shasp as if he were a hot iron and stumbled backward, holding his throat. Shasp rolled onto his side, hacking fitfully, head resting against the floor, and then struggled to his feet. Natu winced at the pain in his neck, rubbed at it, then circled again, but this time cautiously. The screams of excitement deafened the grapplers, and shook the roof of the hall.

Blaquet watched with intense amusement, eyes wide with anticipation.

Shasp brought his elbows in close, leaving his palms forward, hoping it might entice Natu into a clench. Natu smiled broadly at the invitation, certain of his strength, and stepped toward him. Shasp snapped his right hand forward and locked it behind Natu's neck, and the bull moved as he predicted. Natu reached out, locking in classic grappler's fashion, but before Natu's hand reached its destination, the panther sprang his trap.

With his left hand, Shasp struck Natu's elbow from
underneath, raising his opponent's arm then ducked underneath,
coming around behind him. Shasp locked his hands around Natu's
waist, and drove a heel into the back of his knee. Natu's leg folded and
the giant toppled to the floor. Seeking to regain control Natu rolled to
his stomach, but Shasp released Natu's waist. Fast as a viper, he
snaked his arms around Natu's neck and locked his legs in a scissor
around his body. With one arm around the giant's throat he locked a
hand onto his bicep, applying pressure to his opponent's carotid
artery. Now it was Natu's turn to panic. He lurched off the ground,
despite Ironwrought's weight, and spun wildly. Desperate to dislodge
the clinging annoyance, Natu threw himself backward against an
engraved column, forcing a loud grunt from his antagonist. In spite of
the impact and throbbing muscles in his back, Shasp clamped his
scissor-like hold with as much strength as he could muster until the
titan stumbled and fell backwards onto a pinewood bench, shattering
it. Both lay still for several long seconds before Shasp finally shoved

Natu's limp form away, and lay on his battered back gulping air.

At first, the hall fell into stunned silence as its patrons gaped in amazement, but the quiet lull quickly exploded into a roar of hysteria that could be heard in the heavens. Women and men swarmed over them, some trying to revive Natu and others helping Shasp to his feet. Drops of wine splattered him as the over anxious crowd held their cups aloft, and he thought he would be crushed but for a large hairy hand that reached in and dragged him to safety.

"Awright, awright! Calm Yourselves! And yoos lagerts what owes me money...pay up!" cried Navun. He pressed the shirt into Shasp's hands, and then dragged him away to their table where he clumsily dumped wine into a leather jack for his golden goose. Shasp quaffed the cool liquid gustily then gingerly pulled the forest green wool shirt over his head.

"Damn, if I ever saw anything like that! Where did you learn to wrestle?"

"I never learned to wrestle. I just picked up a few tricks here and there."

"Bullshit," retorted Navun.

Shasp had not finished half his wine before Blaquet sauntered up. Her blue linen dress hugged the curves of her voluptuous body and red hair hung in long coiled tresses down her pale shoulders. "That was quite a display of martial skill Sir Ironwrought. No one has ever defeated Natu at hand to hand." She held out a small cloth bag.

He accepted it and felt the large coins through the cloth. "Natu is a stout man. I was lucky, nothing more."

"All is fair in love......and war." She paused and looked long at him generating an uncomfortable silence.

"Whatever you say, my lady," he inclined his head respectfully.

Blaquet turned and wove her way back through the crowd.

Navun's eyes caressed Blaquet's shapely backside as she left before turning to Shasp. He blinked his bloodshot eyes, "I think she likes you," he said, and then fell out of his chair.

Chapter 7

Two days later, in the early hours of morning, Shasp awoke in a cold sweat, fever raging inside his skull. Pain wracked his trembling body as he struggled to his feet and lurched toward the door. When he entered the hall, he was met by a plump servant maid who gasped at his appearance and quickly dropped her laundry to support his sagging form. Shasp's face was ashen and speckled with scarlet blemishes. His hair was soaked from perspiration.

"Sir...you are not well!"

"Water...please," he croaked.

"Come sir, back to bed. You're in no shape to be moving about."

He was dragged back to his room, dropped unceremoniously on his bed then covered with a coarse wool blanket. The maid hustled out, her voice echoing in the empty hall, calling for assistance. Instantly, a gaggle of bustling women teemed, bringing extra blankets, towels, hot water and broth.

Rose heard the commotion and rushed to his chamber, stopping short inside the doorway, her face a mask of fear and anxiety.

He looked up at her through half-open, bloodshot eyes, "I'll be all right, I just need rest and water."

Shaking off the feelings which had frozen her in the doorway, she swept in and supported his head, lifting a cup of cool water to his parched lips.

He gulped and coughed. Shasp saw the concern in her eyes and made a weak smile, "Don't worry, I've had much worse days than this. By tomorrow, I'll be like new."

Rose held back her tears and smiled unconvincingly.

As the next few days dragged by, Shasp slowly worsened until he became unresponsive most of the time. Thrashing about, semi-conscious in his soaked bedding, he mumbled incoherent phrases and gasped for breath. Navun came often, offering what help he could, while Blaquet fussed constantly over his care, ordering maid servants about until they were exhausted. Etgur came in from his post, offering words of encouragement to Rose, who refused to leave Shasp's side, and tried to convince her to eat.

At the end of the fourth day, in the dark hours, Shasp started up out of a nightmare, barely capable of raising himself to his elbows. Sweat coursed down his face as he cast about the room and found Rose asleep in a chair at the side of his cot.

"Rose," he coughed, "Rose, wake up girl."

She quickly came to and took his burning hand, "I'm here......what can....are you...?"

"Rose, get Etgur...quickly," his voice barely more than a dry whisper.

Rose darted out of the room then returned, dragging Etgur by the arm, a look of alarm on his face. Shasp fell back against his pillow and weakly motioned for the youth to come nearer. Etgur knelt beside his bed leaning close so he could hear him.

"Rose...go outside.....please."

A hurt look crossed her face as she stepped out of the tiny chamber. Etgur watched her leave over his shoulder.

"Etgur, listen to me . . . I have seen the shadow of death in my dreams. It waits just beyond my sleep . . . and I fear the next time I close my eyes will be my last."

Etgur stared into his feverish eyes in rapt attention.

"Rose is not mad, Etgur. Her story is true. I have seen the cave of which she has ranted and met the dark force that lurks there in lightless anticipation. It wants her though I don't know why, but I may not live to see her away from this place. I called you here because I have seen the way you stare at her. Am I wrong to think you love her?"

Etgur shook his head, "No. . . you are not wrong."

"Good.   Then you, and only you, must know, because I fear there is some human alliance with this demon. The cave had braziers and chalked runes; some witch or warlock may be masquerading among Blaquet's servants. You have to get Rose away from here, Etgur, or she will face a fate worse than death. There is money in my saddle bags and weapons. Take my horse from the stable. You are her guard sometimes and they would not suspect you. You must take her and ride hard from here as fast and as far as you can go. . . . do you hear me? Fast and far." His voice tapered off and his head lolled as he began staring blankly at the ceiling.   "Send Rose . . . before I lose the will to live."

Etgur nodded and left through the door with Rose returning in his wake. She sunk down next to Shasp and gathered his hand again. Tears streamed in rivulets down her soft cheeks and dripped from her chin. Shasp clenched her hand tightly but continued to stare at the ceiling like a blind man.

"Rose, you must stay with Etgur...he will.....see you away from this evil place. I'm sorry it couldn't be me. Sorry I had to leave you this way." He pulled the stone from around his neck and pressed it into her delicate hand. "Wear this always. Don't let anyone know . . . you have it."

Rose broke down and threw herself over him sobbing uncontrollably. "No!...Noooo! You can't die! Do you hear me? You can't die!" Then softly, "Please...Please don't."

"You have to be stronger . . . now. Fight for . . . yourself." He exhaled a long breath and relaxed under her.

Rose clasped her hands to each side of his face and stared into his unseeing eyes, tears raining on his bloodless face. "You can't go...You can't . . . I love you . . . please." She wailed bitterly. The unseen illness accomplished what scores of warriors could not. Shasp Ironwrought lay cold and rigid in death.

The long train of sad mourners trudged through crusted snow in the cheerless, pale morning light of an overcast sky. Upon the bent shoulders of six men was a wooden platform bearing a body wrapped in strips of linen and twined with cord. They proceeded through the snow-caked woods to a small clearing where they ended their journey before a series of stone cairns. The men, Navun among them, laid the platform on the ground and began hacking at the frozen earth with digging implements brought along by others. After much effort, Navun rested on his pick alongside a depression while the other men lifted Shasp from the plank and lowered him into the shallow grave. They placed the plank over him and piled large rocks on top to keep any mountain scavengers from desecrating his remains. Blaquet stood at the foot of his cairn and spoke several artful words in epitaph. Slowly, the crowd filed by one at a time, tossing handfuls of dirt onto the stones until only Blaquet, Etgur, Rose and Navun were left.

Navun stepped away a few yards and called Etgur over, "I'm relieving you from watching Rose. She was taken with Shasp, and that seemed to calm her but now? I think she is going to be a handful, and I'm not certain you are ready. I'm putting Balam on her watch."

Etgur began to protest but Blaquet's voice arrived before his.

"I do not think that is necessary, Captain Navun.   The boy is energetic and intelligent. Why remove him?"

Navun, surprised by her acute hearing, gave her a grave expression. "Because I'm not sure the boy's head is in the right place. A young man of his age might be persuaded against his better judgment if..." he stammered, "am I captain or not? Since when do you care who is on watch?"

"Careful, Captain," she said with a hint of menace.   "You are in charge but I think that Etgur is near Rose's age and, perhaps, understands her pain. It will be good for her to have someone to talk with who isn't a half drunk, beaten up old warrior. Etgur will continue to guard Rose," she said then turned away and started back through the woods.

Navun glared after her for a long moment before turning a withering stare on Etgur.

"You better not screw up boy or I'll have your ass."

"I won't," he replied defensively.

They walked back to where Rose stood like a forlorn statue in a garden, staring down at the cairn. After waiting in uncomfortable silence, Navun became restless.

"I know one these graves holds Goshun who Shasp slew on the trail, but who is that large one there on the end?"

Etgur looked around the big man, inspecting the cairn he had indicated. "That is Otess, the man you were hired to replace; our last Captain."

Navun raised his eyebrows slightly, "How'd he end up here? Natu drop him on his head?"

"No, he was older than you, though not much. He got drunk one night last winter during a blizzard and insisted that he was going out to hunt, or some crazy thing. Several of us tried to stop him but he was headstrong. I went out with him, thinking he would never find his way back in his condition, but I lost him in the storm. I searched for him until I realized it was hopeless then found shelter under a fallen tree. I nearly froze to death that night. The next day I stumbled into the keep hoping that Captain Otess had found his way back, but he had not returned. A search party found him later that day, near the back of this peak, frozen solid. He was a good man.   Always fair to me."

Navun nodded, "Makes me think maybe I should ease up on

the wine a little."

They lingered, struggling with the loss of the man they had just buried, then silently made their way back to Kulan.

Chapter 8

Before the sun had set on the evening of Shasp's burial, a watchman cried out from the north tower. "Riders coming; a contingent bearing the royal colors!" Word traveled quickly through the keep.

Blaquet, dressed in a swirling forest green velvet gown, glided out through the great portal to the granite steps. Tingling with anticipation, she signaled the gate keepers to raise the portcullis.

As soon as the gate clattered up and out of the way, a mass of horseflesh and riders appeared, pouring through the gap between the towers. Spouting frozen breath, they clopped in row after orderly row. Navun counted fifty.

In the lead was a short, plump man dressed in foppish regalia. Beneath his perfectly trimmed black beard rested a pale round face, almost sickly in appearance, yet with a fixed expression of condescension. His head was capped by a floppy, wide-brimmed hat of black and yellow, and he wore bloused pants of purple linen. A padded black jacket, embroidered with gold thread, finished his costume. The soldiers that followed him were adorned in polished steel caps sporting red horsehair plumes. Each was equipped with the standard issue cuirass and long sword of the Arriginian army, polished to a shining finish. Beneath the armor, they wore the black wool tunics and leggings of the king's royal guard.

The fat little man dropped off his horse, landing amazingly cat-like on his toes, while motioning for his senior officer. "Major Larrick, take charge of the men," he said with a falsetto. The Major's echoed command rang out behind him.

Blaquet waited with the appearance of an anxious servant as the aristocrat waddled toward her. She rushed forward, bowing low before the stunted aristocrat, then took his hand and led him inside, "Welcome Count Durquist!"

Navun, who had no stomach for such high bred people, addressed the senior officer of the royal contingent. "I'll show you where to lodge and fodder your horses then we can make arrangements for your men," he extended his hand, "I'm Captain Navun."

The senior officer looked at his hand as if it were leprous, "I'll find my own way around. Oh, by the way, my men are not to mix with yours nor are their horses, do I make myself clear, Captain Navun? I don't need them picking up any nasty habits or parasites either, for that matter."

Navun retracted his hand and studied the officer for a moment. The surly Captain of Kulan pondered what the repercussions might be for breaking the snob's feminine nose. After a few tense moments, he decided against it. "That suits me just fine. I wouldn't want any of my men picking up any bad habits either; like, suddenly walking around here like they had a corn cobs up their asses."

The officer sneered, grunted something inaudible, and spun on his heel. Navun glowered after him for a while before he realized his fists were clenched. He let his taut muscles relax and yelled for one of his men to call formation.

Count Kaerlo Durquist plopped down on a padded chair before the blazing hearth and was removing his gloves and hat when Blaquet offered him a goblet of hot spiced wine. He rubbed his bald head with his left hand and acccepted the warm, ruby liquid with his right. He gulped the wine, enjoying its warmth as it pervaded his stomach.

"To what do I owe this honored visit Count Durquist?" Blaquet asked knowing the reason full well.

"Do you remember that little business we discussed long ago, concerning your ascension at court? Well, it seems it was overheard by someone with large ears. By the time it was relayed to the king, via the queen of course, it had taken on a conspiratorial tone."

Blaquet paled, "And how did the king respond to this accusation?"

Durquist winced a little, "Not well, I'm afraid but not as bad as he could have."

Her eyes filled with worry, "What does that mean?"

"You have been away for some time now, Blaquet and the king is getting old. He has no stomach for intrigue anymore, though it used to be great sport for him. Now he spends his days delegating his authority and chasing young skirts about the castle the way a farmer chases chickens for the evening meal. I'm afraid there will be no return for you. I am sorry."

Blaquet looked away, scowling in thought as she chewed on

66

her thumbnail. Durquist read her anxiety easily and smiled with understanding.

"There is some good news, Blaquet.

Her head snapped up, "What news?"

"When word leaked out about our little plan, the queen called for me. In exchange for my name being discreetly omitted, not to mention my head, I was to ride here and inform you that the queen would no longer seek your early demise if you gave your word to retire here for the rest of your days and cease meddling in court affairs. I highly suggest that you accept her generous offer."

"Is that why you came with so many men? In case I refused?"

Kaerlo averted his eyes and did not reply.

Blaquet pretended to brighten then straightened her back, "Well Count Durquist, I know when I am beaten. You can tell the queen that I humbly accept her offer of leniency. In the meantime we shall make the most of your stay. I think you will find the hospitality of my home will rival anything the queen has to offer and more." She politely excused herself and retired to her chambers with the ever present Natu.

Durquist's eyes followed her sweeping figure up the stairs until she disappeared through her doorway. "I hope so," he murmured under his breath.

As soon as the heavy hardwood door boomed shut, Blaquet exploded in a tirade, flinging every item within reach. "That bitch! All my work, undone! I can no longer show myself within a hundred miles of his majesty's royal, wrinkled ass! I may as well be dead!" Slowly her rage ebbed and she stood in the middle of the room, panting in spent fury. "I'll get even with that rotting old whore if it's my last act in this world. I just have to move my plan ahead earlier than anticipated. Rose will need to attend Count Kaerlo Durquist back to Arrigin's capital…soon."

By evening, Blaquet had regained her composure and ordered an enormous feast. Music rebounded from the granite walls of Kulan, mingling with the raucous voices of crowded revelers.

Even though Major Larrick refused to let his men mingle with Navun's, he did not refuse them the merriment or mixing with the women of the house. This vexed many of Navun's men, for more than a few of the fickle vixens found their way to the tables and laps of

67

more comely men in uniform.

Kaerlo finished his last morsel of veal, wiped his greasy little hands on a silk napkin and leaned back in his stuffed chair. He was enjoying the fullness of his stomach and the numbing effects of the wine as he listened to Blaquet's minstrel. The man was good but not the best he'd heard. "He's very good," he said to her as he cradled his goblet between entwined fingers.

"Yes he is. I was very fortunate to find him, but he is not the sweetest voice in Kulan," replied Blaquet with a secret smile.

"Oh?"

Blaquet's eyes glittered as she bade Natu to fetch Rose. Moments later, Rose appeared with Etgur dutifully at her side.

"Yes my lady," Rose said coldly.

"Rose, will you sing for Count Durquist? I've boasted that you are unmatched in voice."

"If it pleases the Count . . . but I am not in a singing mood today . . . as you know."

"Well, sing a dirge then."

Rose nodded then stepped up onto the hearth where she immediately became the center of attention. A cheer went up, when they saw it was Rose who was going to sing, but the bard stood at the edge of the hearth and screamed above the din for quiet and a descending silence followed. The minstrel gently dragged his long fingers over the strings of his lute, evoking a soft, lilting tune. Rose closed her eyes and slowly her clear gentle voice began weaving a melancholy series of notes. All eyes were fixed on her, remembering the infatuation of a young woman with a recently passed warrior, and it intensified the songs spell. Her singing echoed through the hall, a reflection of her pain which she easily conveyed to her entranced audience. By the end of the last wavering note many a hardened veteran was wiping away tears from stained cheeks. After a long pause, the hall erupted in applause and Rose returned to Blaquet's table.

"Is there anything else my lady?"

"No, Rose, thank you, you may go."

Kaerlo was awestricken, "Never have I heard such a voice or seen such unmatched beauty!" he blurted, "Who is she?"

"My ward, though I feel her talents will go to waste here among these ruffians. I promised to bring her to court and introduce

68

her, but alas. If only I could have taken her to the capital, to Alem, where she could have married properly and lived a better life more fitting her caste. I am afraid my intrigues have condemned her as well as myself."

Blaquet had created the noose and it took the predictable Count only scant seconds to put his neck in it.

"Lady Blaquet, I would be willing to afford her a place on my estate and introduce her to proper society."

"Oh . . . no, I'm afraid I couldn't burden you with that. It is my problem."

"I insist. Also I could send you regular word of her progress."

Blaquet acted overwhelmed by Kaerlo's offer, "I don't know what to say, sir. You are too generous."

He made a dismissive gesture, "It would be my gain to be certain."

Blaquet had no illusions about Durquist's intentions. He had always been lecherous, in fact, she had counted on it.

After Blaquet dismissed her, Rose tried to appear dignified as she left the hall but once she reached her room, flung herself onto the bed, weeping. It was bad enough, losing someone she loved, but to be forced to perform when her heart was broken was unbearable. There came a gentle rap on her door followed by the sound of groaning hinges. Etgur opened it just wide enough to allow himself to enter, balancing a full, steaming goblet on a platter.

"I could tell you were distressed and I'm sorry about all that's happened. I thought you could use some spiced wine to calm your nerves and help you rest. You are going to need it if we are to escape this place."

Rose looked at him uncomprehending, "What do you mean?"

"I promised Shasp I would get you out of here. I have hidden some provisions and I'll get us some horses. If we leave in the early evening hours while everyone is distracted we can keep a day and a half lead and then take a ship from the coast anywhere you want to go. Here," he handed her the goblet.

Rose looked into the shimmering red liquid, inhaling its tangy aroma. Her smile was barely perceptible but Etgur saw it. "Drink up."

Slowly, she gulped the warm wine to half a goblet and

69

continued to sip on it while Etgur elaborated on his plans. Rose felt the heady effects within minutes and sat the empty cup on her night table. A few moments more and the wine's effect intensified until the room was spinning. She tried to say something, but her words were only slurred gibberish. Etgur rose up from his chair and helped her to lie down.

"Rose, are you all right? You must have drunk it too quickly. Sleep it off and I'll see you in the morning."

Despite her attempt to resist the effects, blackness swallowed her and she was left to wrestle with her recurring nightmare.

Chapter 9

Rose awoke in impenetrable darkness, lying on a cold, wet, stone floor, littered with rotting straw. Musty air invaded her pounding senses. Groaning, she rolled onto her side, and then groped in the darkness, trying to reconstruct the events of the prior night, to separate her tortured dreams from reality. She felt her way across the slimy floor then up a rough, uneven wall. Whimpering mutely, she worked her way right, seeking a doorway, but instead of wood or iron, her hands found warm flesh. A body lurched in the blackness, and chains rattled fiercely against stone. Screaming, she back peddled and slammed into the wall behind her, striking her head. Sparks shot through her vision followed by a hammering pain. She lay crying, broken, and at the end of her sanity. "Please don't hurt me!" she sobbed, "Please!"

The chains ceased their clamor and a long silence followed, then a dry, gravelly voice addressed her.

"Who are you . . . how did you get here?"

"I don't know where I am," she whined. "I fell asleep in my room and woke up here. . . . where am I?"

"I wish I could tell you, but I don't know either. At first, I thought it was hell, but no one has come to torment me yet. Like you, I awoke here, dying from thirst."

Rose sobbed spastically, "I can't take any more of this. I just want to go home! To be rid of this nightmare!"

A long silence ensued before the strange voice sounded again, this time with a note of surprise. "Rose...Rose is that you?"

Rose stopped her fitful crying and sniffed back tears. "Yes, it's me. Who are you? How do you know me? Are you from the Keep?"

"It's me...Shasp."

She hesitated, her mind swimming in pain and residual intoxication, but then anger swelled in her. "Do not mock me! Shasp is dead. I saw him buried! Is it not enough that I am in this place that you must torment me as well?"

"Damn it girl! It *is* me!"

She concentrated on the voice, sensing a familiar tone. Her heart pounded with possibilities, and she scrambled to her bare feet.

With her arms reaching out in front of her, she stumbled toward the opposite wall then stopped when she touched the naked chest of the chained man.

"It's me Rose. The last thing I remember was telling Etgur to take care of you and for you to be strong."

She gasped, stunned, her mind spinning with revelation then threw her arms around his neck and kissed the cracked lips of Shasp Ironwrought. The stubble on his face scratched her cheek as she embraced him. "How can this be? How can you be alive? We carried your body to the meadow, buried you in a cairn."

"I don't know for certain, but I have a theory," he choked.

While Rose clung to him in her relief, a dim glow appeared through the bars of the grated door, unseen until that moment. They waited helplessly in silence while the glow expanded, and with it came footfalls, increasing in volume. Shadows moved under the door and through the grating while the sound of a key turning a heavy lock echoed in the chamber. The door swung wide on complaining hinges, and golden lamplight flooded the cell. Blaquet and Natu entered, while a third figure lingered outside the portal. Blaquet gave a wry look to Rose who buried her face in Shasp's shoulder. Shasp glared back with deadly intent burning in his grey eyes. Blaquet gestured to Natu who ripped the screaming Rose from the chained prisoner and dragged her, cursing and kicking, into the hall.

Smiling absently, Blaquet set the lantern on the floor, "Close the door for a while. I have business with Sir Ironwrought."

The door clanged shut and Blaquet, wearing a wispy red shift which revealed bare shoulders and legs, sauntered to where Shasp hung, his feet barely touching the ground, and pushed her body against his. As she brought her lips close to his, Shasp could smell wine and the odor of opium smoke. Blaquet regarded him with red, dazed eyes then rubbed the side of her face, cat-like, against his neck.

"What do you want with me? Why am I still alive?"

"It's a long story," she purred and wrapped her arms around his neck, beginning to nibble on his ear. It was then that Shasp saw her silver earing, a hoop, dangling only an inch from his nose. To anyone one else, the item may have had no significance, but to him it was freedom.

72

Mike Mino

"Have you kept me for your pleasure, is that it?   Well, you
didn't need to chain me to a wall for that."

His mind churned away like slaves at the oars, and he
reasoned that, if Blaquet had drunk enough wine and smoked enough
opium, her senses would be numb. He nibbled back on her ear then
locked on the earing with his teeth and yanked it free, quickly hiding it
in his cheek. Blaquet pulled back, thinking it no more than an
overanxious love bite.

"Take me out of these chains so you and I can... talk this out."

She stumbled back a couple paces, "I don't think so, lover; too much to do."

"At least tell me what's going on around here, why I'm chained to this wall."

"You are there because you know too much. You see, I know you have met my friend, the being that dwells within the cavern; it told me so. Its name is 'Darok', and he has existed here since before the cataclysms that wiped away the ancients. I guess by now you've figured out that Rose is not just suffering from random nightmares after all."

Shasp thought about lashing out with his foot and knocking Kulan's mistress unconscious, but knew it would do little good with Natu and the other man just outside. "Rose said she saw me buried . . . that I was dead."

"You were but you did not succumb to a sickness as everyone thought, but rather a clever little toxin of mine, carefully mixed with a paralytic from dried puffer fish. Fortunately for you, I got the dose just right. After the burial, I had Natu retrieve you before you froze to death."

"What do you intend to do with Rose?" he asked.

Blaquet went to the door, opened it, and Etgur stepped into the light. Shasp growled deep in his throat, "You traitor!"

Etgur smiled, not the easy, boyish smile of a young man, but an evil, sinister grin, "Easy, Shasp, I wouldn't want you to damage yourself straining against those shackles. I suppose you have a lot of questions." He sighed, "I only get to tell this story once every twenty or thirty years, so I hope you can appreciate how few have heard it. I guess, in that sense, you can consider yourself privileged. Have you ever had a secret that was so fantastic, you wanted to tell the whole world but couldn't? I have a secret like that; an incredible one," he laughed lightly. "You may not believe it, but Blaquet and I are almost as old as Kulan itself."Our story begins many centuries ago with two young lovers," he looked fondly at Blaquet. "We lived in this very range of mountains, for you see, my story not only begins here, it continues here. We were not beautiful people, my lover and I, but rough children of a harsh country. On a warm summer day, we slipped away from our village to be alone and climbed the rocks of this peak," he paused, savoring the memory. "We found a cave and, being curious, explored it, completely unaware of the horror that lurked within. Darok nearly finished us that day and with our last breath we

74

begged for our lives and struck a dark bargain. It could have killed us then and waited another half a millennium for another victim, but instead we exchanged our lives for the lives of others, that was what it wanted, what it feasted on. For many centuries it had been imprisoned by the light, for he cannot even enter into moonlight, only firelight. We became intrigued by the entity, it shared the secrets of other worlds with us, and we discovered its ability to transfer life force from one vessel to another. Our first victims were two travelers, a young man and his wife. We lured them here and, as payment for our service, it placed us into the bodies of our unsuspecting prey before devouring them.

"We left our village and traveled the world, returning here every score years or so with our new forms carefully chosen. It's an amazing thing to always be young, to never grow old or be the same person. We take their names and assume their places in this world, like Blaquet here," he gave her a fond glance as she ran her hands down her body, "she was about eighteen winters when we found her."

Blaquet eased forward, "It's about time to shed this skin for a new one."

"Rose," grated Shasp through clenched teeth.

Blaquet's eyes sparkled with anticipation, "Yes, Rose. Soon, I will be in her body and on my way back to court under the protection of Count Durquist. With Rose's beauty, I'll seduce whoever is next in line for the throne."

"That's right," said Etgur smugly, "and you were wondering why you were still alive. I thought this body of Etgur's would suit me after being stuck as that aging Otess, you know, the old captain of the guard. In truth, I took the boy Etgur out on a hunt in the middle of a blizzard. He would have followed me anywhere. I led him like a goat to the slaughter and left that old shell frozen in a snow bank. It was difficult to call Darok off his meal before he reduced the body to bones. After hundreds of years, one becomes very good at playing the part. But lately, I've been thinking of all the training and work it will take to get this young body conditioned for combat, then suddenly it occurred to me; you have already done the work for me. Besides, Blaquet likes your body better than this one. Sorry."

They turned to leave and Etgur called back over his shoulder, "Don't worry, you won't be lonely for long. I'll send Natu back for you as soon as we are done with Rose."

"Bastard!" spat Shasp.

The door slammed shut, leaving Shasp alone to listen to Rose's receding screams.

Blistering anger seethed through his body like magma, and he grasped the chain with his right hand, pulling himself up enough to spit the silver earing into his palm. Frantically, he worked the heavy silver wire in his fingers until he bent it into an L-shaped configuration. He pulled himself up again, this time with both hands. Shifting his grip, he placed both chains into his left fist, leaving enough slack for his right to work the lock of his left manacle with the bent earing. After the shifting of stubborn tumblers, the lock snapped open. The right-hand was twice as easy.

He could not wait for Natu's return; by then, Rose would become food for the nether world demon. To his utter amazement, he found the cell door unlocked, and exhilaration surged through him. In their haste, with the certainty of large chains binding him, they hadn't bothered to lock the cell. I occurred to him that the cell he was in and hall outside had been hacked out by men and must adjoin the natural cavern somewhere. How else would Blaquet and Etgur come and go at their leisure?

In naught but his loin cloth, Shasp padded down the damp and lightless passageway, silently hoping Rose was still wearing the stone talisman. Perhaps it would buy her precious time. Running recklessly through the darkened labyrinth of tunnels, he occasionally careened into a wall. Periodically, he paused, ears straining for the slightest noise and eventually caught the faint sound of Rose's hysterical sobbing mixed with conversation. Moving stealthily, he eased around a corner until he perceived a faint glow emanating from the distance. Shasp knew Etgur and Natu would both be armed and lamented the absence of his weapons, but at least he had the element of surprise, and that was better than nothing. With his back to the tunnel wall, he edged toward the entrance until he could see the group and recognized the cavern as the same he had been in before, Darok's lair.Rose lay curled up on the floor while, beside her, Blaquet spoke in a forgotten tongue, and chalked symbols on the smooth obsidian dais. Natu poured coal into the faltering fires of the braziers, while Etgur paced impatiently, arms folded across his chest. The brass bowls erupted in flames as Natu stirred them with a long iron poker then laid the implement aside. Shasp fixed on the poker; he had just found his weapon. Darting from the entrance and into the shadows, he moved toward the opposite side of the braziers. Fortunately, Blaquet's theatrics had distracted Natu and Etgur, making it easy for Shasp to slip behind them. Just when he thought the light would reveal his position, he paused, waiting for the perfect moment to lunge from the darkness and snatch the iron rod from the floor. When both men were looking away, he shot from the shadows like a hawk striking for a mouse, and with terrible swiftness, scooped up the poker, and closed the gap between Natu and himself. The giant had scarcely begun to turn at the sound of padded feet, when Shasp whipped the rod across the side of Natu's head. Following the sound of cutting air and cracking bone, Natu spun on nerveless legs, arms dangling loosely at his side, then crumpled, blood leaking from his ear. The attack happened so fast, Etgur barely had time to yank his sword free and deflect a chopping blow that surely would have crushed his skull.

Shasp yelled at Rose, who still lay on the ground frozen with fear, "Get out of here!"

Rose shook off her stupor, clambered to her feet and fled for the labyrinth passage. Blaquet shot after her with a fleetness that belied her femininity and pulled the struggling girl to the ground where they clawed and bit like badgers in a sack.

Immediately, Shasp realized Etgur's skill with a blade as the pretender deftly turned aside every slash and thrust. Shasp fought furiously to work his way past Etgur's guard with the clumsy length of iron but to no avail, then Darok came. The howling wind, accruing from the untold depths of the mountain, rushed toward them, and Shasp, knowing the sound all too well, disengaged from Etgur and ran to help Rose.

Etgur only smiled and sheathed his blade, "There's nowhere for you to run Shasp; Darok will sniff you out. I only hope he doesn't kill you yet, because I have plans for your body."

When Shasp reached the embattled women, he seized Blaquet by her hair and flung her away like a rag doll, provoking a most un-lady-like curse. He jerked Rose onto her wobbling legs and she bolted for the passage they had come in by, so Shasp grabbed her arm, spinning her about. "Not that way!" He ran, dragging her behind him across the enormous cavern to the far wall, scarcely visible from the eerie light of the braziers, and shoved her into a tiny opening. She hesitated at the small black tunnel.

77

"Get going, dammit!" He bellowed in frustration.

Spurred by Shasp's anger, Rose dove into the tunnel and began wriggling her way down it while Shasp scampered after her, cursing a storm. They crawled out of the narrow stretch of tunnel and into the next expanse, but as they shuffled along, Darok overtook them. Cosmic air flooded the cramped space, howling like a trapped wolf, filling their ears with shrieking wind. Immediately, Shasp's body went rigid with bone-biting cold, and he shoved Rose toward the opening, praying it was daylight outside.

Mike Mino

78

Nearly mindless with fear, Rose screamed and fled in panic. Shasp cried out through frozen lips, "Don't run, there's a cliff!" but Rose was beyond hearing. He could feel Darok sucking the life out of him as freezing tendrils penetrated his body, draining his will to live. With brows knotted in grim determination, he placed one unsteady foot in front of the other, driving himself forward. He focused on Rose's fleeing form, silhouetted against the bright entrance, and collapsed in a pool of cold winter light. For a second time, the shadow was driven back by mellow sunlight, deprived of its prey. Shrieking furiously, it spun and boiled just within the shadows of the tunnel. Shasp, with his last ounce of strength, inched forward on his stomach to the edge of the rock shelf overlooking the sheer drop.

Rose had barely stopped at the edge of the cliff and teetered, arms pin-wheeling, then threw herself backward. In her haste, she had nearly plummeted to her death, and now stood, rigid, wide-eyed and gasping with her back to the rough wall.

Shasp clawed his way up the wall, his face ashen, and seized Rose by the front of her bodice. With a wrench, he ripped open the front of her dress, leaving her perfect breasts exposed to the chill elements and gripped the dangling sigil stone. While Rose went from one shock to another, Shasp squeezed the stone until its warmth flooded through his torpid limbs.

"Wha....what are you doing!" she gasped.

"Trying to warm up," he replied through chattering teeth."

Chapter 10

Shasp climbed down the long, treacherous crack with Rose clinging to his back like a tattoo, her eyes clenched shut. By the time both were safely off the rock face, Rose was shaking from anxiety and Shasp was rubbing his strained shoulders. He stood barefoot in knee deep snow, the wind cooling his nearly naked body, and eyed Rose's torn dress. "Aren't we a pair? We better find some shelter, and then I need to find Navun and tell him what's been going on. When the men find out, we'll hang those demons from Kulan's walls."

The events of the last few days had nearly broken Rose, and now she was teetering on the brink of hysteria, "What makes you think they will believe you any more than they did me!"

Shasp took her hand, "When someone comes back from the dead, people usually listen."

"The men on the towers might just fill you with arrows for a demon yourself, especially if Blaquet tells them to!"

Shasp considered the possibility, "Maybe you're right. I could hide you in the woods then climb the rocks where the mountain meets the wall. If I can sneak in and locate Navun, maybe he'll be willing to help us."

Rose took a breath and calmed down, "Navun? What makes you think he's not involved in all this? You thought Etgur was reliable, that didn't work out so well."

Shasp winced at the remark, "I don't think we have a choice. We might die out here with no clothes, weapons or equipment. Navun is our best hope."

Shasp led her down the slope away from Kulan's peak and found shelter in the broken cleft of an outcropping. He broke off the dry limbs from the lower boughs of a pine tree and collected shreds of dry moss. Vigorously, he rubbed two sticks together with his numbed fingers until he created some small embers. Slowly, they became a tiny flame, and then a busy fire and Rose gathered more wood and piled it up. As Shasp's body warmed against the fire, he charred the end of a straight, heavy stick in the flames, alternately rubbing it against a rough granite boulder, until he made a short spear. When darkness fell, Shasp stood, stretched his legs and picked up his improvised weapon. "Stay here and keep the fire small. If they are looking for us we don't need to help them by sending smoke signals. When I come back, I'll have horses and supplies, even if I have to kill Navun and everyone in Kulan."

Rose knew too well, that if Shasp did not return, she would either be re-captured or die in the woods. She decided dying in the woods would be better. "I'll be here. Where else would I go?" She stood and embraced him with a strength that told Shasp she didn't expect to see him again. He lifted her chin, kissed her gently, and started down the hill. With only a loin cloth to gird him and a wooden spear in hand, he was the picture of savage glory. Rose marveled at his courage and watched him striding away through the snow until he disappeared.

Shasp skulked along the base of the peak, working his way over snow-caked boulders and jutting formations until he reached Kulan's looming north wall. Guards paced diligently overhead as Shasp carefully inspected the adjoining rock from within the shadows. Under crescent moonlight, he turned his breach cloth into a sling for the spear, for it would be impossible to otherwise climb with it, and leaving it behind would leave him defenseless if he was caught. Naked, he scaled the frozen rock, silent as falling snow, until he reached the top of the wall. Moving with the grace of a serpent, he eased over the battlement, never taking his eyes off the unsuspecting guard then paused in the shadows to catch his breath. Once his arms were rested, he worked his way along the battlements and down into the courtyard. The stinging cold was numbing his extremities, and, as much as he was tired of being frozen, he was grateful for the frigid weather which kept the sentries close to their fires. Shasp was also thankful that Navun's quarters were not in the main hall. The Captain preferred the privacy of the outbuildings constructed along the inside of the wall, because it kept him closer to the men on watch.

Laughter and the chiding voices of women echoed from inside Kulan, drifting through the chill night air. No doubt, Navun would be drinking himself into a stupor by now, thought Shasp. He waited for the courtyard's patrol to come to the north wall then start back before he glided along its face to the largest structure nearest the tower. When he finally came to Navun's door, he discovered that the latch was unlocked. Of course, who would dare steal from the captain of the guard? Navun certainly knew he would only need to lock down the keep, and then search everyone until he found the thief. Shasp quietly closed the door behind him and was relieved to find the coals of a neglected fire still warm in Navun's hearth. Within moments he had it roaring again, and Shasp thawed his bluish skin. The captain's quarters were moderate in size, built of rough planks and stone. The bed was neatly made and everything was in its place. Shasp mused over the room's tidiness and realized it was only fitting for a captain of the guard to meet the same standards he set for others, though it somehow seemed unlike Navun. Shasp decided he would have to wait for the captain to return and make an on-the-spot decision to take or spare Navun's life. In the meantime, clothing was his priority. As the orange light of the fire flickered across his naked skin, Shasp began a cursory inspection of the room, and his eyes quickly came to rest on a stack of crates in the corner. Curiosity peaked as he opened the top crate and was stunned to see a light, gold-colored helmet with a slit visor and onyx horns, staring back at him. A mixture of elation and bewilderment filled him. "What the hell are you doing here?" he said to the object as he lifted it from the box. Underneath, lay his chain mail, black-lacquered cuirass, cloak, clothes and hard leather knee-high riding boots. The crate was not long enough to hold his sword, but within seconds of scanning the room he located the katana on a high shelf. Fingers moved deftly over familiar buckles and straps, and Shasp was fully armored in minutes. The feel of his armor against his body gave him a sense of completeness, a feeling he had been without for too long. He caressed the black steel of the bracers with appreciation then settled into a chair behind the door and helped himself to Navun's food and wine.

It was a few hours before the red-haired captain wrestled with the door and staggered in. He closed the door and turned to stare into the angry, gray eyes of a ghost; a specter who held a very sharp point to his throat.

"I must have passed out between the hall and my room," Navun said, sounding disappointed, "because this is certainly an unpleasant dream. I sure hope someone finds me before I freeze to death."

"It's no dream, Captain Navun, happy to say. Perhaps you would like to enlighten me on how you came to possess my belongings," Shasp said with a coolness that made Navun shudder.

The captain's voice was hoarse with fear and wonder, "Dead men don't own anything." Navun swallowed, his Adam's apple scraping the tip of Shasp's blade, "besides, I didn't want any of these puffed up pretenders to have any of your belongings. They aren't worthy, so I figured I'd save them for someone who was. Now maybe you can tell me why you're standing in my room, thinking about slitting my gullet instead of in the ground where I left you."

Shasp paused for a long, uncomfortable time before slowly lowering the Tanto point from Navun's sweating throat. A look of relief passed over the captain's face as he dropped onto his bed.

Shasp sheathed his blade, poured two cups of wine then handed one to Navun. He pulled up a chair, faced the bewildered man who sat in rapt, albeit impaired, attention and relayed the events of the last several days. Navun leaned back at the end of the tale, stroking his beard thoughtfully. "And Rose is in the forest as we speak?"

"That's right, she's waiting for me."

"We are in a delicate and dangerous situation. Since you've been dead, Count Durquist has arrived from Alem with fifty royal guards, and he is friendly with Blaquet.   Then there are the men. I don't know how many will be loyal to me and, in case you didn't notice, she throws a hell of a party and pays pretty good too. Perhaps it would be better to get Rose and ride the hell out of here."

Shasp shook his head, "We can't do that. If we don't stop them, they will continue to feed their unwitting victims to that demon, perhaps for centuries to come.   I can't live with that on my conscience. No, we have to stop them."

Navun stood, grabbed his cloak and whipped it about his shoulders. "It's a deadly gamble, but I'll be a son of a bitch if I'm gonna let some court dandy and his concubine from hell make an ass of me. Come on."

Shasp pulled on his helmet then drew his cloak over it, concealing it in the shadow of the hood. They walked briskly to the stable and quickly saddled two horses.   Shasp's black charger nudged him affectionately as he snorted

"Did you miss me, Grimm?"

As they left the stable, Shasp's eyes darted back and forth, half expecting an alarm to be given, then they led the horses across the courtyard to the gate where Navun ordered it raised.   Shasp mounted then paused astride Grimm, while holding the reins of the other mount. "If you betray me, Navun, I *will* kill you."

"Well...I wouldn't want that, now, would I?   Go get Rose.

Keep her face hidden. I'll relieve the sentry here and raise the gate myself when you return. We can hide her in my quarters until we can figure out what to do. Now go on, we don't have all damn night."

Shasp pulled the mare around and trotted out onto the approach where the night quickly swallowed him, leaving Navun alone to work out his plan. An hour later, Shasp returned with Rose and approached the gate but were not hailed from the wall. Shasp cast about for Navun, but the courtyard beyond the portcullis appeared empty. He unhitched the sword at his shoulder, ready for the worst, but then the gate clattered up as the loadstones and counterbalances groaned against one another.

Mike Mino

Cautiously, they plodded forward, stopping at Navun's door, and waited for the portcullis to rattle down behind them. Shasp dismounted and helped Rose from her horse before opening the door to Navun's quarters. Rose immediately moved through the threshold toward the hearth where she held out her palms to the licking flames.

Navun appeared a moment later, "The guards are posting again. Couldn't leave them go for too long, or someone might get suspicious. I've been thinking since you left, and I think I might know a way to get through this."

The three schemed into the night, sleeping only a few hours before daybreak.

Chapter 11

Snow fell heavy on the keep in the hours just before dawn, a thick, slippery layer of powder, accumulating minute by minute. Navun stepped out into the dancing flakes, his hair and beard gradually turning white, and called for a formation with full dress battle gear. His men scrambled for their equipment, exchanging complaints about a day of combat drill in the snow. Slowly, the formation materialized, facing the keep until the ranks were full. Navun stood quietly at the head of the group, counting heads, and then gave the command to rest. Two cloaked figures emerged from the falling flakes and stood by the Captain. Simultaneously, they lifted their heads and threw back the hoods. Shasp and Rose stood in the swirling snow, facing the gathered warriors against a loud collective gasp followed by muttering that ran through the massed men like fire through dry grass.

"What necromancy is this Navun!" cried someone from the ranks.

"Dark magic indeed!" yelled Navun, "but Shasp does not live and breathe before us because of necromancy! He was drugged and buried alive!"

Confused babbling coursed through the men, and Shasp stepped forward.

"Navun speaks true and the reason for this treachery is more evil than you can imagine. For months you have thought this young woman mad for her ravings of nightmares! I also doubted her sanity until I encountered the demon from her dreams!"

Again came the loud chatter of excited voices. Shasp shouted over the din, "It was Blaquet who drugged me to the point of death; even put me in the ground under your very noses, but the rest of the story will freeze your blood! I was investigating Rose's claim when I happened upon a creature of shadows, a soul eater! Blaquet discovered I was about to reveal her alliance with it and poisoned me. I awoke in chains to find she was not alone in her enterprise of deviltry, but was joined by young Etgur. The soul that occupies his body is the same that possessed your former Captain Otess and who knows how many other bodies. They are in league with evil forces to rob unsuspecting victims of their very bodies and souls; the bodies, to

86

inhabit for themselves, and the souls, to feed the demon and seal their bargain!"

Someone from the crowd erupted, "Do you mean Etgur...the real Etgur...is dead?"

"Yes, food for a demon of the underworld."

Now the formation was dissolving and becoming a crowd as men fell out of ranks to form a semi-circle. Angry voices were breaking out on all sides, spewing recommendations about how to deal with this treachery. Some demanded more proof while others simply stood in quiet contemplation.

A lone watchman on the roof leaned over the edge, listening to the exchange. Balam soaked up the words as they floated upward, mulling over the prospects of sedition. Within moments, he finished his contemplation, abandoned his post, and flew down the stairs into the great hall where he found Blaquet and the count politely conversing over tea.

"Forgive me my lady," he breathed heavily, "but grave things are happening outside. Sounds like mutiny among the men, and it seems Captain Navun is in the middle of it."

Blaquet traded surprised expressions with Kaerlo, and then hurried to the entrance with the portly count on her heels. Natu, wearing a long bruise across the side of his head and neck, heaved open the doors for her. They brushed past him into the cold air just in time to hear the ranting of the mob. She pulled flying red streams of wind-blown hair out of her face.

"Captain Navun! What is this insubordination?"

As if on cue, Shasp turned his smoldering gray eyes on her and she stepped back.

"Shasp," she said with feigned shock, "You're alive! How can this be?"

Shasp's eyes narrowed into angry slits, "You know full well, witch, and now, so do your men! Your days of plotting with evil spirits are over!" and he drew his sword. Natu did the same and stepped between them.

"That is a lie," she hissed, "concocted by you and that insane wretch, who I have cared for! What did she promise you? Money? Her body? You are nothing more than a pawn to her."

Durquist was off balance from the sudden exchange, however, he was an aristocrat and the disrespect and accusations of lowly

87

peasants against one of his class infuriated him. "This is an outrage! How dare you speak to your betters with such insolence! Disband immediately, and perhaps, I will see fit only to flog your leaders!"

Shasp turned on Durquist, his rage cool and controlled, "Disband them if you like, Count, but before the sun sets, I will send that murdering bitch and her dog, Etgur straight to hell along with you and anyone else who gets between us."

Etgur had looked for the bodies of the two fugitives after Darok chased them into the tunnel, fearing they might show up, though he had hoped they would simply flee or perish in the snow. When he heard the loud voices, he sought out Major Larrick and escorted him to the front steps. Kaerlo called to the officer as soon as he appeared, "Major Larrick, assemble the men."

Larrick signaled to his second and the man took to his heels, calling his men to arms.

Blaquet saw worry sweeping across the faces in the crowd and seized the opportunity to create a further advantage. "Any who wish to reject this sedition may separate from this rabble and affirm loyalty to me with no fear of punishment."

Balam, waiting in the doorway for just such an opportunity, walked down the steps and stood beside Blaquet. "I affirm loyalty! So will you if you want to live! The Count's men are battle hardened and well armored! Will you give your lives on the word of a stranger and a mad woman?" In truth, Balam did not care if even one man stepped up. Even if all were killed, Blaquet would likely make him captain of their replacements and he smiled inwardly.

Several men made their way from the crowd to stand on the steps next to Balam, eighteen in all. The advantage had just shifted and the others knew it. Navun turned on the remaining men. "Does anyone else want to be counted among witches, warlocks and demons, or worse yet . . . aristocrats? Maybe you won't die today if you side with them, but you *will die* someday! How will you explain to your Creator why you fought alongside evil to save your life? Or, would you rather tell him how you fought against it and died, doing what was right!"

His speech became a tourniquet which stanched the flow of men from his formation. Then came the tramp of boots, increasing in volume with the approach of Durquist's men, until they created a wall of steel separating Blaquet and the Count from the vengeful forces of Kulan's Captain. Kaerlo's tenor voice rang out from behind the royal guard.

"Kill them all!"

The courtyard erupted in screaming, war cries and clanging steel as the royal guard hurled themselves upon the rebels. Amidst the sudden chaos, Navun made immediately for Major Larrick. His hatred for the self-absorbed officer had smoldered from the moment they first met, and he decided, if he was going to die in this melee, the snobby Major was going first. The two met in the middle of Kulan's steps in a crash of bucklers and long swords. Larrick's face was a sneer of disdain as he parried Navun's initial thrust, fueling the red captain's anger. Larrick swung his blade overhead in a motion meant to cleave his enemy's skull. Navun flung up his sword to stop the deadly chop but Larrick's move was a feint, and he stopped his weapon just short, spun in a circle, his sword now coming around to Navun's left. The Captain barely caught the edge on his buckler, saving himself from being hewn in two.

"Oh..., you're a tricky bastard, you are," Navun exclaimed through clenched teeth, now recognizing why Larrick was the senior officer.

They circled, churning the snow, seeking an opening, prodding one another with feints and short slashes meant to draw the other out. Navun tired of the game and came across Larrick's front with a powerful backhand slash. The royal officer blocked it with his shield, but the force caused him to stumble on the stairs, and he fell, rolling to the courtyard floor. Navun, raced down the steps after his tumbling foe. Larrick had scarcely reached bottom before he was on his feet again, shaking blood from a cut on his forehead. He smiled at Navun then made a swipe for his head. Navun ducked and returned with a thrust to Larrick's inside, but the move left Navun over extended, and Larrick dropped on the other's sword with his shield, pinning it to the ground. Navun jerked it free but not before Larrick spun and hacked into his thigh, the blade traveling to the bone. Navun roared in pain and collapsed, dropping his sword. Larrick gave a triumphant cry and stomped down on Navun's buckler, pinning the shield flat with his foot, leaving Navun's left arm trapped in the straps. Larrick reversed his hands on the pommel, point down, and set himself to drive the blade into Navun's heart. As the sword flashed down, Navun rolled to his left and Larrick's sword sliced along his back. The point sank into the hard earth and became fixed between the flagstones. Navun, in a fit of rage, wrenched his buckler from under Larrick's feet, sending the Major backwards. Battle raged about them as blood gushed from Navun's thigh, painting the snow red with clotting droplets. Navun dove for his long sword which lay on the ground, while Larrick grasped the pommel of his own and tried to release it from the frozen earth. The Major's blade came free and he turned to face his enemy, but no sooner had he come around than Navun thrust him through the chest. Larrick stood with his sword raised over his head and a look of astonishment on his face, while Navun continued to grasp the hilt of his impaling sword. Blood boiled out of Larrick's mouth as he crumpled to the ground.

Navun extracted his sword and clamped his free hand to his thigh. "Not so high and mighty now…are ya, Major?" He limped away from the struggling mass to find a binding for his leg before he was as dead as Larrick.

As soon as the Royal Guards surged forward, Shasp seized Rose by her wrist and whisked her backwards, away from the maelstrom. He flung open the door of the nearest outbuilding and shoved her inside.

"Stay there!"

She scarcely had time to protest and, as an afterthought, realized she really didn't want to.

Shasp pulled his helmet down over his head, as he immediately engaged the polished royal troops and killed the first two in as many seconds. The single-edged, katana became a hurricane of steel in his hand and the men who stood before it were swept away in a torrent of blood. His astounding efficiency of movement and precision attacks were catastrophic against Durquist's men, and Navun's men were inspired to renewed fury.

Etgur, wearing a light chain mail shirt, thigh and shin guards, had been watching the battle from the top of the steps with an expression of mild amusement bordering on apathy, until he became aware of the devastation Ironwrought was wreaking on his allies. Casually, he drew his rapier, thumbed the edge, and started down the steps with a swaggering gait.

One of Navun's men, a burly, battle tested warrior, dispatched his adversary and, looking for another, spotted Etgur walking through the carnage. He called out to two others nearby and, screaming battle cries, they rushed Etgur as one. Etgur turned to meet them without showing so much as a look of annoyance. In three strokes, all his opponents were squirming on the ground in their death throes, and Etgur resumed his walk across the bloody courtyard to where Shasp felled another cavalryman. Shasp spun and faced him, evaluating his armor and stance. Something about Etgur's nonchalant attitude and posture generated an instinctive concern. Either he was cocky to the point of being suicidal or he was good and he knew it.

Etgur smiled, "This should be quite an exercise," he said matter-of-fact.

Shasp adjusted his feet and drew the long curved knife from his waist with his left hand.

He bore no shield and neither did Etgur. Shasp rolled and snapped the Tanto tipped blade forward from his wrist and narrowly missed splitting Etgur's head in half.

Mike Mino

91

Etgur raised his eyebrows with a look of satisfaction, gave a brief nod of approval, and unleashed a barrage of slashes and back hand cuts that set Shasp back on his heels. Shasp decided not to wait in the pause that followed the first exchange.

Immediately, he returned the attack with a diagonal slash aimed at Etgur's head, reversed the direction then followed by a spin and a slash from the knife. Etgur deflected each attack with flawless expertise, then stepped back a pace before lowering his blade.

"Impressive, Sir Ironwrought, but I'm afraid I have you at a disadvantage. You see, I have been perfecting the art of swordsmanship for over five hundred years. I doubt you have had so much time to practice."

Shasp was beginning to breathe hard. The residual effects of the poison and lack of sleep were taking their toll, but he refused to show it. "Five years or five centuries, Etgur. It will take more than that to save you today."

"Well Shasp, at least you'll have the consolation of knowing that you were the best I've fought before you die. It's a shame your morals have overpowered your good sense. We could have used a good sword and would have paid well, but . . , " he shrugged and lifted his rapier again, this time taking a more serious stance. Shasp took a deep breath and focused, then, in a whirlwind of steel, the two met, blades flashing so fast the human eye could not follow. Many combatants nearby ceased fighting to gawk in awe at the two masters locked in deadly contest.

Several times Shasp was saved by his cuirass and helmet as the edge of Etgur's rapier glanced off instead of debilitating him. However, the weight of his protection was also becoming a burden and his attacks were slowing while Etgur's were fresh as ever. The two continued to exchange blinding parries and thrusts coupled with masterful feints and footwork. Though Etgur lacked the full physical strength of a mature man, his agility more than made up, and the point of his rapier was regularly finding gaps in Shasp's armor, inflicting shallow wounds, one after another. Shasp slashed at Etgur's neck but was blocked with a clang of steel. In a flash he spun the opposite direction, and aimed another cut at Etgur's thigh. Etgur brought the rapier down and blocked the attack but couldn't be in two places at once. The wicked, curved knife in Shasp's left hand whipped across Etgur's weak arm leaving a painful gash. Shasp was using the supplementary knife attacks to his advantage, and Etgur was also bleeding from several shallow cuts.

The pretender's face bore an intense expression now, his arrogance evaporating, but Shasp knew he could not keep up the pace necessary to stay alive. His mind raced furiously while batting away an artful thrust, and he came upon a risky and desperate solution. He parried three more successive thrusts and returned with a clumsy thrust, purposely exposing his strong side. Etgur dodged the strike easily and, seeing the opening, thrust his sword point through the flesh above Shasp's hip. Once the poorly executed movement had been made, Shasp had already let go of his sword. By the time Etgur's rapier had penetrated his side, Shasp had locked onto Etgur's wrist. Etgur struggled to withdraw the blade but before he realized what was happening, Shasp's left hand came around with the knife and neatly severed his carotid artery. All happened within a split second. Etgur released the rapier's hilt and stumbled back, clutching at the crimson spray which jetted from his neck, then slowly sank into the red slush. Shasp dropped to one knee and swooned.

Several of Durquist's men recognized the opportunity to dispatch the catalyst that had fired the defenders and converged on him but not before Navun, blood streaming from an impromptu bandage, and several others formed a circle around Shasp and beat them back.

Durquist's Royal Guard had dwindled to only half their original number and quickly went on the defensive. The second officer rallied his men and called a retreat to the hall but Navun, hearing the order, immediately dispatch his remaining forces to cut them off. The royal guardsmen had no choice but to fall back and fortify the stables, hoping that Kulan's men would not risk burning them out, killing all the livestock and horses with them. The stables were quickly surrounded and the battle, a stalemate. A little more than thirty of Navun's men remained alive and many were seriously wounded. He knelt beside Shasp in the falling snow and pulled his friend's bloody hand away from the narrow blade that still transfixed his side.

"Guess ya know I have ta pull that out?"

Shasp nodded weakly, "I know, just give me a sec......." His final word had not cleared his throat before Navun jerked the weapon free.

93

"It's better when ya don't know its coming."

Shasp was still trying to catch his breath and when his lungs filled. "Son of a bitch! You conniving old bastard!"

"Aw…c'mon now. Is that anyway to talk to someone who's trying to help you?"

Once Shasp regained control of the pain, he cast about for Durquist or Blaquet. "They're gone! The count and the witch have fled!" Lurching to his feet, he staggered toward the oak doors of the keep. Throbbing pain plagued his side and blood poured through his fingers as he tried to staunch the wound. Wincing against the torment, he cautiously entered the hall and searched the interior. Huddled clusters of frightened maids, nothing more, but when he looked to the balcony, he discovered Blaquet's chamber door was ajar. He clenched the Somerikan long knife in his left hand as he struggled up the stairs and stumbled into the courtesan's bedroom. In an adjoining apartment he found a portion of the wall was offset, a hidden panel left partially open in haste. The door yielded and he peered into stygian blackness. Shasp pulled down a torch, struck flint to it until it blazed, then forged ahead down the cramped passage. After an indeterminable time of creeping through dank passages, he emerged into the infernal chamber of Darok and looked upon a scene of horror.

In the eerie red light of the smoking braziers, Blaquet hovered off the ground inside a storm of freezing nether wind, screaming with blood gushing from a wound in her left breast. Durquist and Balam stood with their backs to Shasp, watching the infernal feast and Balam's sword was wet with crimson. Beside them, Natu slumped on one knee with his left hand clamped down over a gash on his sword arm, his heavy saber on the ground several feet away.

Balam called to the aristocrat, "Count we must go!" They turned to flee but froze when they saw Shasp looming in the exit. He looked past them at the vampiric effects, decimating Blaquet's once beautiful body. She was slowly withering, as if she were aging at an unimaginable rate. As they watched in terror, Blaquet dwindled to nothing more than a clutter of spinning bones, clattering against one another in the frozen vortex like wind chimes.

Durquist cried out in panic, "Please! It will kill us all!"

Shasp turned his attention to Balam and motioned with the knife, "Lose the sword, Balam."

Balam considered his advantage with the sword against the

knife but then recalled the overconfidence of Goshun and let it fall with a clang. "Now can we be away from this evil place!"

Shasp pointed toward the passage and they fled like rabbits down a warren.

"You also, Natu."

Natu looked over his shoulder at what was left of Blaquet, then turned and lurched past him.

Shasp felt the wind ebb and start toward him as Blaquet's bones clattered to the floor. He raised his bloody hand to the stone at his neck and the wind but touched him, sensing the power of the sigil stone, and retreated. Shasp, not knowing how to kill such a creature, casually turned away and strode back down the passage, leaving Darok in his prison.

When he emerged from the keep into the cool wind of the Olloua Mountains, he found the three fugitives surrounded by Navun's men, bristling with weapons and eager to use them.

Shasp motioned toward Natu, "Chain him, and see to his wound." As several men led the black giant away, he turned to Kaerlo Durquist, "Just what the hell happened in there?"

Durquist shook his head and stammered, "I was wrong. I did not believe you because I was blinded by the arrogance of my station. When my men were faltering in the battle, Blaquet told me she knew a secret way out. We fled through her chambers into the cavern. It was there I saw the marks of witchcraft on the floor, and then the black thing came. I was stiff with fear, but she spoke with it and it did not attack us. I realized then what she was; that you spoke true. I commanded Balam to strike her down. Her guard stepped between them, but Balam wounded him and then ran her through. The thing must have been incited by her blood and attacked her. That was when you came in; such horror. Never have I seen anything so hideous, and it will scar my thoughts and dreams for the rest of my life!"

Shasp pointed at Balam with his knife, "I thought you were loyal to Blaquet."

Balam drew himself up, "She may have been the ruler of this keep, but the Count's authority has a far greater reach."

"You mean you saw a chance for a better position and took it."

Balam shifted uncomfortably and cleared his throat. The Count, sensing the enmity between them, interceded, "Sir . . . Uh...I'm afraid I don't know your name."

"Shasp."

"Um, yes, well there is no need to cause further injury to our men by continuing this strife. You have me at a complete disadvantage, but I am still a Count and an important person at court. I will be missed, and people will ask what happened to fifty royal guards."

Shasp wiped the blood from his knife with a rag, "What do you propose?"

"I simply wish to collect the fallen and ride back with my men. I will inform the king of what has happened here and make sure he knows your name."

"I don't care who knows my name, but like you, I don't want any more men to die senselessly. Collect your men, Count, and take Balam with you. His life wouldn't be worth a copper around his former comrades."

Durquist nodded and moved down the bloody steps toward the barricaded stables where he commanded the men to come out. The Royal Guard gathered their fallen, tied them to their horses, and rode out of Kulan.

That night, as the ragged group of survivors sat around a fire in their captain's quarters, Navun and Shasp reclined across from each other while two women stitched their wounds with bone needles.

Navun winced at each prick and, unceremoniously, gulped wine straight from the pitcher.

"Why the hell doesn't anyone want to go to the keep? It's as crowded in here as a whore house in Alem during a rainstorm!"

Rose pushed a needle through the flesh of Shasp's side and the warrior jerked his head and rolled his eyes. She chuckled, "You know why, Captain Navun. They're afraid."

Shasp accepted the flagon proffered by the scowling captain and took a long drink. Wine trickled down his chin. "If you want my opinion, I think you should take what's left of this rabble and go to the Tanyan territories. I hear they pay top dollar to mercenary captains."

Navun raised his eyebrows and considered the advice thoughtfully, "Maybe I will." Then over his shoulder to the drunken band of bloodied soldiers, "What say you worthless jackals? Do want to fight for Tanyan gold?" He was answered by a cheer and smattering of well-meant insults. "Guess that's that. We leave this haunted rat's nest tomorrow."

Shasp struggled to his feet, and Rose wrapped a narrow bandage about his waist. "By the way, I'll bet Natu would make one hell of a lieutenant."

Navun made a pinched expression, "Think so?"

"He has no master now. Maybe his freedom, and the prospect of earning gold, will enlighten him . . . or you could just hang him. Either way, I'm off to bed. I'll take the building next to yours. Maybe I'll finally get some sleep." Rose helped him through the door and into the falling snow.

"Don't count on it," she whispered in his ear.

He stopped and grinned, "Whatever do you mean?"

She looked away, "You know what I mean."

"I don't know," he said gravely, "I might tear my stitches."

Rose slugged him playfully then stood on her toes and kissed him deeply as large snowflakes tickled their faces and bare skin. "If you tear your stitches, I'll just put some more in."

Shasp opened the door for her, "I'm sure it will be worth every single one."

Chapter 12

Alinna enjoyed horseback riding and long trips, she always had, even as a child, though she was little more than that now. The long caravan which traveled with her had brought all the comforts of home, and she lacked for nothing. Without a doubt, court life had been a burden on her freedom lately, and she was ecstatic when Count Durquist invited her to visit the court of Dahoe east of the Arrigin provinces.

She brushed her dancing gold tresses from her face and smiled at the warm August sun as it gently warmed her face. The knock of horses' hoofs against the rocky trail wrested her from pensive thought and she looked at her personal guard, who had just ridden up. The bearded man they called Balam smiled curtly.

"We will be setting up camp shortly and his grace wishes you to ride ahead with him. I think there is something he wants to show you," then he fell back to his place near the center of the line of mules and horses.

Early that afternoon, she left the caravan with the count and her guard to ride up a long mountain trail. When the sun waxed hot, she rode ahead of her keepers, feeling stifled by their presence and stopped to water her mount by an icy stream. She had lost sight of the men but could still hear their horses' hoofs clacking against the occasional rock, and slowed a little as she entered a high mountain meadow and came upon several grave sites. Piled stone cairns lay in an orderly row but one appeared to have been robbed, empty even of bones, and the stones were scattered. An inexplicable chill trickled down her spine and she turned her mount around, hurrying back to where the others waited. As she left the meadow and came back into the forest, she met the count and her bodyguard, who waited on their mounts.

Count Durquist smiled down at her fondly, "Come girl, we don't want to lose the light."

"I am sorry, my lord, but my horse was thirsty and I thought he needed water."

"Just because you are the queen's favorite doesn't mean you can come and go as you please. Not yet anyway."

"Where are we going?" she asked.

Durquist's expression darkened slightly, "A secret place which you must swear never to reveal."

"Is that why you left your guard below with the camp?"

He nodded, "You know how much I love you, and I trust very few people. That is why I have bequeathed my entire estate to you, much to the chagrin of my family and children. I trust you more than them. What I am about to show you will test your loyalty."

She sat erect on her mare, "I will not fail you, sire."

"I know you won't, my dear."

The sun was at its zenith when the trio entered Kulan's abandoned courtyard. Alinna noticed many rust colored splotches on the weed choked flagstones, and the doors to the great hall gaped ajar with squirrels and other vermin moving in and out freely. The riders dismounted and climbed the wide steps to the enormous stone hall where chairs where overturned and dust filled every crevice. Spiders were the primary residents of this once merry place and adorned it with white, gauze patterns of silk.

"What happened here?" she asked as she gazed at the neglect, "Why doesn't anyone live here now?"

"It's a sad story really," Durquist said with a touch of sentiment. "It used to be home to a beautiful woman who sought immortality, but in the end her search was her doom. A knight came here and there was a struggle and she perished. Everyone believes this place is cursed now." He paused; looking around with Alinna, then shook himself as if from a daydream. "Come now, I have more to show you." He led her up dusty stairs to a chamber on the far north end. "This was the woman's room." He motioned to Balam, "The passage door, if you please."

Balam found a seam in the wall and, with some effort, pulled open a panel, revealing a dark passageway. Durquist lit a lantern and motioned for her to enter.

Alinna was loyal but not brave, "Must I go in there, sir?"

"Yes dear, you must."

"It's so dark. I want to do as you say but I'm afraid." Alinna did not understand the instinctive fear that welled up inside her; she only knew it kept her legs from moving forward. "Please don't make me go in; I sense something evil there."

Count Durquist sighed, "I was hoping to avoid this, but you leave me no choice . . . Balam."

99

The bearded captain of the guard seized Alinna by her hair and slammed her onto the dusty plank floor with brutal force, striking her forehead. Never had the slender young woman experienced violence of any kind and was still in shock when he bound her hand and foot. Tears streamed down her face as she sobbed in pain and confusion. Lying with her face in the dust, Balam reached down to lift her.

"Why are you doing this?" she cried, "what did I do?

Rough hands grasp her arms but then she heard the sharp sound of something hissing through the air. She had been lifted only half way from the floor when she felt Balam hesitate behind her, then she fell back onto her face and the bodyguard flopped over her. At first, Alinna thought he had stumbled and lost his balance while trying to lift her but then a spreading warmth oozed across her neck and back and she heard the distinct sound of liquid dripping against the floor. Count Durquist gasped and stared at something behind her. She squirmed and kicked free of her bodyguard enough to see his neck was sheared most the way through. Blood pooled on the timbered floor as his body twitched spasmodically. Alinna screamed.

"That's enough of that, girl," came a keen voice from behind her. She rolled onto her side, looked up at a helmet with a slit-visor and onyx horns and fainted.

Durquist and Shasp stood face to face. Kaerlo took a step toward the door, but the other cut him off. "Well Count, we meet again, or should I say . . . Blaquet."

The other stiffened at the name, and the color drained from the count's face.

Shasp continued, "You must have thought we were going to hang Natu or maybe butcher him. In fact, you were counting on the men's dislike for him. It took me awhile to realize it, but Natu was just being a good slave to a generous master. When he was captured leaving the hall, he thought for certain he was going to die. By the next day, he told me a very interesting tale. A story of how Blaquet lured the Count into a dark cave and how an entity from another world exchange their life essences. Once he was in your body, you had Natu run him through. Then you fed Durquist to your pet demon. In the form of the Count, you instructed Natu to remain still while Balam gashed his arm, to add weight to your story. You might have gotten away with it Blaquet, but you made a fatal error. After you had ridden away to freedom, Natu realized you had abandoned him. He had been

100

wounded for nothing and was most likely looking at a death sentence and that didn't sit well with him. But we didn't kill him. In fact, the last I heard, he was slaughtering Tanyan rebels and making good money doing it. I think he's even made the rank of lieutenant."

Blaquet put on Durquist's most diplomatic face, "Shasp, it doesn't have to be like this, think about it! You can be young forever! You can be like the gods themselves and never die! Don't be a fool!"

Shasp shook his head and continued his narrative, ignoring Blaquet's pleas. "I knew I couldn't just ride into Alem and accuse you before the court. You aristocrats are a tight bunch, but I know you well, Blaquet. I knew you would loath every day you had to stay in the body of a fat, bald noble man. Your vanity would drive you to find a victim soon. Like Rose, you would mentor her, and bequeath all Durquist's wealth to her, before stealing her body."

"Shasp, be reasonable. Think about what you are giving up!" she pleaded, face tight with stress.

"No, I don't think so, however, I do think it's time we paid Darok a final visit."

Shasp's sword flashed out and the flat of the blade caught Blaquet on the side of her head. Blackness followed. She woke to the dim glow of a crackling torch, pain shooting through Durquist's battered skull. Shasp was standing over her. The sound of rushing wind echoed in the cave, and in moments the black shade of Darok hovered before them. It waited, evaluating the situation until Shasp held up the stone talisman.

"Is there a new bargain?" came the invading presence of voiceless speech.

"No...no bargain, I just wanted to bring you your last meal." Shasp thrust his blade through the noble's heart. "Better get it while it's warm."

Shasp strode back down the passage as Blaquet's choked screams died in the roaring wind.

Mike Mino

Alinna woke not a hundred yards from the caravan's campsite with her horse grazing peacefully beside her. She wondered if she had just awoken from a nightmare, but the bloodstains on her dress told her otherwise.

BOOK II

Ancient Whispers

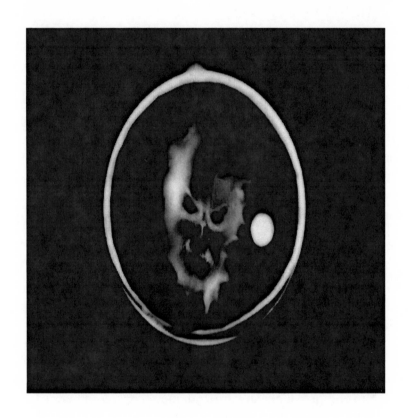

Chapter 1

The rain fell in sheets, thrumming on the roofs and streets of the small Tanyan border town. Night had brought with it an angry thunder storm, bent on driving the inhabitants of Ellings indoors. An occasional figure sprinted through the downpour and across muddy streets, eagerly seeking another dry doorway. One of those thresholds was Farol's Inn, and Farol loved the rain; to him, it was like money falling from heaven.

The inn was a two story affair, blockish and made of prairie stone. Unlike the other simple buildings of Ellings, which were thatched, Farol's was roofed with wood shingles, a symbol of the tavern owner's wealth. Wood was scarce on the open grasslands and had to be floated down from the northwest and fished from the river that ran along the edge of the town; a costly enterprise. Farol's main room was separated from the kitchen by a long bar where he sloshed grog, beer and grain whiskies to travelers and town folk by the hundreds, while the upstairs was reserved for travelers staying the night. The ceiling was low, causing the smoke from the kitchen and uncountable pipes to fill the room with a hanging vapor. Other aromas of roasted meat and baked bread mingled with the smoke, creating an indefinable odor. While the thunder boomed outside, laughter boomed inside, as people from all walks of life packed the establishment. Near the fire, a fat merchant sat surrounded by his bodyguards while he stuffed his face. Several small children ran in and out of a forest of legs as their parents drank themselves into oblivion.

A group of mercenaries in piece meal armor slammed their mugs together in a fiery toast as they chattered excitedly about their last battle. Owen snaked one arm around the plump woman who sat beside him and raised his tankard with the other. "And here's to Blay, who kept me from getting my head chopped off by that big rebel bastard!"

Four heavy cups clanked together and ale sloshed onto the stained wooden table. Blay scratched at an old cut in his grey streaked beard and chuckled, "Well kid, if you expect me to teach you anything, you're gonna have to stay alive long enough to learn; can't watch your back all the time."

A big bald man sitting across from Blay, made a horse sounding laugh, "Are you kidding? I think Owen should have to pay you full wages for all the times you've had to peel someone off his ass."

Blay waved the bald man off, "I've peeled more than a few off your ass, Warron, and I don't recall making you pay . . . much." Warron gave another raspy laugh, slapped the table, then turned his head and buried his face in the heavy breasts of the prostitute who sat astride his lap. Owen ran his fingers through his thick blonde hair and turned a youthful grin to the only quiet man at the table.

Ethur was from the moody northeastern lake lands and like his home, tended to be morose. His hair was the color of fresh mud and shaggy like his beard, but his body was lanky and quick. Ethur peered out from under his mane with slit-like dark eyes, "What's so funny, boy? You nearly met the reaper today."

Owen shrugged, "Just happy to be alive and spending my earnings. True, I didn't kill as many rebels as you or Blay, but I still put down a few, and Blay says I'm getting better."

Ethur snorted and went back to watching the seething mass of humanity that had crammed itself into Farol's Inn. The merciless thunder storm had driven every traveler and local resident indoors and even now, fat Farol was busy pouring ale and slinging food with a zeal that cried out, 'money, money, money.' "When is that fat bastard gonna bring our food? I'm about to cut his hand off and chew the meat from its bones right now." Owen wondered if Ethur was kidding; there were stories of cannibals in the lake lands.

Blay shoved a fresh cup toward Ethur, "You're even more sour than normal. What has your pecker so twisted?"

The lake man was the group's scout and tracker, with a nose for trouble. He had been spending his time preening the crowd with his eyes, looking for anything out of place. The four mercenaries were good at their work and, consequently, made lots of enemies. That made Ethur paranoid, but the others didn't care and even liked the idea that someone was always watching out so they didn't have to. "That guy in the corner over there, leaning against the wall in his chair," he pointed his hooked nose.

Blay lifted his gaze from the table and saw the man Ethur was talking about. He was lean and muscular, wearing a sleeveless white tunic and black leather riding breeches. The heels of his black,

105

knee-high riding boots rested on the table, as he balanced on the rear legs of the chair. His face was mostly hidden in the shadows, but Blay could tell from the cut of his face that he was probably from over the western sea, yet there seemed to be a heaviness to his brow and jaw that smacked of a Nomerikan heritage as well. A sword leaned against the wall nearby and a heavy knife was tucked into a forest green sash at his waist. No armor. "He's probably some traveling forester, by the look of him, Ethur; nothing to get excited about."

Three of the four went back to guzzling ale and pinching prostitutes, but Ethur continued to watch the crowd. A few empty glasses later, the food finally arrived and the crew laid waste to the meal like ravenous dogs on a stray cat. They were nearly finished and Warron was wiping his greasy forearm across his heavy lips when a frigid gust of air swept across the room. A cloaked man slipped in through the alley door, mostly ignored by the robust crowd, and shouldered his way through the press of sweating bodies until he found the counter. Ethur was watching and so, he noticed, was the man in the corner. The cloaked man never dropped his cowl and cloak, only wiped a moist hand over the face beneath, spoke to Farol and turned toward them. Again, he shoved his way through the hooting crowd and stopped, unexpectedly before their table. The four mercs looked up from their ale and Ethur carefully slid his wicked, sharp skinning knife from its scabbard beneath the table.

The man stood for a moment like a water-logged version of the grim reaper, dripping on the table. Blay's usual smile faded, "You want something?"

"Yes," came a strong steady voice, "I was told your crew sometimes takes jobs on the side, when you are between employers."

"Who wants to know?" replied Blay.

The man reached into his cloak and Ethur tensed to spring, momentarily visualizing his skinning knife stabbing into the cowl. But in that tense moment, the stranger withdrew a heavy leather bag, the size of an orange and dropped it on the table. The chime that followed its fall spoke of a tidy sum.   There was a pause before Blay picked up the pouch and weighed it in his hand, "Silver?"

"And some gold," continued the man.

The whole table went silent, knowing that the bag held more money than they would see in a month of hard fighting collectively.

Blay only said one word, "Who?"

Slowly, the cloaked man turned and stared at the lone traveler in the corner. The others followed his gaze and Ethur quickly shot Blay a look of warning. Blay weighed the bag again in his palm and looked around the table. Warron and Owen practically drooled over the money pouch.

Ethur squinted at their prospective employer, "Now that we know who . . .how about telling us why?"

"That's my business, but if it troubles you I'm sure I can find someone else who . . . ."

"No," replied Blay, "your money is well spent. Will you be requiring proof of some kind; a finger, eye or ear?"

"No, but don't underestimate your quarry, my friends." A thin smile surfaced through the shadowed cowl before the stranger turned and shoved his way back through the crowd, out the door and into the arms of the awaiting storm.

Blay dug a silver drago coin out of the bag and waved at the serving woman, "The least we can do is buy a dying man a last drink." The table erupted in laughter.

Shasp quaffed the last of his wine while a local bard banged out a tune on his weathered lute. Although the festive music and fellowship seemed to fire everyone else's core, it did little for Shasp. His already black mood spiraled downward as he glared at the milling throng and contemplated his ill luck. He called over the din to a passing serving maid, and then turned his mug upside down to let her know what he wanted. She nodded and hurried over with a sloshing pitcher as he plucked the last copper from his belt and flipped it onto the table. Her pretty round face, hazel eyes and curly brown hair seared away some of the dourness from Shasp's expression.

She smiled wickedly at his appraising eyes and leaned over to pour the wine, making sure he got an eyeful of her more than ample cleavage. "What's a matter, love?   Ain't you hav'in a good time?"

He shifted his eyes away from the strained bodice and gave her a weak grin. "No, afraid not; I've had a string of bad luck."

"Oh, I'm sorry to hear that love. What happened?"

He took a pull from his cup, "Couple days ago, in Elena, someone cut my purse. I didn't even realize it until I was halfway across the Tanyan territory and now; I'm stuck here in this little backwater."

Lorla ran her hands along her waist and hips, "Anything I can do to raise your spirits?"

Shasp frowned at the seductive gesture, "I wish there was but unfortunately, that was my last copper."

Her face had a simple beauty with an expression of sincerity that was uncommon in larger cities and for an instant she even seemed disappointed, "Well, if your luck changes, love, I'm Lorla."

Shasp nodded and watched her swaying hips beneath the green cotton skirt as she vanished into the throng, but not before she gave him a parting smile from over her shoulder.

Shasp had managed to nurse his wine for nearly an hour before he swallowed the last inevitable drop. He was about to gather his sword and head for the stables where he would be sleeping next to his horse instead of pretty Lorla, but she suddenly appeared through the pressing bodies with another tankard of sour Tanyan wine and clunked it on the table in front of him, "The soldiers from that table sent this over."

Shasp looked around her voluptuous hips, and a mercenary with graying hair raised his cup in salute. Shasp returned the gesture in acknowledgment of the offered drink and nodded once. He was about half way through his tankard when the table of bawdy soldiers got up to leave the inn, and each man gave him a passing glance as they went out the door, but none said a word.

With an uneasy feeling, Shasp finished his wine, wrapped his dark gray cloak about his shoulders and, reluctantly, stepped out into the storm. Rain swept horizontally through the air, pelting his face, and he pulled the hood over his head. Mud plastered against his calves as he dashed for the stables at the far end of town, but Shasp was forced to a premature halt in the middle of the churning street. Two shadows appeared from a side alley ahead of him, blocking his path. As he cast a quick glance over his shoulder, he saw two more behind him, silhouetted by a flash of lightning. Squinting against the driving rain, he watched as they slowly moved toward him, swords clenched tightly in their fists.

Shasp took a deep breath. He was not surprised by the encounter; in fact he almost expected it. He let his cloak slip from his shoulders and, with the swift reflexes of an adder, jerked his sword and knife free in a one fluid movement. Water tinged off the polished steel as he turned and put his back against the wall of a building. As the mercenaries encircled him, their images flashed clear with each crack of lightning and then returned to blue shadows. On his right, a blonde haired youth in leather and scale stood beside a burly bald headed warrior in chain and plate. The old battle leader, and a lanky swordsman with shaggy hair, moved in on his left.

A cruel smile split Blay's scarred face, "Nothing personal!" he yelled over the breaking thunder, "it's just work!"

Shasp's eyes narrowed, "Guess you can't blame a man for trying to make a living."

Rain splashed off armor and flesh as they stood in tense silence, evaluating one another. Shasp had been in enough battles to know it was better to act than react, and he lunged toward the youth on his right, but before the point of the Ayponese sword reached its target, he redirected the point toward the bald man at his side. Owen was in the process of parrying a thrust that would never arrive while Warron was coming forward to aim at Shasp's exposed ribs and caught the katana's point in his eye. The burly soldier clamped his palms over the destroyed socket, and dropped to his knees, howling in pain.

Blay and Ethur closed into the gap Shasp created when he made the lunge. Shasp dropped and spun as their swords whistled harmlessly overhead, then he slipped the Somerikan knife between Ethur's ribs. When Shasp yanked the knife free, Ethur gasped and coughed bloody foam before sinking into the mud where he wheezed like an asthmatic child.

Ironwrought's last attack had placed his back to the street, having strategically forced his last two assailants against the wall. Owen's face grew pale with worry and his eyes widened, while Blay simply shook the rain from his bristly hair, indifferent over the casualties. The battle leader crouched slowly, picking up his lanky friend's fallen sword with his left hand, then called over the wind and thunder to Owen.

"Stay on his back, Owen; it will distract him."

Owen made a wide arc around Shasp until he was behind him, and was surprised that Shasp did not pivot so he could see him, but instead stayed fixed on the older soldier. Like a sudden gale wind, Blay attacked expertly with both swords, but Shasp deftly countered each stroke. Owen, seeing that his prey was engaged with his mentor, lunged for his exposed back.

Shasp heard the splash of mud behind him, made a forward slash with the sword and then reversed the grip just as Owen was arriving for a fatal blow. Shasp stabbed backward, skewering him through the stomach, and then retracted the sword, allowing Owen to crumple to his knees. The youth cried out and clutched at his wound.

For the first time, Blay looked angry, and they circled each other as the fallen writhed in the street. Like angry rams, they crashed together, their blades slashing and blocking in a dance of clanging steel. For several minutes neither could find an opening until fate interceded and Shasp lost his footing in the muck. He slipped and fell onto his side, but immediately rolled away as his opponent hacked at him, leaving deep gouges in the street. Shasp spun on his back in the slippery mud and brought his blades up in a cross that caught Blay's downward chop only inches from his face, but when the old mercenary tried to force his blade through, Shasp kicked him behind the knee, sweeping his legs from under him. As his enemy was falling, Shasp was regaining his feet, and before Blay could get up, he had straddled him. Reversing his grip on the katana, Shasp rammed the blade through his opponent's shoulder, pinning it to the ground and evoking a cry of pain.

Blay lay on his back, squirming against the length of steel with his teeth clenched while Shasp leaned over him. Shasp twisted the katana ever so slightly, causing Blay to hiss with pain. "I've made a lot of enemies," said Shasp, "but I don't remember your face.

110

Why did that man pay you to kill me? Talk, damn it."

Blay was struggling to form words, "He didn't say and we didn't ask. It was a lot of money."

Shasp reached into Blay's belt and withdrew the heavy pouch. "Is this it? Hmm? Guess you didn't finish the job." Blay gave a bark of pain as Shasp jerked the blade out of his shoulder with a grating of bone against metal.

Shasp poured the contents into his palm and examined several gold and silver coins as they sparkled in the stinging rain. He tossed a few onto Blay's chest, "For your trouble. Two of your men might live . . .not sure about the skinny one." With his forearm he wiped the brown muck from his face and shouted to the men who lay groaning in the mire, "I think I'll give this back to your employer with my personal regards!" Snatching up his mud-caked cloak, he slogged toward the stables to collect his gear. It looked as if his luck was changing after all, and his poor charger would have to sleep in the stall by himself, but Shasp never noticed the cloaked stranger who had watched the fight from a shadowed doorway. The man waited until Ironwrought had disappeared before he allowed himself a curt chuckle and stepped into the brackish water of the street.

Chapter 2

Shasp woke late the next morning and squinted against the glaring light that poured through the second story window of his small room. Lorla had just pulled open the shutters and was bustling about, gathering her clothes from off the warm plank floor.

Shasp groaned, sat up and ran his fingers through his dark brown hair. Smiling at Lorla's bare backside, he feigned annoyance. "What are you buzzing about for? I paid Farol for your entire day's wages, or would you rather clean tables?"

"No I wouldn't, but that doesn't mean I want to spend all day in bed," she said, her round face beaming. She sat next to him and started to tie the straps on her sandals, "Besides, I'm starving!"

Shasp threw his arms around her and pulled her down onto the bed. "You'll always have food, but you won't always have me," he said, kissing her neck.

"I suppose your right about that," she purred, dropping her clothes.

The serving hall of Farol's Inn seemed cavernous after most of the patrons had finished their breakfasts and moved on. Only a few still loitered, most nursing hangovers. All the windows had been opened, allowing the musky smell of the evening crowd to escape. Early light filled the hall and dust hung in the sun beams, dancing a slow spiral.

Shasp appeared at the balcony overlooking the stairs with his white linen tunic unlaced at the neck and hanging over his pants. Slowly, he ambled down in a lazy, carefree gait and stood a moment in one of the many bright rays, enjoying the sun's warmth on his face.

Farol was sitting on a wooden stool catching his breath and wiping his greasy bald head with a dirty rag. When he saw Shasp, he hurried over to him, "Anything I can get you this morning, sir?"

Shasp was a little surprised at Farol's immediate attention and was beginning to think he had overpaid him, but Farol had evicted a guest in order to make room for him. "Eggs, meat, bread and some fruit, enough for two. Lorla says she's starving.....Oh, and some mead," he said before strolling toward a table.

112

Farol waddled away, cursing Lorla's good looks and his lack of help.

Before Shasp made it two steps, he saw the stranger from the previous night, still cloaked and hooded while sitting at a table, watching him with his back to the wall.   Given the warmth of the room, it was clear to Shasp that the cloak served but one purpose; to hide the face of the man who had paid to have him killed.

Shasp marched across the room, placed his boot against the edge of the table and shoved it into the man's chest, pinning him to the wall.

"Easy friend," wheezed the man as he struggled to suck air into his compressed lungs, "you're not carrying that sword this morning."

"I don't need a sword to kill a bag of guts like you," Shasp growled as he lifted a brass candlestick from the table, "Why did you send those mercs after me?"

The man reached up and slowly pulled the cowl and cloak away, revealing the weathered and scarred face of a middle-aged fighting man with a neatly trimmed beard and closely cropped blonde hair. Unlike Shasp, he was of medium height with stocky build, and he flashed a smile full of large, white teeth.

Ironwrought blinked in astonishment, "Vargos? . . . Vargos! . . . It is you! I don't believe it!" Shasp threw the table aside as Vargos leapt to his feet and they embraced, laughing and bellowing sarcastic greetings.

Shasp stepped back, holding the man at arm's length, "I thought you were dead. We went looking for your foraging party when you didn't return to the ship, and found them hacked to pieces. The natives took their heads and everyone thought you were among them."

Vargos rolled his eyes, "Sit down, we have a lot to talk about."

Shasp pulled the table back and dropped into a chair.

Vargos took a deep breath and sighed, "How long has it been, five years?"

Shasp nodded, "Yes, about that since that old merchant vessel we were paid to protect was blown off course." Shasp laughed, "I remember the captain spent a good deal of time trying to figure out where the hell we were and the whole crew was about to mutiny."

Vargos leaned forward over the table, "Well, after we dropped anchor at that island; the one not on the map, we had the misfortune of taking charge of foraging parties, since most of the ship's water went rank."

Shasp dropped into somber thought, "I took my party into the interior. We were deep in stinking jungle; hacking our way through vines and undergrowth unlike anything I had seen before; slow going. When we finally broke free of it at the edge of a glade, we were attacked."

"Same as mine. The natives ambushed us from the brush alongside the trail, killing most of the men before we could even arm ourselves; must have spotted us when the ship came in."

Shasp drummed his fingers on the table top, "Only Deluet and I returned to the ship. When you didn't come back we gathered more men and went looking for you."

Vargos leaned back in his chair, "When I saw that we couldn't fight our way free, I fled into the jungle. Three savages gave chase and after several minutes of running, I hid in a thicket and waited for them. When they passed, I came out from behind and killed one before he even knew I was there. The other two weren't much of a chore. I tried to make my way back to the ship, but every time I got close, I crossed a group of the devils hunting me. So, I decided to go the long way around, but by the time I made my way to the cove, the ship was on its way over the horizon.

"I hid in the jungle for weeks, but they eventually caught me and brought me back to their village. It was a picture of hell; fires, human sacrifice, cannibalism. It didn't take a genius to see what was going to happen to me. They led me out to an open area in the middle of the village, in front of the chief's throne. He was a fat brute of enormous size, covered in bone trinkets, wooly hair to his back. I figured what the hell; if I was going to die, I might as well take him with me. I pretended to be desperate for my life, crying for mercy, blubbering, all that shit. They all thought that was pretty funny, but when I was brought closer, with a guard on each side, they threw me onto the ground in front of the fat bastard. He was still laughing when I snatched a spear from the guard nearest me and thrust it through his fat gloating face. I fully expected to be overwhelmed and slaughtered, or worse, tortured. But, when I

114

turned, ready to trade my life for many more of theirs, no one came on. They stood like statues, staring, and then fell on their faces. It seemed they considered their chief a god and therefore, anyone who could kill him must be even more powerful. I healed up and used my new found position to abolish their nasty customs. After a while, it became quite a peaceful little island. Nearly a year later, a lookout spotted a ship, and I took a canoe so I could get close enough to catch someone's attention. It was a Kalyfarian warship, and it turned out there was a nobleman on board who found my story so intriguing that he brought me to his court to tell it to his king. The King was so amused by the account that he made me one of his agents."

Shasp sat in amazed silence until Farol plunked down a plate of food and a cup of mead. Shasp shook his head, "If I had known you were still alive, we wouldn't have left."

Vargos looked him in the eye, "I know. We were fast friends, you and I."

Shasp smiled, bit into a pear then suddenly made a confused expression. "If you and I are such good friends, Vargos, then why did you pay those men to kill me?"

Vargos waved his hand in the air and scoffed, "Oh please, do you really think, for one second, that I believed those louts capable of killing you? Spare me; I just needed to make sure you were still handy with a blade."

Suspicion seeped into Shasp's voice as he leaned forward, "What for?"

Vargos raised a finger, "Patience."

"Well, I hope I met your expectations."

Vargos' eyes lit up, "Absolutely, even better than I remember." Vargos glanced down at the table, allowing a long pause while Shasp chewed his food. When he spoke again, it was low and serious. "Shasp, I've spent six months tracking you down. You don't stay anywhere for very long, do you?"

Shasp shrugged and took another bite, "Never did, but I don't suppose you came all this way to catch up on old times."

Vargos fumbled with his cup, gazing into the liquid, "No, I didn't. I need your skills."

"Come on Vargos, you know me. Maybe you think it's amusing to watch men slaughter each other but I don't. You have always been indifferent about killing. Just because I take pay to fight for this duke or that count doesn't mean I'm not particular about who I'm killing. We have always been at odds over that."

Vargos acted hurt, "You make it sound like I would kill an old woman for her shawl."

"No Vargos, that's not what I'm saying. I know you're not a penny paid cut throat. You have your standards too; they're just not the same as mine. And another thing; you are reckless, getting us into dangerous predicaments that we usually had to carve our way out of."

"I'm a changed man now, Shasp. I'm older and wiser because I have never faced death so near as I did on that island. My current mission is one of dire importance, and his majesty needs you."

Shasp laughed, "He's not my king; what do I care about his problems, or any king for that matter?"

Vargos smiled, "He pays well."

"How well?"

"Very well."

Shasp leaned back in his chair and rubbed his chin, "Well . . . maybe I *do* care about your king's problems, but I warn you Vargos, the first hint of treachery and you'll be left to fight your battles alone."

"Have I ever stabbed you in the back?"

"Well....there was that courtesan in Breska."

"Are you still pissed about that?"

Before Shasp could answer, Lorla appeared and pulled his plate away.

"Thanks love." She smiled at Vargos, "Friend of yours, love?"

Shasp reached for his mead, eyes narrowing, "You could say that; we were just catching up."

Vargos smiled and lifted his cup.

Chapter 3

Hammering hooves shook the ground of the golden prairie, sending waves of kinetic force through the rippling stalks of golden grass; parting like waves before the storm of horses. Thirty armored troopers bounced and rolled with each powerful contraction of animal muscle as they thundered down on a small farmstead.

Two young boys, toiling under a relentless sun, looked up from their chores. Seeing the mass of cavalry bearing down on them, they ran toward the sanctuary of a stone hovel, screaming for their father. A gaunt man with dusty brown hair appeared in the doorway scratching his beard and scowled as the lathered mounts drew up on the packed earth surrounding his home, but his face remained stern, hiding the fear that welled up in his breast.

Weary soldiers dismounted in a clamor of plate mail and swirling dust while horses shook sweat from their manes. A slender young man emerged from the troop and approached, lifting his helmet to reveal a narrow handsome face and straight thin nose. Wide blue eyes regarded the farmer from under tangled auburn hair, and he extended his hand.

"Lieutenant Lecasc," he said, almost friendly.

Relief flooded through the farmer as he accepted Lecasc's hand, "Rymand. What brings you here, lieutenant?"

Lecasc wiped the sweat from his eyes with the back of his gloved hand, "We are looking for a man called Vargos that came through this territory. Our Captain thinks he may have stopped here."

Rymand's eyes flitted over the blue etching of a winged serpent insignia on the right side of Lecasc's breast plate. "Long way from Kalyfar, aren't you?"

Lecasc seemed anxious as he nodded and glanced back at his bustling men, "Yes sir, we are. Please, did he come through here?" Before the man could answer, another soldier appeared at Lecasc's shoulder. He was a head taller than the Lieutenant and much wider with thick, ape-like arms as hard as carved rock, hanging from under the tarnished steel shoulder plates. His insignia was red, denoting a higher rank and his cold dark eyes stared through Remand, as if searching his thoughts. Lecasc fell suddenly silent. Reaching up with hands like great bear paws, the man removed his helmet, revealing closely cropped black hair. Scars crisscrossed the painfully brutal face but one scar overshadowed the rest; a large puckered remnant of an old burn on the left side of his face which began near his forehead and burrowed into his beard.

"Well Lieutenant," he said in a low rumbling growl, "was he here?"

Lecasc swallowed hard before clearing his throat, "I was just getting to it, Captain Kaskem," he turned back to Rymand, "Has a man called Vargos been through here?"

Rymand was taken aback by the Captain's dangerous appearance, but he was also aware that his young boys were watching the exchange and drew himself up. "Why? Is this Vargos a fugitive?"

Lecasc looked at Rymand with pleading eyes and his voice quivered slightly as his superior appraised his progress from over his shoulder. "Yes sir, he is. Has he been here?"

Rymand made the unfortunate mistake of misinterpreting the anxiety in Lieutenant Lecasc's voice as weakness, and it lulled him into an unrealistic belief that he was safe, causing him to remain aloof. "Do you have a writ of passage from the Tanyan magistrate to bring armed men into this territory?"

Lecasc felt a large hand on his shoulder slowly pushing him aside, and his face fell as Captain Reth Kaskem stepped forward. Kaskem boomed out with a voice like cracking rock. "Which direction did he go!"

Rymand shuddered and his eyes widened a little, "Southwest . . . to Ellings. He was looking for someone there."

Reth grunted then turned to Lecasc, "Butcher the livestock to feed the men." After the order was given, Reth turned away from Rymand and started away from the house.

The crusty farmer shook off his fear and followed the captain into the yard, yelling at his back. "You can't just come here and kill all my stock! You'll starve us!" Rymand shook his finger at Kaskem, "I'll report you to the garrison at Bitterwood!"

Kaskem moved with such speed that Rymand had no time to duck. The heavy fist streaked into his jaw with an explosion of blood and teeth, and the farmer went down like a sack of grain. Reth Kaskem reached down, seized him by the hair, and dragged his limp body into an out building. When he emerged seconds later, blood was dripping from his heavy short sword. Wiping it clean with a rag, he called to his subordinate, "Lieutenant Lecasc! Bring out the others!"

Lecasc went cold. 'Not again,' he thought, as his stomach knotted. "But Captain, do you think . . . ?"

"Lieutenant, I will not discuss my orders with you."

Lecasc nodded in defeat, called to three of the men and relayed the order. The two boys and a screaming woman in a brown wool skirt were brought out into the yard. Lecasc stood by while Kaskem slowly ambled toward them and stopped, inspecting each of the horrified captives. "What do you think we should do with them, Lieutenant?" he asked, as his eyes burned into the pitiful faces.

Lecasc already knew what the captain had in mind, "Why do we need to do anything with them sir?"

Reth stood with his hands on his hips, appraised the horizon for a moment, then shook his head and spat. "We're in foreign territory, Lieutenant . . . with no writ of passage. What do you think will happen when word gets back to some Tanyan outpost that foreign troops have breached their border?"

"We could tie them up.... leave them here....inside."

"Right . . . where they would starve to death or worse, some neighbor would come calling and our presence, again, would be reported."

"If I had known that we were, somehow, required to kill every person we came across on this mission, I would have declined!"

Reth was not angered by the Lieutenant's outburst. He never got angry. If he did, it never showed and that just made the man seem all the more dangerous. Instead, Reth just stared at him with eyes as cold and black as a shark. "Explain to me why I have a lieutenant if he isn't going to follow orders?"

"War is war, Captain Kaskem, but this is not war and these are not soldiers! I feel it is my duty to remind you that it was your reckless exuberance that led us to this homestead in full force, knowing full well what the outcome would be, whether they cooperated or not!"

Kaskem rested his withering shark's eyes on Lecasc. Regret seized his already agitated stomach while he awaited a

119

lightning fast death stroke for his insubordination. The blow never came. Instead, Captain Kaskem's cool voice came back to him with eerie calm.

"Alright Lieutenant, we'll play it your way from now on, but in the meanwhile," he snatched a spear out of the hands of a nearby trooper, "take care of our current problem," and tossed him the weapon.

Lecasc caught it clumsily, "I won't be part of this."

"You'll obey my command, Lieutenant or I'll summarily execute you where you stand for sedition and if you think your being a general's son will stay my hand, you had better think again. Now do it!"

Three hours later, Lecasc returned from the burial detail. His eyes were fixed when he walked by his captain to his horse. He fumbled absently through his worn leather saddle bags, removed a rag and began wiping the blood from his hands. He tried to make their passing as painless as possible, and did not blame himself for their fate, it was fixed. Instead, he assuaged his guilt by reassuring himself that he had shown them mercy when they could not have expected any from Kaskem. Likely he would have let the men have the farmer's wife first for their morale. 'No,' Lecasc thought, 'I'm not the demon here,' and swore in his heart that Kaskem would pay if it took his last breath.

Mike Mino

121

Chapter 4

Shasp and Vargos left Ellings at the onset of an orange sunset. Both rode partially armored, compromising between readiness and comfort. Shasp wore a black leather jerkin with steel banded sleeves reaching to his elbows. Heavy, black, engraved bracers were clamped around his forearms protecting him from wrist to elbow, and the long Ayponese sword, as always, was slung loosely across his back. Vargos preferred a light boiled leather cuirass with wide metal studs that left his muscular arms and broad shoulders bare.

Vargos insisted on traveling at night, northwest out of town and avoiding heavily-traveled roads, though he refused to give Shasp an explanation. Ambiguously, he stated that all things would be revealed when they reached Delane, a city in central Dahoe on the Oshintan border. Once there, they would contact a scholar who specialized in dead languages. Shasp was perplexed and a little uneasy at the secrecy. Again, Vargos insinuated that he was not capable of giving a worthy explanation and begged for his patience.

For a week they rolled through oceans of golden grass which reached to the horses' shoulders before arriving at the foothills of the Bitterwood Mountains. Ten more grueling days waxed as they negotiated passes laden with massive glaciers. There were easier ways around the Bitterwoods but Vargos did not want to become embroiled in the current rebellion and Shasp had agreed. Time was spent with the casual ebb and tide of reminiscence, conversing over anecdotes from their past and since they last parted company. Eventually the Bitterwoods released them into rolling forests of pine and fir, parched from the summer heat, cracking twigs announcing every fall of the horses' hooves. Another two days and the forest gave way to the Acadea Steppes, a land stingy with water and populated by a hearty, drab scrub brush and tough dry grasses, springing up tenaciously in tufts amidst the dusty earth. The duo turned north, and at the end of a long dry day, entered the bustling city of Delane.

Delane was pinched between the forested mountains to its east and an enormous lake, referred to as the 'Sea of Delane' to its west. Rolling, verdant hills gave relief to travelers coming north through the dry steppes.

Dusk descended, casting a fiery orange hue against the many buildings, and men on stilts were just finishing the task of lighting the tall oil lamps along the main street. The ordered rows of flaming pole lamps revealed multi-storied buildings of painted timber. Architecture varied widely from buttresses and multi-gabled roofs to blocky facades of simple construction. Most structures flaunted balconies to hold the overflow of sightseers, merchants, mercenaries and locals. Shasp and Vargos waded on horseback through the press of bodies and beasts of burden, absorbing the cacophony of laughter, screams, and fierce bartering jumbled with an assortment of complaining animals. Shasp, remembering his penniless journey to Ellings, untied his purse from his belt and tucked it into his leather jerkin. Painted harlots called down from overhead to the handsome men of war, and one or two even called to Vargos by name. Shasp looked at his companion with a raised eyebrow; but Vargos just shrugged.

At the north end of town the energetic crowds gave way to sullen figures, murmuring and lurking in the dark. There were only a few lamps to reveal the clumps of rugged, dirty men clinging to the shadows of alleys, waiting for any drunken victim, and the city guards who patrol here held their spears at the ready as they patrolled past. This was the poor quarter. Again Shasp cast a questioning look to his friend who received it with a wan smile.

"Just a bit further."

When Shasp thought he had seen the worst that Delane had to offer, the cobblestones gave way to packed earth and the taller structures degenerated into dilapidated tenements. The typical pole lamps vanished, leaving the streets at the end of town in utter darkness. Vargos drew up in front of a small house with heavy shutters and lamplight squeezed out from cracks in the doorway and windows. Shasp imagined a winter wind blowing through those wide cracks and wondered at the misery of the tenant. They swung out of their saddles, pausing to stretch cramped and aching muscles, and then tethered the horses to a post beneath the porch overhang.

Vargos drew a leather satchel from his saddle, hesitated, and turned to Shasp, "Maybe you should stay with the horses until I can find a place to stable them. This place is teeming with thieves."

Shasp smirked and glanced over his shoulder at Grimm, "I

wouldn't worry too much about your horse while it's tethered next to that son of a bitch." The horse snorted and jerked its head as if responding to the insult, and Shasp walked passed Vargos to the door. "Is this the place?"

Vargos stepped onto the creaking porch and nodded, "Yes," then rapped lightly with his knuckles.

The escaping light shifted as someone moved inside, then footfalls padded toward the door and a woman's small, frightened voice called out.

"W...Who is it?"

"It's Vargos, Ella. Open up."

Chaffing wood answered as a heavy beam slid back and the door creaked open on complaining hinges. Shasp studied the slight figure silhouetted against the lamplight as she moved to let them in. Vargos greeted Ella softly before stepping into the cramped room and Shasp followed.

The gray, rotting walls were lined with dusty books and scrolls, many adorned by cobwebs. Furniture was sparse, only a rickety table holding an oil lamp, and a couple wicker chairs cushioned with faded pillows. Stairs went up through a square hole in the low ceiling to what Shasp assumed was her bedroom. An adjoining doorway led to a poorly stocked pantry. Once Shasp's eyes had finished sweeping over the contents of the room, he turned his attention to the tenant of the sorry house.

Ella was young, with straight, pale blonde hair, but Shasp could tell that she was thin even under her bulky dark brown robe which gave her the appearance of a hanger more than a person. Her face was narrow and a little gaunt with purplish circles under her icy blue eyes which made her seem slightly cadaverous. Overall, she was as sad and depressing in appearance as the rundown shack she lived in, and Shasp sensed some tragic history in her.   She sniffled and returned Vargos' greeting without looking up from the ground.

They stood in awkward silence for a moment and Vargos laid his satchel on the table.

"It is good to finally meet you, Ella. Obviously the courier arrived with the message of my coming." Ella only nodded and Shasp's eyes narrowed.

Vargos pulled out a chair and motioned for her to sit down, but she shook her head.

"No sir, I can stand. I'm sure your friend would like to sit after riding all day."

Shasp smiled, "Not even if I rode a thousand miles." He pulled out the chair for her and she hesitated before sitting down, but still kept her eyes averted. Shasp came around to the center of the table and stood by while Vargos opened the satchel and eased out a square shape wrapped in cloth.

"I sent word I would be bringing something of great interest to you. Before I left I spoke with a man you met long ago, Willan, a scholar. Do you remember him?"

Ella smiled weakly for the first time, "Yes, I was ten years old. My father and I lived in the merchant's quarter."

"That's what he said. He also said he was amazed by your understanding of dead languages, and that you were particularly fond of the study of the language of the ancients. He said that if anyone could speak that language, it would be you . . . if you had continued in your study."

Again she nodded. Vargos unwrapped the cloth revealing a gray stone tablet riddled with complex runes. Immediately, Ella perked up and slowly reached out to receive the artifact. Her eyes widened as her frail fingers lightly traced each stenciled character.

"This is a script from the pre-ice times, maybe twenty thousand years old. It is said by some ancient philosophers that the language had not changed from the time of the cataclysms until then."

Vargos leaned closer, his voice excited, "Could it be a copied script? Something handed down from the time of the cataclysms?"

She chewed a thumbnail while scraping away some debris, "It depends on the content . . . I think." Her eyes narrowed in concentration as she studied the tablet.

"Can you read it?" Vargos asked.

"Most of it perhaps; 'An ancient house...no...fortress. Locked in the desert south of the Great River and....west of the ...teeth. The power of the ancients. Vexgos.' Well, the script is not a copy of the ancient language but is near enough to the time to be written in the same language. The writer refers to the ancients and is therefore not one himself. The tablet is carved from basalt, a rock found in the valleys bordering mountainous regions."

Shasp felt he had been silent long enough, "This is the part of the conversation, Vargos, where you explain to me what the hell is going on."

"Yes," said Ella quietly, "the courier only said you would be arriving from the palace of Angelis with a matter of great importance."

Vargos leaned back in the creaking wicker chair and folded his hands behind his head. "Nearly a year ago, Willan, a friend to the king's vizier, stumbled across an old manuscript describing a relic from ancient times called Vexgos. The tablet you hold Ella. Further research revealed nothing but the possibilities of seizing some ancient form of power was overwhelming to Willan.....and King Mellal.   We all know the fables of ancient powers. Calling down lightning, controlling mighty rivers and even harnessing the heat of a volcano from empty air. What if Vexgos is something like that. Imagine what a benefit it could be.   What we could learn."

Shasp brooded during the discourse then turned to Ella, "This Vexgos...is it sorcery?"

Ella shrugged, "Who knows? Maybe sorcery and maybe science."

"Science; what sort of science?"

She withdrew her hands into her robe and sank a little in her chair, "I once read a dissertation by Tractos Philipas. He suggested that the ancients were masters of the natural world. They came to understand things not seen; where the wind came from; how man's body worked; even what was beyond the stars. Philipas thought that man had learned more than he was ready to learn. In the end their knowledge created the cataclysms." Ella got up and removed a dusty book from a leaning shelf, opened it, and thumbed to a page. She read out loud, "'In the deepest part of the pit we call time, even before our fathers left the caves to build cities; so long ago, even the rocks would scarce remember; the Ancients lived. We know little of them except what we have pieced together from glyphs carved into crumbling stone and long buried artifacts of curious design and purpose. They hungered for knowledge and power; gained for themselves godhood but without mortality or wisdom. They mocked the true power of creation and like foolish children, brought fiery destruction and plagues on the world. Even the earth and seas rebelled against them until all of humanity was nearly wiped out. I have studied them most of my life and marveled at what they must have known . . . and cringed with fear. For man will always be man. He will always strive for power rather than wisdom. What will come of him should he uncover the secrets of the Ancients? If man fulfills his desires, will we survive again? I am filled with dread.' This was written by Philipas long ago."

Shasp shook his head, "If they weren't ready for such knowledge, we certainly are not."

Vargos shot out of his chair, his face a mask of disbelief, "I can't believe what I'm hearing! We are not seeking all the power of the ancients, just one relic! What if it is something that can heal or create food or warmth?   Wouldn't it be worth it?"

Ella shifted uneasily, "I...I would give almost anything to see something from the ancients."

Vargos laughed loudly, "Good, because you're coming. We will need you to translate anything else that we may encounter."

Shasp became perturbed, "Go where? We don't even know where this relic is."

Ella stood up, slowly pushing her chair back, "Actually, we do; south of the Great River and west of the teeth."

"Riddles."

"Not riddles, directions, although vague. The 'Great River' in ancient times refers to the Olumbria River of today. The 'Teeth' are the mountains separating the current Tanyan and Oshintan territories, the great Cascans. So the mentioned fortress must be southwest of here."

Shasp eyed her sternly, "That's a hell of a lot of territory to cover."

Ella reached out and ran her fingers over the tablet again as if finding comfort in its antiquity. "Yes it is, but perhaps we may find clues along the way. Some believe the pillars of the Olumbria are the remains of an ancient bridge. There may be something there and it's on the way, near the ferry at Utilla."

Vargos became anxious and excited, "Let's leave tonight! What do you say Shasp, are you still game?"

Shasp threw his arms wide in a gesture of capitulation, "Whatever, Vargos, as long as it pays in the end."

Ella got up and started toward the stairs, "I'll need to gather a few things and some tomes to research on the way."

Within the hour they were on the way out the door. Ella held the lamp for Shasp as he carried her bag of belongings down the porch but she halted and let out a stifled cry at the sight of a man lying on the ground behind Shasp's charger.

Shasp knelt to examine the horseshoe imprint on the corpse's jellied skull. "It seems he tried to steal my horse, but I guess old Grimm wasn't having it. I told you not to worry about the mounts." Shasp secured Ella's bag then swung into the saddle. He reached down to take Ella's hand but she hesitated. "Come on, girl, we don't have all night."

"What about him?" she pointed at the man lying in the dust.

"What about him? Leave him."

Shasp took her thin hand and lifted her easily onto the saddle behind him, "You don't weigh any more than a house cat! Don't you eat?"

She didn't respond, but sat quietly behind him while Vargos mounted, "We'll get Ella a horse in town and pick up some more provisions. I'm not at ease here with . . . well with what we know."

Shasp didn't like the tone in his voice, "Is there something you're not telling me?"

Vargos scratched his beard, "Well . . . Ah, as a matter of fact, there may be others interested in the relic, but that's why I have you," he said with a tense smile.

Shasp rolled his eyes, turned the charger about and started toward the brighter side of town. Vargos brought his chestnut mare alongside and they rode silently into Delane's bustling and much brighter merchant quarter. Shasp sensed uneasiness in Ella as they rocked and swayed on Grimm's back, as if she was uncomfortable with his proximity, and he wondered again about her past. Delane was a harsh place for a poor frail girl. If that didn't give his mind enough to chew on, there was Vargos' comment about others being interested in this elusive relic, and he remembered how easily his old friend had always gotten him into trouble.

Chapter 5

Lecasc brought up the rear of two columns with Captain Kaskem at the head. He resented the position of rear guard, but Kaskem never missed an opportunity to humiliate him in some small way. Most of the men disliked the captain, but none had the stomach to stand up to him, that is, no one but himself and now he was paying for it. Even though they all feared Reth Kaskem and sometimes hated him, everyone respected him. Some of the older veterans in the group had been through ugly scrapes with Reth before he had been promoted. The tales of his ferocity would give children nightmares, but Lecasc knew they were not just stories. The man was unstoppable and merciless.

Ten days past, Lecasc had convinced his captain to let him go into Ellings alone during the night. The lieutenant had pulled a heavy gray robe over his armor and started into town, but not before Kaskem made it clear that, if he did not return by morning, he would assume Lecasc was captured and come for him. Translated: he would wipe out the town, and so the burden of the entire existence of peaceful Ellings rested on Lecasc's shoulders.

He had listened at Farol's Inn and made some discreet inquires which led him to some injured mercenaries. They didn't know Vargos by name, but told him about a cloaked man who had paid them to kill someone . . . someone they had underestimated. Farol himself described the man with the cloak and the description was exact, but there was more. Vargos was traveling with an experienced swordsman. Lecasc even discovered the direction in which they had left. With a great sense of pride, he had returned to the hidden camp and informed his superior of what he had learned . . . without having to kill anyone. Smiling to himself, he rode across the night-blackened steppes, remembering the satisfaction of proving to Kaskem that it wasn't always necessary to kill people to get information. Once Kaskem had mulled over the details of Lecasc's report, he ordered the men to mount up and ride.

Ten days of hell followed as they lived, ate, and slept in their saddles, crossing plains, passes of gargantuan glaciers and the burning steppes of Acadea. Like a contingent of rag dolls, they flopped on the backs of dying horses with dried mouths and tongues swollen for lack of water, all but Kaskem. He still rode tall in the saddle like a figure of carved marble, eyes sharp and sword arm perpetually taut. Lecasc was beginning to think Kaskem was not even human. The man was as tense as a notched arrow. Several hours before dusk the columns approached Delane and Lecasc rode to the front to consult with Reth.

"Lieutenant, we'll take the men around to the west end of town. As you can see from here there's little movement and even less light there. We'll have the men hole up in that large barn over there while you and I prowl around."

Lecasc, grateful for the opportunity to rest the men and stunned that Kaskem would want to take him along, replied, "Yes Captain," and rode back to pass the word. The men muttered as excitedly as those on the edge of total exhaustion were able. Against the backdrop of shadowed mountains, they dismounted and led their horses through the scrub to the dilapidated barn then collapsed in exhaustion. Though he knew he did a poor job of hiding his fatigue, Lecasc tried to make himself appear as stalwart as Kaskem. The men soon found a watering trough and were trying to squeeze as many heads as would fit into it and though Lecasc longed to do the same, he waited until the last man was filled before dipping his dusty face into the tepid water.

Kaskem threw a black leather cloak over his mail and tossed his tarnished helmet to one of the weary sergeants. "Let's go, Lecasc, the moon won't stay up forever. Vargos will need the woman scholar, so if we find her we'll find him."

Lecasc pulled a brown robe out of his kit, drew it on and followed the looming shadow of the captain into town.

Blackened streets received them as they wandered past gaping alleys and rickety facades. Lecasc was uneasy and clenched at the saber under his robes, but Kaskem seemed completely undaunted, chin level and eyes ripping at the darkness. Lecasc steeled his nerves. The dwindling lamps of evening were sputtering in their death throes as the two approached the only tavern still radiating the laughter and curses of hardened revelers.

Kaskem stopped, "Maybe somebody in here will know something."

They climbed the brief steps and threw open the heavy door. Lamplight washed over them and at the same time, revealed a dingy rectangular room with a low soot-smeared ceiling. The plank floor was littered with the casualties of drink and perhaps a few from combat. Clustered around the bar sat a group of six rough-looking men, dressed in gaudy rags and dirty leather. Most of them were armed with knives but a couple had swords and a woman, painted in a manner reflecting her profession, languished in the lap of the largest man. Everyone turned at the sound of the scraping door and Kaskem advanced to the middle of the room, grunting as he took in the scene. His entrance appeared to have interrupted the band's sport of knife throwing. A thin, sweating barkeep stood framed by daggers which were pinned in the wall around him, and he bled slightly where one of the blades had nicked his arm. When his antagonists turned to face Kaskem, the horrified man ducked behind the bar and disappeared.

The leader, a black haired man as large as Kaskem, shoved the harlot off his lap and stood up, "What do we have here? Two late comers?"

Kaskem grunted again, but this time with a hint of disgust that did not go unnoticed. "We're looking for someone; a woman who sells books and speaks other languages. Know where she's at?"

A rangy, greasy-haired thug chirped up, "Here that, Forice? They're look'in for books." and laughed.

Forice placed his hands on his hips and smirked, "I know most of what goes on in Delane, but information is never free, especially not in this town."

"How much do you want?" growled Kaskem, annoyed at the game.

Forice stroked his stubbled chin and looked thoughtful, "A hundred silver dragos," an outrageous request.

Kaskem did not even pause, "Done, now where is she?"

Surprise washed over Forice's face. Maybe this man really had that kind of money. "I don't think so, my good man; money first, information later."

"No," was Kaskem's only reply.

Lecasc leaned over his captain's shoulder, "Sir . . . we don't have that kind of money," he whispered.

Kaskem whispered back, "I know," then louder to the others, "Make up your mind we don't have all night."

Forice looked to his crew and reviewed the nodding heads

before turning back to Kaskem. "Alright then, but don't think you're leaving this room without paying for my services."

Kaskem shrugged, "I'm waiting."

"She's a mousy little prude who lives in a two-story building across from the dung peddler; about a hundred yards back down this very street. Now, how about our money?"

Kaskem snorted, "Eat shit you worms."

Forice's eyes bulged with sudden rage as he made a sweeping gesture toward the door. Like trained soldiers his men leapt from their seats and encircled Kaskem and Lecasc, cutting off their escape. Lecasc jerked his saber free and put his back to Kaskem's. Kaskem did nothing, only stood with his arms folded. Mirthless laughter rose in his thick throat, "What are you sewer rats planning to do, huh? Tell ya what, get out of my way and I'll call it even."

His answer was the sound of steel sliding from their sheaths. Forice gripped a heavy cutlass in one fist while he pointed accusingly at Kaskem. "You're about to find out what you look like on the inside."

He slashed murderously toward Kaskem, but the blow lost momentum when his stomach folded under the Kalyfarian's heavy riding boot. Forice flew backward into the bar, cracking the wood with his head. Kaskem spun with the kick, drawing his sword and slashing open a thug on his right. A third brigand thought to bury his long dagger in Kaskem's back, but the brutish captain twisted and caught it in mid-strike. In the same instant, he buried his short sword to its hilt in the thief's stomach. Still holding the man up by his limp arm, he used him as a shield to soak up another blade meant for his back. The long knife penetrated clear through, but Kaskem threw the corpse like a doll, entangling his attacker, and then split his skull while the man fought to free his knife.

Lying on the floor with a ruffian on top, Lecasc struggled over a knife, while his sword laying several feet away.

Kaskem faced the last brigand standing, who's eyes darted, looking for an exit, knife held out defensively. Reth cast a quick glance at the struggling Lecasc, "Lieutenant, hurry up and finish him, we are running out of time!" Suddenly the nervous thief made a lunge for the door, but Kaskem met him half way and caught him with a backhand slash that nearly left the man in two pieces.

133

The captain walked over to where Lecasc fought desperately to keep the needle sharp point of a knife from penetrating his throat. Kaskem casually hacked through the spine of his assailant, splashing Lecasc with gore then reached down with one massive hand and jerked the body aside. "Get up, Lieutenant."

Lecasc was so entangled in his own fight for survival that he only now witnessed the devastation wrought by Reth and was horrified.

Eventually, they found the bookseller's home and ransacked it, but found no clue to her whereabouts. After an hour or so and a few silver coins in the right palm, a scrawny, toothless drunkard spun the tale of two formidable looking warriors who had stopped at the bookseller's house and then left with her the night before. Kaskem wanted to know who this bookseller was, but the drunken skeleton didn't know, however, he gave them the name of a man who might. Poluntis Ilka; a fat merchant from the wealthy quarter who had taken her as apprentice sometime back.

On the way into the lamp-lit merchant quarter Reth realized more people were appearing as the paling of the sky warned of dawn's approach. "We have no time for pleasantries, Lieutenant. We sneak into the villa, find this Poluntis Ilka and beat whatever information we need out of him."

Lecasc might have argued in favor of not beating the merchant, but knew it was pointless. They located the villa with little difficulty. A two-story, alabaster building sprawled like a sleeping giant behind granite walls twice as high as a man. Its red clay roof stood prominent in the creeping dawn's blue light.

Kaskem considered the walls, "This Poluntis has done well for himself. Men like that are treacherous at best.   I'll boost you to my shoulders so you can secure a rope from that tree on the other side."

Lecasc stepped into Kaskem's cupped hands as the burly captain heaved his lieutenant up like he was a child. Lecasc was lean, but a head taller than most men and managed to seize the edge of the wall and pull himself atop its narrow width. Balancing in his riding boots, he eased his way over to the brooding oak tree that crowded the inside face. Soon, the hemp rope dropped before Kaskem and he flew up the cord faster than a monkey on a vine. They darted across groomed gardens to a tiled courtyard with a walkway of intricate mosaic design, then through a high archway and into a hall. Distant laughter rode the warm morning air and Reth wasted no time locking in on its point of origin. A few more strides brought them to a smaller cul-de-sac with several adjoining doors and only one had a guard. Reth Kaskem slid a heavy poniard from his belt and silently glided behind a row of ornamental shrubs, effectively flanking the unsuspecting guard. Rigid and disciplined the man stood, his spear pointing skyward in front of the large oaken door, oblivious to the encroaching danger. The poniard flew with expert precision, transfixing the guard's windpipe and severing his artery. Unable to make a sound, he clutched at the blade, staggered and fell. Taking full advantage, they sped to the door where Reth listened with his ear pressed against the painted wood then held up two thick fingers and nodded. Lecasc drew his saber and Kaskem, his short sword. For a moment Lecasc mused over Reth's disdain for the standard issue cavalry saber, boasting that it was better to be close to your enemy. Reth took a step back and slammed his boot against the door next to the jamb. Wood shattered and flew as the men burst into the room beyond.

Elaborate furnishings of expensive wood cluttered the large chamber while red silk curtains adorned plaster walls. The floor was richly carpeted in assorted animal furs and in the middle was the fattest man Lecasc had ever seen. He was bald and his clean shaven face glistened with perspiration. The rotund body was swathed in green silk, gold chains draped his thick neck, and jeweled rings adorned his plump fingers. Eyes like a fish were set in the heavy bags of his lower lids and stared at the intruders, with an air of indifference. Sitting on his lap was an attractive young girl with brown hair, wearing a gray cotton shift, who was immediately horrified by the sudden explosion of the door.

The fat merchant only seemed mildly surprised, "Well, this is unexpected. I suppose I should assume my guard is no longer with us? Well, I guess he wasn't worth what I was paying him. What can I do for you gentlemen?"

Kaskem thoroughly expected to scare the man to death and then torture him if needed, but was taken aback by the unexpected calm in the merchant's voice. "I'll assume you are Poluntis."

"Yes, as a matter of fact. To what do I owe this . . . visit? Oh, I hope this isn't a kidnaping. As you can see, I would be quite impossible to carry and though I can walk, not too quickly as you might have guessed."

Reth Kaskem leapt over the table like a panther and landed before Poluntis, his sword tip pressed dangerously into the folds of his chin. "The woman bookseller from the far end of town, who is she? Think before you answer," came his malevolent warning.

"Ah...Ella. Yes of course," he said, undaunted by the uncomfortable point. "There is no need to be uncivilized, gentlemen. She was an apprentice of mine until a couple years ago. Her father, captain of the Delane Guards, was killed in a fight that broke out between some mercenaries who were passing through. She was about twelve at the time and showed great promise; always had her nose in a book or a scroll. She would have been destitute without him because there was no mother, so a friend of her father came to me and asked if I would take her in to learn the trade. How could I refuse such a poor, little wretch?"

Lecasc placed a careful hand on Kaskem's shoulder, "What kind of books did she read?"

Poluntis slowly reached up and, with a single finger, directed the razor-sharp blade away from his throat. "She read ancient languages. I have no love for the little vixen. She finished her apprenticeship and immediately left to open that miserable excuse for a book shop in the most dangerous part of town. I treated her well but she turned her back on me, and even though I tried to persuade her to come back to be a part of my enterprise, she refused; the gall!"

Lecasc had no doubt that Poluntis wanted more from the woman than a partnership but had no interest in his relationships.

"*Dead* languages?"

"That was her favorite subject."

Kaskem presented a wicked grin, "Thanks for the information and hospitality, but we have to go now and I wouldn't want the city guard hard on my ass, so . . ." he raised his sword.

Poluntis raised his arm and squealed, "Wait! I don't care about the guard nor am I angry about the intrusion. In fact, gentlemen, I am always on the lookout for new talent. You see, I sometimes come across unwanted competition and nosy inspectors. I could use men like you and I pay very well. Killing me would only limit your opportunities."

Kaskem slowly lowered his short sword, "Well, if there's one

136

thing I've learned it's never burn your bridges. Remember this, if I so much as smell a city guard on my trail, I'll be coming back for you. It will be messy and painful. You don't move so fast, remember?"

"I wouldn't want to make an enemy of a man like you. No indeed. Good journey my friends," and he held up a golden cup.

Lecasc was a little slow following Kaskem out of the room, so surprised that the fat merchant wasn't lying in a pile of his own guts. They crossed the garden, climbed the oak tree, and sprinted to the barn where the men were sleeping. With dawn nearly upon them, they kicked the sleeping forms awake and quickly prepared to ride. If possible, the company would need to be in the forest by daybreak, just in case the merchant lied and word of their presence was shouted from one end of Delane to the other.

Chapter 6

Shasp rocked in time with Grimm's rhythmic stride, enjoying the breeze that played across his skin while Olympian islands of white and silver sailed across the vast sky like an armada on its way to war. Casually, his fickle gaze shifted from the clouds and settled on the curious Ella. When they left Delane, she had insisted that her wool robe was sufficient for travel, but Shasp would have none of it and acquired leather rider breeches, boots and a cotton tunic for her. Embarrassed, she admitted she had no money to repay him, but Shasp dismissed her concern. For days, they had rambled through the forests near Delane, heading southwest to avoid the steppes, and eventually, the trees thinned to rolling grass hills, similar to those in Tanya.

Lately, Ella's doleful condition seemed to dissolve slightly, and the savannah sun had tinged her pale skin to a shade of light brown. Her eyes seemed to spend more time admiring the scenery and less time studying the ground. She had even smiled a little when Shasp pointed out a descending hawk landing on some unfortunate vermin nearby. Large tawny cougars and wild bison always gave her a reason to stop their progress so she could admire the beasts. The change from Delane's seedy streets to the wild southwestern grasslands had done wonders for her and as her depression evaporated, Shasp saw that Ella was truly beautiful.

Shasp suggested they stay on the plains for as long as possible, where game and water were abundant, but sooner or later they would have to head due south and enter the Acadean Steppes. Vargos grew inexplicably more anxious as time passed, and Shasp surmised it had something to do with the other party Vargos had mentioned. In spite of the casual travel and pleasant weather of the cooling fall, Vargos never missed an opportunity to ride to a high vantage point where he would scan the horizon.

"Why are you constantly checking our trail?" asked Shasp one afternoon when Vargos returned from a nearby hill.

"Just keep your sword sharp and ready," Vargos answered with none of his usual quips.

Shasp snorted, "Is there any other way to keep a blade?"

By the time the sun reached its zenith, pouring out its heat, they had reached the Kennawar River, where its snaking waterways wound through deep gorges hewn from sandstone and basalt over thousands of years. They dismounted and led the horses down a treacherous narrow trail to a gravel beach below, which seem to run along the river for as far as the eye could see. Ella admired the unusual colors weaving through the layered rock of the cliff walls, and her warrior companions stretched their legs in the cool air near the calm water.

Vargos looked about with his usual concern as the horses gulped noisily, "Let's not stay too long. I don't like the look of this canyon."

139

Shasp nodded, "It's narrow, alright. If we were ambushed here, we couldn't go back the way we came and swimming the river would leave us exposed to arrows or crossbow bolts."

Vargos grabbed some empty water skins from his saddle and called to Ella. "Come on girl, get your water replenished and let's get out of here."

"Why, it's cooler down here and peaceful. Couldn't we camp here for a few days?"

"No, I'll explain later."

No sooner had the words cleared his lips than came the distant sound of gravel trickling down from the trail above. Seven swarthy men on horseback were carefully descending the narrow path, and quickly poured out onto the gravel beach barring the way of return. Ella shrank behind Shasp as the sickening odor of bodies long unwashed pervaded the air and she suddenly felt ill. Some wore tattered leather breeches and wool while others wore cotton with compliments of fur from a variety of animals. Ella could see glimpses of fractured armor under the collage of clothing and a lean, wiry man, wearing a steel cap with a spike ambled forward away from the rest. A long uncomfortable silence followed as Vargos stood with his arms folded, appraising the hard-looking crew.

Eventually, the leader showed his blackened teeth in a broad smile that spread slowly under his hatchet nose. "I thought I heard voices down here. Normally we use the path a quarter of a mile east of the canyon because it's a little easier to get down. I'm the leader of this band of scabs."

Vargos gave back a grin that belied his apprehension, "I hope we're not intruding. We will be moving out of your way as soon as we finishing watering our horses."

The rotten toothed man dismounted, "Oh, no intrusion at all, friend. We were on our way to the wars in Tanya to sell our services to whoever pays more. Rebel or king, it makes no difference to us." He extended his hand, "Name's Assant."

Vargos accepted his hand, "Vargos, and these two are Shasp Ironwrought and Ella of Delane."

"Ella, huh? Well dear, you are a vision of loveliness on this lonesome plain." Behind him, his men snickered and murmured.

Shasp came around Grimm's flanks, flashing a broad smile and extended his hand to Assant, "It's always good to meet a fellow

140

soldier of fortune."

Assant took his hand and Shasp gripped it hard for a moment, still smiling…then jerked the man across his body, spinning him around, chest to back, and with his free hand drove his Somerikan knife hilt deep into Assant's neck. Before his crumpling corpse hit the ground, Ironwrought had already covered the short distance between himself and the other riders. His blade was out on the fly and the nearest man died in his saddle before he could even clear his weapon from the scabbard. The shock of the unexpected attack left all stunned for moment, but the filthy brigands shook off their surprise, screamed in unison, and quickly maneuvered their mounts for a counterattack.

By the time Vargos lunged for his crossbow where it dangled from the saddle, Shasp had already hamstrung a screaming horse. Vargos aimed the crossbow and its bolt sang from the frustrated cable, punching a hole through a charging horseman then disappearing into the distance beyond.

Shasp quickly dispatched the man from the injured horse, nearly cutting him in half before he fell from the saddle. An iron spear head ripped through Shasp's jerkin and laid open his back. The rider retracted the spear for a second stab, but when the wicked point flashed down again, Shasp side-stepped, caught the haft and jerked his foe out of the saddle. The air whistled from the man's lungs as he impacted the beach; lungs which Shasp promptly impaled.

While Shasp was fighting his battles, Vargos was surviving his own. He ducked under a horse's neck when its rider tried to split his head with an axe then reappeared on his assailant's unprotected side and sank his long sword into his ribs. The mercenary cried out in pain and shock, then slid from the saddle into a heap. Little did Vargos realize that he was between the trail and the last of the wolf pack, who was trying to flee. By the time Vargos heard the churning hooves against the gravel beach, it was too late to dodge out of the way. Instinctively, he thrust out his sword and the blade penetrated deep into the horse's chest as the mass of flesh blasted him off his feet, wrenching the hilt out of his hand. The horse's forelegs immediately crumpled, catapulting the rider headlong into a boulder, and with a sickening crack of bone and cartridge, the brigand's neck broke like a twig.

Vargos struggled to his feet, pain shooting from his bruised

141

thigh, and glared at Shasp, who was striding toward him, bloody katana in hand.

"What the hell was that? Are you stark raving mad! You don't pick a fight with a band of armed men three times our number because you don't like the way they look, or whatever the hell your reason was! Have you taken leave of your senses?"

Shasp reached out and steadied Vargos, then helped him to a rotten log near the water. "Do you think it's broken?"

Vargos gave him an incredulous look, "I don't know. I don't think so. The horse caught me in the thigh as it collapsed. Now, if we are done discussing my injury . . . why in the hell did you attack a friendly group of riders?"

Shasp called soothingly to a spooked horse, coaxing the animal as it cautiously approached. He stroked its muzzle until it calmed, then moved to its side and lifted a flap of dirty leather under the saddlebag. Black cast iron manacles clanked as they dangling from sturdy chain links. "Slavers," said Shasp.

Vargos grew grim and stumbled to the horse where he fingered the shackles. "That doesn't mean they were interested in us. We might have departed without incident, so I still say you were reckless."

"Is that right?" Laughed Shasp, "*You* are calling *me* reckless? What about that time in Alem when we nearly got hung over that hussy that turned out be married to the magistrate, remember that? Now listen to me! Maybe you haven't had much experience with slavers, but I have! After they waved a warm farewell they would have tracked us until nightfall and fallen on us in our sleep, and if they did not kill us, we would have ended up slaves on some fat nobleman's estate pruning grapes! I certainly don't need to tell you what would have happened to Ella! Those bastards are the lowest form of insect. Becoming buzzard shit will be a step up in the world for the likes of them!"

Vargos rubbed his leg, "I'm sorry, I sought you out for a reason and this will serve as a reminder."

Over the next hour they sifted through the dirty belongings, searching for anything useful. Ella screamed and recoiled when she drew a necklace of human ears from one bag, a confirmation of what Shasp had spoken. When they were finished, they waded the Kennawar and climbed a path on the south side.

142

Soon, twilight washed over the deepening sky, and they made camp again in somber quiet. Shasp was still smoldering over the slavers presence and silently wondered if they were only a contingent of some larger band sent ahead to scout out villages. When Vargos rode off to a low rise, looking for fires on the horizon, Ella sat down on a saddle next to Shasp. He had removed his steel-sleeved jerkin and was trying hard to reach the gash on his back.

Ella took the wet cloth from his hand, found a medium sized bottle from her pack and doused the cloth.

Shasp sniffed the air, "Is that vinegar?"

"Yes, it will prevent infection." She swabbed the long cut and smiled when Shasp hissed at the stinging needles of pain. "I shouldn't think this would bother a born killer like you."

Shasp raised an eyebrow, "That sounds a little like an insult. By the way, I wasn't born a killer; I was made one, and I didn't have a choice in the matter."

"I'm no stranger to violence," Ella said with sadness in her voice, "though I have never been on the giving end of it as you are.

Shasp pulled on a greying linen shirt and noticed Ella staring at him, her lip was trembling and tears began to stream from some hidden pain. The brush with the slavers had dredged something from her fears and Shasp immediately understood Ella's association to violence; she had been on the receiving end.

Ella saw the doleful sympathy written on his face as he sat in awkward silence.

"My father was a man like you, on the giving end; a captain of the guard in Delane. Those who tested his mettle were sorry for it. That muddy pit I live in did not exist when my father protected that undeserving city. He would use his moderate pay to buy me books and scrolls because he knew how much I loved them. I was his only love after my mother died of the fever." A long silence hovered before Ella spoke again, "When I was fourteen he was backstabbed while breaking up a fight in a local tavern. I had nowhere to go, so a friend of my father kept me for a while but he couldn't afford to take care of me and his family. To his credit he tried to do better for me and secured an apprenticeship with a merchant who lived in the wealthy quarter; Poluntis Ilka. For the first month I thought I had gone to heaven. I had everything I needed or wanted and strangely, he didn't have much work for me to do. I was too young to realize what he really wanted from me." Tears continued to flow but her sad expression became a twisted mask of hurt and rage. "I tried to hide, to fight, but it only made things worse and the inevitable happened anyway. I endured that hell for four years, until my apprentice contract expired, because if I tried to escape, and I did, then the law allowed him to punish me. I had become his slave. Only two years ago I left his house and came to live on my own, but now . . . I can't sleep . . . and I live with this crushing spirit of shame and . . . fear. I'm afraid of everything!" Her voice cracked and she fell into uncontrollable sobbing. "Except... except when I'm near you." She waited for a response but Shasp only sat looking uncomfortable. Ella cast her eyes down in embarrassment, "I'm sorry, I shouldn't have said that. Someone like you would never want anything to do with someone like me. Someone who has been . . . I'm sorry," she choked.

Shasp's knelt beside her and gently took her chin in his hand, redirecting her gaze back into his own. "Did I ever tell you how much the wild favors you? Back in Delane you seemed a ghost among your books, but since then, you have grown more beautiful with each passing day. Another few weeks of this sunshine and fresh air and you'll become a goddess. Who will resist you then?" He bent forward and, feeling the wetness of her cheeks against his own, gave her a lingering kiss.

Vargos returned to find Ella reclining against Shasp's chest and she smiled up at the agent.

Vargos gave a knowing grin, "Well, I'm glad to see your spirits have improved, Ella."

Chapter 7

The blinding heat of the midday sun poured down upon the narrow river bank where Lecasc knelt to examine a bloated corpse. The stench seared his nostrils and he gagged involuntarily. He stood and scanned the scintillating water of the Kennawar. Covering his mouth with a rag, he turned to see Captain Kaskem nudge another of the seven bodies with the toe of his boot.

Lecasc cleared his throat and spat the stench from his mouth, "What do you think, Captain?"

"What do I think? I think these slavers thought to make a pretty penny on the wrong men and became prey instead of predators. Vargos chose his friend wisely." Kaskem bent to examine a footprint and dragged his fingers lightly over the textured indentation in the sand where it sponged water from the river. "Or . . . maybe they just wanted the girl."

Lecasc looked at the small footprint, "Do you think it was Vargos and the girl, Ella?"

"Whose trail have we been following, Lieutenant?   It would be a hell of a coincidence if it wasn't."

Hoof beats and clattering pebbles from the other side of the river stole their attention as a lone cavalryman thundered down the slope and splashed into the river. He rode his dripping horse out of the water and up to Kaskem.

"Just as you said, sir; three sets of hoof prints on the other side, heading south."

Kaskem glanced around at the scattered corpses and two dead horses, "It *was* them. It doesn't look like any of the gear was taken from the dead and the extra horses were freed and sent back up the path."

Lecasc nodded gravely, "How long?"

Kaskem shrugged, "These bodies are none too ripe and the scavengers haven't had much time to work them over. I'd say a day and a half at most, which means, if we push hard we can overtake them in the next two days. No doubt Vargos has pushed a little himself. He must suspect we are trailing him."

Lecasc glanced around at the faces of his men. Some sat astride their mounts while others milled about the grotesque bodies, searching for anything useful. Smeared with the dust and grime of a hard trail and exhausted, he absently wondered if they would be worth a spit in combat after two more days of hard pursuit. Lecasc knew Vargos had left Kalyfar five months ago with a ten day lead. Now it was narrowed to a day and a half, but at what cost. Did he dare plead for rest so the men could recharge? He looked again at their hardened faces and decided they were sturdier than he gave them credit. Perhaps it was he alone who was tired. He who really wondered if he gave a damn whether or not Vargos disappeared with the King's prize, but then he remembered his father, the general and consummate soldier. He could not return a failure; it would mar his family name forever. He secretly envied Kaskem's undying stamina and irresistible strength, his single-minded focus. The man wasn't even Kalyfarian, but a creature of the Somerikan Mountains much farther south where the weather turns cold. Reth had worked his way up through the infantry to the cavalry and finally officer, a legend. The more Lecasc thought about Kaskem, the more he realized he did not envy him but hated him. He snapped out of his reverie and mounted his gelding. He wasn't about to let his men know how tired he was.

"Shall we go, Captain?"

Kaskem swung into his saddle, "Absolutely."

The Olumbria River created a fertile band through the otherwise cruel Acadia steppes. Ella rode ahead a little, anxious to reach the cool water after a day of riding under the blistering August sun. "Come on you two, I want to cool off," she laughed and trotted ahead.

Shasp leaned over and rubbed Grimm's neck, "I've wanted to talk to you about something."

Vargos wiped sweat from his eyes, "What?"

Shasp sat up again, "This Vexgos, power of the ancients, what if it *is* some weapon of devastation? What do you think your king will do with it?"

Vargos shrugged, "Who knows? Keep it to protect the country from invaders I would think."

"You have more faith in royalty and aristocrats than I do. The idea of a power hungry potentate with something so powerful makes me uncomfortable."

"The king is a good man, Shasp. I wouldn't worry about him."

"What about his successor? Just because the current king doesn't want to use it to make war doesn't mean the next will not."

Vargos sighed with frustration, "You worry too much. I'm sure it will be some kind of benevolent power and if it isn't, maybe we can use it as such."

Silence reigned for a moment before Shasp spoke again, "Fine and well, Vargos, but if this thing is capable of great destruction, we destroy it, agreed?"

Vargos smiled, "If we even find it."

By the time Shasp and Vargos wound their way down the long switch back to the broad Olumbria, Ella was already treading water in her cotton shift, her riding clothes piled on the rocky shore near her gulping mount.

Shasp cast his gaze over the sun-splashed river toward the other side nearly a half-mile away. Waves lapped lazily against the rocky shore, pushed by an easy southern breeze. They were just east of the Umbrian Sea, a place where the river widened to thirty miles across for a length of sixty miles, but here the sea narrowed again to this broad span of river where Ella capered about.

Shasp unsaddled Grimm's lathered back then led the stallion down to drink and rest. He called to Ella, "What is this place east of here that you want to look for?"

She stopped treading water and walked out of the shallows toward shore, wincing and stumbling painfully on the sharp rocks. Dripping and shivering from the cool water, she dropped onto a large boulder and wrung out the hem of her garment. "There are several ancient pillars about a day or two from here. They border this river, but are out of the way, not near the main road. Tractos Philipas wrote that he believed they were the pillars of a mighty bridge that once spanned this river. The structures were embedded with many ancient characters but he was unable to decipher them all."

Shasp gazed across the river and contemplated a bridge massive enough to span it, "Impossible."

Vargos dropped his saddle next to Grimm's, "So you think they will lead us to the relic?"

"Maybe," she said, now squeezing the water from her hair.

Shasp interjected, "But if this Tractos person couldn't

understand them, how are you going to do it?"

"I've been studying his work and the works of many others and I think I have deciphered at least some of the rudimentary elements of the language. Why do you think I was so anxious to go? I've been wanting to see these pillars all of my life."

Vargos grunted, "I hope so, because if you can't decipher them or if there are no writings, we'll be forced to scour the steppes."

Shasp found a level place along the shore, heaved a few large rocks out of the way and set out his supplies. They ate a meager meal of salted pork, hard, crumbling bread and some dried fruit before settling down to a small fire. Vargos made his nightly jaunt to the horizon just before sunset to calm his paranoia and Shasp used his leisure time to oil his weapons and armor. Ella watched him quietly as he worked the heavy oil onto the blade of his Ayponese sword.

"Where did you get that," she asked?

"Aypon, across the western sea."

"I have read about that place. Is it true that they are consumed by the pursuit of perfection?"

"Yes, but they are also hopelessly cruel and impersonal," he added with a tinge of disgust.

"Is that where you learned to use that," she pointed at the sword.

"Most of what I learned about combat, I learned there, but I was exiled, so I had to leave and since then I've continued to learn what I can."

Ella dragged a string of pale blonde hair out of her eyes, "That knife doesn't have the same look as your sword."

Shasp pulled it from the scabbard, revealing its heavy hilt and heavier blade. "That's because it's Somerikan. Somerikans are some of the world's best knife fighters. It's true; they would often scorn taking a sword into combat even if it was against an enemy who had one. I learned quite a lot about the knife while I was there."

Ella marveled as Shasp spoke, "I've only dreamed of going to the places you have been."

Shasp shrugged, "The world is not a prison, Ella…go where you want."

"It is not a prison for a well-trained warrior…but for me; it's

148

like being a mouse in a room full of cats."

Shasp was suddenly saddened by her response and began to understand her fear, why she caged herself in a miserable hovel, slowly starving to death. They sat silently while he moved from the care of his weapons to that of his armor, slowly buffing the tarnish from the pale yellow metal of the helmet.

"Can I see it," asked Ella and Shasp tossed it to her.

Her fingertips moved over the short onyx horns of the forehead and down the slit visor. Truly it was an intimidating mask.

Shasp, sensing her curiosity, answered her unspoken query, "The Ayponese design their armor to strike fear in their enemies. That is the most important aspect of the armor; protection is secondary. This suit was made by a master of metals for my instructor when he was young. It is without equal, though I have made some modifications. He wore it and gave it to me when I left Aypon."

Ella handed the helmet back to him, "It looks like gold, but lighter in color."

Shasp chuckled, "It's not gold. It is folded steel with just enough Iron Pyrite to give it a light golden cast. I've killed more than one fool who tried to take it from me."

Again they fell to silence while he continued his work in the flickering light. Ella rolled onto her back, gazing up at the clear, sparkling sky and her bare legs gleamed in the firelight below her cotton shift. Polishing absently, Shasp rested his eyes on her, finding his mind locked in a mild trance by her beauty. He mused over the change in her, from shy and withdrawn to bold and brown. In his heart he knew she had a long way to go before she would be free of her fear . . . if ever. He set his buffing aside and crept, tiger-like, to where she lay until his face hovered over hers.

She gave him a serious, concerned look, "Promise me something."

"Anything," he replied.

"Don't get killed over me."

Her response took him by surprise. Had he known her so long that she would make such a selfless request out of love? Or was it simply a sense of worthlessness created by her own tortured feelings?

Shasp returned her grave stare, "I would never die for a

foolish cause but some people *are* worth dying for Ella, and you are one of them. No, I won't make that promise."

Tears welled in her eyes as she pulled his face to hers, lingering in a long and delicate kiss. He loved her gently, carefully, and afterwards lay with his chest to her supple back, his arm draped over her as she faced the fire. They lay quiet and content in each other's warmth until Vargos returned.

The next morning, they set out early while the dew still adorned the grasses which thrived along the river, then headed east along the Olumbria toward the ancient pillars. Late in the day, when the sun was sinking into a fiery horizon, Vargos spied the columns in the far distance.

They discussed whether to camp or continue, but Ella's excitement won the consensus. Late in the evening the troop cantered up to the nearest monolith, black and looming against the moonlit sky. Shasp marveled at the girth and height of the ancient structures. Round smooth columns of stone so big around, ten men holding hands could not encompass one. They reached, easily, two hundred feet high. The tops were jagged, which suggested that they were much taller when initially constructed. Shasp ran his gloved hand over the surface as his mind reeled over the speculation of manpower it must have taken to build those giants. As he gazed over the sparkling water to the other side, he could see similar spikes silhouetted against the far shore and began to grasp the size of Tractos' bridge.

Ella chattered with excitement, running from pillar to pillar in a fit of abandon, so Shasp shook off the nostalgia and started to set camp, knowing Ella would not be able to find the symbols she sought in the dark.

Vargos came alongside him, "No fire tonight, Shasp. I have an ill feeling in my bones."

Shasp nodded, knowing Vargos' premonitions well enough. They had saved him before and he respected what others might refer to as an old woman's superstition. "Should we take turns watching?"

Vargos stood silently for a moment, thinking, "Yes, we should."

A long night of broken sleep followed before the welcome rays of morning greeted the bleary-eyed warriors. Ella was sharp and smiling, eating only a little fruit and some nuts before striking out among the lonely, titans with lead marker and onion skin paper in hand.

Shasp suggested that Vargos keep an eye out while he helped Ella gather what information she could from the silent stone.

"Just make sure it's work you're helping her with and not something else. There will be time for the other later."

Shasp shot him a withering stare, "You're one to talk."

Vargos just smiled and rolled his eyes as he turned his mare toward the ridge bordering the river.

Shasp and Ella spent the afternoon copying weather blasted engravings onto onion skin. She was careful to map the pillar positions and number the corresponding lists of markings. By the time the sun waxed hot overhead, Ella had completed her work and the two sought the shade of the giant pillars. Her excitement over the find, mixed with the heat of the day, awakened her desires and, in spite of Vargos' admonishment, they unleashed their passions in the comfort of the tall grass. Afterward, Ella sat with her back against a column, Shasp's head pillowed in her lap.

"Have you been able to make anything of those writings?"

"Most of them." She pointed across the river to the sister columns, "Those columns were the base for the bridge on the far side. If you line them up with these, then you can see the direction of the ancient road."

"So if we go in that direction we will find this fortress?"

She wagged her finger and laughed, "Not so. The markings on the pillars suggest that, in ancient times, there were crossroads south of this bridge. Alem is built on ruins to the west and there were probably settlements to the east. I think the fortress of Vexgos could be near that junction."

Shasp shook his head, doubtful, "The road doesn't exist anymore. How are we to know where this junction is?"

"Have you ever heard of Avisen Dabis?"

Shasp shook his head.

"I didn't think so. He was a scholar from the southern Arrigin, and he noticed that many hillsides had irregularities, one face rounded and the other flat."

Shasp's eyes widened slightly, "Yes, I've seen hillsides like

151

that often."

"Everyone has, but Dabis noticed that those deformed hills ran in patterns. In the plains territories he mapped them and found they ran mostly in a straight line. On the coast they would wander but still maintained a predictable course."

"I'm not following you."

"Dabis believed those hillsides were cut by the ancients to make way for roads."

Understanding dawned on his face, "So if we find the cut hills east of the straight line of this bridge, we will find our ancient road and somewhere near it will be the fortress."

Ella beamed with a pride she had not known since before her father's death. It ran through her like light through a window.

Shasp saw it in her eyes and seized the moment, "Never, in all my years, have I known a woman so beautiful and so brilliant."

When the afternoon cooled and Ella was convinced she had missed nothing, they mounted and rode out. They found Vargos leaning on his pommel, dressed in full armor.

"I think we should be ready for anything from here on," he said, responding to Shasp's inquiring brow.

Shasp carefully donned his black and gold Ayponese armor then hung his helmet by its chin strap from the pommel of his saddle. Silently, they started back toward the ferry a half day's journey west.

Chapter 8

Dusk spread its wings in the distance as the three riders descended a tall berm and trotted toward a sandy stretch of beach where the river washed fickle on its shore. At the edge of the water was a stone dock, not so neatly constructed as a pile of rocks cast into the water, but functional. Two large flat rafts, capable of holding ten horses and their riders, bobbed gently against the sides of the dock with the soft sound of creaking wood. A rough plank one-room shack stood on sturdy poles, a man's height off the ground to allow for the ebb and flow of the Olumbria. They had stopped at the ferry the day before while on the way to the columns, intending to return and purchase passage to the other side. The old ferryman and his son were hospitable enough and had shared a quick meal with them.

Shasp started off the berm when he spotted the old man and his son descending the rickety plank stairs of the shack. They eased off the horses and Vargos clasped the ferryman's hand as his son stood by quietly.

"Would you like to come in for some food before you cross? I have plenty."

Vargos clapped his hand on the old man's shoulder, "Yes, by the buttocks of Ariess, I'm getting tired of salt pork. Do you have any wine left?"

"Yes . . . yes of course," replied the ferryman, "come in."

Shasp thought he sensed some strain in the man's voice but surmised it was from the battle dress. Commoners were usually distrustful of armored men.

The old man led the way up the stairs to the entrance of the shack, beckoned for them to follow and disappeared through the doorway. His son followed the troupe up the stairs, and as soon as the three of them cleared the threshold, the door slammed shut behind them.

Shasp turned intending to ask the ferryman's son a question but did not find him there. Instead, eight calvary soldiers in full plate armor bearing the winged serpent of Kalyfar, stood with swords drawn. The soldiers had been standing with their backs against the front wall, and Shasp had entered, oblivious to their presence. Now he realized the anxiety in the old man's voice and reached out to push Ella behind him as the soldiers began to circle. He and Vargos backed up to the rear wall as Shasp drew the heavy, eighteen-inch Somerikan knife. In just a few seconds, he had assessed the room and quickly calculated that it was too small for swords. In such close quarters the knife would be a strong advantage.

Lecasc stepped forward, sword wavering, "We just want the girl, Vargos, no one needs to die today."

Vargos slowly drew his long sword, "Lieutenant Lecasc, how nice of you to come all this way just to see me."

"Captain Vargos," he replied formally, "the king is not pleased with you."

Vargos grinned broadly, "What else is new. Who did he send with you Lecasc? I know you didn't come alone."

"I didn't; Captain Kaskem is in command of the company."

The words had scarcely left his lips when the thundering of hooves shook the little hovel. Shasp heard shouts as men surrounded the shack and realized they had been hiding behind the berm on the opposite side of the beach. He cursed himself for not heeding the signs when he saw them.

When Lecasc mentioned Kaskem, Vargos paled slightly and his confident grin took on a nervous aspect. "So, Captain Kaskem has been dogging my trail. I'm flattered that his highness thought it necessary to send an entire company through foreign lands just for me."

"It wasn't just for you, Vargos. He wants the relic. We know that you need the woman to interpret the tablet and the signs leading to Vexgos. Give her to us and surrender and we'll take you back to the king. Maybe he will be lenient; your execution might be brief and painless. As for your bodyguard, we have no quarrel with him."

Shasp was never one to talk when his steel could speak for him. He knew they needed Ella and as far as he was concerned, she wasn't going anywhere. In one fluid motion, he flung Ella to the floor and lunged to his right. Side stepping a sword lunge, he plunged the knife into the soldier's neck, sending the man to the floor gurgling and choking. Before the cavalryman next to him could maneuver, Shasp stepped into him, entwined the other's sword arm and plunged the knife up under his cuirass. The soldier shrieked and slumped as the blade punctured his heart, but Shasp did not let him fall. Instead he draped the armored corpse across his back and drove into the knot of scrambling men. The weight of the body added impetus to his rush and fouled the movement of at least three of his foes. He drove home again with the knife, evoking a cry of pain from yet another victim and then quickly leapt back before an enemy on his left could skewer his exposed flank.

Vargos battled with a soldier over his sword while another lay at his feet in a spreading pool of blood. Two were still struggling to get into the fray when Lecasc lunged for Vargos' exposed ribs, but Shasp earned his pay and caught the lieutenant with a side kick that sent him off his feet and thudding into a wall where he slumped to the floor. Shasp quickly put himself between Vargos and the last two opponents. He stood facing them resolutely with the Somerikan blade dripping in a reversed grip, and after a long tense moment, the braver one dove forward with a wicked downward slash. Shasp ducked under his arm, spun and hammered the blade into the soldier's armpit as he went by. The man stood frozen in shock from the strike, holding one hand under his arm, then fell to his knees and finally his face. Shasp backed the remaining man toward the door where the soldier opened it and eased himself down the stairs. Shasp stepped up to the threshold, thinking to follow him out, when a crossbow bolt hissed into his helmet and ricocheted into the shack to rattle against the wall. He ducked back and slammed the door. Vargos had wrenched his hand free, dispatched his adversary and now stood silently regarding his blood-smeared bodyguard.

Shasp moved to the shack's only tiny window and carefully peaked out, "We're trapped, Vargos."

Vargos fumed and spun on the old ferryman, "You son of a bitch, you sold us out!" He started toward the cringing old man, blade extended, but Shasp yelled.

"Vargos, don't do it! He had no choice."

Vargos lowered his blade and spun away, "What now!"

Shasp continued to appraise the situation from the window, "I don't know." He left his position and kneeled over the dazed Lecasc. Seizing him by the collar of his breast plate, he jerked the young man forward and touched his throat with the keen knife point. "How many men are with you?"

Lecasc roused from his stupor, eyes darting about. Amazement took him when he realized his situation and the point of the knife quickened his pulse. "Thirty," he looked at his fallen men, "twenty-four."

Shasp pushed him down, stood and began scanning the room, "We're in a real fix this time, Vargos."

A voice boomed from outside, "Well Lecasc. . . .do you have them?"

Vargos yelled back, "Not quite, Reth! It seems we have him instead! Care to make deal!"

Outside, Reth Kaskem stood on the berm surveying the trap, "I don't think you're in a position to make deals, Vargos! Send out the girl!"

"Go to hell!" was Shasp's reply as he drew his sword, shifting the knife to his left hand.

"Look Vargos, we just want the woman. If you send her out we'll be on our way."

"I thought the king wanted my head!" Vargos called back.

Shasp eased to the door and faced Vargos, "I thought you were the king's agent," he hissed.

Vargos waved him down, "I was...we'll talk about it later."

Shasp was feeling that familiar twinge in his guts; the one he had every time Vargos got them into a similar situation, but this one was the worst. "You're damn right we'll talk later."

Again, Reth boomed, "I'll tell the king I left your rotting corpse in Oshintan. No one needs to know you walked away. Be reasonable, Vargos."

Vargos became agitated, "I have a better idea! I'll trade you Lecasc for our freedom! His father is a Colonel, right?"

"General actually, but Lecasc got himself into that pot of stew, he can get himself out." Kaskem gave a quiet order to a man standing next to him. The soldier darted away and returned with several men bearing bows, knocked with oil soaked arrows. Kaskem nodded and the arrows were lit. "Last chance Vargos. What's it going to be? Freedom or death?"

Ella stood slowly, walked to the door and called out, "Captain Kaskem! It is Ella! If I come out, do you promise not to harm these men!"

"I do!" was the reply.

Shasp shook his head, "No, Ella., you are not going out there. He'll kill us anyway."

"I have to take that chance, Shasp. . . for you."

156

"Ella you're not going!" he said firmly. "I won't argue with you!"

"Don't you tell me what I can and can't do, Shasp Ironwrought! I am a free woman and I did not starve in that rundown rat's nest so someone could give me orders. I was free when you found me and I'm free now! I'm going out."

He softened, "Please Ella, don't do it."

"There is no other way." She turned and looked down at Lecasc, "Lieutenant Lecasc, will Captain Kaskem keep his word?"

Lecasc believed he would not, but also understood that he would not fare well in this shack if he gave a fool's reply. "Yes my lady, he will and you can add my word to his."

"Lieutenant, will you escort me out?"

Lecasc scrambled to his feet, slowly collected his saber from the floor and sheathed it, lest the killer with Vargos make worm food out of him.

Ella reached for the door handle but Shasp's hand was already on it. "Please Ella."

She cupped his face in her graceful hands and kissed him, "I don't want you to die because of me." She lifted his steel-shod hand from the handle and pulled the door open. Lecasc slid through the opening behind her, never taking his eyes off Shasp.

Outside, several troops escorted her away from the shack and over to Reth where he gave her an approving look. "A wise decision, lady. Lecasc, are you still whole?"

The lieutenant turned away ashamed, "Yes captain but the others are not."

"Lieutenant, take this lady down to the ferry and start loading the gear." Then he called out to the archers, "Fire the house!" Flaming arrows thudded into the dry wood which immediately gave succor to the fire.

Ella screamed, "No! You gave your word!" Tears gushed from her eyes as the shack slowly became engulfed in ravaging flames.

Men with crossbows kept aim on the doorway until one screaming figure lurched out of the inferno. Smoke trailed from the singed beard of the ferryman as steel bolts shot through his body ending his misery. The son ran to his dying father, cradling him in his arms only moments before he met the same fate.

Kaskem bellowed orders to retrieve Vargos' mare and Shasp's stallion. The mare went easy enough but Grimm neighed, reared and bucked, sending one cavalry man off his feet, before he bolted away.

Ella started to run for the shack, but Lecasc seized her arm. She tried to pull away from him but he held her fast. "You promised!" She cried, collapsing on the sand, sobbing spasmodically while the acrid smell of smoke filled the air, and she pounded the earth with a tormented fist.

Kaskem watched until he was content the structure was wholly consumed in crackling flames then gave the order to board the ferry. With military efficiency, the rafts were filled to near sinking and the ponderous crafts eased out across the water. When they were nearly halfway to the far side, Ella heard the building collapse, saw the orange flames still feeding on the ruins, and wanted to die.

Chapter 9

Shasp heard the order to fire the house and the thumping of arrows into the wooden planks of the exterior. "They're going to burn us out!"

Vargos looked around helplessly, "We have to get out!"

"There is no way out, Vargos. We can't go through the door or we'll be riddled with bolts."

"Then we knock out the back wall, it's flimsy enough."

Shasp shook his head, "You're not thinking. The house is surrounded. It's no good."

"Then the floor!" he persisted.

"The floor is at least six-feet off the ground. They would still see us." Shasp's eyes consumed every aspect of the tiny room; a wooden table with a pitcher of water; two low bunks with wool blankets and straw mats; a few crates and chests. Suddenly Shasp darted to the beds and ripped the blankets off. "Vargos, knock the legs off that table!" Then he snatched the large pitcher from the table, dousing the blankets even as the odor of smoke filled the air.

Vargos hacked at the wooden legs, removing them in seconds. "What are we doing?"

Now, Shasp was using his knife to pry stubborn planks from the floor. "We are going to put one of those wet blankets over the table and one over us. The table will go over us while we lay on the floor. We can breathe through this hole in the floor because the smoke and heat will rise. If we're lucky, maybe we can survive under here until your friends are convinced we are ashes. Then we can escape through the floor. Ferryman, help me with these planks." The old man set quickly to work.

"That's the best you can do?"

"Unless you have a better idea, yes and we better hurry."

A few more minutes passed as they pried up several planks, creating a hole large enough for them to drop through. Shasp used the majority of the water on the upper blanket, lamenting the lack of dampness on the other.

Suddenly a clump of flaming thatch fell from the ceiling, landing in the ferryman's wooly hair. It immediately ignited, sending the man into a panic. Shasp tried to help him, but in his alarm the ferryman bolted through the door and into the midst of the awaiting archers. Shasp slammed the door and returned to their desperate plan.

They stretched under the table, holding themselves just above the gaping hole. By the time the plan was implemented, fire had chewed through to the interior spewing stinging tendrils of smoke and licking flames. The sounds of shouts and milling horses carried over the raging fire above, warning that it was not yet time to vacate their crematorium. Flames spread out greedily over the walls and the heat intensified until rivulets of sweat poured from their faces. Wood beams collapsed, thundering to the floor in a shower of searing sparks and still the horses and men tromped outside. Shasp was beginning to doubt his reckless plan and silently wondered if they may have to face bolts and arrows anyway. As the seconds ebbed away, they began to cook in their armor, leather straps began to smoke and hair singed. Shasp's blood felt like it would boil and he strained, shaking, against the hell that blazed around them until he could hear only the snapping fire. Suddenly the building lurched and groaned.

Vargos cried out over the din of the inferno. "I can't stay here any longer!"

Shasp saw the desperation in his face and nodded, "Very well," and let go of the floor to free-fall onto the sand with Vargos landing across his back. He lurched to his feet, armor smoking, and stumbled out from under the burning hut. They reached the berm a few yards away before the roof crashed through the floor, creating a pile of spouting flames. Singed and smeared with soot, they stood fixated by the fire while contemplating their narrow escape.

Vargos turned toward Shasp and laughed, "That is without a doubt the tightest fix I have been in yet! Once again you saved my. . . ." Before he could complete the sentence Shasp's steel fist slammed against his mouth. Vargos reeled backwards and fell as Shasp stepped over him, fist still clenched and pointed down at him with an accusing finger.

"You son of a bitch! What did he mean, 'the king is not pleased with you,'?" Aren't you the king's agent? That's what you told me! You better tell me the truth, Vargos, or I swear by all that's right, I'll beat it out of you!"

160

Vargos rose up on an elbow, wiped the blood from his lip and regarded the red stain for a moment. "I *was* the king's agent. Everything was true about Vexgos and about Ella, but I had a better offer. A spy in the court from Dahoe approached me one night during a banquet. Someone had leaked the information of the expedition and the power of the ancients. He promised me an irresistible sum for Vexgos and a place of honor in the court of Boycee. Hell, I was getting sick of Kalyfar anyway, I couldn't turn it down. Unfortunately, my friend made some fateful error and was discovered. Lucky for me, he held out long enough for me to get away from Kayfar with a good head start. I figured the offer would still be good in Dahoe and I was going to split it with you. Think of the money! No more taking orders. No more scraping out a living by risking my life for some fat aristocrat with a lap dog!"

Shasp had quietly listened to Vargos, "I should have guessed as much because I know you so well. I don't even mind saving your ass as long as the pay is good, but this time your antics have placed Ella in danger! What do you think will happen to her when they have what they want?"

Vargos sighed, "We'll get her back, Shasp, somehow."

"You're damn right we will and if you pull another fast one, Vargos, I'll run you through!" He walked away from his prostrate companion to the top of the berm where he gazed out at the horizon and made a shrill whistle. Soon the clomping of hooves beat toward him and Grimm hove into view. Vargos gathered himself and staggered down to the stone dock where he cursed the absence of both rafts. Shasp walked beside him, leading Grimm by the reins.

Vargos rubbed his short, blonde hair in agitation, "How are we going to get across? By the time we double back and find another ferry, they will be long gone."

Shasp gazed across the mile-wide river and slowly began unbuckling his steaming armor, "We're going to swim."

"Swim? It's a mile across, Shasp!"

"Grimm will carry our armor, and we can re-equip on the other side. If we get tired we can hang on to him."

Vargos spat, "If he doesn't drown, leaving us in the middle of a vast plain, naked and defenseless."

Shasp stripped and tied his gear to Grimm's back. Vargos followed his example, but amid a barrage of curses and pessimistic oaths.

Darkness draped over the river as they eased into the cold, easy flow of the Olumbria. Orange firelight from the burning hut danced on the waters creating an eerie glow as they swam alongside the horse toward the other side.

Chapter 10

The troop had a full night's rest, but sleep did not come to Ella. She had lain awake contemplating Kaskem's demand to know what she had discovered, and from spite and self-preservation, told him only enough to keep him content. She had considered refusing the bestial captain altogether, hoping he would just kill her in his frustration, but her instincts warned that death would not be quick. Besides, Ella wasn't ready to die just yet.

After the morning muster, she rode silently as the column of cavalry waded through a sea of golden grass. She did not look up at the peaceful blue sky with its sailing silver clouds nor to the sun-drenched horizon beyond. She just stared blankly, her mind folding inward, while a cool breeze played over her. She was infused with pain, anger and hopelessness from suffering so much, but this last blow had left her as hollow as a gourd.

The burly captain pulled his gray mount around to his right and ambled back along the column until he turned alongside Ella's mare.

"The scout said there are pillars ahead, just as you predicted. Where are we going from there?"

"I won't know until I examine them," she said, her tone filled with acid.

Reth grunted and gave her an appraising look, "I hope you're right, girl. Just don't keep anything from me. Not that I would mind forcing it out of you." With his incentive still hanging in the hot air, he rode back to the front of the column.

By mid-afternoon, they spotted the jagged teeth of the ancient monoliths where they stood clustered together the same as their twins on the far side of the Olumbria. With little daylight left to work with, Ella began making copies of the ancient symbols, noting the positions of the pylons, and like their brothers, found they possessed the same markings.

Lieutenant Lecasc approached her with a worried expression, "May I interrupt you, lady?"

Ella did not lift her eyes from her onion skin diagrams, "Who am I that you should even ask?"

Lecasc cleared his throat, "I was just wondering if you have discovered anything."

Ella straightened her back and gave him an icy stare, then held out her papers, "The inscriptions on that column," she pointed at one to the south, "are the same as those on the Olumbrian columns. There are more, yet different symbols on the columns to the west and east. I believe they are the names of the ancient roads that once spanned this land."

Lecasc perused the diagrams, "Amazing."

She stood and brushed the dust from the back of her riding breeches and pointed to the southern horizon. "Do you see that hill, the one that has the misshapen side?"

Lecasc shaded his eyes, "Yes."

"That is the direction we need to go. When we reach it, we will watch for another and head for it. Your scouts should spread out ahead of us and look for anything unusual in the terrain."

Lecasc gave a satisfied nod, "Ella, I think I should warn you against angering Captain Kaskem. The man is a brute."

"And a liar," she shot back.

Lecasc paused, "Yes, he kills without thought or remorse. I will do what I can to protect you but. . . .," he cast his eyes to the ground and exhaled sharply, "I will do my best to keep you safe." He turned and stalked away, leaving Ella in a tangle of emotions she wanted nothing to do with. She stepped back and let her eyes take in the ancient giants. Awe crept slowly into her burdened soul and she realized why she needed to live; to see the power of the ancients.

The sun was low on the horizon and they had been leaping from one distorted hillside to the next for most of the day when one of the scouts road back to the company. The dusty rider reined in next to Reth Kaskem and saluted, "Captain, there's a shallow canyon about two miles ahead, full of cave mouths and fissures. Nothing is alive there, sir, not a single blade of grass or even an insect. The vegetation grows up to the edge of the canyon walls and stops. I've never seen anything like it."

A grin creased Kaskem's mouth, "Bring the girl forward. I want her next to me."

Soon the lines of horses were descending a narrow rocky switchback of natural origin between looming walls of reddish rock. At the bottom, the air was slightly cooler and the lengthening shadows of the high walls lent a menacing and eerie aspect to the canyon. By the time the group reached the bottom, the sun had settled and their surroundings were bathed in darkness. Ella shrank as the looming shadows caused fear to well up inside her and suddenly, Shasp's absence became a yawning abyss that threatened to swallow her sanity.

Jason Stone

Lecasc came up alongside Reth, "Captain, should we make camp?"

"Yes, and double the sentries. We'll look for anything significant tomorrow."

That night, Ella's dreams were restless. Messengers of destruction visited her in red nightmares and she bolted upright, covered in a film of sweat. Her old fears were returning, gnawing away at the strength she had accumulated over the last weeks. She cried fitful tears of hopelessness and, at dawn, woke in a fog, haunted by strange premonitions. Men clamored about the camp, rummaging for food and preparing for the day's excursion through the canyon.

Kaskem had his men divide into several groups, and sent them out to scour the desolate canyon. It was nearly midday and Reth was returning to the mouth of a dusty cave, which had turned out to be a dead end, when he saw Lecasc trudging up the slope toward him. Lecasc pulled his hand through his sweat-soaked auburn hair. Kaskem could see the fatigue in Lecasc's sunburned face, but felt no pity, "What is it Lieutenant?"

165

"Some of the men think they may have found something; an entrance of some kind, perhaps." Kaskem brushed past him on his way down the slope and Lecasc trailed behind. "Over by that outcropping, sir."

Lecasc directed him to a narrow cave mouth on the opposite side of the canyon where several men waited, and Kaskem was forced to turn sideways to squeeze his bulk through the hole. It opened into a musty passage wide enough for him to walk straight for a hundred yards then terminated in a wall of loose stones. The air was dank and an odor of ancient dust pervaded his nostrils. Slowly, carefully, he ran his hands over the stones, examining their position. They had been stacked neatly by hands long since dead. He turned to Lecasc who had come in behind him, "Lieutenant, bring me an axe."

Before the sun reached its zenith, Kaskem stood, sweating and bare chested, before a gaping hole. There had only been room in the cave for one man to work and Reth had easily removed the piled rocks; a job that normally would have exhausted three men. He pulled on his black linen tunic and began buckling on his steel cuirass, "Go get Vargos' bitch. I have a feeling we're going to need her."

Lecasc returned with a sullen Ella in tow. Kaskem drew his heavy short sword, took a torch from a nearby subordinate and trudged into the blackness. In a passage that was just wide enough for Ella to reach out and touch both walls at the same time, ten men stumbled downward in the flickering torchlight. As the minutes crept by, the warm air turned cold, and the dank walls began to show signs of fungal growth. The scraping of their feet against the dusty floor and the labored breathing of the men became a rhythm that checked Ella's fear as they continued their descent. It seemed like hours before Kaskem finally halted, and they found themselves teetering on the verge of an abyss. Their tiny torchlight was swallowed by the great vastness of a monstrous cavern. At their feet, the dirt floor of the tunnel gave way to a metal platform, crusted with antediluvian limestone, and the silence conceded to the scattered dripping of water as it rained down from countless stalactites.

Lecasc knelt on the deck, astonished, "Captain Kaskem, this entire platform is crafted of some strange metal I have never seen before. It couldn't be iron or steel, the water would have destroyed it long ago." He turned to Ella, "Do you have any idea how many

166

blacksmiths it would take to construct something of this magnitude? An army of them would take years."

Reth grunted and started for a staircase adorned with small stalagmites, created a drop at a time over the millennia. Booted feet rang on the metal case as they descended into the abyss. Hundreds of feet below the staircase dropped to a floor littered with the ancient limestone formations, yet strangely level. Again Lecasc examined the floor and felt the patches of grey flat rock that appeared to be congruous for as far as the torchlight would reveal. He wondered if it was a single, massive cut stone and began to fear the ancients more than ever. Reth's voice broke the monotony of the dripping water, echoing back to one of his men. "Go back and get as many torches as you can carry and lamp oil." The soldier hurried off, leaving the awestruck group to ponder their surroundings.

Ella hugged herself to ward off the cavern's chill, her linen shirt thin and inadequate. Her dreams from the night before threatened to take substance in the ominous and brooding depths. The men returned with lighting equipment, their torches flaring and several lanterns were also lit. Kaskem carried one to the front and gave the order to move. Men spread out on the lake of stalagmites, their puny lights defiant against the inky blackness. As they pressed forward, a gray shape slowly materialized against the firelight and rose steadily until it towered over the insignificant intruders. A wall of greyish stone stretched as far as they could see, both up and to the left and right. Calcium and limestone coated the bastion periodically in thick layers of pastel colored minerals. The men worked their way along its surface for many yards before finding the place where the wall adjoined the cavern, but soon realized it was not built against the cavern wall but embedded in it as a contrast of geometric structure melded with the natural formation of rock. Lecasc peered at the juncture and slowly moved away from his men, and toward a gaping hole in the natural rock next to the wall, big enough to fit a ship through. Water snaked out from the ominous cave mouth, disappearing into the shadows, and an indescribable stench exuded from the darkness causing him to nearly retch. He quickly returned to his men.

"What is it, Lieutenant?"

"I don't know, but stay clear of it."

Kaskem walked along the man-made wall, "Get moving you

167

slugs."

The far end of the wall did not end in an embankment of rock, but came to a sharp corner. As they rounded the corner, Kaskem faced a crusted door and tried to work the latch but it was caked in limestone and welded to the frame. He slammed his axe into the door, creating a small tear in the metal when the same blow would have shattered one made of heavy wood. "Bring up some men with axes and get started on this door," ordered Reth.

Axes fell on the ancient portal with a staccato of thundering blows that echoed in the cave amidst the constant drip until the threshold was finally battered down. Kaskem eased through into a hall that ran left and right. Slime and mold clung to the floors and walls, and he moved a short distance ahead to make room for Ella and his apprehensive contingent.

"Lecasc, take half the men and go that way. I'll send a runner to find you if we locate the Vexgos." Then he turned to Ella, "You're coming with me."

The anxious men wove their way through a labyrinth of shadow-shrouded halls and rooms. Decayed remnants of old furniture and other reminders that men had once lived in this fetid place created the unnerving perception of ancient ghosts. The hall made one final turn and converged on a wide passage which brought them half-circle and face to face with the other party. Flaming torches appeared ahead as Lecasc and his group approached. "A huge door of solid metal lies at the end of the corridor, captain, and there are several symbols over its mantle."

With faces masked in shadows of fickle light, they walked back down the hallway to the door Lecasc described. It was mammoth, spanning the height of two men, and just as wide with a wheel set in the center instead of a latch, perplexing the officers. There were no mineral deposits to inhibit progress, but when Kaskem attempted to turn the wheel he found it frozen. He heaved back with a heavy axe in his powerful fist and hacked at the door with Olympian strength. The axe fell with a resounding clang of metal against metal, leaving his arm numb from the reverberation of the impact. He had barely scratched the door's surface. "Woman, this is where you make me glad for keeping you alive. How do we get in? What do the symbols say?"

Ella edged forward among the men and held a lamp up to see

above the door. The ancient symbols were eradicated by time, but the symbols for Vexgos were clear. "This is the place. Vexgos is here," she paused with a puzzled expression, "but, there are three other characters. I don't know the word they form....unless...maybe.....fume? I don't know, it doesn't make sense to me."

"What about the door!" Kaskem growled.

Ellas studied the wall around the door and found a strange box with nubs and more symbols imbedded in the frame that held the door. "It's some kind of puzzle key," she said, astonished. "Not like we are used to seeing, but much more complex. See," she pointed at the metal pad of buttons, "those are numeric symbols, and I think you must have to know the order of certain numbers to open the door."

Reth pointed at the door with his axe, "Then open it!"

Ella backed away, frightened, "I don't know which numbers to push."

"The code must be here somewhere!" shouted Reth.

She looked around at the condition of the floor and walls, "I don't think we will find it here. It would have been memorized, not carved in stone for all to see."

Kaskem purpled with rage, "I did not come all this way to turn back! If I have to tear this fortress down with my bare hands, I will!" He threw the axe at the wall adjacent the impenetrable steel door. The blade bit into the wall, hung a moment, and then clattered to the ground with a shower of crumbling mortar. Everyone paused in calm surprise, while Ella eased over and inspected the hewn cleft. Though the wall appeared as solid as the exterior, it clearly was not.

"Eons of moisture must have eroded the wall here while the wall outside is reinforced by the buildup of mineral deposits. Perhaps this entire fortress is nothing more than poured mortar of some kind. In its day it would have been as hard as basalt, but now...."

Reth Kaskem picked up the fallen axe and roughly shoved Ella aside, then raged against the wall, sending chunks of mortar flying in all directions. The indomitable man did not stop until he had hacked his way through four feet of the crumbling masonry, and into the vault beyond. He snatched a torch from Lecasc, thrust it inside and stepped in, but Lecasc did not follow as eagerly as Ella.

The gaping vault was large enough to hold a company of men with steel shelves lining the walls. The inside was as dry as the steppes high above, and Ella realized it must have been air tight for there was no sign of moisture or mold. Dusty steel cases of various sizes and shapes rested upon the shelves in ordered rows, untouched by time.

Kaskem motioned for Ella, "Are they all Vexgos?"

She shook her head, "I don't know." Ella wiped the dust from the surface of one and read the symbols. "I recognize the symbols but I don't know what these words are. Look for symbols that are similar to those on the door."

Lecasc and Reth systematically dusted and examined the cases until Reth called out, "Here, I think I have it!"

Ella examined the box and recognized the symbols for Vexgos but they were followed by another ancient word she knew quite well and her blood froze. "That word is translated to the same as weapon in our language," she choked, "Its purpose is destruction."

Kaskem grinned broadly, "Of course it's a weapon. Did you think we would come all this way for anything else?" Slowly he opened the case and gazed upon several rows of glass spheres cushioned in a strange grey substance similar to sea sponge. Ella and Lecasc peered over his shoulder with intense curiosity. They could make out a swirling black, oily substance within the sphere, like an evil cloud straining at its bonds. The power of the ancients was at their fingertips.

Ella shuddered at the thought of certain death being held in so fragile a container. It was as if it were meant to be so. Like the container's purpose was to break and release whatever sort of hell that lay within.

Lecasc unconsciously drew back as if someone had dumped a viper at his feet, his mind weighted by the thoughts of hideous death.

Kaskem, however, was fascinated at the prospect of such deadly power at his disposal and the grin on his face made Ella's skin crawl. Gently he closed the lid and secured it in place with the strange silver catches. "Sergeant Orem!"

A man appeared in the opening, "Sir?"

"Get five men and bring out these other cases."

"Yes sir," Orem said and called to the corporal behind him.

Kaskem carried the case through the gap with Lecasc and Ella behind him, and handed it to one of the men. "Have someone go up and bring down more men. We have a lot more to bring out."

Sergeant Orem pulled down a heavy case and rested it on the floor, while Corporal Seget hovered over him.

"Are you going to open it?"

Orem shrugged, "Why not? The captain did." With that he pried the metal green lid open, revealing a few dozen curious shapes. He lifted one out and examined its round body about the size of a small apple. On the top was a head with a metal ring and a long lever along the side.

Seget shifted nervously, "I don't think you should touch that Sergeant. We don't know what it might do."

"Stop whining, coward. I'm not going to damage anything." He turned the ancient device over in his hands, and accidently hooked his little finger in the ring, pulling it out. The lever flew from the steel apple, sailing across the room. Sergeant Orem and Corporal Seget held their breath for a tense moment, and then exhaled a sigh of relief. They were completely unaware of the explosion that followed, scattering their remains.

Reth Kaskem was knocked flat from the concussion of air escaping the vault, as were Ella and the others. Shocked, but not dead, the crew stirred in wonderment and fear, brushing the dust and debris from their bodies as mortar continued to fall and clatter. Ella's deafened ears could only hear voices as if from far away, but her instinct to run invigorated her limbs enough to flee the abysmal tomb. She lurched down the hallways, head spinning and was nearly to the door when she felt the shuddering under her feet. Dull screams pursued her and grew with strength as the troop of men swarmed up behind her with Kaskem and Lecasc in the lead. Behind them boiled a great cloud of grey dust and cascading mortar as the fortress began to implode. She flew through the opening into the cavern and was knocked flat by the soldiers bursting out behind her. A blast of hot air shot out, filling the area around them in an impenetrable cloud. The only remaining light was from the glow of torches held by a few soldiers who waited outside. Men coughed and hacked from the dust then called to one another, but Kaskem's voice boomed over all, ordering the troops to get back. They stumbled out of the choking

171

dust cloud and into the damp, but breathable, cavern air. Reth breathed a sigh of relief when he found the Vexgos case was intact.

"Lecasc, head count!"

The soldiers sounded off as Lecasc kept a running total in his head. "All present except Sergeant Orem and Corporal Seget, sir."

"Fools!" yelled Kaskem. "All that weaponry . . . destroyed!" He fumed momentarily enraged over the loss, "Gather the men, we're leaving!"

Kaskem had scarcely given the order when a loud scraping sound emanated from the darkness. Lecasc turned toward the stinking tunnel mouth near the ancient wall as he realized the noise was coming from there. It was the grating sound of two hard surfaces chafing together, loud and rhythmic. Instinctively, the troopers armed themselves and moved cautiously toward the inner cave. As the scraping sound grew louder, the same insufferable stench from before, intensified until Lecasc vomited, and the men backed away. The Kalyfarian cavalry did not breed cowards but none were prepared for the horror that emerged into the waning torchlight.

The lizard, if that is was what it was, was a mountain of reptilian flesh, large enough to sink a trireme battleship. The nightmarish beast, awakened from its immemorial slumber by the shaken cavern, ceased its ponderous amble, and leered down at them from a lofty height, regarding the curious insects with gargantuan spheroid eyes. Long horns protruded from its snout and above its swiveling, armored eyes, while thick pale green scales, caked in mineral, covered the emerging body like the overlapping shields of a battalion. Suddenly, the leviathan lurched forward, dragging its sledging tail behind. A cavalry man flung a spear at the armored skin but the voracious animal ignored it, and before he could draw his sword, a huge elastic tongue shot from the gaping mouth. It slapped against his body, engulfing his entire front side, then just as violently, jerked him off his feet and he jetted through the air and into the awaiting pink maw. He did not even have time to scream. The others stared, frozen in horror as the beast ground its jaws together in a posture of indifference to the life it just took. Armor rained from its mouth to bounce and ring onto the stalagmites below as it tilted its terrifying visage again to consider another morsel.

172

The stalwart contingent broke and ran. One soldier, having just turned his back when the tongue lashed out a second time, adhering to him, screamed as he shot through the air and into the lizard's mouth. Ella, who was familiar with similar looking small reptiles, stood paralyzed with fear as the victim's helmet bounced and rolled against her feet, covered in sticky slime. By sheer will, she forced her limbs to move and turned to bolt into the darkness when she felt the slam of reeking flesh against her back. Time slowed, as it often did when one's life was about to end, and Ella felt the absence of gravity as she was jerked through the air, but at the apex, her impetus was cut short and she fell crashing to the floor, impaling her calf on a stalagmite. She fought for consciousness and

173

for air. Slowly she reached back to feel for the tongue, but realized someone was holding her, ripping the disgusting flesh from her back. In dwindling torchlight and amidst pandemonium, she looked up at the face of a demon. A golden face with horns and a cyclopean eye which stared back at her, and she feinted, her mind overcome by horrors.

Vargos kept an eye on the feasting lizard from earth's dawn while Shasp carefully worked Ella's impaled calf off the small stalagmite. The creature seemed more perplexed by his shortened tongue rather than pained and Shasp knew its appetite would arouse it to action soon enough. He gathered Ella over his shoulder and they bolted for the platform, following the stream of fleeing soldiers toward the exit.

Reth Kaskem was unaware of his enemy's presence, too busy bellowing orders for retreat. Hardened soldiers rushed up the staircase and Reth followed the last man, oblivious to the three hidden figures in the shadows below, awaiting their chance to escape.

The armored reptile finished considering its pained tongue and whipped its gargantuan body around. With its giant claws screeching against the stone floor, it lurched forward at frightening speed and quickly closed on the stairs. Splayed toes as long as a man climbed the wall and as it reared up on hind legs, its mammoth head overlooked the trail of fleeing warriors. A man lashed out helplessly with his saber, slashing at the creature's nose only to feel the blade rebound. The lizard plucked him off the platform as if he were a fly while his comrades stared down the huge throat of pinkish slime, the man's boots visible for only an instant before disappearing. As fate would have it, the beast's next target was the soldier carrying the Vexgos case. The scaled snout shot out to snatch him, but quick reflexes saved the trooper's life. He threw himself sideways against the stair rail to avoid death, but the impact numbed his arm and the case skipped away over the edge. Reth watched in horror as his prize spun away toward the floor, expecting to see it shatter on impact. To his amazement a figure darted out of the shadows, caught it, then disappeared, but not before Reth recognized Vargos as the savior and thief of his prize. He screamed at his men, "Stand your ground, the case is lost below!" Half a dozen of the more experienced

veterans turned back into the face of death and followed their
commander down the stairs into the cavern while the insatiable titan
swallowed yet another man.

Shasp saw the case fall from the platform and started to yell,
but Vargos was already in motion. He cleared the distance and leapt
through the air like a panther, intercepting the case on its way to
certain destruction. No sooner had he caught it then Kaskem's voice
boomed out. Shasp scooped up a fallen torch and bolted away from
the terrible scene with Ella over his shoulder and Vargos on his
heels.

"Make for the fortress!" yelled Vargos.

Shasp was thankful for the lead they had as he ran through
the murky shadows toward the looming wall. At the entrance they
clambered over piled rubble and into the collapsed interior.
Torchlight revealed large chunks of grey rock and gaping-holes
overhead where other compartments were on the next level. A steady
stream of water poured out and fell into the hallway below. Shasp
climbed a pile of tumbled rock and hefted Ella onto a fractured floor
overhead before pulling himself up behind her. He turned and
received the Vexgos case then took Vargos' hand, pulling him up
before kneeling and shaking Ella into confused wakefulness. She
blinked in the darkness then winced at the pain in her leg. "What is
happening?"

"No time, Ella! Get up, I'll help you!" Shasp snapped.

Ella rallied herself and gave a clipped cry as she tested her
damaged leg. They started for a flight of stairs, the origin of the
stream of water, when the sound of tramping feet warned of Reth's
imminent approach. The captain spotted them just as they were
turning away from the hole and barked for his men to follow.

With the hounds on their heels they took to the staircase, but
water flowed over the crumbling stairs making the climb precarious.
Ella limped as fast as she could, slowing their progress more than
could be afforded. Shasp's torch burned away cobwebs from a
threshold at the top with a heavy steel door hanging neglectfully ajar,
and he dragged Ella through the opening. Vargos was nearly to the
top of the stairs, with Kaskem's close behind, when fate showed its
fickle nature. Vargos slipped on the top stair and fell backward, still
gripping the case, and tumbled to the bottom, semi-conscious. As
quickly as fate had placed Vexgos into their hands, it had taken it

away again. Reth regarded the stunned man for a moment before reaching down to retrieve Vexgos, and chuckled mirthlessly, "I'd kill you now, fool, but I think maybe I'll make an evening of it." He motioned to his men, "Bind him and bring him out."

Shasp drew his blade and started down the stairs, but a hail of bolts sent him scurrying for the safety of the room.

"You three! Take crossbows, go in there and kill that pest!" roared Kaskem.

His men re-cocked the bows and slowly began ascending the stairs. Shasp immediately knew he could not defend against them, though he might kill one or even two but not before he was pinned to the wall. He dove across the portal and put himself behind the heavy steel door. Grunting, he bowed his back against the stubborn thing until it groaned and slowly swung closed with the sound of its rusted latch snapping into position. While his enemies banged on the door outside, he surveyed the interior of the room. The ceiling had collapsed revealing a shaft that disappeared overhead and from somewhere far above came the faintest hint of light. Suddenly the door shuddered with a resounding bang. Reth's axe had sheared off the exterior latch and light faintly penetrated through the hole that had been the latch release.

Reth's voice boomed from just outside the door, "You have chosen your tomb, mercenary! You should have minded your own business!" With a laugh Reth quit the stairwell, and the sound of retreating footfalls confirmed their departure.

Shasp held his torch to the ruined latch-assembly, "Damn!" Taking a step back he kicked at the ancient door and found it as resolute as the day it was made. "Just wonderful." He sat next to Ella on the pile of rubble that used to be the ceiling while she nursed her punctured calf. Tears of pain and fear trickled down her face, and he put a reassuring arm around her. "We'll get out of here...somehow."

Captain Kaskem and his men emerged from the fortress for the second time to find the cavern in relative silence, save the sound of scales sliding across the stone floor in the dark. Reth knelt and opened the Vexgos case then stared momentarily at the boiling substance trapped within the glass globe. Gingerly, he lifted one out. "Perhaps it's time we saw what the power of the ancients is capable of. Corporal Arik, you are officially promoted to sergeant. Now lead these men toward the stairs on the double."

"Captain…," he swallowed, "Maybe if we put out the torches we would stand a better chance of reaching the platform."

Kaskem smirked, "Sergeant, that beast lives in the dark. It doesn't need its eyes, only its nose. While you are bumbling your way to the stairs, if you can find them, it will be feasting on you and your men at its leisure." He snatched the crossbow from Arik, "Go, sergeant!"

Arik inclined his head toward a groggy Vargos, "Sir, what about him?"

"Well if he doesn't want to get eaten, he'll run faster than you."

Arik nodded and left at a run across the sea of stalagmites.

Reth slung the crossbow and hefted the case before jogging out at an angle that separated him from his men. The torchlight pushed at the blackness ahead of him as he ran forward dodging the mineral teeth that sought to send him sprawling. Suddenly the scrape of claw on stone warned him of the monster's presence and instinctively he twisted around to face it. A rubbery mass of the lizard tongue slapped against the floor next to him where he had stood only a split second before and then retracted back into its mouth. Reth dropped his torch and brought the crossbow to bare as the looming head emerged from the shadows and into the flickering light. The bow snapped and the bolt shot out, sinking just below the armored eye. The goliath recoiled with an unearthly trumpeting, and Kaskem seized the opportunity, streaking toward the snake of torches which was, even now, climbing the stairs. He was appalled by the littered armor below the platform and realized he had lost several more men while he was pursuing Vargos. By the time he reached the platform the beast had shaken the bolt from its eye and was bearing down on him once again. Reth's troops disappeared through the tunnel exit, but he lingered on the platform and when reptilian death swarmed up the wall, he held out his hand and let the fragile glass ball drop. It shattered onto the plated back, releasing the inky coils which slowly washed over the body of the creature, tendrils winding around it, caressing the beast with menacing intent. When they reached its head, it choked and hacked pathetically and returned to the cavern floor where it thrashed amidst snapping stalagmites. Kaskem watched in amazement as the hardened scales

177

began to liquefy and run in putrid rivulets even before the beast ceased to live. In his morbid fascination, he was almost caught unaware of the black gas reaching out for him, and bolted for the tunnel, running like a man leaving hell. A few minutes later he burst from the tunnel entrance, "Seal it up! Quickly damn it!" Men set to work immediately, piling rock and earth over the tunnel mouth. Reth held Vexgos up before his eyes and an evil grin spread over his face.

Lecasc met Kaskem as he was leaving the cave, case in hand. The lieutenant was less than pleased to see that the captain had survived, but struggled to hide the fact.

Reth barked, "Lieutenant, call formation."

Lecasc broke off and repeated the order to the men, and the troops quickly gathered while some wrestled with bits of armor they had removed for the sake of sealing the tunnel. In a few short minutes the ranks were formed outside with Lecasc in his place at the front corner and Kaskem pacing before them. Vargos sat on the ground with his hands tied behind his back, leaning forward in an uncomfortable position while the commander addressed his company.

"A few months ago we set out to find the power of the ancients for our king and the traitor who betrayed his trust. We have accomplished both. Half of you also remember that you were hand-picked by me for this mission. I spoke to each of you to determine the depth of your loyalties to make sure you were the men for this job. For those of you who were picked by me . . . it is time for you to speak to those who were not."

Without warning, sabers sang from scabbards as calvary men suddenly turned on their bewildered comrades and quickly cut them down in a merciless flurry of steel. Lecasc stood frozen for an instant before one of his own men lunged at him. The lieutenant twisted at the last instant and his back plate deflected a slash meant for his neck. He ducked and drove into the man, knocking him off his feet, and ran for a cleft in the rock as speeding quarrels hissed by. No sooner had he found sanctuary in the womb of the canyon wall, a bolt shattered on the lip of rock behind him. His heart pounded and his skin went cold from the shock of sudden events. Outside, his men, the ones *he* had picked, were screaming and dying. Tears welled up in his eyes as he clenched his teeth against the clamor until all was silent. The sound of boots crunching on pea gravel drifted through the winding rock to where he crouched at bay.

"Lieutenant!" bellowed Kaskem, "Come out and die with some honor! Don't cower in the rocks like a child!"

"Come in and get me you bastard!" screamed Lecasc, enraged. "Besides . . . how can a man die with honor at the hands of a man who has none! I'll live to see you hanged, Kaskem!"

Reth Kaskem laughed loudly. He knew Lecasc would have a deadly advantage against anyone who came in after him. There was no room to maneuver in the narrow cleft, and there would be no way of knowing which bend Lecasc was hiding around until the pursuer found a dagger stuck in his neck. "Suit yourself, Lecasc!" He turned to one of his veterans, "Keep your crossbow trained on that cleft. If he comes out, put a quarrel in him." The trooper nodded.

Reth walked over to where Vargos leaned on the canyon wall and drew his short sword. Vargos stiffened, expectant of the imminent thrust that would end his life. Reth grabbed his shoulder and flung him face down in the red dirt then pressed the sword point against the base of his prisoner's skull, preparing to sever his spinal cord with one violent thrust, but Vargos cried out. "Wait, Reth! I just want to know one thing before I die."

Reth stepped back, amused, "Why not, Vargos?   Ask away."

Vargos twisted his head around to see Kaskem over his shoulder, "What do you plan to do with Vexgos?"

Captain Kaskem chuckled, "I intend to sell it to the highest bidder and make us all rich men. What kind of stupid question is that for a man who is about to breath his last?"

Vargos shook his head, "Problem with you Reth is you think way too small," and he bent his neck submissively.

Reth's smile faded, "What do you mean, 'too small'? Wasn't that what you had planned before I intercepted you?"

"My plan was more involved than that. I have an entire network of agents waiting and I was going to make my buyers pay until it hurt, but not for Vexgos; but enough of this. Fate doesn't seem to favor me anymore, so just get on with it."

Reth put the sword point to his neck again but then lowered the weapon and sliced the cords that bound him. Vargos brought his hands around, rubbed his bruised wrists and stood up to face Kaskem.

"Let's hear it, Vargos."

Vargos gave a sly grin, "Imagine having the capability to wipe out a fortress full of nobility in one fell swoop. That's the kind of thing that the shirt tail relatives of kings and princes will pay any price for. And they will pay when they come to power, because they will have seen the devastation worked against our victims and they will know what awaits any who refuse us. I've spent years putting this together, building a network of spies in various territories in anticipation of finding Vexgos. You're thinking that the king has only known about this for a few months, but Willan and I knew about the tablet a long time ago. The king was a means to an end. Money and equipment, that is, until that bumbling ambassador from Dahoe fouled my plans."

Kaskem rubbed his chin thoughtfully, "Assassination and extortion. I like it, but why do I need you?"

Vargos smiled, "You need my network and my guile. There's a lot more to this than you realize. Let's face it Reth, you lack the fineness for this sort of undertaking. Sure, you may get top price for Vexgos itself, but you can get a whole lot more for what Vexgos *can do*."

Reth Kaskem grunted, "So be it, Vargos, you and I just became partners. There are a dozen Vexgos globes in that case, more than enough to extort all the northwest countries."

Vargos smiled, "If only we had talked before. All this strife could have been avoided."

"Perhaps we should go back for your bodyguard. I locked him behind a steel door in the fortress."

Vargos thought for a moment and then shook his head, "I don't think so. Shasp Ironwrought doesn't see the world the way I do. Besides, my story fell apart when you put us at bay by the ferry. I was planning on parting with him soon and hoping I wouldn't have to kill him. We were friends of a sort, but I'm not so sure he'll stay where you put him, anyway. We should take his horse just in case, at least put him afoot. Also, we will need to test Vexgos as soon as possible to make sure it meets our expectations."

Reth laughed, "No need, that giant lizard that killed six of my troopers in as many seconds is now soup at the end of that tunnel."

Vargos extended his hand, "Then it's a deal."

Reth ignored his gesture and clapped a hand on his shoulder,

"Lucky for us, you didn't burn up in that shack on the Olumbria."
He called over his shoulder to Sergeant Arik, "Sergeant, have the
men mount and prepare to ride. Strip the dead and bring all the
excess weapons and armor."

Vargos pointed toward the opposite end of the canyon, "His
horse is tied a few hundred yards from here.

"We still have your horse if you want it," Reth said.

Vargos wound through the milling men and mounts until he
found his mare, still saddled, and swung onto its back.

In the time it takes a man to dress, the disciplined contingent
was mounted and riding back out of the canyon. Vargos motioned to
an outcropping at the bottom of the canyon pathway. "His horse is
behind that rock." They swung around the feature and stopped, but
only gravel and an empty alcove greeted them. Vargos ran his
fingers over his bristly blonde hair, "It's gone," he said flatly and
spat in consternation.

"It could not have been your bodyguard. He would have had
to pass through the gas on the way to the tunnel, which was also
sealed. Perhaps it simply got loose."

"Captain, I know this man and he is quite capable of being an
enormous thorn in your ass, trust me. Tell your men to stay sharp."

Reth showed his huge white teeth, "If he did escape, he
would be a fool to try and attack a large force like this. He and the
girl would have fled."

They rode up the steep canyon pathway and out into the
awaiting savanna, turning east. Vargos had spent enough time with
Shasp to know the man could always be a danger and an unsettled
feeling came over him.

Chapter 11

Water slowly filled the dilapidated room. The flow, no longer free to wind through the fortress, pooled and gradually crept up the slimy walls. As freezing water swirled around his waist, Shasp lifted Ella onto the pile of rubble from the collapsed ceiling, then returned to the door and yanked hard on the latch. When he was convinced it was hopelessly jammed, he leapt up beside Ella then grasped the ragged edge of the hole overhead and heaved himself up. Once he had climbed out of the room, he realized the space above the ceiling was not a shaft but a chasm with the unmistakable glow of daylight penetrating from high above.

Kneeling, he called down to Ella, "Give me your hand." Ella stood, hopping on her good leg and held up her hand. Shasp caught her wrist and carefully lifted her up beside him. "There's light above. That means a way out but we're going to have to climb and I don't have any rope."

Ella prodded her calf, "I don't think I can do it."

"You don't have a choice Ella. It's that or stay here and die slowly. Give me your shirt."

Ella gave him a cynical look but removed her linen tunic, leaving her bare from the waist up, and handed it him. He tore the cloth into strips then quickly wove them into a linen cord that would reach nearly six feet and secured one end to his waist. The other end he tied to the front of Ella's belt.

"I'm going to climb a few feet until I can brace myself, then you'll follow, understand?   If you slip, I'll hold you." Ella's brows wrinkled with fear and doubt but Shasp spoke to her with calm assurance. "You can do this Ella, just trust me. I haven't let you down yet." She nodded and Shasp tucked his gauntlets into his belt, rubbed some dust on his hands, and then dug his calloused fingers into the shale of the chasm. He searched desperately for every crack and nub of rock the stingy defile would allow, heaving himself up only a few feet at a time, and occasionally, only a few inches. Sharp cries of pain drifted up to him as she used her wounded leg, but Shasp continued to encourage her, allaying her fears.

J.L. Stone

Nearly a hundred yards up, the chasm narrowed and he was able to create enough pressure with his feet against the opposite wall to hold Ella's weight. Slowly, the dim light grew brighter until Shasp could make out the shape of an opening overhead. "We're almost there, Ella, hang on." Ella clung to a small ledge while Shasp moved upward, and his fingers were just digging into a crack when the fickle rock under Ella's toes broke off. With a startled scream she fell and her weight jerked against the cord, pulling Shasp from his perch. His heart leapt into his throat as he plummeted downward, and with panicked desperation he lashed out for the wall and caught a protrusion of rock. Their weight slammed against his shoulder with joint-wrenching force and he cried out in pain. Muscles screaming against the strain, Shasp managed to pull himself up enough to hook his arm around the jutting rock and catch his breath. Ella's screaming diminished to frightened sobs as she slowly twirled on the length of linen rope. "Ella, can you get a hold of the wall?"

She wiped her damp eyes with the back of her hand and half-heartedly examined the surface next to her. "Yes, I think so." Reaching out, she seized hold of a knife-like edge of shale and discovered that it would hold her weight. Shasp, feeling the pressure

183

release from his harness, locked his hand into a crack above his head and started up again. For many tense minutes, the climb continued until he finally climbed out of the chasm and hauled Ella into the glaring light. The chasm had released them onto the top of a small plateau in the center of the canyon, overlooking its depths. They lay panting from the exhausting climb, neither speaking for several moments, until Ella rolled over, pressing her bare breasts into the front of his cold, steel cuirass and kissed him passionately. Shasp propped himself up on his elbows and grinned, "You're welcome."

A teasing wind cleansed the stale cavern odor from their skin as they regained their strength but their rest was suddenly interrupted by shouting from below. Shasp and Ella flipped onto their bellies and wriggled to the edge of the rock table. With his finger to his lips Shasp put a hand on Ella's back, warning her to stay flat, then looked down into the canyon. With their bodies pressed against the warm shale, they beheld a scene of bloody betrayal as Kalyfarian soldiers massacred their comrades in cold blood, and Lieutenant Lecasc fled into a cleft in the rock to escape a shower of quarrels. Then Shasp saw Vargos seated against the shade of the canyon wall, and cursed when Kaskem dragged him into the sun and shoved him to his knees, preparing to kill him with a sword. Shasp clenched his teeth so hard he thought they would break in his mouth, but at the moment he expected to see the blood spray from Vargos' neck, Kaskem sliced his bonds instead. Ella and Shasp exchanged confused looks, then continued to watch the scene until Vargos pointed in the direction of Shasp's horse.

"That son of a bitch! He's taking them to my horse. What the hell is going on?" Ella and Shasp scooted back from the edge until they could stand without being seen. "I have to get to Grimm before they do, but you won't be able to keep up on that leg, so stay here and I'll come back for you." Turning away, he sprinted across the plateau until he reached the side opposite the Kalyfarian camp, and without breaking stride, leapt from the edge and landed in the loose, flat shale which littered the slope. Dust rose around his feet as rocks clattered down the face ahead of him. Ella, not content to wait behind, tightened the bandage around her calf and eased down the slope. Shasp had scarcely reached the bottom when he noticed the sound of cascading rocks still falling behind him and knew Ella was following him, but he also knew that if he waited for her, his horse

184

would soon be in the hands of his enemies. He wondered, did that include Vargos now? Normally he wouldn't worry about Grimm but he had hidden him in an alcove with only one way out, and if the Kalifarians couldn't subdue the stallion, they might just kill him. Either way, it was obvious that Vargos wanted to leave him on foot. He waited for Ella to pause in her descent before giving her a disapproving look then motioned sharply for her to wait at the bottom before turning away and continuing his race toward Grimm.

Fortunately, Shasp had arrived just ahead of Kaskem and was able to lead the snorting charger out of the alcove without being seen. Taking a path that would keep him clear of the cavalrymen; he circled back for Ella and found her sitting on a large flat rock, nursing her swollen leg. Shasp pulled a spare tunic from his saddlebags and handed it to her. "Here, put this on before you get burnt."

Ella pulled the green shirt over her head while Shasp dug for bandages and salves.

"Shouldn't we find another way out of this canyon before they come looking for us?"

Shasp shook his head, "I don't think we'll need to. I'm hoping they'll find Grimm gone and assume we've already cut our losses. They would never expect us to return to the canyon. In an hour or so, we'll leave, and to hell with Vargos and Vexgos. We'll go west to Attle or maybe East to Oma."

Ella flinched as he took away her make-shift bandage and applied water and salve to the bleeding hole. She winced and placed a small hand on his shoulder, "I have to tell you something. Vexgos *is* a weapon."

Shasp paused, sat back on his haunches and turned his face toward the sun where it began its downward journey. "I guessed as much. How else could Kaskem have made it through that cavern without becoming lizard food?" He let out a sharp sigh and faced her again, "I'm not sure I care, Ella."

She reached out and caressed his sweat-soaked brown hair, "We don't know the extent of its power. What if they sell it to the wrong person, someone who would use it to launch a war or kill innocent people?"

Shasp began winding the clean cotton strips around her shapely calf. "Why should you care about the people that left you in

185

squalor, who couldn't give a damn if you lived or died?"

"Not everyone is bad, Shasp. What about the good ones?"

"I've come to believe that most people are bad but still, you're right." He tied a knot in Ella's bandage, tugged at it, then lifted her onto Grimm's back and swung up behind her. Shasp pulled the reins around and turned Grimm toward the remnants of the Kalyfarian camp.

"I thought we were leaving," said Ella with a hint of surprise.

"Soon enough, but it might be worthwhile to have a word with the lieutenant first. Perhaps he could be of some use."

They rode around the base of the plateau and went toward the narrow end of the canyon where a scattering of bodies lay naked and cooling. Lecasc sat in the dirt among the dead, contemplating the knife in his hand with its tip touching his abdomen.

Shasp dismounted and approached the forlorn Lecasc, "What do you plan on doing with that blade, Lieutenant?"

"Don't know yet...my men are dead...those who were loyal, and my mission is lost to betrayal. I can't go home . . . can't face my father?"

Shasp surveyed the eight naked bodies, spattered with blood, spat, then picked his way through them to stand directly in front of Lecasc. "One thing's for sure, Lieutenant, your captain appears to have gone rouge with a very powerful weapon and many treacheries to answer for. I, for one, do not intend to let him have his day. So, you can stick yourself with that knife and prove to Kaskem that you are as weak as he thinks you are, or you can put it away and help me track those traitors. When we find them, we'll figure out a way to repay them and retrieve the Vexgos."

Lecasc stared at Shasp through red, tortured eyes, and then looked down again at the knife in his quivering hands. Slowly, he turned the knife away and sheathed it, then stood with an effort that reminded Shasp of an old man struggling to his feet.

Lecasc gave the dead another long, sad look before turning back to Shasp, "Maybe I'll die trying to kill Kaskem for his betrayal of my country and my men; just promise me that you will tell my father, General Alracasc, that I died fighting. Maybe that will mean something to him."

Shasp nodded, "I will."

Only Ella rode as they left the canyon and walked into the

186

savanna, following the tracks of the renegade troopers. As they went, Lecasc relayed the conversation between Kaskem and Vargos which he had overheard while under cover of the canyon wall. Shasp was not surprised that Vargos had changed alliances to save his skin, but it stung him to know that the man, whom he had considered his friend, may have been plotting his death.

They moved slowly into the deepening hues of dusk until nightfall swallowed them. Shasp set up a meager camp and, in the flickering firelight; the trio discussed the need for horses to close the gap between them and their prey.

Ella sipped some stale water, "If the tracks continue north, we can follow them and, if they cross the river, we can go a few miles west to Utilla and buy mounts to follow."

Shasp knew it was the best option, "I agree, they'll disappear long before we can catch them on foot, but I still have no thoughts of how to take back the power of the ancients."

"Why not have the Magistrate at Utilla send for a garrison?" Ella asked.

Lecasc shook his head, "No, the weapon would only find its way from one selfish hand to another."

Shasp raised an eyebrow at Lecasc's statement, "Why... Lieutenant, are you suggesting that we destroy the very thing you were sent to retrieve?"

Lecasc nodded solemnly, "It will be enough for me to rid my King of a traitor, and Kaskem's death will be a fine restitution. No one needs to know that Vexgos was ever found or destroyed."

The next day, the tracks wandered north, as expected, and stopped at the Olumbria River where they found the docks for a ferry, but no raft or ferryman. They turned west and made their way along the river until they came to the township of Utilla where many ferry men vied for business. They negotiated a fare price for transport and, an hour later, off loaded on the bustling docks of the river city. On the way to find a horse trader they passed a smoking blacksmith shop with an open roof. Several men in leather aprons sweated over red hot work, hammering out iron and steel from molten metal as fumes of acrid smoke filled the air. Over the din and clang of hammer against anvil, a soot-stained man with a round belly shouted at the workers around him.

Lecasc paused at the shop and motioned for Shasp and Ella to wait. He called to the proprietor and, when he had his attention, waved him over. The blacksmith approached the counter, wiped the sweat from his receding hairline and his palms across his apron. "What can I do for you?" he said in a booming voice with a hinted lack of patience.

Lecasc reached around his waist, unbuckled his cuirass and dropped it on the counter in front of him. "How much will you give me for this?"

The smithy lifted the breastplate and inspected it carefully, "Kalyfar Calvary. Good quality and the insignia is still intact. Give you seventy-five dragos."

"Done," Lecasc replied.

The smithy stiffened, a little surprised that the owner would part with the piece so easily and for so little. Quickly, he took out his moneybag and counted the coins, worried that Lecasc might change his mind.

When the three of them were on their way again, Shasp questioned Lecasc. "Why did you sell your armor when I feel you're going to need it?"

"The insignia places me in danger of being reported to some local guardsmen or magistrate. Besides, I need money for a horse. I'll find some replacement armor later."

Shasp shrugged, "You won't get much for seventy- five in silver. You should have bartered for more."

"I'll make due."

By the early afternoon, Lecasc had purchased a reasonable mare and a jerkin of hard leather with fringe along the shoulders. Supplies replenished, they rode out once more across the golden savanna.

As they rode through the waving grass, a feeling of impending doom settled over Ella and she tightened her arms around Shasp's waist.

Chapter 12

Vargos and Kaskem rode up the long rocky slope that brought them out of the grasslands and into the foothills that bordered the Acadean Mountains. For days, they traversed the savanna, avoiding the city of Akan then crossed the Sea of Delane. In spite of the long ride, the troopers remained vigilant, and maintained their staggered columns as they wound their way through draws and valleys. It was clear to Vargos that their cautious behavior was a sign of distrust but he only smiled at their discomfort. By the end of the day, they were winding along a narrow road to the top of a knoll, and finally stopped before a wall surrounding a lonely manor house. The old manor was made of cut stone and three stories high with heavy oak shutters; all that remained of an ancient estate that Vargos had come to possess. Kaskem studied the structure and the surroundings, musing that, perhaps, the owner had chosen the location for the sake of a hasty retreat into the foothills beyond. It would certainly remove any advantage of surprise if anyone approached and gave the owner plenty of time to disappear if need be.

As the anxious mounts began to stamp and shake their manes, Vargos called to a sentry who wearily approached the gate. "It's me," he grunted, "Open the gate and tell the others to meet me in the main hall. We have guests." The sentry nodded as he opened the lock and pushed the heavy iron gate aside. Vargos gestured for Kaskem to enter.

Reth rocked lazily in the saddle, like a man without a care, as his horse sauntered through, its hooves clopping on the flagstones. His men, however, looked around uneasily, expecting a trap, but their captain did not share their fear. He had never been in a trap he couldn't cut his way out of.

Vargos jumped off his horse in front of the main door and tossed the reins to the sentry, "Find fodder and room for the others," then turned to Reth Kaskem, "Follow me."

They passed through finely crafted doors of redwood and came into a large foyer with a main hall on the other side. Reth was impressed with the furnishings and tapestries adorning the rustic manor, "Who lives here?"

189

Vargos gave Reth a mischievous half smile, "I do. Dahoe and Oshintan pay well for secrets concerning their neighbors, but the real trick is playing both sides and not getting caught; a trick which failed me in Kalyfar and set you on my trail."

Kaskem laughed, "Your luck hasn't left you yet. After all, I didn't kill you in that canyon."

Vargos gave only the briefest snort before opening the door to the hall. The chamber was sunken with several other doors along the adjoining walls. In the center rested a long, rectangular table of polished wood, and a strange array of people sat around it. They were from every age group and gender, some wearing filthy rags or common clothing and yet others were dressed in expensive attire. Vargos noted the starnge look that Reth gave the gathering. "They are spies and cutthroats, some of the best and all are here, like you, for the promise of great wealth." Reth silently counted ten men and two women and began to wonder if Vargos hadn't brought him here to kill him and lighten his overhead.

Vargos seemed to read his thoughts, "Relax, Reth, you and your men are safe here. I consider you a welcome addition to our twisted little family and if you're worried about money, you needn't be; there will be more than enough to go around, I can assure you of that. We will squeeze the gold out of the northwest kingdoms first, and then turn our gaze on Kalyfar."

"Good idea, the sweetest plumb for last," Kaskem responded, "but I will maintain control over the weapon and my men will guard it."

"If that makes you comfortable," Vargos replied. He turned to his men who waited for an explanation of the burly soldier's presence. Gentlemen, we have a new addition to our company, Captain Reth Kaskem, formerly of the Kalyfarian military." Vargos smiled at the hushed exchange of muttering and wide eyes, and hoped that the captain's infamy would generate more confidence than fear.

An older spy stood up, "How do we know we can trust him. What proof of loyalty does he have to offer?"

Vargos laughed, "The same proof as the rest of you . . . his greed.

Vargos filled the next few days with details of potential clients in various kingdoms vying for power. He spoke to Reth at length about his company of spies and their functions which included gathering money and carrying out assassinations. It was in the cool of the evening, shortly after one of these conversations that Reth was walking among the shrubs and flowers of the garden behind the manor. He rounded a neglected hedgerow to a crumbling fountain surrounded by a courtyard and looked across at a man in a dark grey robe. He was sitting on a stone bench and tossing crumbs to the schooling coy. A draped hood shadowed his face in the waning light and Reth had a feeling he was not one of the regular riffraff.

Without looking up the man addressed him, "Captain Reth Kaskem, please join me."

Warily, Reth sat on the bench across from him and tried to peer into the hood, "Have we met or are you a new arrival?"

A soft laugh answered him, "Yes, you could say that.   I only recently learned of your addition to our. . . . family."

"Family... that's what Vargos calls it too; an odd word for this collection. What do you do here?"

"Well, it used to be a greater role than it is now. I'm afraid our friend, Vargos, has not dealt very fairly with me."

Kaskem sat up slightly at this, "Really, how so?"

"I was supposed to be his partner for half when we first arranged this conspiracy. Since then he has found others to take my place. You for example; I passively accepted my demotion because if one angers Vargos he may just find a drop or two of poison in his ale."

"Ha!" scoffed Kaskem, "He'd better not try that shit with me or I'll cut him into crow food."

"What makes you think he has not already made plans for your removal?"

Reth leaned forward and lowered his voice to a menacing tone, "What plans?"

The stranger held up a hand, "Easy, friend, I am a listener and I hear things because I am quiet and unobtrusive. Vargos intends to unleash his men on yours when they least expect it. Knowing Vargos, he is probably hoping some of his own die in the process. No doubt he feels there are too many people in his organization to trust or keep track of loyalties and wishes to whittle it down to a manageable few. You and I, of course, will be of the pieces peeled off."

Kaskem's jaw tightened, "Let me guess . . . you are telling me this because you hope to use me to rid yourself of Vargos and rise to your former position."

Again the gentle laugh, "No, I'm no fool," he tossed some more bread to the teeming goldfish. "The man on top has to have the nerve and wit to stay there. I am not that brave. I would be glad to serve as your second, though, or even third; less responsibility and risk. Also, it is my way of showing good faith. I would not want you for an enemy, for I have heard tales of your cold brutality and do not wish to be on the receiving end of that."

Reth stood up, "How do I know you are telling the truth?"

The robed figure shrugged, "You can always wait and see what happens. Of course by that time it may be you who are crow's food. I remember a proverb from an Arrigin general, 'Victory is for those who act, not those who wait.'"

Kaskem nodded gravely, stood and spun away. He called over his shoulder to the man as he left, "You had better be right my friend or my wrath will come to you."

As Reth disappeared through the bushes the robed figure muttered to himself, "You'll see soon enough."

Vargos was in his chambers examining reports from his spies when one of his men knocked at his door. Vargos dropped the papers on the table with an exasperated sigh, "What is it?"

A hunched man opened the door a crack and poked his head through, "Ah, excuse me, sir, but that new man, Kaskem, he's demanding everyone meet in the hall at once; thought you would want to know."

Vargos, vexed by the thought that Reth was already testing his position among the men, began to wonder whether snake venom or hemlock would work best on someone of Reth's vitality. He belted on his sword and knife and pulled on a studded jerkin; standard precaution when moving about a den of self-serving assassins. Men, muttering to one another, flowed through the halls and from doorways into the great hall where Reth waited at the head of the table.

Vargos was the last to enter amidst the confusion, "What is it Kaskem?"

Reth sat in Vargos' chair, feet propped on the long table in a careless repose, "I thought it would be a good idea to discuss the fine points about who is running this show."

Vargos struggled to appear indifferent in front of his men and smiled, "I thought we already had an understanding. We are to share power over this organization...equally."

Reth appeared pensive as he dug in his bristly, black beard, "Is that what it was? Because I have heard that you intend to resume full control, and you know what that would mean for me."

Vargos shifted uncomfortably. Perhaps he would need to deal with Kaskem sooner than he thought. "Who have you been talking to, Reth? It sounds like someone has misinformed you."

"Really? Or maybe you just underestimated me, Vargos. You have always thought of me as a simpleton. Perhaps that will be your downfall," he leapt up suddenly, "Now, Sergeant Arik!" At his command, nine of his remaining ten troopers flooded into the room, swords drawn. "I'm taking control, Vargos."

Vargos looked at the men seated around the table. "Well, I guess I'll just relinquish all my hard work to you, Kaskem." As he finished his sentence, Vargos whipped out his long sword with blinding speed and slashed the soldier nearest to him. The blade cut through the man's neck just above his armor, showering the assembly in crimson. Immediately, the hall erupted in violence as Vargos' men exploded from their seats, knives and short-swords materializing from under their clothes. The rogue calvary-men were outnumbered now, eight to thirteen but with armor and heavier weapons, they were still an easy match. However, the cutthroats of Vargos' house were deadly in close-quarter combat and the hall soon ran slippery with the blood of the dying. Swords smashed together and chairs flew as the two forces howled for blood. Men grappled over weapons, hands on one another's throats, and feet kicking. The air was thick with the stench and groans of death. Amidst the screams and roar of battle Kaskem hacked his way across the room toward Vargos. Cagey as he was, Vargos was not going anywhere and he had no intention of leaving his budding empire of assassins to an usurper like Reth, regardless of his reputation. They met in the middle of the hall in a vicious flurry of steel. Vargos was light of

193

foot and experienced with the long sword. He knew he would need to stay well out of Kaskem's reach, for the heavy short sword in the captain's iron hand would be devastating. Steel rang and rebounded in endless arcs and parries as the plotters circled and sought the opening that would secure the leadership of the band. Reth swung his sword in a close arc meant to clear Vargos' sword and allow him inside the guard, but Vargos leapt back just as the shorter blade sheared through his jerkin to his skin. Kaskem grinned over first blood, but his arrogance cost him. The cut fueled Vargos' anger and he slashed with such tenacity that Reth was forced back several feet, nearly slipping on the bloody floor. Slowly, the din of battle ebbed around them as men fell and died. Only a few remaining combatants still struggled, but Vargos and Reth were oblivious. So caught up in their own life and death struggle, they did not even notice when the last spy went down leaving only a mortally wounded cavalry man who was slowly bleeding out. Their forces were decimated but neither man cared. Vexgos was still waiting for a victor. Sweat and small wounds trickled as each man puffed and wheezed. Then, suddenly, they became aware of a sound so completely opposite that of combat that it rode through the air, piercing the clamor until the last two combatants eased away from one another to look at the source. The sound was applause; a loud clapping of hands as if to show appreciation for a fine performance, echoing from the entrance of the main hall. They drew apart and stared at the doorway as a gray robed figure emerged, the same man who had warned Kaskem of Vargos' coming betrayal.

Reth boomed out, "So, you have come to see if I am worthy to be called master! Only a moment longer and I'll have this whelp begging for mercy!"

Beneath the hood he shook his head, "Not quite, I came to put an end to this game." He reached up and withdrew the cowl, revealing a horned helmet of light gold with a cyclopean visor and black plume.

Kaskem's face purpled, "You, the bodyguard! I'll carve my name in your liver!"

Vargos lowered his sword and laughed loudly, "You never cease to amaze me, Shasp, but why? Why come all the way here and risk your neck? What is it you want?"

Shasp reached behind him and lifted the case with the

Vexgos spheres, "I came for this, but unlike you, I intend to get rid of this blight."

"Over my dead body," blurted Kaskem.

"Shasp, be reasonable," pleaded Vargos, "You can't defeat us both. Join us instead and you can be rich, maybe even a governor someday. How about it?"

Shasp was silent, leading Kaskem to believe he was contemplating the offer, but Reth quickly calculated what would happen if the two joined forces against him. "Be damned!" he yelled and lunged toward Vargos' unprotected side. Before the master of spies could bring his long sword up to defend himself, Reth's heavy short sword ripped through his ribs and lung. Vargos cried out, clutching his shattered torso and crumpled to the blood-soaked floor. Before Reth could deliver the killing blow Shasp had leapt off the steps, Ayponese blade out on the fly, and blocked the downward stroke inches from Vargos' skull. A side kick sent the stout cavalryman stumbling back.

Kaskem grinned wolfishly and gave a short laugh, "So . . . It's just you and I. I've seen your handy work and I must say, I've been wanting to test your mettle. Been so long since I had any real challenge, though I must admit, Vargos was giving me some exercise. Even so, he was running out of wind. It was only a matter of time."

"Don't worry Kaskem. You'll get more than just exercise from me. I've heard of you, when I was traveling in Somerika. They called you the Butcher of Kilea. Fortunately, I have no such title."

Reth shrugged, "Titles mean nothing. Now, steel..." he held out his blade, "that has all the meaning you or I need."

"You are Somerikan, Kaskem, so let's finish this the southern way."

Reth snorted in disbelief, "Knives? Clearly you don't know what you're getting into." Reth tossed his sword aside and drew his heavy Somerikan knife with a slow hiss of steel against leather. He flipped it a few times adjusting his grip, "No northerner is a match for a Somerikan with a knife, especially when the Somerikan is me."

Shasp pivoted and threw his katana imbedding it into a wooden column with a thud and a ring of steel, then slid his own heavy Somerikan blade from its sheath. "We'll see soon enough."

Reth sneered, "You're going to find out that just because you

195

own that blade doesn't mean you know how to use it."

Kaskem shot forward wielding the knife with a reverse grip. The flashing inside cuts were so fast that Shasp scarcely had time to deflect as he withdrew, but managed to stall Reth's advance by

blocking with his bracer and countering to his enemy's legs, causing
Reth to retreat. Shasp used the brief respite to set himself properly,
feet shifting position and knife blade held defensively in front, grip
reversed. Reth was annoyed by Shasp's unexpected skill and
adjusted his own stance, dropping into a crouch. Like a bolt of
lightning, Shasp darted forward with a complex combination of stabs
and sweeping slashes. Reth ducked sideways and caught a deflecting
blow off his steel cap. The razor-sharp edge bounced and sheared
through the top of his ear. Blood streamed down the side of his face,
but the animal from the Somerikan Mountains only smiled. Shasp
stepped in for another swipe, but as his knife slashed down, Reth
blocked it on his own and spun inside. Before Shasp could re-align,
Kaskem's heavy blade slammed into Shasp's back plate. The point
penetrated the stout armor and sank an inch or more into the flesh
beneath. The blow nearly knocked the wind out of Shasp as he
twisted away, and Reth wrenched his knife free as they parted.
Warm blood oozed from the stab wound, running down the inside of
the cuirass. Shasp steeled his mind and focused, ignoring the pain.
Truly Kaskem was turning out to be a warrior worthy of his
reputation. Both bled now with renewed respect and circled again.
This would be a battle of wits as well as steel and Kaskem was
turning out to be no dolt. Simultaneously, they lunged, hard edges
grating and sliding as they pushed and parried, slashed and stabbed.
Back and forth the battle ranged across the blood splattered room of
cooling corpses. Reth's mocking smile faded into a grimace as he
used every trick and technique to penetrate Shasp's defense with
only the slightest gain. Armor became gouged and nicked, the blades
chipped. Shasp was desperately trying to keep Kaskem on the
outside while seeking openings in the solid Kalyfarian armor.
Dozens of cuts and shallow punctures covered both men as they won
their small victories, but neither showed any sign of fading strength.
Kaskem desperately wished to see his opponent's face through the
visor, to read his eyes and expressions, the slightest telegraph of a
movement, but instead only received the black stare of the menacing
helmet. It was evident that he was not going to find a way through
Shasp's guard so he placed his bet on one crucial action. Reth
shuffled back a step, cocked his arm and flung the knife with
expertise.   The heavy blade flashed through the air with Reth
leaping after it. The tactic caught Shasp off guard and he was barely

able to deflect the flying blade before it could pierce his throat, but he was not able to bring his weapon to bear on Reth before he was inside his guard. One massive hand gripped Shasp's wrist holding the knife hand while the other seized him by the throat. Immediately his air was cut off by Reth's powerful grip. Shasp slammed his free fist under Kaskem's cuirass, evoking grunts of pain, forcing Reth to let go of his throat in order to stop the assault on his ribs. Shasp was powerful, but Kaskem was a beast. Normally, Shasp could have rolled against a man's thumb and freed his hands easily, but the immense strength of this enemy refused to yield. The rogue captain twisted his wrist and slowly began to force the knife toward Shasp's throat. Sweat streamed down their faces as wills battled and the deadly point crept within a hair's width and then drew blood. So focused was Reth on Shasp's knife that he did not have time to react when Shasp drove his knee into his groin. The pain did not break the titanic hold on his wrists, but it weakened it enough for Shasp to roll the knife away from his throat. He thrust his helmeted head into Kaskem's face, and sent him reeling backwards, but Shasp did not lunge in to finish him. Instead, he stepped back, hooked Reth's knife with the point of his toe, and kicked the weapon into the air. Reth caught it with a look of surprise on his face; a look that smacked of floundering confidence. Shasp leaned his head to one side then the other, stretching his neck, and came back to his normal stance. Then, like a sudden storm, he flew forward. Kaskem saw the movement and lunged sideways to block the anticipated slash to his head, but it never came. Instead, Shasp dropped into a forward roll, slashing backward to the inside of his adversary's thigh. Arterial spray erupted from Kaskem's femoral artery. The captain from Kalyfar watched dumbly as his life blood arced across the room. He dropped his knife and clutched at the gash but it was like a man trying to stop the flow of a mountain stream with only his hands. He staggered and slipped, crashing backwards over a toppled chair. Shasp stood over him as a shocked expression settled on Reth's face. The flow of bright blood slowly ebbed to a gentle welling as Kaskem's hue changed to chalky white. Slowly, his head sagged and he fell over onto his side.

Shasp turned away from the lifeless captain and knelt by Vargos who coughed splatters of blood onto his chest. Shasp reached behind his neck, gently holding his head. Wheezing and pale he lifted his hand to Shasp's shoulder. "S…Sorry for all those times I . . . got us into tr....trouble," he laughed weakly, "You were always true . . . even when . . . even when I wasn't. We're still friends . . . right?"

Shasp knew Vargos had only a little time left in the world, "Yes, Vargos, we are."

"That's good, I'm ...." Vargos' eyes glazed over and he sank down with his last escaping breath.

Shasp stood, wiped the blood from his knife and sheathed it. When he turned toward the doorway, he saw Ella standing there, her face a mask of horror at the nightmare scene of the bloody hall.

"Ella? What are you doing here? You were supposed to stay with Lecasc."

Lecasc stepped from the shadows of the threshold, a crossbow leveled. Cautiously, he walked forward and lifted the Vexgos case then motioned Ella into the room where she hid behind Shasp.

Shasp clenched his teeth, "All this time . . . all that self-righteous talk but all along you intended to exploit it like the rest."

"Oh no, nothing of the kind. In case you haven't noticed, I'm not much of a soldier. In fact I detest the chaos and blood of war as much as I do living in the dirt and taking orders from self-absorbed officers like Kaskem."

"What then? Why do you want it?"

"You might remember me telling you that my father is a General in Kalyfar. It seems he has plans of his own. He chose me for this mission, not because I was the best soldier, but because he knew he could trust me. You see, I have a stake in all this; a rather large one."

Shasp eyed the crossbow, "So your father wants Vexgos so he can be the one to present it to the king; to be his second?" Shasp was buying time, looking for an opening.

"No, not quite; he is already the ranking officer in the military. He plans to wait until the nobility have their annual gathering and then deploy it."

Understanding dawned in Shasp's eyes, "He wants to be king. And you? A prince?"

"And heir; much better than a paltry lieutenant."

"And us?"

Lecasc shook his head, "Sorry, but you have shown me that you simply do not give up. My guess is that you wouldn't leave me alone to return with the weapon. That only leaves me one avenue. I'm sorry."

Shasp saw the tendons in Lecasc's hand tighten as his fingers constricted on the stock. Shasp twisted as the bolt jetted from the crossbow, and in one fluid motion, he threw his knife straight from the scabbard. The steel quarrel caught Shasp's breastplate at an angle with a resounding clang and ricocheted. Shasp staggered backward from the force then regained his balance.

A crimson stain spread over Lecasc's jerkin just to the right of his heart. A pinched expression crossed his face as he looked down, and the crossbow slid from his fingers to clunk against the floor. Body leaning, he gripped the edge of the doorway as trembling fingers reached toward the imbedded hilt and lingered there. Lecasc contemplated the futility of its removal before his hand dropped listlessly to his side, and he raised his eyes to lock with Shasp. Shasp removed his helmet to show his face to the dying man. The lieutenant coughed flecks of bloody foam onto his chin, then managed a weak smile. "It seems…you are the winner of this game," he croaked.

"No, Lecasc, there are no winners here. I never intended for you or Vargos to die here today."

"Would you tell my father I…well…maybe you could make something up," and he toppled forward with his arms at his sides.

Shasp regarded the sad youth and his wasted, short life, but then a moan from behind him caught his attention and he spun around. His heart froze when he saw Ella propped against a piece of toppled furniture with Lecasc's quarrel jutting from just under her collar bone. He sprang across the room and dropped beside her, his hands reaching out to touch the bolt. She searched his face, hoping to see a sign reflected in his worried eyes that would tell her the truth about the severity of the wound.

"Ella . . . don't move," he said as he reached carefully behind her back to see if the quarrel had exited. It had not.

Tears began to flow down her cheeks, "Am I going to die, Shasp?"

"I won't let you die, Ella, but I have to remove the bolt. It's going to hurt."

200

Her lips trembled and she nodded. Shasp slowly wrapped his fingers around the shaft and pulled. Ella shrieked as he increased the pressure, straining to remove the stubborn missile from where it was lodged in the bone. Finally, he could not take her tormented cries any longer and relaxed his grip on the shaft. Sweat ran down Ella's face in rivers.

Shasp lowered his head and slammed his armored fist into the floor, "I can't get it out! It's lodged in your shoulder blade. I have to get you to a healer."

Ella shook her head, "We are days from the nearest town. You have to do it," she sobbed, "don't listen to my screams. Don't stop . . . do you hear me?"

Shasp raised his eyes to hers. He seized the shaft a second time and Ella nodded slowly. With his left hand he pinned her shoulder on the floor then pulled on the shaft. Ella's screams ripped through him and she begged him to stop, but he did not. She clawed at him and cursed him, but he hauled on the shaft until beads of sweat broke forth on his forehead and spittle flew from his clenched teeth. Then, after Ella had lost consciousness from the overwhelming pain, the bolt tore free in his fist. Shasp eyed the bloody iron quarrel with disgust and flung it away.

When Ella awoke, it was to the sound of roaring flames. She was bundled tightly on a make-shift stretcher, tied behind Grimm. She tried to move, but the pain in her chest was excruciating and she moaned. Rolling her head to the other side, she saw Shasp standing with his back to her, silhouetted against the manor as it was engulfed in ravenous fire. Cleansing flames upon the crest of the watchful hill scoured the earth free of blood and evil, and then blackness overtook her again.

The next time she woke it was to the worried, lined face of a bearded and balding old man as he inspected her wound. Behind him she could make out a low wooden ceiling and plank walls. A lamp burned low near her bed and she was covered in blankets.

Jason Stone

"You are awake, good," he said in a wavering voice. Ella felt as if she was on fire and perspiration dampened her face and soaked her pale blonde hair.

The old man ran his thick hand over her head. "Someone will want to talk to you." He left the small room and a few moments later returned with Shasp behind him. The old man gave Shasp a grave look and left them alone. Shasp sat down on the edge of her bed, his face looking haggard, as if he had not slept in days. Dirt from the trail still clung to his brow and hands.

Ella labored at her breathing and fought for enough wind to speak, "What is it, Shasp?"

"I rode two days and a night to bring you here, to Cheni, but I dared not take you any farther. I am told this man is one of the best healers there is but . . . your wound has become infected," he choked, "he has done all he can. The rest is up to you, he says."

Ella smiled weakly; her voice was dry and distant. "I feel so tired, like I'm floating on water. I just want you to know… that I have lived more in the last few months… than I ever did before, thank you for that." She reached out and touched his face, her fingertips warm on his cheek.

He pressed her hand to his face, "Stay with me Ella, please."

She rocked her head slowly back and forth on her pillow, "Know this, Shasp of Aypon, I love you and even when I leave this body, I will still love you. I will always love . . . y…" Slowly, her eyes closed as her head tilted away and Shasp knew Ella was gone, but his mind could not accept it. His eyes widened and he grasped her shoulders, shaking her gently, "Ella?" He shook her harder, as if trying to wake her from a deep slumber, "Ella! No, Ella! Don't go . . . Stay . . . please . . ." The first tears he had known since childhood leaked out as he wrapped his arms around her lifeless body and crushed her against himself. "Ella…Ella no…" he whispered in her ear as he cradled her.

Chapter 13

Poluntis Ilka bolted upright in his bed of fine silks, greasy sweat oozing from every pore. Beady eyes peered into the shadows, searching for the sound that jerked him from the world of slumber. Had he dreamed it? Only blackness stared back. "Who is there?" No reply. Slowly, he lifted his massive bulk from the bed and waddled to the nearest window. He opened the shutters, allowing pale blue moonlight to spill in. Poluntis glanced outside then turned back toward his bed only to find the way blocked by a demon with a golden head and black skin. The creature regarded him with a single slit eye resting below two black onyx horns. Black plumes sprouted from its head and it held a straight sword in its fist. Ilka screamed, stumbled backwards and fell, his blubbery body pressing against the cold stucco wall. The demon lowered the sword point and touched the quivering flesh of Poluntis' neck.

"W...who are you? Wh...What do you want from me?" he squealed.

"I am the reaper. Your sins have overtaken you," came a deep and menacing voice, thick with hate and disgust.

"Please! I'll give you anything...anything!"

The golden head swung from left to right. "I do not think so, Poluntis. Will you give Ella back her childhood, which you ripped from her? Will you give her back her life? No! Payment is due and you can't afford the bill." The blade rose and arced down. Poluntis screamed and closed his eyes, but the pain of the stroke did not come. Slowly, he opened one eye, fearful that the thing would still be waiting, instead, only the moonlight and an empty bed chamber. Suddenly, there came a loud banging at the door, followed by a guard's voice. "Sir, are you alright? Sir!"

Ilka raised his obese form from the floor with great effort and lumbered toward the door. He found the bolt in place, slid it back, and stared into the face of the worried watchman.

"Sir, I heard a scream coming from your chamber! Is all well with you?"

Poluntis was silent. Was all well? He shook his head as if to clear it. "Yes, I'm fine. Too much food and drink before bed, that's all. Go back to your post . . . and have the guards check the grounds." He slammed the door in the watchman's face and started back toward his bed. He was about to reach for the shutters to close them when a voice hissed from the darkness outside.

"Time to pay your debt!"

An object arced through the window over his shoulder and shattered on the flagstones behind him with the tinkling of fragile glass. Immediately his flesh burned like molten fire. His eyes and throat felt as if they were drenched in acid and he screamed the scream of a man on his way to hell.

No one knew what happened to Poluntis Ilka. Two guards died trying to enter the room. Eventually it was sealed with brick, mortar, and wax, and then forgotten, as was the passing of the most powerful man in Delane.

Chapter 14

Skerick and Lexac did not understand why the man would want to rent their boat only to sail out several miles from shore only to return from where they came. No journey, no destination. No fishing. It was odd, but he paid well, and the brothers never questioned good fortune, especially when they made so much for so little work. The sun burned down and the wind snapped the white sails as the small skiff coursed over the waves.

Their client stood in the prow watching the horizon, the breeze ruffling his brown hair and white cotton tunic. Turning, he dropped onto the deck and signaled to the brothers, "This is far enough!"

The dark haired, brown skinned men moved around the rigging and dropped the sail as the boat continued to scud along. Their client lifted a large sack, large enough to hold a man. It was the only thing he had brought onboard. He turned it upside down and tugged the bag away revealing a large iron cage and inside it were an odd looking case and several large rocks. Shasp hefted the cage onto the rail then looked all the way around. When he was certain he could see no coastline, he shoved the cage into the choppy waters and watched as it sank out of sight amidst a fountain of bubbles. No one would be finding the Vexgos spheres any time soon. The brothers looked at one another, bewildered, until Skerick shrugged. Lexac mimicked his brother in reply.

Shasp wondered as he watched the waves slap against the side of the boat. In the end, Vexgos held a power much more sinister than the poison within its glass spheres. It whispered down through the ages and infected the dreams of men with promises of wealth and power. Suddenly, the true reason for the destruction of the ancients became crystal clear. Like the shattering globes released black death, promises of power released the darkness in men's hearts and laid waste to all they touched.

The sail was hoisted again and the skiff was soon on its way back to shore, a speck on an eternal horizon. Shasp tilted his head back to feel the warmth of the sun on his face, closed his eyes, and thought of a blonde-haired, pale-eyed lover.

BOOK III

RAGING SANDS

PROLOGUE

Thunder heads rolled over the lush jungles of the Azon, booming with lightning followed by powerful winds. Palm and Banyan trees bowed to the gale force. Moans and wails lifted skyward as people lay dying in the streets of the jungle city, covered with sores and filth. No longer was Xochotol the vibrant teeming center of powerful warriors and industry. In just weeks it had deteriorated into a haven for specters and ghosts. A small contingent of bald priests followed a creaking chariot through the listless dying, and along the stone streets toward a towering pyramid at the heart of the necropolis. A tall, dark-skinned man held the reins, his physic, marvelous as the rain washed over him, clearly their leader.

At the first signs of plague, the people had turned to him for answers. Why were their gods angry? Had they not invaded the southern kingdoms and wrested their wealth? Didn't they do what their head priest commanded, even as Mal had commanded him?

The high priest, Lord Tabeck, had thought so too, but a few weeks ago he learned otherwise. While he lay in fitful slumber, his master, Mal himself, visited in a dream and blasted him for his arrogance and misinterpretation. Yes, he had ordered Tabeck to take Xochotol's armies north and invade the southern kingdoms of Nomerika, but, not for wealth or blood, but rather, to force their submission and spread his dark rituals. Tabeck woke the next morning and heard the news of the first few plague victims.

Now, he rode through a thunderstorm on his way to the great pyramid to make amends to his god and save his people. It was the only thing he could think of which might appease the dark entity who demanded blood.

At the foot of the ziggurat, he drew rein, stepped off the chariot and began his long ascent to the apex. His servant priests followed close behind, chanting and wailing. At the top waited a slab of blackest basalt, stained with the blood of a thousand sacrifices, and Tabeck hoped he would not be the last. An acolyte held out a clay jar and Tabeck reached into it. He drew out a handful of black flower petals and placed them in his mouth, 'enough to kill ten men,' he thought. Then he lay down on the cold wet surface as drops of rain pelted his eyes making him blink and nodded at the man closest

208

to him. Some of the lesser priests came to hold him down but he shook his head and they backed away. Another priest, his second, drew a sharp curved knife from his robes and hovered over Tabeck, chanting loudly while looking skyward.

Suddenly, the structure began to rumble and shake as an earthquake shrugged beneath the surface and Tabeck's face showed the first traces of fear. Without warning, a dark cloud burst from the entrance at the top of the pyramid, just behind the sacrificial slab, and snaked around the base of the dais. The knife wielding priest began to shake with unspeakable fear at the first cold touch of the black fog but still Tabeck did not move. Their eyes met for a split second before the knife flashed through the glistening rain and plunged into Tabeck's chest. Tabeck's back arched with pain and he opened his mouth to cry out as his subordinated carved into his torso, but the black fog filled his mouth, choking his screams. Pain engulfed him but he gripped the edge of the slab obediently until the other reached into his chest and pulled out his beating heart. Now it was amazement and fear which creased Tabeck's face as he stared at the bloody organ clenched in the other's fist, blood streaming down his forearm. How could he still live when his heart pulsed in his servant's hand, and what of the fog? Had it entered him?

Then the cluster of priests lifted him from the basalt rock and carried him into the pyramid. Tabeck complied, though it was not what he expected. He expected to die. They descended the long flight of centuries-worn steps and entered a dark passage which led ever downward into the clammy heart of the earth. The musty smell of eons filled Tabeck's nostrils as the priests stopped in front of a doorway, bound his arms and feet then gently laid him inside.

His servant stepped in and knelt above him, shaking his heart in his hand, "I have also had a visitation from Mal. Your punishment is not to be as easy as death. You are to live . . . in here, until it is time for Mal to come forth again and bring his reign of blood to the world. You and he are one now and in his mercy, he will share your cell and teach you his powers until you are ready." The priest stepped out again as several large slaves began to mortar massive blocks in place. For the first time, Tabeck screamed.

CHAPTER 1

Under a scorching sun, the gray horse limped into the dusty desert town, its right foreleg infected and teeming with flies. Lexia lay draped across the animal's back; her long brown braid hanging in defeat against the mare's lathered shoulder. Gleaming, sticky sweat covered her sunburned skin, and dusty armor clad her breasts, shoulders and shins, a testament to the spirit-crushing trek across the burning Abi desert.

Although she was at the edge of town, its voices seemed distant to her wind-worn ears. Instinctively, the horse found its way to a stone trough near a clay brick porch and dipped its dry muzzle into the tepid water, gulping noisily. Lexia raised her head slowly and cast about as if she had only just woken; unaware of her surroundings, then, seeing the trough, rolled off the mare's back, and fell into the dust. She staggered to the edge of the trough and plunged her head into the water. Bubbles sparkled as they eased to the surface in tiny bursts, and lingered until she jerked her head up in a cascade of flying water, gasping for air, revitalized. With her one good eye, she scanned the village and saw it as nothing more than a cluster of adobe buildings a hundred yards across, devoid of moisture. Like the rest of the Abi, not so much as a scrub weed grew along the streets. Laughter caught her ear as a group of children, ages ranging from toddler to teen, kicked a leather ball in the talc-like dust of the street. They spat chiding insults and challenges from dry mouths until one kicked the ball and it shot toward her. She reached out with her toe and stopped it. Dark, round faces studied Lexia's pale, blind eye, the scar bisecting it from eyebrow to cheek, and her strong arms and thighs. She was taller than most men and carried a confidence in her posture equaling any soldier they had ever seen. They gaped at the anomaly, the ball forgotten, until Lexia bent down and picked it up. She gestured with her chin for them to step back, examined the ball briefly, then drop-kicked it skyward where it rose steadily to the excitement of the pack. Eventually, it made a slow descent into their midst, bounced over their heads, and rolled away. Immediately, the dirty crew attacked the leather sphere again, jostling against one another as they worked their way back down the street, occasionally darting a wary glance toward Lexia.

Turning her attention to the gray's foreleg, she splashed some water over the wound and wiped off a crust of caked blood. The mare whinnied and jerked back. "Easy girl, just trying to help; come on, let's have a look." The mare rolled its eyes and shied away, the pain too recent in its mind to allow further examination. "Fine, I'll look at it later. Just hope you don't die from infection and leave me on foot." She unbuckled the saddle and threw it over her shoulder, evoking a snort of gratitude from the gray.

As she walked, she noticed, apart from the group of children, the town seemed barren. A vortex of white dust spun between the stark, white-washed buildings, assaulting her nose and eyes, but Lexia staggered through it until another sound reached her ears, a sound different from the wind. People laughing. As she followed the distant cackling through crooked alleyways, she tilted her head to find her bearings. She walked on until she came to a squat two-storied structure in the center of town with a row of horses tied out front with a wagon. Through an open door that faced the dusty street, riotous music and laughter poured out and Lexia grinned. It had been a long while since she'd had a good time, long before she entered the Abi to escape bounty hunters.

She stepped across the threshold and dropped her saddle next to the door as she took in the room. Inside the tavern, eight men with thick, black hair and beards, laughed and drank, spilling ale and wine over their black, lacquered leather armor. Easily, a hundred men and women, in drab tunics and dusty hair, filled the small space and Lexia wondered if the entire town was at the inn, quaffing liquor. As bawdy laughter peeled, Lexia leaned on the stone counter and flipped a copper onto its surface, "Wine and water." The painfully thin barkeep grinned at her, placed a dark bony finger on her coin and slid it back.

"Your money is no good here, my desert flower," he poured the wine into a wooden cup then handed it to her, "Everyone is leaving tomorrow with these men to join the rebel army, myself included."

Lexia raised the cup, saluting the barkeep's generosity, then gulped it dry, enjoying the burning sensation as it ran down her parched throat, "Lucky me; in that case, I'll have another." He dumped another dram and she swallowed the second one even faster, "Where is this army headed, and how much are they paying?"

211

"Pay?...Pay?" he laughed, "More than money dear, much more. We get paid with black petals."

"Petals?"

"Yes, black flower petals."

She scoffed, "I don't fight for flowers or ideals; only gold or silver."

One of the big hairy men turned when he overheard this, "Then you haven't had one." The crowd erupted into laughter and cat-calls. "Give her one!" called out a young woman, then the crowd, "Yes, give her one!"

Lexia raised a suspicious eyebrow, perplexed, her hand easing toward her sword hilt. "What the hell are they talking about?"

The man smiled gently, then lifted a wicker basket from beside him and removed the lid, showing Lexia a bushel of dried flower petals, blacker than midnight. "Take one."

She had never been one to refuse anything truly free and the crowd of emaciated townsfolk seemed eager enough. She reached in and withdrew a petal larger than her thumb.

"Now, put it under your tongue, but don't swallow it." His easy manner seemed genuine enough, so Lexia dropped the petal into her mouth. At first, it tasted bitter, but quickly turned sweet as she worked it around under her tongue. Suddenly, a spreading warmth ran from her mouth down her body until her feet tingled. She tensed, surprised, and the tavern howled. Her pulse hammered, face flushed, and strength, long absent, flowed through her again as her muscles quaked, and a heat invaded her loins and breasts. Never had she felt so strong, with such a sense of radiant confidence. There was clarity in her mind like none she had ever experienced and an intense euphoria. The feeling was so perfect, in fact, despite her trek over the Abi desert, she felt regenerated, no, reborn. Laughing, she took the man by his broad shoulders and kissed him fiercely as the overwhelming sensation poured through her, evoking another roar from the revelers. Gold had purchased wine and comfort sometimes, but it had never brought a feeling like this one. She was a goddess and knew from then on, she *would* fight and die for the black petals.

CHAPTER 2

The army of the Black Tide came together in Southern Attah near the border of Kulunata. Under the black flower's powerful influence, streams of people from all walks of life poured into the desert hills, dyed their clothing and hair black, then took up battle gear issued by task masters.

Whenever the Tide entered a town teeming with life, it was desolate when they left. Those who did not take the petal willingly were forced to take it by hairy, olive-skinned Somerikans. They were separated into fighting units, and marched west across the burning sands. A large force broke off early before leaving the border, and traveled north to lay siege to the Attahn capital of Salsida.

The army was unique, in that there was only marginal rank and file. Groups of men and women were assigned to Somerikan task masters, who gave them instruction in combat and directed daily tasks. Beyond that, the flower was incentive enough to ensure one did as one was told. Every evening, the task masters reminded them of the righteous goals of the Black Tide; to unseat the despotic kings of the southern lands and return freedom to the people. Lexia and most of the others could have cared less about the daily rhetoric and just did what they were told as long as the petals kept coming.

Along the way a man refused to obey an order, and they watched him squirm and contort when he did not receive his allotted dose of the black flower. By nightfall, he was begging his masters to kill him, which they did, leaving a deep impression on the rest. Over the next months, Lexia had come to live only for the black petals. Eating became a grueling chore and, sometimes, had to be enforced by the lash. It wasn't long before apathy took root in her and she didn't care if the person next to her lived or died; only that she received her pay.

Eventually, the black horde arrived at the Tetas River to find the far west bank fortified by the Evatan army. The Tetas, meaning red for the color of its water, flowed south between the jagged Keddi Mountains from the northern Crimson Sea.

Now dusk was upon her, and as the dying sun waxed behind the jagged peaks of the Keddi, Lexia crouched behind a sand dune bordering the river. Her eyes scanned the opposite shore, watching as men labored like ants over bulwarks and ditches and horses whinnied against their riders. Her drug-honed senses strained at the desert wind, attempting to retrieve any morsel of information they might pluck from the air.

The Tide task masters had not failed to notice her aggressive nature, specifically, after she had killed three of her comrades in combat. Lexia never cared for unwanted advances. Under the cover of darkness, she was to infiltrate the enemy camp; not a highly desired mission as the last ten men had discovered. None of them had returned.

She inspected a pouch hanging from her leather harness where a single midnight petal waited. Confidence leaked from her, strength ebbing as she waited for nightfall. Soon it would be time to slide the silky flower under her tongue again. She would only have until morning to complete her task and return or she would be writhing in pain like a sand adder, pinned to the ground by a spear. Gently, she took the petal from the pouch and placed it in her mouth, feeling the surge of confidence and warmth, strength and perfection. After she regained her composure from the drug's initial rush, she eased her naked body into the cool waters of the Red, nipples tingling from the heightened sensation of the liquid's touch. Once she was up to her neck, she checked the buckles and straps of the warrior's harness that graced her bare form and struck out for the far shore. She surmised that by the time she reached it, darkness would have fallen and she would be at leisure to haunt the camp of the Evatan army, collecting information at will. After half an hour of treading water, Lexia stepped up onto the sandy banks of the west beach only a hundred yards from the enemy pickets. She opened a sodden pouch of charcoal, dipped her fingers into the black mush and spread it over her arms, legs, body and face to help her blend with the shadows. There was no fear in her, the drug saw to that. Boldly, she slipped into the camp, moving through shadow and flickering half-light while armed men paced and ate just a few feet from her.

Anxious talk over the sudden appearance of the black army mixed with campfire smoke among the pressing tents. Stones sang against sword blades, honing them for the coming fight while older soldiers reassured the younger ones.

Lexia's heart hammered from the drug and she suppressed an urge to draw her long knife and kill. She lingered for a few moments then, realizing there was no useful information to be had, crept away. Wearing the darkness like a garment, she glided through the camp, counting unit flags and war engines. The danger coupled with the hot night air added to her excitement causing her loins to burn with unexpected passion. She closed her eyes and controlled her breath and, when she opened them again, was surprised to see a large red tent propped on a rock bluff overlooking the camp. Given the unique color and its position, she reasoned that it must be the command tent of the Evatan forces and smiled through her charcoal smeared lips. Warm, soft sand whispered beneath her bare feet as she crouched low and sprinted across the open space to the bluff. When the bark of a guard echoed overhead, she dropped to the ground, whipping her long knife free. For several long minutes she waited until the man atop the bluff, who had called, was approached by another guard; a change in shift. Once the replacement strode past the front of the tent and circled away, she continued to the bottom of the bluff. Calloused hands moved over the rock as her practiced eye examined the surface for cracks and ledges that would hold her weight. Her white teeth clicked on the knife blade as she began to spider up the short bluff to the tent thirty feet above. Fingers and toes bit into crumbling shale as wiry muscles heaved against her weight, pulling and pushing upward. Once she reached the tent, she would slit the guard's throat then listen for as long as she liked, but Lexia was only halfway up when she stopped to rest her toes on a narrow ledge of loose rock. The eroded gob broke off and she plunged into the soft sand below. The impact left her stunned and breathless, yet no cry of surprise escaped her lips; nevertheless, the sound of breaking rock and clattering gravel did not escape the notice of the guard above. Thumping footfalls echoed and two helmeted heads peered down at her, followed by shouts of alarm. "Spies in the camp!" More running feet and calls, but Lexia had regained her wind and forced aching muscles to respond. She started to run, but too late, and was cut off by a wall of armed men. Standing with her back to the bluff, she waited as they encircled her.

From above, a low, heavy voice called down, "I want him alive!"

She jerked her head up to see a big bodied man in a red robe with a bald head, clutching a goblet. Of course, he would assume the spy was a man. She snorted with disgust.

Lexia did not wait for the circling men to strangle her chance of escape. As long as the juice of the petal was still flowing through her, she was invincible, and there was no doubt in her mind that she could cut her way through the mob and swim the river. She drove forward in the torchlight, ducked under a swinging shield and slashed a soldier across the neck. Before the one behind him knew what happened, she had hamstrung him and started on another. Bodies pressed in as she spun and darted among them, fighting her way through the throng of sweating men as they clawed and pummeled her. A fifth and a sixth went down from her razor-sharp knife and, finally, she created enough room to break and run. The muscles of her legs contracted as she bolted toward the river, but she had only sprinted a short distance before a figure emerged from the shadows ahead of her. A warrior, clad in a cuirass of black steel stamped with cryptic runes, and the same odd armor covered his thighs and shins. Steel bands riveted to black leather protected him underneath and gold spaulders* and bracers guarded his shoulders and forearms. On his head was a full-faced helmet of light gold with black onyx horns protruding from the forehead, and a black plume cascading from the top. From behind the blackness of the slit visor, he regarded her, yet did not reach for the blade strapped across his back. Lexia, not waiting for the men behind her to catch up, decided she would cut her way through this fool as well and lunged, but the man was too quick. He stepped aside and let her momentum carry her off balance. She twisted at the last moment and slashed backward catching the edge on the breastplate with her blade, the sound of grating metal echoed. The man only thumbed the scratch her knife had left then leapt in front of her again. She shot forward, stabbing expertly with the knife, but a mail-clad fist trapped her wrist, twisting it upside down and bending her forward. Before she could roll out of the hold, his booted foot snapped up into her jaw three times, lighting fast, and Lexia sank into oblivion.

     *Spaulder: Armor that protects the shoulder also known as an Epauliere or Pauldron.

CHAPTER 3

Pain burned in Lexia's battered head as she lay still, afraid to move or open her eyes. Sand grated beneath her skin and all was black behind her lids. Carefully, she opened her eyes and realized she was on her side staring at an earthen wall. Moaning, she rolled onto her back and immediately vomited, coughing and choking on the foul acids of her stomach. When her guts finished bucking like an angry horse, she looked around, confused and stunned, trying to locate an opening in the tiny, round dirt chamber. Where was the door? How did she get here? She closed her eyes and felt the deep pain in her body from the tips of her toes to the end of her hair, a terrible ache sweeping through her like a firestorm. Muscles contracted, folding her over and she retched again, but this time the pain was worse and her stomach long since empty. Dragging her forearm over cracked lips, she tried to pull fractured thoughts and memories into a single cohesive thought. She failed miserably. Then the flower called to her from deep in her mind and body, the need gnawing at her soul like a lion on a bone. As the withdrawal wrung her out like a rag, her desperate screams slowly gave way to bitter weeping. While her body convulsed with spasms of regret, tears streamed down her face and rained onto the sandy floor. Not since she was a babe in arms had she cried so. It was forbidden in her tribe, a sign of weakness and, now, here she was, weeping like a child over the death of her mother. But her dead mother was the black flower.

A voice called down from above and for the first time Lexia understood why there were no doors in this cell. She was in a deep pit, like a well, deep enough to keep out the light.

A soldier's face leered down from high above, "Thirsty darling? Have some water!" then he spit and laughed before disappearing. Lexia collapsed against the wall, shaking uncontrollably. She hugged her knees and screamed again, and continued to scream until her throat was dry and hurting. The day passed like a day in hell and so did the next, one after the other, days into nights and nights into days. Unconsciousness would come upon her like a blessing, easing her pain, and then she would awaken once again to her nightmare. Occasionally, food came down in a basket, but she couldn't eat; the very idea caused a surge in her stomach. Sometimes she could take water but wondered why she bothered, knowing only torture awaited her, or perhaps, this was the torture, but no one asked her anything.

As she lay in her own filth she absently crushed a scorpion, one of many that fell in, attracted by the effluence of her body. After an undeterminable time, the pain eased, the need weakened and Lexia was able to form thoughts and memories again. Silently, she asked herself if she would ever take the flower's petals again, after feeling the pain and regret its absence caused, but could not answer. She combed bony fingers through her matted hair then stared at its flat, lusterless strands. She had dyed it in homage to the black flower. She felt the hollows of her cheeks and looked at her thin arms, for the first time realizing the toll the black flower exacted from its followers.

A grunt resounded down the shaft and Lexia gazed up at a wide, round face with a flat nose, broad mouth and a tassel of black hair from the middle of his shaved head hanging past his shoulder. A corded hemp rope dropped along the wall. She picked up the dangling cord and examined the knot tied at the end for her to put between her feet. For a moment, she considered the torture that awaited her above. It couldn't be worse than what the drug had already done to her, she thought as she trapped the knot between the soles of her feet, and gripped the hemp in her hands. Whoever the odd-looking brute was, he was powerful enough to pull her up like a bucket of water. When she reached the top, he seized her arm in a vise-like grip, spun her around, and lashed her hands behind her back. She twisted a little to get a better look and squinted in the harsh sun. He was thick with a large round belly and huge arms. The spindly legs which held up the bulbous body seemed inadequate, but in spite of that he moved with grace. His only clothing was a flap of leather covering his groin. The man wrinkled his nose at her smell then smiled wickedly; revealing sharp filed teeth, and shoved her toward the river. They plodded down to the Tetas where the strange man handed her over to a group of rough looking soldiers who loitered near the sandy bank. They carried the miss-matched armor and weapons of mercenaries instead of the red cloaks, banded leather, turbans and scimitars of the regulars. Most of them were not even desert people.

219

"What's this, Molgien, a gift?" asked one of them.

The dark-skinned man with the tassel did not reply, but only shoved Lexia toward them and pointed at the water. With beaming smiles, the soldiers swarmed over her, lifted her bodily and dropped her into the brick colored water. Hands scrubbed her, dunked her head and groped her body, but she was too busy coughing up water to be offended. When the brutal bath was over, she was hauled out onto the beach to dry. They eyed her naked body as she lay in the sun, looks betraying the thoughts behind them. "Haven't had a woman in a long time. What say we have some fun?"

Sergeant Albis smirked, "I don't think so Pieter, the lieutenant will peel the skin off yer ass. He said no foolin around with her." The others averted their hard stares after the admonishment. Albis, a stocky Oshintonian with brown hair and a beard, hefted Lexia off the ground by her arm and pushed her up the slope toward the bulwarks. They walked around the fortifications and up to an arched opening of adobe brick that led down to a bunker under the bulwarks. "Lieutenant, I have the spy."

"Send her in," came a smooth hard voice, "and wait outside."

The burly man pushed her forward roughly and she descended a short flight of dusty steps into a shallow, dim, low-ceiling room filled with crates, barrels, weapons and armor. Sitting on a crate with his back to her was a lean, sun-tanned man, naked from the waist up. He sat with forearms resting on his knees while the sharp-toothed man trimmed his dark brown hair with a knife. Black leather pants and knee-high riding boots covered his long powerful legs. A raw, red stone, dangled from his neck by a leather thong. Stacked on a crate nearby was the armor of the man who had kicked her unconscious and recognition flashed across her face.

"Were you mistreated?" he asked.

She paused, surprised, "No, nothing serious," she replied hoarsely.

Molgien finished cropping the man's hair close against the sides and back of his head. The brute tousled the longer hair on top to remove the excess clippings, and then poured water over the lieutenant's head. He stood and stretched his lean, muscular frame, then turned to face Lexia. Intelligent gray eyes regarded her diminished form, and she wondered at their modest slant.

He smiled crookedly at her nakedness as he toweled off, but Lexia did not shy away or turn her head. She was not ashamed of her body and the officer was aware of it. He crossed the small dirt chamber and rifled through an open crate. He tossed her a pair of horsehair trousers and a white linen shirt. Moments later, he found a pair of low boots only slightly too large for her. She faced him, undressed and defiant, but with a hint of concern in her voice. "Does this mean you aren't going to torture me?"

"Do I need to? Or do you still feel some loyalty to your

army?"

Lexia shook her head, confused. "I don't understand."

The Lieutenant pulled on a gray linen shirt and tucked it into his pants. "You aren't the first spy caught in our camp. I've done most of the interrogating and discovered some interesting things about the army called the Black Tide. Like the drug they feed all the soldiers and camp followers. Whatever it is, it's powerful. The other spies died within a few days of interrogation, not because of torture, but from the aftereffects of the black flower. It was my decision not to question you while you fought off your addiction. I wanted to see if you were going to live, then I could worry about getting information."

Lexia threw back her head and stuck out her chin, eyes flashing. "So, it is torture!"

He waved his hand in a dismissive gesture, "Normally, yes, it would be. However, I don't believe you have any valuable information. Even if you did, what allegiance do you owe them? Look at yourself, at what you've become." Lexia's proud chin dropped as she examined her gaunt figure.

He continued, "Ten spies have been brought into this room, raving like fanatical lunatics and not one could tell me who was in charge of their army, who the generals were, what their goal was. Why should I think you would know anything more?"

Lexia dropped her eyes, "It's the petals. No one cares who is in charge or where they're going, whether they live or die. Only that they have the drug. There is nothing else for them."

"Are you free from it now?"

She shrugged and turned away from him, suddenly ashamed, but not from her lack of clothing, "I don't know.   I hope so, but it hasn't left my thoughts."

"Tell me what you know." He turned to Molgien and made several complex hand gestures. The savage nodded and left.

"Who are you?" she asked.

"Shasp Ironwrought. I'm the officer in charge of the foreign cavalry… and interrogations. And you?"

"Lexia of Bretcombia."

"Well Lexia, I suggest you dress and tell me what you know. If I believe you, torture won't be necessary, but if I think you are holding back, I'll have Molgien eat your hand while you watch."

Molgien returned bearing a platter of smoked fowl with pomegranates and a bottle of wine in a braided leather bottle. Lexia pulled on the clothes and sat on a crate across from Shasp. He tore apart the fowl and held a leg out for Molgien, but the big savage only wrinkled his nose in distaste and shook his head. "Molgien is a cannibal from somewhere deep in Somerika, as far as I can tell. He doesn't care for much except fruit and human flesh. As you can imagine, he's not too popular with the other men, due to his eating habits, but I find him to be an excellent attendant and bodyguard."

"Why do you sign to him? Is he deaf?"

Shasp took a bite and shook his head, "No, I just don't understand his language, but fortunately, I do understand Somerikan sign language. It was developed by merchants to allow trade to spread throughout Somerika. Most peoples in the southern land know it, basic as it is, and he and I communicate well enough." Shasp leaned back against a sack of grain, clay cup of wine in hand. "Now…you were about to tell me everything you know."

Lexia nodded and carefully relayed her story from the time she entered the lonely village at the edge of the Abi, and her first taste of the black flower, to the time she was captured.

Shasp sat quietly sipping wine, absorbing each word. He considered Lexia's face and found her handsome if not beautiful, in spite of her scars, sightless eye and emaciated form. It was easy for him to see how she might be attractive once again, should she ever regain her former self.

"I believe you," he said. "Your voice was steady, you didn't look away or seem stressed at any time; besides, I've already received word of the siege on Salsida." He turned to Molgien and signed. The cannibal caught Lexia by the arm and jerked her off the crate.

"He'll be taking you to a cell until I decide what to do with you. The general may have an interest, other questions he may want to ask. I don't recommend you struggle."

Lexia's eyes narrowed and instantly Shasp knew she wasn't going to take his advice. She let her arm fold behind her back and struck Molgien in the throat with the blade of her off hand. He grunted as she pulled free and leapt for the door but not before he caught her by the hair and yanked her off her feet, sending her flying over the improvised table. She landed upside-down on a pile of

223

sacks, stunned. Molgien, rubbing his throat, started for her, but Shasp held up his hand. "I think you need to reconsider you relationships, Lexia of Bretcombia. You may be better off as a prisoner of Evata rather than a slave of the Black Tide." Lexia regained her feet as Molgien caught her again by the arm and started to usher her out the door.

Suddenly, Sergeant Albis burst through the doorway, "Lieutenant, Bolis is at it again," concern edged his voice. Shasp cursed and walked toward the threshold, drawing his Ayponese blade from its scabbard. Molgien smiled his evil smile and followed him out the door, dragging Lexia behind.

The group crossed an improvised street and wound through a labyrinth of tents, eventually pouring out onto an open training area of packed, earth. A ring of more than two-hundred cavalry men surrounded a single rider who was preaching loudly. Horses stamped, sensing the anxiety of their riders. The instigator was blonde, tall, wiry and handsome.

"I'm telling you, Ironwrought is no cavalryman! I could ride circles around that lout and yet here he is, telling us how to train in some foreign way, instead of the way we was trained! He's going to get us all killed!"

Men were grunting their agreement when Shasp broke through the circle, "Starting the training without me, Bolis?"

Bolis glared down with pure contempt, "We've decided you're full of shit, Lieutenant, and we aren't following you anymore. We're gonna do things my way."

Shasp nodded and frowned, "I see, so you think you can do a better job of training the men? In that case, you won't mind a little exhibition to prove your competence." He whistled two sharp, shrill notes. Seconds later, thunder sounded behind him as a huge black stallion knocked riders aside and forced its way into the center, dust boiling from beneath anxious hooves. Shasp caressed the brute's neck. "Grimm here has no saddle and I have no armor. You, on the other hand, have both." He looked around at the men, "If Bolis can beat me in a contest of cavalry combat, then you will follow him. If I win, there will be no more dissension. Agreed?" The men nodded and shouted their agreement.

Shasp grasped Grimm's mane in his left hand and jumped onto his back, still gripping the blade in his right. With the black mane tight

224

in his fist, he goaded Grimm out to the center of the circle while Bolis turned his white mare around to face his adversary, a wicked smile of certainty twisting his lips. Both raised their swords in salute to their comrades then trotted away from each other and toward the edge of the horseflesh barrier then turned. Bolis jabbed his spurs into the mare's flanks and she lunged forward. Grimm needed no goading and exploded from the sideline on his own. Shasp rode high on his shoulders as they shot forward, sword held out away from him, wind whistling past. The horses slammed together in the dry heat and their riders attacked one another with razor-sharp steel. The spectators screamed their best war cries for whomever they favored and cheered for the embattled men. Shasp wheeled Grimm to the right as Bolis pressed his mare, hoping to cause the black stud to rear and unhorse his rider, but Grimm was too experienced and kept his hooves down. Shasp deflected several slashes meant to decapitate him, waiting for an opening, but Bolis was good, one of his best, and Shasp hated to have to kill the man. Steel rang and crashed over the horse's heads, slash and parry, parry and slash. Bolis hissed through clenched teeth as he fought to beat his way through Shasp's guard, but the lieutenant was formidable even without a saddle. Shasp's features were focused and stolid, as if studying a puzzle, with no sign of fear. Then in an amazing display, Shasp backed Grimm up a space and tugged up on his mane. The stallion reared slightly and spun to his left rolling around the front of the mare and coming along Bolis' weak side. Instantaneously, Shasp whipped his blade over his head in the opposite direction of Grimm's turn and lashed out. Bolis' head flew from his body in a spray of crimson rain. The body sat atop the saddle briefly in a morbid display, sword still dangling loosely in hand, blood jetting, then toppled from the back of the stained mare. The clamor of yelling spectators fell away as Shasp slowly dismounted and the mare milled uncertainly around its fallen rider.

He strode to the edge of the arena and looked squarely at Lexia, "I wonder if the Black Tide has this problem." He turned to his men, "It's bad enough I have to risk my life in combat with the enemy then to have to risk it fighting my own men. From now on, if you have any bitching to do, you'll do it there," and he pointed to the center of the training ground where Bolis' body twitched.

225

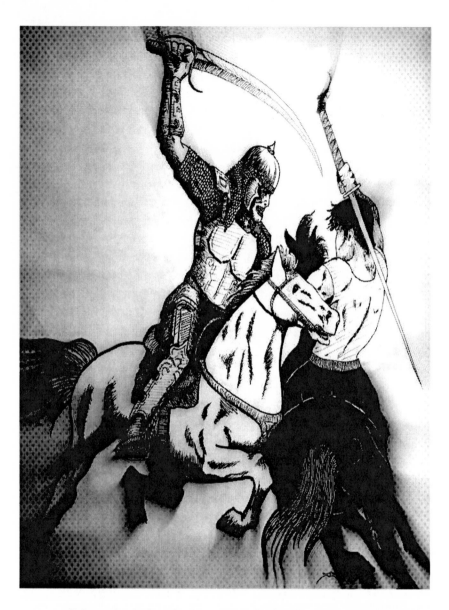

Grimm had already forgotten the battle and nuzzled the white mare affectionately. One of the men dismounted to stop the beach in horse etiquette but Shasp stopped him. "Leave him alone! He's earned his prize! The rest of you haven't earned anything yet!" He turned away, Molgien following, and wound through the tent maze again until they came to a row of mud brick cells and he motioned at the door. A guard opened it and Molgien shoved Lexia inside then locked it.

"I told you everything!" She cried.

"Did you?" Shasp replied as he removed his blood-stained shirt and wiped his face.

"Yes! I'm not going back! I have no allegiance to them!"

"Hmm, I'll give it some thought," he said as he turned away.

"Wait . . . please," she screamed at his back, "let me out of here! I told you everything!"

He walked away, leaving her demands to dissolve in the afternoon breeze.

CHAPTER 4

The guard snorted, squatting next to the door and gnawing on an apple. The sight of food suddenly made Lexia's stomach ache with hunger, and she even longed for a piece of hardtack bread. Later that evening a camp follower came around with watery porridge for the prisoners and Lexia devoured it with great relish. She slept fitfully in the cell, cooling off after nightfall and woke again with the heat of morning as the clay walls absorbed the sun's energy. By late morning, sweat ran in rivulets down her neck, back and breasts, soaking her linen shirt. She stripped off the horsehair trousers to let her legs breathe and visited a shallow basin of lukewarm water placed in the corner for her thirst and hygiene. By evening of the second day, she languished, waiting for anything to happen, when the lock of her cell clattered and snapped open, the door swinging wide.

Lieutenant Ironwrought stood silhouetted by the setting sun, "Get up. It seems the general trusts you more than I do," and he tossed a bag at her feet, "though I can't imagine why."

Lexia pulled the trousers over her long legs, catching Shasp as he snuck a sidelong glance. At least he didn't stare, she thought, as she hefted the bag over her shoulder and stepped past him, finally feeling the breeze on her skin. Shasp started to turn away.

"Wait," she called, "what now? What am I supposed to do?"

He shrugged, "What do I care, I'm just a lieutenant. The bag has some gear and food. More than you deserve."

She cleared her throat, "I can't cross the desert with just a bag of meager provisions. I need water, a horse, and weapons."

Shasp wiped his face on the hem of a green cotton tunic, an agitated expression painting his face, "You're lucky you're not dead, and in case you didn't notice, we are about to fight a war and can hardly afford to be giving away supplies and horses to wandering spies! The only reason I gave you those supplies was because the general ordered it. He seems to think the drug is the only culprit in your crime . . . I don't agree."

"I'm not a spy, not anymore, not for them."

He laughed sardonically, "Oh . . . is that right? You'll forgive me if I don't believe you," and turned his back. Striding away, he called over his shoulder, "It's a big camp, find a place for yourself."

"Sonofabitch," she muttered under her breath as she hefted the bag again and wandered through the camp, looking for a secluded corner. She fumed at the arrogant officer for not even giving her a paring knife to defend herself with, and skirted the main body of men finally finding a place under a wagon followers' camp. "Arrogant prick," she muttered. She hated him, yet no matter how hard she tried, could not seem to dislodge his face and slanted gray eyes from her mind. Dried ox dung smoked as she started a small cook fire and soon discovered it was impossible to cook anything over dried dung without it tasting like dung. She gagged on the half cooked fish pilfered from another wagon. Camp followers, smithies, armorers, cobblers, boot makers, cooks and prostitutes teemed around the fringes of the camp, their fires and activities bringing forth a vast array of odors and sounds. The noise of laughter, screams, chatter, hammers banging and pots boiling filled the air. What was she doing here? She was a warrior, not a whore or a cook. Self-loathing filled her, stinging her ancestral pride as she flung the half-eaten piece of fish away. A dog quickly snapped it up. She knew she was stuck in the camp. She couldn't go back to the army of the Black Tide and she couldn't cross the desert, and she sure as hell was not going to live under a wagon eating handouts from the camp followers she once disdained. There was only one way out, one way back to being the person she had been before the black flower raped her soul. It would be risky, but her ancestral pride demanded restoration.

CHAPTER 5

Night hung with moonless oppression over the streets of Salsida while the panicked residents prepared for another assault under a cloud of anxiety. The sounds of wailing and shouted orders blended in a cacophony against the constant drumming beyond their refuge. Archers and soldiers rimmed the walls, while workers reinforced the gates with timber and marble from their own homes.

Outside, an army of madmen, and mad women, hemmed them in on all sides. A sea of campfires illuminated massive siege engines, looming like evil giants throughout the enemy encampment. The soldiers of the black army worked tirelessly, fighting and openly copulating between tasks. To the defenders it seemed a picture of hell. They would never have guessed the creatures beyond their walls were once the same as them.

It was among the demons of this hell Atawar Lackeddi walked, following the black robed acolytes through the throng of gaunt, wide-eyed warriors. Men and women were dressed for battle and performing functions regardless of gender. They appeared to him, somehow, less than human, acting much like animals with indifference to civilized custom.

His dark guide stopped in front of a large tent and drew back the door cloth, revealing the red glow of a brazier within. Atawar ducked through the opening and was silently greeted by more acolytes. Their leader stepped behind the smoldering brazier, greenish smoke wafting with an acrid odor, and pulled his hood back, revealing an emaciated head like a skull with skin stretched over it. "Our master has foreseen your arrival. He will speak to you."

Lackeddi began to sweat from the muggy heat of the tent, or was it fear? He ran his shaking fingers through his curly black locks. "It is as well he does, for my liege would be greatly angered if he did not."

The priest's mouth spilt into an amused grin, "The relationship is mutual; I am sure." He closed his sunken eyes and began to chant in a long forgotten tongue. The green smoke seemed to respond to his monotone voice, thickening and boiling, the odor intensified. "Come closer," beckoned the priest, "look into the bowl."

Atawar moved cautiously toward the bronze vessel as his eyes darted around the tent at the meditating ring of acolytes, then rested uneasily on the glowing embers. A wave of heat rippled and waxed before his eyes then suddenly faded, changing into a watery surface. Only, instead of seeing his reflection, he saw a hooded figured robed in coarse red cloth, reclining on a throne of blackest obsidian. Atawar peered into the pool trying to penetrate the darkness of the cowl, but could not. It spoke to him in a deep, dripping voice, thick with menace, "Speak, messenger."

He was stunned by the unnatural communication, unable to form words at first but managed to croak out his reagent's message. "My master wants to know why you have routed such a large force north to Salsida instead of staying with the plan which was agreed upon."

The hooded image sat up slightly, "Tell him it was necessary to divide Attah's and Evata's forces. They are, after all, allies. With the bulk of the Attahn forces at bay in Salsida, it will be easier to break Evata's armies."

With sweat dripping from his face, Atawar pressed further, "But can the Black Tide overcome the army of Evata under General Holkerm? He is an accomplished tactician and brilliant officer. Your army is nothing more than a mob. How will it stand against seasoned veterans?"

The red figure's voice dropped an octave, adding to the already dangerous tone, "Do not underestimate the power of the Adder blossom. Its petals will keep the Black Tide together; besides, I have alliances within the enemy's ranks. Tell your master he has nothing to fear, the plan will proceed and our agreement will stand."

Atawar nodded, "It is well that it does, for he has instructed me to inform you, he will cease to fund this venture if it deters again." No sooner did the words leave his mouth, Atawar felt a sharp pain, as if a knife had been thrust into the pit of his stomach and he cried out. Two acolytes reached out and held him so he would not collapse. Then the voice came again.

"Perhaps you should inform your master, he is too deep in the pit to leap out now. Our alliance must not be broken, otherwise he will forfeit his life and our efforts will be for nothing."

Just as quickly as the pain had come, it left and with it the image of the robed man. Atawar Lackeddi had always considered himself to be a courageous man, but now, cold fear gripped his heart.

CHAPTER 6

Morning's gentle rays had scarcely splashed upon the Tetas when Shasp saw an exhausted rider speed past him. Hooves thrumming, the lathered mount charged by surprised soldiers on the way up the sandy slope to the general's tent. Something important was happening and Shasp didn't need to wait for orders. "Corporal Pieter!" The lanky, young mercenary with shaggy blonde hair leapt from his vantage point on a rock and ran to him.

"Sir?"

"Spread the word, tell our troopers to rally at the training field immediately. I want full battle dress and formation. Go!"

Pieter sped away, kicking up sand as he went. Shasp was hurrying along the Tetas on the way to his tent when he spied an object bobbing in the water, slowly spinning with the current. He stopped and stepped closer to the water's edge; it was a body. As he pondered it, three more slid by, then six, then ten, until the river became choked. His amazed wondering ended abruptly when he realized most of the bloated forms were dressed in the red Evatan navy uniform. The rest were dressed in the dyed leather of the Black Tide. The Evatan navy held the Crimson Sea to the North, keeping the army's flank protected while scouts along the river watched for enemy crossings. The bobbing corpses could only mean one thing. A vicious battle had been fought on the Crimson Sea, and the Tetas had brought the dead here. Shasp considered the scout who had just rode in, and his instincts warned him something was wrong. Could the enemy have defeated their navy and crossed the Crimson? He dashed to his tent and quickly strapped on his armor. Grimm, sensing the growing electricity in the air, appeared at the opening, snorting and huffing. Shasp hefted a saddle over Grimm's back, cinched the belly straps, fitted the bridle and leapt onto the saddle. They bolted toward the training ground where his unit of three-hundred, battle-hardened mercenaries slowly filtered in from the camp. By the time the mismatched cavalry formed ranks, a runner from the general's observation post galloped across the front and skidded to a stop.

"Lieutenant Ironwrought, the general has reports of enemy troops moving south along the Tetas on our side of the river. The scout said they were infantry and some archers, about a thousand, less than a day's ride out. The general wants you to take your auxiliary unit and hold them until he can form up the infantry to reinforce you."

Shasp thought a moment. "What about the rear, who's holding that?"

The runner looked over his shoulder at the river, "The regular cavalry and most of our archers. He doesn't think they will attempt a crossing here as long as they have to take heavy fire."

Shasp sighed. Three-hundred poorly trained cavalry mercs against a thousand blood crazed addicts. "Story of my life," he muttered to himself. He faced his men, "Column of three!" The horses jockeyed and bumped into their respective positions as he turned Grimm along side of the right column. He lifted his arm then dropped it in a cutting motion, "Forward!"

The tramp of hooves beat out a rhythm on the packed sand as they started upriver, dust roiling up from the churning legs. Shasp considered the time it would take for the Evatan infantry to equip and move out. His cavalry would be twice as fast at a walk, which meant the foot soldiers wouldn't catch up until dusk. He would have to hold back the pace of his troopers to keep down the dust; let the enemy tire itself as it came south, and leave the distance between his troopers and the reinforcements as close as possible.

By midday, Sergeant Albis returned from a scouting expedition, drawing up alongside him. "Just as they said, about a thousand infantry, loaded with pikes and archers, just waiting for cavalry, almost a quarter-mile from here and coming along the river. It's as if they knew they were going to face heavy horse." Albis' face looked grim as he frowned through his scar-crossed brown beard and scratched his thick mane.

Shasp held up a fist and called a halt. He rode with his sergeant to the crest of a high dune where he pulled open a spyglass and searched the northern horizon. Dust hung in the distance, foreshadowing the enemy's approach. His vision swept the area, resting on a depression along the shore with a ridge of sand to the west. He collapsed the glass and looked into Albis' sunburnt face, "Do you trust me, Sergeant?"

Albis thought a moment then grunted with a brief nod, "Aye, enough I guess."

"Good, I want you to take the first column and lead them directly at the forward ranks."

The sergeant's eyes widened, "Suicide, that is."

Shasp smiled, "I don't want you to commit, just keep their attention. Before you get to the lead rank, break and take the column toward the river."

"What are you going to do?"

He slapped Albis on the shoulder, raising a puff of dust, "Trust me."

Even though the black army had marched south for days, the troops seemed as fresh as when they left, and though most appeared gaunt from lack of food, they did not lack energy. The black flower kept their bodies moving forward with ease, and there would be time enough for eating after battle. Black-armored soldiers marched forward, a mass of pikes resting on their shoulders while bowmen brought up the rear, trudging through the stinging dust. Suddenly, the ground began to tremble with a low drumming vibration and the men anxiously scanned the sandy rises around them. Without warning, a forest of steel-tipped lances broke over a wind-lashed dune directly to their front, bearing down on the forward rank like a tidal wave of thundering horseflesh. Black-bearded men screamed orders and obscenities as pikes clattered and fell level, creating an impenetrable wall of razor-tipped death to welcome the Evatan cavalry. Row after row and shoulder to shoulder, the battalion of the Black Tide stood on the butts of the ten-foot spears, the points eager for the onrushing horses. Quickly the gap narrowed as arrows zipped from string to rain on the advancing troops. Long cavalry shields snapped up as clothyard shafts splintered against armor and barding. Two horses screamed, crashing to the earth, bearing their riders with them, as the deadly broad heads shot between chinks in their mail. One rider flew from his mount, an arrow in his neck, and two more received wounds but continued their reckless charge, shafts jutting from leg and chest like quills. The cavalry bore down within feet of the waiting pikes, sand flying and dust blinding as men roared their defiance of death, but their lances stayed skyward. Then, just before beast and rider collided with prickling death, the rank of cavalry veered right along the wall of pikes. Black Tide soldiers mocked them and laughed at how easily they had warded off the troopers with not so much as a snapped stick. Suddenly, a cry of alarm

236

sounded from the flank opposite the river. Men swiveled their heads to see more cavalry thundering down on them from the rise to their left. Before the jostling infantry could swing their pikes around to cover the other side, Shasp crashed his half of the unit into their unprotected flank like an iron avalanche, sweeping men aside like grass in a field. Bodies flew from the driving shoulders of armored horse and bowled into their comrades wreaking havoc. Albis took his que and drove his men along the beach on the opposite flank then turned into the confused infantry with the same devastating effect, avoiding the long spears as they waggled uncertainly overhead. The two wedges of cavalry knifed toward each other, slowly cutting the black battalion in half. Shasp's Ayponese katana scythed through infantrymen on his left and right, slinging sticky ropes of blood as arms and heads flew from their screaming owners. The horses strained forward as their impetus slowed in the quagmire of the enemy's surge. Albis whipped his cavalry saber in a blood frenzy as men sought to tear him from his mount. He reined the animal around sharply, knocking soldiers off their feet and creating room for another lunge forward. With a final push, the wedges came together, dissecting the mass of tangled, fury spitting infantry.

Shasp yelled at Pieter, who had just cleaved a man who was trying to impale him, "Sound the horn!"

Pieter raised a bull horn, which hung from his neck, inhaled deeply and gave a long, low blast. Instantly, both columns of cavalry rolled southward and horses screamed as they reared and leapt forward, their masters whipping them mercilessly with the flats of their sabers. Hooves drove downward, crushing skulls and shattering bones as they dug into the southern ranks of the divided Tide battalion. Black soldiers fell back on one another like dominoes as the Evatan mercenaries ground them up, slowly dissolving the forward ranks. Tide soldiers watched in horror as their comrades were reduced to bloody, whining pulps. The press gradually ebbed as the enemy ranks fell apart and the cavalry broke free, running down the scattered men who fled before them and leaving the intact northern ranks behind as they rode away.

At the top of the rise, Shasp signaled for his unit to regroup and greeted Albis, "Good work Sergeant, but we have to hit them again before they can reorganize, full frontal assault, Pieter, sound charge!"

The doleful horn blasted its loud message and once again the hurricane of steel and flesh poured down from the rise to wreak havoc on the milling Black Tide battalion. Horses stormed through the crowd of painted Tide in a clash of clanging steel and screaming men. The stench of blood and excrement filled the dust-choked battlefield as the cavalry pierced the heart of the formation and slowly stalled. Horses spun and churned in the chaos as men stabbed and hacked, clawed and wailed. Cavalrymen were dragged from the saddle and drowned in raining knives, while horses were hamstrung and impaled. The forces were locked in the throes of finality and Shasp hoped his men could stay in their saddles long enough to break the spirit of the battalion's remnants. Trained chargers danced a terrible jig as riders slashed down from above with vicious sabers, loosening the strangling squeeze of men and allowing their horses freedom of movement, then slaughter. Like the slow thawing of ice, the northern ranks of the tide finally melted and fled in panic. Ironwrought's men were sweeping down on the fleeing soldiers when a trooper cried out. "Look to the horizon!" A cloud of dust rose lazily into the air north of them, signaling the approach of a second force.

"Pieter, ride ahead, we'll reform and await your news!"

In a flash, Corporal Pieter wheeled his mount and dashed northward, disappearing over a dune.

"Head count, Sergeant."

Albis busied himself calculating the casualties while Shasp watched the horizon for Pieter's return.

Albis finished his count and trudged through the sand to Shasp's side, "We have two-hundred and thirty-one men; more than a third of those are wounded."

Shasp nodded, "Gather as much gear from the dead as you can without burdening the horses or encumbering their riders, then form up."

Albis dashed back down the hill, relaying the orders as Shasp continued to anxiously search the distance. Long minutes passed as the sand twirled in the desert's capricious wind, and hot rays slowly roasted them in their armor. Shasp had removed his helmet and was wiping the sweat from his brow when he saw a rider in the distance. Snapping open the spyglass, he quickly brought it up and made out Pieter's form whipping his horse desperately.   Before Shasp could question why, the answer swarmed over the distant hill behind his corporal. Black-armored cavalry, about a dozen, rode hard on his back.

"Sergeant Albis! Get everyone behind this ridge and don't stir the dust. Pieter's coming in with a squad of cavalry on his ass. I want lances ready with a right and left wing to wrap around as soon as he clears this ridge."

Seconds later, Pieter's mount soared over the ridge leaving a trail of flying sand. His heart leapt as he saw the waiting column of fellows, lances ready and visors down, wheel and explode over the bank behind him. Two more columns galloped away to his left and right to out flank the black riders, who were oblivious to the trap.

The first four Black Tide cavalrymen were instantly impaled and slammed out of their saddles while the others were quickly surrounded and cut down, with the exception of one. Shasp had made it clear that he wanted at least one alive. The man's horse circled and pawed the ground as its rider, eyes wide in a crazed stare, held his scimitar out defensively. The mercenaries backed away and circled him.   Shasp rode forward. Grimm trotted head to head with the other horse.

"Drop your weapon and surrender and you might yet live."

The Tide rider answered by heeling his mount and slashing at Shasp's head. The lieutenant parried the cut, twisted his blade and neatly severed the man's wrist at the joint. Blood sprayed and the cavalryman howled, but only for an instant as the flat of the Ayponese blade quickly snapped against his skull, knocking him out to the ground. Two soldiers leapt from their saddles and tied his arms behind his back, then flopped him over his own saddle.

Shasp rode back to an exhausted, but grateful, Pieter, "Well, Corporal?"

"More cavalry and infantry . . . a lot more, maybe three battalions marching and two on horse.

"Sonofabitch!" Shasp huffed, "We can't hold that many and our infantry reinforcement will be overwhelmed.   Sergeant Albis! Form the men, we ride hard!"

239

CHAPTER 7

Shasp's mercenary unit had only been gone an hour when the
sound of wailing horns reached Lexia's ears. The blasts were a
mixture of short and long notes, sending a coded message to the
Evatan camp. Followers eyed each other with worried expressions as
the camp broke into a teeming mass of men and beasts. Evatan
soldiers, archers and cavalry swarmed, running to their respective
gathering points, carrying armor and gear. Red capes and trousers of
the regulars fluttered in the warm breeze as they went, men shouting
orders and encouragement to comrades.

Lexia ran from her place under the wagon, where she lay in
the shade, to the bulwarks facing the Tetas and climbed to the top of
the raised earth mound. Her breath caught at the sight that filled her
view. For as far as she could see, up and down the river, large rafts
with protective shield fronts, lined the opposite shores. Black garbed
men and women were pouring onto the crafts by the thousands, each
bearing a shield to hold overhead, then launching in unison. Some
were small enough to carry only a dozen men and others large
enough to bear whole platoons of cavalry.   Aboard three of them,
huge siege engines tottered over the disturbed waters. Lexia now
realized the reason for the battle's delay. The Tide army had been
waiting for logs to be brought up from the timbered south lands.

Runners streamed off the general's knoll and soon archers
and infantry were marching to their allotted positions on the
bulwarks. Bowmen took the forefront, standing in ranks three deep
for the width of the protective mound, three hundred yards long,
while mercenary infantry and cavalry waited anxiously with the
brightly dressed regulars behind them. The remaining cavalry
regulars swept north and south along the Tetas to keep the main
body from being outflanked. Obviously, the general didn't trust the
ragged mercenaries with his flanks. Other than the bulwark
construction, which had been built prior to the Black Tide's arrival,
there was no protection from arrows.

Slowly, the mass of log crafts surged across the river until
within range of the Evatan bowmen's deadly skill. In the trembling
hands of a young man the signal flag hung on its pole, and with a
nod from the general he waved it energetically. The archers, with

eyes on the flag, anxiously turned to their work. A thin, swarthy battalion commander in a red cape and turban screamed the orders, "Ready . . . Loose!"

Hissing from their strings, a thousand wooded shafts blackened the sky. Out on the Tetas, razor-sharp broad heads thudded into the wood rafts and upheld shields, occasionally finding a gap and sticking into flesh and bone. Here and there a body rolled into the river and bobbed in the water while the armada pushed relentlessly on. The commander of archers, stunned by the lack of effect for so many arrows, screamed again, "Loose at will!" That was the favorite command of this company of archers, and arrows sped from creaking longbows. Each man, proud of his skill at hitting a peach pit from fifty yards, drew down now with intense focus. Whistling arrows found every tiny hole and crack between the Tide shields with renewed success. Bodies dropped into the river by the dozens, bumping against the sides of the lumbering vessels as they pushed on apathetically. The distance was quickly shrinking and as they came closer, the archer's aim improved. Hundreds of dead Black Tide now choked the river as their rafts grated against the Evatan shore. Hordes of screaming soldiers stormed off the planks and into the lapping water of the beach. Another red flag waved, and with a common shout, the Evatan infantry displaced the archers, who fell back to another bulwark structure, seeking vantage points to fire down from. Ranks of red-turbaned soldiers stood shoulder to shoulder, their small round shields overlapped, spiked-steel caps gleaming and scimitars waving with anticipation.

From where she stood, Lexia could even see the familiar faces of whip masters and old comrades, if that's what she could call them.   Quickly, she decided she could not.

Howling addicts in black leather armor flooded toward the bulwarks, their mismatched weapons gripped in angry fists, eyes bloodshot and crazed, they attacked with the ferocity of ravenous wolves.

With a long trumpet blast, and the infantry fast on their heels, the mercenary cavalry rode down the slopes of the bulwarks, screaming the unintelligible war cries of a dozen foreign tribes. The opposing forces slammed together like storms born on separate winds, generating a clap of thunder made from flesh and steel. The ring and clang of sword and axe resonated through the desert heat as

241

cavalry horses stomped and crushed men and the infantry clashed all around. Ever growing numbers of Black Tide horsemen reached the beachhead and crashed into the fray, screaming like madmen. Tactics were forgotten as the battlefield became a seething mass of bloody humanity. Clusters of cavalry broke apart as footmen ducked and darted between the deadly hooves. Arrows zipped down into the fray by the hundreds, seeking their targets, before a flash of movement changed someone's fate. The last wave of craft brought the Black Tide archers aground. They immediately drove the Evatan bowmen behind cover, slowing the relentless bite of broad heads.

The sandy shores of the Tetas quickly became a red paste, greedily drinking the blood of the vanquished, who struggled to hold onto life beneath the kicking, stomping legs of the victors. Lexia's blood surged as she beheld the horror of the battlefield. In the midst of the chaos, she made out the half-naked figure of Molgien. Though he was valet to Lieutenant Ironwrought, he must have been attached to the mercenary infantry, she thought. He swung a long spiked club, against the swords of several soldiers who sought to surround him. His bulky body exuded power as he expertly employed the huge weapon among his enemies with devastating effect. A sword swinging addict ducked in for a thrust, then fell back again with a crushed skull. Nevertheless, Molgien was but one man who was quickly becoming overwhelmed like a lion against jackals.   Lexia knew it was only a matter of time before he went down under a wave of flashing blades. She dashed along the bulwark, ducking arrows and dodging spears as she moved along. Without breaking her stride, she snatched a scimitar from the hand of a dead Evatan soldier and plunged into the struggling mass, blade slashing and thrusting. The Black Tide had become her enemy and, as far as she was concerned, that made Molgien her ally. If the Black Tide swept over Attah in a few short months, how long would it take for them to conquer the rest of Nomerika? The memory of her humiliation in the pit boiled to the surface of her tortured emotions and rage filled her. Enraged at the flower, at the Black Tide and furious, as only a woman can be furious, with the force behind it. Molgien was not her enemy and he had not hurt her, though he may have considered it. Whether Shasp or Molgien realized it, they had saved her and now it was time to take back her dignity. Her fierceness was rekindled and she drove forward through the spitting, clawing, hacking mass, cutting down anyone who wore black. She could see Molgien's head bobbing in the fray ahead, but he suddenly faltered and disappeared. In a few short seconds, she carved her way through and found the cannibal on his back, leg deeply gashed. He was desperately warding off the soldiers who thrust down at him, trying to put an end to the stubborn savage. Lexia, slashed one across the neck with the tip of her sword, blocked another and stabbed him in the pelvis. Her unexpected presence allowed the surprised Molgien to regain his feet, though awkwardly, and they stood back to back against the endless surge of black armor. The Evatan forces were slowly eroding under the overwhelming numbers of Black Tide, crowding the beach. Between sword thrusts, Lexia wondered why the officers had not given the order to pull back to the bulwarks. She glanced about for a lieutenant or captain but saw no one. Red-swathed helmets were becoming fewer and fewer while black leather was quickly filling in the gaps. It was beginning to look as if she wasn't going to see the sunset. Blood caked her face and clothes as a dozen new cuts bled afresh over her body. Joining a desperate battle without armor was not one of her wiser moments. Molgien, drenched in enemy viscera, fought like a demon as he smashed, clawed and bit. Bodies piled up at his feet. Then came the sound of a cavalry horn. Not the brass trumpet squeals of the regulars, but the lowing ebb of a mercenary bull horn. It seemed strange to her that someone from within the battle would be sounding retreat; there was nowhere to retreat to. Her heart sank, as she felt the creeping tendrils of fear burrow into her heart, and she decided she wasn't ready to die.

The ground beneath her feet began to tremble as a low thundering drifted over the bloody field from the north. She hazarded a glance from the corner of her eye and hope surged through her. Suddenly, a flood of steel-clad horses swept over a low ridge and into the north flank of the Black Tide. The racing mounts collided with the enemy, knocking soldiers into the air as their riders slashed those still on their feet.

Shasp Ironwrought was at the tip of the spear, his armor a ghoulish blend of red, black and gold. The frightening mask of his bloody helmet struck fear into the Tide infantry as he cut them down like wheat in a red harvest. Lexia could tell his unit was not fresh, and by the looks of them, they had already seen hard fighting, but still, his sudden appearance gave her the strength to fight on.

243

Slowly, the heavy horse drove a wedge between the enemy and the fortified bulwarks and as they neared the place where Molgien and Lexia fought, the enemy withdrew. Shasp stopped in front them, Ayponese blade dripping, and paused not knowing what to think of Lexia standing next to Molgien covered in blood.

She smiled a wicked grin, "Where the hell have you been?"

"There are another five battalions of Black Tide on their way here. We have to retreat or we'll all be slaughtered. Where's General Holkerm?"

Lexia shrugged, "By the look of things, I'd say he's either on a fast horse north or hiding because he sure as hell hasn't given any orders. This is the saddest stand I've ever seen. I saw the regular cavalry go south to cover our flank and I assume you picked up the units that went north."

"Yes, what was left of them," he said as he stood in his stirrups, looking around for the familiar garb of a superior officer and seeing none. "Damn! Go find a trumpeter and sound a route, but first spread the word; I want all the foot soldiers and wounded to make their way to the Keddi foothills. I'll gather the southern units and create a rear guard. We can hold them off in the rocks. Don't just stand there...move!"

Lexia bolted toward the bulwarks and disappeared into the trenches. Shasp leaned out of his saddle and clasped Molgien's hand. "Good to see your still here." He eyed the cannibal's gashed leg and Molgien signed to him. Shasp looked over his shoulder in the direction Lexia had gone.

Word of the retreat spread through the trenches and bulwarks like the desert wind and soon soldiers were fleeing southward toward the Keddi Mountains, three miles away. Many were helped along by their fellows or rode on wounded horses, while the ragtag cavalry withdrew from the littered battlefield a little at a time, skirmishing with fractured Tide infantry and horse soldiers.

Albis rode south along the river with a hundred cavalry and managed to bring back four hundred of the two thousand that had left then rejoined the rear guard.

General Holkerm had greatly underestimated the number of Black Tide forces which had gathered on the Tetas, Shasp thought, or perhaps they were reinforced during the night.

For hours, Shasp's men surged and retreated under the

glowering eye of the sun, cutting off flanking efforts and feints while the black army slowly regrouped. Under the protection of the exhausted cavalry, the Evatan foot troops finally found sanctuary in the jagged Keddi range while horse soldiers followed them in under the cover fire of deadly Evatan archers. The enemy stalled at a narrow pass and was forced to withdraw with arrows in their backs. The pass belonged to the red army now. Shasp set a troop of cavalry at the mouth of the pass with infantry support and lined the heights with every available archer.

The Tetas River cut its way through the Keddi range, leaving deep gorges flanked by sheer sandstone walls. On the west side of the river, the rocks were riddled with natural columns and deep gashes leading to the peaks above, similar to streets and alleys but cut by eons of running water and blasting wind, instead of human hands. It was among these the troops found respite and Shasp was finally able to pull the soaked saddled from Grimm's lathered back. He examined several cuts on the black charger's shoulder and flanks, "Good work today, my friend. I appreciate the way you took care of me." He removed some salve and was applying the stinging mixture to Grimm's wounds when Lexia appeared carrying a bundle.

"I hope you don't mind, but I sent some runners to climb the peaks and watch the enemy's movement."

Shasp dragged the sweat out of his hair with his fingers and sighed, "Enemies? I thought they were your cohorts."

Lexia looked away, a little embarrassed, "Were . . . they *were* my cohorts."

"You could have gone back to them, why didn't you?"

She shrugged, "Just didn't think I wanted to fight for that side anymore. I realized, in that pit, that they took something from me. Now I want them to pay for it...but still..."

Shasp raised an eyebrow, "Still what?"

"I can't help but feel sorry for the men and women fighting for them. They didn't know; couldn't have known the price . . . that they were being deceived, just like me."

"It frustrates the hell out of me, not knowing who is behind this army," Shasp spat.

Lexia dropped her weary body onto a large rock and stretched her long legs. "The Black Tide army doesn't use officers or sergeants, just task masters. I think they know who is behind it."

245

"How's that?"

"They're not like the others; they're Somerikan. We all took our orders from them and they gave us our allowance of petals. Someone has to be giving them orders." She leaned forward and drew off the horsehair pants, bloodied linen shirt, and the boots which were too large.

Shasp was slightly surprised by her bronzed nudity, but then remembered how unabashed she had been in the bunker. Old and new scars crisscrossed her muscular body, a story of past contests. In spite of them, her physical beauty still shone through with great force and his pulse rose slightly in spite of the post-battle fatigue.

"Molgien said you saved him today, why?"

Lexia pulled on a pair of red silk trousers and a chain mail byrnie, "I had to show you where my loyalties are . . . that I'm a warrior and not a spy."

"I see. Molgien is thankful nevertheless."

She drew on some infantry sandals and brass forearm bracers then checked the nicked edge of her scimitar. "I hope you don't mind, I took these from a soldier who didn't need them anymore."

Shasp nodded his consent, "If you're from Bretcombia, what are you doing in the Abi desert. Shouldn't you be carousing around the northern climes?"

She smiled, almost a sneer, "Shouldn't you be in Aypon?"

He laughed, "I'm not Ayponese . . . not exactly."

"I see . . . but your armor and fighting style are. How do you explain that?"

"It's a long story and I'm too tired to tell it," he parried

She leaned back against the sandstone wall, not missing his long look, and playfully bit her lower lip, "I found a nice place to sleep just up that draw; a little depression in the rocks, up high. I think it's going to get cold tonight, and two sleeps warmer than one."

Shasp glanced away, slightly unsettled at her directness. He was about to answer when he heard the sound of scraping sandals drift over the moans of the wounded. Shasp faced a panting boy, sweating in his red attire.

"Sir, the enemy is surrounding the range and cutting off the passes. Looks like they are blockading us."

"Have Sergeant Albis post watchers on any other potential access points. I want to be informed of any movements."

"Yes sir," and he sped off between the rocks.

Lexia lost her playful look, "Do you think they just want to keep us here?"

Shasp snorted, "How the hell would I know? They can't come in and get us, but we don't have any food. Water, yes, but we won't be able to hold out for long. The only one who could last around here is Molgien."

"If I die, you better not let him eat me!"

He laughed again, "I don't let Molgien eat anyone but the enemy, because it doesn't sit well with the men."

She smirked again, "I'm hungry enough to eat someone."

Shasp bent down, dug in his saddle bag, took out some dried beef wrapped in leather and handed it to Lexia, "Enjoy, but make it last."

"Bless you," she said just before biting into it.

He plopped down beside her, "Any idea where the black petals come from?"

She swallowed hard and wiped the grease from her shining lips. "I saw a caravan come into the camp once and watched the task masters unload baskets which were kept guarded. The drivers were Somerikan."

Shasp sat in quiet thought while Lexia continued to chew the stringy meat. She forced herself to leave a portion and wrapped it up. She leaned toward Shasp's scarred yet handsome face and studied his icy gray eyes, her lips hovering inches from his. The smell of the meat on her breath was not unpleasant to him, hungry as he was, but he eyed her questioningly, and decided a liaison was not prudent at the time.

"Aren't you exhausted from the battle?"

"Yes, but fighting always gets my blood up, I can't help it," she grinned.

"You Bretcombians are a strange lot."

"A passionate tribe, yes, and to us life and death are twins and the lines between the thrill of battle and the thrill of lovemaking are not so defined as they are for you soft-skinned southern peoples." She stood, collected her weapon and war harness then swaggered away.

"I'm not from the South," he called after her.

Shasp scratched his head, wondering if he'd made her angry,

247

and decided he couldn't tell. His mind fell back to the current dilemma; how to get three thousand, poorly equipped, mostly wounded, men through a blockade of ferocious, drug affected warriors and across a desert to Laveg, almost a hundred miles to the west.

It certainly wouldn't be one of the easier tasks he'd undertaken, but if they didn't do something soon, they would all die in the Keddi Mountains.

CHAPTER 8

Shasp waited a day for the severely wounded to die and the living to become anxious before setting his plan into action. At first, the regulars were apprehensive about a mercenary leading what was left of the army, but they were quickly reminded about who had saved them.

The Keddi range ran along the Tetas and curved toward the West on its southern end. If he could keep his men among the rocks, they could follow the ravines through the mountains and come out in the Trabic desert pass, two days march from Laveg, the capital of Evata. The army broke into companies of five hundred and began the treacherous march through the lifeless, jagged peaks. Shasp lead what was left of the combined cavalry forces in a rear guard that could move forward quickly in the event of an ambush farther up the line.

At the top of a high pass, Shasp paused and looked down at the endless line of dusty, haggard men who struggled up the trail ahead of him. Albis was coming along the rear to take care of any stragglers or seditionist and drive them on. Shasp looked toward the west at the vast peaks stretching away and led Grimm into the next ravine.

For days they marched as many men weakened and others succumbed to their wounds, leaving behind scattered markers of piled rocks and helmets. On the morning of the eighth day the remnants of the once great Evatan army came to the end of the Keddi range and looked out over the sprawling Trabic desert. Although he could not see the peaks of the Akis Mountains on the other side, Shasp knew they were there, two days away with Laveg at their base.

Water was low and the men were getting worse. There was no way he could allow them to rest, just getting weaker without food or water.

He brought his scope to bear on the horizon as the sun rose behind him, but saw no scouts from the Tide or any other movement below and sighed with relief. The task masters of the black army must still believe his forces were holed up miles away.

Either that or they thought the Trabic would finish the Evatans and save them the trouble. Silently, he wondered if they were right.

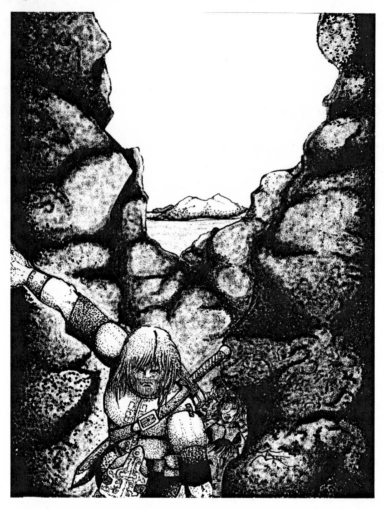

Either way, it was only a matter of time before the Black Tide came to Laveg.

There was no water in the Trabic, no game, and no life. Its sands were as scorching as the Abi and it was just as hostile to the living. The men took shelter from the gnawing sun and rested until nightfall. At least they could avoid one day of marching in the heat. When darkness came, they started out of the mountains and into the wasteland. Minutes merged into hours as they trudged through the blowing sands and shifting dunes. Men ducked their heads and wrapped their faces with the blood-crusted silk of their uniforms. Sand stung the eyes and filled every crack and crevice of body and armor until it grated painfully with each movement. Suffering became a constant, hated companion, there with each miserable step and forced breath. When day came, the cold desert wind vanished and the air turned into a stale, hanging heat. By evening, many men had collapsed from exhaustion while their comrades staggered by, too tired to help them, and expired under the sun. Lexia kept pace with Shasp, who refused to ride his horse or allow others to do so, not wanting the army to become fractured. Her lips were split and sore from the hot wind and her tongue felt like the tail of a sand lizard. She wondered why Shasp refused to drop his armor and leave it on the dunes like the rest, wondered how he kept from baking alive in the leather and metal. Slowly, day dissolved into night and the winds returned to torment them again. On the second day, the army approached Laveg's fifty foot walls, their limestone finish glaring in the morning sun. Two massive statues of female warriors stood on each side of the gates, their heads even with the top of the wall. Hewn from beautiful white marble, they stared down impassively at the army of ants who approached. Shasp formed the men up into disciplined ranks a mile out, explaining that the citizens wouldn't want to see their men return in haphazard streams, and then led the Evatan army into Laveg.

The men drew themselves up as much as possible before the mumbling throngs who came out to see them as they half stumbled, half marched into the city, one battered company after another. An officer rode down the red brick streets and reigned in.

"What happened? What battalion is this?"

Shasp barely croaked a reply, "It's not a battalion, It's what is left of a brigade. Water and food for the men . . . then we can talk."

The officer looked surprised then worried as he sent his second back with the order.

An hour later, Shasp and a few sergeants from the regular ranks briefed the officer who immediately sent a runner to the king's palace. Before Shasp could finish his water skin and choke down a crust of bread, a messenger galloped down to the city well where the men teemed, vying for water. Even though the well was large enough for fifty people to comfortably draw water, it was too small for an army dying of thirst.

"His majesty, the Sultan, commands the officer in charge to the palace at once."

Shasp looked around lazily, stood and stretched.   His vision swam from fatigue but cleared. "I guess that's me. The palace, huh?" He motioned for Lexia, Molgien and Albis to mount up, which they did with only minimal complaining. Shasp didn't blame them.

The messenger appeared vexed, "The sultan only requested you."

"They go where I go," Shasp said flatly.

Past whitewashed buildings of molded clay, the group meandered along the brick streets toward the towering palace, resting high in the city center. As it slowly loomed larger, the buildings became more extravagant with spirals and buttresses, balconies and vaulted windows, all stark and bright. Turbaned lords and veiled ladies gazed down from their heights at the dusty travelers as they ambled past on dirty, snorting mounts. Blinding light reflected from the white palace wall in the morning sun as they approached, lending it a golden sheen. They moved through the gates under close scrutiny before reaching the main building of the royal court. It was a gargantuan structure so large that Shasp contemplated riding around it would take a good ten minutes. Capping the structure was a proud dome of shining, plated gold. The wealth in the roof was a staggering thought as they craned their necks to drink in its brilliance. On through courtyards of tinkling fountains and endless gardens they rode, through mighty pillars and along polished marbled walkways, until they came to its center. It was an island in a sea of crowding architecture. Shasp dismounted and tossed his reigns to a waiting servant. When the others started off their horses, he turned. "Stay mounted, I won't be long...at least, I don't plan to be." He followed the messenger through a tall, arched threshold and into a cavernous room, girded with massive marble pillars. A dozen dark-skinned eunuchs, adorned with blue silk and shining mail, guarded the doorway with needle-tipped spears. Shasp and his guide proceeded along the polished floor of forest green marble, a rare stone, and stopped before a raised dais. An entire platoon of royal guards stood before it, arms folded and tulwars at their sides. On the dais, a thin, swarthy man reclined on a pile of cushions. He studied Shasp with sharp eyes beneath shaggy gray brows. One finger twisted the hair of his pointed beard as the herald bowed low and made introductions.

"My lord, Sultan, Lieutenant Shasp Ironwrought of the Foreign Calvary Company of the Second Brigade, as you requested," and he withdrew. Shasp made a halfhearted bow, and the eye of the Sultan did not miss the hinted lack of respect. Shasp was too exhausted to care. He had heard wild tales of Sultan Alafar's wealth and now, realized they were true. In a long silence they exchanged impassive expressions and Shasp sensed the cunning in Sultan Alafar's eyes, a cunning honed from a life of palace politics and intrigue.   Shasp had no stomach for such diversions.

Finally, the monarch spoke in a liquid tone, "So . . . you have come from the Tetas. Where is General Holkerm?"

Shasp shrugged, "I don't know; I believe he fled when the battle went sour but..." he paused.

"You may speak your mind, Lieutenant."

Shasp paused, choosing his words carefully, "I think we have been betrayed. Either that or someone promoted the most incompetent officer he could find to general."

The Sultan leaned forward on his cushions, a tone of annoyance played in his voice, "I *appointed* General Holkerm, and he was never incompetent. The man is a brilliant tactician and has proven himself time and again.   Do you think me a fool, that I would make just anyone the leader of my armies?"

Shasp noticed the eunuchs shifting slightly at the Sultan's irritated tone, "No, I don't think you are a fool, and I'm not saying that to placate your anger. If Holkerm is as competent as you say, then he has clearly betrayed you."

Alafar leaned back into his cushions, "Why do you think so?" he asked.

"Because, only an idiot would split his cavalry up and leave the infantry unprotected. I don't know what happened to the divisions of cavalry he sent out, but obviously both ran into ambushes. Then, just as the battle was beginning, he fled, leaving the men leaderless. The Black Tide specifically targeted all the Evatan officers and wiped them out to a man, but I wasn't at the battle when it started. Holkerm sent us north to stop a battalion of Tide infantry coming south on our side of the river. We were nearly overwhelmed, so we fell back to the camp in time to break their lines and created a rear guard for the retreat.   There were too many enemy soldiers crossing the river.   We didn't stand a chance. How could they have massed so many men and the general not known? Why didn't he send for reinforcements?"

Alafar sat like a statue, absorbing these words, then roused himself from his thoughts. "You are a mercenary. Why didn't you simply flee and save yourself?"

"My men needed me. Only cowards leave their fellows to die on the field."

"You fight for gold. What do you care about the dying?"

Shasp sighed, "I came south for personal reasons. Fighting is what I do. When in battle, I rely on my men and they have to know I will risk my life for them before they will risk their lives for me."

Sultan Alafar nodded, "How many men survived of the ten thousand sent to the Tetas?"

"About three thousand and the Black Tide are on their way here."

Alafar sat forward suddenly, eyes widening at the stated number. Slowly, he regained his composure and fell back into the cushions. "Lieutenant, my palace is at your disposal," he said absently as he stared off in thought. "I will speak with you again in the morning."

"I appreciate your hospitality but I have comrades waiting outside."

"They are welcome here. You may go."

Shasp bowed, this time with slightly more sincerity, and left the hall with a court servant on his heels.

The servant was a slight man in green robes. When Lexia saw him, she speculated that he'd probably never seen a real day's work in his life. Yet he was capable enough when it came to allocating rooms and body servants to care for their needs. Such was the hospitality of Alafar's house.   Their private chambers were spacious and extravagantly furnished with silks and statuary, water basins and colorful wall hangings, contrasting with the pale marble, and they went their own way for the evening. Molgien's servant was terrified of him. If the cannibal wished to eat him, was he obliged to concede? Molgien sensed the man's fear and showed him a toothy grin of predatory teeth.

Shasp gorged himself on food and drink before his caretaker suggested he may want to bathe. When the man tried to assist him with the buckles of his armor, Shasp shoved him off roughly, undressed and took a towel.

"Have my armor and weapons cleaned, polished, and

255

sharpened. If anything is missing, I'll feed you to my friend."

The servant gulped and carefully gathered Shasp's equipment.

Soon, Shasp was soaking in hot scented water. At first his cuts stung from the salts added to the water, but eventually the pain eased to a dull throb. The bath house wasn't far from his room, and he imagined there were several such steam-choked places in the endless spans of the palace. Lying back, he gazed absently at the

vaulted ceiling, his body melting against the marble of the sunken tub. The distant sounds of bustling court life were his only connection to reality after he closed his eyes and slipped into a state of semiconsciousness. After soaking for awhile, he thought he felt the water lap slightly against his
chest, or did it? Then the current in the tub stirred ever so slightly, moving where before it was still. Suddenly, his instincts jerked him from his sedation and he lunged to his feet, the water surging away from his body with a sucking sound. Standing naked in thigh-deep water, he stared blankly at the cause of the disturbance.
Lexia reclined on the other side of the steaming bath, smiling as she appraised his naked figure. She bit her lower lip and her eyes narrowed with mischievous contemplation. Shasp, feeling foolish, was too tired to be annoyed by her prankish behavior and slid back into the water.

"Aren't there any other baths for you to haunt?"

She rubbed her calloused fingers over a crusted wound on her shoulder, "Probably, but I like the view in this one."

He rolled his eyes, "Suit yourself," but he was having trouble pulling his eyes away from her bobbing breasts. Lexia noticed him staring and Shasp averted his eyes.

Lexia became irritated, "Don't you find me attractive, or do you think I am, somehow, inferior?"

He looked into her good eye, "Neither, in fact, you impress me, it's just..." but he could not finish.

They reclined quietly in long silence before she spoke again. "So, who is this woman who enslaves your affection?"

"There is no woman . . . not anymore."

"She left you?"

"You might say that," he said, "She died about a year ago."

Lexia nodded her understanding, "Aahh . . . and that's why you came south, to fight in Evata's army?"

He nodded slowly.

"Did she give you that," she asked as she pointed to the raw stone hanging from his neck.

"No, it came from an old hermit in the mountains of the Arrigin."

"It looks primitive, like something you would find among my tribe in the north. Those sorts of talismans always have some meaning or other import, so...what is the purpose of that one?"

Shasp fingered the reddish stone and felt the carved runes beneath his fingertips, "It is not a passive one; I will tell you that. I was traveling through the forest when I met the hermit, his name was Ormund, and he made known to me that the place I was headed to was evil. It was a keep, high up in the peaks. Things went bad, real bad, and this talisman...it saved my life." (A Thorn for Rose)

Lexia gave a look that was not committed to belief, yet not completely cynical, "Interesting. It has the look of something very old. Where did the hermit get it?"

Shasp sighed, "He didn't say. I spent the night in his cottage, drank with him, talked of all sorts of things, ate breakfast and left...but I returned much later, when winter broke, to thank him." Shasp paused like he was finished, but also like there was more to say.

"And did you tell him it saved your life?"

Shasp looked away from her, still thumbing the talisman, "When I came back, I found that the cottage was in ruins. Not like someone came through and burned him out, but like the place had been uninhabited for decades. The roof fallen in, vines creeping over

257

everything, leaves a foot deep on the floor. All was in heavy decay, but…near the window a heavy table of stone and wood still stood…and on it, two wooden vials of spice I gave him before I left."

"So you are saying he was a ghost?"

Shasp shook his head, "I don't know. I have thought about it at great length and I think he was something else; A messenger perhaps. I think I was destined to meet him there; to receive this talisman. He said it held a single drop of blood from the One God."

Lexia let the subject soak with them for a while before prodding Shasp further, "And this woman you morn for; did you find her in these same mountains too?"

"I met her quite a bit later," and he stared off again like he was seeing a vision, "She was something to behold."

Lexia felt the sting of jealousy. She knew she was not beautiful the way most civilized women were. She was not soft and pale skinned, nor did she smell of jasmine or roses. She was scarred and calloused, and smelled of campfires and blood, the way all the women of her clan did. To a Bretcombian man, that was beauty. But she was not among her clan, she was among the civilized. Her voice broke slightly as she ventured forward.

"In our land, when a man loses a wife, he does not wait so long to take another. We believe it is easier for him to forget when he has the help and warmth of a woman."

"It's a good philosophy, but I'm not . . . ." His mouth clamped tight as he looked away again, and Lexia thought it wise not to press him. They soaked for a long while, saying nothing before Shasp climbed out of the tub and wrapped his towel around his waist.

"Where are you going?"

He sighed deeply, "To get drunk," and walked away, wet feet slapping against the marble floor.

By early evening, Shasp was well into his cups and brooding over his constant misfortunes. He decided he should consider himself lucky to be alive, and drained another crystal goblet of Alafar's fine wine, satisfied with his intoxication, suppressed memories and dulled discontent.

A knock interrupted his brooding, and he crossed the room, pulling open the heavy door to find Lexia. She wore a white silk robe that halted at the top of her thighs, revealing long brown legs. Her hair was pinned on top of her head, and riddled with fragrant, colorful flowers. Sweet-smelling oil shined on her bronze skin and she flashed a white smile.

Shasp gawked silently for a moment, too surprised to speak, and then quickly found his old military bearing.

"What do you want, Lexia?"

She brushed past him, "I'm not in the mood to drink alone," she said.

Shasp raised an eyebrow, "Maybe I am."

Undaunted, she glided to the table and poured a goblet of wine for herself, gulping it down as fast as any barroom better Shasp had ever seen. Soft lilting music suddenly floated in from the balcony next door.

"Your doing?" he asked, jerking his thumb toward the window.

She nodded, sat down at the dark mahogany table and poured another glass. "You and I have unfinished business. Where I come from, women and men are required to be the same. It's necessary for survival in a land full of wild beast and even wilder tribes, where life is uncertain.   We all learn the way of arms and combat. We all tend to our homes and our children. When there is war, we all ride and we all fight."

"I've heard stories of Bretcombians even before I met you and I've even known a few. I don't doubt your fierceness or your loyalty, Lexia."

"Aahhh, but you shunned my womanhood," she said stabbing her finger in his chest, "and I have to prove that as much as I have to prove my skill at arms."

"I don't understand."

"You will. Among my race, men and women are the same except in one way. Women are also expected to learn how to awaken passion, but we don't do it with perfumes and fine clothing or feigned weakness. Those things are nonexistent in our world. No, we have the extra burden of learning another traditional art. I want to show it to you, and then I will not bother you again."

Shasp nodded and sat next to her, "Very well, Lexia, let's see this art of yours."

Lexia smiled and rose in the fading light of a setting sun. It poured through the open window and splashed over her as she walked out onto the balcony and waved at the musicians hidden from Shasp's view. Lightly tapping cymbals began to beat out a methodical rhythm trailed by the low drone of a wavering pipe. The music caressed his weary wine-soaked brain. Soon, a harp joined in, then a lute and a drum. Lexia swept into the center of a large ornate rug and stood silently with her eyes closed. Slowly, she began to sway with the ebb and flow of the strains floating on the warm air, and the music rose in volume as the warrior woman began to dance. She danced with elegance and beauty, as if drifting on the notes like a leaf upon the wind. Her arms and legs moved with the serpentine grace of a constrictor winding its way through warm desert rocks. Shasp watched, impressed by her remarkable skill, as the music slowly changed and Lexia's dance with it. He poured another goblet of wine. Gradually, the beat intensified and quickened, the drums taking the lead with the pipes coming forward while the harp receded causing the sound to grow wilder, bolder. Lexia spun now and gyrated her hips, her robe slipping from bare shoulders and parting in front, revealing a hint of her firm breast.

Shasp felt his face flush and pulse quicken as he tried to follow her mesmerizing limbs. Gleaming thighs and calves moved with reckless abandon and in the next instant, the robe slipped to the floor, but her dance continued, wild and feral. She leapt and twisted, revealing her bare back then bare front in a flashing twirl, muscles flexing and releasing with each new movement. She began to spin on one foot with the other tucked behind her knee, while her buttocks, round and perfect flashed by with each rotation. Shasp fully understood the meaning and purpose of Lexia's art as blood hammered in his temples and his muscles tightened until he thought they would snap. Never had he felt himself spiraling out of control as he did at that moment. The music pounded against his ears as the dance sped to a climax and Lexia thrashed her hair in time with her naked gyrating pelvis. It was all too much for Shasp and before the last note slammed home, he was on his feet. He tossed back his head, downing the last of his wine, and smashed the crystal goblet into a corner. Lexia dropped into a crouch and backed away like a cornered animal, panting with a playful grin mocking him, eyes wild and wanting. She was pleased with herself and the effect of her dance. Shasp eyed her hungrily, her gleaming limbs, slick with sweat, his head swimming from too much wine. He surged toward her. Before she could move, he wrapped her in his unrelenting arms, lips hovering so close they shared each other's wine-soaked breath. He crushed his lips against hers with savage fervor, and she wrapped her arms around his neck, her skin like a flame against his chest. Lexia's heart pounded and her loins ached with need as she gave back his lust in equal doses of passion. Together, they tumbled onto the rich furs and silks of the large bed, and made love with the wild abandon of their natures. Outside, the musicians blushed and sweated from the sounds which emanated from the chamber next door but continued to play the slow sweet music Lexia requested. When they finally staggered away, they were wondering if any palace servant girls were still wandering about. Not one could remember the last time the palace walls had heard such passion.

CHAPTER 9

In the dark morning hours before dawn, Shasp woke suddenly. The scuff of leather against stone brought him out of his sleep, though the sound was only slight, and he turned his head toward the noise just in time to see a knife blade flashing down toward his chest.

Before the knife could strike home at his beating heart, Shasp flung up an arm and rolled into his assailant. The keen edge slashed open his forearm, but before the assassin could redirect the blade; Shasp crushed his groin and throat in his iron grip.

Lexia flew from the bed and seized the hilt of her scimitar as two more shadowy figures emerged from the dark corners of the room, their knives glinting. One leapt toward Shasp while the other rushed at Lexia, trying to get inside her sword's reach. She slashed at him. At first the assassin thought he had avoided the swipe, until he went to thrust with his knife only to discover it lay on the floor still clutched in his twitching hand. As he stared dumbly at his severed limb, Lexia ran him through.

Shasp shoved the first attacker off, dropping the corpse in front of the other assassin, fouling his legs. In the time it took his enemy to avoid the obstacle, Shasp kicked him, artfully, in the knee, stomach and head. The assassin crumpled.

For a long moment they scanned the shadows of the room before Lexia trimmed a lamp. The scattered bodies were dressed in jet black silks from toe to crown, and their faces were swathed. Lexia knelt and unwound the black cloth from a swarthy face, as his dead eyes stared blankly.

"They are southerners," she said.

Shasp noted uniformity in their dress and weapons, "Professionals." He was glad for the years of training and combat which had made him a light sleeper. "There seems to be a conspiracy to keep me awake," he joked darkly. "I think someone doesn't want me talking to the Sultan."

Lexia, seeing blood streaming from his forearm, snatched a linen towel from a stand and bandaged it, then called for a servant. Footsteps padded hurriedly down the hall, but when the girl arrived she took in the scene and fainted. Lexia made a throaty sound of disgust, "Damn soft bellied city dwellers." She turned her attention back to the wound, "Do you think the blade was poisoned?"

"I doubt it; either that or the bleeding has washed it out."

A groan from the corner caught their attention as the surviving assassin began regain consciousness. Shasp stepped over a corpse, caught the man by his shirt and jerked him off the floor. "Who sent you?" The man's eyes widened and he began to chew on something. Before Shasp could knock him out, the assassin went into convulsions. Spittle flecked the assassin's lips as Shasp struggled to hold him down.

"Guards!" Lexia yelled. In the few seconds it took for the palace guards to arrive, the prisoner stopped shaking and exhaled a dying breath. Shasp dug in the dead man's mouth and took out a piece of dark red plant material.

A guard's eyes widened, "The Kahlanata," he breathed.

Shasp stood over the quivering form, "I know that cult. Guard, I'll need another room."

Morning came too early and fatigue weighed heavily on Shasp. It seemed, after the long march, he could have slept for days, but there was too much afoot. Servants brought fine foods for Lexia and him to breakfast on, and when the meal was done, they brought in his armor. He inspected the cleaning and noted several straps were replaced and chinks repaired. The nicks had been worked out of his sword and it was razor sharp again. He complemented the anxious servant for thoroughness. By the time he dressed, the Sultan had sent a eunuch. Shasp followed him through the extravagant halls, but not to the king's court where he had been the day before. Instead, they wound up a long flight of stone stairs to the top of a tower. The chubby eunuch panted in front of a heavy oak door with two guards on either side, and rapped gently on the wood. The door swung inward on oiled hinges, revealing a wiry, middle-aged man standing in the threshold, dressed in black silk trousers, tunic and turban. He regarded Shasp briefly with narrow brown eyes while stroking the point of his silver-streaked beard. His thin lips were frowning. "You must be the lieutenant," he said with a deep liquid voice, "do come in."

Shasp eyed the man's deep lined face then stepped past him to see the Sultan seated at the end of a mahogany table. To his right sat two younger men. One was in his late twenties with oiled, curly black hair and trimmed beard. His clothes were blue lightweight linen with a fancy gold sash. The other was a tawny-haired youth with a shaven face in a gold embroidered tunic. On his left, a wizened old scholar with a pile of books and scrolls shuffled papers. Other than the table, there were no furnishings or decor and a solitary window was the only source of light. The room was clearly reserved for secret conversations, as it would be impossible to eavesdrop on the lofty place.

Shasp bowed, "Your majesty."

Alafar smiled pleasantly, "Please, sit down, Lieutenant.   I heard of the unfortunate event this morning.   It seems the Kahlanata underestimated their prey."

"So it seems," replied Shasp, "thankfully. But why me?"

Alafar folded his hands on the table and leaned forward slightly, "I think we are about to find out. Tell me what you know of the Black Tide?"

Shasp sat down and leaned back in the chair, "I know they don't have a normal chain of command. Their army depends upon black flower petals, a powerful drug that enslaves the soul and will. Most of the prisoners we captured died from the withdrawal."

"Except the woman," interjected the lean man in black. "She lived."

Shasp paused, quickly considering what else the man might know. "Yes . . . except the woman. She told us the task masters control the army and someone gives them orders but no one knows who."

The Sultan turned to the old man on his left, "Harrau, if you please."

The old man rifled through some papers and pulled out a yellow parchment with some illustrations and writing, "This is an old script from Somerika. It tells of a flower, which grows near the great river, called the Adder Blossom." He handed the paper to Shasp. "The blossom is very rare and fragile. The natives who live there consider it poisonous."

Shasp rubbed his chin thoughtfully as he studied the page, "And you think this is the black flower?"

The Sultan shrugged, "It is the most likely candidate."

Shasp nodded, "The woman we captured, Lexia, said the

petals came to them on caravans driven by Somerikans, but if the flower is fragile and rare, then someone would have to be cultivating it to have so much."

The old adviser drew out another dusty sheaf and handed it to him. "It's not the first time the black blossom has been farmed, nor the first time a black army has descended upon the civilized world. As you can see, it happened about four hundred years ago."

The black-dressed man interjected, "My spies inform me there are caravans coming north through Teksika and Sona. More than usual and they carry the petals to the Black Tide."

Sultan Alafar read the questioning look on Shasp's face, "Bakarath, my chief spy."

Shasp put the papers on the table before him, "That is all I know, and what I know, General Holkerm knows too. Maybe he sent the Kahlanata assassins after me."

Bakarath placed his manicured hands on the table, "The situation is grave. The Black Tide grows daily. Each new town captured or city sieged adds to their numbers. Our military is severely reduced, thanks to Holkerm's betrayal, and now we will be surrounded by the Tide in a matter of days. Word from Salsida says they cannot hold out for more than a few months and, Kalyfar will not come to our aid."

"It seems to me, you already had the information I gave," said Shasp, "so what do you want from me?"

Bakarath turned away when the Sultan smiled wanly. "I'm afraid my court is thick with spies and intrigues, as you may have guessed."

"Which ones aren't," snorted Shasp.

"Yes, of course, but you, a man who should have no loyalty, returns the remnants of an army instead of saving himself. For you, it is not *all* about gold. For that reason, I wish to employ you further, to seek out the source of the Adder Blossom and destroy it. If you succeed, you will be compensated quite generously, I assure you."

Bakarath turned and leaned over the table, "My liege, do you really think it wise to entrust so important a mission to a mercenary, especially one who keeps with the enemy?"

Shasp's temper flared and he pushed away from the table, coming nose to nose with Bakarath, but before he could challenge the chief intelligence officer, the Sultan held up his hand, "I have spoken Bakarath! It will be as I have said, but if it chaffs you so, then accompany him."

Bakarath did not avert his hard stare, only inches from Ironwrought's own, "I would see it as my duty, my lord."

"Good, it is settled. Bakarath, you will take the lieutenant to the armory and see that he and his men are provisioned."

Bakarath gave the Sultan an incredulous look, "And his men?"

"Yes, what is left of the foreign company."

Now the tawny haired youth with the gold embroidered tunic broke in, "Father . . . I must agree with Bakarath. This is far too important to entrust to mercenaries. We should send our regular corp."

The Sultan ignored his son and addressed Shasp, "You must forgive my son, Prince Terafar, for being so direct. I'm afraid he has much to learn."

"Your heir?"

Alafar shook his head, "No," then motioned to the older youth, "Prince Alafar is next in line and will carry my name. Now, would you like to discuss payment before you leave or on your return?"

Shasp did not miss the hate-filled look which Terafar gave to his brother, "At the return. I'll trust in your wisdom, it seems to have held this long." Shasp bowed curtly and ducked out the door with an exasperated Bakarath following behind. They descended the stairs and strode through the hallways saying nothing.

When the two men emerged into the courtyard, Bakarath stepped in front of him. "It does not matter that the Sultan trusts you, I do not, and if you try to slither away when this mission becomes dangerous, I'll kill you."

Shasp considered cracking Bakarath's skull but thought better of it, "If I think for one minute you are scheming or endangering my men, it will be you who dies

"Very well," replied Bakarath, "but the woman is not coming."

"She is if I say so, and I say so."

"You're a fool!"

Shasp shouldered past him and continued to the other side of the courtyard where Lexia, Albis and Molgien waited. "Albis, rally the men but only those who can ride or heal in the saddle, then meet us at the armory." Albis nodded and hurried through an archway.

Lexia raised an eyebrow above her sightless eye, "What's going on?"

"We have a hard ride ahead of us."

Soft velvet boots scuffed lightly against the stone of time-worn steps as they spiraled downward into blackness. The youth held up an oil lamp to ward off the encroaching shadows with its weak light. Walls of sandstone loomed as he plunged into the bowels of the palace, struggling to time his steps against the stairs until he reached the bottom and emerged into a low-ceilinged room. He touched the lamp's flame to a torch mounted in a crescent then lit a large brazier with the torch. Embers burned slowly, emitting a pungent fume. Sweat dripped from his forehead as he leaned into the coals, brown eyes wide and searching. As he watched, the air above the glowing embers became strange and liquid, then solidified into his reflection, but the reflection rippled again, turning into a robed man seated on a black throne.

He spoke uncertainly, "Can . . . can you hear me?"

The black vault of the hood replied, "Of course. How can I be of service?"

"I must warn you, a hundred soldiers have been sent to find the source of the blossom. You must be ready for them."

The robed figure touched his fingertips together in thought, "Who are these men?"

"Foreign cavalry; capable, but not trustworthy. They will be crossing the Trabic on the way to Fenic for resupply, then south."

"I see. Not to worry, I will take care of them. I have an ally in Fenic. In the meanwhile, you will need to send more gold on the next caravan. My preparations here are nearly complete and soon your investment will reach its fruition."

The youth rubbed his shaven face, "Smuggling gold out of the city is becoming risky. This must be the last time and I hope I have not trusted you in vain. Has the general arrived yet?"

"Soon, and I must say, he should be pleased. I will send your regards."

The youth nodded, "Good, your gold will be on the way tomorrow."

The hooded head dipped slightly and the burning embers ate away the vision, leaving the young man to ponder in the flickering light.

CHAPTER 10

For twenty days, the company of cavalry trekked across the southern Trabic, avoiding Black Tide scouts. Alafar provisioned them well with camels, supplies, weapons, and maps before they began the arduous journey south. Of the three hundred men under Shasp's command, only ninety-seven were fit enough or willing to ride with their lieutenant. Lexia nearly worked one blacksmith to death, forging and hammering out a cuirass that fit her curves, woman warriors being non-existent in the south. She traded her silks for good, lacquered leather breeches, girdle and boots. Under her new breastplate, a quality chain mail hauberk clung, and a horned steel cap, won in a dice game, protected her head. Just before leaving, she cut the dyed strands of her hair away, leaving only nape length brown locks.

Shasp was amused to see how Lexia seemed to grow stronger in the saddle while others grew weary; the raw wild was her element.

The horizon shimmered in the distance as they plodded through the stifling heat and over tawny dunes, hoping to reach Fenic within the next day or two. By early afternoon, scouts returned, anxiously bearing news of giant red rocks a few hours ride south where the troop could rest in the shade and find protection from the night winds.

Bakarath, who now wore white linen robes and a turban, stretched on his desert mare, holding his lower back, "I could use a rest." Shasp smiled inwardly at the man's discomfort.

Before late afternoon, the long column started down off a plateau toward the distant rocks. Like jagged teeth, they ran in rows, thrusting through the sand. Between them, welcome shade waited, thwarting the sun's rays. Haggard men filed into the rift, their skin cooling, and sighed with relief. Most had covered their armor and heads with white linen which was quickly removed in the wan shadows to allow the pleasant air to flow over their sweat-slick skin. Shasp ordered them to dismount and they flung themselves down on the sand which pillowed against rock that was the color of dried blood.

Molgien, seemingly unaffected by the heat, left his linen in place and wandered around, examining the wind-pocked walls. A primitive instinct pricked at the giant Somerikan's mind, making him uneasy.

Lexia sensed his agitation and sauntered up beside him, "What has you so jittery, man-eater?"

Molgien looked at her dumbly then returned his gaze to the rocks. She returned to find Shasp gulping tepid water from a skin. "Your friend doesn't seem as relaxed as the rest of the men." She pointed her chin toward the savage, "Why do you think he's so bothered?"

Shasp shrugged, "How would I know?" He stoppered the skin and walked with Lexia to Molgien's side. Shasp tapped his shoulder and they exchanged signs. Lexia peered up at the ribbon of blue that stretched overhead, hemmed in by sharp edges.

Suddenly, a trickle of tiny pebbles caught her attention. She turned to see a few grains of rock pepper the sand, and then heard the noise again to her left.

Several soldiers began peering up into the rocks, hands hovering near sword pommels. Then the raining pebbles began falling in dozens of places, followed by the faint sounds of scratching. Men who were leaning against the rock moved away from it, brushing pebbles and grit from their hair and shoulders. All eyes became fixed on the rock walls.

Suddenly, there came the dull thud of objects dropping on the sand nearby. As one, the troop of cavalrymen recoiled in horror when they saw the source of the mysterious noises.

Several white, semi-translucent scorpions, as large as dogs, started toward them. Deadly stingers as long as a knife dripped steaming venom as chitinous pincers reached out to seize their prey. Shasp, Molgien and Lexia bolted for the horses as hundreds more dropped from their perches in the rocks or popped up from under the sand, shaking it off.

Men screamed in alarm and leapt to their saddles, spinning their mounts around, but so many were trying to flee at once, that the mouth between the teeth became plugged. Shasp yelled, "Get the hell out of here!"

Horses and riders bumped and thrust against comrades as the clattering wave of scorpions bore down, thirsty for the moist nutrient hidden in man and beast. Shasp, Molgien and Lexia were mounted now but were behind the struggling contingent. He turned and his

270

blood ran cold at the sight of the white carpet of dripping, clattering death. Instantly, he knew there was no way to fight this menace. In a few seconds, they would all go down under a wave of poisonous daggers and die painfully as they were eaten alive.

CHAPTER 11

There was no time to waste; if they were going to live, it would take a great risk. Shasp wheeled Grimm around and cried out, "Ride through them! Now!" He dug his spurs into Grimm's flanks and the massive charger exploded. If the tiny brains of the invertebrates could have sensed surprise, they would have, but only just before the crushing impact of steel shod hooves trampled the thought into oblivion. The teeming arachnids randomly flicked out their stingers, timing skewed by the horse's impetus, and their bodies shattered in an explosion of yellow gore. Lexia and Molgien watched in disbelief, but quickly followed, there being no other sane options. Like a knife through flesh, they cut their way through the hungry, snapping, creatures. Bony stingers tinged off barding and thigh plates. Occasionally, the tip of a needle sharp injector pierced flesh or found its way through chain mail, but the momentum of the horses simply snapped off the brittle tips before any significant amount of venom could be injected. Scorpions locked onto mounts with pincers, but were instantly cut away, leaving only the dangling appendage and slinging sticky ribbons of foul-smelling blood. If the horse stumbled or took a direct hit of poison, beast and rider would face certain death. After an eternity of storming through a white hell, the trio broke free of the pressing rock walls and burst onto the open sands. They were pasted with reeking yellow gore and galloping at full speed, until Shasp was certain they had left the nightmarish horde behind. He reined Grimm in, swung off the saddle, then began pulling the broken stingers from Grimm's legs as well as his own. Already, both were showing signs of swelling lumps where the stingers penetrated. Lexia and Molgien followed his example and plucked out the bony injectors.

Lexia dropped her leather breaches to her knees and probed a red welt on her thigh. "I don't think we have to worry too much. Usually, the bigger an animal is, the less deadly the poison."

Shasp winced as he pulled out a deep one, "Why is that?"

"Larger animals have more; smaller ones don't, so the venom has to be stronger."

Her logic made sense to him, but already he felt like he wanted to vomit and knew it was the residue of venom moving through his body. "I hope you're right. Mount up. We need to circle back around these rocks and see how many men we lost, but give it a wide birth."

A few minutes later, they encountered the troop coming around the rocks toward them. Albis rode out with Bakarath to meet them.

Albis, shaking his head in disbelief, reigned in, "I can't believe you're alive!"

"Me either," said Shasp. "How many did we lose?"

Bakarath answered for Albis, "Three camels, eight horses, and ten men."

It chaffed Shasp to hear the count in that order, "I guess it would be wise to avoid any other rock outcroppings. It seems the scorpions prefer them."

Bakarath shifted in his saddle, "I do not think it will matter, Lieutenant. White scorpions are generally solitary creatures and very rare."

"Obviously not. There were enough in those rocks to populate half the Trabic."

"Lieutenant, I do not think you are seeing my point. The Aricknawar, that is what we call them, do not congregate except in mating season. Even then, a male will seek out a female and after mating, she will kill him. They do not tolerate each another."

Shasp's eyes narrowed, "What the hell are you saying?"

Bakarath gazed out over the horizon, "I sense evil at work here. Some malevolent force pervades the very air."

"Never figured you for a seer, Bakarath."

Bakarath raised his nose, "In my responsibilities, it is critical to be many things," and he started off the crest of the dune toward the beckoning desert.

Shasp felt the cramp of poison in his stomach, swallowed some water, then plodded after him with the columns falling in behind. That night they camped in the open desert, and crossed the Tetas River the next day where it entered the province of Sona, a satrap of Evata, then they rode southeast toward Fenic. The landscape changed slightly as rock and low hills resisted the relentless sands. Some signs of moisture even showed in the form of hardy scrub weeds and flitting lizards. By evening, the haggard columns approached the walls of Fenic, and torches flickered along the battlements as guardsmen relayed the message of their approach.

Shasp dropped back until he rode alongside Bakarath, "Has the Sultan made arrangements for our resupply?"

Bakarath wiped sand out of his eyes, "He does not need to make arrangements. The governor, Hamed Akkadi, is his nephew and Fenic is under Laveg's rule."

"Keep your eyes open anyway, Bakarath."

An uneasy quiet choked the city as the train of riders shuffled through the gates. Perhaps it was just the presence of the foreign troops, or maybe it was just that time of evening when the workers rest from their chores, but the silence and lack of activity caused a nervousness to rise in Shasp. Many of the city's lamps were not yet lit, leaving the streets in a wash of heavy shadows. An occasional figure would start to emerge from a doorway, then dart back inside.

Shasp held up his hand, halting the group at the city well, "Albis, have the men fill their skins quickly. I don't like the feel of this place." He turned to Bakarath, "Not a very warm welcome for the friends of a beloved uncle."

Bakarath muttered his agreement, "I have been here before and never has it been so quiet."

Scarcely had Bakarath spoken when a clanking squad of guardsmen came jogging up the dirt street toward them. There were only ten men armored in leather with steel caps swathed in blue silk and holding spears. Hamed Akkadi was wise not to send so large a force as to create tension. The leader approached Bakarath, "Lord Akkadi welcomes Bakarath to Fenic and requests your presence at the Palace."

Bakarath showed a tired smile, "Tell Hamed, I would be honored. Lieutenant, will you accompany me?"

Shasp shot a quick glance to Lexia who shrugged then nodded, "Of course, but the men need to supply soon."

The guardsman bowed, "We will see to your needs."

As they rode behind the running group of guards, Shasp had to remind himself they were in a friendly city and there was no reason to be uneasy. He wondered if the many days of combat and stress had made him overly cautious. Then again, his caution had saved his life more than once. The packed dirt street sloped gently upward to a large building of whitewashed brick, capped with spires, and buttresses broke the monotony of the architecture, giving it an added dimension. It was an impressive structure, but compared to Alafar's palace, it was a hovel.

They dismounted and handed the reigns to the guardsmen before climbing a wide set of marble stairs to a heavy arched doorway of red mahogany. As they were led inside by a eunuch with the guardsmen marching along on either side, the corridor opened into a vaulted hall with a pillared ceiling. When they emerged into the hall, Hamed Akkadi left his throne on the dais and waddled toward them with a gash of a smile on his obscenely round face. A bright silk robe of crimson hugged his short, fat body, and in one pudgy hand he gripped a slopping goblet of wine while the other pushed greasy black locks out of his eyes. A razor-thin beard framed his repugnant face. Hamed's physical appearance was a testament to years of debauchery, and Shasp almost winced at the sight him.

"Welcome Bakarath," Hamed said in a lisping falsetto while clasping his hand. "Welcome to my humble palace. I received word, by pigeon, quite some time ago about your arrival. You must rest and join me for dinner. How is my uncle?"

Bakarath bowed his head gracefully, "The Sultan is well, but I'm afraid we cannot linger. Our mission is far too important."

"Of course, of course," replied Hamed, his tone dropping off, "this must be the officer who saved the battalion at the Tetas from Holkerm's betrayal."

Shasp cleared his throat, "I didn't save much."

"That is not what I heard," countered Hamed. "I could use a man like you."

"Sorry, I have current obligations, as you can see." Shasp was too tired for the polite small talk that infested all royal conversation and was about to become discourteous when Bakarath stiffened slightly.

"Lord Akkadi, please forgive my lack of courtesy, but the lieutenant and I have been on horseback for many days. The grime of the desert is thick upon us and I am embarrassed to be in your presence, knowing our odor must be offensive. If we could just freshen ourselves, I am sure conversation would be much more tolerable for you."   Shasp was about to protest but Bakarath laid a hand on his shoulder.

"Of course, how thoughtless of me." Hamed beckoned to the eunuch, "Take our guests to their quarters.   If there is anything you need, Bakarath, please let my servant know."

Bakarath bowed, Shasp did not, and they turned toward the corridor following the slope-shouldered eunuch.   When they reached the doors of the guest quarters, Shasp faced Bakarath, "We don't have time for . . . !"

Bakarath gave him a hard look and held up a finger for silence, then addressed the servant. "That will be all. We can find our way from here." The man bowed and left. When Bakarath was certain he had gone, he opened the door and motioned Shasp inside, then closed it. Shasp watched him, perplexed, as the sultan's chief intelligence officer moved curtains, checked the balcony and closed the shuttered doors which overlooked the courtyard. He hurried across the room until he was inches from Shasp's face and whispered, "We have to get out of here immediately."

Shasp found Bakarath's sudden concern unnerving, "What is it?"

"Did you not notice? Hamed's pupils were dilated and he

276

was sweating. It was not warm in the hall."

"So? The man is a pig; pigs sweat; especially royal ones."

"Perhaps, but I also saw the thinnest line of black stain on his lips."

Shasp stiffened, "Adder Blossom?"

"I think so," said Bakarath, "and that means . . ."

"The Black Tide has already been here," Shasp finished. "Why didn't we receive word of a siege or a battle?"

The swarthy Evatan cracked the door and whispered over his shoulder, "Because there has not been one. Hamed has betrayed the Sultan and taken the petal willingly."

Shasp cracked the balcony window and peered out. Men waited in the shadows at the edge of the courtyard, hushed whispers giving away their location. "There are men hiding outside, I can hear them. I say we cut our way through the courtyard and link up with the unit before we get surrounded in here."

Bakarath closed the door gently, "I have a more subtle plan."

When Hamed Akkadi saw Shasp and Bakarath strolling down into the court chambers, still dusty, he was surprised, but Bakarath's disarming smile made him relax.

"Is everything all right gentlemen? You have not washed."

Bakarath came within arm's reach of Hamed and stopped, "Your excellency, all is well, it's just that I thought of something of grave importance and I did not wish to delay in informing you."

"Yes?"

Bakarath stepped a little closer, looking around suspiciously as if he needed to whisper the urgent message to Hamed. Akkadi, sensing this, leaned in, but Bakarath, quick as a viper, lashed out with his index finger and poked Hamed in the neck. The governor recoiled, clasping the spot which now stung, then withdrew his fingers to examine a few drops of blood.

"You dare draw royal blood!" Hamed's guards rushed from their places along the wall at their master's angry tone, but Shasp spun, whipping the long Ayponese Katana from its sheath and stood guarding Bakarath's back. Bakarath slowly raised a steel-tipped index finger and wagged it at Hamed.

"You have been entertaining the Black Tide in your fair city, yes, Hamed?"

Hamed and his guards exchanged guilty glances. "What

madness has taken your mind, Bakarath? I am loyal to his majesty."

"You lie!" exclaimed the chief of spies, "The effects of the black blossom are written on your face!"

Hamed touched his neck, "What have you done?"

"I have injected you with a fast, lethal poison. A poison with an anecdote," he pulled a vial from his dusty robes, "which I always carry. I know what you are thinking, Hamed, 'I'll just have my men kill him and take the antidote,' but that would be foolish. The vial is fragile and I would crush it first."

Hamed felt pangs twisting his guts and stumbled. Bakarath was not lying. He was, after all, the chief spy and assassin of Evata. "What do you want?"

"You have little time, Hamed. If I do not give you the antidote within a half hour, you will die horribly."

"What! What do you want!" he screamed, the pain intensifying.

Bakarath's face was stoic, "Take my arm and walk with me, as if we were brothers, to the gate. When we are free to leave, you will have the antidote."

Hamed stood with his hand on his stomach, eyes darting as if searching for another option.

"Time is wasting, Hamed, and time is something you do not have."

Hamed quickly staggered toward the exit as Bakarath came alongside him, engaging in the ever present small talk of the court. Hamed was not saying much. Shasp sheathed his sword and followed them out. When they reached the street, they walked through a formation of guardsmen who weren't there when they came in. Shasp guessed they were awaiting orders to come in and seize Hamed's guests, but now they just stared, dumbfounded, as their regent waved them back and escorted the two men down the street.

"Tell me, Hamed," asked Bakarath, "why the ruse? Why not attack when we came through the gate?"

"Lord Tabeck wanted to offer you an opportunity to serve him, to take the petal. I told him you were fanatical about your loyalties to the sultan. If you would not join of your own free will, I was to force the petals on you."

"Who is this Lord Tabeck?" asked Shasp.

"You will find out soon enough, if you live," choked Hamed.

Within a few minutes, they reached the city well and found their entire cavalry troop surrounded by city guards and Black Tide soldiers. Both forces stood, weapons out in a standoff, waiting for the order to attack. Hamed gave Bakarath a fierce look, but the spy held up the light green vial.

"Were *you* forced to take the petal, Hamed?" asked Bakarath in an almost compassionate tone. Hamed turned his paling face away in shame. "So," said Bakarath, "you were not. Tell your men to get back."

Hamed, clutching at his stomach, stayed silent.

Bakarath wrapped his fingers around the vial that represented Hamed's life and made a fist as if to crush it. "We can all die here, right now, or we can all live to fight another day."

Hamed Akkadi vomited in answer and, after spitting the last of the bile out of his mouth, shouted hoarsely at the surrounding warriors. "Get back! Put your weapons away!"

The men froze in bewilderment, eyes questioning the governor. "I said get back, damn you all!" His anger sparked a response and swords slid back into sheaths as the strangling circle of men slowly backed away. Shasp leapt on Grimm's back and held the reigns of Bakarath's steed. The craggy faced spy smoothed his beard as if he were in no hurry, studying Hamed, then placed a foot in the stirrup, and swung onto his saddle. "Walk with me to the gates."

Hamed clung to the horse's stirrup as he stumbled alongside Bakarath, and the soldiers of the Black Tide followed behind at close distance. When they were outside Shasp turned to Albis, "Take the men and ride hard toward the Ile River. We'll catch up."

Albis nodded and gave the order. The mercenaries turned toward the east, reluctant to leave their lieutenant, and spurred their horses. When Shasp could see only the cloud of dust which marked their passing, he turned to Bakarath and nodded.

The spy made certain he was out of bow range then tossed the vial to Hamed, but the sickly regent was not prepared, and the container bounced on his fingertips as he juggled it. The elusive vial slipped through his plump hands and shattered on a stone at his feet. He stared at the spreading liquid in horror, as he watched the thirsty desert sands drink up the antidote. Stubby legs crumpled as he dove to the ground, stuffing muddy sand into his mouth and sucking at the

279

stones which held traces of the potion. Bakarath laughed in amusement and Shasp screwed up his face in curious disgust at the spy's humor. He was anxious to ride, and scolded the old spy, "Let's go, Bakarath! We have no time to watch this man die! His hounds will be on our backs when he comes to his senses!"

Hamed looked up, his lips caked with dirt, "You are a liar! You promised me the antidote but instead, you have killed me!"

Bakarath chuckled, "You will not die yet, Hamed. I would not steal the pleasure of watching your death from the sultan."

"But the poison, it burns in my blood!"

"Bakarath waved a dismissive hand, "a toxin, yes, a poison . . . no. You will live Hamed . . . for a little while."

Hamed gawked stupidly, then rage swept over his face as he turned toward the gates and screamed at his men, "Kill these swine!"

The soldiers were like dogs hovering over a slab of meat, only a leash holding them back. Now the leash was off and the furious army exploded from the gates on foot and on horse, screaming and running toward them. Shasp and Bakarath dug in their heels and rode with the demonic Black Tide at their back. The powerful Grimm and the relentless desert mare easily out distanced the howling pack of mismatched soldiers as they made for the Ile River, scarcely slowing down. Not an hour had passed when they overtook the rest of the troop. Shasp and Bakarath rode to the front where Albis and Lexia still trotted their steeds to maintain a decent pace.

Albis shook his head; a dour expression pinched his face. "We hardly had time to fill any water skins when the soldiers fell upon us. Good thing Pieter was watching and warned us when he saw some movement between the buildings. But now, we have no supplies and little water. Fenic was the only city in this forsaken land. How are we going to reach the Ile River?"

Shasp really did not know but smiled at Albis anyway, "We'll think of something Sergeant, we always do," but when he looked out into the twilight of the vast hard earth and its rocky, dead horizon, he felt the cold dread of their reality settle on him. They wouldn't last more than a couple of days in the heat without water and returning to Fenic was out of the question.

Lexia saw his poorly hidden concern and leaned close as they trotted along. "We're going to need a miracle. You know that."

Shasp nodded.

CHAPTER 12

The step pyramid of Tabeck was ancient and as big as a mountain, hewn from grey volcanic stone thousands of years earlier, with twisted figures of ancient gods and demons carved in nearly every inch of the massive structure in stark and unsettling reliefs. Its base was nearly two hundred yards wide, and by the time Holkerm had climbed the stairs to the entrance at its peak, he was exhausted. He stood at the top of the ziggurat and took in the broad valley floor stretching away beneath him. Verdant jungle hemmed in a sea of black flowers, flourishing in the humidity. Ragged, dark-skinned natives with wooly black hair seemed like ants from the height as they moved among the Adder Blossoms in the quadrant fields, pruning and weeding under the suns staring eye.

The general walked around the stone veranda and mused over how it would take several minutes to walk around the base to see the same view. On the opposite side, he gazed down at a level floor of brickwork, far below, stretching to the valley's edge; the foundation of an ancient city. Upon its sunbaked surface, thousands of black-armored soldiers drilled in vast formations. These were not the unruly Black Tide regulars, intoxicated and crazed by the blossom's stimulant effect. These were Somerikan hoplites, mercenaries, bought and paid for with desert gold. Full, open-faced helms with cheek guards and black horsehair crests protected their heads. Breast plates of boiled leather, dipped in bronze, covered torso and metal greaves covered them from knee to ankle. A large round shield barricaded bare legs while the strong arm wielded spear and sword. All was lacquered to a shiny black finish. The formations moved as one, struck as one and echoed the drill chants as one.

A wicked grin split Holkerm's face as he rubbed the black silk of his cape between his fingers and appraised his armor, the same as the others, shiny and black but with intricate designs and bosses. He turned toward the pyramid's entrance.

The low ceiling capping the edifice forced him to duck before starting down the worn steps and into the awaiting darkness. Steep, narrow stairs whispered under his sandaled feet, as the adjoining walls pressed against his shoulders. He required no light for the darkness, feeling his way along the descending stairs as they twisted and dropped for a very long time. Holkerm finally emerged into a long hallway, perceived the distant, faint glow of lamplight and continued toward his meeting. He ran his clammy palm over his slick bald head, wiping the humidity from his broad scalp. Even

though the inner chambers of the ugly temple were swept clean, the stench of an ancient evil still hung in the trapped air. He was a big man and barely fit through the age-old corridors, reasoning that the people who built them must have been of smaller stature.

He hesitated before an archway etched with twisted figures and was about to clear his throat and announce his presence when a deep voice spoke.

"Come in, General. I have been waiting for you. How was your journey?"

Holkerm sensed no sincerity in the question and answered in his own blunt way, as he stepped into the low room. "Uneventful."

As he entered, he saw the same figure seen before on the liquid surface of burning coals.

Coarse red robes and a hood hid the features of Lord Tabeck as he reclined on an obsidian chair. "Good, and the troops? Are they to your satisfaction?"

"They seemed to be, but I haven't met the officers yet."

Tabeck nodded slowly, "Soon enough, General, but for now I

wish to discuss other matters. As you may have guessed, I did not choose to attack Evata randomly."

"Of course," said Holkerm, "there is great wealth in Laveg. Enough to finance a war."

"That is a small matter, General. I have enough gold to finance my army, but I needed someone to lead it; a man who was capable of gaining great prizes. I have watched your distinguished career under Sultan Alafar. Without you, he would be only a second rate potentate. He does not realize your full potential, but I do."

Holkerm stood silently, contemplating Tabeck's words, "As you have said, and thus the handsome offer which caused my . . . defection. But I must admit, I still don't understand why you feel the need to spend so much on these mercenaries when you can enlist soldiers with the Adder Blossom and pay them nothing."

A short silence preceded Tabeck's answer, prelude to some important secret. "The Black Tide is a storm, and like a storm, comes on with great fury, wind, rain and thunder. But . . . storms do not last forever, do they, General? Like all other tempests, this one too will lose momentum and fade."

Holkerm's expression was one of confusion, "I don't understand. The black army has swept across the desert kingdoms of Sona, Evata and Attah only gaining strength and making warriors with each victory, turning the vanquished into loyal servants. I *wish* I had known about the black flower."

"True, but the Adder Blossom is also deadly. Once a man is enslaved to it, he will live only for the flower. Food and water become secondary until he has starved himself to death. Reports from the field are already showing such signs of decay. Task Masters are having more and more difficulty getting the army to eat. Food is rotting in the camps for lack of consumption. Time is running out General, we need to move soon before the army dissolves. This new army of Black Tide soldiers will need to be on its way to the field by the end of the month. We will keep the flower moving north until it gets there."

General Holkerm thought a moment, considering the logistics of moving so many men on short notice and nodded. "It can be done. I wonder Lord Tabeck, would you indulge me by answering one question?"

"Of course."

"You do not dress in regal robes, though you have great wealth. You hide your face yet seek glory. You live in seclusion in the middle of a jungle yet bring great nations to war. What is it you hope to gain from all this? What *do* you want? It isn't fame, wealth or power that much is clear."

Tabeck did not answer, but only sat quietly for an uncomfortable amount of time, regarding Holkerm from the depths of the cowl, then his deep voice changed slightly. "If I answered you, General, I do not think you would grasp my reasoning. Suffice to say, mine are not the ways of most men. You will have Evata and all her wealth when we are finished. Then, we will talk about what I want and you *will* give it to me."

Holkerm shuddered at the menacing confidence in Tabeck's voice and nodded curtly. "I will begin the preparations for departure. Is there anything else you wish to discuss?"

"Only a reminder, General. Do not forget your alliances. We have wagered everything on our venture, you and me. We must see it through, there is no way back. No redemption."

Holkerm, sweating even more now, turned and left the chamber. Unconsciously, his feet moved faster as he left the pyramid than when he had arrived and he wondered at the sudden, inexplicable fear.

CHAPTER 13

Arid desert air sucked the moisture from their bodies like grapes drying in the sun. Horses stumbled and dusty riders lurched in the saddle. Tongues swelled and lips cracked open, but the blood dried before it could run. Skin pealed, becoming leathery and eyes dried up, full of sand. There had been no water for three days and at least a few men had succumbed and were left on the burning earth of the Sona desert. Unlike the Trabic with its rolling sands and wind, the Sona desert was hard and flat with growths of jagged rock springing chaotically from the merciless ground.

It seemed to Shasp that, since the defeat at the Tetas, misery had been his constant traveling companion. He had hoped to bring his troops to a tributary of the Ile River the day before, but when they arrived, they found only a dusty chasm where the narrow vein had been. Some of his men had even wept. There was nothing else to do but press on and pray they did not come across enemy scouts. In spite of his bravado, Shasp knew it was unlikely they would live to see the Ile another two days east. He no longer felt the sting of dehydration, or the ache of the saddle, or the burning of the sun. Life had become a numb panorama of repetitious scenery and intense heat. He aimed Grimm toward a ridge of red earth, his eyes hypnotized by the shimmer of a distant heat wave. When his horse staggered over the top, he saw one of his forward scouts ambling back. Pieter waved weakly from the distance, and a few minutes later the young corporal reined in before his lieutenant.

Pieter's excitement was subdued by fatigue, "Lieutenant Ironwrought, there's a caravan," he motioned behind him, "two miles east. Black Tide guarding them, maybe fifty."

Shasp felt a puny strain of hope rising as he checked the horizon, "Sun's going down. They'll camp soon." He held up a fist, bringing the column to a halt then spun his finger overhead, signaling the men to circle around him.   Normally, the reaction to all hand gestures was immediate, but it took several minutes for the column to react and face inward. Shasp addressed them as loudly as he could with his mummified throat.

"Pieter spotted a caravan two miles east of here, guarded by about fifty Black Tide soldiers. I don't think I need to tell you, it's our only hope. Now is the time to discover what you are made of; find strength in your souls because I know it's no longer in your bodies." He turned and started east and the silent column fell in behind.

An hour later, the red sun was melting into the horizon as the cavalry troop dismounted behind a mammoth rock, sticking out of the ground like a hog's back. Shasp ordered his men to strip off their armor and anything that could make noise. They waited, naked save for footwear and breechclouts, glinting swords gripped in their fists. Silently, as the light dissolved into darkness, Shasp led his men out across the cooling ground. Even though they had the guards outnumbered, his troopers were tired and weak. There were also the other members of the caravan to consider. How many of them would fight? Shasp's mind sharpened, as it always did before killing. He would give no battle cry and had ordered the others to attack silently, stalling the enemy's alarm to those who were sleeping?

Campfires flickered from the raised mesa where the caravan had made camp, allowing their sentinels a better view from the higher ground. Ten of the Black Tide guards patrolled the camp perimeter, gaunt men with black hair, peered into the blanket of night. Their vigilance was a disappointment to Ironwrought who was hoping for a surprise attack, but undaunted, he silently signaled his men to divide and fan out, then crept forward on his stomach with Molgien at his side. Lexia took a group to the right and Albis split off with another to his left. As soon as Shasp believed the others were in place, he sprang from the night, appearing suddenly, like a desert ghost in front of a surprised soldier. Before the Tide warrior could bring his spear up to defend himself, Ayponese steel hissed through the air and sliced through his neck. Blood sprayed Shasp's naked flesh, but before his enemy hit the ground, he was sprinting forward to engage another. There was no way to silence the next guard and he screamed a warning just seconds before he fell under the thirsty Katana. Shasp could not see through the clustered tents, but he heard shouting and the ringing clash of steel on all sides. He came upon Pieter, struggling just to defend himself from another sentry who hacked at him like a demon. In a single fluid movement, Shasp sliced through the Tidesmen's spine, and Pieter fell onto his knees, relieved. The din of battle continued to fill the air with a cacophony of chaos, waking servants and drivers alike, and they

287

swarmed from their tents. Some darted back inside to cower, while others sprang out with knives, swords or clubs and joined the Black Tide in their defense. All around him the battle raged and Shasp set himself on the run, cutting down anyone who was not one of his own. Donkeys and camels brayed, honked and spun in the tumult as his men poured into the camp, having thoroughly breeched the perimeter. Fighting became individual struggles among the tents and everywhere he looked crimson sprayed and splattered the white canvas walls. Shasp was glad the enemy did not have time to group because if they formed a collective resistance, his men would be slaughtered. At least, now, there was a chance of winning. He threw himself into the fray anywhere his exhausted men faltered, giving them respite so they could endure. He regretted the lack of armor, but it had been necessary for surprise. Suffering from many small wounds, Ironwrought fought on until the desert dust became muddy rivers of blood, and the defenders slowly dwindled. One at a time, they dropped their weapons onto the slippery muck and begged for mercy. Most of the Black Tide guards had been cut down, but Shasp had also lost a lot of men, and his stomach churned at the sight of his dead comrades littering the ground. Nevertheless, it was better for a warrior to die in combat than a slow death in the desert. When the last of the caravan were dead or surrendered, he called what was left of his cohort together and sent them among the tents in search of food and water. The men never gave the gold or gems a second look, but only grabbed at water skins and pouches of meat as they rifled through the tents and wagons.   Ironwrought mused over the way priorities changed when death walked at one's shoulder. Eventually the horses were brought into camp and the men collected their armor, then drank and ate with a fervor known only to the starving.

Molgien had not seen combat since the Tetas river and, in the past, had not had time to collect his prize from battle. This night would be different. To the disgust of his comrades, he artfully butchered the best cuts from some of his enemies and put a campfire spit to work. Even Lexia wrinkled her nose at Molgien's grinning satisfaction and the stench of burning flesh. Only Ironwrought seemed indifferent to his valet's eating habits, having seen it many times before. The survivors from the caravan sat horrified, wondering which of them would be next on the cannibal's spit.

Dawn broke over the low, rocky mountains to touch Shasp's cold face with warm tendrils of light. Fatigue still weighed on him, but he felt much better after a few hours of sleep and a skin of water. Only sixty-three of his men survived from the night before, but it was more than he had hoped for. He cast about the smoldering camp and his eyes fell on the circle of captives, tied together, back to back. One wept and called on his gods as Molgien squatted and began poking him with a stick, evaluating him as if he were a fat goose. Shasp cleared his throat, gaining the cannibal's attention and made a curt sign. Molgien gave a petulant snort and moved away. Shasp moved to the circle where the prisoners were tied together in pairs. He seized a bearded old man's face between his thumb and fingers and turned his head from side to side, looking for signs of the drug. When he was satisfied, he pushed him down roughly.

"What's your name?"

"Caddi, I am . . . was the master of this caravan," he said, his voice quivering with fear.

"Caddi," said Shasp with some disdain, "where were you going with this caravan?"

The man tied to Caddi twisted around, "Tell him nothing!"

Caddi hesitated and his eyes darted, revealing the lie he was about to tell, "North to the main army at Salsida. We were bringing . . . " Before he could finish his sentence, Shasp had whipped the katana from its sheath and lopped off the head of the man he was tied to. A fountain of blood erupted overhead, bright in the morning light, soaking Chaddi's white robe with warm sticky fluid. He screamed, trying to wriggle free from the corpse he was bound to, wanting to remove himself from the nearness of death. Shasp stood, arms crossed with the dripping blade still in his fist, jutting from behind his shoulder. He waited patiently for Chaddi to stop whimpering before he spoke again.

"I'm not a patient man, Caddi. This caravan is carrying gold and gems, not food and supplies. You are carrying a payment for something, now . . . where?"

Caddi was horrified and his mouth worked like a fish out of water until he was finally able to form words, "South . . . we were going south to bring the gold to a place down river."

"In Somerika?" asked Shasp.

Caddi hesitated again until Shasp put the point of his sword

289

against his throat, "Yes, Somerika, down the Ile to the Azon River, then down another tributary to a place."

"They wouldn't happen to grow black flowers there . . . would they?"

Caddi nodded.

Shasp continued, "Does anyone else among your men know the way?"

"Only me," said Caddi, his blood-smeared turban now crooked on his head.

Shasp cut the old man loose with a clean swipe that barely shaved his wrists, and then hauled him to his feet, shoving him away from the other prisoners. "Sergeant Albis!"

Albis appeared from a tent, already buckling on his gear, "Sir!"

"Sergeant, get the men together. Bundle up all the armor and keep it hidden. Have the men dress in caravan robes and any other clothing they can find, then break down the tents and pack up the camp. Give the prisoners enough water to see them back to Fenic, all except Caddi there."

Albis squinted an eye in confusion but nodded. Shasp perceived Albis' question and smiled, "We're going to finish taking this gold where it was headed."

Arbok Castella leaned his large body into the rudder as the wide barge slowly responded in the muddy current. Brackish water coursed away from the hull with a whispering noise that had become part of his everyday life. He watched as the clumsy craft with her crew of five slid along the rocky shore of the Ile River. The crew was busy jabbing long poles into the murk, testing the bottom and occasionally pushing the bow away from a place they thought too shallow. Arbok pulled back a greasy string of hair that had fallen across his balding forehead and into his brown eyes, and then searched again for the docks. He spied the rickety structure in the distance, defiant against the current, and the milling caravan of white robed men he was contracted to pick up. A swarthy fellow with a pointed salt and pepper beard, waited at the edge of the docks on the back of a large black horse. Several black-haired men wearing the armor of the Black Tide, waited along the banks. Castella anxiously pulled his sweating hand over his heavy jowls and yelled at his men,

"Bring us in you lazy dogs! And watch the sand bars!" The barge was wide and flat of bottom, but sturdy, and made a groaning sound as it slid along the pier, much to Arbok's displeasure. "Fools! Are you trying to sink us before we are even underway?" The anchor plunked into the water and ropes flew to waiting hands which secured the vessel. Arbok Castella swaggered to the edge of his boat and dropped his squat bulk heavily over the side onto the dock. He approached the man on the horse, "Caddi?"

"Of course, who else would I be?" replied Bakarath with a smile.

Arbok wiped his sweaty hand on his bare thigh then offered it to Bakarath, "Captain Castella. I'll be taking you down river. I'm told you know where we are going."

Bakarath considered the hand for a moment wondering what sort of foul things it may have touched, then shook it grudgingly. "So you are, and yes I do. Here is the first half of your payment, as agreed." He tossed a swollen leather pouch to the fat captain who caught the jingling bag.

Castella smiled broadly, revealing several missing teeth and nodded, "Welcome aboard, Master Caddi. I was told the last barge that took you down was sunk by Evatan troops on its return. I hope nothing happens to my boat, or I might have to come looking for payment," he turned to his men who idled about the deck, "Get off your asses, you lazy bastards and get these animals and supplies loaded!"

The sailors sprang into action, leaping over the deck rail and swarming into the caravan. Bakarath figured he should also keep appearances and barked loud orders rivaling Castella's. Soon, white robes and bare backs mingled in a swarm of activity. Shasp, used to being in charge was standing next to Grimm, whom Bakarath rode, and watching the bustle. Bakarath reached out with his booted foot and shoved Shasp toward the others. "You lazy slave, get busy before I have you whipped!"

If looks could kill, Ironwrought's would have severed Bakarath in two. But the old spy simply grinned out one side of his mouth, an unspoken sentiment of mischief.   Arbok saw the exchange and smirked, "If that slave were mine, I'd have his legs flayed for such a look."

"I have considered as much, but I paid a considerable sum for him. Perhaps later, if he does not come around, I'll have a torturer break his spirit."

Arbok laughed, opened the rail to a gang plank, and then waved Bakarath on board.

Shasp hefted a bale onto his shoulder and joined the line of men and horses as they boarded the massive craft.

Lexia, dressed in Black Tide armor, chuckled over the prank, but reached out and ran her hand across his back as she rode by. Shasp couldn't help but smile. Within minutes, the barge was crammed to capacity and its bulk was shoved out into the current again. When Castella was not watching, Shasp approached Bakarath and bowed low for appearances. "Master, may I speak?"

Bakarath looked away toward the shore and sighed with annoyance, "Speak, slave."

Shasp leaned toward him and whispered menacingly but with a humble looking expression, "If you ever kick me again, I'll break your leg . . . Master Caddi."

Bakarath raised an eyebrow and laughed inwardly.

Slowly, the Ile River wound ever south, through wind blasted steppes and jagged, haunted cliffs that reached for the heavens. Sunlight sparkled on the rippling current, scattering as it touched and blinding anyone who gazed toward the river's surface. The men performed their menial duties then languished in the heat or fished for the long Ariana; a carnivorous fish which sometimes reached eight feet in length. Bakarath and Shasp caught a moment to discuss further plans and argued briefly over the possibility of killing the crew of the barge before they reached their destination, but decided none among his troopers were capable of manning the boat or negotiating the river.

On the fourth day, the Ile cut through the southern desert and saw fertile ground. Small villages of low mud huts stood no more than a hundred yards off with irrigation ditches running beyond to green fields and orchards. Dark-skinned people looked up from the shore, some waved and others only stared cynically. In all, the slow drift toward the Somerikan jungles had been restful and Shasp was grateful his men had time to heal and replenish their bodies after a grueling ride through two deserts.

Shasp plied the real Caddi for information at every

opportunity, much to the old man's distress, for he had not forgotten how close he had come to being a headless corpse. Neither was he able to move more than a few feet from whatever guard was assigned to him. Secretly, he wished he could get but a moment alone with Captain Castella to reveal the plot, believing his life would be forfeit upon reaching the clearing in the jungle. Caddi told Shasp about the clearing of the pyramid and in spite of his prattling, Shasp was not completely certain what awaited them. The old caravan leader said the last time he was there, mercenaries had been flowing in from all over the southern regions. Great preparations were underway. Why? Hadn't the Black Tide already swarmed over Sona, Attah and Evata? As long as the flower went north, the Tide would continue to devastate the desert kingdoms, wouldn't it? Shasp leaned on the deck rail, and contemplated the brackish water as it washed along the barge's hull. He was hoping to find the source of the Adder Blossom mostly unguarded, far from its influence on the war. Now, it seemed he would have to do the impossible; wade through a growing army of mercenaries and destroy the fields of flowers with only sixty men. He shook his head in self-doubt not realizing Bakarath was watching him. The old spy came alongside him at the rail and watched the verdant vegetation slide by, clinging to the river for its life, the desert just beyond.

"I see your thoughts are as plagued as mine," said Bakarath.

Shasp turned his head just enough to see him out of the corner of his eye, "Is it so obvious?"

Bakarath nodded solemnly, "To a trained eye, yes."

"Then you've been wondering how to pull this off too; any ideas yet?"

"A few."

Shasp turned toward Bakarath and searched over his shoulder for Arbok Castella. It wouldn't do to have the captain see him speaking to his master in such a relaxed state. "So, let's hear them."

Bakarath frowned as if he was about to say something very profound, took a deep breath and exhaled. "There can be no head to head battle this time. If what Caddi says is true, we will be hopelessly outnumbered. We must act covertly, silently, unexpectedly." He waited a moment to let his words sink in then continued. "Caddi has been there before, so when we arrive, my disguise may be compromised. The fact that Castella believes me to

293

be Caddi, complicates things even further. However, Castella has not been to the clearing before, therefor, if another assumed his place," he nodded at Shasp, "none would be the wiser. Then I could claim to be Caddi's successor."

Now it was Shasp's turn to frown, "Except his crew, which would mean . . ."

"Killing everyone," finished Bakarath.

Shasp remained silent, staring down at the water again then, "I don't think so, Bakarath. War is war, but slaughter is another thing."

Bakarath drew himself up, looking annoyed, "Have you forgotten that Caddi, Castella and every member of his crew are conspiring with our enemies? Besides, you didn't hesitate to lop off the head of a prisoner when Caddi failed to answer your questions. I believe I even remember hearing that you were Holkerm's battlefield interrogator, but now you are squeamish about cutting a few throats."

Shasp sighed at Bakarath's logic and responded to the spy's angry expression with one of his own, "I know what you're getting at, and maybe it's a fine line I draw here, but I still find the idea of assassinating men in their sleep distasteful. When the time comes, we'll maroon them somewhere."

"That is a mistake!" hissed the chief intelligence officer.

Shasp shrugged, "So you say, and I have killed men in their sleep before, but only those who richly deserved it. Conspiring or not, these men are just river sailors making a living. We will maroon them in good time, when we are close."

Bakarath sputtered a moment over Shasp's stubbornness, then threw his arms into the air and walked away.

Caddi huddled against the rail in the dead of night, the glow of a brazier barely lighting the rigging and door of Castella's cabin. The rest of the men lay strewn about the deck like so many casualties of a battlefield. Fidgeting with his chains, he adjusted himself to become more comfortable against the rubbing wood and let his eyes settle again on the warm brazier's glow. He had wracked his brains for a way out of his predicament but nothing came to mind. However, there in the night, while his guard waxed against the weight of sleep, he gave birth to a revelation. Slowly he rose up and crawled toward the brazier, carefully cradling his chains to keep them silent. When his guard felt him stir and questioned him, Caddi answered that he only wished to get warm. The trooper seemed satisfied with that and returned to his half-sleep status. Caddi reached carefully into the brazier and drug his chain over a coal until it dropped onto the deck in a tiny shower of sparks, then began to cool. He hovered over the small coal and spat on it to help, then tucked it into a fold of his robe and returned to his place against the rail. The next day, when Arbok Castella ordered one of his men to swab his cabin out, Caddi volunteered to do the work for a tiny ration of the sailor's bread. Castella agreed and Caddi's guard grudgingly escorted him after much debate. He was pushed inside to clean while his watchman waited outside with the door open. The cavalryman knew Arbok was at the helm and saw no reason why Caddi shouldn't be put to use as long as he was not near enough to blurt out the truth about the mission. The little old man seemed to scrub the floors with enthusiasm, but when the guard looked away, Caddi pulled out the lump of charcoal and quickly scribbled a message on the wall near Arbok's bed, relating what had happened and who he really was in as few words as possible. It occurred to him that the captain may not even know how to read, and he silently prayed the man was at least slightly educated. Once his note was done, Caddi hurriedly finished his work and backed out of the cabin door with mop in hand. His guard escorted him back to the rail, and the sailor tossed him the extra ration of bread. Caddi dropped onto the deck, heart thumping, and held the bread in his hands. How quickly had he gone from being the wealthy master of his own caravan to a slave whose life hung in the balance, like a spider dangling above a flame.

CHAPTER 14

King Nachmed gazed down from atop Salsida's
battle-blasted walls and into the darkness. Nearby, the fires of the
Black Tide burned as they had since the siege began, casting an eerie
orange glow. Yesterday he had been a prince, but yesterday his
father, the King, had been crushed by a clay jar of flaming oil, flung
over the wall by a catapult.

The young man's face was narrow and clean shaven, but
strong.   Dark brown hair of tangled locks hung dirty and tired
against his scalp. Lanky arms were folded across his chest while
brown eyes stayed fixed on the ground below and his general,
Momad, filled his ears with the problems of the day. The heavyset
man of waxing years spewed out issue after issue through his curly
black beard, his rumbling tone low and concerned. The west wall
was starting to weaken and needed to be shorn. Food and water
rations were running low and morale was falling. Many within the
city were resigned to their deaths.

Nachmed nodded somberly, still eyeing the darkness. How
could he blame them? He understood the despair of the soldiers and
citizens behind the gates. Emissaries had been sent to Breska and
Kulunata, but those kingdoms were far removed and disinterested in
the wars of the west. Why should they send troops? He was not
surprised by the response stating none of them would intervene. His
last hope waited somewhere below; a messenger he'd sent out to slip
through the enemy lines. Laveg may be faring well enough against
the Tide and perhaps would be able to send a force to break the
stranglehold on his city.

As the general continued to rattle on about the condition of
the walls and dwindling forces, Nachmed glimpsed movement in the
shadows. He shushed the officer with his raised hand and leaned
cautiously over the wall. Silently he hoped it was his man, but also
knew it might be a sniper with a crossbow looking for a target of
opportunity. Now that he was king, he would be exactly that.

Then the signal came, the light of a small candle revealed
three times from under a cloak.

"That's him. Bring the rope," said Nachmed.

Two soldiers in tarnished scale armor flung one end of a rope over the wall where a small man hurried to slip his foot into the loop tied at the bottom. The men heaved on the rope as fast as they could until the mousey man wearing a black cloak tumbled over the edge of the battlement. Before the messenger could gather himself, the king was upon him, grasping the tattered leather tunic under his cloak.

"What news? Will Alafar come to our aid?"

The man's sunken eyes fell, "Ill tidings my lord. Laveg is also under siege by the Black Tide. All her soldiers defend the city. We are alone in this fight."

King Nachmed stumbled back, shock and despair etching his face as he shook his head. General Momad looked away while they stood in silent grief, each considering what their fate would be when the provisions gave out . . . or the walls. Suddenly, Nachmed lifted his head and threw back his shoulders, the look of horror erased and replaced with one of fierce resolve. He turned to Momad with stony eyes, "General, I want every piece of metal in this city, that isn't already being used for warfare, melted down, all of it. Put everyone to work smelting it into swords, shields, knives, and armor. Once that is done, I want everyone from children to old crones training for combat. That means marching, formation, hand-to-hand, spear and bow. When the last of our supplies are gone, we will march out and meet the Black Tide, and if the walls give first, we'll grind them up in the gap. The price for our lives will be expensive.

General Momad nodded, "Prince, ah, King Nachmed, I knew, even when you were a child and I swung you around by your heels, that you would grow to be a fine king someday. Your father would be proud, and it will be my honor to fight my last battle at your side."

Nachmed placed his hand on Momad's shoulder, "As will I."

The general turned, hurried down the stairs leading to the city below, and disappeared between the pock-marked buildings. Nachmed watched after him then placed his hands on the rough stone of the battlements. He had known the time to be king would come, but was never in a hurry to be one. He had loved his father and missed him desperately already, but now there was no time for grief. What would he have done? Nachmed wondered if he had missed some avenue of assistance or escape and sighed.

In the distance, the drums of the wild Tide soldiers began to thrum and mix with mad revelry. It did not look as if he would be king for very long.

CHAPTER 15

Lexia had just beat Molgien for the third time in a game of knucklebones when Arbok Castella called down from the upper deck.

"All crew muster for a foraging party!"

Molgien gave her his typical, 'I don't understand,' look and she stood, motioning to him. He heaved his massive torso up onto the spindly legs she found so comical. She gestured to him with a hand near her open mouth as if to eat then pointed toward the crowded trees and thick vegetation. They had left the desert behind a couple days ago when the Ile River flowed into the mighty Azon. Since then, they drifted past massive deciduous trees with sprawling canopies choked with vines and heavy underbrush. Light broke through in chaotic beams creating a collage of shadows. In contrast to the constant silence of the desert, the jungle was always alive. Roaring cats, howling monkeys, and bird chatter were ever present. The water of the Azon was also teeming. Snakes, fish and enormous crocodiles nearly as long as the barge itself, swam around their refuge. One of the big crocks actually snapped a good sized fish off Molgien's pole just as he was bringing it over the side. Lexia would never have guessed that the dark-skinned cannibal could turn so white.

They wove through the men on the deck and found Shasp standing with his arms folded. Lexia slid her hand down his back and he responded with a wink. "Castella thinks the water on board is going foul. He wants us to look for a fresh source."

"It is beginning to taste a little stale," she replied.

When everyone was assembled, Castella addressed them again, "With Master Caddi's permission, we will be breaking up into five foraging parties to replenish our water and take whatever game you happen to find. Is that acceptable Master Caddi?"

Bakarath thumbed his hooked nose, "Of course, Captain."

Castella continued, "I will head a party of ten from your caravan and you may appoint the others. We'll head inland, but no more than an hour walk. Will you be heading a party?"

Bakarath feigned fear and held up his hands, "Oh no, not me. I'll stay on board after I divide my men. Do you mind taking this troublesome slave with you?" He pointed at Shasp, "I would be more comfortable sending him with you, knowing you were in charge, you know . . . if he tried to run away or do some other foolish thing."

Castella bowed, indicating his acceptance. Bakarath turned to Shasp with a serious look and whispered, "I sense something is afoot. Watch him closely."

"Don't worry; I'll wear him like skin."

Bakarath turned and called to Castella as he started down the stairs from the bridge, "Will your men be coming, Captain?"

"Only a few, the others will need to tend to the barge and keep a look out for trouble."

The spy nodded and bowed with mock respect.

Momentarily, the barge's boarding plank was lowered and men spewed out into the jungle's waiting maw. Nervous eyes scanned the shadowy canopy of broad leaves and the thick brush before them. Bakarath sent Lexia and Shasp with Castella and Molgien with another group. Shasp made it clear to Molgien before disembarking that he should not go far from the boat. The foraging parties fanned out, hacking at vines and twisted saplings which barred their way, slowly working away from the boat. Mosquitoes and other unpleasant insects swarmed and bit. They slapped at their sweating necks and arms then continued to chop through. Hack then slap, hack then slap. The repetitious defense was nearly maddening and when those clearing the trail became exhausted, others stepped up to relieve them. All except Arbok, of course; he stood behind them yelling orders and pointing out the direction they should go. When Shasp's turn came, he stepped up to the work, hacking at the stubborn vines, splattering their sticky milk along the length of his katana. After he mowed down the brush for several minutes, he

300

suddenly realized he had not heard Castella yelling his usual string
of purposeless orders and turned to look for the plump captain. He
searched over the heads of the men but could not see Arbok, so he
waved for someone to continue in his place. Shouldering his way
past the others, he moved toward the back of the column, looking
around.   There was no sign of Arbok, nor did he see Lexia in her
Black Tide attire.

"Lexia!" he called. Only the sounds of the jungle responded.
"Lexia! Damn it, answer me!"

"I'm here, blast it. Can't a woman piss?" she said as she
emerged from the foliage, buckling her black leather kilt in place.

"Where's Arbok?"

Lexia shrugged and looked around, "I don't know?   I
thought you were watching him."

They called Arbok for a few seconds, but Shasp's instincts
told him the captain had returned to the boat. Realization dawned
suddenly. Not only was Arbok gone but so were the four men from
his crew. The gold and gems from the caravan raid were still aboard
ship while he and all his troopers were in the jungle on a trumped up
excursion.

"Damn!" Shasp swore. "You, you and you," he pointed, find
the others and get them moving back to the barge immediately!
Lexia come with me!" He spun and darted into the trees, leaping
logs and ducking branches. Vines whipped their faces and thorns
tore at their skin as they blasted through the thick jungle. As he
negotiated obstacles, Shasp wondered what Arbok was up to. Was it
a typical ploy he had used to seize wealth from unsuspecting
passengers in the past, marooning the helpless victims in the jungle?
Or, was there something else. Had he discovered the truth about who
they were? Shasp's mercenaries were trying to keep up with their
leader, but he and Lexia were slowly out distancing them. Castella
was fat and would move ponderously through the tangled growth,
but Shasp had no idea how much of a head start he had. After what
seemed an eternity, the enfolding arms of the trees finally released
them onto the river bank where the barge had been anchored.   But
now, the ship was casting off and a good twenty feet from shore.
Bakarath was on the deck with his back to the forward rail, scimitar
in hand as six crew members surrounded him. Shasp cursed and
stamped his foot; what a fool he had been. Desperately, he scanned

301

the bank down river and saw a massive banyan tree, its roots reaching into the water and its branches stretching over it. Mud and rock flew from his feet as he sped toward the tree with Lexia on his heels. He reached the banyan, scampered up its trunk and into the branches with the dexterity of a monkey. He shuffled along the tree's largest arm and stopped where it tapered dangerously, bobbing in the wind. The barge was just beginning to slide by below when he dropped nearly ten feet onto the bow next to Bakarath. The old spy was as surprised to see him as the crew and both stopped waving their swords at his sudden appearance.

Bakarath shook off his amazement and smiled, "Why didn't you bring the men," he jested.

Lexia had taken a few seconds longer to reach the end of the banyan's branch and at that moment, dropped onto the upper deck at the opposite end. The sailor next to her barely had time to open his mouth before she cut his scream short and sent his perforated body into the river.

Shasp pointed his sword at Lexia, "We aren't fighting Arriginian cavalry, Bakarath, just a handful of river rats. I decided to give the men a rest."

He raised a graying eyebrow, "But not the woman, eh?"

Before he could shrug a reply, Castella called out, "Drop your weapons, you fools, and I might spare your lives. There is no need to lose deck hands over a brawl which can only lead to your deaths. Throw down, I say!"

"I don't think so, pirate," yelled Shasp. "How many others have you left to die in the jungle?"

Castella pretended to be surprised, "Pirate? Was it not you who slaughtered a caravan and sought to deceive me? The question is; what were you planning for me?"

Bakarath snorted, "I told you we should have killed him."

"Shut up."

"Caddi . . ." said Arbok, "the real Caddi, left a message, written on my cabin wall, warning me of your treachery, and you stand there and call me a pirate; now, over the side with you!"

"I don't think so," answered Shasp, "but you should know, we could not make you an offer yet. If you would have refused, there would have been no one to man the craft. We had to wait. If you want to test that bargain now, it's not too late. As you said, no one

302

needs to die."

Castella thought for a moment, "Why should I deal with you at all? Why take a chance that you would have a change of heart once your men are back on board? Besides, I have all the money now and I don't think I need to take that chance."

Shasp laughed, "You mean Caddi's money."

"No," said Castella, "I mean my money."

Shasp's eyes narrowed, "So, you are a Pirate."

Castella smirked, "Kill them . . . now!"

Before the first sailor even flinched, Shasp threw his katana, piercing his chest with a thunk. Sailors dropped from the rigging and swarmed toward them, heavy knives and wide cutlasses in their fists. Several ran up the stairs to the bridge where Lexia waited with a wolfish grin on her face.

Bakarath thought Shasp had lost his mind when he threw away his weapon until he saw him knock his next adversary out with a kick to the head. The spy drove in, side-stepping a cut meant for his head, and skewered a deck hand through the ribs, leaving the man in a gasping huddle. Then, he spun to his right and came alongside another, but this man was more experienced. The sailor knocked away several thrusts and returned the attack with better than average form. Bakarath tightened up his position and unleashed a barrage of slashes and thrusts that sent the sailor reeling backward until he was against the rail. When the sailor raised his blade to stop a downward cut, Bakarath kicked him in the chest, sending him over the rail and into the river. He spun to engage another and realized Shasp was not where he had been. Instead, five sailors lay on the deck. Two lay sprawled and unconscious, one was dead and two more were cradling fractured limbs. Ironwrought was speeding across the deck with the retrieved katana in his hand on his way to meet Castella.

The two met in the middle of the lower deck in a clang of steel. Arbok, though fat, was surprisingly agile in spite of his bulk and stronger than he looked. Nevertheless, Shasp received his flurry of crisscross slashes, banging them back in time, and then ducked under the last. He seized Castella's wrist as he went by, pulling him off balance then kicked him in the back. The captain's momentum was already propelling him toward the rail before Shasp kicked him. He sailed into it and toppled over the side, landing in the murky

303

water with a splash. Shasp turned to make for the bridge and help Lexia, but she was already standing at the rudder painted with flecks of blood. When Castella went overboard, she turned and watched as the barge slid by. The captain sputtered curses, promising revenge, but was suddenly jerked underwater. Blood boiled to the surface followed by the thrashing back of a huge crocodile. It rolled over twice then vanished beneath the dark surface with its prey. For a moment they watched silently until Bakarath remembered to throw out the anchor. He ran across the bridge and heaved it into the river. Slowly, the boat eased to a stop with the river washing around it.

Shasp met his comrades on the bridge and they looked around uneasily.

"Well," he said, "who's taking the mooring line to shore?"

CHAPTER 16

Major Rodreeg adjusted his helmet. The heat and humidity created the most uncomfortable itching on his scalp, forcing him to constantly adjust the steel headpiece. He hoped it wasn't jungle lice or some other debilitating fungus so common to the interior regions. The day grew long and its remnants lay smeared in the sky above the spreading canopy in streaks of violet and orange. He watched General Holkerm survey the line of ships amongst the clamor of wooden mallets, saws and various tools of the carpentry trade. Behind them, the dock stretched back to the wide clearing of the pyramid, torches placed at intervals. Holkerm insisted Rodreeg accompany him to oversee the construction and refitting of hundreds of vessels on a nightly ramble while debriefing issues of mobility and logistics. It was the way Holkerm liked to function, constantly juggling tasks and subsequently, accomplishing more than any five men.

The general stopped to inspect a barge modified with a second deck to hold more troops, "Any sign of the caravan yet?"

Rodreeg decided to remove his helmet and hold it under his arm, "Not yet sir, but they are expected any day." His speech was thick with a Somerikan accent. So much so, that Holkerm sometimes found it difficult to understand him.

"Good. How are the men progressing," he asked as he stooped to examine a fitting.

"They're anxious to see battle and the spoils of war."   The major scratched his beard and gazed off into the tree line, "May I ask you a question, sir?"

Holkerm stood up, still looking at the ship, "What is it, Major?"

"Lord Tabeck, sir. What do we know about him? I mean . . . I have gone to war many times, from small border disputes to the survival of nations, but this . . . ?"

Holkerm sighed, a sharp noise hinting at irritation, "Out with it, Major. There are more important matters at hand other than your idle speculation."

Major Rodreeg shifted his feet in a moment of discomfort, "Sir, I mean when there is a border war, there is normally just a

305

wealthy baron buying swords to get his way. When there are this many troops, in a war this great, I'm used to seeing many generals, kings, princes and other nobility behind its construction, its movements and its funding . . . Tabeck is one man and you are one general. Who is this man? None of us have seen him and we only hear from his . . . what are they, priests?"

"Major, the men are stout and fearless, their training superb. Probably one of the finest units I've ever seen, thanks to you and your peers. Maybe Tabeck is only one man, but he's brought this force together and currently has the richest desert kingdoms on their knees, almost singlehandedly. We have but to march this army up and take it, so what is it that disturbs you?"

"Apologies, General. I just feel uneasy, like there is some evil here. I have sensed it from the moment I arrived. Other men have complained too. Like a shadow hanging over us, eyes watching from beyond the leaves. Something ancient and wicked and I think Lord Tabeck knows something about it. I don't trust him."

Holkerm remembered that he also felt the unease from the moment he met Tabeck face-to-face, but wouldn't voice his feelings and create a stir among the men that might turn into sedition. "Major, I think the jungle heat has worn on you. Tabeck has to be a genius. If I would have thought of this . . . well, I'd be a king already. Fortunately for me, Tabeck has promised me that anyway. I just have to wait a little longer."

Rodreeg nodded, "Yes, sir but what does he require of you? He hasn't planned this just to give it all away when it's done."

Truly Holkerm did not know the answer to that question as Tabeck had refused to answer it. He had considered the prospect of just killing Tabeck and completing what he started but some instinct told him to wait. He was considering a response when he heard the scuffing of many sandaled feet coming down the dock.

Shadows stretched long from the gaunt, black robed figures huddled together as they shuffled towards him. Their shaved heads bobbing reminded Holkerm of eggs in a basket, but he resisted a smirk. In their midst was the blood red robe and hood of Lord Tabeck. When the priests (for that was what the general believed they were) halted, they moved apart and Tabeck glided forward. Only the bottom of his chin was visible beneath the hood and his hands were folded under his arms.

Holkerm gave a curt bow, respectful but not self-degrading, "Lord Tabeck, I'm surprised to see you." In fact, it was the first time the eccentric had left the ziggurat that Holkerm was aware of. "What do you think of our progress," he said sweeping his arm over the boats cramming the narrow tributary.

"Impressive," came the low menacing tone of Tabeck's voice, "I knew you were the right choice, General, but I have some reservations about your choice of officers."

Holkerm looked surprised, "The officers I chose from among the men have proven to be reliable. What is your concern?"

"Loyalty, General. Loyalty defined by trust and discipline. How would you deal with a man who questioned your authority, who spread dissension among the others?"

Holkerm made a grave face and stared directly into the folds of Tabeck's hood, "I would have him tied to a pole for spear practice. His own comrades would deal out his sentence. It brings the reality of such punishment closer to home and they will remember it."

"Indeed," said Tabeck. He turned his hood toward Rodreeg, "Indeed." Like a viper striking, Tabeck's hand shot out and stopped inches from Major Rodreeg's face, held out in a claw as if clutching an invisible pomegranate. Holkerm nearly gasped at the unnatural grey hue of his forearm. Slowly, the tendons stood out as Tabeck began to squeeze his fingers together. Rodreeg's helmet clanged to the dock as he clasped his hands to his head and screamed. The two stood within arm's reach; Tabeck continuing to hold his hand out with his fingers straining while the major sank slowly to his knees. Blood oozed from Rodreeg's nose and ears, his screams increasing in pitch as Tabeck chuckled.

"So Major, you think I am some weakling. You believe me to be naive of the fire of conspiracy which passes beneath my temple. Know this, I am no man!" With that, Tabeck made his claw into a fist in one quick movement. Rodreeg's head crumpled in on itself like a crushed melon and he toppled to the dock like a doll.

Holkerm stared in horror as blood and grey matter oozed from Rodreeg's shattered skull.

Tabeck turned on him, "It is a good thing you trust in my abilities, General. I regret the major's demise but it was necessary."

Holkerm shook his head, "Necessary?"

"Yes. I could not have the major creating sedition among the men."

Holkerm's face reddened as his fear subsided ever so slightly. "Disciplining the men is my responsibility, Lord Tabeck."

"Then I recommend you do your job, General. I hope this small demonstration will renew your respect and deter any thoughts of removing me from this great venture." Tabeck turned his back and moved gracefully down the quay to the beachhead with his gaggle of acolytes at his heels.

Holkerm looked down at what was left of Major Rodreeg and an icy finger slid down his spine. What did Tabeck mean, 'I am no man.' Silently Holkerm began to fear the price Tabeck would exact for a kingdom.

CHAPTER 17

The four crewmen left alive on the barge were only too eager to show Shasp and his troopers how to sail the river. As if the value of their lives were not enough, Shasp offered them much more gold than Castella.

Lexia found Caddi hiding in a barrel near the aft deck and when she pulled him out, the little man screamed as if a demon had him by the neck. Shasp assured Caddi he would not be killed if only he would cooperate, however, another misstep like the last would mean a painful death. The old caravan leader had fully expected to be executed in a most unpleasant fashion and blubbered his repentance.

For three more days, they continued to glide along the Azon under the white blossoms of the dripping Banyan trees, before Caddi finally pointed out the tributary leading to their destination. A mile up river from the clearing of the pyramid, the barge eased to the shore and its crew cast mooring lines over branches and around tree trunks.

Shasp ordered his men to don their armor and weapons. He divided them into two groups then called Lexia, Bakarath, Albis and Molgien aside.

He stood in his black and gold armor, legs braced and arms folded, "Bakarath and I have long considered our next move. Castella has never made this trip before, so no one should suspect if I pose as him. Caddi *has* been here before and he *is* expected, but there's no way I would trust him to play a part in our little ruse. Therefore, Bakarath will pose as his replacement. When they ask, he will say Caddi fell deathly ill and is currently recuperating at a village upriver. Half the men will stay with us on the barge, concealing their armor and weapons under caravan robes. Lexia, I want you and Molgien to bring the others through the trees and wait in the jungle about a hundred yards from the clearing. I'll take Albis with me. We'll make an assessment and then I'll send for you. Take as much oil as you can find on board, I think there are three barrels in the hold. When the time is right, we'll destroy as much of the Adder Blossoms as we can, then run for our lives. Any questions?"

Lexia shrugged, "It's the best plan I've heard so far." Albis nodded his agreement while Molgien waited patiently for Shasp to translate. Bakarath only stood at the bow; chin in hand, in thoughtful repose, "If I am going to pretend to be related to Caddi, I'll need a name. I've always liked Agrafar."

Shasp's lips curled in a wry smile, "You know, for a stoic old spy, you're sort of a crazy bastard."

Bakarath raised his eyebrows with new contemplation, "Hhmm . . . One would have to be a little mad just to be a spy, don't you think?"

The afternoon sun sparkled on the water as the barge slid past the long line of boats moored against make-shift docks. Nearby, Shasp could see a vast force, thousands of soldiers drilling relentlessly and beyond that, fields. Boat wrights and carpenters looked up briefly from their work to watch the new arrival and then returned to their labor. Near the middle of the line, a dock sat empty and a contingent of armored hoplites waited upon it.

Shasp examined them from the helm as they stood in a disciplined formation, spear points fixed skyward. The armor and weapons were uniform, their bearing professional. These were not the same wild creatures from the Tetas River battle.

Carefully, he guided the barge in and ground it against the dock while his men tossed mooring lines to the waiting soldiers. A few moments later, the leader of the squad crossed the gang plank to the deck. Bakarath met him and bowed, "Welcome aboard."

The black clad warrior eyed him, "The general has been waiting for you, Caddi, isn't it?

Bakarath bowed again, "Sorry, but it is not. I am Agrafar, Caddi's cousin. I'm afraid we had an unfortunate chain of events. You see, Caddi fell ill and we had to put to shore at a village on the river for a while. When it became apparent that he was only worsening, he commanded me to continue with the cargo so it would not arrive any later. I still fear the worst for him and we are all anxious to return. Please give the general my most humble apologies. I will have my crew offload the cargo immediately."

The squad leader nodded, "My men will assist you," and he motioned to the ranks of men, who left their spears on the dock in an orderly fashion. They marched onto the plank and into the hold where they returned with crates and chests. Shasp grumbled and shouted at his men in a way that he hoped would seem like Castella then approached the hoplite.

"Sir, would it be possible for me and my men to rest our legs on land for a while? We've been on the river a long time."

"Just stay away from the training grounds and out of the way of the construction. The general deals harshly with troublemakers, so warn your crew."

Shasp nodded and returned to yelling orders. As the unloading neared completion, a runner came down the docks and hailed the squad leader.

"Sergeant Serano, Lord Tabeck wants to see the caravan leader. I guess he wants to know what took so long."

"And where is Lord Tabeck?" Serano asked.

The messenger pointed to the pyramid, "There."

Serano turned to Bakarath, "You heard him, Agrafar, let's go."

Shasp and Bakarath exchanged worried glances, but the old spy gave a nod of assurance and left the ship with the squad falling in behind, feet tramping down the dock.

Shasp caught Albis by the shoulder, "I'm going to look around. Have the men work on the ship, put on a good show. I'll be back as soon as I finish checking the area." He patted his sergeant on the shoulder, "Any sign of trouble, you get the hell out of here, understand?"

"Aye, Lieutenant."

Shasp dropped off the gang plank and made his way south along the shore, past the nearly completed armada, until he left the practice field behind. The clearing was enormous, almost four miles wide and deep. Rock and gravel gave way to grass, and eventually, fields. Here, a few downcast natives labored, picking the few remaining black flowers. The rest of the fields were remnants of golden stalks all the way to the jungle's edge. He looked around, not sure what he expected to see, but saw no more of the Adder Blossom. Moving through the whispering stalks he approached a haggard, swarthy woman dressed in only a grass skirt and naked from the waist up. Stooping under a coarse bag of petals, she stopped her labor and gave him a frightened look, as if she expected to be struck. Shasp tilted his head and spoke in Somerikan. "Where are all the flowers?" The question was simple enough, but the old woman only shook her head and backed up, causing Shasp to wonder if she even understood him. The old woman appeared to be part of a native jungle tribe and most likely spoke some dialect far removed from Somerikan. He plucked a blossom and held it up, then shrugged while looking around in a gesture he hoped would convey his question. With suspicious eyes she pointed a gnarled finger toward a large outbuilding near the docks. Shasp nodded his understanding and headed for the structure. As he left, he checked over his shoulder, half afraid the slave would bolt for the nearest guard, but saw she had simply returned to her work.

Shasp approached the out building from behind, trying to shield himself from view, and eased around the corner. More of the natives were dumping sacks of the flowers into the building. So the harvest was over, he mused. Shasp looked back toward the drill field and again the contrast of the two armies played on his mind, but he could not solve the puzzle. One army, a seething mob of addicts and another of professional mercenaries. There did not appear to be any more planting of the blossom to continue with a second harvest. The drug was still going north, but it seemed the building held the last of it. Why? Then realization came. The Black Tide in the field against Salsida and Laveg would come apart without a steady flow of Adder Blossom. The ships under construction were, obviously, meant to bring the new army north to replace the old one. "So," he said under his breath, "the old army was expendable. The drug swept through all the towns and villages of Attah creating a rebel army so fast the nobility couldn't react. But it was never meant to last." Shasp flushed with anger as he realized the injustice done to all those who fell victim to the Adder Blossom. Their lives were over from the moment the petal touched their lips, just as certain as if they had been executed on the spot.

The structure was the only storehouse he could see near the fields and he assumed all the flowers were there. A quick reconnaissance of the docks told him the ships were only a few days away from completion. The new Tide would soon be underway to attack the weakened cities of the desert, but the stock of Adder Blossom must leave first to bolster the army in the field until the fresh troops could arrive. Silently, he pondered the force behind the war's inception as he had a hundred times before. Someone had paid Holkerm to defect, but the general was long gone, and with him, any answer to that question. He considered the name Sergeant Serano repeated, 'Lord Tabeck,' but it never rang in his memory. Shasp found his way back to the barge where an anxious Albis waited. Ironwrought stiffened at his worried expression, "What is it, Sergeant?"

"Bakarath hasn't returned and I have a feeling in my bones that something is wrong."

"I better go find him. In the meantime, send Pieter to find Lexia. About a quarter mile down the beach there's a large outbuilding where the Adder Blossom is stored. Tell her to wait until dark then work their way along the edge of the clearing and come in from the south. Burn it and get back to the barge."

He turned to go, but Albis stopped him, "What if you're not back?"

Shasp smiled, "I'll be back . . . but if I'm not, get the hell out of here and have a good life." He strode down the dock, his white robe fluttering in the humid breeze.

Bakarath climbed the steps of the ancient pyramid with a sense of trepidation and entered the doorway at its apex. Cool, damp air greeted him as they descended into the bowels of the structure. He studied the stone steps, worn by centuries of scuffing feet, and wondered what civilization had created it. Slowly, the squad progressed down a narrow corridor, shouldering past Black Tide officers on their way out, until they came to a deep, low-ceilinged chamber. The guard outside the door made them wait for long minutes before another came to take them inside. Within, several men, wearing lacquered breastplates and greaves, hovered over maps strewn on a long table. Behind them, a robed figure reclined on a chair of carved obsidian. Oil lamps were stingy with their light, refusing to reveal all the details of the room and leaving most of it in shadow. The robed man addressed Bakarath from under his hood with a condescending voice of disapproval. "So . . . you are the master of the caravan?"

Bakarath nodded, "Yes, I am."

"Where is Caddi and why are you so late in arriving?"

Bakarath cleared his throat, "I am Agrafar, cousin to Caddi. I came with him at his request but he grew gravely ill along the way.

We had to harbor at a village, but he insisted we leave him there to recover so we would not be any later with the cargo. My most humble apologies."

A deep chuckle came from behind the robed man and a large figure emerged from the shadows, "You always could spin a fine story, Bakarath."

Bakarath's eyes narrowed as General Holkerm stepped to the side of the obsidian throne. He knew the general well. Many times they had sat across from one another discussing the security of Alafar's kingdom. Now the traitor was standing next to . . . who? He shook off his surprise and retorted, "General Holkerm. I would like to say it's nice to see you again, but . . . ," he shrugged. "This must be your new benefactor. I can't say you have moved up in the world. A sultan's palace for this?"

"This is only temporary. Soon, I *will* be the sultan, but you . . . . I think you will be dead. I must admit, I was surprised to see you standing on the dock with Sergeant Serano. Why are you here?"

Bakarath realized if Holkerm had found out about him, he might also suspect the crew and order them killed before they could complete the mission and get away. Shasp was wise to keep the others hidden in the jungle. Quickly his mind worked, "I came to find the source of the Black Tide's power. The sultan insisted I bring a force of men, but I convinced him I should come alone. I found out about Caddi's part in transporting the blossom, killed him, and then hired this crew to bring me here. I thought the fewer who knew I was coming the better. I was to return and inform the sultan so he could plan an attack."

Holkerm's smile faded, "Your luck isn't too good these days."

"So it would seem, but I'm curious," he said turning to Tabeck, "are you the one behind all this? I could never believe Holkerm was ambitious enough to imagine a scheme of such grandeur."

Holkerm growled and started forward but Tabeck held up a hand, "You would be correct in your assumption. I am Lord Tabeck. I tell you that because you will die soon."

Bakarath put on his best diplomatic face while his brain continued to form a plan of escape, "Since you feel so inclined to indulge my foolish questions, perhaps you would also be so

314

generous as to enlighten me as to how all this began. The sultan certainly did not see it coming." Bakarath chose his words carefully, hoping his humble demeanor mixed with acknowledgment of Tabeck's superiority would keep the man talking long enough to buy some time.

The officers had stopped their examination of the maps when Tabeck first spoke and now stood by anxiously hoping to hear Bakarath's question answered.

Tabeck leaned forward, "So you wish to hear my story. Very well, it is time to tell it. I am sure General Holkerm will appreciate what I am about to say, and I doubt the conscience of these officers will keep them awake as long as the gold flows.

"A long time ago, in this very place, a vast city thrived and this temple was its center. The people were all warriors, a fierce and proud race who dominated all those around them. They invaded new lands and brought back wealth and slaves to lavish on the source of their strength, the guardian of the gates of the underworld, Mal. Mal spoke to his warrior-priests in visions and dreams, bending them to his will and giving them strength. They considered it an honor to be sacrificed and as part of the ritual, would take the Adder Blossom to assist them on their journey to the underworld. One warrior-priest, their greatest, had a dream; a vision. He would take the armies of the jungle north to conquer the kingdoms of the desert. He was told to show them the might of Mal. This priest assembled the armies and planned with great care. When the time came, he sent the Adder Blossom north to enslave the minds of their unsuspecting enemies. He controlled them from afar through agents until all the great kingdoms were in chaos. He led his forces out of the jungle and swept over these nations like a storm. Oh, it was a glorious time; a time of conquest and blood. When his enemies were decimated, he brought their wealth and people back here and made a great sacrifice.   He believed in his heart he had done a great service, but that night, as he dreamed he met his enraged master. Mal told him he was a failure for misinterpreting his will. The priest was supposed to have enslaved the desert cities and brought them the religion of the underworld. Instead, he had destroyed them. Mal, in his anger, brought a great plague upon this place slaying nearly everyone. The priest, knowing the fault was his, ordered himself sacrificed in atonement. He took a lethal dose of the Adder Blossom and commanded his acolytes to remove his heart. The knife plunged down and he felt them reach under his ribs and pull the beating organ from his body. As the light of life was fading from his eyes, a black cloud poured from this temple and filled his lungs. In his death throes he hardly realized what was happening when the other priests dragged him into the depths of this pyramid where they sealed him in a tomb, still alive. It seemed they also had dreams that commanded them; dreams he knew nothing about. Centuries passed and with them, madness. Madness you could never begin to imagine. Madness which slowly turned in on itself and became a component of the mind. When a jungle native stumbled upon the tomb seeking treasure and opened it, he found me instead.

"I will not fail again. I will bring the religion of Mal to all the northern kingdoms and redeem myself." He turned to Holkerm who stood in wonderment, sweat beading his bald head. "That is the price of your kingdom, and you will keep your bargain if you do not wish to become as Major Rodreeg."

Bakarath was a rational man, but Tabeck's story was insane, "Are you saying it was you who was responsible for the destruction of the desert kingdoms four hundred years ago? You are mad." As he listened, Bakarath realized there was no way out of the pyramid and he was facing a torturous death. Better to kill this madman, destroy his plans in one fell swoop and be cut down mercifully in the bargain. Slowly he sidled near the obsidian chair as he continued his dialogue, "Yes you have mimicked the plan of your ancestors, if that's what they were, but still you are only a man, for you could be nothing else. And, like any other man, you can die, and your plans with you."

Like a flash of lightning, Bakarath ripped his hidden scimitar from under his robes and leapt at Tabeck. Before anyone could stop him, the blade thrust out and pierced Tabeck's chest. Bakarath stood frozen like the others looking at the sword which ran through Tabeck's sternum and chipped the back of the throne. Tabeck's head dropped to examine the blade which should have ended his life, and then he looked up, allowing Bakarath to gaze into the folds of the hood. Slowly, Tabeck raised his hand and drew back the hood, evoking a gasp of horror from every man in the room. His skin had the grey pallor of a corpse and his black hair bristled like a boar, but that was not what froze these men with terror. Indeed, it was his glowing red eyes; eyes of malice and hate. He held his hand up and Bakarath felt himself lifted off his feet, unable to let go of his sword. Slowly he drifted backward, hanging in the air, until the scimitar came free of Tabeck's body, as cleanly as the moment it had left the sheath. The priest of Mal stood, holding Bakarath in his giant, invisible hand, "Now you see, don't you, spy? Only here, at the moment of your death, do you understand the power of my master and the futility of your mission."

Bakarath, frozen, spat out his reply, "You can tell Mal to go to hell!"

Tabeck laughed, "I don't need to. You just did.   Don't you understand? I am Mal and Mal is Tabeck."   Slowly he squeezed his hand closed and Bakarath cried out under tremendous pressure. His ribs were pressed in, snapping as the air was forced from his lungs as if he lay under a massive stone. His vision blurred and all became agony. Through the haze of pain he sensed a sudden commotion and the supernatural grip was released. He crumpled to the ground, blood dribbling from his lips, ragged breaths escaping his tortured lungs. Bakarath shook his head and looked around the hazy room, blinking. One guard lay outside the door while another lay inside, prone and bleeding. Two men dressed in Black Tide armor exchanged vicious sword thrusts; one was quickly vanquished and fell to the floor holding the stump of his sword arm. Bakarath's head cleared a little more and he began to see differences. The victor wore the crested open-face helm and his armor was black, but with gold pauldrons and reliefs. His sword was the unique Ayponese katana. Shasp tore the Tide helmet from his head and came between Tabeck and Bakarath, sword wavering. "You couldn't have picked a worse time, old friend."

"Lieutenant Ironwrought?" came the surprised voice of General Holkerm, "What in the hell are you doing here!"

"Well, well, if it isn't the traitor from the Tetas River," said Shasp.

Tabeck's voice rang out, "Silence! Is this another of your loose ends, General?"

"He was the lieutenant in charge of one of the foreign cavalry units at the Tetas. I thought him dead."

"Happy to disappoint you, General," said Shasp.

Tabeck roared and thrust his hand out toward Shasp.

Ironwrought was forced back, feet sliding against the stone, but he remained upright, growling in anger. Tabeck made a frustrated grunt and brought up his other hand. For the first time, the warrior-priest saw that something was clenched in Shasp's other hand; a leather thong hanging from his fist. Holkerm screamed at the officers, "Don't just stand there you fools!"

The first officer to shake off his amazement was also the next one to die under the katana. Immediately it became apparent to Tabeck that the talisman Shasp held was powerful, but not strong enough to completely break his power. The two were in a stalemate. The rest of the Black Tide officers crowded together in an attempt to bring down the infiltrator, but the confines of the room made it difficult for them to attack. Shasp cut them down one at a time, but Tabeck's continued force was like a great weight on his chest and his breath became labored. "Bakarath! Get up, damn it; let's get out of here!"

Bakarath struggled to his feet, "Shasp, run! Leave me!"

"No, damn it! Come on!"

But instead of fleeing through the door, Bakarath lifted his scimitar and slashed at Tabeck, hoping his power would leave him with his severed head. The blade arced down and bit into the priest's neck, but Tabeck was quick to redirect his power and keep the weapon from slicing the rest of the way through. Shasp felt the weight lift from him and saw Bakarath trapped once again in Tabeck's crushing power.

Bakarath screamed in pain, "Run, you dammed fool!   Run!" Then the sound of bones breaking and the sickening gush of fluids carried across the room and Shasp knew his friend was dead.

Shasp heard the tramp of feet coming from behind him. If he was caught in this narrow room, between two forces, he would surely die. He made a parting slash, splitting open an officer's eye socket, then spun and ran. At breakneck speed, he vaulted down the dusty corridors toward the opening and collided with four guards coming the other way. His momentum bowled the group down into a cluster which he scrambled through. The pursuing officers had to untangle themselves to follow, and Shasp made some headway as he sprinted out through the exit. Two surprised guards exchanged confused looks as he bolted past them, but it wasn't until he was halfway down the steps that the enraged officers also poured out and one snatched a spear from the guard's hand.

Shasp felt the steel warhead bite into his hamstring and he toppled down several steps, dislodging the spear from his leg. Without missing a beat, he was on his feet again at a dead run, blood oozing inside his armor, pain stabbing his mind with every footfall. In the distance, toward the beach, he saw smoke and flames rising into the deepening sky. Lexia had done her job and the last of the Adder Blossom was blazing away, its ashes rising. As he approached the shore, he could see a tangle of ships clustered in the middle of the river, two were ablaze. Just a few yards up river he saw the barge, still tied to the dock, and all his men fighting to keep the Black Tide soldiers from swarming aboard. More soldiers were pouring into the fray. Lexia hung from the yard arm searching the clearing and he knew she searched for him. Shasp landed on the docks, hacking through the backs of the unsuspecting warriors until he made it to the ship. Lexia yelled over the clamor of battle and ringing steel to push off. Shasp leapt across the span of water which opened between them and barely caught the rail when another spear hit him like a hammer just below his pauldron. He cried out and his grip slipped from the rail but Molgien's massive hand shot down, snatching him from a certain drowning. The cannibal hauled him aboard with one hand as if he were a child while two others protected them with overlapped shields. The rest heaved on the oars with all their strength and the ponderous boat slowly surged into the center of the tributary, then north.

Lexia was on the deck in a flash, rolling Shasp onto his side to examine the spear jutting from his back. She parted the torn chain mail around the warhead's tip and tested it by moving the shaft slightly. Shasp cursed, "Damn it, Lexia! Either pull it out or leave it, but don't play with it!"

Lexia leaned over his shoulder to whisper in his ear, "It's in your shoulder blade and a good thing too or it might have punctured something important. It may have anyway." She sat back on the deck and placed her feet against Shasp's back, then seized the spear haft and pulled. Shasp screamed through clenched teeth as the spear held for a few seconds then came away. Lexia tossed the weapon aside and examined the wound to see if there was any bright blood flow. Then she placed her ear to his back and listened for wheezing or gurgling. She sat back and Shasp rolled onto his back, blinking at the

319

fingers of spreading canopy.

"You'll be ok, I think. Just make sure you keep the wound clean. That fancy armor saved your life. A long silence followed before she spoke again with concern in her voice, "Where is Bakarath?"

Shasp groaned and struggled to sit up, "Dead. The sonofabitch killed him. I would be dead too if not for . . . ," he fumbled with the stone at his neck then looked back over the stern to see the flaming ships dwindle as the barge pulled away. Lexia frowned and sighed, then looked toward the clearing, "I liked him," was all she said.

Shasp shared the silence with her for a long moment and pointed toward the confusion of ships, "Nice work.   Bakarath would be proud."

"I knew they weren't going to just let us leave after we torched their stock of petals, so I had Albis and Pieter lead a band to take a few boats out and block the river so we could get away. They only had to contest with a few carpenters."

He smiled at her, "Good thinking," he said, "but now we have to get to Salsida as fast as possible. Holkerm and Tabeck will know they have to step things up and that army of addicts might come apart about the time we arrive. If the desert kingdoms are going to stand a chance, we will need to act quickly. The old spy gave his life for his king and country and we need to make sure it wasn't in vain."

Her eyes narrowed, "Holkerm? General Holkerm?   And who is Tabeck?"

"Is there another Holkerm? And Tabeck is some kind of . . . I don't know . . . creature, necromancer or something.   He's behind all this. I saw Bakarath give him two mortal wounds, but he didn't die." He unstrapped his thigh guard and unlaced the mail legging beneath it, revealing the gaping wound in his hamstring, "How are you with sutures?"

"What do you mean; he didn't die," asked Lexia, "what the hell is he?"

"Exactly . . .what the hell."

Days passed on the Ile River to the sound of dipping oars or the snap of wind in the sail. Slowly, the jungle thinned and the banyan trees were left behind as the barge moved toward the desert regions. Trees became twisted and the vegetation scarce until finally there was no green at all save that which clung to the river's shore or along the irrigation canals of small villages.

The sun burned down on the cavalry troop as they took turns bending their backs to the oars. Shasp rowed with them, but pulled only with his left arm. His shoulder needed to heal for battle and that would come soon enough. Eventually the Ile conceded to the strength of the Tetas as they heaved the vessel north into the broadening body of water.

Caddi had been marooned in a small village near the fork, life intact.

The quiet of the surroundings, wind and water mixed with time, gave Lexia ample opportunity to reflect on the past months. She finished her turn at the oars and lay down on the deck in the shade of the sail which hung limp. Sweat glistened on her strong limbs as she lifted her head and glanced around to find Shasp watching her. They traded shy smiles and he came over to sit next to her, saying nothing. In all the time she spent with the man, he said little to her about who he was, where he was from or why he involved himself in someone else's fight. He was an enigma, not the massive, brawny axe wielding man her tribe spawned, but there was no doubt in her mind, he could master them all. The armor and sword were like nothing she had ever seen and neither was he. She had always known, from the moment she first met him, there was a fascination. She had tried to convince herself she disliked him at first, but could not deny the intense attraction. Shasp lay down next to her, looked up into the blue sky and placed his hand on hers. It was a tender gesture that surprised her and she felt a stirring warmth in her chest, a feeling that frightened her just a little. Then a loud crack filled the air and the sail snapped taut. The rowers cheered over the welcome rest the wind would bring.

More windy days came and went, propelling them up the Tetas until they came to the Keddi Mountain range. The men became quiet as they remembered the place where they barely escaped annihilation.

Large jagged precipices of reddish rock loomed overhead, making the massive barge seem like a tiny insect. A ribbon of blue sky was all that was visible from within the narrow chasm, cut by the mighty Tetas. By the end of the day, the melancholia of the men peaked as they glided by the remnants of the battlefield where they had been betrayed by General Holkerm. Twisted piles of the dead were mixed with the faded red rags of Evatan uniforms and the scraps of black armor left behind by the Tide. Vultures and jackals had picked the bodies clean, leaving only grinning skulls and pickets of bone. As the macabre scene slid by, the men stood silently at the rail and each of them wondered if a particular skull might be an old friend or former officer. Each knew that the memory of this part of the voyage would return to haunt them for the rest of their lives. Pieter suddenly jumped up on the rail and dove over the side, swimming for the shore. Shasp yelled to strike the sail and toss anchor but they were a hundred yards gone before the ship halted. He leapt up to the stern and looked back for the lanky corporal in time to see him in the distance. Pieter made the shore and ran up the beach between the wrestling dead, stopping in front of a standard still upright in the sand, a ragged red banner flapping in the breeze. He pulled it free and ran back along the shore, past the barge and then swam again for the boat, letting the current carry him out and toward his awaiting comrades. A line dropped into the water and Pieter caught it, handed up the standard, and then climbed back on board. Shasp thought about scolding him, but couldn't bring himself to do it. Instead he clapped a hand on the corporal's wet shoulder and nodded his understanding.

CHAPTER 18

Nachmed strode among his citizen soldiers as they sparred and drilled in the square. Any of the buildings which had been flattened had been removed to create room for the transition from frightened town's people to a trained force. Here a guardsman showed an old woman how to step on a spear butt. There, another soldier showed a boy of no more than fourteen winters how to stab under a shield. The king was amazed to see the frightened rabble evolve over the last few weeks. Every waking moment was spent in training for war and everyone was slowly forgetting who they had been.   Baker, shop keeper, blacksmith, washing woman or street urchin, they were all warriors now. Momad said he had never seen any group of men train with the intensity and seriousness of these men and women. No doubt, because the reality of death knocking at their gates had motivated them with a fury.

Most had armor now, though gray and ill fitting, for the smithies had been working feverishly to smelt all the metal they could find and make at least a few pieces for every citizen.

Some of the people who were too old even to lift a sword had busied themselves sewing uniforms for the unorthodox army; the colors of Attah, blue and white, though they were a patchwork. Even now, the majority wore the colors of their nation. Nachmed's heart filled as he watched them. Here near the end, he found a pride in his people he had never known before.

A high-pitched voice cut the air, "Sire! Sire! Lord Nachmed!"

Nachmed turned to see a child running toward him, a runner from the walls. "What news?"

"General Momad asks for you on the southern wall.   He says to come quickly."

Nachmed scooped up the child and moved to the foot of the wall, then ran up the stairs to the battlements where he found Momad leaning on the stone lip with a spyglass stuck to his eye.

"What is it, General?"

Momad shook his head, "Not sure, Majesty. Maybe you should take a look. My eyes aren't what they used to be, but I think something is happening in the enemy camp."

323

Nachmed took the glass and peered through it. In the oval of the lens he saw smoke and horses churning with the men. It seemed some of the camp was in a disorder greater than usual. Some Tide soldiers were riding in force among their own, striking down men where they clotted together in knots. As he continued to watch, he realized there was some level of sedition in the camp and not a small amount. He snapped the glass shut, "Looks like they are having some difficulties holding their men together, General. What say we give them some more trouble?"

Momad wrinkled his forehead, "Do you think our forces are ready for that?"

Nachmed was already walking away, "I doubt if there will be a better time. The Tide is in disarray and our own rations are nearly gone. Better to hit them now while our people have strength and the enemy is confused. They will never expect it."

"Our people or the enemy," asked Momad?

"Either."

The Attahn forces marched out through the gates of Salsida in twenty-one tight phalanxes of three hundred soldiers each. Momad mixed the veterans with the citizen soldiers to bolster their resolve, hoping that, with a veteran next to them, they would not flee. Nachmed had no doubt they would stand and fight. Six thousand were infantry as most of the horses had already been eaten and there could be no cavalry. Long pikes bristled along the front and flanks to slow any cavalry onslaught while five hundred archers were mixed into every third row. When the battle ensued, they could fire nearly point blank. When those ranks went down there would always be a fresh barrage of missile fire. As the infantry receded the archers would fall back through the ranks and become more concentrated, bringing on a deadly hail of broad heads.

The force moved out rapidly, taking advantage of the Tides confusion. The drums beat a quicker rhythm and the tramp of feet kept up with the staccato until the huge grid of Attahn soldiers were nearly to the Black Tide Camp. Skinny, bare-skinned runners looked up from their chores, saw the force and heard the drums, then ran.

Tide warriors scrambled for gear and weapons, making small, hastily constructed cells which quickly formed into larger ones, but without leadership. They swarmed out, eyes wide with reckless abandon. Unkempt hair flying, they threw themselves against the wall of pikes, dragging the tips down. One after another, they slammed into the clattering spears, screaming hateful death cries.   Nachmed's herald waved a flag at his signal and arrows whispered through the air.

The black army began pouring out, but not in the force Nachmed had seen before. Streams of howling maniacs condensed into a wall along the Attahn front, but the citizens fought with a ferocity matching the madness of the Adder Blossom. With a wave of another flag, the Attahn archers fell back through the ranks while General Momad led several forces out from the rear to attack the east flank. Within minutes three quarters of the Tide force had been surrounded and, with no clear front, the blue and white began to force a wedge through their sides and front. The herald waved the flag again and Acharis, one of Nachmed's colonels, took another force around the enemy's west flank. It had nearly arrived and finished the encapsulation when the thunder of hooves shook the ground beneath their feet. Black tide cavalry burst through the canvas walls of tents and impromptu structures to crash against Acharis' troops. It appeared that some of the Tide soldiers finally had the sense to gather a force of cavalry before entering the fray. The Attahn line folded under the irresistible storm of horseflesh and sabers. They fell beneath the churning hooves and were thrown against their comrades as the black cavalry surged in and quickly split the Attahn infantry apart. A large hairy man in the middle of the horses, apparently their leader, signaled for part of the force to break off and intervene at the front. Nachmed whispered under his breath, "No. No." But the painted black horses were already pushing through their own men and grinding his front beneath their steel-shod hooves. His citizen army was slowly falling back beneath the superior power of cavalry. 'No matter', he thought, 'we will fight to the death and take many of these howling demons with us.' The crush continued and blood soaked the earth beneath feet and hooves. All, it seemed, was lost.

Nachmed forced his way through the ranks to the front. His command no longer had any meaning in the battle, so he split a hairy head with his scimitar. At least he would die a king and a warrior. Blood splattered his armor and face, matted in his tawny hair. To his left and right, man after man fell, but he stayed and new comrades came to his side. His arm ached, the stench of blood and excrement filled his nostrils, but the killing went on and on. Glancing around him, he quickly saw his phalanxes dwindling, dissolving into a mass. It wouldn't be long now. Suddenly, a horn blasted over the din of battle, then another. He risked another glance and saw more horsemen crest a low ridge near the city's west wall. It could only be more black cavalry, he thought, and felt the sinking resolve of certain death, however, something unexpected happened. The small force of cavalry smashed into the Tide's west flank and began trampling and hacking. The enemy milled uncertainly, unaware of the newcomer's presence until hoof or sword ended their lives. The unit formed another wedge in the heart of the Black Tide infantry and trampled its way through to the Attahn front where it drove into the back of the Black Tide cavalry. At its head, a figure in black and gold armor spun his black charger and whirled a long narrow blade overhead. His small force broke through to the Attahns, dividing the enemy's cavalry line.

Nachmed recognized the opportunity and called his men to form up behind the troop of horsemen. The riders spun back toward the fractured Tide front and struck spur to flesh. The horses lunged in, crushing the foot soldiers under hoof while Attahn infantry filled in behind. The wedge came together again and stabbed once more into the heart of the enemy army, dividing the mass. Occasionally, Nachmed caught sight of the black and gold armored rider. His blade flashed like a scythe, streaming a trail of blood and bone. The Tide horses milled among their own dissolving into pools as the Attahn phalanx began to regroup.

Momad's men had made good progress, but floundered when the Black Tide riders appeared. They brought all the pikes forward and formed a barrier, hoping Nachmed's and Achris' forces would push the enemy into them. When he saw the friendly horsemen arrive and felt the release of pressure from the line, he ordered his men to swords and they hacked into the mob. Now it was the Black Tide who was in trouble, their force breaking up into smaller cells which were quickly overwhelmed. The raging madness which drove its warriors into combat was slowly transformed into extreme fear. Men dropped their weapons and fled into the deadly arms of the parched Abi desert, while Attahn archers used them as target practice. When the rest were routed, Shasp ordered his men to run down the cavalry and bring back as many horses as possible, then he rode back to where Nachmed waited. The king was leaning on his knees, panting as gore dripped from his armor.

"Just when I thought all was lost," he said. "Who are you?

Shasp lifted his helmet from his head revealing his scarred face, "Shasp Ironwrought, lieutenant in charge of the Evatan Foreign Company."

Nachmed straitened, "Evatan regiment? I have heard nothing from Laveg. I thought them overrun by the Tide after the battle of the Tetas. We would have come to your aid there, but were under siege."

Shasp looked back at the cloud of pursuing men, "For all I know, Laveg is still under siege, but things are about to get worse. There is a force of about fifteen-thousand more Black Tide on its way here. Not the crazed fools we fought here today, but a trained and disciplined army."

Nachmed was awestruck, "How do you know this?"

"I saw them," said Shasp, "coming out of Somerika, led by a madman and with General Holkerm. We need to mobilize what's left of your army and march to Laveg."

Nachmed shook his head, "Army? What army?   This force is comprised mostly of old men and children. Only a third of them are tested soldiers and most of them are half-starved. Now you want me to tell them we have to march across the Trabic to Laveg to protect Sultan Alafar's kingdom? He laughed.

"If you don't, your people will be slaves to a dark cult and your city destroyed. You have no choice! At least let me talk to your father, the king. Maybe I can reason with him."

Nachmed's face fell, "I am the king now, Nachmed. My father is dead, killed during the siege."

Shasp threw up his arms and turned his back on Nachmed, who didn't seem to notice the affront or else did not care. "Well Nachmed, your army may be old men, women and children, but they certainly did a hell of a job today," and he began to walk away.

Nachmed called out, "Wait, Ironwrought! I will reason with you . . . as, I know, my father would have. It's just; I don't know how they can make it to Laveg."

Shasp turned and smiled then swept his arm across the smoking Black Tide camp, "There will be plenty of food and water

327

there. Between that and what is left in the city, we can make it. Laveg is well fortified and Alafar will welcome you."

Nachmed nodded, "What choice do we have?"

"None," said Shasp.

Shasp's men brought back another fifty horses, and Nachmed turned them over to his cavalry commander. They walked through the enemy camp when the others returned from the pursuit and saw what had caused the commotion among the enemy. Bodies lay piled in various stages of decay, white skin-stretched corpses. Shasp explained the effects of the Adder Blossom to Nachmed and what happened when the user had no more drug. Shasp thought he should have been pleased by the impact his raid had on the enemy by cutting off the supply of the black blossom, but instead he felt pity for the hapless victims who fell under its power. When Nachmed left to rally his forces and make arrangements for the logistics of the march, Shasp continued to wander through the camp. As he ambled on, he spotted Lexia standing at the edge of the battle-strewn field, looking toward the desert. He eased alongside her, already knowing her thoughts and placed his hand around her blood-splattered waist. She had fought ferociously beside him that day.

"I was almost one of them," she said, "one of those starved soulless soldiers . . . not soldiers . . . people."

"Almost," returned Shasp, "but you aren't now."

She turned and brought her blood-flecked face close to his and kissed him, "I'm not because you saved me. You gave me back my dignity and let me be a warrior again."

"No Lexia, you gave that to yourself. Come on, we have a lot to do, and a long way to go."

She shook her head, "Is there no end to this?"

"There will be soon enough."

CHAPTER 19

The stench of smoke and blood hung heavy in the haze of the battle's aftermath. Corpses and debris littered the ground for hundreds of yards in all directions. The desert vultures circled and dropped, feasting on a sea of bloating humanity.

Tabeck had traded his red robe for the armor of the Black Tide, yet still wore a red cloak to distinguish himself. He strode among the dead and apathetically kicked a limb away with his booted toe. Bright, blood-red eyes swept over the seen. He breathed in the odor of death and smirked with satisfaction. Holkerm's face bore a pained expression, a mixture of surprise and disgust. He was surprised at Tabeck's indifference over the destruction of the camp and their vanishing quarry. He was disgusted because the general understood he would lose men in combat, but Tabeck gloried in it.

Tabeck knelt on one knee, closed his eyes and let his hand hover over the ground. "Your lieutenant has been here, Holkerm," he hissed then slowly straightened. "Who is this mercenary that vexes me so?"

Holkerm shifted uneasily, "I don't know much about him. He wandered in looking for a commission and proved to be capable enough; never talked much."

"I see, and have you any inkling where the inhabitants of Salsida went?"

"He might be organizing them to ambush us in the desert, but there's always the possibility the king decided to seek refuge in the North."

Tabeck snorted, "North? North!" he waved his grey arm, "and all this? Wouldn't the king naturally assume he'd won a great victory here? Why is he not in the confines of his city, feasting and drinking?"

General Holkerm was silent for a moment, "Because he knew we were coming," he said flatly.

"Yes, General, he knew. He knew because your former cavalry commander told him after he arrived and assisted with the slaughter of our army."

Holkerm was certain he would feel the crushing force of Tabeck's evil power upon his skull. He sweated in expectation, but instead, Tabeck chuckled.

"Put your mind at ease, General, before you faint. The Salsidian army is on its way to Laveg and we will crush it there just as easily as we would have defeated it here. That is, if you are half the tactician my sources say you are."

Holkerm felt the weight of his impending death lift, "I . . . I will send scouts to determine their lead. We may be able to overtake them before they make it to Laveg."

"It doesn't matter. We will strike for Laveg in the morning, commander." Tabeck walked away leaving Holkerm to his tasks.

It was the middle of the night when Ababul rode in from the desert. He was tired and pissed, the way he always was when he didn't receive the flower on time. The presence of an unknown army marching across the Trabic toward his camp did not help his sense of humor.

When the last caravan failed to arrive, the taskmasters began rationing the black flower and, for the last several weeks, had trouble managing his tumultuous Black Tide brothers and sisters. Many had been killed as examples to keep the army from exploding with mutiny. As far as Ababul was concerned, it only worsened the problem. They all needed more of the flower's strength and many of them were prepared to take it. It called to them, day and night, and the lack of it only made the call that much stronger.

The walls of Laveg loomed in the distance several hundred yards from the Tide camp. Its marble guardians watched their every move as soldiers hovered at the shoulders of the giant statues, watching with them. It unnerved him more than he liked to admit, and added to his difficulty in concentrating. Inwardly, he knew it was the blossom which had reduced him to the savage he had become, but he didn't care anymore. Life had become a constant desire for the flower and the pleasure it promised. A desire which he could no longer fulfill; a promise that evaporated like water on a desert rock. It hurt his head to think about it. Now he needed the petals just to feel alive or some semblance of life.

He made his way through the mob of fighting, copulating male and female warriors, through the disordered maze of dirty canvas tents. The constant odor of unwashed bodies and feces, which he had become accustomed to, hung thick in the air. Sitting in front of a large red tent, a taskmaster ate slop from a wooden bowl, never bothering to look up at Ababul. "What is it, scout?"

Ababul scowled at the condescending tone, "Nothing much, just an army of over four thousand troops, only a day out."

The taskmaster stopped eating and slowly leered up at Ababul through his shaggy black mane, "An army? Heading toward us now," he stated more than asked. "This had better not be some kind of joke."

Ababul bent and lifted a dusty crust of bread from the table, "No joke, master," he said nibbling at it with crumbling teeth, another gift from the flower. "I saw them near the Keddi pass, coming in from the northern Trabic."

The burly officer stood so abruptly, his chair tumbled over. He swatted a fellow task man next to him, "Sound assembly and divide the companies! Move you worthless bastards!"

Ababul was smirking to himself as he discarded the impenetrable crust. Companies? Hah! More like mindless mobs, he thought. The head master became annoyed at his presence and slapped Ababul's skull, "Get your ass back on that horse and out to the desert. I want constant reports!"

Ababul shot him a dangerous look, but did as he was told. Soon he and his family of blossom slaves would engulf the nuisance of an army and when they were finished, they would turn on these miserly taskmasters and take what they were owed. Then, when they were full of the beloved poison, they would scale the walls of Laveg, fly over its gates and slaughter the miserable inhabitants. Ababul knew where he was going when this war was over. He would find out where the flower came from. He would grow it, nurture it and lay in it for the rest of his life . . . which he knew wouldn't be much longer.

As he rode into the gusting night wind, dust stinging his eyes, he heard Black Tide horns sound the assembly.

CHAPTER 20

Shasp made sure the scouts had seen their approach, knowing every one of them would be flying back to the Tide camp with word. He was counting on it. Tiny lights twinkled on the horizon, torches from Laveg's wall and the surrounding Tide camp. Sergeant Albis and Corporal Pieter returned from spying on the enemy and reported that nearly eight thousand Black Tide surrounded Laveg. The Attahns would be slaughtered if they met them in battle. Somehow, he would need to link up with Laveg's forces. It was risky but, as usual, the only avenue.

Up to that time, each member of the army of Salsida had carried a torch or candle to make their presence known. Now, with the Tide assembling for battle, all the flames were extinguished. King Nachmed and General Momad prepared to double back, planning to sweep wide and slip past the enemy under the cover of darkness. Shasp and his cavalry of a hundred would harry the enemy front and make a good show of it while the main force made for the gates of Laveg. He only hoped the sultan would recognize them as allies and not some trick by the Tide. If the plan failed, everyone would die between the black army and the walls of Laveg, ground up, like so much flour in a mill. Only then would Laveg realize, too late, what devastation their refusal would bring.

The main force broke off quickly. In the sands of the Trabic, even a few thousand soldiers made little noise when their gear was tied down and wrapped. Shasp stood in the stirrups, felt Grimm shift nervously under him, and made a cutting motion with the torch in his hand. The rest of his hundred troopers, half mercs and half Attah's best horsemen, waved their torches in response and started forward. Shasp brought Grimm to a slow trot at the center of the line when he saw the first signs of the enemy moving toward them. The plan was working so far. They had lured the enemy farther into the desert, but they still had to survive long enough to race back to the walls once the Attahn force was safely inside.

Shasp glanced to his right and saw the grim look on Albis' face, "Well Sergeant," he yelled, "at least you'll have one hell of a story to tell if we live through this!"

Albis, also standing in the stirrups, smiled and nodded at his commander, "One hundred against eight thousand? There'll be no doubt about it, Lieutenant! And if I live through this, I'll make sure I have a houseful to tell it to. The story of a suicidal lieutenant!"

Slowly, the speed built as horse muscle bunched and relaxed in a steady, powerful rhythm, rolling and then exploding into a thunderstorm. They felt the power and shock of hooves against sand, reverberating through their mounts. The madness of their suicide mission spread among the horsemen, evoking fierce battle cries, cutting through the darkness as they fell on the enemy front like a tidal wave. Hooves and sword crashed into the enemy infantry before the milling mass could even bring their pikes to bear. Metal slammed into metal as barding met breastplate and quickly crushed men underneath. Blood sprayed and the dying screamed their final farewell as the diverse cavalry reaped a bloody harvest until Shasp called them back. Even though the plan appeared suicidal, he didn't want his men bogging down in the infantry's line, becoming separated and surrounded. Then there was the problem of pulling back too far and opening themselves to missile fire. He would need to stay close enough to engage, but not too close. The men pulled back and some Tide soldiers gave chase, but were quickly mowed down when the horses turned again. The game went on and on as Shasp and his men attacked, then retreated into the darkness only to return and assault another position in the enemy ranks. The poor leadership of the Black Tide was showing as the cavalry picked away at it, like a vulture on an elephant's corpse.

Shasp was calling another retreat into the dark, luring the enemy away even further, when an Attahn rider returned from Laveg. The horse reeked of sweat, its flanks heaving with exhaustion. The scout looked no better. It was his task to notify the cavalry when the gates of Laveg were open.

Shasp lunged toward the panting horse, "Is it time!"

The scout shook his head, "No sir, the Evatans will not open to us. Lord Nachmed is trying to reason with the prince on the wall, but to no avail."

"Which prince?"

"Terafar, sir."

Grimm spun under Shasp's rein, "Head back, we'll be along in a moment." The scout turned and loped off. Shasp waved for another line formation, and then charged toward the mob that doggedly pursued them. Again his troopers bit into their ranks, then wheeled and ground along the black front, disappearing into the darkness a final time. Thrumming hooves drove north away from the infuriated enemy, then headed west in a wide circle. Ironwrought hoped he could make it to the gates of Laveg in time to reason his way inside before the Black Tide taskmasters discovered his tactic and maneuvered the unwieldy bulk of their men back toward the city. If not, they would be crushed between the enemy and the walls. The sorties he led had baited the mob nearly four miles from camp, but it would still take time to get everyone inside.

With Lexia ever on his right and Albis on his left, they galloped up to the bronze portals. Slowing to a trot, they moved between the rank and file of Attahn troops, standing before Laveg's marble mistresses. The statues glared down from on high as if it were they who would make the final decision about who could enter.

Shasp felt a surge of admiration for Nachmed as he brought his cavalry through. The new king wisely kept his troops formed and did not allow them to turn into a surging mob before the gates. It gave him credibility before the Evatans, would allow an orderly entrance if the gates were opened and better prepared to face the enemy if they were not. He reined in alongside Nachmed, who was calling to someone atop the wall. Grimm snorted catching his attention, and Nachmed glanced over his shoulder.

"He will not open the gates He thinks it is a trick of the enemy."

"The scout said it was Terafar."

Nachmed nodded, "Yes, he is a difficult royal brat."

Shasp stood in his stirrups and lifted the steel helm from his head, "Prince Terafar, open the gates! We came to help, will you see us all slaughtered out here!"

A distant voice called down, "Well, well, if it isn't the mercenary who cavorts with enemy spies! You are not bringing this alien army inside my walls to rape and pillage!"

"Prince, listen! This army defeated thousands of Black Tide and crossed burning sands to stand with you against this horde. Even now, thousands more Black Tide, better trained and equipped are on their way here. Let us in or we will all die!"

After a short pause, Terafar called down, "If what you say is true then where is Bakarath to substantiate your claim?"

Shasp cursed, "He's dead, killed by the demon who leads the enemy! We finished our mission and destroyed the flower, but the new army does not require it. Open, I say! At least call for the Sultan or Prince Alafar!"

Suddenly, from behind him a soldier called out, "They're coming!" Shasp turned in the saddle to see the torches of the Tide returning from the desert, their echoing screams of rage carried on the cool desert wind. "Damn you, Terafar, open these gates!"

The young prince only watched from the wall with apathy as his soldiers shifted nervously around him. It was then fate smiled and Shasp saw the face of Prince Alafar look over the wall. Immediately, Alafar took in the scene and yelled to the gate towers, "Open the gates, now!" Slowly, the gears and counterbalances clattered and rumbled as the enormous bronze portals began to part.

Shasp looked back again with horror as he realized the Black army would wash over them before they could get inside. He spun his mount and bolted back through the ranks until he and his men poured out behind them. Signaling for a rank, he waved the ends back, creating a wall of cavalry to hold the enemy until the army could get inside, but his horse troops were too thin.   General Momad recognized what Shasp was attempting and yelled an order, "Left flank, south, march! Right flank, north, march!"

Instantly the columns broke away and filled in the empty wings of the capsule as the main body marched through the partially opened gates. The majority of the Attahns were inside when the enemy fell upon their rear. Shasp's foreign cavalry backed up just before the clash then lunged out to meet the wall of axes and swords. In the half-light of a coming dawn, blades flashed and hewed, blood was slung in purpling strings and splashed its warm stickiness over armor and hair. The horse soldiers slowly retreated under the onslaught as the Attahn soldiers seeped through Laveg's door. Arrows hissed down from above by the hundreds, felling row after row of the painted maniacs. Under the rain of warheads, Ironwrought finally backed the remnants of his troops through the opening and heard the clatter of gears as the huge doors swung ponderously shut and clanged together.

Prince Alafar was already descending the stairs of the whitewashed walls, "My apologies, gentlemen. My little brother lacks perception. I am grateful for your assistance." He held out his

335

hand and Shasp clasped it, gratefully. Alafar turned to Nachmed, "Prince Nachmed, I remember you from my childhood, welcome."

Nachmed clasped his hand and gave a sad smile, "Sorry to say, I am king now. My father was slain in the siege of Salsida."

Alafar nodded his condolences. Shasp dropped from Grimm's back, "We need to speak to your father."

Prince Alafar waved to an officer, "Get these soldiers food and water," then he turned to Shasp and Nachmed. "Follow me."

The streets of Laveg were no longer warm and bright as they had been on his first journey. The violet of the cresting sun lent a purpling aspect to the walls, while the streets remained dark and quiet with the city's inhabitants huddled in their homes. They progressed a short distance to a tall, fortified building, shaped like a large block. It was in contrast to the elaborate architecture which most of the city boasted. Shasp guessed it had been constructed to hold up under ballista fire, strictly for military purposes. He slipped through the door behind Prince Alafar and down a short hall until they came to an archway, and beyond, a wide large room. Oil lamps smoked and candles flickered with the slight movement of air. Sultan Alafar was bending over a set of plans, murmuring to one of his generals. The old sultan had exchanged his court robes for an armor typical of the Evatan army but much more expensive. Deep engravings and tracers of gold and silver ran throughout the cuirass and weapon girdle. A filigreed scimitar hung at his waist, while red silk pantaloons covered his legs. His turbaned steel cap even sported a gold spire. When the sultan looked up at the sound of his son's entrance, he smiled at Shasp, "Lieutenant, you have returned."

"And with friends, Father," added the prince, "nearly five-thousand troops from Attah, though Terafar nearly left them outside to be ravaged by the enemy. I give you King Nachmed."

The sultan raised an eyebrow, "King? I see. I always liked your father, Nachmed. We are grateful for your support. I hope you understand why we could not come to your aid. We were under siege ourselves." Nachmed nodded in agreement. The sultan turned an eye on Shasp, "I am anxious to hear your report, Lieutenant, though I must admit, I wondered whether I would see you again. Where is Bakarath?"

Shasp told the entire harrowing tale from Prince Hamed's treachery in Fenic to Bakarath's death in the valley of the Adder

Blossom and the breaking of the siege of Salsida. He gave a clear description of the *new* Black Tide army, coming out of the south and the evil necromancer who led them. The sultan slowly lowered himself into a chair. "Perhaps we should strike the mob outside these gates before it can link with the army coming across the desert."

Shasp shook his head, "We could, but we would lose valuable resources. We've destroyed the last of the Adder Blossom. I think Tabeck was hoping to fortify the mob until he arrived. With the drug supply cut, the thousands of Black Tide outside will soon fall to complete madness and die. Maybe even do some damage to their replacements when they come. Then we will only need to contend with Tabeck's hoplites, whose numbers are estimated at over fifteen-thousand."

Sultan Alafar nodded, "But we must also contend with General Holkerm's strategies. The man knows the city's defenses and will bring siege engines."

Nachmed cleared his throat, "How many fighting men do you have?"

Prince Alafar responded before his father could, "Including the remnants from the Tetas River, about six-thousand."

Nachmed shook his head solemnly, "My troops are a mixture of hastily trained citizens and veterans. They are no match for seasoned mercenaries."

"Maybe we could outlast them," said General Momad, just entering the room.

"Perhaps," said the sultan.

Suddenly, a young Evatan officer burst in, "Forgive me majesty, but another force is approaching the city."

Everyone came to their feet, flooded out, and dashed to the top of the walls. Shasp snapped open his spyglass and scanned the horizon. A tall cloud of dust boiled up in the distance, a brown smear moving north with the wind. Morning sunlight glinted off armor and weapons. The army from the Azon was coming. Slowly, the first divisions appeared, a black line emerging from the dust, wavering behind the morning's first heat wave. Other ranks followed then spread out, birthing more of the same until hundreds upon hundreds were visible. The first to take shape as they neared were the cavalry units flying icons of snakes and panthers. Thousands of hooves stirred the lighter particles of sand. Then, the infantry appeared, protected by black armored breast plates and greaves, and carrying the large round aspis shield of the hoplite. Their order and discipline was evident even from far away. Spears stood straight and even like the trees of a forest. Nor did the standards falter or phalanxes waver, as if they were units cut from blocks of wood. Even with the muffled effects of sand, the sound of their approach intensified, the hooves and feet beating a perfect rhythm against the backdrop of the desert. In their midst towered monstrous catapults, ballista, ambling like wooden giants over the oxen that pulled them by long ropes. The sight of the siege engines sent a wave of fear through the men on the walls. Beneath the wall, the mob of the old Black Tide cheered at the arrival of their brothers-in-arms with hoots, yips and other calls. Shasp surmised the combined force would number nearly twenty-five thousand men. Eventually, the horizon melted in a sea of black, like the shadow of a great thunder head.

Sultan Alafar, who looked as if he had the wind knocked out of him, slowly turned toward the stairs, "Gentlemen, I suggest you get some food and rest. You will need it," and he withdrew down the staircase. The others followed, leaving Shasp on the wall with the nervous sentries.

It occurred to him he had not seen Prince Terafar, but decided it was just as well. He probably would have beaten the ignorant dolt for nearly costing them their lives. As he was leaning on the wall, Lexia brushed up against him and gazed out over the enemy camp, "I hope you don't think I'm a coward, but . . . I really don't want to die in this place."

Shasp turned to her, "Me either. Don't worry Lexia, I won't let you die."

She smiled at him, "Are you my guardian now?"

He shrugged, "I doubt you'll need one, but I'll be there to watch your back anyway."

CHAPTER 21

Tabeck reclined on a wicker chair in the shade of his tent. Servants had rolled up the walls so he could watch the preparations of the siege. A stifling heat followed the cool breeze of the morning. General Holkerm seemed capable enough, bringing the siege engines within range and placing regiments where they could be easily directed. Taskmasters were placed under the supervision of the officers from the hoplite corps, but there was still the problem of the addicted Black Tide soldiers. There was no surplus of Adder Blossom, the last of it being destroyed by the troublesome mercenary. Tabeck knew the man was behind Laveg's walls and contemplated what forms of torture he would visit upon him after he had him dragged from the burning city. He also pondered over the talisman the warrior wore around his neck.

Holkerm ducked under the rolled up canvas wall, sweat pouring from his bald head. He mopped at it with the back of his hand and dropped onto the edge of a camp table near Tabeck.

"I have the siege engines in place but the old corps of Tide troops are becoming unruly, causing trouble with the hoplites."

"You are the general . . . what do you intend to do about it?"

Holkerm cleared his throat, "The taskmasters say there is only enough Adder Blossom in reserve to last for a few more days. After that, the old corps will begin dying but not before they wreak havoc. The Evatan army may use that moment of weakness against us so . . ."

Tabeck drummed his fingers on his cuirass, "What is it, General?"

Holkerm continued, "When I was in Laveg, I was privy to all the city defenses. Her most exploitable weaknesses are the gates. Yes, they seem impenetrable, but the hinge mounts are set too near the outer edge of the wall. We can focus our ballista attacks there, breaking through the outer edge of the wall and destroying the hinge mounts, collapsing the gates."

"It sounds promising, general, but what has that to do with our old Tide corps?"

Holkerm scratched his head and began to pace, "Well, I thought we would lose our first corps anyway, so why not give them double their ration of Adder Blossom. After we destroy the gates, we'll send them in ahead of our hoplites as shock troops and if we lose the majority of them at the threshold, so what? The drug will keep them fighting, won't it?"

Tabeck nodded with his chin on his fist, "It certainly will. The toll it will place on the defenders will be devastating; brilliant general."

Holkerm gave a curt bow before leaving, "We should be ready by evening."

From the height of Laveg's walls, the men watched the teeming masses below with morbid curiosity. Massive catapults were dragged within range of the walls and staggered with malevolent intent. Shasp and General Momad estimated their range and calculated the target. The city gates. Momad shook his head as a dark foreboding pervaded his thoughts. The gates were laminated oak encased in nearly an inch of solid bronze. It would be easier for Holkerm to knock down a section of wall, so why was he targeting the gates unless he knew something they did not? Though no one shared his concern, they still agreed to bring up extra beams and stonework to re-enforce the gates. Extra men were shifted from other duties to relocate in case the gates were somehow breeched. Shasp, Molgien and Lexia waited atop the walls to help repel the scaling ladders they had seen in the distance. General Momad insisted on leading the companies behind the gates while Prince Alafar took charge of the wall. King Nachmed remained in the fortified headquarters with the sultan to plan wall fortification and troop movements. Upon Nachmed's suggestion, the sultan ordered out every able bodied person from within the city, from youths to old men and women. Everyone was assigned a task. Throughout the burning day, people milled and bumped along at their work, knowing the first assault would come soon.

Lord Tabeck attempted a parley and rode to the gates, but the proud sultan ordered an archer to reply with steel. The cloth yard shaft whistled through the air and transfixed Tabeck's body, but he ignored it as one might a fly, turned and road back to his camp, leaving the spectators on the wall stunned with disbelief.

Such was the scene when the white sun became orange and slowly simmered on the horizon in a wild display of fading color.

With its demise came the violet and blues of desert dusk.

Shasp honed his katana to a razor's edge and was inspecting it against his thumb when he heard the first faint, whistling of a massive rock cutting through the air. He looked up, barely making out the blurred shape as it soared toward them.

"Move!" he screamed a second too late, and the boulder smashed into a section of the wall near the gate. An explosion of rock and mortar showered outward just below them. The shock of the impact knocked them flat against the battlement, at the same time causing the wall's corner to collapse in an avalanche of rock. The section Lexia was laying on began to slough away. Shasp saw the horror in her eyes as she slid away with the crumbling rock. He spun on his belly and grabbed for her, catching her wrist as the wall disappeared, leaving her dangling over empty space. Shasp cried out at the sudden strain on his unhealed shoulder and clenched his teeth against the shot of pain. He tried to pull Lexia up, but the damaged muscles from the spear wound would not respond. Clutching at the battlement with his free hand, he stared into Lexia's panic-stricken face, unable to pull her up and refusing to let her go.

"Lexia, climb up!"

She reached up with her other hand and grabbed his elbow, heaving against her weight and the weight of her armor. Shasp gasped with pain but it melted into stinging fear when another rock came screaming overhead. There would be no leaping away from danger this time. Both were trapped like flies in honey. The second impact struck the wall adjacent to the gate just below them. Lexia was clawing her way past Shasp's shoulders when the shockwave jarred her loose and she fell again. Shasp clawed blindly, miraculously catching the back of her collar. Rock dust billowed up, choking them as their ears rang. Lexia tried to reach overhead for Shasp's wrist but she was twisting back and forth. The movement wrenched at Shasp's fingers and he screamed in agony and anxiety as his fingers slipped, leaving only two tangled in her chain mail byrnie. Time stopped in that moment when he knew he would hold her for only a second more; when he knew he would have to watch her plummet to her death among the rubble. As their eyes locked in disbelief, Lexia knew it too.

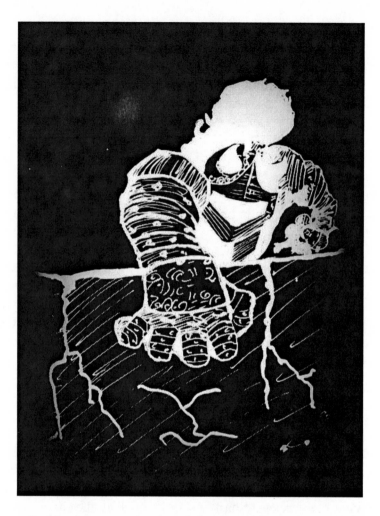

Suddenly, a massive hand shot past him and caught Lexia by the scruff of her byrnie. Like a child, she was lifted out of harm's way. Shasp was reeling under the shock and pain, his head swimming, trying to grasp what had just happened. Then that same hand was upon his breast plate collar, dragging him back. Men screamed and ran back and forth. Shasp sat up and blinked the dust from his eyes as Molgien squatted in front of him. A trickle of blood ran from his top knot down the side of his face and he gave a sharp-toothed grin. Shasp smiled back and slapped his shoulder while Lexia, still on her hands and knees, tried to clear her head of the near death experience.

More stones whistled through the air, hammering against the

bronze portals and the wall adjacent to them. Rock and dust spewed outward with each of the deafening concussions. Shasp picked a moment between the hail of stones to return to the gates and peer over the edge. When he saw the exposed hinge mounts, Holkerm's tactic became clear.

"Get below, the gates are coming down!" Kicking and shoving, he drove men from the battlements leaving only enough to repel the ladders.

Lexia caught a runner by the arm, "Go to the generals and tell them we need every able-bodied fighter at the gates . . . go!"

Against the cacophony of hailing rock and shattering chunks of mortar, the string of warriors rushed to the broad cobblestone avenue before the gates. More soldiers poured onto the entranceway from the adjoining streets as word reached their commanders. Shasp stood with Molgien and Lexia in the forefront and glimpsed Sergeant Albis as he slipped in with some mercenaries. Men winced with every shattering strike against the gate and wall. Rock rained down, and the gate to the left suddenly sagged and twisted, coming loose and banging into its twin. For a breathless moment, the massive bronze doors teetered uncertainly, and then toppled outward in a deafening crash followed by billowing dust. Hell swarmed in.

The roar of eight thousand voices reached through the hanging cloud of pulverized stone and, following the din, materialized into crazed, wide-eyed sons of the black flower, more insane than Shasp remembered. Like demons they frothed and screamed horrid battle cries as they poured through the gap, a horde straight from a nightmare.

The defenders leapt to the challenge with a matching fury borne from desperation, and the forces clashed in a swirling mass of steel and blood. Shasp fought like a whirlwind, his Somerikan knife and Ayponese katana sliced and stabbed in choreographed movements, practiced thousands of times. The gaunt brutes of the Tide were no match for his machine-like skill and fell one after another, second by second, until he stood upon a mound of bloody corpses. Each thrust found the exact organ it aimed for. His razor-sharp steel slipped through ribs to find heart and liver and glided across limbs to seek red fountains just beneath the surface. Everywhere, chaos reigned as men hacked and bashed, their minds lost to battle fervor. Lexia fought shoulder to shoulder with Molgien and Shasp, her scimitar bright with crimson while Molgien cleared great swaths with his massive spiked club. Ringing steel and screams filled the air as men died and fought to stay alive. The Black Tide soldiers threw their lives away without so much as a blink, each believing in his own drug saturated mind that he could breech the city single-handed. Each one believed he had no need for the thousands behind him. The sheer weight of the attackers pressing forward through the gap caused the defenders to waver, but they stiffened against the onslaught as the two armies smashed together like sea against cliff. Arrows hissed down from on high, burying sharp broad heads deep into neck, thigh and chest. Like a rainstorm, the missiles fell upon the intruders by the hundreds, as fast as the archers could notch them. Slowly the cobblestone avenue filled with blood and bodies.

Shasp fought to maintain his balance as gore crept above the soles of his boots and he tripped over corpses. He dodged the swing of an axe and returned with a backhand slash, leaving his opponent to spew red from his shoulders. Another replaced him and died seconds later from a thrust to his heart. Yet another stepped up and on it went until Shasp's shoulders ached from the slaughter and he struggled to hold on to his sword. The pain of his wounds stabbed at his mind and conspired with his fatigue, but he fought on. A heavy scimitar flashed toward him and he raised his katana to deflect it, a fraction late. The enemy blade raked along his own and struck his helmet. With ears ringing, Shasp stumbled backward, tripped over a corpse and fell. His foe smiled over the advantage and hacked downward but quickly gasped when Shasp rolled onto his hip, avoided the stroke and slid his katana through the man's lungs. The stinking Tidesman collapsed on him but Shasp was too spent to push him off. He did not know if he lay among the dead for seconds or hours but finally gathered enough strength to shove the body away and regain his feet. Blood oozed down his face inside his helmet as he staggered, waiting for his head to clear and was surprised that no one attacked him.

The roar of combat was still deafening but had moved away as the defenders had pushed the enemy back toward the fallen gates. Though the bronze doors no longer barred the way, a new impediment was slowly forming. Thousands of corpses piled up in the gap, forming a hill higher than a man seated on a horse. The

344

defenders of Laveg climbed this gruesome slope by the hundreds to meet the onslaught of Black Tide.

Shasp stood a moment on wavering legs, took a step forward and collapsed. Cursing, he struggled to his feet, lurched toward the fighting and climbed the macabre pile. Bodies rolled under him and tumbled to the blood-soaked avenue below while arrows continued to hail down into the mob along with thrown chunks of stone and mortar.

Almost to the crest, he saw Lexia just ahead, blood splattered and faltering. Some remnant of adrenaline spurred him up the hill as she exchanged blows with a broad-shouldered, taskmaster, gripping a raised shield. She was exhausted and trying desperately to get behind her enemy's buckler. Shasp reached her just as the taskmaster lunged forward, bashing Lexia with his shield. She reeled back and nearly fell, but Shasp caught her, simultaneously thrusting his katana through the Somerikan's open mouth just before his victory cry. The man teetered for a moment then crumpled and fell to become part of the hill. Lexia dropped to her knees gasping and soaked in gore.

For the first time, Shasp saw the far side of the hill. It was alive with movement like ants on a ripe pear, black with crawling figures. Before he could right himself, another enemy surge pushed up the mound and Shasp killed the first two men he faced. But the slippery bodies beneath his feet made for terrible footing; he staggered and was born down by several soldiers.

On top of the pile, the giant Molgien swept his huge club like a man reaping his field. When he saw Shasp fall, he cleared a path to where his lieutenant struggled to survive beneath stabbing swords.

Shasp lay on his back in the sucking pile while Tide soldiers hacked at his guard. Again and again Shasp's armor turned poorly placed cuts as he slashed at a forest of feet but, even more of the enemy had clawed their way up the hill. It was only a matter of time, he thought, but by the time he felt the bite of the first well placed thrust, Molgien had thrown himself against the knot of enemies, bowling men back down the hill. Shasp felt the mass of foes fall back and rolled to his feet but before he could reach the cannibal, a spear shot through Molgien's leg. Lunging, Shasp slashed the culprit across the throat as Molgien dropped to one knee. Three more screamed and leapt. Ironwrought cut down two, but the third threw a spear, piercing Molgien's chest. The spear man died with Shasp's katana in his heart the instant the weapon left his hand. Molgien stumbled to his feet and ripped the spear from his chest with an angry cry that should not have come from the throat of a man. Like a predator that becomes wounded, the Somerikan giant released his rabid fury, bashing heads and sinking his sharpened teeth into anyone unfortunate enough to get too close. In spite of the blood pouring from his chest, he lifted men off the ground as if they were children and flung them onto their comrades.

On and on, the armies clashed until all that was left of the eight thousand Black Tide soldiers were a few hundred bunched toward the top of the bloody pile. As Shasp took in the horror, he realized the true evil of the Adder Blossom. Every single man and woman of the Black Tide had thrown themselves into the breach, believing they were invincible, and had died. Even now the remnants were being picked off by archers and surrounded by groups of defenders to be slaughtered.

Molgien bashed a lingering opponent with his huge fists then stood over the vanquished man like a strange and forlorn jungle idol with his chin resting on his chest. A feeling of dread stirred in Shasp when he saw his comrade and remembered the spear wound. He plunged toward him, stumbling, "Molgien? . . . Molgien!"

Just as Shasp reached him, the cannibal silently sank to his knees. Shasp knelt in front of him, placing a hand on his shoulder to steady him, and then stared down at the horrific wound, and the steady flow of blood running down his stomach. The giant Somerikan's eyes narrowed as he grinned a blood filled smile. Suddenly, Molgien pitched over backward, and Shasp ripped off his helmet, reaching for him. He leaned over Molgien, cradling his head. Lexia appeared and knelt across from Shasp with a weary sadness on her face, and gently placed her hand on Molgien's chest. Molgien coughed a few flecks of blood onto his chin and made a weak animal sound, then raised his arm, signing weakly. Shasp gestured back with his fingers forming the words, "And you have been a good friend to me. I will honor you." Molgien signed again but Shasp did not answer him until the cannibal gripped his shoulder with a bloody hand and squeezed, grunting for a reply. Slowly, Shasp gave a defeated nod and Molgien's anxious expression melted into a smile. As he released his dying breath, his eyes filled with a faraway look and Lexia felt his body relax under their hands. For a long while they

346

knelt atop the bloody heap, holding their comrade. Lexia wondered what Shasp had seen in the cannibal that others could not and silently grieved for both of them. Without warning, Shasp lifted his Somerikan knife and carefully cut a slice of muscle from Molgien's leg.

Lexia's eyes widened with shock, "What are you doing?" she asked, incredulous.

Shasp gave her a sad look, "I promised him."

CHAPTER 22

General Holkerm stood just inside the shade of his tent with his back to his charts. In the distance, hundreds of vultures circled over the fallen gates, anxious to glut, and their numbers were growing. It had been his intention to follow the old corps with the new once the gates were under assault. He even had them in place, but when the first wave floundered and were forced back into the gap, he knew his plan would not see fruition.

"General, a word with you," came Tabeck's voice.

Holkerm turned, surprised to see the sorcerer seated at the table behind him, "Of course."

Tabeck pitched his fingers, "Why are we not in Laveg? I thought you planned to follow the first wave of Black Tide through the gates with our hoplites. Why didn't you do it?"

The beads of sweat on Holkerm's head increased, "They would have been slaughtered. There was no foreseeing the buildup of dead in the gates. I knew it was possible but thought it unlikely and now the mass has created a secondary barrier. We could have taken Laveg by sending in the new corps, but we would have lost too many and that would leave us at the mercy of Kalyfar. We must have a substantial army in order to hold on to what we have won, however, I don't think we need to be concerned."

"And why is that?"

"Because the corpses will rot in this heat and bring sickness to Laveg, weakening the defenders' resolve.   Besides, throwing the old corps at the gates has served its purpose. The defenders have been severely weakened and we are rid of the old corps and the problems it posed."

Tabeck leaned on his elbows, his blood red eyes glinting with menace, "You still have not explained how you intend to take Laveg, General."

"Simple. We work on a section of wall where it is the weakest and either break it down or wait for the plague ridden city to surrender. Either way, Laveg is ours; it's only a matter of time."

"Time, General? I am not as patient as you may think. I have waited too long, and I am too close to fulfilling my purpose. Find a way in, now!"

Holkerm was stuttering his reply when a smooth young voice interrupted, "I can get you inside."

Two hoplites stood on either side of a handsome, tawny haired young man. He was dressed in a simple white linen tunic and wore an easy smile on his shaven face. "I know a way into Laveg."

Tabeck raised an eyebrow, "Prince Terafar, welcome, though I must admit your presence here is a surprise."

The youth grinned, "What reason have I to remain within Laveg's tortured walls? I think it is only fitting her new regent should enter with the conquering army . . . you know . . . the one I paid for."

Holkerm scowled and started to speak but Tabeck shot him a look that demanded silence.

"Please tell us," Tabeck asked, "how can you get us inside?"

Terafar strode across the carpeted floor, plopped lazily into a chair and helped himself to some of Holkerm's wine, "Easy, the same way I got out. There's an old tunnel which starts in the mountains above the city. It runs under the wall and comes up in the poor quarter. You see, when I was a child, my father took my brother and me to this labyrinth as part of our education on the city and its history.   Our family has used it for centuries, finding it handy for acts requiring secrecy. And it certainly has been useful. I moved a lot of gold and silver through there. Only my father, my brother and I know of it."

Holkerm cleared his throat, "How do you know this is not a trap? He might be leading us into an ambush."

Terafar looked annoyed, "I did not risk my neck sending caravans loaded with gold to Lord Tabeck so I could throw it all away by leading the army I funded into an ambush!"

Tabeck leaned over the table, "You will show us the way?"

Terafar paused as he examined the gray skin of Tabeck's face and blood red eyes. Until he approached the tent, he had only seen his hooded figure. He was frightened then, but dared not show it. Still the inhuman appearance of the face was unsettling, "Of course, we have a deal, remember?"

"Of course, Prince Terafar," said Tabeck before turning to Holkerm, "General, collect a large force of your worthiest men. Have one of your most trusted officers go with Prince Terafar after dark."

Holkerm was still wondering why the undeserving upstart prince should expect to be king when Tabeck had already promised Laveg to him.

"General! The men?" said Tabeck, raising his voice.

Holkerm looked up and nodded, "Of course. We will have to swing wide to avoid being seen and leave a substantial force here to distract the defenders.

"Why should we concern ourselves?" scoffed Tabeck. "They can't even get out."

Shasp and Albis had spent most of the morning wrapping Molgien's body and preparing him for cremation. That evening Shasp built his friend a funeral pyre, and with fire, sent Molgien on his way to the other world. After the fire died down, Lexia followed Shasp to the battlements where he withdrew a bloody cloth and built a small fire. He sat quietly with his knees against his chest, watching the sliver of meat sizzle over the fire, his eyes were distant. Lexia sat with her brown legs hanging over the castellated battlement, watching the enemy camp as she stitched a gash in her thigh. It was strangely quiet in the desert heat and most likely the enemy had escaped to the shade of their tents until nightfall.

"Why did you do that . . . cut Molgien," she asked?

"Because I …I promised…," stuttered Shasp, still not looking at her, "…to make him part of me."

Lexia's expression bordered on confusion and disgust, "Make him part of you? You mean you intend to eat that? Why?"

Shasp glared at her, irritated, "In his culture, when a comrade or family member dies, the others eat them. The body of the dead becomes a part of the living and, in their minds, continues to live in them."

"Then why did he eat his enemies? Wouldn't he want them to stay dead?"

"No," answered Shasp. "Molgien did not look upon his enemies the way we do. He did not hate them, and by eating them, he believed he added their strength to his own, making him even more powerful. When I refused him the meat of fellow soldiers, dead from battle, it bothered him because he saw eating them as paying homage and giving life. He didn't understand why we would refuse that for our own."

350

Lexia nodded, "You don't actually believe that? Molgien is dead and it makes no difference if you keep that promise."

"It does to me!" Shasp leaned over, prodded the strip of meat and wished it had been a smaller one. He lifted the small spit and pulled the strip loose, considering his duty. Lexia swung her leg off the battlement and came to kneel next to him.

"Do you think Molgien would be offended if some of him ended up in a woman?"

Shasp shook his head, "Not if that woman was you," and he tore the meat in two, handing half to her. With wine in hand, they toasted Molgien and fulfilled a promise.

CHAPTER 23

When the scorching sun finally sank below the horizon and a cooling dusk waxed orange, the Black Tide crept from their tents, and the defenders left the comforting shade of walls and doorways. Once again the city wall filled with anxious soldiers, still sore and battered from battle. All that day they tore down buildings and constructed fortifications behind the festering remnant of the evening's slaughter. More than four thousand defenders lay tangled in a heap with eight thousand of the enemy dead and the stench was already unbearable. Vultures swarmed over the pile, speckling it with the black of their wings. Angry men stared down from the battlements wanting to use the deplorable birds for target practice but fought the urge. Each arrow would be worth its weight in gold when the enemy came again.

When night fell, it brought the chill desert wind and airborne sand. In an abandoned apartment near the wall, Shasp untangled himself from Lexia's naked form, stood and stretched his complaining muscles. He regarded her natural beauty for a long time and smiled to himself, then painfully, pulled on his black leather pants and steel-sleeved jacket. Lexia stirred and woke, smiling at him through the moonlight as he leaned over to pull on his boots. They had nearly died in last night's battle and both knew their lives hung by a thread with no guarantee of tomorrow. It only seemed right to enjoy each other while they could. Even small pleasures were rare in a siege, so they sought out the empty room and spent the hot afternoon together in the cool apartment.

Lexia knelt in front of Shasp, took his thigh guard and laid it in place, buckling it. Carefully, she fitted his armor and checked the straps, "Careful about exposing your left shoulder, you have a tear between the links and the plate."

Shasp nodded, and then helped her into her chain mail byrnie and plated mail skirt. He buckled her leg guards and greaves then repaired a cut strap. When finished, they faced each other in silence.

Shasp reached out and pulled her to him, "We are not going to die here, Lexia. If the city falls, we will find a way out."

She nodded, "Stay close today, please."

"I will and you do the same."

Both were still exhausted from the fighting and would have liked to stay in the small room for another week, but that was only a passing desire, like a dying man in the desert that wishes he had some ice. They made their way into the streets where people had begun bustling in anticipation of another thrust from the Black Tide. Everyone knew the next wave would not be the screaming, starved madmen from the last battle, but instead, the disciplined hoplites drilling in the distance.

They stopped at the gate fortifications, gagging at the smell of heated corpses and quickly made for the wall where fresh air would drive away the stench. Woe to the soldiers stationed down there, thought Lexia.

As Shasp gazed out, toward the enemy encampment, he noticed little activity and the moon did not give sufficient light to allow his spyglass much detail. He gave a hopeful sigh, "Maybe we'll get a reprieve tonight." The words had barely cleared his lips when he heard a commotion and saw the soldiers below swarming toward the city center.

Lexia and Shasp traded worried looks. "You spoke too soon I think," she said as they leapt from their place on the wall. Women and children flooded past them as they ran toward the sounds of ringing steel and screaming men.

Shasp seized one by the arm, "What is going on?"

The trembling old woman, eyes wide, croaked out a reply, "They're in the city!" she cried and wrenched her arm away.

They ran on, freeing their weapons as they went, until they came to a cluster of soldiers near a dead end alley.   The way was filled with black armored hoplites, hundreds of them fighting shoulder to shoulder toward the street. Immediately, Shasp knew that if they reached the end of the alley they would be able to disperse, and he wondered how they got there. The defenders were being mowed down like grass by the Tide phalanx as it crept toward the alley mouth and there was no time to teach his comrades how to combat locking shields in the middle of a battle. Even his skill was no match for a rank of seasoned mercenaries. He looked around, desperately seeking some means of stopping the irresistible push of the hoplites when his eyes fell on an abandoned oxcart, full of straw. He grabbed a young man headed for the fray and spun him around, "Oil! I need oil now, as much as you can find, move!" Not too anxious to throw himself into the hoplite machine, the youth darted off with his new orders.

Shasp snatched a torch from another and tossed it into the straw, igniting it. He snatched up the yoke, "Lexia, the other side!" She grabbed the other yoke and together, they turned the cart and shoved it toward the alley mouth. As flames burst overhead in showering sparks, they screamed for men to get out of the way, and rammed the blazing wagon through their own line, knocking their comrades aside. The front rank of defenders opened as the cart roared past and slammed into the upright shields of the hoplites. The hell cart became the center of a pushing contest as each struggled to move it from center, but it quickly became engulfed, forcing everyone back. The cart wasn't wide enough to block the entire alley and several hoplites came around the sides but could no longer form a rank and were quickly cut down. More carts and wood were brought from the market square and piled behind the wagon. Shasp grabbed another man, "Get me some archers on those roofs! Where the hell is that kid with the oil?" As one was running to organize the archers, the youth was returning with a heavy keg of oil, "I have it, sir; it's the largest I could find!"

Shasp snatched it out of his hands, "Get these men busy finding buckets for water before these buildings catch fire, but don't throw a single drop until I tell you! Do you understand?" The boy nodded and ran off. Shasp followed a group of archers into the building adjoining the alley with Lexia close behind. He hefted the large keg onto his shoulder and carried it up two flights of stairs to the rooftop. The archers were already firing on the enemy below, but were having little luck against the large stout shields. From his vantage point, Shasp could see a square hole in the pavement of the alley below and a discarded stone tile which, he presumed, had capped it; a secret entrance into the city. Even as he watched, more of the Black Tide poured into the alley, waiting for the flames to die down so they could push forward again. He lifted the keg overhead and threw it down on the raised shields. With a shattering of wood, the keg exploded, raining oil. He was about to turn and order more to be brought up but as he did, two more men with kegs emerged from the stairwell.

"Over the side," he yelled. The kegs crashed down, soaking the hoplites' armor and flowing underfoot. The Tide officer began screaming for his men to get back and struggled toward the secret entrance. He almost made it. The oil found the fire and, with a whoosh, it ignited, turning the alleyway into a firestorm. Men screamed and stumbled toward the opening only to find it plugged with others seeking escape from the inferno. For a moment, Shasp regretted the means necessary for securing the alleyway; soldiers should die in combat. He called down from the roof, "Bucket brigades! Get moving!"

Soon, a steady stream of men was arriving in the street and on the roof top. They doused the carts and rubbish and wetted the wood works inside. Others brought up buckets of dirt to drop on the oil. The fire was not quite out when Shasp headed down the alley for the secret opening, tiny flames still licking at his boots. No sooner had he reached the discard tile lid, a helmeted head popped up and he quickly cut it off. Curses and profanity floated up from below and were answered in kind. Because the opening would only allow one man at a time to enter Laveg, the enemy plan had depended on stealth and had failed. Fortunately, someone must have spotted them coming through. Shasp ordered four spear men to replace the stone tile and stand guard with a runner in case the enemy attempted another entry, and then he headed for the command barracks. He and Lexia found Sultan Alafar and King Nachmed as they were leaving the building.

Shasp stopped them, "It's under control," he said. "They found a secret entrance in the north end but we managed to stop them before they could get out of the alley and form ranks."

Sultan Alafar and his son exchanged shocked expressions.

"What is it," Shasp asked?

The sultan turned to the prince, "Find your brother." After the prince sped away, Sultan Alafar turned to Shasp, "I know of that entrance, but never thought it to be a liability. It is well hidden at both ends. The only people I have ever shown were my sons."

Shasp remembered the look Terafar had given his brother when the sultan briefed him on his mission to find the adder blossom. The sultan waved them inside, returned to the planning chamber, and dropped into a chair. "We will be hard pressed to withstand this siege, I think. The arrival of my guest and his army is welcome of course, but has also placed a strain on our food stores. I am also concerned about the dead at the gates. Soon, sickness will sweep over Laveg if they are not buried or burned. If the enemy were not prepared, I might feel better, but I have seen the long baggage train which followed them here. They will outlast us."

All stood quietly thinking when Lexia broke the silence, "Does the tunnel run under the city wall where it might be undermined?"

Alafar shook his head, "No, it runs back into the mountains, which form our rear defense, about a mile and comes out in the slopes."

She looked at Shasp, "Do you think the Tide would try the tunnel again?"

Shasp thought a moment, arms folded, "I wouldn't. If the wall can't be undermined and with the opening guarded, there would be no reason. Why?"

"She shrugged, "Maybe we could use it to our advantage. Sneak out with some troops and go plead for assistance from Kalyfar or some other ally."

The sultan shook his head, "No, I'm afraid Kalyfar will not help and Dahoe is too far away. Teksika and Attah have fallen to the Tide and Breska is also too far north and indifferent."

Again the chamber fell into silence until Shasp broke it, "Well, if we are on our own and not likely to outlast the invaders, perhaps we should attack."

Immediately, the room came alive with stuttering and snorts. Nachmed threw up his hands, "Are you mad? Have you taken leave of your senses? Since last night's battle, we are down to about six thousand men and they have cavalry!"

"So do we," said Shasp, "and though we only have six thousand soldiers, we do have several thousand citizens."

Nachmed pointed toward the gates, "How do you expect to get hundreds of horses over that pile of bodies? Even if you could, you would still be outnumbered three to one in cavalry alone."

Shasp took a step toward the king of Attah, "There are only two ways to die, Lord Nachmed. On your feet or on your knees. I would have thought your father would have taught you that."

Nachmed turned away, "You are right. We will forfeit our lives either way. Better to die fighting rather than wasting away in here from disease and famine. Do you have some kind of plan?"

Shasp was about to answer when Prince Alafar burst through

the door, "Father, Terafar is nowhere to be found."

The sultan's head sank into his hands and there fell an uncomfortable silence. The prince began to wave everyone out but his father held up a regal hand, "Stay! I have lost one son to this evil and I will not lose another! Lieutenant, what is your plan?"

Shasp put his chin on his fist, "It's coming to me."

CHAPTER 24

When the failed secret incursion was reported to Holkerm, he moved the war machines forward and hammered the walls of Laveg. Rocks and flaming jars rained down continuously in the city, blasting apart homes and buildings, punishment for their stubborn resistance. At the north end of Laveg, however, the defenders were hard at work, building scaffolds and constructing hoists amidst the destruction. The city's catapults were moved out of danger and collected near the rear while fighting units were reassigned. When the moon climbed to its zenith, every available fighting man eased down, one at a time, into the secret exit.

Shasp led the way through the arid tunnel, and a ghostly breeze played with the flame of his torch. A hundred yards behind came the host of Evata and Attah, their boots scuffing and echoing down the long sandstone corridor.

He stopped and knelt to inspect the corpse of a Black Tide sentry with a smiling gash across his throat. Shasp had been fortunate enough to hear about some Badowan nomads who were trapped in Laveg when the siege began and quickly enlisted their skills of assassination and desert warfare. He sent them ahead to silence any Tide sentries prior to the emergence of the army. It seemed they were living up to their reputation.

The tunnel ramped upward at a constant but gentle incline until it opened into a cool sandstone cave. Under a crescent moon, men filed out, forming a shadowy worm which wound its way down the barren slopes. In the dark, they quietly collected into their respective companies, while their leaders met to confirm plans and countermeasures. General Momad would take his remnant of Attahn troops, two thousand, out of sight to wait for their signal. Prince Alafar, although he argued against it, was assigned to the citizen forces inside the walls. Throughout the day, the people of Laveg had stripped the bloated corpses of their dead soldiers, removing armor and weapons. Prince Alafar was angry over his assignment to lead a rabble, but the sultan soothed his pride by reassuring him that only a gifted leader could hold such a frail collection together in the face of danger. Besides, every aspect of their plan was critical and the sultan was too old to father any more heirs. He would ride with Shasp in the cavalry while Nachmed led the rest of the four thousand Evatan regulars into a ravine just below the cave. That left Shasp with about eight hundred who could ride.

After the other units dispersed, Shasp led his men to the base of the wall where it merged with the rock of the Akis Mountains. Nearly a hundred feet overhead, he heard the muffled clatter of wood and the whispers of engineers on the battlements. The day's labor was about to be tested, and the first neighing horse swung out over the sand, dangling from a beam of wood and an impromptu sling. The poor beast struggled, legs thrashing as counter weights and sweating hands eased it to the ground. As soon as its hooves touched the sand, it was consoled by its rider, removed from the sling, and the contraption sent back up. More of these beams swung out with their frightened loads and slowly, the cavalry's mounts descended, four at a time, like spiders descending on strings of silk. It took most of the night for the process to be completed but before dawn broke, Shasp and Sultan Alafar were leading their battalion of cavalry out across the sands. They had to swing wide for a long distance to avoid sentries before vanishing into a low depression in the dunes.

Shasp, Alafar, Albis and Lexia would each lead a troop of two hundred to keep the units flexible and allow for decisive movement. By the time the first warm rays of sunlight caressed their cool skin, the entire force was well hidden and waiting for the prince's opening move in the deadly game of chess. Lexia, sitting astride a fine chestnut mare, sidestepped the animal toward Grimm where she looked at Shasp with her one good eye. She did not need to say anything, the look on her face said it all and Shasp nodded. Sultan Alafar drew a deep breath and sighed, as if considering the passage of old memories. He turned to Shasp, "I am very glad we did not have to eat the horses."

Shasp chuckled, "So am I. Grimm would have been too tough to eat anyway."

Holkerm was splashing lukewarm water over his freshly shaven face when he heard a croak from behind him.

Prince Terafar raised his battered head from his chest and glared through swollen eyes, "You think you are something," he rasped, "a great man?"

Holkerm turned nonchalantly, padded his face with a towel

then grinned, "Well, Prince, you are the one hanging from a post. I think I can safely say I am greater than you at the moment."

Terafar spat a wad of coagulated blood which landed on Holkerm's polished boot, "You're scum and so is Tabeck! It was I who funded the Black Tide, and without me you would both still be nothing! Lying, deceiving snakes! If you were of true noble blood, you would honor the agreement."

Holkerm stepped closer to Terafar, reached up and tested the chains holding his wrists overhead, "You are no more honorable than I. Wasn't it you who betrayed your father and countrymen so you could be sultan? Hhmm? It wasn't enough to be the second most powerful man in Evata when your father dies. No, you wanted it all, and I can't fault you for that but you were stupid to be so trusting. Fool, Tabeck already promised me Laveg. You didn't have the foresight to see that he would no longer need you once the city was within his reach."

Terafar shook his blood-crusted head, "I think you are the fool, because Tabeck will cast you aside when he has what he wants. He will not share power."

Holkerm sneered, "We'll see, but at least I won't play the fool. Perhaps you might have at least lived, Terafar, if you had not tried to betray our men in the passage."

"I did not betray them, slime! The entry was risky and you knew it!"

"Does it really matter?" asked Holkerm. "Tabeck wants your father and brother to witness your death and know who betrayed them. It's the only reason you aren't dead already."

Terafar's head dropped and Holkerm was gloating over the man who thought to take his prize when a sentry entered the tent.

"General, there is movement near the city gates."

"What? What kind of movement?"

"They are clearing the dead away, sir."

Perplexed, Holkerm pushed past the man and threw open the tent flap. In the distance he saw hundreds of soldiers dressed in the Evatan uniform with cloth wrapped around their mouths. Most of the bodies had already been moved which meant they must have been at it all night. He scratched his head. Why would they clear one of the barriers from the city? Unless . . . Holkerm spun and called to his second, "Get the men formed up and bring the cavalry to lead!" So, the defenders decided not to wait for plague and famine to finish them off. Instead, they meant to take as many of the enemy with them as possible. He had always known it was a possibility and had even hoped it would end this way, though he would regret the loss of a few thousand troops. At least he wouldn't have to wait out a long siege sweating in his tent. He would crush the starving army and be in the sultan's palace by evening, enjoying the old man's harem and wealth.

By early morning, before the heat had even come, the Black Tide hoplites were spread out over the desert before Laveg's walls, a sea of squares made of thousands of men. Holkerm had his three thousand cavalry stretched out in front of his infantry units, hoping to mow down the pathetic force which was, even now, pouring out of the gates and forming ranks. Before them, pranced a white gelding with Prince Alafar astride, calling out directions and orders. From his vantage, Holkerm could see the confused and disorderly way the phalanxes came together. He considered just ordering his cavalry to trample them before they were organized but decided it would be better practice for his horsemen if they waited. When Laveg's ranks were formed and began marching into the open, Holkerm turned to a group of squires on his right and nodded. The first one held up a blue flag, waved it, and the line of Black Tide cavalry started forward, stirring the dust.

Prince Alafar screamed orders until his throat was raw, managing to get the horrified citizens herded into their respective companies. They wore the bloodstained pantaloons, armor and weapons taken from the dead at the gate and he hoped his adversary, General Holkerm, would not be able to see the aged faces and piss stained crotches of his force. Alafar had placed the oldest in the front of the formations and the youngest in the back, children from ten to fourteen, with the hope some would survive to tell the story. Fifteen and older went out with the other forces. When they were in order, the prince brought his gelding around, adjusted his turbaned steel helmet, and rode ahead of his sad army.

They had managed to scrape together enough of the city's elders, mothers and children to create a force large enough to lead Holkerm to believe he was facing everything Evata had left. When he saw the way the general brought out his troops he knew, at least, this part of the plan had worked. Now they just had to survive long enough to spring the trap.

With a wave of his hand, a bull horn sounded three blasts; the signal was sent. Prince Alafar brought the horse to a trot when he saw the Tide cavalry start toward them. When he moved past the white marker arrows jutting from the sand, he held up his hand and the army came to a disordered halt. It was time to stand before the storm.

Slowly, the Black Tide horses increased speed, hooves drumming against the sand, until they were charging full on with a thundering clamor. The stoic professionals on their backs never gave a battle cry but only leveled their lances with practiced choreography, leaning forward in their saddles. Prince Alafar had prepared for combat his whole life but never against anyone but a court-paid tutor and now he was seeing the reality of war and nearly lost control of his bladder. He remembered the royal blood in his veins and spurred forward just ahead of his running army of grandparents, women and children.

Spears and arrows flew from the Evatan ranks, thwacking into the Tide cavalry. Dozens of horses crashed to the sand in a spray of grit and blood while riders tumbled under the hooves of their own comrades. Before another volley could be sent, the wall of horseflesh and steel collided and cut through the Evatans like hot steel through butter. Foot soldiers were slapped aside and cut down in a single instant. The cavalry plunged clear through, raking the phalanxes and coming out again. Prince Alafar cut a rider out of his saddle and was astounded that he still lived. When he finally shook off his amazement, he screamed for his soldiers to regroup. Hundreds lay scattered like fallen stalks of wheat under a scythe but his forces quickly reorganized. They knew as well as he did, there was nowhere to retreat to, nowhere to run. Fighting was all that was left to them. Surprisingly, their fear seemed to evaporate, leaving only hatred and resolve, especially the old ones. Many of the soldiers in this army were their children and grandchildren. The prince came to the front again and this time the soldiers held their ground, standing on their spear butts. Again, the Tide cavalry regrouped and circled around. The enemy infantry had been hard on the heels of their cavalry and the horsemen were hoping to get another run before their brothers on foot reached the line and ground up their sport.

For the second time, the cavalry tore through the defender's ranks leaving rows of broken bodies in their wake. Again, Prince Alafar survived the raking but no sooner had he pulled his battered force together, when the Black Tide infantry slammed into their front. Immediately, the first three ranks went down under the onslaught but the fourth held. Alafar found himself trapped behind the first enemy rank and reined his gelding in a hard circle. Men fell under the beast and others were knocked aside unable to attack before Alafar thrust back behind his own ranks. Now, the Tide regulars were face to face with their opposition and could see the wrinkled faces of old men and soft features of young women under helm and corset, and they smelled victory. Slowly, the Evatans were pushed back under the irresistible pressure, giving ground as the hoplites stepped over the bodies of the vanquished. When Prince Alafar saw the flag on his right go up as the Evatans retreated past the marker, he waved his arm and a horn sounded.

For long minutes they struggled to hold the enemy in place and Alafar saw the Tide cavalry working its way back along the enemy rear. Once they had come around, the Black Tide infantry opened up, allowing the horses to rush headlong toward the front. Ten columns of Tide cavalry churned the sand as they charged between their infantry ranks, intending to cut through his front line and allow the footmen deep into his phalanx. Prince Alafar smiled and looked over his shoulder to the walls. High above, the last catapult rolled back into place and already the creak and groan of their counterweights reached his ears. Like comets from the heavens, massive rocks and chunks of masonry whined overhead and crashed down among the shocked Tide forces. Dirt erupted skyward with deafening noise as man and horse were crushed to pulp. The missiles, some as big as a soldier's tent, rolled and bounced, cutting great swaths in the enemy formations. Again and again the massive stones touched down like the thumb of an angry god, smashing ants.

Engrossed with his coming victory, Holkerm saw the movement on the wall too late. Only when the first rocks began to scream overhead, did he realize he had been baited into a trap and howled for a retreat. But, his phalanxes were packed too close together in anticipation and were slow to respond to the bull horn. He turned again and signaled for his northern and southern reserves to move inside the range of the devastating weapons and squeeze the

Evatan flanks. Holkerm squirmed over the fact that nearly two-thirds of his cavalry was trapped among the milling infantry. He cursed and called to a flagger, "Signal a hard cavalry retreat!" The flagger hesitated, knowing what the order meant. Holkerm reddened and backhanded the man, "Do it, damn it!" The soldier raised the yellow flag and waved it energetically.

The Tide cavalry columns, now only shattered fragments, responded to the flag, turned their mounts and charged through their own men, trampling them under hooves until they cleared the rear.

By the time they reformed, Tabeck had appeared at Holkerm's side, "What is happening General! I thought you had matters in hand!"

Holkerm, though aware of Tabeck's deadly powers, was still in no mood to take his berating while trying to fight a battle, "It's only a minor setback. Their forces are still no match for ours and they are well outnumbered. The catapults were not on the wall this morning, and I thought them mostly destroyed by our ballista yesterday."

Tabeck regarded the floundering ranks and flying rocks, "We do not appear to have things in complete control, General."

Holkerm pointed, "There. Our reserves are coming in from the north and south. We'll squeeze them in the middle and either cut them off or force them back inside. Either way, our men will be out of range of their catapults, close to the wall." Holkerm turned to his signaler and made a curt hand movement. Two green flags waved and the returning cavalry split, half going north and the other, south. Tabeck rubbed his cadaverous chin, "What are they doing?"

Holkerm folded his arms, "I sent them to reinforce the reserves. They'll chew up the Evatan flank, letting the infantry inside. They'll be ours soon enough."

"They had better be, General, or you will know the meaning of pain."

No sooner had the words cleared Tabeck's grey lips, there came a rumbling from behind, and they turned to see a wave of cavalry charging toward them, lances lowered and swords raised with deadly intent. Tabeck cocked his head, "That does not look like our cavalry."

Holkerm was already running for his charger, "Move! Signal the cavalry to rally!" Most of the signalers scattered and a few waved the flags but the waving was short lived as Shasp and his troopers tore through them with screams of vengeance. They drove on through the ranks of archers, and various support officers, bodies crushed underneath or sent spinning from a decapitating slash.

Shasp smiled under his helmet as he led his men into the back of the milling Tide infantry. With the command platform overrun and the signalers dispersed and killed, Tabeck's army would be in chaos.

Holkerm and Tabeck managed to get mounted and were racing to regroup with their cavalry before they were caught between the Evatan charge and their own infantry. The general fumed when he saw that only half of his cavalry had responded to the flags; the others had not had time to see the signal and were still pressing the Evatan flanks. He checked over his shoulder and saw Shasp and his troopers drive into the back of his infantry, unaware of death riding into them. Tabeck rode around the right flank at Holkerm's side and they drew up face to face with a young major, his force reining in behind him. His horsehair helmet was missing, knocked off when a mammoth rock bounced in front of him and careened over his head. Blood ran down his face from the gash in his scalp, hinting at how death had breathed in his face.

"Sir, your orders."

The general hesitated and twisted in his saddle to take in the scene. The major's force was only slightly less than Shasp's.

"Major, take your troop back behind our lines where the enemy cavalry is attacking our rear. Have two men break off and split our infantry ranks through the center, then give them an about face. We'll pinch him between our cavalry and infantry."

The major saluted and heeled his mare's flanks with sharp spurs and his men thundered behind him.

"Lord Tabeck, would you ride to our far flank and take charge of our foot and horse troops? I'll take this flank and we will meet in the middle before the city's opening. We can cut off their retreat and fight where the catapults cannot reach. You did say you were a warrior once."

Tabeck sneered, "I still am, General, as you shall see." He jerked his mount around and kicked it into a gallop. Holkerm looked after him a moment before doing the same, hoping there would be no more surprises, but as he closed on the north flank and regrouped with the rest of the cavalry and infantry, another bull horn blasted.

General Momad lay under the desert sand, licking his dry lips as the moisture was wicked away from his body. Only his face was exposed to the sun's approaching glare, the rest of him was buried, as it had been all morning. Throughout the night he had led his Attahn troops behind the enemy lines, circling around the sleeping Black Tide. By the time dawn stretched its arms, they were dug in and waiting. When he heard the second blare from the horn, he was relieved to rise from the burning sand. With a fierce cry akin to a roaring waterfall, the two thousand soldiers erupted from the ground, sand pouring from their helms and armor, and sprinted toward the unsuspecting north flank. With nearly a mile to cross before they reached the enemy, the haggard men pumped their legs as fast as their armor would allow.

By the time Holkerm realized he had been flanked, the Attahns were only a hundred yards away, and such was the din of battle. He yelled for his horsemen to turn but before the order moved down the line, it was too late. They poured into his cavalry at close quarters, hacking at horse and rider. Beasts went down with their burdens while others formed tight groups and fought from the saddle. The rest of the Attahns slashed through his position and into his infantry rear. He had thought to squeeze the Evatan force, but now found himself squeezed between the Evatans and the Attahns. He screamed at the horsemen nearest him to circle and fought for his own survival as his forces slowly dissolved into a mass against the north flank.

King Nachmed led his foot soldiers out of the ravine at the sound of the horn. The sound of catapults unleashing their fury against the Black Tide and the screams of the dying carried through the still desert heat. In spite of the roar of war being so close, he held his men near the mountain where it met the walls. Warriors kneaded their pommels and wiped the sweat from their foreheads, tensed like a savannah cat hovering only a leap away from its prey. When the second horn sounded, Nachmed imagined his countrymen under Momad bursting from the sand and closing on the north flank and he leapt into a dead run, the Evatan contingent following behind.

Sprinting, they followed the curve of Laveg's wall and quickly raced out into the open space where they fell on the southern flank. Like maddened wolves they sprang upon the backs of the Tide cavalry under Lord Tabeck with the same devastating effect as their allies on the north side. Cavalry was caught off guard as Nachmed's forces poured over them like a spring flood. Men were swept from the saddle and cut down as the Evatans broke their formations and melded into their force.

Shasp's plan had accomplished what he intended. The discipline and order of the Black Tide army had been reduced to a chaotic mass. There were no longer any fronts or flanks. No phalanxes or locked shields. Only the blending of opposing forces like two rivers flowing into one and now there was only to hack and kill, to live or die on one's own merit and luck, just the way Shasp liked it. He was deep into the back of Holkerm's infantry as they faced toward the gates. So far, Prince Alafar was holding them at the entrance and slowly drawing them in so the archers could wreak havoc from above, as they had before. Grimm was caked with blood and viscera from the work of his hooves and the sweeping arc of his rider's katana. Shasp was drenched in the blood of his enemies as red fountains opened under his blade, turning his golden helmet into the mask of a cyclopean monster. He heard the distant thrum of horses approaching his rear and hazarded a glance. A troop of nearly seven hundred Tide cavalry was closing on his rear and he quickly assessed the danger. With a cry he called a retreat and rolled Grimm around. Sluggishly, his troop responded and charged back to meet the new threat. Like a catapult missile against a fortress wall, the two cavalry forces collided with the clamor of steel against steel. The Tide cavalry were solid fighters, tight and disciplined and they ground to a halt. Men screamed their hatred and pain as blade and lance thrust and cut in arcs of red ruin. Bodies thumped against the ground as they fell from the saddles to be churned under hooves. Like a man possessed, Shasp hacked and spun, parried and thrust, his pain forgotten, his fatigue beyond consideration. He had become a machine of war, his sole purpose to slay and slay, and slay. Man after man went down before him and his fierce charger, facing Ayponese steel and shod hooves at the same time. Like a unit of destruction, man and horse plowed through their black armored adversaries. He was only vaguely aware of Lexia's presence beside him, her berserk fury wreaking havoc on all who met her. Each cavalry man who closed with her was betrayed by his notion of feminine weakness and in that moment her sword arm cut through their air of superiority, leaving another bloody hulk to slake the sand's unyielding thirst. Soon, the lines of formation were gone and organized combat deteriorated into the seething chaos of war. Each man sought out his own enemy, one at a time and lived or died with each new engagement. Such had become the contest for Laveg and the southern desert kingdoms beneath the burning eye of an indifferent sun. The sand became a red paste of blood and urine, scattered bodies growing in number with each passing moment.

Slowly, the field began to shrink toward the walls of Laveg as the two forces consumed one another with savage appetite. Lord Tabeck turned at the sound of the approaching Evatan force as they appeared from around the wall and rushed into the Tide cavalry. His enemies quickly streamed into his company, cutting soldier from saddle. With his great sword held easily in one fist, he hewed through the first man to face him and laughed with a psychotic smile twisting his evil lips. He felt the familiar rush of killing and it pleased his black heart to sense the splitting of muscle and bone under his sword. More soldiers surrounded him as he cut through them like jungle grass, and he imagined a mass sacrifice where his victims ran to him in great numbers, pledging their lives. A spear tore through his corset but he simply hacked through the shaft and then its owner. Blood did not flow from him as it did others and pain did not trouble his dark mind. He had come to Laveg to bring ruin and rule and to force the admiration of his dark being. The same evil that made him live for centuries reveled now, in massacre, and he considered tossing his weapon aside and using his power to subdue his enemies, but could not yet give up the pleasure of feeling their death under his own hands. No matter how many times a spear thrust through him or sword gashed him, he did not falter and continued to slaughter all who came on. Finally, it was Nachmed's turn but the reluctant king had seen the damage wrought against Tabeck's grey body and decided on a different strategy. With all the force he could muster, he hurled a six foot spear into Tabeck's black mare. The horse screamed in pain as the warhead punctured breast then heart, and it reared back and fell. Tabeck was thrown clear but rolled to his feet, agile as a cat, and faced the rushing men with a smile. Nachmed closed with him, and parried Tabeck's great sword as it slashed down. Like the hammer of a giant, it slammed home, the shock numbing Nachmed's arm all the way to the shoulder. Before he could bring up his guard again or thrust forward, Tabeck had already swung for his head. He ducked a split second too late and the great sword caught the edge of his helmet and sent the steel cap flying. Nachmed reeled backward, unconscious and fell, blood streaming from his scalp. The sorcerer stepped forward to deliver the death blow but a wave of Evatans swarmed over him, and bore him to the ground under a pile of stabbing swords and knives.

Sergeant Albis paused between engagements long enough to find a milling Black Tide horse that had lost its rider. His own horse had been cut from under him long minutes earlier leaving him to fight on foot. This animal didn't care who he was, but wanted only some human guidance in this sea of disorder, as any good war horse would. Albis, rolled up into the saddle and patted the grey mare's neck, then kicked her forward toward Holkerm's fighting cell. He remembered Holkerm's betrayal at the Tetas River and the loss of many of his friends there. Albis had always taken orders well enough from the right commander, but never could stomach generals, especially one who was a traitor and he would test this one's metal. His mare was just reaching a full gallop when another horse flew past him. He was relieved it had not been a Black Tide cavalryman or his head would now be rolling on the sand and cursed himself for his inattention. But who had charged by? He heeled the mare harder and she responded, bringing him closer to the back of the other rider. It was then he recognized the back of Sultan Alafar's armor and helm. The old man's scimitar was held high overhead and he stood in his stirrups, bearing down on Holkerm.

Holkerm watched in horror as his army's rank and file broke apart. His advantage had been neutralized and he wondered incredulously, how Laveg had managed to get an entire army outside her walls undetected. Yet, he still hoped for victory; his forces still outnumbered the defenders and were more skilled in arms. He may not have as many left when the battle was done, but he would still have Laveg's wealth. With that, he could easily build another, much larger, war machine and continue his conquests. All this he considered as he hacked at a soldier who reached for his leg to pull him out of the saddle. As the man went down, Holkerm looked up just in time to see Sultan Alafar's horse crash against his own. Eyes crazed with anger and face painted with blood, the sultan slashed murderously leaving Holkerm to parry desperately to save his life. The general flung up his shield catching the other's blade and turning it aside. He thrust from underneath, piercing the old man's sword harness near his waist.

Alafar doubled over as his scimitar fell from weakened fingers and he cried out in shock and pain. A sickness immediately settled into him as he realized the depth of the wound.

Holkerm smiled with satisfaction. How very fortuitous to come face to face with the sultan of Evata in combat, he thought, as he brought his blade up for the killing blow. But when his arm arced down, and he expected to feel the yielding bone of the old man's skull against his scimitar, it resounded instead against steel.

Albis caught the general's flashing blade only inches from Alafar's head and turned it back. He reined his grey around and thrust alongside Holkerm's beast, bashing him with his shield at the same time. Holkerm nearly fell from the force but managed to right himself in time to knock away Albis' thrust. Their horses danced and bounced, reeling as riders adjusted their position and hacked with equal hatred. Sweat stung their eyes as they exchanged blows, shields ringing and slowly disintegrating under the punishment. Holkerm's face became a visage of consternation as he attempted to work his way under the old veteran's guard, but Albis would have none of it. The sergeant only smiled grimly and returned each stroke he received, unable to look away to check the sultan's condition.

Albis tired of the game and as was his nature, made a bold move. He drove his grey into Holkerm's mount and sliced across the animal's nose. It reared from pain, forcing Holkerm to lean forward to control it and maintain his balance. Albis chose that moment to drop his guard and thrust over Holkerm's shield. His long sword pierced the general's throat just above his collar. Albis quickly backed away as the other sat dumbfounded on his horse with blood pouring down his breastplate. Holkerm swayed then toppled to the sand where he struggled to his knees, clutching the wound. Albis thrust back in to finish him but was forced aside by two Tide horsemen who had seen the battle and rushed in to save their leader.

Holkerm's eyes blurred as he tried gain his feet and failed.

Suddenly, his plans were forgotten as he contemplated whether the wound would cost him his life or not. He coughed up gouts of crimson and spat, growling through the bloody foam in his throat. Just when he thought he had suffered the worst, a voice creaked from behind him.

"You have betrayed my trust, General Holkerm, and the trust of Evata. You will know justice." Still on his knees, Holkerm twisted around to see who had spoken these words of accusation and stared into the pale face of Sultan Alafar, his blade again in his hand. Holkerm started to reach for his fallen sword but never made it. The sultan's steel hissed through Holkerm's neck and the bald head rolled away, eyes bulging and lips trying to form words with no voice.

Alafar's legs gave out from under him and he crumpled to the ground. He felt strangely cold and disconnected as he gazed up at the sun and the clear blue sky around it. His own life began to flow like a river through his mind as he considered all his rights and wrongs, weighing each in a flash of thought. He did not know how long he lay there, feeling his life ebb from him, but then the bearded face of Sergeant Albis obscured the sky.

Albis pried the sultan's hand from his stomach and quickly turned his head away, "Lord Alafar, what can I do?"

"I am dying, Sergeant. I can...accept that..," he wheezed. "Does my son still live?"

"Last I knew my lord. I saw him fighting like a sand cat."

Alafar smiled, "He will make a fine sultan...tell him I am proud."

Albis nodded as the sultan's smile slowly faded and his head lolled. Albis gently reached up with blood-caked fingers and closed Alafar's eyes for the last time. He looked around and saw that word of Holkerm's death was already spreading among the Black Tide and some were falling back to regroup.

When Tabeck went down under the avalanche of human bodies, he let go of his great sword. When the knives and swords began to pierce him in a hundred places, his capricious killing attitude changed to wrath and he called on the dark powers he served. With a cry of hot anger he surged under the weight and the mound of men heaved upward. Suddenly, a wave of air followed by an unforeseen force pushed up and out with the strength of an elephant. As if struck by a battering ram, men flew from him in all directions, leaving Tabeck to stand alone. Another twenty Evatans clustered together, believing they had brought him down once, they could do it again. With a war cry they rushed the lone figure but before they reached him, he swept out his arm and an invisible force swatted them aside like flies. Most lay on the ground bemoaning their broken bones and ruptured organs.

Slowly, the Black Tide withdrew from the city entrance, consolidating their forces, leaving more and more of the defenders free to deal with Tabeck. Spears flew at him, some sticking through his body, but he plucked the shafts out and tossed them aside with a laugh. It wasn't long before the horrified soldiers realized there was no fighting the demon, and Tabeck was encouraged to take the battle to the Evatans. He lifted his hands again and slammed them down with a shout, leaving dozens of men crumpled on the sand. Wading into the defenders, his invisible force smashed them like a man would swat mosquitoes. His maniacal smile returned to his twisted face and the Tide soldiers, though frightened, were heartened by his power and renewed the battle for Laveg.

Many Evatans fled from him as he continued to cause mayhem, cackling all the while over the terrible expression of his power and the fear it inspired in his enemies. But then, in the midst of his revelry, something slammed into his back and he sprawled, face down with his mouth full of sand. Unaffected, he leapt up, snarling and faced the black charger which had ground him into the desert floor.

Shasp sat on Grimm's back, his left hand clenched around the talisman, the right holding the katana. When Shasp had used the talisman in the pyramid, he wasn't sure it would work even though it had saved his life in the Olloua Mountains of the Arrigin. So far, it had kept Tabeck's power at bay, and now he would use it to put an end to this plague who scourged all the southern kingdoms.

Tabeck sneered and waved his hand at Shasp with no effect. With a disgusted grunt, he held his hand out toward a fallen spear and made a motion as if throwing it. The spear shot from the ground and flew toward Shasp just as he goaded Grimm forward. His charger leapt up, catching the missile in his chest. The mighty Grimm screamed in pain, rearing and threw Shasp from the saddle.

The black war horse tried again to lunge at Tabeck but was no longer under the stone's protection. The jungle priest dropped his hand and Grimm fell, crushed as if by some giant hand.

Shasp rolled to his feet and closed with Tabeck, his katana rolled menacingly in his hand. Tabeck bent and picked up his great sword then stood with legs braced, inviting the attack. Shasp crouched, holding his blade along his shoulder in classic Ayponese fashion then darted in like an asp. Before Tabeck could bring his weapon down, Shasp rolled through and slashed his stomach and legs but Tabeck only sneered, feeling no pain and leapt at his opponent, slashing with the massive blade. Ironwrought brought his steel up to block but the force behind the slash was far beyond what he expected and it battered him to the ground, breathless.

Tabeck, enjoying the game, stepped back, tilting his head, "Lieutenant Ironwrought, how nice of you to come out from behind your walls."

Shasp wasted no time returning to his feet. It was clear this would be a game of cat and mouse. Except, he was the mouse and this cat was invincible. "Well, Tabeck, if you refuse to die, then I'll just have to whittle you down a sliver at a time."

"Come then, little man, let's see what sport you have to offer," said Tabeck, grinning through black teeth.

Shasp answered with steel. He anticipated the swing of the great sword and spun away, letting it chop into the ground. He then cut through Tabeck's left wrist, nearly severing it. The priest held up the nearly severed stump and gave it an annoyed expression, then replaced the hand which fused itself. The great sword swept up again and Tabeck worked it into a mighty figure eight pattern, forcing Shasp to back pedal before the swishing blade. Shasp dove to the left and rolled, coming back to his feet, but he underestimated Tabeck's ability to handle the large weapon. As if it were light as a rapier, Tabeck spun the opposite direction at the last moment and the tip caught Shasp between his cuirass and girdle, slicing through his leather jerkin and biting deep into his flesh. He cried out and lurched away as blood flowed down his armor. Hissing at the pain, he forced his body on and fell back into his attack stance, blade wavering. For the first time he realized many of his Attahn and Evatan allies had formed a semi-circle around them on one side, unable to help, while a large group of Black Tide mercenaries formed the other half,

373

wary of their enemies but holding great stock in the outcome of the fight. Everywhere else, the battle still raged but in this small forum it was only Shasp and Tabeck.

The warrior priest laughed again, "I will consider you my first sacrifice to Mal, Lieutenant. You will be a worthy one."

Shasp answered through his teeth, "Go to hell, Tabeck. You'll be talking to your demon face to face soon enough."

He hacked at Tabeck's leg but instead of completing the attack, feinted and drew the tip of his sword up through the underside of his jaw, hewing the lower mandible in half. The priest lashed out with his free hand striking Shasp across his helmet with a clang. Ironwrought crumpled as pain shot through his neck and skull. He tried to rise but fell, rose again and staggered barely in time to catch the great sword with the katana. He flew from his feet, landing on his back a dozen feet away, still clenching the amulet in his hand but unable to rise. He sensed Tabeck was approaching and, though the voice in his head screamed for him to get up, he could not bring his body to obey. Shasp struggled to lift himself on one elbow and watched through blurred eyes as Tabeck stalked toward him, sword resting casually over his shoulder.

"Come now, Lieutenant," he said through his grotesquely disfigured mouth, "surely you have more fight left in you than that."

Shasp rolled to his knees and fought his way to his feet, lurching to one side, "I'm just getting started." Fighting Tabeck was like doing battle with an avalanche and Shasp struggled desperately to think of a strategy to defeat him. The great sword lashed out and Shasp staggered as it clipped his pauldron. Another swipe knocked his katana off guard and rang against his helm spinning Shasp around. He shook his head trying to clear it as Tabeck came in again. When the blade sliced through the air, Shasp ducked inside Tabeck's guard. With a reversed grip he stabbed his katana through Tabeck's skull until the hilt was against his forehead. Tabeck backhanded him and Shasp flew back yet again, twisting and landing on his face. Sounds came to his ears but only mutely, and he was vaguely aware of his limbs lying askance in the sand. Still, he could not bring himself to stand. His mind screamed again, 'get up, get up, fight,' but this time his body refused to move. Tabeck reached up, slowly withdrew the katana from his skull, tossed it aside, and ambled to where Shasp lay crumpled upon the sand. He reached down and lifted him off the ground by the collar of his cuirass. Shasp could smell the fetid breath as Tabeck held his face close.

"You have been a nagging canker on my plans, Lieutenant. I'll be glad to be rid of you." Tabeck stabbed his great sword into the sand leaving it upright then grasped Shasp by the throat and slowly squeezed. Shasp kicked and twisted in the iron grip, clawing at Tabeck's face with no effect but when the stone brushed against the dark priest's skin he heard it sizzle, followed by Tabeck's surprised curse. Only half conscious, Shasp pressed the stone into Tabeck's skin, evoking a cry of pain from the juggernaut. Tabeck pushed him down and snatched his sword from the sand, raising it overhead. Time slowed as Shasp tried weakly to crawl away, knowing there was no escape from the inevitable down stroke of the huge blade. But just before it fell, he heard Lexia's war cry and the slashing of steel across Tabeck's shoulders. The unexpected attack caused the demon to pause long enough for Shasp to roll away but Lexia was caught in the invisible vise of death, suspended from the sand and screaming as the force slowly crushed the life out of her. By sheer will alone, Shasp dove for his katana, fought his way to his feet, and with his last ounce of strength hewed through Tabeck's extended arm. The priest twisted at the sound of whistling air just as the blade flashed through his limb. The grey arm hit the ground at the same time as Lexia's limp form. Tabeck stared at the stump then snarled through black teeth and spun to finish his nagging enemy but Shasp was already in the middle of his second cut. Tabeck barely had time to impose his will on the thirsty katana, stopping it only inches from his neck and leaving both fighters suspended as if in amber.

Poised on the tips of his toes with sword hovering, Shasp strained to push his way through the force while Tabeck struggled to hold it against the stone talisman. Shasp growled in frustration as his eyes bulged behind the slit visor.

A dim memory from his childhood training floated back from the grey recesses of his mind, a lesson on the power of the will. Slowly, he understood the source of Tabeck's power and knew he could not match the will of an immortal but, with the talisman....? He calmed his mind and reverted to the focus technique taught to him by his aged instructor many years past and pressed his will against the unseen wall.

Tabeck held the great sword in his fist but could not move it, requiring all his concentration just to keep the razor-sharp edge from decapitating him. The Evatans shook themselves from their fascination and remembered the magnitude of the struggle between the two champions. They came howling in for a third time, hoping to help put an end to the necromancer, but the black hoplites also understood the stakes and cut them off. The ring of spectators erupted into violence once again and raged around the living statues. A young warrior managed to slip though the pandemonium, came within knife throwing range, and hurled his dagger with all his might. The knife tumbled through the air and sank into Tabeck's lower back.

Shasp felt his opponent's will tear open like papyrus and he stepped through. The katana came free with all the pent up strength he had left and sheered through Tabeck's neck. The grey head dropped to the sand and rolled while the body stumbled in a circle. "This is for Bakarath," he said, hacking off the arm holding the great sword! With another backhand slash he cut through both legs, and then stood swaying over the fallen parts. Evatans cheered and ran toward Shasp, hands waving triumphantly while Tide soldiers began to break off and flee at the sight of their dismembered leader.

Tabeck's head swiveled on the ground and his bright red eyes leered up at Shasp, "You believe you have victory! Instead, you will despair at the sight of my full power!" His hideous laughter cut the air and suddenly, his torso and limbs levitated above the sand. Slowly, they circled in a sluggish vortex as if floating in water, then fused together again. His head rose from the ground and floated through the air, gently settling atop his shoulders like a raven on its perch.

Shasp stumbled back as shock and hopelessness wrenched his stomach. The Evatan soldiers drew up short, gasping, and began to fall back. The Tide mercenaries halted their flight, calling to their comrades and pointing at the floating form of their resurrected warlord.

Tabeck drifted toward Shasp like a feather on the wind and settled on the sand a few feet away. Shasp crouched on his aching muscles, holding the katana before him as his arms trembled with fatigue under the weight of the blade.

Tabeck stepped forward and Shasp tried to hack at his head, but he simply swatted it away with his own sword as if Shasp were a child. His grey fist shot out grasping Ironwrought by the throat and, with a smile on his lips, he slowly squeezed off his air. Blackness hovered over the residue of Shasp's consciousness as he fought to stay alive. He dropped the katana and clawed at Tabeck's eyes but the priest took no notice. Then, from the depths of impending death, a strand of rational thought pierced the darkness and Shasp opened his bloodshot and bulging eyes. With a strange calm, his right hand fumbled at his belt, came away with the Somerikan knife, and plunged it into Tabeck's chest.

The black warlord laughed and shook him by the throat, "Fool, Do you still not realize I am immortal!"

Shasp, feeling his knees buckling, withdrew the knife and, before the wound could close, jammed the stone talisman into the cavity.

Tabeck felt a strange sensation spreading through him, "Wha...?" Absently, he dropped Shasp and stood back staring at his chest. The flesh near the wound began to sizzle and slough off. Tabeck screamed in panic and clawed at his torso but his fingers only hissed and dissolved at the touch, causing him to scream even louder. He was being consumed from the inside out.

Shasp rolled onto his side coughing fitfully through his tortured throat and watched in horror as his nemesis began to smoke and fume. Tabeck's grey flesh sputtered and popped, his screams becoming hysterical as if aflame and unable to find water. His legs collapsed sending him to his knees and he called on every foul spirit he could think of to save him, but already his body began to liquefy. A black fog slowly seeped from Tabeck's melting torso, seething intelligently as it prodded with smoky tendrils. The howling diminished with the decoction of Tabeck and soon, his armor and sword were all that was left upon the sand.

Shasp stared weakly at the milling cloud of smoke. As it probed and twirled, dim realization surfaced and he knew he was seeing the remnant of the entity, Mal. Slowly, the fog drifted across the sand and flowed toward Shasp. He rolled over and crawled on his stomach, trying to escape the thing as he remembered Tabeck's story of possession by the evil force. The tendrils stabbed at his flesh, eyes and mouth but Shasp shook his head violently and poured all his energy into escape. The noxious cloud became increasingly aggressive, tearing at his face, choking his airway and at the same time a different force probed his mind, demanding entrance. Shasp clawed forward as he felt the gates of his mind crumbling before an irresistible onslaught of psychic energy. Elbow over elbow he went toward Tabeck's pile of black armor as thoughts of promised immortality seeped into his brain, promises of godhood and he fought off the unnatural desire to concede. He reached the remains of his foe and dug in the slimy breastplate until his fingers found the stone and clamped around it. The dark fog recoiled from his body as if blown by a strong wind and Shasp hauled himself up to one knee. Mal hovered near him, wanting in, but Shasp held up the stone and tore his helmet from his head. "Foul, stinking demon! Be off! You'll find no rest here!"

The fog hesitated then spun into a howling whirlwind, and vanished.

Shasp took in a deep breath and lurched toward Lexia's lifeless body. Collapsing on his knees, he hovered over her, "Lexia? Lexia?" He reached for her but his world spun out of control. Blood dripped from his wounded face and body as he tried to shake off the pain from the brutal damage. Blackness rushed over him like a wave and his vision winked out. 'So this is what it is to die,' he thought.

CHAPTER 25

Through fog and images, his consciousness drifted, like a
boat on an angry ocean. Thoughts of a childhood, long forgotten,
floated to the surface and dove under again. Familiar faces of friends
and lovers peered down from leaden skies then dissolved. The
waters calmed and faded into clouds, then sand. He walked now but
did not feel the earth beneath his feet or the sun on his neck, then the
dunes poured out beneath him and he sank into a void. Voices darted
in and out of the darkness; pleas, promises, words of encouragement
and blasts of condemnation. He twisted as he hung over the abyss
and screamed. Suddenly, a soft light burned away the void and he
felt firmament under his feet. A strange calmness pervaded his soul,
and a feeling of comfort flowed through him. Slowly, the light took
on the shape and color of a woman's face, beautiful beyond belief,
and she spoke with a powerful, yet sympathetic, voice, "Awake,
Shasp of Aypon!"

Shasp stared at her, awestruck, "Who are you and why
should I wake?"

"Because you must. Wake up!"

He shook his head, "No, I won't."

"Wake up!"

"No!" But suddenly pain filled him and the light became
harsh, stabbing at his eyes.

"Shasp, wake up."

His eyelids fluttered and his body became racked with pain.
At first, he could only see light, and then blurred images, a face
hovering close to him.

"Wake up," came Lexia's voice, soft and encouraging.

His vision cleared and he looked into her good eye. He
remembered the battlefield and thought he still lay on the sand. He
raised himself, expecting to see the bloody havoc of war strewn
about him, to learn if they were victors or slaves. Instead, his eyes
were greeted by a finely decorated room of marble with expensive
trappings. He looked at himself and was surprised to find he was
lying naked, covered by a linen sheet. Illusion slowly gave way to
reality, "Where am I?"

Lexia handed him a chalice of pure water, "Drink this.

You're in the palace."

"How long?"

"A week," came a thin voice near the door. A dark skinned man with a white beard walked in and held Shasp's face between his palms, looking into his eyes for some sign. "I have never seen a man take so much punishment and live. You nearly lost your intestines through that gash in your stomach. Your skull was badly cracked and most of your ribs were broken. I reset the bone in your forearm, so don't move it."

Lexia, covered with half-healed cuts and bruises, pushed the court physician away and leaned over Shasp, her lips pressed against his. She combed his tangled hair out of his eyes, "You should stay in bed for a while, until you're healed."

Shasp sat up but groaned at the pain in his stomach and the physician gently pushed him back down, "Please! Your stitches will tear! Another week, sir, at least."

Lexia gave a smile that betrayed her joy, "Don't worry, I'll be here if you need me."

"That is certain," complained the old physician. "I haven't been able to get rid of her since you were consigned to my care. Remember, no moving around!" He gave Lexia a disapproving glare then left the room.

Shasp lay back against a propped pillow, "So, we won."

Lexia nodded, "When you killed Tabeck, the Black Tide soldiers withdrew to their baggage train to take stock of their numbers. Alafar took the opportunity to seize their war machines. Without them, all hope of a siege was finished."

Shasp smiled, "The old Sultan is crafty, that's for certain."

Lexia shook her head, "No, 'Prince' Alafar. The Sultan was killed and Prince Alafar is now Sultan Alafar."

"I hope he was wise enough to re-fortify the gates. As soon as the Black Tide reaches Kalyfar, word of Laveg's condition will inspire Angelis to hire the mercenaries, combine them with their army and send them right back!"

Lexia laughed, "You don't give Alafar enough credit. His father taught him well. He foresaw exactly what you did."

Shasp raised an eyebrow, "He pursued them?   Wiped them out?"

"No," she said, "we didn't have the resources nor did the

381

prince think it was wise to destroy what was left of the city's population to do so. These Black Tide soldiers are mercenaries. The prince held a parley with the senior officers and cut a deal."

Shasp shook his head, "No."

Lexia nodded, "Oh yes. Even now, the soldiers of the Tide patrol our walls and help to reconstruct the city. In Alafar's own words, 'never underestimate the power of gold.' however, he did insist their armor be re-colored to reflect their new assignment in Laveg. Gold and red."

"I guess it was the only reasonable action," said Shasp soberly, "Laveg needed more soldiers to deter the surrounding territories from racing to pluck her like a fig. I hope Alafar was wise enough to take precautions against any insurrections."

Lexia was about to answer when another voice interrupted, "I have," said Alafar as he entered through the doorway. "The new mercenary forces have been broken up and merged with the Evatan regulars. I also make sure they are paid well and regularly. So far, there have been no signs of trouble."

Shasp nodded to the new sultan, "but doesn't it bother you, having them so close, inside the walls after all the destruction they caused?"

"My dear Shasp, Champion of Laveg, a mercenary is like a sword. It does not swing itself. Should I hate the blade which cuts me or the man who wields it?"

"Your logic is flawless, Sire. I am sorry to hear about your father."

Alafar lowered his eyes, "I am sorry you missed his entombment. It was worthy of him and I will never forget his wisdom." Alafar crossed the room and plucked a grape from a bowl near Shasp's bedside. "I hope you don't mind, but I stole your sergeant."

Shasp looked confused, "Stole him?"

"Yes, he's been promoted to captain of my personal guard. I thought, if he was loyal to you through all your trials, then he would be trustworthy with my life."

Shasp laughed, "If I tell him to."

Alafar frowned at the jest but then broke into laughter, "No doubt! I hope to inspire loyalty such as you do, my friend!"

Shasp winced at the pain his chuckles caused. Alafar became

serious, "I know you have not yet healed, but when you have, I wish to ask a final favor of you."

Ironwrought nodded, "Not because you are the sultan, but because I consider you a friend, name it."

Alafar began to pace, "A contingent of the hoplites departed before I could begin negotiations. I learned why later. My brother, Terafar, still lives. He promised them great wealth if they guarded him and returned him to Fenic where he hoped to find refuge with my cousin, Hamed. I'm afraid, together, they pose a threat to our weakened condition. Terafar is a blood prince of Evata. With Hamed's support, they may gather allies from Kulunata, Teksika and Kalyfar." Alafar paused for a long while and Shasp thought his eyes were beginning to water, perhaps thinking of a childhood memory of his little brother. "Shasp . . . will you kill my brother?" Shasp's eyes narrowed, "Gladly."

CHAPTER 26

Prince Terafar lounged on a low couch in an elegant chamber, nibbling on a pomegranate. His battered face had healed but his bitter resentment had only flared hotter. Holkerm and Tabeck were dead and with them, all their plans. He considered his fortune so far. Luck and a smooth tongue bought him a platoon of black hoplites and bore him safely to Fenic. During the painful journey, he wondered whether his cousin, Hamed, would have him put to death or receive him graciously. Again luck favored him. Upon his arrival, he found Fenic devastated by the old Black Tide. Without the Adder Blossom, the army went insane and turned its inconsolable wrath against the citizenry before the lack of drug finally ate away the last man. Smoke was still rising from burned out buildings. When he sought Hamed, he found him in the palace, screaming profanity and foaming from the mouth in the grip of withdrawal. By evening, Hamed was dead and Fenic was looking for leadership, a role he gladly accepted. Now he was regent of Fenic and Laveg was nothing more than a bleeding wreck many days travel away. Terafar smiled to himself. He would be sultan of Evata yet. Even now, there were emissaries from Kulunata and Teksika waiting to speak to him. He would bring together another force before his brother could strengthen Laveg. He would learn from Holkerm's mistakes and show patience when it came time to lay siege again. Fenic still retained a substantial force of regulars who could be supplemented in a short time. The treasury was well provisioned and Terafar was quite content, believing complete power to be a certainty which required only a little patience and some smooth talking.

He jumped to his feet, called for the guard outside to prepare to accompany him to the hall, and threw a regal purple cape over his shoulders. He must appear confident if he was to convince the delegates to commit their troops. Suddenly, he realized he had not heard a reply from the guard.

"Guard, did you hear me? We go to the hall." No reply. Terafar stepped through the threshold and gasped in horror at the two hoplites that lay in pools of spreading crimson. He looked down the hall, saw no one, and called out, "Guards! Guards!" With fear twisting his gut he retreated to his chambers, found his scimitar hanging from a partition, and pulled the sword free, hands shaking. He eased back through the door and started down the corridor. Twenty paces along he found three more hoplite corpses, their bodies pierced and cut, lying in blood. Terafar backed away then turned only to find a cloaked figure standing behind him. He let out a startled scream and lashed out with his blade but a lightning fast reflex batted it away. The prince stumbled and fled back down the hall casting a glance over his shoulder at his pursuer, but the man had disappeared. He ducked into his chambers, slammed the door, and threw the bolt. With his sword held out before him he backed away from the door, eyes wide with fear. A voice from behind startled him and he spun around.

"You should lock your windows, Prince Terafar."

Standing on the ledge of a tall narrow window, the cloaked man reached up and drew back the hood. Terafar shrieked at the sight of the horned head and slit visor, turned toward the door and grasped the bolt. Before he could unlock it, he was caught by the shoulder and thrown backward.

Shasp walked forward slowly, backing Terafar into a corner. The prince's terror overtook him and he slashed with the scimitar over and over but the katana parried every thrust expertly until Shasp finally hooked the point of his blade in Terafar's hilt and wrenched the scimitar from his grasp. The weapon flew across the room and clattered against the floor. Now the prince faced a menacing point as it hovered inches from his chest. "Wait, Lieutenant, I'll give you anything, wealth, power!"

"It doesn't interest me, Terafar. I came here at your brother's request."

Terafar's face reddened with anger, "I am his blood and yet he sends you to assassinate me! He is not worthy to be called sultan!"

"You are not worthy to live, Terafar, let alone be called prince!"

"Even my brother would not allow a common soldier to draw royal blood!"

Shasp pressed the point into his flesh, "Don't be so sure. Still, he has not forgotten you are his blood and royalty." He reached into his cloak, drew forth a vial of green liquid and held it out. "Your brother offers you this as a token of his mercy."

"And if I refuse it?"

Shasp sank the tip through the first layers of skin, evoking a hiss of pain, "I'll split you open and leave you to collect your organs from the ground at your leisure."

For a long time, Terafar stood facing Shasp then slowly reached up and took the vial from his hand. He held it up to the light and gave a wisp of a laugh. "Alafar always was the lucky one while I was the one who always tried to force fate." He uncorked the vial, holding it near his lips, "It was all so close; almost mine."

Shasp gestured for him to drink, "It's too bad you won't live long enough to realize wealth and power are not the most important things in life."

Terafar smirked, "I'm beginning to see they mean little," and he tipped the vial into his mouth. Shasp stepped back and lowered his katana. For a few seconds Terafar stood waiting, then stumbled, shaking his head, "It works quickly." Terafar took a single step and pitched forward onto his face, dead.

Shasp considered his prone body, "They mean nothing to the dead, my prince."

EPILOGUE

Shasp leaned forward and stroked the neck of the black stallion then sat back to study the sun's position in the sky, his hand shading his eyes. The horse was expensive and the chief of the Badowa tribe was hard pressed to give him up. Fortunately, Alafar insisted on filling his saddlebags with gold and expensive gems. Shasp was able to make the desert chief an offer he couldn't refuse.

He was not Grimm, with his long legs and neck, but the horse's physique was impressive nonetheless. The handlers insisted he was tried in battle, and the beast had the scars to prove it. To say the least, his gait was as smooth as glass and he seemed capable of trotting forever. They chose the route through the northern Trabic, across the Snake River to Ceddin on the coast.

Shasp smiled at Lexia as she rode alongside, "What do you think? Is he worthy of a name like Grimm?"

Lexia shrugged, "Why don't you let him prove himself before you give him that name."

Shasp nodded, "I think I will."

She laughed, "When we get to Ceddin, I'm going to get the most expensive room I can find and bathe in wine. You can join me."

He returned her smile, "I think you've gotten spoiled, all that time spent in the palace. Maybe you should have stayed."

"And miss all this," she gestured at the wide, empty desert. "Actually, I'm ready to feel the north wind on my skin again."

Shasp was suddenly quiet, "I'm tired of all this intrigue. Maybe I'll go with you to Bretcombia."

"I don't know," she chuckled, "you're too small for a Bretcombian."

"I can hold my own; besides, I think I would enjoy the calm of the northern mountains."

She threw her head back and laughed loudly, "Calm? In Bretcombia? We fight hard and play harder. The word calm is not part of our language."

He shrugged, "A few raids might keep me in good form and at least your people are straight forward. I can appreciate that."

They rode along for the rest of the afternoon, accepting the silence of each other's company. For two wayward mercenaries, fair company was worth more than all the gold in Evata and it never tempted men to evil.

Shasp considered the heat of the sun again. The west coast would be a welcome sight.

BOOK IV

BITTER

RETURNS

Chapter 1

Emperor Muhara waited impatiently as his food taster sampled the delicacies spread out on the low table. Candied meats, vegetables and delicate cakes glistened in the light of a thousand candles, the scent making his mouth water with anticipation. General Hatsuro sensed his frustration and sought to distract him before he executed another taster.

"Great emperor, forgive me for interrupting, but there are grave matters requiring your attention."

The regent smoothed the yellow silk robes over his lanky frame with long-nailed fingers. "What is it General?" he said tersely, hovering over his meal.

Hatsuro paused, examining his superior's lean face and carefully oiled hair. It seemed there were more grey streaks than last they spoke. "I believe the threat of rebellion is no longer just rumor from the streets. A growing animosity for your lordship has been demonstrated and our barracks in the waterfront district have been burned."

Without moving his eyes from the table Muhara waved a hand. "So, you are the general. Go crush them and have the instigators impaled in public. Why are you bothering me with such trifles? Do I need to replace you? Are you not competent enough to deal with a handful of rioters?"

Hatsuro stiffened in his armor at the insinuation, "No, your eminence, I have already done these things, but my agents have found scripts of condemnation nailed on nearly every business. Someone is inciting the people with lies; claiming that their poverty is caused by the endless squandering of the palace and fraudulent corruption of the government officials under your control. I merely wished to inform you that we are seeking this lying traitor."

The food taster finished his duties and considered the interior of his mouth, seeking any sensations of burning or bitterness. He closed his eyes and tilted his head, opened them and checked his balance. He was stable and his stomach felt no ill effects. With a wan smile he bowed toward the emperor indicating that it was safe for his master to have his meal.

Smiling, Muhara took a delicate bite of candied pheasant.

General Hatsuro stood quietly with several other body servants as the emperor ate, knowing it was dangerous and pointless to disturb him at that time.

Hatsuro was average height for an Ayponese man, but stout. His grey hair and beard testified to his age as did the weariness in his almond-shaped eyes. His family had served the masters of Aypon for ten generations though he could not think of a single emperor as indifferent as the current one, no matter how hard he searched his memory.

Hatsuro squinted at the taster when the man shook his head as if clearing it from a fog. Suddenly, the taster's eyes widened and he lurched forward. "Eminence, do not eat!" Three steps from the table the taster's knees buckled, he choked and flew into convulsions. The emperor's face paled with horror and he waved his arms frantically, "My apothecary!" but his screams turned into a choked attempt at breathing. Foam flecked his lips and his eyes rolled up as Muhara reeled backward on his cushions in a spasmodic fit. The palace dining hall erupted in panic as guards ran from their posts and tried to hold the thrashing man.

"Find the apothecary!" screamed Hatsuro as he held the emperor down against the bucking protest of his flailing limbs.

Immediately, the guards sprinted from the room and returned, dragging the apothecary by his elbows. The fragile little man glanced at the emperor and flew into a panic. He nearly dropped the wooden box he was carrying as he flopped down beside the thrashing emperor. His knobby hands shook as he sorted through various vials of colored elixirs, uncorking them and forcing the extracts between Muhara's bluing lips. Seconds passed slowly and eight vials lay emptied and scattered before the regent's body began to relax. The apothecary was frozen with fear as he waited to see if the relaxation was from death or the effect of his elixirs. A rhythmic rise and fall returned to the emperor's breathing and both general and old man fell back on their haunches, breathing a sigh of relief. Slowly, Muhara returned to consciousness and stared about him with a bewildered look.

"Eminence," said Hatsuro, "are you well?" and he helped Emperor Muhara to sit up.

Muhara looked around as his expression slowly changed from one of confusion to rage. He grasped the edge of the dining table and flung it over, sending the tainted food flying. "I want this assassin's head and I want it now! Do you understand me, Hatsuro! Now!"

"My lord, we are using all our resources. Our most worthy soldiers and inspectors have combed the city and the country side, but found nothing. Even the warlord, Tetsushiro Ishaharo, has failed to find even the smallest clue."

Muhara's face grew red as his temper exploded, "Then find someone better! Better than you and better than Tetsushiro! I will have no more attempts on my life! This vermin has come within a hand's breadth of killing me five times in the last eight years and I will have no more of it! Bring me Tetsushiro . . . .and Kamira Gami; he has trained nearly every Kyamurai warrior in Aypon over the last thirty years. Maybe he will know of someone more competent."

Tetsushiro Ishaharo strode through the palace corridors with an arrogance seldom seen within a mile of the emperor. The leather of his Ayponese armor creaked with the rhythmic movement of his powerful legs and arms. His long black hair swayed against his back and his wicked black eyes stared straight ahead, as if the courtesans he passed were nothing more than insects. He stopped before the massive portals to the throne room and turned his head just enough to regard the two men on either side of the doors. Both were Black Tigers, the personal bodyguard to the emperor. They were Kyamurai, the very best, and wore the dark red lacquered armor of their caste. Kyamurai armor was a layered affair, with thick padding beneath laminated leather and bamboo. A heavy apron of woven leather and steel chain protected the thighs below which thick greaves ended in a bronze instep. The helmet was a steel cap with a skirt covering the neck and a mask to protect the face. The mask was hinged on the side of the helm as a visor and molded in intimidating reliefs to draw out their enemies' fears. Every Kyamurai had a different mask, usually molded in the form of a spirit or animal representing their family. All but the Black Tigers, who proudly displayed the mask of a tiger's face and the image of a black tiger's leaping figure on their breast plates. Even though both men were highly trained warriors, Tetsushiro took pleasure in their discomfort as he halted before the doors.

One stepped forward, "Your weapons, Lord Tetsushiro, if you please."

Tetsushiro had handed his long, sleek Kyamurai sword over countless times before when called to the emperor's presence, but he never tired of pausing before relinquishing the weapon, just long enough to make the guards wonder if he might refuse. With a hint of a smile he slid the strong narrow blade from the sheath on his back. He admired the perfection of his sword for a moment, its strong narrow blade with a tanto point and its simple round guard, just big enough to cover his hand. He flipped it over and laid it across his forearm, pommel toward the edgy bodyguards. "You will treat it with sacred care." The guard nodded and bowed before accepting it. Both knew full well how many men had died beneath its edge.

The huge golden doors swung silently open and the warlord, Tetsushiro, passed into the great hall, the emperor's throne room. The ceiling was vaulted, ten times the height of a man, with enormous wooden beams plated with gold leaf and engraved with thousands of tiny reliefs. A man could spend a lifetime admiring them all. Square pillars of rare wood held the massive roof aloft and a polished wood of light yellow shined under his feet. Large braziers emitted even warmth and the perfumed smoke of incense. He sniffed, 'Sandalwood,' he thought. He continued across the length of the chamber, casually glancing to the row of Black Tiger guards on each side and eventually halted before the raised dais of the Emperor of Aypon, the most powerful empire in Azia. He slowly lowered himself onto his face, "Oh worthy emperor, your servant has come as you have bid. Your will is my command."

Muhara left Tetsushiro in his prone state, "I have called you here because I have grown weary of your lack of progress. As you know, the assassin nearly killed me . . . again."

Tetsushiro raised his head slightly, "Lord, I have been . . ."

"Silence, I have commanded the city inspector to investigate the incident. I think you will find what he has to say very interesting. Rise, Tetsushiro."

The warlord came to his feet, wincing over the length of time Muhara had kept him prostrate. It was meant it to humiliate him.

Muhara inclined his head toward a thin, middle-aged man on is left, "Inspector Pok Cho."

The man bowed deeply, arms folded with his hands inside the wide emerald sleeves of his silk robe. Pok Cho wore his jet black hair in a top-knot and kept his face cleanly shaven save for a long

393

wispy mustache. He turned his gaze on Tetsushiro, his narrow dark eyes showing as much humility as possible. "A few days ago, I discovered the means by which the emperor nearly perished. After hundreds of needless interrogations and tortures, I learned that a stranger brought a cow to the royal stockyards for sale. The stock keeper claimed that the cow appeared healthy in every way. There were some remnants of the animal still in the palace kitchens, so I took samples of it to a local chemist, whom I sometimes employ. After hours of exposure to a variety of chemicals, and various other concoctions, he discovered which type of poison it was. A rare, slow-acting toxin found only in the deepest jungles far to the east. It seems that the cow had been fed the toxin before it was sold to the palace. The substance is extremely expensive, so whoever is behind the assassination attempts has money and patience."

Emperor Muhara nodded and the inspector withdrew, bowing. "I told Inspector Pok Cho of my disappointment over your inability to bring this assassin to justice. On his advice I have had Kamira Gami brought here. He waits without."

Tetsushiro clenched his jaws, a sign he knew the regent would not miss, "Lord, I will bring this man to you. I only need time."

"You have had time and you have accomplished nothing. Meanwhile, this snake poisons my food under our noses! Bring in Kamira Gami."

In the vast golden hall, the aged instructor of the Kyamurai walked quickly to the base of the ivory throne and threw himself down before Muhara, his long, thin, white beard dusting the floor beneath his wrinkled face. With his eyes focused on the floor, as was required when in the emperor's presence, Kamira waited for the ruler to speak.

"Kamira Gami, do you know why you are here?"

Kamira answered with a raspy voice, "I do not, my lord."

"You are here because my general and my warlord are incompetent. I have nearly lost my life on several occasions and no one can find this assassin who vexes me. Is there another who can find this man and bring him to me?"

"Tetsushiro is the greatest warrior in Aypon. After his brother was killed, he trained with a zeal rarely seen in any other. He is our best."

"Then our best is not good enough!" fumed Muhara, "Is there no one else?"

Kamira was silent for a long moment, fearful of affronting the ruler of House Ishaharo. "Perhaps there is another; the one who fled in exile after killing Tetsushiro's brother. Masatsuo Tekkensei."

Muhara rubbed his chin, "I have heard that name. Where is he?"

"I do not know, Eminence, the killing of the first son of the house of Ishaharo was a death sentence to him, for he was not of noble birth. He fled fifteen years ago to the land across the great ocean."

"Ah, it was he who slew Matashumi, I nearly forgot. Do you think he is capable of doing what my warlord and general cannot?"

Kamira answered with his face to the floor, "I do not know, Eminence, but he was a talented student. Perhaps . . . if he continued in the ways of the Kyamurai."

The emperor nodded, "You may go, Kamira."

After Kamira Gami had bowed his way out of the hall, Muhara motioned to Pok Cho. He quickly moved before the throne and threw himself face down, "My lord."

"You will go to Nomerika to find this Masatsuo Tekkensei, and bring him to me." Muhara turned to Tetsushiro, "When Masatsuo Tekkensei arrives, you will extend him every hospitality of your house. You will put your feud aside for the greater good of protecting your emperor. Anything less will be considered treason."

Tetsushiro bowed low and backed out of the hall. He retrieved his sword and strode from the palace, smiling with satisfaction. It would be good to finally meet Masatsuo again.

Chapter 2

"He's been in there a long time," whispered Harkin as he peered over his employer's shoulder.

Morgit, annoyed at Harkin's large head hovering so close to his own, shoved his second back behind him. "Patience, fool," he said as he turned to look around the corner again. The coastal rain had subsided to a mere drizzle and Morgit's back was beginning to ache from standing and watching for so long. It was very late and would still be dark for several more hours. Behind him, his six hired thugs shifted and fidgeted with the handles of their knives and swords. The short eaves high overhead had kept most of the rain off, but the wind had kicked up and began to blow the misty sprinkle into the narrow alley where they were becoming soaked.

Harkin was a big man with a protruding stomach and a deep rumbling voice. "We should go in after him," he suggested.

Harkin was big, but not bright. Morgit turned, folded his arms and looked into Harkin's scar-puckered face. Harkin's left eye was completely covered in scar tissue, adding a fearsome aspect to his already intimidating frame. "We haven't hunted this bounty for a year just so he could escape or worse yet, kill us all. And, I'm not going to lose a thousand gold coins just because you're impatient." Morgit returned his attention to the street and to the tavern door down the block.

He shivered as the cobblestones sucked his body heat out through the soles of his feet and cursed the cities of men. He didn't mind the leaden skies overhead or the constant presence of rain. He had been a tracker for over twenty years, the best there was, but he was getting old. He scratched in his red and silver beard, wondering how long he would have to stand there.

He had pursued his prey southeast through Dahoe and then south again into the Evata desert, where he was nearly captured by an army of madmen. Then they went west again to the city of Ceddin on the northern Kalyfar coast where he found out he was only days behind his quarry. The trail turned northeast to Bretcombia and he and his crew followed but were set upon by the barbarians which inhabit those mountains. He barely escaped with his life and only Harkin survived the slaughter, such as he was. They were forced to hole up in Tanya to re-supply with a fresh batch of eager mercenaries. Their presence was not reassuring to Morgit. His prey left bodies everywhere he went . . . lots of them. Now the trail had finally ended and for the first time since he had been paid to track this man down, he caught his first glimpse. Morgit was surprised to find him traveling with a woman, but was even more surprised at his appearance. From all the stories he had accumulated on the long track, he'd expected the man to be as tall as a lance with muscles like an ox. Instead, he was only slightly taller than average and, though of an athletic build, he was no lion. It was even more peculiar that his trail ended in the very city where Morgit had accepted his commission.

Harkin leaned down again, "Why we gotta stand here all day? We done our job, let's just tell those slant-eyes where he is."

Morgit spat and huffed, "Because, idiot, if they are willing to pay a thousand in gold just for information of his whereabouts, then what do you suppose they will pay for the man himself?"

Harkin was silent; thinking on it longer than a normal man might have, and then smiled with understanding. "So, what are we wait'n for? Let's go get 'em."

"He's dangerous, Harkin. I want a clean advantage."

Harkin placed his huge hand on Morgit's chest and shoved him out of the way, "I seen'em, Morgit, he ain't nothin. I'll go get 'em." The giant strolled away from the alley toward the tavern door with his feet slapping in the shallow pools of the cobblestone street, and his long mace bumping against his side.

Morgit cursed, "You fool, come back!" but Harkin had made up his mind. The tracker spun on the men behind him, "Leu, you and Addis get around the back. Load your crossbows and if he tries to escape out the rear, take him in the legs. I don't want him dead."

Leu stepped on the bow of his weapon and heaved on the string, using his back, until it clicked into the trigger assembly. "What about the woman?"

"I don't care about her, if she gets in the way, kill her." Morgit turned to two more of his men, "Blith and Adel, get to the corner opposite the tavern, keep your bows ready. Verner, stay with me." Morgit signaled to his last man on the roof who nodded from above and notched an arrow.

His pack was still in the process of dispersing when the

tavern door across the street exploded in shards of wood and Harkin stumbled backward into the street, blood streaming from his mouth. A figure stepped casually out onto the tavern's raised porch and Harkin lurched toward him, his horrible battle cry echoing off the stone buildings of the crammed streets, his mace swinging overhead.

Shasp had no idea what the behemoth wanted with him, but he barely escaped being brained by his club. Instinctively, he had struck him in the face, creating enough time and space for a more devastating kick to the chest, the force of which sent him through the tavern door and down the steps of the entrance. The ungainly warrior was big and slow, but he took the punishing blows as if they were only slaps. Shasp walked out onto the porch just as the goliath gathered himself and launched a second attack. He hadn't come to Attle for trouble and was hoping to avoid the officers of the local magistrates, but enough was enough. He slid the katana from its shoulder scabbard when he caught the movement of men out of the corner of his eye. There was no time to look further; the mace came down like a meteor, shattering the wooden porch where Shasp had stood a split second before. Harkin was overextended for a moment and Shasp seized the opportunity to hack through his spine, causing the man to go limp as a wet rag. Men ran to his right along the wall of the building across the street and to his left were two more. All had bows or crossbows. He ducked back into the building with his back against the wall and peered out. Lexia looked up from her stew, still drunk from the late-night binge.

"Lexia, did you piss somebody off yesterday?"

She swallowed her food and raised the brow over her good eye, "Me? What about you?"

"I think you better finish your meal, we have company; lots of it."

Lexia scooped another mouthful of stew into her mouth, and then pulled a cavalry saber from the sheath beside her.

A voice called from outside, "Drop you weapons and come out. I promise you will not be harmed!"

Shasp kicked a table over in front of the door, "If it's all the same to you, I think I'll stay here. The food's not bad and the ale is good! What do you want?"

Morgit cursed Harkin's stupidity and stubbornness. A

standoff was exactly what he was trying to avoid. Well, it was the last mistake Harkin would make and Morgit did not intend to duplicate it. "There is a man who very much wants to meet you! How can I convince you to come out!"

Shasp laughed, "You are missing the point! I'm not going to separate myself from my sword. I suggest you find another tavern to occupy!"

Morgit spat and made several complex hand signs to the man on the roof, who quickly disappeared from sight. He turned to Verner, a crusty old veteran, "Bring Leu and Addis through the back entrance and we'll come in the front. Be careful of the crossfire." Verner nodded and sprinted around the back of the tavern. Morgit signaled for Blith and Adel to move forward. If only this game could have been played out in his native Oshintan forest, then things would have been easy. He was at home in the woods, but here in Attle? He was out of his element.

Lexia moved toward the back door but Shasp called after her, "No! It will be covered. Check the roof."

Lexia started up the narrow staircase, thankful that the patrons were still sleeping . . . though not for long. She ran up the stairs to the landing and stood face to face with the archer who had come down from the roof. "Where the hell did you come from?" At point-blank range, the arrow hissed from the ash bow and the missile tore through Lexia's left lung. The impact spun her around, but she reeled forward. The man's second arrow was only half out of his quiver when she hacked into his neck. Wheezing, she turned and stumbled back down the stairs, her saber limp in her hands. When she reached the first landing, Shasp saw the arrow in her chest, the blood on her lips.

"Shasp," she wheezed, "I'm. . . I'm . . ." Lexia collapsed, tumbling down the last few stairs, and flopped on her back, lifeless.

"Lexia!" he shouted as he bounded toward her, but before he could reach her, he heard the back door shatter and the stomp of boots against the plank floor. Men were coming into the kitchen on the other side of the bar. He kicked over another table and piled it on top of the first in front of the porch door, then turned toward the bar just as Verner, Leu and Addis burst through. Leu and Addis leveled their crossbows as Verner stood behind them with a black -toothed grin on his face and his long sword in hand. As he faced the three bounty hunters, Shasp could hear the clatter of the tables being moved from the front entrance behind him. There was no time to think, only to act. He leapt forward, twisting in the air like a court dancer, his katana cocked across his body. Addis was an inexperienced youth and fired his crossbow before his target was certain. When Shasp landed, his arm uncoiled with the added force of the spin and cut off Addis' head. Leu was older and a cool-headed fighter. No sooner had Addis' head left his shoulders, than Leu sent a bolt through Shasp's thigh. With a loud thunk, the steel bolt slammed into Shasp and pinned him to a wooden support beam. Shasp cried out and grabbed the bolt, but it wouldn't budge. Leu smiled at his expert shot and Verner called out to the men who were trying to get in through the barricaded front door.

"We got him boss! Take your time!" Verner ambled over to where Shasp hung limp with pain and in his confidence prodded him with his long sword. "You're not so damn tough after all, are ya?"

His words had barely left his lips when Shasp came to life, his katana snaking around Verner's long sword to its hilt, where it instantly severed the hand holding it. Verner fell back and screamed at his red stump as Shasp lurched forward with a scream of his own, ripping the bolt through his leg, fletching and all. He left the dripping missile in the post and limped toward Leu, who was scrambling to tear his short sword from its sheath. Shasp pierced him through the heart before Leu's blade was halfway out.

By the time Adel and Blith had made it through the door, Addis and Leu were dead and Verner was useless. Adel lifted his bow, but Shasp flung a chair and fouled his aim, sending the arrow into the wall where it hummed with vibration. Blith released his broad head from the frustrated string just as Shasp threw himself sideways. The shaft pierced the meat of his right shoulder and passed clear through, but his left hand was already throwing the Somerikan long knife straight from its scabbard. Blith cried out and clutched at the blade projecting from his pelvis as he fell over. Adel had another arrow notched and was just bringing the broad head to bear with deadly intent when Morgit stepped through the door behind him and thrust his short sword between Adel's shoulder blades. The bow and shaft clattered to the floor and Adel fell forward with a look only the betrayed could truly appreciate.

Morgit stepped over the spreading pool of blood, "You see? I

400

really *didn't* want to harm you."

Shasp pushed himself up with his good arm and fought his way to his feet, carrying all his weight on his uninjured leg. He shifted the katana to his left hand and limped to where Lexia lay unmoving at the bottom of the stairs, blood oozing from her mouth. He leaned down with disbelief in his eyes, stroked her brown hair and kissed her forehead, "Lexia." He placed his forehead against hers and squeezed his eyes shut as he fought against the rising despair that sought to overwhelm his senses. His body felt weak with the sudden onslaught of grief and he started to weep, but then something snapped in him. Some instinct recognized the futility and danger his sadness was creating within the perilous situation and siphoned it away to another feeling that was much more functional. The emotional strain finally burst apart, and when Morgit saw the look of burning retribution carved on Shasp's face, his blood ran cold with fear. Shasp stood and started for Morgit, dragging his disabled leg behind him.

Morgit backed away slowly, collecting Adel's bow and shaft as he went. "Don't be insane, you're too wounded to fight me and I don't want to kill you."

Shasp stopped and hovered over Blith's writhing body before kicking him over and jerking his knife out of the moaning man. "Really? That's too bad, because I intend to butcher you like an ox." He started toward Morgit again, "Your men killed my friend and since they are all dead, I'm holding you responsible." Shasp backed Morgit all the way to the middle of the street. Lamps were being lit in the windows below and overhead. The clamor of battle had awakened the residents of the tavern and the surrounding apartments. Morgit was running out of time. Soon the watch would come and he might lose his life as well as his prize. "Drop your weapon!"

"I don't think so."

Morgit fired an arrow point blank into Shasp's good leg. Shasp barked and fell over sideways, but he hauled himself upright again, legs quivering. He lurched toward Morgit again. The tracker fitted another arrow and was taking aim. Shasp was about to throw his knife when a voice called out in a familiar accent.

"I see you have found my friend."

Recognizing the voice, Morgit released the tension on the arrow and lowered the bow. "I....I have."

401

Five figures emerged from the shadows of a nearby alley and came into the dim lamplight of the street. Shasp immediately recognized the armor, as it was very similar to his own, Kyamurai, but that wasn't all. They wore the Black Tiger mask and emblem. Their leader was slender, with black hair carefully pinned into a top knot and a long, limp, black mustache hung under his nose. A chain graced his thin neck and at the end of it, the golden disc of a Hung Lai inspector.

The inspector turned to Morgit, "I believe our agreement was for you to locate this man and inform me, but here I find you in the middle of the street putting arrows into him. Per chance, were you planning on changing our agreement?"

Morgit was caught and he knew it, "Maybe I was, but he's here now and he's alive. I've upheld my end and lost all my men doing your work, so pay me what you promised."

Pok Cho frowned, "Hhhmm . . . I wonder, if the man I had sent to follow you had not returned when he did, we might have arrived to find you both gone. I do not appreciate your dishonesty."

Morgit turned suddenly and drew the bow, aiming it at Pok Cho, "I want my damn gold, and you better get it before my arm gets tired!"

Pok Cho appeared unaffected by the threat to his life and shrugged. "As you wish," and he looked over his shoulder at one of his men. The kyamurai stepped forward with a medium sized chest and placed it at Morgit's feet, then returned to his place. Morgit slowly laid the bow on the ground beside him, arrow still notched, deciding he could still kill the slender Ayponese man if his soldiers moved. He removed the clasp pin and opened the hinged lid. Instantly, yellow powder erupted into his face, blinding him and causing him to cough uncontrollably. One of Pok Cho's men started forward, drawing his sword, but Pok put up his hand staying him. Morgit began to cough blood and it leaked from his eyes and ears. He screamed in rage and defiance and stumbled away down the street, seeking to escape, but only made it a short distance before he collapsed, twitching.

Pok Cho walked over to Shasp and, with his hands clasped together in his sleeves, bowed low and spoke in Ayponese. "My lord regent, the Emperor of Aypon, graciously requests your presence in Hung Lai. Will you attend us?"

Shasp felt himself weakening with the loss of blood, as he tried to remember the long unused words of his native tongue. "What if I refuse?"

The Black Tigers fanned out around Shasp. They were not average men and Shasp knew it. The inspector lifted a slender straw to his mouth and exhaled. Shasp felt a tiny sting in his neck and immediately, his limbs became like water. He sank to the cobblestones.

Pok Cho smiled down at him, "The emperor has expressed his desire to meet you . . . Masatsuo Tekkensei."

The world faded to black.

Chapter 3

The small boy ran across the deck of the galleon toward the bow of the ship. He liked the way it moved under his feet with the rolling waves and keeping his balance was a game he never tired of. The sky was bright blue and the wind was crisp against his face, tossing his brown hair. Rough looking deck hands strolled back and forth on their way to assorted duties, mopping, changing the rigging, handling the ship's rudder. He never tired of pestering the good-natured men, constantly asking what it was they did and why they did it. He skipped over a bucket and mop then ran up the short flight of stairs to the bow.

Standing against the rail and looking out over the blue was a tall man with brown hair and beard. His grey eyes searched the horizon as his powerful hand rested on the pommel of his sheathed long sword. He turned and looked down when the boy tugged at his sleeve, smiling through his beard as if he had just received a wonderful gift. Lifting the child in his arms, their grey eyes met, sharing and lingering in paternal warmth; warmth which spoke of love and satisfaction.

Shasp awoke to the crack of thunder and the flash of lightning. He blinked against the pounding of his head and tried to lick away the taste of metal that lingered on his lips. He became increasingly aware of a growing cold, spreading over him, and the presence of water as it dripped from above. His wrists ached. He blinked again, clearing the haze from his vision and peered into the dark. He looked up as lightning snapped a second time and saw a grid of iron bands above him; his arms were tied to it. The room lurched and the floor dipped down, leaving him hanging in midair until he felt a mild impact and the floor tilted the other way. Tiny voices could be heard through the howling wind and crash of water. 'So,' he thought, 'I'm aboard a ship and chained in the hold.' Another flash of lightning illuminated the hold, revealing several prisoners and in that split second, Shasp recognized the face of the Hung Lai inspector, only a few feet from him. The man's hair was soaked and his red silk robe was plastered against his body, and he was also tied, but smiled politely anyway.

404

"You are awake, good. I must apologize for the accommodations, but an unfortunate chain of events has complicated our journey. I am truly sorry."

For the first time, Shasp realized he was naked from the waist up. He still wore his black riding breeches and boots, but everything else was gone. Clearly, the man did not expect to find himself chained in the bowels of a ship, but that did not mean he had not intended it for Shasp. He glanced around at the other prisoners, making out the faces of several sailor types and then concentrated on his Ayponese tongue. "Who are you and . . . if you did not intend for us to be tied up down here, how did we get here?"

"I am Pok Cho," he inclined his head, as he could not bow while his hands were tied overhead, "I am the Chief Inspector of Hung Lai, sent by the Emperor to find you. We were a day out of Attle when the ship was taken by pirates, and we were thrown down here. You were resting comfortably in a decent cabin until then."

The ship nosed into another wave and once again the floor angled away from their feet, leaving men to moan as they dangled from the ropes, waiting for the floor to return. When Shasp felt his feet against the rough wet planks again, he resumed his conversation. "I find that hard to believe, as you had four Black Tigers with you, more than a match for a ship full of sea rats."

Pok Cho, with water streaming down his face, nodded, "True, but I did not say the ship was taken by force. You see, the captain hired a new crew while in Attle and, in his ignorance, did not realize they were not actually looking for work. The men above are the crew of a pirate . . . what was his name? Oh, yes, Captain Jake Bulyford. It seems his own ship was nearly lost to rot and barnacles, so once we were out of port, he drugged the wine and the water. Not a very brave way to take a ship, but if one does not wish to jeopardize his crew, it is efficient."

"Where are your men now, I don't see them here?"

Pok appeared as apathetic as ever, "Thrown overboard with most the others. I would have gone too, but they believed I was probably worth a ransom to someone, my clothes perhaps. They were going to throw you over until I told them you were worth much more than me. The rest of the men are bound for a slave port, at least that is what I overheard them saying."

Shasp looked up to examine his bonds, squinting against the

pouring rain as it pelted his eyes. The ropes had been looped through the iron grid overhead and then wrapped around his wrists, holding them together. He grasped the rope and began to drag it back and forth in short strokes against the iron bands, sawing at the wet strands. The moisture would impede his progress, but there was no other option. If the vessel broke apart in the storm while they were still lashed in the hold, everyone below deck would drown. Harder and harder he whipped the rope, his shoulder wound causing him intense pain. Seconds grew into minutes and minutes dissolved into an unknown quantity before Shasp could tell the sturdy rope was sawn most the way through. However, his shoulder was fatigued beyond its limits and the storm was beginning to let up. He pulled his feet off the planks and coiled up, placing them against the iron grid, hanging upside down, and pushed against it. At the same time, he pulled with his back. Corded muscles and veins popped out from under his skin as he strained against the diminished fibers of the rope. The pain in his pierced legs and shoulder was slowly sending him toward madness and he screamed with the tormented voice of a man who refused to give up against all odds. Suddenly, one of the ropes gave with a snap, and Shasp thumped against the hull on his back. He lay against the rough wood waiting for the throbbing to subside and touched the bandages on is thighs. The extreme exertion had opened his wounds and his fingers came away red with blood. Slowly, he stumbled up and then fell again when the ship pitched forward. Cursing, he climbed to his feet and stood before Pok Cho, who seemed impressed.

"It would take me all night to try to untie everyone, so I'm going for a blade. I'll be back soon." Staggering, he made his way to some stairs and started up toward the main deck.

As soon as Shasp opened the hatch, he was blasted by freezing ocean spray. Thunder boomed and lightning flashed into the water as he struggled to stay upright against the bucking ship. He snatched up a length of rope and a wooden mallet, something that was always found in great supply on any ship. Quickly, he tied the rope to the handle of the mallet, twisting it tightly to deny slippage, then he lashed the other end to the mast and wound some of it around his ankle. At first, he was not noticed by the frantic pirates who ran to and fro, lashing down gear and moving the sails as they drove away from the winds. It was only a matter of time though, and eventually a sailor stumbled by in the dark, stopped and stared at the man who held the dangling mallet. The sea rat recognized him as one of the men he had personally tossed into the hold and ripped his cutlass from his sash, lunging at Shasp. Shasp whipped the mallet around his head then sent it flying at the sailor's head. With a crack that could be heard above the raging winds, it smashed into the man's skull and he flew backward. The deck heaved as a rogue waved slammed into the port side and washed the unconscious pirate overboard. Another buccaneer had seen the contest from where he tied down a piece of rigging and called to several others who started down off the bow.

Shasp had lunged for the fallen cutlass, but too late, and it was swept over the side with its owner. Now, four more men, soaked with salt water, moved across the deck, knives and short swords in their fists. Shasp peered through the wind-swept darkness, let out some slack from his make-shift weapon, and twirled it overhead again. Two men came at him simultaneously from his left and right, but he jerked the mallet out of its orbit and slammed it into the closest man's face, breaking his nose. The other darted in, but before he could get within reach, Shasp had jerked the mallet back the other way and clunked it against his skull as well. The two prone bodies sloshed about on the planks with each new crashing wave, but the pirates who were still standing were more mindful than their comrades and eased forward with care. Shasp was about to send his missile out again when he realized the ship had just crested a tall wave. In the background, he saw its twin looming like a black mountain beyond the bow and knew they were about to dive into a deep valley of water.

The ship's nose dropped violently as it caromed down the slope of the wave and both of Shasp's assailants slid down the deck away from him. Pain lanced through his leg as the rope became taut around his ankle and he dangled from the mast by his foot. The bow crashed into the trough at the bottom of the waves, foamy water surging over it, then sprang up to meet the next challenge. Wood groaned loudly against the wrenching forces of the ocean and the mast complained as if it were threatening to snap. Pirates tied themselves to barrels and rigging, giving up on trying to do anything that might save the ship.

As the galleon's fore deck lifted and the monstrous wave tried to shrug the vessel off, Shasp seized the opportunity and loosed his ankle from the rope. He would have to move quickly if he was to avoid being swatted into the water by the hand of an angry wave. His balance was poor due to the injuries in his legs and his muscles rebelled against his commands, faltering. He lunged toward an old pirate who had twined himself against an empty barrel, praying to some unknown sea goddess, and ripped the man's cutlass out of its sheath. The old sailor never even noticed or else did not care. Shasp staggered side to side under the bucking of the ship, toward the hatch which led to the hold and stumbled down it. Water rained off him and glistened on his skin in the dim light as he found Pok Cho and sawed at his ropes.

"Impressive," he said without emotion, "thank you for your efforts."

Shasp grinned, "Don't thank me yet. You might change your mind once you're topside." He glanced around, "Can anyone here sail this ship?"

A short, stocky man with wooly, black hair and beard nodded, "Aye, I can. Jus gae mi a chance!"

Shasp sliced through his bonds and then another's. He turned to the second man, a golden haired youth, "Cut everyone else loose and get above!" Then he turned to Pok, "You and the would be captain, come with me."

Pok threw off his silken robe, leaving it on the floor of the hold. He was thin, but the muscles beneath the pasty skin were taut. In only his red silk trousers and slippers, he followed Shasp and the wooly-headed sailor back up the stairs and into the awaiting storm. Shasp squinted against the stinging wind as his eyes swept over the ship to the aft end. There, behind the rudder wheel, the pirate captain leaned hard against the steering rungs. Against the protests of the lurching ship, they struggled up the short stairs to the steering platform on the aft deck. Just above them, Captain Bulyford and his first mate fought with the ship's rudder wheel. Shasp reached the top stair when the captain's first mate abandoned the wheel and met him there. The pirate was tall and lanky with a long reach which he immediately used to his advantage, weaving a deadly web of slashes. Shasp's wounded shoulder was all but worthless after breaking the ropes that had held him and he was forced to fight left-handed. The cutlass felt clumsy in his hand until he reversed its grip and began to employ it the way he did his Somerikan knife. He and the first mate battled on the stairs and tiny sparks from the banging steel winked in and out of existence until Shasp was finally able to press the pirate back enough to gain access to the deck. Now, with much of his advantage gone, the first mate attacked out of desperation, a move that quickly left him open and allowed Shasp to get inside his reach. Shasp blocked a downward slash and spun inside the pirate's guard, punching the cutlass through his sternum. Groaning, the first mate pitched backward over the rail and disappeared. Free from further attack, they surrounded the captain and Shasp touched the cutlass to his throat. The captain's face was a mass of matted brown hair and scars, and he laughed like a lunatic. His hip-high boots were water-logged and a dark purple waist coat covered his drenched linen shirt.

"Not a wise move, killing me! Who'll steer the ship through this storm?

The wooly-headed sailor stepped up, "I will!"

The captain's pinched expression darted from one wet face to another and he stepped back from the wheel, "It's all yours lad, but someone should see to the sails, for my men have lost heart and aren't worth a whore's promise now!"

The sailor quickly grasped the spinning wheel and heaved it back over, "He's raight! We hav' ta trim tha' sail or we'll lose tha' mast! Ge' tha' men outta tha' hold!"

Shasp turned to Pok Cho, "Watch the captain! I'll get the others!"

No sooner had Pok nodded agreement and Shasp turned to go, than the captain drew his knife and lunged toward the sailor's back. Pok's hand shot out, as he plunged his rigid index finger into the captain's armpit. The pirate immediately froze as if in ice and fell over, still locked in the same position with his arm extended and the knife clenched in his fist. Pok turned back to the sailor as if nothing of significance had occurred, "Sail on." Nervously, the man looked at Pok then put his bulging shoulders back against the wheel, straining under the rudder's resistance.

Shasp and the prisoners from the hold surged up onto the deck and set to trimming the sail, tugging at the securing ropes and climbing into the mast nets. Knowing little about sailing, Shasp took to disarming the rest of the pirate crew amidst the slamming wash and wind. Most did not resist, and those who did, died quickly.

All through the night they fought the tempest and wrestled against the mountains of crashing waves. More than once, Shasp thought the ship would break apart and leave them to a watery death, but she held fast to her timbers and planks. Some of the pirates were kicked into life and helped once more with the ropes and gear. Near the early hours of morning, the storm giants lost interest in the tiny ship and moved on. With the rising sun came a fair, calm wind and an easy rolling surface for the hull to glide upon. The wooly-headed sailor slumped over the wheel, his back and shoulders beyond exhaustion, while Pok Cho wrung the water out of his favorite robe. The pirate captain, Jake Bulyford, still lay on his side like a living statue and most of the original crew took the time to put at least a few bruises on him.

Shasp had spent most of the morning cracking open crates in search of his gear and finally found it in the captain's cabin. The fool probably thought the helmet and shoulder guards, or pauldrons, were real gold. He looked around the spacious cabin and took in the elaborately carved reliefs on the mahogany beams and the view looking out from the wide cabin window and decided to make the room his own. He boxed the armor back up and left it, but secured the katana to his back. Wearing armor at sea was like strapping a large rock to your chest and strolling around the rail. He didn't want to walk or move anymore, his legs were throbbing after last night's ordeal, but there were things that needed to be done. He limped out of the cabin and up to the steering platform where he prodded the wooly-haired sailor.

"Wake up."

The man raised his head slowly, "Aye, a'm awake. Wha' is it?"

"What's your name?"

"Gyle A'Creshec, wha's yurs?"

Shasp smiled, "That depends on who you ask, but you can call me Shasp."

"Ya' saved our arses last night, I'm beholden ta ya."

"I wouldn't have lived long without you steering the ship through that storm. I just wanted to let everyone know that I've decided to be captain until I get back to Attle. After that, the ship is yours, Gyle."

Gyle stammered, "Ma...Mine?"

Pok Cho overheard the conversation and knew that without his Black Tigers he had lost all leverage with his charge. "Excuse me, Masatsuo, but did I hear you say you would be returning to Attle?"

"That's right, I'm going back."

Pok Cho became agitated, "But your emperor needs you. How can you go back?"

Shasp scowled, "He is not *my* emperor."

"You are Ayponese! It is your sacred duty as a Kyamurai to serve him! You must come to Aypon!" Pok demanded.

Shasp took a step toward Pok Cho, mindful of the man's skill and reach, "Oh, how convenient for you to call upon my duty as a patriot of Aypon, now that your emperor wants something from me, whatever that may be. Look at me! My hair is not black and my eyes are not brown, though everything else about me says I am Ayponese. Others living in Aypon, with the exception of one man, saw me only as a mongrel . . . mixed blood. I was nothing to them and I would have been nothing to your emperor, so do not tell me about my sacred duty! My duty is to survive in this pitiless world and that is all!" He started to turn away, stopped as if he had forgotten to say something then spun around with his katana hissing from its sheath. The blade stopped just below the first layer of skin on Pok Cho's neck. "I almost forgot. You sent men to hunt me down. Give me one reason why I shouldn't push this blade in half an inch deeper and end your life."

Pok's heart was in his throat, but he managed to appear as indifferent as always. "I did not send men to hunt you down. I sent men to find you and that is all. That foolish tracker was supposed to tell me where you were, nothing more. He simply decided I would pay more for a ransom. If only he knew who he was dealing with, he may have been happy to collect his fee and go his way. It was my intention to convince you to return with me to Aypon."

Shasp laughed, "With four Black Tigers? Yes, your narcotic dart was very convincing. Need I remind you that your friends killed someone who was very important to me?"

Pok swallowed as he felt the razor-sharp edge press ever so slightly into his neck, "I had no knowledge of that. Truly, I am most sympathetic to your loss. Your pain is my pain."

"I wonder." Shasp dropped the sword to his side. "If your emperor wants something from me, then he is going to have to pay for it like everyone else . . . but more."

Pok Cho brightened, "Of course, please state your terms. I am authorized to make any offer."

Shasp sheathed his weapon, "First; a full pardon. I assume you know why I left Aypon when I was only fifteen."

Pok nodded, "I do, please go on."

"Second; my fee; two pounds in cut rubies and diamonds; one now and one when I have completed whatever the emperor requests."

Pok nodded again, "Agreed, and your last?"

"I want answers."

"Answers? I do not understand."

"I want to know who my mother was . . . who my father was and what happened to them."

"This I do not know, but I will find out. Is that all?"

412

Shasp nodded and started toward his cabin when Pok called after him, "What do you suggest we do with Captain Bulyford?

Shasp looked down at their prisoner, "Hmmm . . . Shaylinn nerve lock. I thought that was a forbidden practice."

Pok smiled wanly, "It depends on who you work for," he tilted his head toward Bulyford, " . . . the captain?"

Shasp shrugged, "We will show him the same mercy he showed your Tigers. Throw him overboard."

Bulyford gave a pitiful moan.

Chapter 4

The plump old woman wrung the blood-soaked rag over a bowl near the bed, turning the mixture of water and vinegar to a pinkish color. She sighed and turned toward the bed, slumping with exhaustion.

Nadel was a poor woman, in fact she was as poor as one could be, but had decided a long time ago that she was not going to let her poverty affect her the way it had those who became thieves and prostitutes. She laughed to herself, 'prostitute,' and mused how maybe she wouldn't mind that part time, but old as she was it wasn't likely.

Two days ago, she was ambling up Market Street, collecting the laundry she would be washing that day when she stopped near the White Owl tavern. At least a dozen of the City Guardsmen were milling about on the street outside as their captain stood with his arms folded. He was questioning several people, including the owner, Owen, and a man with the bandaged stump of a wrist. Eight bloody corpses lay in the street, placed in a neat row, all facing the same direction with steam rising off the bodies as they cooled. Nadel's morbid curiosity got the better of her and she moved a little closer to get a look. Her breath sucked in at the sight of one corpse that caught her attention. A woman; but not the sort of woman Nadel was used to seeing in Attle, but a woman who, even in death, still exuded an aura of confidence and intimidation. A warrior. Her brown braid lay askew and limp on the wet cobblestones. There was a scar running through one of her closed eyes and an arrow jutted from her chest. Nadel knew she should be going about her business, but something about the woman intrigued her and so she stayed.

She heard the captain say it was some sort of a barroom brawl and one of the tavern's occupants was missing. Once he had gathered the information that the magistrate would require, he ordered his men to drag the corpses out of the street and into the alley behind the tavern where the local undertaker could pick them up with a wagon. It wouldn't do to have them lying about in public. His men, of course, picked over the bodies, removing weapons and anything else of value before discarding the dead. Eventually, everyone went their own way . . . everyone but Nadel. She looked around to see if anyone was watching her then hurried into the alley, checking over her shoulder as she went. When she was sure no one was watching, she approached the piled corpses and dragged two off before she found the woman beneath. What was it about the woman that was so fascinating? Was it that she was just so different? Nadel leaned close to examine her face, so many fine scars. Suddenly, she caught a movement out of the corner of her eye; a movement so small and faint that at first she doubted she had seen anything. It was the shaft of the arrow. Turning her face away from the woman, she stared at the arrow sticking up from her chest, stared at it with intense expectation. There! A tiny movement only perceptible at the end of the rod near the fletching. Now that she knew what she was looking for, it was easier to see; a rhythmic tiny movement amplified along the shaft; a heartbeat. Could it be? She dropped down on one knee and placed her ear close to the woman's mouth, feeling for the faintest hint of breath. "Dear me!" she gasped. At first she thought about running and telling the captain that he had made a terrible mistake and one of the corpses was not a corpse at all, but then she remembered the penalty for a disturbance where blood is shed and people lay dead in the street. The captain would simply allow the woman to heal up so that the magistrate could order her to be hung, and that did not sit well with Nadel. She could only imagine what sort of attention the woman would receive in the jail while she awaited execution, handsome as she was. No, that would not do. Nadel chewed on her thumb and glanced around until an idea surfaced. She laid out several bed sheets, then grabbed the wounded woman by the heels and pulled her off the bloody heap and onto the spread linens. Nadel grasped the arrow close to the wound and held it as stable as possible before taking hold of the top and snapping it off. The woman never made a sound. She was about as close to death as one could be without slipping over to the other side and that would happen soon enough if Nadel didn't do something quick. The warrior woman would probably die anyway.

A few minutes later, Nadel was dragging her huge load of laundry up the street behind her. Fortunately for her, she didn't live far from the tavern. At one point the butcher stepped out from his shop, "My, Nadel, but you have your work cut out for you today. That has to be the largest load of wash I have ever seen you bring by!"

"Oh yes!" she answered with her heart in her throat, "I

415

believe it is."

Nadel's home was just a one room apartment off a narrow, back alley; one of those places that never got any sunlight, due to the height of the walls outside, but it was her home, such as it was.

The next two days would be hard on her, sleeping on the floor and caring for this anonymous person, yet still needing to accomplish her cleaning and make a living. Fortunately, the broad head was narrow and small, only requiring a small incision to remove it, but it had gone deep into the lung and fever was setting in; that meant infection. Nadel hoped the woman was strong because on her wages there was no affording medicine. She cleaned the wound and kept fresh bandages on it with wax paper underneath to keep the hole from sucking in air when the woman breathed, but it leaked a yellow fluid and required constant attention. She laid the bowl on the ground and gathered the woman's hand into her own, caressing it. It did not seem like so long she had sat on the same stool holding the hand of her daughter when she burned with fever nearly ten years ago. Now, here she was again, but maybe this time, this woman would live. That would give her some redemption wouldn't it? Redemption for saving this life when she had failed to save another? A small tear wound its way down Nadel's cheek as she gazed at Lexia's unconscious face and remembered her daughter.

Chapter 5

The boy shot up from his shallow bed, looking around. The loud slamming of a door had jerked him from a deep sleep and now he listened as booted feet beat out a staccato on the wooden floor of his home. Men were yelling, but there were no men in this house, only mother and the old lady. Father was gone . . . .had been gone. He slipped from his covers and went to the door, slowly pulling it open. Lanterns wove back and forth across the hall and his mother screamed, demanding an explanation. The old lady also came into the hall, adding her voice of disdain to the other, but a large shadow came out behind her and stabbed her with a knife. Mother screamed again, but this time with fear, and when one of the men turned toward him, she became insane with maternal rage. Two of them grabbed her arms and two more, her feet. Another swept him up over a burly shoulder and carried him down the hall. He screamed for his mother until his lungs ached, and though she strained against her captors, she could not help him. He bit, kicked and clawed until the man had enough and knocked him unconscious with the back of his hand.

He awoke to the jogging motion of a cart and found himself alone in a small cage mounted to the deck of the wagon. He was no longer in the city and watched as lonely green hills slid by, creating a sense of finality and isolation in him as he was drawn ever farther away.

The smell of old fish and human refuse began to interfere with Shasp's sleep and he awoke from his light slumber. He sat up in the bow net, folded his arms across his chest and considered the feeling of deja vu created by the odor. He had never stepped foot in Hung Lai, but he knew all about it. The city of wealth, some called it. Others called it the city of deception, and Shasp conceded that the later was a good title for most cities. The sun emptied out its warmth as he cast his gaze over the horizon, taking in the many Azian fishing boats or 'junks' and merchant vessels from Aypon, China and Honguk, scattered over the water. They tacked and bobbed, some fishing, others headed for the docks. Hung Lai, a center for trade, welcomed them all.

Slowly, the galleon coursed through the waves, and the city grew steadily before the ship. As they closed, Shasp could make out the images of the warehouses which lined the docks and the many roofs of homes, temples and businesses. The bay was wrapped by level land which gave way to a steep, verdant hillside beyond. The earth there was carved into a multitude of terraces and upon each was perched a long row of houses which crowded one another, like a branch full of birds.

The ship eased into the bay, dwarfing all other craft, and scudded along the wooden wharves until the sails were dropped and it ran out of momentum, bumping against the dock. Deck hands tossed down heavy tether ropes to awaiting almond-eyed men who threw the loops over the protruding posts of the dock.

It had taken a month to reach Hung Lai due to the storm which had blown them off course, and Shasp's wounds had mostly healed, but he still felt an ache deeper inside the muscle. He had strapped on his armor just before arriving and tested his shoulder and legs with several sword katas. When he was satisfied, he went back to his cabin and sat on his bunk.

There was so much wrong inside him, so many things that pricked at his soul, destroying his focus. Most of all, there was Lexia. Shasp had tried to keep from falling in love with her. Ella's death had left him determined not to be vulnerable to another, but Lexia's free spirit and constant companionship had worn down his cool exterior. She never asked him for anything and was always careful to read his moods, because she cherished their friendship. How could he not fall in love with her? Now, like Ella, she was gone. It wasn't as if either of them died because of something they had done. No, both deaths were because of him, because of his entanglements. He dropped his head into his hands and clawed at his scalp as he fought to keep his anguish inside. Emotions of loss and guilt blended with his anxiety of returning to Aypon. So many memories, jumbled together, and with them the same plague of tortured feelings. Hatred, pride, sadness, guilt and yes . . . love. What was he doing here, really? Wealth was not the issue, though most of his gold was probably claimed by a tavern owner in Oshintan. He needed to know who he was and *why* he was.

Outside he could hear the lowering of the gangplank and the voices of sailors calling down to the men on the docks, asking about the local brothels and opium houses. Then came another sound; the sound of many horses galloping down the wharf. Outside, sailors and deck hands dove out of the way as the indifferent riders barreled over the worn planks.

Pok Cho stepped off the gangplank and bowed low as the double column of mounted warriors drew reign. "Master Tetsushiro, I am honored that you have come to welcome me."

Tetsushiro ignored Pok Cho's greeting, "Where is Masatsuo?"

Pok cleared his throat and smiled nervously, "I beg patience on his behalf. He has been among the barbarians for many years and . . . ."

"Do not make excuses for me, Pok Cho," called Shasp from the top of the gangplank, "The barbarians have nothing to do with it." In full armor, Shasp descended to the dock, walked past Pok Cho and stood before Tetsushiro's horse, his eyes locked with the warlord's. "It is not rudeness which kept me. I was considering the implications of my return."

Tetsushiro smiled warmly, "Welcome Masatsuo, the emperor has bid me make my home and all its comforts available to you. Will you accompany me?"

Shasp noted his smile, but did not miss the poorly hidden malice in Tetsushiro's black eyes. "I will." Already the tension between them was almost tangible.

Shasp called up to the sailors on deck, "Let my horse out of the hold."

The sailors exchanged a few worried glances then turned reluctantly to the port door. One flung it open and leapt back as a lean black stallion burst onto the deck, slamming the door the rest the way open with a loud bang. Men moved away as the beast pawed uncertainly at the deck, listening and turning his long neck.

Shasp whistled. The horse followed the shrill sound down the gangplank and stopped next to Shasp, snorting and rubbing his muzzle against his arm. "There you are Tempest."

Tetsushiro was clearly impressed with the mount, "A magnificent beast!"

Shasp took pleasure in the praise, "He is that. Pok, have his saddle brought down." Pok Cho bowed and walked up the plank. Shasp had been surprised to find his mount in the hold of the

419

galleon, but Pok Cho made it clear that he had taken great pain to bring everything which belonged to him, including his horse.

"I want you to understand, Masatsuo; I harbor no ill will over my brother's death. It was a long time ago and my emperor needs you."

"Very well," said Shasp, still wondering about the emotions behind his eyes, "but you should know that it was your brother who challenged me. I had no choice in the matter."

Tetsushiro nodded, "He was always strong willed."

Shasp watched as the warlord's eyes shifted briefly from hatred to sorrow. Clearly Tetsushiro's words were not consistent with his feelings. Silently, Shasp wondered how great a danger the man posed. Tempest was finally saddled and Shasp came along side of the warlord as was appropriate for a man of his status.

"I heard you call the horse 'Tempest,' what does it mean?"

The name had been spoken in Nomerikan so Shasp explained it in the Ayponese. "It is the word for a great storm. He has a habit for being unpredictable and will outrun a good northern gale."

Tetsushiro laughed at the obvious stretching of the truth. The Ayponese mounts tended to be slightly shorter and sturdier than their Nomerikan cousins, but were just as agile if not as fast. But Tempest was an anomaly, just as his last horse, Grimm, had been and Shasp considered himself blessed to come by not only one such horse in his lifetime, but two.

Flocks of seagulls wheeled chaotically overhead, as Shasp checked the sun's position, their unique calls echoing against the hillside. It was afternoon. By the time they left the wharfs and entered the markets, Shasp's senses were overwhelmed by the sights and smells of the pressing carts and houses. Vendors and buyers locked in debate over the value of wares. Open crates of produce expressed a spectrum of colors and textures. The scent of fish, kelp, sweat and spices clashed, creating a confusion of odors.

They pressed on through the low laying markets and began the long climb up the wide flagstone street of the hillside which snaked back and forth across the terraces. Intermittently, wide rows of stone steps cut between the houses, allowing foot traffic to flow smoothly, and relieving the congestion of the main road. The typical Ayponese dwelling was a single story affair, constructed in the shape of a horseshoe, with a ribbed roof dipping slightly in the center like an inverted fishbone. The interior doors of the houses did not open on hinges, but slid from side to side in a shallow wooden trough cut into the threshold. The walls within were usually made from a simple wooden frame covered with rice paper laid against intricately carved panels of geometric reliefs. They were a necessity in a land plagued by earthquakes. A heavy wall of wood or stone could collapse and kill the resident. Not a single nail was used in the construction, rather all the frame work was jointed and locked together. This allowed the building to shift, and flex with the shaking ground. Heat came from a fireplace under one end of the house, which allowed the hot smoke to flow under the floor, yet kept it outside the home. The Ayponese were simple people who liked a simple decor, but the temples were another story altogether. Brilliant colors and intricate murals covered every temple in Aypon, and various artist competed for the opportunity to gain favor from their ancestors by adding their imagination to the walls and ceilings.

Shasp looked upward toward the top of the tall hill. Silhouetted against the sky, the palace rested like a bird of prey on the edge of its nest.

High walls encompassed the massive structure and the outbuildings which surrounded it. The walls were easily twice as tall as the roof of a common house, made of cut granite, and patrolled by guards who glared down from above as they leaned on eight foot naginatas. The naginata was a pole weapon with a razor-sharp sickle on the end and a long pointed blade for stabbing mounted just above

421

it. Other forms of naginatas were similar to a meat cleaver or a long heavy knife fixed to the end of a pole. In skilled hands they could be devastating even to mounted Kyamurai.

The palace was constructed in the same cultural shape as any other Ayponese home but with multiple stories, a hundred times the capacity, and made from expensive cedar. It rested at the apex of the city's loftiest hill.

The Ayponese horses were snorting and huffing as the columns of warriors reached the gate, but Tempest was as fresh as ever, anxious to be out after being kept in the hold of the ship. The gates of the palace were made of thick oak and painted with the red and black, yin and yang symbols which contributed to so much of local life. A guard with a Black Tiger mask leered down from the wall adjacent to the gate, carefully inspecting the men below. Tetsushiro lifted his chin so the guard could see his face. After a moment, the sentinel looked back over his shoulder and called down to others hidden behind the gate. Massive pin hinges groaned under the enormous weight as the gates moved ponderously aside, and they urged their horses through.

Shasp marveled at the beauty within. Tall deciduous trees waved in the breeze, all showing signs of careful pruning and many held fruit or nuts. All along the flagstone path, manicured bushes and hedgerows had been coaxed into extraordinary shapes and patterns. The path split apart and curved off at angles, offering different avenues through the sprawling gardens. Flowers of every conceivable variety bloomed and swayed in the breeze, their perfumes filling the fresh, cool air; air which was very different from that of the docks. As they continued, Shasp saw several large, shallow ponds of crystal blue water filled with shining coy. Eventually, the garden released them into the area immediately surrounding the palace. Dozens of smaller buildings sprawled beneath it, the homes of all the servants who cared for the needs of the emperor and the outbuildings which housed his stock and goods. The area within the walls was over two square miles and all of it was immaculate. Even though the palace of Hung Lai was not as enormous or extravagant as the palaces of Nomerika, its beauty and natural rhythms were beyond compare. Almond-eyed commoners bustled about a cobbled square in their earthen hued clothing. The women wore kimonos of pastel colors mixed with dark brown, green or black while the men wore a tabard that reached to their knees with a robe underneath and belted at the waist. All Ayponese clothing was a heavy affair of layers and folds that allowed one the option of shedding a skin of cloth as the temperature climbed and then replacing it later as it cooled. Both the men and women kept their black hair combed and pinned up, though in different ways. The woman's hair was always coiled and kept on top while a man would put part of his hair up in a knot and allow much of it to hang at their backs. Seeing these peasants again in their modest dress and honest daily lives gave him a sense of pride, but Shasp remembered that these were only one aspect of the Ayponese culture. The warrior and ruling classes were keenly deceptive and hard on these folk. As they moved through the little village toward the palace, he noticed that not a single person looked up at him.

Before he realized it, they had reached the palace entrance and Tetsushiro was dismounting. Shasp swung off as servants hurried to take their horses. Tetsushiro's men waited outside as the palace eunuchs led Shasp and the warlord up the broad stone steps and through gold leafed doors. Their footsteps echoed down a long corridor, flanked by columns of cedar, the scent of which was intoxicating. At the end of the hall two Black Tigers stepped forward and collected their weapons. Beyond the guards were another set of golden doors which one of the Black Tigers cracked open and whispered to someone on the other side. Long seconds passed in silence as Shasp and Tetsushiro waited. The doors opened without protest on well-oiled hinges and a court eunuch waved them inside. Shasp had difficulty keeping his eyes fixed ahead, so breathtaking was the workmanship and artistry of the golden hall with its honey-colored floor and vaulted beams covered in decorated gold leaf. At the far end, a figure reclined on a large ivory throne, also intricately carved. To his left and right, standing like statues along the walls with their naginatas, were rows of Black Tigers, at least forty. The two closest to him stepped out and crossed their pole arms, barring any further advancement.   Tetsushiro slowly lowered himself to the ground, face down.   Shasp knew this moment would come, knew the culture and its requirements. He bowed at the waist, then stood with his arms folded.

At first, the guards didn't know what to make of it. No one had ever dared to stand in the emperor's presence without his permission. Only the Black Tigers were allowed to stand and then only out of necessity. Their anger at this transgression quickly shook them from their shock and they leapt forward fully intent on skewering the infidel when a loud command from behind stopped them.

"Hold your weapons!" called out Muhara, "I did not send for this man and wait for an entire year to see his face so you could kill him when he got here!" The sharp blades of the naginatas were only a hair's width from Shasp, but he had not flinched. Like trained dogs, they heeled at the sound of the emperor's command and returned to their places. A tense silence hung over the room as the emperor considered the man who stood before him. "Why do you refuse to bow before your emperor?"

"It's simple," replied Shasp, "You are not *my* emperor, and I prostrate myself for no man."

"All bow before me in Aypon. To refuse is to invite a torturous death."

Shasp nodded understanding, "If I was one of your servants or vassals, I would throw myself down. I am not. I did not initially choose to return to Aypon and I have long since ceased to consider myself as Ayponese. I will not degrade myself by being prone on your floor. If you wish me so, then your guards can kill me and arrange my limbs however you like."

Muhara stared through Shasp for a moment, and then gave a sardonic laugh. "I will allow you stand. Rise Tetsushiro!" Muhara motioned to a servant who ran forward, holding a platter with a cup. The emperor took the goblet and sipped the warm rice wine. "So, you are the slayer of Matashumi, first born of the house of Ishaharo." Shasp winced at the name. Muhara continued, "Do you know why I sent for you?"

"I do not, though I pried at Inspector Cho for weeks, he revealed nothing."

"It is good that he did not. Otherwise I would have dealt harshly with him. It is not a servant's place to do more than he is told. Pok Cho's only directive was to bring you to me. We thought you might be living off your Kyamurai skills and so I also gave him the authority to negotiate any fees. Has this been done to your satisfaction?"

"It has, but there are some things not so easily given.

424

Inspector Cho will inform you, I am sure."

Muhara nodded, "Of course; now to business. Over the last eight years, I have been plagued by attempts on my life. Normally such things are but minor inconveniences, but one particular assassin has proven to be most resourceful and has nearly killed me on several occasions. I must admit, my sleep is not what it used to be. Every flicker of light, every shadow receives my undivided attention now. At first, I sent out inspectors and Kyamurai to investigate but shortly afterwards, their bodies began to show up in the strangest places. General Hatsuro and Tetsushiro have tried to find this man, but their efforts have returned nothing. It became clear that I needed someone who was more capable. Kamira Gami was the one who gave me your name, Masatsuo Tekkensei."

At the mention of Kamira Gami's name, Shasp's eyes flicked up, "Kamira Gami lives?"

Muhara nodded.

Shasp stood silently for a moment. "I will do all I can. I am not unfamiliar with the ways of assassins. I would not be so sure it is the work of a single man. It could be a guild."

Muhara froze for a second, his confidence evaporating, but his demeanor returned. "Very well; Tetsushiro will see to your needs," and he waved for the eunuch to escort them out. They bowed and stepped backward toward the door.

Outside, Tetsushiro mounted his chestnut gelding, "We will wait for General Hatsuro at my home," he said as he reined the beast around and started back along the path to the gate. Shasp chose to speak as little as possible, feeling awkward beside Tetsushiro. It was clear that he still harbored malice for the killer of his brother and Shasp did not resent the notion. But, Shasp realized it was not only Matashumi's brother he should be concerned with. "What of your father, Tetsushiro?"

"He was slain six years gone; an arrow through the neck when we were putting down a rebellion in the southern regions. He died well as was befitting his station. I am master of my house now."

Thinking to show respect Shasp replied, "I hope to die so well."

Tetsushiro smiled, his eyes sharp as they trotted along, "I hope to live for a long while."

Within the hour, they arrived at house Ishaharo where it lay south of the palace and inland a few miles. It too was surrounded by smaller buildings built in the ever present U-fashion with raised porches and multiple entrance ways. The main house, like the palace, was larger and stretched out with several stories and larger rooms. Next to it was a soldier's barracks with stalls for horses, and a communal bakery. Beyond the estate were fields of rice paddies and tiered vegetable gardens.

People went about their business with an unusual languor, and Shasp felt uneasy at the lack of general conversation one normally finds in the streets as neighbors pass by and children play, but in this place all was quiet. In the eyes of the people who went by, he sensed something; fear. He had seen it enough to know the look of oppression.

The columns stopped before the main house, a three-storied structure with several gabled roofs, and servants swarmed them, taking the horses and gear to its proper storage. Tetsushiro clomped up the stone steps and across the porch, gesturing Shasp to go inside. A wide foyer with a high ceiling awaited them as they were greeted by the head servant, an old man with his head partially shaved from the ears back. He bowed and took Tetsushiro's gauntlets.

"Send for General Hatsuro, Lau. My guest and I will wait in the tea room."

Lau bowed deep and scurried off without a word. Shasp was about to say something when he heard a crash to his left. Both men spun toward the sound, hands flying to their hilts, but quickly relaxed when they saw the cause of the distraction. A woman in an exquisitely decorated kimono of red silk was kneeling and collecting shards of broken ceramic from the floor. Though her hands felt for and lifted the broken pieces of tea cups, her eyes were locked on Shasp. Shasp studied her for a moment and as recognition dawned, his heart froze in chest. All had happened in an instant, but Tetsushiro missed nothing. With a smirk and narrowing eyes he stepped toward the woman, gesturing for Shasp to follow. "Do you remember Kumi; Kamira Gami's daughter."

Kumi left the remnants of the shattered cups on the floor and bowed. Shasp returned her bow, "I remember her well." It was an understatement to the most extreme. She was, indirectly, responsible for Matashumi's death. It seemed she had changed very little since Shasp last saw her. The wide dark eyes still had much of their sparkle and her lips were as full and pouting as he had remembered. Her silky black hair was bundled up, held in place by jade pins, and Shasp knew from experience that if he were to pull one out, the long tresses would flow to her waist. He swallowed hard.

Kumi did not reply, leaving a vacuum of uncomfortable silence. Shasp was beginning to wonder what sort of game Tetsushiro was playing.

Tetsushiro placed his hand on the back of her head and stroked her hair, "We have been wed now for eight years, though I am yet to see sons from her."

In another culture the small quip might have gone unnoticed but in Aypon it was the equivalent of a backhand across the face. Kumi's expression darkened, her pain stabbing at him, as Shasp sought to relieve the tension. "I am sure it will happen. The best of things always take time."

Tetsushiro snorted, "So I'm told." He turned to his wife, "Kumi, take Masatsuo to the tea room and serve him. I will be in as soon as I have changed."

She bowed and turned slowly toward the adjoining room. Shasp glanced over his shoulder at the warlord before following her. The dimly lit room was only a short distance down the hall, a small cozy place with a low table and piled forest green cushions. The scent of jasmine and spices were pleasantly strong. Kumi motioned for him to sit and Shasp lowered himself, cross-legged, onto a cushion. She lifted a bamboo tray from a nearby hutch and laid it gently in the center of the table. Pouring tea was an art and Kumi had mastered it well. With unmatched grace she set a delicate cup before him and ladled tea into it then poured her own. She rested the ladle back in its place on the top of the kettle and lifted his cup and plate, holding it out for him to receive.

Shasp sipped on the scalding drink, savoring the mixture of tea and sweet herbs. If his mind had been a jumble when he arrived in Aypon, it was a whirlwind now. Never had he expected to see Kumi again, though he believed the possibility was one of the underlying reasons he chose to take the emperor's commission. "You are as beautiful as the day I last saw you."

"It is not proper for a man to speak so to a married woman . . . but I thank you for the compliment." The reply seemed cold, but he caught a hint of a repressed smile.

427

As they sat in silence, Shasp could not bring himself to take his eyes off Kumi. Memories of time spent with her flooded back to him, creating a confused and contrary mixture of anxiety and warmth. Without warning she broke the stillness, unable to keep the edge of pain from her voice.

"I thought I would never see you again. I waited for years, but you never came back. Now you sit with me drinking tea in my home."

Shasp stared into his cup, "I wanted to come back. You have no idea how much I wanted to . . . but after Matashumi's death, I realized I would never be good enough for you. I would always be a half-breed slave to Aypon, and I could not bear to bring that disgrace upon you or your father, though I know you would have accepted it."

"That was my decision to make, Masatsuo . . . mine. You said you loved me. You said you would come back."

"I wanted to, but . . . " his sentence trailed off, "I have never forgotten you." When she did not reply, Shasp turned the conversation, "How are you treated? Are you happy?"

Her eyes became wet and her lower lip trembled but she nodded her head, "As happy as can be expected. I live well and . . . no, I am not."

He did not believe his heart could sink any lower than it had. At least if she would have been happy, he could have accepted the result of his inaction, but now . . . "I'm sorry, Kumi. If I had known. . . ."

The door opened and Tetsushiro walked in with Pok Cho and an older, grizzled Ayponese man. Shasp stood and bowed to the elder.

"Masatsuo, this is General Hatsuro, and you know Inspector Cho." The stocky general bowed, but hesitated as if he recognized something in Shasp, a stirring of an old memory. He straightened with a serious attitude. The general eyed his brown hair and the unusual cut of his armor.

"Your armor appears to be Kyamurai, but it has been altered. Why?"

Shasp knew Hatsuro had only said what others had been thinking. "I removed the face mask because I have no family icon. The slit visor is more practical. The riding boots are from Arrigin, they give added protection to the greaves. The shoulder pauldrons

428

are from Dahoe and are reinforced with steel and shaped to fit my body."

Tetsushiro grunted, "If a man's skill is good enough, he has no need for extra metal."

"True enough," returned Shasp, "but in a fierce battle, a man cannot watch everyone . . . as your father discovered."

Tetsushiro reddened slightly and Hatsuro interrupted before the warlord said something he regretted. "What of that large knife? It looks heavy and slow . . . unwieldy."

Shasp drew it with a hiss of leather, "It is much heavier and wider than the Ayponese tanto, but I have studied Somerikan knife fighting and found the weapon to be superior in many ways."

Both men grunted at the presumptive nature of Shasp's claim. They sat around the table and Kumi served tea. At no time did Tetsushiro acknowledge her presence. She excused herself and slid the panel closed behind her.

"So, you are the man who is going to find the leader of the Shadow Foot," said Hatsuro.

Inspector Cho set his cup down and cleared his throat, "Forgive me, General, but we do not know that the Shadow Foot are behind these attempts."

"Who else could it be? Only they have the skill and resources to come so close."

"Hatsuro is right," said Tetsushiro, "it has to be them, but why? They must know that trying to assassinate the emperor would not be worth any amount of money. It would bring far too much attention, endangering their organization."

Shasp had heard of the Shadow Foot. Old men whispering over chess, and fearful stories told by mothers to frighten children into behaving. One had never been caught and to Shasp's knowledge they were only a myth. "Are you saying, the Shadow Foot really exists?"

The men looked at each other as if not wanting to be the one to answer. Pok Cho finally accepted the challenge. "I am not a man who gives weight to fanciful stories, lord Tekkensei, but I must believe my eyes. When I began my investigation into the assassination attempts, several of my colleagues had already been killed making the same inquiries. I was determined not to meet their fate and took strict precautions to protect myself; building

immunities to certain poisons, wearing armor under my clothing and other things. One night in the Tan Fu province, I was following a lead on a shred of evidence I found on one of my officer's corpses. A bit of lemon grass found in abundance there. I believed there was a possibility he had been killed near Tan Fu and his body had been carried back. After questioning several townspeople, I went to my room at the local inn. Late into the night, I was reviewing my notes when I realized I had left my shutter open and got up to close it. I stuck my head out to look around and felt a sudden sting on the back of my neck. At first, I thought I had been stung by a hornet or spider, but when I reached back to wipe the insect off, I found a dart instead. I began to feel ill and knew immediately it was poisoned.
Fortunately for me, I carried several anti-venoms with me. I ingested the vial I felt was the most likely to help. By the time I began to recover, a figure swept into my room on the third floor. He had to have come in from the roof. He was covered in black silks with a katana similar to yours, Masatsuo, and tried to finish the job. His blade slashed me several times but the heavy leather armor under my robes turned the edge away. I managed to get inside his guard and we struggled violently until the noise woke the other residents. When he heard the others coming down the hall, he fled out the window."

Shasp shrugged, "So, that doesn't make your assailant a Shadow Foot. It could have been any hired killer."

Pok Cho reached into the folds of his robe and produced a small, black, iron symbol, dangling from a broken chain. "He lost this during the fight. I tore it from his neck."

Shasp held out his hand, took the necklace and held it up to the light. It was a small round disc with the shape of a bare footprint in the center. Hatsuro and Tetsushiro looked at him expectantly but Shasp just tossed it back to Pok Cho. "Maybe you are right, or maybe it's just coincidence."

Hatsuro intervened, "Clearly, Inspector Cho got close enough to prompt an attempt on his life. That and the symbol should account for something."

"True," replied Shasp, "but like you said, why would even the Shadow Foot risk the attention? What is it they stand to gain? They must know the emperor suspects them and would stop at nothing to destroy their organization. Royalty in most countries function under the mutual assumption that assassin guilds are left alone as long as they do not try to kill the elite. It guarantees mutual survival. Did the emperor seek to destroy the guild before the attempts began?"

They all shook their heads. "No," said Pok Cho, "I do not think he believed they existed until recently."

Shasp finished his tea and stood, "Well, Pok Cho lured them out before. Maybe we can do it again."

Tetsushiro stood also, "I will make arrangements for your accommodations."

"That won't be necessary," said Shasp, "I will find a place near the harbor where I can keep my eyes and ears open. I hope you aren't offended."

Tetsushiro bowed curtly, "As you wish. I will have your horse brought around."

As Shasp left the main house and walked out into the courtyard he wondered if Tetsushiro really wanted him to stay so he would be tormented by Kumi's presence.

With all his heart, Shasp wanted to sweep her up in his arms and pretend that fifteen years had not passed but knew that was impossible. He leapt onto Tempest's back, glanced at the house and found Kumi staring down at him from a window above. He gave her a long look then reined Tempest around and headed back toward Hung Lai.

Chapter 6

Lexia knew it was foolhardy to be moving around so soon. It was even more foolish to be moving around in the squalid parts of Attle. She still had difficulty breathing and there was a lancing pain from her upper left breast to her back. For over a month she lay bedridden in the old woman's apartment, plagued by feverish dreams and infection.

A week ago, under Nadel's scathing protests, Lexia had begun looking for Shasp in every inn and drinking house in Attle. She had been with the man long enough to know he would never have left her laying on the floor of an inn, even if he did believe she was dead. Something was wrong.

Last night, she had finally run down one of Attle's seedier characters, a mousy little man named Delert. Delert's specialty was knocking over drunken sots and signing their names to sailing contracts before they woke up. When they did, they were usually out to sea and had better live up to their contract or go overboard. Of course, Delert collected a reasonable fee from the ship's captain. He was also connected in Attle, with his greasy little fingers in nearly every underhanded scheme on the waterfront. When Lexia found him and asked if he knew anything about Shasp's whereabouts, the rat had demanded payment for information . . . and not in coin. Lexia was patient with him and only removed three of his fingers. Delert, clutching his bleeding little stubs, had given her a name; an Azian name, Sun Shi, the owner of an opium house in the Azian quarter.

The Azian quarter was home to all those from the Azian continent who had landed in Attle for whatever reason; Chinese, Ayponese, and Honguks. Their common ancestry gave them a bond on the Nomerikan coast that they would otherwise not have shared. Lexia wove her way through the quarter, through the haze of cook fires and market odors of fish and spices to the long row of opium houses on its far end. Buildings crowded together with hundreds of articles of clothing hanging overhead in the damp air and grey light. She thanked her strong Bretcombian blood for her survival and pushed open the rickety grey door of the opium house. In the dim light of paper lanterns, grey ghosts of opium smoke hovered over prone bodies and the air was thick and cloying, smelling of sweat and fornication. A burly, bald-headed man with a shaved head and slanted eyes stepped into her path. "What do you want?"

Lexia hunched over in her tattered brown robe to make herself appear smaller and coughed a small amount of blood onto her hand. "I want to see Sun Shi."

"Get out of here; we don't need any more whores, especially sick ones."

He reached out casually to shove her back through the door but Lexia's hand shot out from under her robe and pressed the edge of a dirk tight against his upper thigh near his groin. "I suggest you get Sun Shi because if you don't, you'll be in a real fix. You see if I go right, you will lose your manhood and if I go left, you will lose your life. I think to most men it is pretty much one and the same.

The house guard all but held his breath as he called over his shoulder to a prostitute who lingered nearby. "Get Sun Shi."

"What is it?" the girl asked.

"Do not ask stupid questions, you miserable cur!   Go and get her or I will flay the skin from your body!"

The girl squeaked in horror and dashed off through the crowded cots, her silk shift fluttering behind her. A moment later, Lexia saw a woman approaching. She was middle-aged with deep slanted eyes and black hair hanging down her back. A dark blue robe with flowered prints reached to her ankles but was open in the front, allowing glimpses of her nude body as the material shifted with her movements. "What is the meaning of this interruption, Loi?   It had better be important or I'll have you castrated!"

"A thousand pardons my lady, but that is exactly what I am trying to avoid," said Loi through clenched teeth. The brief exchange had taken place in Chinese, so Lexia did her best to read the expressions on their faces, attempting to gauge the emotional content there.

Sun Shi directed her gaze to Lexia's hand, saw the knife pressed against Loi's femoral artery and raised her brows. She spoke in broken Nomerikan, "Clearly this is an important matter, but somehow I doubt it actually involves you, Loi. My dear, if you would be so kind as to release my servant, I am sure we can resolve whatever it is that has brought you here."

Lexia smashed the top of her head into Loi's face, breaking his nose, and then shoved him down. She tossed off the robe, revealing her molded cuirass and leg armor underneath. "I have questions."

Sun Shi smiled, "Don't we all? Please, follow me." She turned nonchalantly and started back through the sprawl of addicts.

Lexia regarded the prone bodies as she passed with a mixture of disgust and sympathy, having been like them once. She followed Sun Shi up a flight of stairs and into a hanging loft which looked down over the sprawled men and their professional female companions. Rich silks and furs covered nearly every inch of the loft floor. Hand carved tables of Azian design lined the walls and held a variety of eastern art, from vases and fans to brilliant scroll work. In the back of the room a large low bed was pushed against the wall and a man reclined under the silk sheets. He was a young Caucasian man, and when they entered, he sat up, running his fingers through his black hair.

"Sun, it isn't like you to introduce another woman into our play."

"I don't think that is what she is here for, Captain Markis." Sun Shi sat on the bed next to him. "Please sit. It isn't every day I meet a woman, or a man, who could handle Loi so easily. Are you looking for work?" Lexia jerked her head around at the comment and her eyes flashed with malice. Sun Shi laughed, "Oh, I don't mean that, my dear! I meant guarding my guests. One is extremely vulnerable when using opium. They pay me well for protection as well as the drug. In return, I pay my guards a good wage."

Lexia relaxed, "That isn't why I'm here. I'm looking for someone . . . someone important to me."

"I see, but why do you think I would know where this person is?"

"Delert gave me your name, with some coaxing. I've drawn a blank in every other quarter of this city. The Azian quarter was the only place left to look, and according to Delert, you are the one with the connections here. The man's name is Shasp."

At the mention of the name, Captain Markis and Sun Shi glanced at one another. Lexia was no fool; she understood the implications of a high-ranking city guardsman lying in the bed of a woman who made her living through criminal enterprise.

Markis lunged for his long sword and had it in his hand before Lexia could stop him, but she managed to trip Sun Shi as she darted for the doorway. The Chinese madam hit her head against the wall, and one of the many expensive vases toppled onto her, shattering. Lexia and Markis faced each other with naked steel as Sun Shi moaned softly on the floor. Markis' steel wasn't all that was naked.

Lexia took a step back. The sudden burst of energy she expended sapped what little strength remained, and she struggled to maintain her facade of confidence.

Markis ignored his nudity, crouching, "I thought I recognized you. You were one of the bodies we found inside the White Owl. Everyone thought you were dead. You have a lot to answer for."

Lexia laughed, "Ha! And you don't? I'll bet the magistrate would be interested in knowing what kind of schemes you and Sun Shi have been cooking up. I hear he's a very forgiving man."

Captain Markis knew that was a jest. The magistrate was anything but forgiving. "You won't live to tell anyone."

"Use your head, Captain. You have no armor . . . I do, and I did not get all these scars or lose this eye fighting with serving wenches, but if you wish to throw your life away, by all means, come on." Lexia tried to control her breathing, hoping desperately that her bluff would work. In her condition, she wouldn't be able to defeat a skilled man like Markis, armor or not.

Markis lowered his sword, turned and sheathed it. "What do you want?"

"I told you, I lost someone, and judging from the looks on your faces when I mentioned his name, I'm guessing you both know something. I will pay for the information."

The captain's eyes flicked up, "Pay? How much?"

"Collect your woman from the floor and we'll talk."

Markis laid Sun Shi on the bed and rubbed her head, bringing her back to consciousness. When Lexia questioned her about Shasp's disappearance, Sun Shi spilled her story.

"An inspector from Hung Lai, a city in Aypon, came to me over a year ago bearing the name of Masatsuo Tekkensei. He had four guards with him, skilled warriors, I knew their ilk. I had never heard the name before, but for a generous fee I found out about the man he sought and discovered that the name had been changed years ago. I knew a reliable bounty hunter with a reputation for tenacity named Morgit, and if anyone could track this Masatsuo, it was him.

435

I helped to negotiate the contract between Morgit and the Inspector. I was paid, he left, and I thought that was the end of it until Captain Markis came to me with the story of a tavern brawl where several bodies lay strewn around the White Owl. One man was missing . . . Masatsuo Tekkensei, or should I say, Shasp Ironwrought. That is all I know."

Lexia nodded, "Thank you. I didn't come here to cause trouble, I just wanted information. Captain Markis, if you want your money you'll need to come with me, but I suggest you dress first." The captain grunted and grabbed his blue trouser from a nearby table.

Sweat beaded heavy on Owen's forehead as he answered Captain Markis' question. "I've never stolen anything in my life, sir. It's just bad business!"

Lexia snorted, "Yes, but stealing from the dead is acceptable. You must have been shocked when you found out how much money my friend and I were holding."

Owen's eyes darted around, "I don't know what you're talking about."

Markis gave Lexia a look that said he was beginning to doubt her claims. For safety sake she had insisted Markis come alone, lest he be tempted to take all her money when she found it. She walked over to the bench where Owen and his wife sat together and leaned over them. "Last time, Owen. Where's my money?"

Owen chuckled nervously, "Really I don't . . . ."   Before he could finish his sentence, Lexia kicked over their bench and stomped on Owen's groin. Owen curled up on the floor with a moan and Lexia knelt beside him, tangling her fist into his thinning hair. She wrenched his head back, exposing his throat and placed the razor-sharp edge of her dirk against his pulsing jugular. She at the tavern keeper's wife with her hard, cold eye, "For your husband's sake, where is my money?"

Tears ran down the plump woman's creased face, "It's under the larder in the back. There's a loose board under it."

Markis raised his brows then walked to the kitchen where Lexia heard him prying up the boards. He returned with a large sack, dropped it on the floor and opened it. His eyes popped at the wealth within. Lexia had told him she had left a substantial amount of money in her room the night of the fight, but he never imagined it was so much. She tore off the old woman's apron and tossed it to Markis, "Take a third and don't even think about getting greedy."

Markis stared into the bag again, at the rubies, gold and emeralds there. Greedy? A third would make him wealthy beyond his dreams. He scooped up his share, wrapped it in the woman's apron, and bowed. "Nice doing business with you," then turned and walked out the front door.

Lexia scooped out a few gems and placed them in the hand of the keeper's wife who stopped sobbing and stared at Lexia in disbelief. She flung the bag over her shoulder and disappeared out the back door, not fully trusting that Markis wouldn't be waiting to waylay her out front.

A few minutes later she staggered into the tiny apartment, tucked into the narrow alley. Nadel came off her stool like a startled dove, dropping her sewing at her feet.

"I've been worried to death about you! Are you crazy, running around this city in your condition. All that trouble I went through getting you well just so you could run off and ....and....die in the street. Have you got rocks for brains? Lay down, right now!"

Lexia didn't argue as she dropped onto Nadel's bed. A wicked cough wracked her body and red sputum speckled her hand as she covered her mouth. When her coughing fit subsided she sat up. "I've lived through the worst of it, Nadel. I think I'll survive."

The poor old woman looked exhausted and fearful, "I suppose you will, but still, no more running off 'til your well." She lifted Lexia's feet onto the bed and pulled her boots off, then her armor. "What are you wearing this armor for? Looking for a fight in the shape you're in? Are you crazy? I can't keep doing this Lexia! Taking care of you and working to keep us fed, not if you're just going to go running around and get yourself killed!"

Lexia reached into the bag lying on the bed beside her and pulled out a handful of gold coins and rubies. "I think your washing days are over Nadel."

Chapter 7

The fortress teemed with monks and Kyamurai, doubling as a martial school and monastery. From the time his captors hauled him out of the cage, he had not rested. From that moment, the boy was handed buckets, brooms, scrub brushes and other implements of drudgery. If he did not work fast enough, he was beaten. If he looked wrong, he was beaten and he didn't dare say a word. That had been his first painful lesson.

He pressed his weight onto the scrub brush as he scoured the blood from the wooden floor. Casually, he glanced at the boys who were training in the courtyard only a dozen feet away, boys his own age, but they wore the grey garb of students, loose-fitting tunics and pants of canvas while he wore the drab ragged garments of a lowly servant. With wooden Katana in hand, they called out the number of the choreographed movements, stepping and swinging, blocking and retreating, over and over again. Their master, an older man with greying hair, moved through them with a sure eye, occasionally stopping to correct one with a stiff cuff to the head.

After a few more drills, the master gave them a rest and walked through a door adjoining the courtyard while the boys milled around, calling names and laughing. The slave boy looked up from his work for a split second and caught the eye of one of the students. "What are you looking at, slave!" the student yelled and walked toward him. The boy turned his eyes back to his work, saying nothing, but it made no difference. A sandaled foot slammed into his ribs evoking a cry of pain from him, and laughter from the group. Their voices encouraged the angry student as he kicked him again and again. "I see you watching us all the time! Why don't you keep your eyes on your work instead!" The others joined in, punching and stomping him with their feet, laughing all the while. Suddenly a loud voice called out, "Matashumi!" The instigator froze and the others backed away. The master stepped out of the doorway and into the courtyard. "Does this servant belong to you?"

"No, master, he is yours."

"Then why are you vandalizing my property?" Matashumi hung his head and the old man began the repetitious drills once again, never giving the boy another look. The servant boy rolled

onto his knees, spat some blood into the wash bucket and continued with his scrubbing. When the sun had set and the work was finally done, the boy climbed the ladder to a loft in the horse stalls. He had long since grown accustomed to the stench; in fact he preferred it because it kept others away. The loft had plenty of room, and he liked having the extra space to move around, though it was freezing at night. From under a pile of hay, he withdrew a broom handle, broken off just above the straw head, whipped it through the air a few times and slowly went through the katas he had watched that day. He shifted his feet, swung, stepped forward, blocked and retreated, quietly calling out the number of the movement and paying close attention to the small errors the master had taken time to correct. Over and over again with an intense focus, he practiced the movements late into the night. It was all he had, this time alone practicing with his make-shift sword, imagining what this stroke or that thrust would do to a body. It made him feel their equal.

Shasp awoke to a single rap against his door, causing his hand to jerk instinctively toward the pommel of the katana which hung from the bedpost. Deputy Inspector Shau Lan had struck his door only once as he passed and would be waiting in the main hall, having tea. Shasp sat up and rubbed his neck while glancing around the grimy little room. A rusty washbasin sat on a rickety wooden table, grey with age. His armor hung on pegs near the door and a chamber pot sat beneath the shuttered window. He took a deep breath, inhaling the unpleasant odors of the inn that slipped through the generous gaps in his door. The inns near the docks were cheap and shabby, but that was where Shasp believed he would find the speck of information that would lead him to his quarry. Quickly, he rose, splashed some cloudy water on his face and dressed. He tied his katana around his waist with a sash, and then pulled a brown, tattered cloak around his armor, leaving ample space for his hand to reach his weapons. The musty robe reached to his ankles, concealing the fact that he was Kyamurai. For the final touch, he placed a wide coned-shaped straw hat on his head; the hat of a peasant.

Bustling crowds began to pour into the foyer of the inn. Dock workers, sailors, merchants and guardsmen all filed in when the doors opened. The scent of warm bread and cooked fish wafted up to the balcony where he overlooked the clustered tables, causing his stomach to complain for lack of food. With his chin lowered just a little, Shasp made his way down the stairs and through the chattering crowd. He walked past the Deputy Inspector, who was reading a scroll layed out beside his soup, found a table on the far side of the room and sat with his back to the wall. One of the keeper's eight sons laid a platter of bread, rockfish and tea on the table and Shasp, not wanting to draw attention, paid him in the coin of the realm.

Lan was a younger man, slightly on the heavy side with a long black braid. He wore the brimless, black, tight-fitting cap of the merchant class and a long yellow silk robe with intricate designs. Shasp considered his appearance and decided that Cho's assistant did a fine job of looking like a man with money.

Even so, Lan was not out of place because most of the merchants from China and Honguk preferred to stay near the docks where they could keep an eye on their investments until they were shipped.

Pok Cho had said that several inspectors and Kyamurai had turned up dead after making the rounds and asking questions about the Shadow Foot. Pok Cho himself had nearly fallen victim and that fact did not sit well with Deputy Inspector Shau Lan. Nevertheless, the man had accepted the assignment in spite of the danger it could pose for him. Of course, Shasp had promised to watch his back and his superior, Pok Cho, insisted it was Lan's duty. But Shau Lan would not be making inquiries as an inspector investigating an assassins' presence, but rather as a merchant wanting to take out a contract on a competitor.

It was important for them not to be seen together or speak in public, though they had met in secret a few times. Lan mostly complained about the lack of progress. It seemed anytime he so much as mentioned the name of Shadow Foot, people's eyes would widen and they would shake their heads and move away, fearful of any residual retribution.

For a week, Shasp had watched him from a distance, staying just close enough to rescue the inspector if the need arose. But, after seven days, he was having difficulty keeping his attention on Shau Lan as he contacted captains on the docks, went over false ledgers and looked for a contact who could introduce him to the Shadow Foot . . . if they even existed.

Shau Lan finished his breakfast, rolled up the scroll and

441

headed out into the market area, but Shasp waited until he reached the door before he went after him. Outside leaden skies released a light shower of morning rain onto the gathering vendors as they set up their carts and wares. Shasp knew the route Shau Lan would take and, trying to blend in, paused to buy an apple from one of the stands. All morning they moved through the warehouses and waterfront inns, past brothels and opium dens, Shau-Lan pretending to be a wealthy business man and Shasp watching the landscape around him for any sign of trouble. It was noon by the time Shau decided to start back toward the inn for a meal but, to Shasp's chagrin, he didn't return by the regular route. Instead, the plump inspector took an alley between the warehouses, working his way diagonally through the waterfront. Shasp cursed under his breath as he tried to keep him in view, difficult as it was with so many turns among the packed stone buildings. His feet slapped at the dampened flagstone as he hurried to overtake his charge.

Shau Lan had just squeezed between a stack of crates and an alley wall, emerging into a wide space where the backsides of several buildings came together. Only two narrow alleys led back out. He scrutinized the three dockworkers who lounged on a stack of wooden crates, drinking rice liquor, and then quickly walked toward the nearest alley, until one of them piped up.

"You there!"

Shau turned slowly, his stomach tightening, "Yes?"

A big man pushed himself onto his feet and swaggered toward him, "I think you are looking for me."

Shau appeared confused and shrugged, "I don't believe I am. Why?"

The big man rubbed his bald head with a meaty hand, "You're the merchant looking for someone to remove his competition, right?"

"I was looking for a Shadow Foot assassin. Do you know how I can contact one?"

The big man laughed, "Shadow Foot? They don't exist. I'm the man for your job, and I've killed plenty."

Shau Lan laughed nervously, "Oh, ah well . . . I really prefer the Shadow Foot, you see, this job is complicated and delicate, but thank you." Shau started to walk by the brute, but a large hand on his chest stopped him. The big man shook his head.

442

"I don't think you understand. I'm the best." He turned his head toward his friends, "Ling . . . Chinsuto." The other men, muscular from the heavy labor of the docks, left their perches on the heap of crates and joined their friend. "What have you found, Xang, a fat wharf rat?" called Ling.

Shau swallowed and nodded, "I see," he said trying to distract the big man, Xang, "and what do you charge?"

"What do you have on you?"

Shau was sweating now and checking the alley behind the thugs who barred his way, searching for a glimpse of his guardian, but seeing only the shadows of crates and walls. "I don't carry much. Do you think me a fool?"

"I think you were a fool to come down this alley. We've been watching you; came down here to make sure we met." Xang's hand lashed out, striking Shau in the eye with the power of a thunder clap; the shock sent the inspector reeling backwards into a wall, and he was unconscious before his head hit the ground. His assailants grabbed hold of his silk robe and tossed him unceremoniously onto an empty cart where they rifled through his robes. Xang shook some silver coins out of Shau's money bag and into his palm, and then spat. "Not bad for a few minutes work, but we aren't done yet." He pulled a long Ayponese tanto knife from under his tunic and glanced around, "Time to earn our pay," he said as he laid the edge across Shau's throat but that was as far as he got.

A hand from behind caught his collar and a foot kicked in the back of his knee, causing Xang to fall hard on his back with a loud grunt. A hooded peasant in a tattered brown robe hovered over him, one foot pinning the big man's knife hand to the ground.

"Now, why would you think killing this merchant was necessary to earn your pay when you already have his money? That is, unless someone was going to pay you more after he was dead."

In response, Xang rolled his legs up and kicked Shasp in the chest, knocking him backward and freeing the pinned knife. Instantly, Xang was on his feet and slashing murderously with the knife as Shasp ducked and dodged the weapon. Ling and Chinsuto quickly joined in the fray, Ling pulling a length of chain from his pocket while Chinsuto snatched up a discarded length of board. Shasp watched their movements from the corner of his eye as he blocked a knife thrust meant for his heart then slammed his mailed

443

fist into Xang's face, crushing his nose. Eyes watering and unable to see, the big man staggered back as his friends moved in.

Chinsuto swung the board at Shasp, catching him on the shoulder and shattering half its length while Ling whipped the chain around Shasp's ankle and jerked him off balance. Shasp crashed against a pile of crates, smashing them into splinters and hit the ground like a sack of wheat, the air whistling from his lungs. Quickly he surmised the martial skill of his attackers, realized he wasn't up against common thieves, and cursed himself for underestimating his opponents; a violation of his training. Fortunately for Shasp, that was exactly what Xang had done when he made a lazy attempt at attacking what he believed was just some blundering beggar.

Chinsuto swung again, but Shasp rocked back onto his shoulders and delivered a powerful kick to his head. Jawbone cracked as the man spun and flopped face down onto the flagstone. Ling whipped the free end of his chain around and brought it down, but Shasp had raised his arm to protect himself. The lashing steel was the equivalent of a metal bar and if not for the steel bracer under his robe, Shasp was sure it would have shattered the bone beneath it. Upon impact, the chain coiled around his forearm. Numb from the lashing, Shasp grasped a length of the chain and, bracing himself, jerked Ling off his feet. Ling was forced to let go of the chain and flung his arm up to protect his face as he flew into the wall. That was all the advantage Shasp needed and the timing couldn't have been more crucial because Xang was on his feet again. Shasp shook off the length of chain that was twined around his ankle, snatched it up and whipped it around Ling's neck before he could regain his balance. With a murderous wrench, Shasp tore the man off his feet, and with the sound of crunching vertebra, Ling spun in the air and crashed onto the unconscious Shau.

Now it was only the big man and Shasp, but Xang didn't seem to care, believing that a man with sharp steel couldn't help but defeat an unarmed man. But his leering smile faded when Shasp reached into his robes and unsheathed the big Somerikan blade hidden beneath. The massive knife dwarfed the tanto blade of his opponent, but Xang was determined to finish the fight and crouched low, spinning the weapon and switching hands to confuse the robed interloper.

Shasp, disdainful of the playful knife handling, flipped the hilt into the comfortable reverse grip required for its use. They circled each other warily, feinting and slashing. Once they had tested one another's skills, they came together in a whirlwind of spinning steel. Knives plunged and slashed only to be blocked and redirected. Limbs were a blur as they moved with blinding speed. Shasp blocked a slash meant for his eyes and returned with a cut to the groin. Xang caught Shasp's guard against the blade of his hand and redirected his tanto for Shasp's throat but Shasp dodged out of the way. He caught Xang's forearm when he redirected the tanto toward his abdomen. Shasp feinted for the man's face but then shifted his position, spun inside, and went for his armpit. The big man twisted away at the last second, receiving only a slash across his back instead of the intended punctured lung. Shasp was sweating slightly now as he realized that his opposition was not a thief at all, but rather, a man who was highly skilled in the art of the Ayponese knife. Shasp was about to test the theory of Somerikan knife handling against the thousand-year-old art of the tanto. Both men suffered from multiple lacerations, bleeding in a dozen places, and Shasp knew it must be evident that he was not what he appeared to be either, for his armor had already saved him from grievous wounds many times. Again they threw themselves back into the swirling, hissing steel, blocking and kicking as they sought to find a way past the other's guard and into flesh. Shasp leapt back and kicked at Xang's knee, receiving a slash across his greaves for his trouble, but while the thug was attacking his shin, Shasp rolled away to his left, throwing his knife just out of arm's reach.

The big man had no time to redirect or deflect the flying blade as it sank to the hilt just below his ribs. Xang stiffened, reaching toward the imbedded hilt but could not bring himself to touch it. Staggering toward the alley's exit, he placed a hand on the wall to hold himself up, but his knees buckled and he slid to the ground.

Shasp walked over to the man's fallen tanto and kicked it away then reached down and jerked his own knife free, allowing the blood to flow more rapidly from Xang's wound. The big man's face grew ashen as Shasp hovered over him, "You're no ordinary thief. Who sent you after the inspector?" But the only answer Shasp received was the death rattle of Xang's last breath. He cursed and walked back to where the only living assailant lay prone on the flagstones. Shasp hefted an old barrel half full with stagnant rain water and upended it on Chinsuto's face. He awoke in a sputtering fit and immediately clamped his hand around his broken jaw, groaning.

"Who sent you?" demanded Shasp as he held the bloody Somerikan knife against Chinsuto's throat. Chinsuto began to mumble a reply when Shasp caught the faint hiss of a missile from behind and pivoted out of the way. Suddenly, a steel dart, no doubt meant for him, thudded into Chinsuto's forehead. Whoever had thrown the dart had been as silent as a cat. Shasp dropped the corpse and spun, crouching behind his uplifted forearm bracers. Though he searched the shadowy alleys and the roofs with his eyes, he spied only circling gulls, nothing more. The assassin had vanished.

"Damn it!" Shasp shouted as he straightened. He checked the alley a second time then came back to Shau and splashed some water on his face. The deputy inspector groaned and struggled to his elbows. His eye was already swollen to abnormal proportions, causing his purplish cheek to meet his brow.

"What happened?" Shau asked.

Shasp bent and retrieved the inspector's trampled hat, "You didn't stay on the agreed route, that's what happened. I lost you for a moment and that seemed to be all it took for you to get into trouble."

Lau winced as he poked at his cheek, "I thought maybe the assassin would be more likely to try something if I left the busy street."

Shasp glanced around, "I think it worked, but not like you expected."

For the first time, Lau saw the carnage from the fight, "Well, they *are* dead. I would say our work is done. We lured the assassins out."

Shasp shook his head, "I don't think that's what happened."

Lau touched his eye gingerly, "What do you mean?"

"I think it was us who were drawn out, Shau. These men weren't your average street thugs, they were trained killers."

Shau glanced at the bodies again and at the blood dripping from Shasp's many wounds. "Speak plainly."

Shasp spat and nudged the fellow with the dart in his head, "I'm saying that the Shadow Foot already knew you were an inspector and that I was watching your back. This fight wasn't just about killing you, it was meant to test me."

Shau Lan raised his working eyebrow as understanding dawned, "Ah, I see. You were the only real mystery to them . . . until now. They wanted to know what you were made of."

Shau eased himself off the wagon, rubbed his eye again and chuckled. Shasp stared at him, annoyed by his strange behavior. "What's so funny Shau, you were almost killed."

"They wanted to know what you were made of . . . Tekkensei."

Shasp nodded with a slight rising of his lips. His name, Tekkensei, was Ayponese for Iron.

"What do we do now?" Shau asked, "There is no point in continuing this charade."

"True enough. We will just have to try something else."

Chapter 8

Pok Cho reclined on a cushioned chair in his official chambers, though it had more the appearance of a comfortable flat than a place of government business. Delicately carved doors of flowery design; expensive looking vases; rich dark wood furniture and thick rugs of oriental patterns gave it the appearance of wealth. Cho leaned forward, placed a splinter over a candle and lit his ceramic pipe.

"So, my friend, you believe it was the Shadow Foot who tried to kill you?"

Shasp took a sip of rice liquor from a sturdy green porcelain cup. "I do, but what I don't understand is, why the deception? The men in the alley were experienced murderers pretending to be common thieves, but they were not the quality of fighters I would expect to see in an assassin's guild, too brazen. If the guild wanted us dead why not use one of their own?"

Shau Lan sat quietly holding a cold compress over his eye, "Perhaps they did not want to get too close, maybe test the waters and see who they were up against."

Shasp leaned back and put his feet on Cho's desk, a very western habit, "Your subordinate and I have managed to find out that much, and at the cost of some of my blood. Have you come up with anything, or have you just been lounging around your fancy government chambers?"

Pok stared at the bottom of Shasp's boots for a moment, irritated at the lack of respect but maintaining his ever present indifference. "Actually I have been quite busy."

"Really," said Shasp sardonically, "with what?"

"Fulfilling our agreement. It was extremely tedious work, going back through all the twenty-five-year-old ledgers and sorting through literally stacks of government documents. Your memories of your childhood were vague at best, but I found a reference to a soldier from Arrigin named Lyan Morgenon, who came to Aypon near the time of your early childhood. It seems he came over as a military advisor. Some old ship's ledgers showed he arrived here with his wife and child. Interestingly enough, the mother's name was Ikuru Hashita, an Ayponese name. The child's name was not listed as is sometimes the case in arrival ledgers. But, the coincidence and timing is truly remarkable."

Shasp was listening silently and though he appeared calm, his heart was racing. Slowly he dragged his boots from Pok Cho's desk and leaned closer. "Perhaps General Hatsuro knows something. Is there anything else?" he said in a dry voice.

"It is all I have for now, but I will pursue this information and see where it leads. I must admit that, while I was looking through all those names, I began to think of you. Most men only have one name but you have two. I am curious, why."

Shasp snorted, "Humph, most westerners couldn't pronounce Masatsuo Tekkensei, besides . . . it wasn't my real name anyway. It was the one Kamira Gami gave me when I was ten. Only my parents knew my real name. So, I took a name of convenience. As you know, 'Masatsuo' is the name we give for the sound a sword makes when it clears the sheath. Only the Arriginians have a word for that sound and it is the 'shasp'. 'Tekkensei' means made of iron. In common Nomerikan when something is made it is 'wrought'."

"Pok Cho smiled politely, "Ah, I see, you simply converted your name to the most common Nomerikan expression, a simple explanation, but a man without a past is a hollow thing."

Shasp snapped out of his reverie, "I would appreciate anything else you can find out; what happened to my parents and why I ended up a slave at the age of five."

Pok bowed his head, "Of course. In the meantime, do you have any thoughts on the Shadow Foot?"

"I'd like to know who is behind them. I fear that smoking out the assassin will only temporarily take care of the symptom and not cure the illness."

Cho took another pull on his pipe, "I have been wondering that same thing. About a year ago, we began finding sheets of rice paper with seditious rhetoric tacked to the doors of public offices and inns all over Hung Lai."

"What kind of rhetoric?" asked Shasp.

Pok Cho waved his hand in dismissal, "Questioning the emperor's use of taxes for selfish ends and corruption of government officials. That sort of nonsense."

"Is it true?" asked Shasp.

Pok Cho chuckled, "Of course it is true, but what difference

449

does that make? Our government has always struggled with these issues, that does not give one the right to cause rebellion. The emperor is the center of Aypon's spirit. To betray him is to betray the country and its people. You should know that."

"I've seen governments turned upside-down over less than excessive government corruption. Perhaps the emperor should minimize his expenditures and not give his enemies those weapons to use against him."

Shau Lan became uncomfortable with the direction the conversation had gone. "Excuse me gentlemen, but I am quite exhausted after my beating today. I believe I will try to get some sleep."

Pok and Shasp nodded as Lan walked out of the office, still holding the compress against his swollen eye. Pok finished the tobacco in his pipe and dug out the ash with a tiny spade. "What action do you propose now, Masatsuo?   Have you any ideas?"

Shasp sat quietly spinning the thick sweet liquor around in his cup then downed it and reached for another dram. "Obviously, the Shadow Foot are on to us. They easily figured out who Shau Lan really is and, not doubt, who I am as well. Yet, we still have to lure them out because we have no idea who or where they are."

Cho sighed in exasperation, shaking his head, "That does not leave us in a very good position. The emperor is not a patient or forgiving man and he demands results."

"The emperor," scoffed Shasp, "can go . . . wait."

"What?"

"That's how we will lure the Shadow Foot. By giving them what they want most...the emperor."

Pok Cho leapt to his feet, hands flat on his desk, "Are you mad! We cannot endanger the emperor and to even think of it borders on treason!"

Shasp smiled and settled back into his comfortable chair, "With brilliance sometimes comes insanity, Inspector Cho, but we must keep this secret. Obviously, the Shadow Foot have informants or they wouldn't have seen through Shau Lan's disguise so quickly"

"What about Tetsushiro? He must be informed."

"No, he must not," answered Shasp. "Not yet."

Chapter 9

The waterfront of Hung Lai was a dangerous place at night, as many a man had discovered just before becoming a corpse. Crowded warehouses of wood and brick, opium dens, drinking establishments and brothels clung to the waterline from one end of the bay to the other. Many of the buildings were built on poles along the water's edge in an attempt to create businesses without paying for property. Here among the unlit streets and sewage of the city, the dregs of Ayponese society eked out their parasitic existence. Under a cloud-shrouded moon, bands of men roamed in the shadows, looking to strip wealth, and sometimes life, from some unfortunate sailor or drunken merchant.

"Stay outside," Tetsushiro ordered his captain in a low tone. The older man nodded and turned to a handful of other Kyamurai who lurked the shadows of the street.

Tetsushiro stepped smartly up the plank stairs to the front door of Dreck A'meragin's drinking house and brothel. The Arriginian merchant had arrived years ago with a bounty for piracy on his head. He had used the loot he scraped together from his dubious trade to buy the business from an aging madam. Tetsushiro knew that liquor and prostitutes were not the primary source of Dreck's income. Murder was.

Tetsushiro, wearing a blue robe, black sash and Kyamurai sword, paused before the heavy, salt-laden door and listened to the bawdy western music as it vibrated through the planks, accompanied by the raucous laughter of the patrons. Dreck did not cater to the Ayponese, feeling they were somehow inferior to westerners, but rather to the host of sailors bringing trade vessels east to Aypon. Consequently, the men under his employ were generally from Nomerika. Tetsushiro wrinkled his nose at the odor of unwashed bodies seeping through the cracks in the door and realized it would be much more unpleasant inside. He slammed his palms against the doors and walked in. The laughter and music came to an abrupt halt as several of the revelers looked over at the Ayponese trespasser. Drunkards with harlots on their laps and drinking mugs in their fists gawked, astonished that an Ayponese man would dare to show his face in Dreck A'merigan's place. With disgust etched in his face and

451

malevolence in his narrow eyes, the Kyamurai looked over the crowd until he spied Dreck in the back of the room, watching the crowd from his usual corner. The Arriginian was an older man in his fifties, with a greasy streak of salt and pepper hair raked over his bald forehead. Jowls, heavy from years of sordid behavior, hung nearly to his chin. His body, once barrel chested and solid from seafaring, was now fat and soft, but Dreck's eyes had lost nothing of their original diabolical character. Small and shifty, constantly roaming, looking for any conceivable way to make money, honest or otherwise . . . but usually otherwise.

Dreck hefted himself out of his chair and waddled to the middle of the room where he met Tetsushiro. Neither exchanged a word, but Dreck motioned toward a door and ambled toward it. When the door had closed behind them, the muffled sound of music and laughter burst forth once again. Dreck trimmed a lamp, revealing his dank and littered office. Clusters of scrolls and coins covered one table while crates and boxes filled another. Similar items filled all four corners and a moldering rug of Kalyfarian design covered the rotting planks of the floor.

Dreck dropped onto a rickety chair, "So, what brings the head of house Ishaharo to my humble establishment?" he said with a raspy voice.

"Your men failed yesterday," spat Tetsushiro.

Dreck shrugged, "There will be other opportunities."

Tetsushiro began a slow walk around the small room, eyeing various relics and documents as he passed. "I don't think so. Masatsuo Tekkensei will be more cautious than ever now."

The warlords ramble around his room made Dreck uneasy and he shifted in his chair. "I hope you don't expect me to pay back the money you gave me. I'll make sure the job is done, that's for certain, but the money is mine."

Tetsushiro stopped his inspection of the room and stared at Dreck. As the former sailor stared back into those evil black slits, he felt the icy fist of death grip his heart, but then Tetsushiro smiled unexpectedly. "It really does not matter. I had the opportunity to see Masatsuo's skill, though I had to kill one of your men with a spike before he revealed the truth about us."

"That's good," said Dreck, breathing easier, "We certainly don't need the emperor finding out about that, do we."

"No, we certainly do not," replied Tetsushiro. Like a flash of lightning, the warlord's sword sang from its sheath and, in a single fluid motion, hissed through Dreck's neck as if it were no more than a wisp of smoke. Blood sprayed the walls in pumping jets and rained down on Tetsushiro Ishaharo's head before Dreck's body slumped and fell off the chair. Tetsushiro reached out with the tip of his sword and flipped an oil lamp over onto the scattered dry scrolls, creating a sudden inferno.

The crowd outside the office had heard nothing over their carousing but all went silent when Tetsushiro walked out, drenched in the blood of their host and with his sword in his hand. Slowly, men reached for their cutlasses and boot knives. One sailor reached out and dropped the bar across the door as the angry mob swarmed out from behind their tables, bristling with steel.

Tetsushiro smiled and spoke in broken Nomerikan, "You fools believe you have locked me in here with *you* . . . but it is *you* who are trapped."

A brawny armed youth held up his cutlass, "There are fifty of us and only one of you, my little Azian monkey. You killed our friend and now we're gonna flay the meat off yer bones!"

Like a seething mass of locust, thugs and sailors leapt toward their waiting prey, but soon found out they were not the predator.

Tetsushiro's moves were fluid, as he ducked and spun, leapt and somersaulted; each time he moved, his blade took another life with surgical precision. The western men banged into one another clumsily, each fouling the other's attack, allowing the Ayponese swordsman to slip between them easily. He seemed to know where everyone was at all times. One attacker thrust toward Tetsushiro's back, only to find that the warlord had reversed his grip on the Kyamurai blade and pierced him through his heart without even looking. The Ayponese steel hissed through the air again and again, thrusting and slashing with perfect aim as men howled in their fury and frustration every time one of them went down. Tetsushiro's face was emotionless as he calculated his movements with the speed of a darting arrow. The razor-sharp steel, coupled with amazing velocity and skill, sliced through bone and sinew as if it were paper. Arms and legs came lose, heads leapt from shoulders and bodies littered the floor in a swamp of viscera. In the end, the last man standing, one of Dreck's own thugs ran for the door and hefted the wooden bar out of its cradle. The doors had barely cracked open when Tetsushiro pinned him to the planks. The warlord turned back toward the room and surveyed his bloody work. Bodies spattered with red gore, both male and female, lay piled on the floor and draped over tables and chairs in macabre poses of death while orphaned limbs lay strewn about the room. The walls and ceiling were likewise painted with blood, a scene from a nightmare.

He pulled his sword from between the shoulders of Dreck's henchman, allowing the corpse to slide down the face of the door, and then pushed his way outside and into the cold fetid air. His captain waited at the bottom of the stairs, the sight of Tetsushiro covered in gore was no longer a shock to him, having seen it so many times before. "Are you wounded my liege?" he asked flatly.

Tetsushiro wiped his blade on the hem of his robe and sheathed it, "None of this blood is mine."

"Are there any prisoners, my lord?"

"No, just another den of thieves." He smiled at the sight of eager flames reaching upward from Dreck's window.

Chapter 10

The boy is older now, almost ten and mopping up some blood from the wooden floor of the main exercise room, spilt during an earlier session. The young students milled around, taking a rest while the master tended to the one who was wounded. That was when trouble always started and the tallest student was always the one to cause it. He saw the boy mopping up the blood with a worn rag and elbowed one of the others as he started for him. The slave pretended not to notice, like always, that the older student was coming to cause him grief. It was always when the master stepped out, that Matashumi took the opportunity to abuse his property. "I think I still see some blood on the floor. Why don't you lick it up?" Matashumi grabbed the boy's neck and forced it toward the floor, but the boy resisted. Several of the students watched closely for the master while Matashumi had his fun. "Lick it up, I said!" The slave boy began to breathe in ragged breaths, not from physical exertion but from the tremendous struggle to maintain his calm. His eyes bulged and teeth clenched. Then he snapped. With a yell, he reached up and caught Matashumi's tunic by the sleeve, then rolled under him, pulling the student off balance. They tumbled and the slave boy came up on top, driving hard punches into Matashumi's face. But the victory was short lived as the other students dragged him off. Bleeding, Matashumi lunged for his wooden practice katana, "Insolent slave! I'll teach you to lay hands on your betters!" The hands which had pulled him off now thrust him out into the open space of the exercise floor. Matashumi lunged, slamming the end of the wood katana into the boy's stomach. He doubled over; feeling like he would retch, then the practice sword came down again across his back, prostrating him. The slave boy rolled onto his back and lashed out with his foot, striking Matashumi in the jaw, knocking him back. Before the student could regain his balance, the boy was on his feet and dashing for the mop he left leaning against the wall. In one motion he seized it and swung it against a ceiling post, snapping off the mop head and leaving only three feet of wooden handle. Matashumi came at him again but stopped short when he saw the boy holding the broken mop handle in Kyamurai fashion, his left arm ninety degrees across his body and handle parallel to his head.

455

There was a brief pause followed by a burst of laughter from the crowded students. The boy could feel the heat of anger and humiliation as it rose from his neck and spread across his face. "So," said Matashumi, "you think you are a Kyamurai. Let's see how good you are, slave." He came in fast, cutting downward, but the slave boy blocked him and answered with a devastating series of expert blows to Matashumi's nose, groin and knee. Matashumi, bleeding from his nose, hauled himself from the floor and attacked again, mindlessly and the slave boy put him down a second time with even less effort. It was then the master returned, stopping short to take in the scene of his best student lying on the ground with the slave boy straddling him, a broken mop handle in his fist. The boy watched the master with trepidation as the older man stalked toward him and snatched the handle from his hand. "Who taught you to use this," he said with an accusatory tone. The boy looked up and locked eyes with the master for the first time in five years. "You did, master."

     Shasp dangled under the eaves of the tall building like a spider, a length of rope wrapped around his leg and foot. The deep shadows of night enfolded him, concealing his presence from the spectators below. In keeping with his desire to remain unseen and move quickly, he had exchanged his armor for heavy leathers, lacquered black, and boots with thin leather soles. His katana remained slung across his shoulder. As the din of celebration floated up, the cool spring breeze tousled his hair and gently pushed him like a child on swing. He had chosen his perch carefully, where he would be able to quickly gain the roof, or repel to the ground, should an attack spring from either direction.

     The flared roof he hung from belonged to the Hung Lai city offices, a four story affair with tiered floors, with each story slightly smaller than the one it rested on. Of course, it was closed for the evening. Below, a long parade snaked through the city streets like a river of fire. Everyone in Hung Lai had turned out for the annual festivities marking the year of the dragon, and hundreds of cheerful participants danced through the streets holding candles and torches. Paper lanterns, decorated in an endless progression of possibilities, swayed over the crowd on long poles.

Drums and whining lyres created a melody of Azian music which clashed with the sounds of a thousand voices. Even the outlying villages had emptied out with their populace pouring into Hung Lai for the occasion.

Below him and across the cobbled street, the emperor of Aypon reclined on his padded throne atop a raised platform. Wide marble stairs, slowly shrinking in size as one ascended toward the top, terminated nearly forty feet above the procession. The dais was a permanent fixture, like a low ziggurat with only one side, from which the emperor presided over a variety of festivals. This was the first time in many years the regent had shown his face outside the palace walls, adding to the public euphoria.

Ironwrought scanned the surrounding roofs, only slightly lower than his own, then the streets below for any suspicious behavior or movements. It had taken little effort to convince Muhara to give up one of his many changelings, bait for the trap, but Shasp had insisted that only the most trusted officials be informed, reducing the possibility of word getting back their prey. His conscience stung him at the prospect of the innocent double being killed for the sake of drawing out an assassin, but he consoled his guilt by reminding himself that it was the man's duty to take risks for his king. Nevertheless, Muhara still sent three dozen Black Tigers to keep up appearances and they lined both sides of the stairs to the platform. Tetsushiro stood to the emperor's right, arms folded and watching the jubilates as they waved and hailed the emperor in passing. Somewhere below, Pok Cho, wearing a traditional paper mask, was stalking the crowd.

The bogus emperor smoothed an eye brow, then the wrinkles from his emerald robes. He appeared as indifferent as Muhara, a

457

good actor, for certainly his heart was racing, wondering when death would strike.

The trap had been open for over an hour, but Shasp was not concerned. He knew the temptation would be too great for the Shadow Foot; it was only a matter of time. And if they did not come tonight, that meant the assassins had an insider working in the palace. Either way, he would not come away empty handed. He would either have an assassin or a traitor.

The smoke and heat of the fires wafting up caused an acrid film to coat his tongue and Shasp spat, certainly causing someone below a little consternation. Suddenly, he heard the snap of a bow string, somewhere to his right, and the hiss of a shaft as it took deadly flight. He jerked his head around, eyes tearing at the shadows upon the rooftops, while the crowd near the dais changed its tune from one of adulation to a cry of horror. Slumping on his seat with a crossbow bolt protruding from his sternum, the emperor's double gave a long death rattle. The Black Tiger guards, not knowing the wound was fatal, threw themselves over the body, protecting it from further injury while the other half of their comrades swarmed, screaming, out into the crowd, hunting the culprits who were responsible for such an unthinkable affront.

Shasp was sure the attack had come from above and quickly scurried up the rope, gaining the sharply pitched roof of the government building. Silently, he moved to the crest and surveyed the lower structures. Three figures, scarcely discernable in the darkness, flitted noisily over the baked clay shingles at astonishing speed. He marveled only for a split second then leapt over the ridge cap and ran down the opposite side of the roof. Without stopping, he vaulted over the narrow chasm, landing on the next building with the grace of a cat. His long legs churned up the next roof line to the apex, and then he turned along it and ran along the top to the end, taking another leap. The assassins had been on the clustered buildings to his left and the street separating them was much wider than the narrow alley he had just gone over. He would need some height and some luck if he was going to make the next jump uninjured. Breathlessly, he hung in the air as he fell to the next roof, his muscles contracting with the impact to absorb the energy of his fall. Shasp slammed into the tiles and started to roll, but flung himself out wide and slid to a halt. Then he was on his feet and moving again, ahead of him the fleeing shadows appeared and disappeared with the rolling shapes of the roof lines, jumbled as they were. He knew he must continue his silent pursuit until he was upon them; else they would melt into the labyrinth of clustered homes and warehouses. With the power of a leopard he sprinted across the tilted surfaces of Ayponese architecture, feeling the clay tiles under the soles of his feet. When one of the figures stopped and looked back, Shasp ducked behind a smoking chimney, only allowing himself the vantage of a single eye as he peered out from behind it. The man paused; still looking then turned and continued after the others. When Shasp believed the assassin had gone on, he left his concealment and resumed the chase. Slowly, the gap between them closed as his prey slackened their retreat. Shasp grinned, knowing that they slowed because they believed they were well out of harm's way. Well, he thought, harm was coming to them. Careful not to give himself away, he slowed a little, paying more heed to his need for silence now that he was closer. When one of the assassins stopped a second time to check their rear, Shasp hid behind another chimney, its smoke curling around the top and temporarily blinding him. He stifled a cough and wiped his stinging eyes, then ventured another glance but the men were gone. Cursing under his breath, he loped down to where the roof hung over the street and peered down. Nothing. A three-storied building with a tiered roof was the only way they could have gone, but the distance was significant. Standing slightly higher than the opposing structure's second-story roof, he calculated his odds of a successful jump then ran back up to the crest, took a deep breath, and hurled down the slope, springing at its edge and soaring across the dizzying space. He landed with such force that one of his legs broke through the tiled surface and penetrated the hollow interior of the roof. Pain shot through him and the air was blown from his lungs, but in spite of the shock, he hauled himself out, whipped his katana free and glanced around. Surely they must have heard him, but no other sound reached his ears save the whispering breeze of the blue evening. Cautiously, he eased around the corner of the building only to see another empty section of roof, then the next corner . . . nothing. Shasp dropped his blade to his side and spat in frustration; they were long gone, he thought. He was about to turn back when he felt a drip of moisture touch the back of his neck. Reflexively, he started to reach up to wipe at it but a sudden realization froze his blood. The night was mostly clear and he was standing on the roof of the second story with the roof of the third story above him. Instinctively, he knew it was not a rain drop that had landed on his neck, but a drop of sweat.

Shasp spun, bringing his blade up at the same instant the assassins dropped from their hiding places in the rafters overhead. With a deafening clang, his katana rebounded from a fierce slash meant for his skull, carrying the impetus of his falling antagonist. Shasp was knocked to his back and the assassin slashed again, but he kicked at the man's knee, and the killer stumbled backward, pausing before his comrades. For the first time, Shasp had the opportunity to get a good look at the legendary Shadow Foot. They were draped in loose silks so blue as to appear black at first and their heads were cloaked in dark cowls with yet another wrap around their faces, allowing for only the briefest hint of eyes to show through. Their feet were sandaled with the laces weaving back and forth over the leggings of their pants, no doubt to keep them from snagging. Black sashes belted their tunics, holding tanto knives in place.

One was taller and heavier than the other two and he motioned them forward with a gesture of deadly intent. Blades drawn, they advanced, spreading out as much as possible on the

460

sloping roof. With his left hand, Shasp jerked the Somerikan knife free. He would need it to tip the balance back in his favor. The dreaded Shadow Foot were a complete mystery to everyone and that meant their skill at arms were equally unknown. Shasp moved up the roof and put his back to the second-story wall to hold a height advantage. This tactic forced one assassin to move to his left while the other stayed on his right, but the leader simply stood off with his arms folded, watching the preliminaries to combat.

With the speed of a darting hawk, Shasp lashed out at the man on his right, who brought up his guard to fend off the stroke. Just as he had planned it, the assassin on his left thrust toward the opening of Shasp's exposed side, but was unprepared to defend himself when Shasp redirected his knife. As the heavy Somerikan blade knocked the longer, but lighter sword aside, Shasp spun away from the wall in a full circle and with a back hand slash, sliced cleanly through the man's leg. Without a grunt, his attacker collapsed on the roof, clutching at his stump and slid toward the edge where he disappeared over the side. There was no time for even a breath, for the other wasted not a second at the loss of his partner and immediately released a vicious flurry of cuts and thrusts which rocked Shasp back on his heels. Desperately, he countered each stroke, slowly losing ground as he retreated before the madman's suicidal onslaught. Nevertheless, Shasp kept his head against the hail of blows, awaiting his opportunity and it came to him in an instant. The fierceness of the assassin's attack did not allow for his defense or the perfection of an armed Kyamurai of Shasp's skill and in a fleeting moment between the fall of the blade, Shasp made a simple thrust through the man's unprotected heart. The twinkle of astonishment glittered briefly in the eyes above the scarf as the assassin still held his sword aloft but disappeared as he, too, collapsed and rolled over the edge.

Now Shasp stood face to face in the pale moonlight with the leader, arms still crossed over his chest and legs braced.

Shasp flicked the blood from his katana, "You can surrender or . . ." he glanced over the edge, "join your friends."

The tall man gave a short laugh, "Not tonight, Kyamurai. I intend to celebrate my victory over Emperor Muhara." His voice was deep and hearty, no doubt like the man behind it, but that did not amuse Shasp. If he couldn't capture the man and was forced to kill

461

him, it would only leave the legless assassin for interrogation . . . if he didn't bleed to death first.

"There's not going to be any celebrating." Shasp stepped forward and the leader drew his katana and tanto knife, dropping into a crouch. They circled cautiously, careful of their footing yet staying focused on one another. With blinding speed, they came together in a tempest of steel. Blades rang and hissed as they slid and slammed together, locked and unlocked. Like masterful dancers, they ducked and leaned, thrust and slashed, blocked and returned, neither giving an inch. Shasp received a slash against the guard of his knife, simultaneously returning with a stab of his sword. His opponent was flawless in his defense and, like a true student of war, understood that his defense was more valuable than the attack. This was not the sort of combat that would allow for the swashbuckling kicks and punches of an open brawl with lesser foes. It was a technical game of chess and Shasp knew he was playing with his life. He always had, but this was Aypon and the warriors here were perfectionists in their skill, not like the bawdy braggarts of the west who relied mostly on size and strength. Back and forth they battled, toe to toe, as cuts opened in various places on both, and blood dripped onto the already precarious surface. Shasp finally found an opening and thrust his knife at the assassin's ribs, but the man twisted at the last moment and received only a deep slash for his inattention. His blood flowed more generously now, running in a tiny rivulet and dripping onto his feet. The wound spurred something in the assassin and, tightening his defense, he began to counter to Shasp's legs. Shasp missed blocking a slash to his thigh and the razor-sharp katana cut through his thick leather leggings and deep into his flesh. If not for the thickness of the hardened leather, it certainly would have gone to the bone. Still, Shasp knew it would slow him down and he forced himself to rethink his position. Stepping back, he switched to a different defense, one that would favor the wounded leg. The head assassin came forward again, his breath ragged as he took in gulps of air. Shasp was also winded but not as badly. The leader was tiring and Shasp grinned at the thought then unleashed a storm of hacks and thrusts, whirling and throwing away all consideration of his defense. The assassin backpedaled to the edge of the roof where he stiffened against the onslaught, but Shasp battered him, forcing the man to constantly redirect his weapons in order to stave off certain death. Slowly, his guard was disintegrating, barely catching the intended jabs and slashes as they bit again and again into his muscle, yet the manic Kyamurai continued to attack him with complete abandon. When the assassin knew he could no longer maintain his guard, knew that any moment his opponent's blade would find a way through his defense and end his life in a fountain of blood, fortune changed her fickle mind.

As Shasp stepped forward for another thrust, his foot slipped on the blood soaked clay shingles and he shot down the roof, greased by his own leaking fluids. His momentum built as his feet shot out over the edge and he twisted, reaching for the roof. His fingers barely caught the edge of a decaying wooden gutter and his body jerked to a halt, dangling above the roof of the first floor, thirty feet below. His weapons slid past him and clattered under his feet. Glancing over his shoulder, eyes wide, he saw the prone bodies of the first two assassins. One lay askew on the alley floor while the other with the severed leg groaned on the roof below him. He looked up to see the assassin leader hovering over him. Shasp knew that if he let go, he would probably break something in the fall and that would leave him hard pressed to defend himself, nor could he stay where he was.

The man lowered his sword until the tip hovered near Shasp's eye, "Looks like I *will* be celebrating my victory after all."

Shasp was about to let go and drop to the next roof when the assassin suddenly stiffened and dropped the sword to his side. He turned sideways and dropped to a knee, balancing against the pitch of the roof. In the light of the large moon, he leaned down, looking closely at Shasp's face. With a gasp, he muttered a hushed expletive, came to his feet again and looked around, then looked at Shasp again as if he were torn with indecision. With a decisive flourish, he sheathed his katana and disappeared around the corner of the building.

Shasp clung to the gutter in wonder for several long seconds before he finally dragged himself back onto the roof. Was the assassin playing games with him, now that he was unarmed? Warily, he moved up the roof to a shuttered window and kicked it open. The room beyond was empty but for some scattered furnishings and he clambered through. Quietly, he made his way through the hall to a flight of stairs and then down to the first floor. As Shasp found his bearings, he realized the structure contained apartments. He checked over his shoulder as he rapped on the door to a room adjoining the roof, expecting the assassin to leap from the shadows at any moment. When a creaky voice answered the knock Shasp called out, "Open up for the emperor's agent."

"How do I know you are the emperor's agent and not just some thief trying to rob me?"

Shasp sighed in frustration, "If I am a thief, you'll just get robbed, but if I am the agent, I'll come back here with the city guard and haul you and your household off to prison, now open up." Shasp would do no such thing even though he could, but there was no time to debate with the old crone. Following a muffled curse, the door opened and an old Ayponese woman peered out. Shasp pushed past her, went to the window, unlatched the shutter and stepped out onto the roof. He returned a few minutes later with his weapons sheathed and the wounded assassin over his shoulder; a bloody bandage made from the man's scarf entwined his severed thigh. The old woman gawked in wonder as Shasp made his way back outside and into the street. As he limped through the quiet alleys and back toward the clamor of the crowded square, his mind was shaken by the bizarre actions of the Shadow Foot assassin who had fled. What was it he had seen in Shasp's face to startle him so? What farce was being played out? Shasp's eyes narrowed as the man over his shoulder groaned. Whatever it was, he would not want to be this assassin when morning came.

464

Chapter 11

"Two-hundred and fifty pieces!" exclaimed Lexia as she clapped a hand to her forehead, "Your ship is a rotting hulk and your crew is a scabrous lot! One-hundred and twenty-five and that's more than generous!"

Captain Belico grinned though his wiry black beard, "Aye, it is, but you would have us leave immediately without cargo and that, my sweet lass, is the rub. With a full hold and clear skies, I usually make two-hundred and fifty. Besides, you make the men nervous. It's bad luck hav'n a woman on board, though I must admit, some of the men have taken a like'n to the idea.

Lexia could easily afford the money; she just didn't like the pirate vermin believing he had got the best of her. "One-hundred and seventy-five and not a copper more. Take it or go to hell. I'll swim to Aypon before I'll pay you more."

Belico plucked an insect from his beard, examining it thoughtfully then flicked the squirming creature into the water beneath the groaning docks. "Awright lass, but don'cha be expect'n no special treatment for that kinda money."

"Fine by me," Lexia replied, "and if your crew tries to give me any *special treatment*, I'll turn them into fish bait, understood? Nor will I pay for any worthless hides I send to the sea."

"Awright, awright lass, we'll leave in the mornin but I'll need half up front for provisions and such."

Lexia tossed him two small bags, "One third, unless you think I'm a complete idiot, and be careful how you answer that captain. I've killed men for much less."

Captain Belico showed his checkered smile again and adjusted the knot on his head scarf, "Awright, but only cause I likes ya. We leave at daybreak. Don'cha be late."

Lexia gave the stocky man a stern look and without a word, turned and strode back down the docks toward town. Most of the pain in her chest was gone as were her bloody coughing fits, and she had begun the slow process of exercising her body back into fighting condition. In fact, she was finally beginning to feel prim once again. It had been weeks since her brush with Captain Markis and her healing had been slow. While she was recuperating, she had plenty of time to reflect on Shasp. Even though the pain from her wound had vanished, it had been replaced by a different kind of hurt. The pain of absence. For nearly a year she had been with the mysterious and amazing man, scarcely leaving one another's side and only recently did she realize how much he meant to her. Her heart was being wrung out in her breast, a pain she had never experienced before, but then again, she had never truly been in love before. Yes, she had been in relationships with other men, some even good for a while, but they could never accept her for what she was; a woman who fights. One would try to protect her, another would be intimidated by her, yet another insisted she settle down. Shasp always treated her as a partner, an equal. He never complained about the risks she took and even said they were hers to take. He was full of wanderlust, like her, and when the heat took them . . . she felt a shiver in her legs at the very thought. Turning, she looked back down the docks at the ship that would carry her to Aypon. Tomorrow was not soon enough.

Chapter 12

Unlike most empires, the Ayponese did not keep their dungeons below the residence of the local warlord. Instead, enemies of the state were held in a prison near the outskirts of the local communities. Hung Lai's was one of the largest and the people simply referred to it as, "The Caves." Sequestered in a depression not far from the shore, the structure resembled a military block house. A thick wood and rock building with natural and hand cut caverns sunken beneath, like veins, reaching deeper and deeper into the bowels of the earth, branching out as one descended.

The puny lamp light stretched into the blackness, fading just before the next fixed lamp relayed its rays. Claustrophobic walls scraped against Shasp's shoulders as he followed Pok Cho down a steep incline into the bowels of the prison. Ghostly moans and quiet weeping drifted on the dank air like cobwebs, creating a growing sense of unease, while the smell of sweat and excrement were so overwhelming that Shasp wondered how Cho could seem so unaffected. Intermittently, the narrow walls widened and Shasp could see a forlorn skeleton huddled in a corner. Now and again, a hoary-headed man would lunge toward the rusted bars of his cell, eyes wide and hands thrust outward, begging for food or water. They had passed so many branches during their descent that Shasp was beginning to wonder if the inspector would actually be able to find his way out. After many long minutes of listening to their footfalls echo off the walls of the plunging corridors, the tunnel finally leveled out and a stronger glow beckoned them toward a roughly cut archway. Pok Cho, hands clasped behind his back, walked through the opening as if it were his home. Red-hot braziers were clustered near a fire pit and chains dangled along the walls at various intervals. Here and there were machines of torture, some shaped like tables and others standing upright, equipped with straps and buckles.

Seated on a tall stool nearby; a soot-streaked man hunched over a tray of tools lay out on a table. His hair was black, wooly and unkempt, looking as if it had not been washed in years. He was naked except for a simple leathern apron, stained with rusty blotches of dried blood. Big for an Ayponese man, he was nearly as tall as Shasp but his body was soft and rubbery with an unhealthy pallor.

As they entered, he looked up from his knives and picks with a slack expression.

Cho smiled politely, "Hugasaro, so nice to see you. We came to see if you have made any progress with our new prisoner."

Hugasaro wiped a forearm across his sweaty brow, "Progress? I cannot make progress until he is healed. When you brought him to me, he was barely alive. If I torture him, he will die before he can say a word. It will be at least two weeks before I can start. In the meantime, he will need herbs and extra rations of meat and water. He scoffed again, "Have I made any progress." and sneered.

Pok turned to Shasp, whose lip was curled in distaste. "Hugasaro is the finest torturer in Aypon or China, though the Chinese will argue that. Consequently, he is also the best healer. Anytime I feel ill, I come see Hugasaro. He's particularly good at sewing wounds and treating burns. You can imagine why."

Hugasaro raised a smile, "With the right methods, a good torturer can keep a man alive for months or longer. You see, getting information and exacting punishment works best over time." He picked up a long thin scalpel and examined its edge.

Shasp mused that the man was just like any other Ayponese . . . a perfectionist at his art. "Where is the prisoner now?"

"Down the hall, in his cell. Where did you think he would be; dining with the emperor?"

Shasp didn't like Hugasaro when he came into the dungeon and he liked him less with every passing second.

Pok nodded, unperturbed, "I see, when should we return?"

"Two weeks, then we will see."

Pok Cho thanked him and left the chamber with Shasp at his elbow. By the time they made their way up to the ground floor and the guarded entrance, Shasp was starving for fresh air. He stepped outside, leaned back against the door jamb of the block house and looked out over the ocean.

"So, what did Emperor Muhara have to say about the capture?"

Pok twisted his mustache, "Oh, he was very upset at the death of his double. Not that the emperor cares about the man, but mostly because it is difficult to find a replacement. It is a long process sometimes requiring physical changes to be rendered to the prospective candidate. However, he was generally pleased. It is the first progress we have shown toward finding and defeating the Shadow Foot."

Shasp pushed himself off the door, "That may be true, but I think the Shadow Foot will be making extra efforts to deal with us. If they tried to kill you just for snooping around, imagine what they will do now that we have one of their own."

Pok Cho nodded, "Indeed. So what do we do now?"

Shasp stepped away into the night, "I've been wanting to visit General Hatsuro."

Tetsushiro wandered among the pungent cherry blossoms in his garden, arms folded and brows knitted together in thought. Overhead, stars twinkled for the first time in weeks, and in the absence of the ever-present spring clouds, a cool wind came to fill the vacuum. He strode along the tile walk and around a sculptured tree, coming face to face with a dark clad figure. Deep blue silks swathed his body and head. Tetsushiro leapt back, drawing his sword.

"Good evening, Lord Ishaharo," said a deep voice.

Tetsushiro sheathed his blade, "I'm glad you came. I need to speak with you."

"And I, to You."

"I thought you would," replied Tetsushiro. "You must understand that I had my reasons for not informing you of the trap," he said, irritability rising in his voice.

The assassin folded his arms, "Are you playing games with me, warlord? According to my sources, it seems the emperor has been miraculously resurrected from the dead. But, I don't believe in miracles, Tetsushiro. Why did you let me waste my time on a double?"

Tetsushiro began pacing, "I had to. The Kyamurai that the emperor had brought here from Nomerika insisted on using the double, keeping the trap a complete secret. If not for my spy, I would not have known myself. I had to let you make the attempt because if you had not, they would have known someone was working with you."

The assassin snorted, "Even if it cost me two men? Your new Kyamurai is good. Who is he?"

Tetsushiro could not hide his fury as it leaked out into his voice, "His name is Masatsuo Tekkensei, trained by Kamira Gami. He arrived at the school when he was a small child . . . as a slave. After a few years, the old master brought him into the circle and taught him alongside us. When my older brother was nearly ready to leave the training grounds, he and Masatsuo got into a fight. My brother, Matashumi, was killed and Masatsuo fled to Nomerika."

"He is not Ayponese?"

"No," replied Tetsushiro, "he is mixed blood of some kind, a bastard. He doesn't know who his father or mother is. Pok Cho tells me part of the reason he agreed to the mission was so he could find answers about his past. I would kill him myself, but the emperor would have my head. Besides, he's not an easy man to kill. We will have to tolerate him awhile longer."

The dark clad man nodded, "It seems your tolerance for Dreck was short lived."

"Dreck was a fool. I hired him to kill Masatsuo and his men failed miserably. He could not be trusted."

The assassin chuckled, "You are a traitor and I am an assassin. Trust is not in the cards for us, only mutual goals."

"Our goal is still the same. When it is achieved, we will go our own ways. In the meantime, I will continue to fund your guild."

The assassin stood quietly pondering what Tetsushiro had said, then took a step toward the warlord. "Very well, but if you deal falsely with me again, I will kill you, Tetsushiro."

The warlord ripped his blade free, holding it a fraction of an inch from the assassin's nose. "Do not threaten me! I will not cower behind the walls of a palace when I am emperor! No one has ever defeated me in combat and no one ever will, especially an assassin."

The assassin chuckled briefly then took a step back. "I may not be able to best you in a fair fight, but I have other talents, equally lethal." Another step backward and he disappeared into the shadow of a nearby shrub. His voice came again but from behind Tetsushiro, "How can you fight that which you cannot see?" Tetsushiro spun, nervous sweat standing out on his forehead. Then, from his left, "How can you fight that which you cannot hear?" The warlord spun again, sword tip quivering. The next time he heard the voice it was distant and moving away, "We are shadows . . . you cannot kill shadows."

470

Tetsushiro lowered his sword and walked in the opposite direction towards the main house. As he drew near, he thought he heard the scrape of leather against stone. His adrenalin pumped through him and he wondered if the assassin had circled around for him, but when he came to the front of the manor, he saw a slight figure dart through a side door.

He hurried over and looked into the shadowed recesses of the hallway beyond, then stood back looking to the windows above. Only Kumi's window showed the glow of a lamp and within seconds the lamp was doused and her window, dark. His eyes narrowed as he digested the possibility that Kumi may have been in the garden and wondered at the things she may have heard.

Chapter 13

It was late when Hatsuro finally rolled up his last procurement order and handed it to the youthful runner. The boy sped away toward the logistics office. The general left his chambers, legs stiff from another day of paperwork, and he longed for the outside air. Sandaled feet chaffing against the flagstone stairs, he descended to the first floor of the military complex which housed most of Aypon's elite officers. He crossed the broad u-shaped porch to the courtyard, past the springs and manicured bushes toward the broad avenue that would take him to the heart of Hung Lai. There was a jar of sake waiting for him. When he reached the gate of the complex, two soldiers broke away from their post to escort him, but the old general waved them back. He ran his stubby fingers through his bristly hair and rubbed the back of his neck. It seemed that lately, every part of him was stiff and sore, and he cursed growing old.

It was a weeknight and the area of town around his favorite drinking house was calm with only a few pedestrians wandering by. He crossed the street and jogged up the creaking plank stairs, loosening the top of his tunic as he went. The owner, a skinny man with only a tassel of hair, received him warmly, for the general was one of his best customers, and seated him at his usual table where a jar of sake was already waiting. Hatsuro had only finished his fifth cup when someone dropped onto the cushion beside him. He looked up from his drink to see Shasp pouring a cup of his own.

"Masatsuo . . . Uh, welcome."

"How is the sake here, General?" said Shasp as he sniffed at the cup.

Hatsuro grinned, "Cheap. I quit worrying about the taste a long time ago."

Shasp smiled at the jest, "I was wondering if I could ask you some questions?"

Hatsuro's smile faded, "People ask me questions all day long, now you want to ask me questions when I'm trying to drink."

"Nothing requiring much thought, General. As part of my agreement with the emperor for my services, he promised to help me fill in my past. Inspector Cho told me he was going through some ledgers a week ago and found the name of a man who came here

472

from the Arrigin about twenty-six years ago. He was a soldier and military consultant to Aypon who brought a wife and child with him; an Ayponese wife."

Hatsuro shifted uncomfortably and shrugged, "What has this to do with me?"

"I understand that you were a commander back then, and I thought you might remember the name, Lyan Morgenon.

Hatsuro's cup was to his mouth and he choked on the sake at the mention of the name. "Damn Inspector Cho! One should leave the past *in* the past." He leaned back and sighed, "This is no place for this conversation." Waving to the owner, Hatsuro struggled to his feet.

The owner bowed, "Of what service can I be?"

"A private room where my friend and I can have a conversation away from itching ears," slurred Hatsuro.

The skinny man led them to a side room with a sliding door, "This is my personal quarters, gentlemen. There are chairs and a table and a window if you require fresh air. I will bring you another jar."

Shasp and Hatsuro waited until the owner returned with the sake, then Hatsuro closed the door, settled into his chair and poured two more cups.

He leaned back, the cup resting on his chest, "Yes, I knew Lyan Morgenon. He is one of the reasons I am a general . . . he is also one of the reasons I drink so much."

Shasp was surprised by the answer, "Who was he?"

The general emptied the cup and poured another, "Aypon and Arrigin were just opening relations after years of isolation under Muhara's father. The old emperor passed away when Muhara was only nineteen. Muhara wanted to make sweeping changes and sent emissaries to Arrigin. Arrigin sent back a ship full of scholars, statesmen and soldiers. Lyan Morgenon was the highest ranking. He was chosen by the western king because he had lived in Aypon and understood the language and culture. He even had an Ayponese wife and a son by her. His mission was to show the Ayponese western battle tactics. I'm sure his king also expected him to return with Ayponese ones." Hatsuro fell silent, staring at his cup.

Shasp let the old general collect his thoughts for a while then prodded him onward. "What happened to him? Is he still alive?"

473

When Hatsuro looked up again there was sadness in his face, "No, he is dead. Back then, the Honguks were invading our southern border. They had already burned several garrisons and taken the city of Nagasato, where they dug in when our forces came to meet them. Lyan Morgenon led a battalion of infantry to attack the gates."

Shasp's curiosity perked up, "The gates? Why would the captain of a battalion be leading any of his troops against a city's gates. It's suicide. One does not throw his officers away so lightly."

Hatsuro kept his eyes downcast, "Because . . . because I ordered it."

Shasp was stunned by the answer. He was familiar with General Hatsuro's many victories over the years and had learned of even more after his return to Aypon. "Is that how you won all your victories, General; by throwing your men away?"

"No!" was his immediate reply. "I did not. But I was not so versed in war then. Your father and all his men were caught against the gates by the press of men from behind, and then the Honguks rained down flaming oil. The gates became an inferno and hundreds were killed. Consequently, the gates burned to the ground and we were able to breach the walls."

Shasp was feeling the tumble of his emotions as he digested all that Hatsuro had told him. Still, there was no concrete evidence that this Lyan Morgenon was any relation, yet something in his stomach said otherwise. "The emperor made you general for your victory?"

Hatsuro nodded but said nothing more. Shasp was beginning to believe there was more that Hatsuro wanted to say. "What about Lyan's wife and child? What happened to them?"

"I . . . I don't know. Back to Arrigin maybe."

Shasp got up and started for the door but turned just as he was leaving. "Was this Lyan Morgenon a good officer?"

Hatsuro took a drink, "One of the best I ever had."

Shasp nodded and left Hatsuro to his drinking. On the way back to the waterfront inn, Shasp let his thoughts roll over. Every instinct told him that Hatsuro was keeping something from him and he became increasingly annoyed at the likelihood of deception. It was late when he arrived at the inn and he had to rap on the inn doors to get the owner's son to open up. Once in his room, he removed the robe he wore over his breastplate, then the cuirass.

474

Naked from the waist up, he poured a pitcher of tepid water into the old basin and splashed it on his face. He was wiping the water from his face with his hands when, suddenly, he felt a touch on his shoulder. Spinning he seized the wrist, locking the intruder's arm out straight and struck the back of the shoulder with his free hand, driving the sneak thief to the floor. It happened so fast that Shasp had no time to examine his attacker. With a whimper, the prone face turned as much as was possible given the restriction of the arm lock, and looked over the stressed shoulder at Shasp. Immediately releasing his hold, Shasp breathed a surprised curse, and helped a shocked Kumi to her feet.

Eyes watering from the pain, Kumi forced a weak smile, "I'm so sorry I startled you."

Shasp took her gently by the shoulders, set her on the edge of his bed and poured her a cup of rice wine. He took in her beauty, the perfect olive complexion of her skin and wide sharp eyes. Her raven hair was loose and flowing, and though she was not smiling, he could imagine the large white teeth behind her full lips. "I hope I didn't hurt you, Kumi, but what are you doing here?"

"I had to come . . . to warn you. You are in danger," she whispered.

"Really, I had not noticed," he said smiling at his own sarcasm.

"I'm very serious, Masatsuo. I was wandering the gardens behind our home late tonight as I often do when I cannot sleep. I heard voices. It was Tetsushiro and a man wrapped in dark blue silks. They mean to kill you."

Shasp hid his surprise, "This man . . . was his face hidden also?"

"Yes. Tetsushiro means to be emperor."

Shasp finished her thoughts, "The emperor has no heirs and as Tetsushiro is the only heir to house Ishaharo, he would be the logical replacement if Muhara died."

Kumi's eyes began to tear, "Muhara may be a foolish and apathetic ruler, but Tetsushiro is cruel beyond imagination. He cares only for power; Aypon will be steeped in war if he gains the throne."

"What did the assassin have to say?"

"He was angry at Tetsushiro," said Kumi, "for not telling him that the man at the celebration was an imposter . . . and he asked about you."

At this, Shasp stood and began pacing. It had perplexed him that the assassin did not try to kill him on the roofs when he had the chance. At first he thought it may have been because he was needed as some kind of pawn in this conspiracy. He shook his head as if to clear it, "It doesn't make sense."

"Of course it does," whispered Kumi, "he hired the Shadow Foot to kill the emperor."

"Not that . . . the assassin had a chance to kill me. If I am in the way of their plans, why didn't he do it?"

Kumi shook her head, "I don't know." She dropped her face into her palms and wept. Shasp took a knee beside her, placed his hand on her head and began stroking her silken hair. "You took a great risk, coming here. If Tetsushiro finds out, there will be hell to pay."

She looked up and sniffed, "I don't care about that. I can't hold my feelings in any longer, Masatsuo. You promised to take me from here once. You can still keep that promise."

Shasp had to admit, his past had been haunting him and nearly every moment, thoughts of Kumi pricked at his mind. But, he had not forgotten Lexia and Ella. It seemed whenever love found him, death was never far behind. "I will Kumi," he said dryly, "but I have work to do here; questions that need answers."

She straightened, finding some composure, "Why? The emperor does not care for you, he cares for no one. There is nothing in Aypon but pain and loss. This country has always been a haven for deceit, you know this. You owe them nothing, but you do owe me. You promised me and I have never quit loving you, even when I thought you were dead."

"How did you come to marry Tetsushiro if you loved me so much?" he asked sardonically.

"I had no choice. My father wanted you to have me, but when you left, Tetsushiro began asking for my hand. My father refused, of course, but when Tetsushiro came to control House Ishaharo after the death of his father, he threatened Kamira. He said he would have him charged with treason, because Ayponese law demanded a lesser servant of the country to concede to higher authority. There was nothing he could do. If it means anything to you, Tetsushiro has not visited my bedroom in years. He prefers the

476

company of his concubines."

Shasp sat on the bed beside her, "I'm sorry, Kumi. I'm sorry I left you. I always believed you were so beautiful, so perfect, that you could have any man you ever wanted; someone who could really make you happy."

"You *are* the only man I ever wanted, Masatsuo." She stood before him and, reaching up, pulled her robe from her shoulders, letting it fall to her ankles. Shasp drank in her naked loveliness, the perfume of her skin, and slowly stood to face her. Gently he reached out with his calloused hands and placed them on her silky shoulders. Her skin was flushed with anticipation as he pulled her body against his own. Their eyes locked, lips hovering a breath apart. Kumi ran her hand down his hardened chest and stomach, fingertips skipping over the raised surface of countless scars. Shasp smiled down at her, "I'm a little worse for wear since last I was in Aypon. I hope it doesn't bother you."

She brought her hands to his face and raised up on her toes to kiss him, "I will only love you, Masatsuo, for as long as I live." Their lips met in a deep kiss that fanned the flames of their passion. The accumulation of years' worth of longing and loss poured out of them as they became entwined, drinking from the vessel of a forbidden love.

Hours later, Shasp lay back with Kumi's head pillowed against his chest. The fulfillment of his long neglected needs gave way to other considerations. He didn't like being used, in fact, he had a long-standing debt to settle with Aypon, and the more he learned about his past, the more he wanted to collect it. Gently, he shook Kumi awake and she moaned softly.

"Kumi, you need to get back before you are discovered. Come on, I'll take you."

She smiled up at him, "When will we leave Aypon?"

"A few more days, Kumi. There are just a few more things I need to do. I took the emperor's money and he has kept his half of the bargain, so I must keep mine. Come."

Shasp watched her as she dressed, amazed by her grace even when doing something so mundane. Outside, he saddled Tempest and helped her up onto his mount then jumped up behind her.

As the clopping of Tempest's hooves disappeared into the night, a silhouette emerged from the bushes beside the inn. Tetsushiro smiled his wicked smile and led his horse out from the shrubbery.

Chapter 14

Menacing skies rumbled overhead as the clumsy merchant vessel crested a wave, its groaning timbers complaining against the sea. A strong eastern wind filled the sails to overflowing and harassed the bustling crew as they pulled the woolen collars of their coats tightly around their necks. Lexia lay in the net of the prow, feeling momentarily weightless as the foredeck fell between the waves, then heavy again as it coasted up the next watery slope. The taste of misty salt air filled her mouth as she considered the horizon and what lay beyond.

In their long travels, Shasp had said little of Aypon, leading her to believe there was resentment in his soul. She had gleaned as much information as possible from Captain Belico, but couldn't stand to be around the man, or members of his goggling crew, for very long; a predicament aboard a small ship. Nevertheless, she felt reasonably prepared for what might lay ahead. Every passing day, her heart seemed to increase a beat, the expectation of seeing her lover becoming more intense until she could hardly sleep; not that it would be wise to sleep aboard a ship of ugly, sex-starved sailors.

She left the net, dropping onto the foredeck, and strode toward the water barrel. The salt air and wind always gave her such a thirst. She had barely raised the lid and took her first drink when she saw three of the crew ambling toward her, muttering in low tones to one another. Two were average sea rats, but the third was a hulking giant of a man. His skin was black and scarred, and his eyes held the steady emotionless aspect of a great white shark. He said nothing as his shipmate sidled up to the barrel, smiling with hidden mischief. Lexia knew the look and the swagger.

"How do you like sea life so far, lass?" one said through broken teeth as he scratched his dirty blonde hair.

"Don't you three have work to do?" she scoffed in her thick Bretcombian accent.

They chuckled and exchanged looks of encouragement. "All work and no play is bad livin, lass, you should know that."

Lexia took another drink, "What I know is none of your business, now shove off."

The sailor feigned a shocked expression then glanced over

his shoulder toward his comrades, laughing. "Come now, lass, no need ta be so bitter ta old Keshak. We just wanted ta know if you were interested in mak'n a little coin whilst we made our way. Me and some of the lads have solid money and your be'in on ship riles a man's loins someth'n fierce. What do ya say?" He held up a money pouch and shook it.

Lexia sneered, "You wouldn't live through the experience, little man."

Keshak eyed her muscular bronze arms and shoulders, "Perhaps not, but old Batala there could soften you up enough ta make it easier on me when the time comes."

"He's not my type," answered Lexia, "Maybe you three could net a seal. It would be closer to your own kind, other than the seal would probably smell better." Lexia turned to leave but Keshak laid his hand on her shoulder.

"Hold on there Lass. There's a whole ship full of crew here. I only offered to pay for the sake a be'in polite.   We could just take what we want from you . . . and we will if that's the way you want it."

Lexia half turned, raising an eyebrow at his dirt crusted hand, "So, that's the way it is then?"

Keshak and his friend smiled, "Aye, Lass, that's the way it is." The last thing Keshak saw was a flash of steel just before it sheared through his neck. His smaller friend never even cleared the cutlass from his sash before Lexia stabbed him through the waist. With a shriek he collapsed onto the deck, writhing in pain. Big Batala managed to arm himself just in time to parry the first two slashes to his head, but even then he found himself terribly outclassed. Lexia ducked his clumsy thrusts, dodging aside gracefully before slipping in for another cut. She toyed with the giant sailor, nicking him here and there, poking her saber into his legs and arms only a few inches, over and over, until the man bled from dozens of minor wounds. He howled with rage and swung his huge cleaver with powerful intent, but like an evasive fly, Lexia always managed to avoid his devastating swipes. Finally, Balata, winded and nearly bled out, stopped fighting and stood amid ship, arms hanging limp and breaths coming in ragged gulps. Lexia snapped the tip of her saber under his chin as his cutlass clattered to the deck.

She turned toward the watching crew, "Who else wants to

bed me!" she screamed in fury. She launched herself at the meanest looking sailor she could find, "What about you! You look like a hard man, care to try!" The sailor raised his hands and backed away. "Who else, I said!" None answered. "The next man who approaches me without proper respect will *die* where he stands!"

Captain Belico stumbled down from the poop deck, his hands on his head, "Aw, Lass! Did ya have ta kill me crew! I needs these men ta manage the ship."

Lexia was already headed back to her place in the net, "I left you the big man. Next time I leave no one and you can crew this ship alone."

Belico shook his head in disgust and turned to the bystanders, "Well! What are ya wait'n for? Throw this shark bait overboard and clean up this mess!"

Lexia climbed into the prow net and lay back again, watching the horizon. Absently, she rubbed at the speckled blood on her arms then shot an angry glance back at the gathering men.

She had known this time was coming, but it had worked out well. Clearly, Batala was the deadliest man on ship and with him soundly defeated, the others might just become much more amiable. With a sigh, she crossed her arms, laid her head against the net and slept soundly.

Chapter 15

The spring rain fell heavy, thumping the roof of the inn with a chaotic thrumming. Shasp lingered over a hot cup of rice liquor, thinking on his rendezvous with Kumi only a few days before. His heart was troubled by tangled emotions for his loss of Lexia and the reunion with Kumi. Her absence of late gnawed at his mind, creating a deepening concern. Perhaps he should just leave her be . . . it might save her life, seeing as just about every woman he involved himself with ended up dead. He took another gulp of the warm liquid, enjoying the sweet taste and burning sensation as it ran down his throat.

The rain had driven most wanderers of the late evening indoors and he scanned the scattered customers of the inn, looking for anyone out of place. Nothing at first, but all of a sudden, the doors were thrown open and a Kyamurai stepped inside, his cream-colored robe dripping from the heavy rain. He was a slender, older man with a greying top knot and Shasp recognized him as one of those generally seen at Tetsushiro's shoulder. The man gazed over the crowd until his eyes settled on Shasp and he started toward him. Shasp carefully raised his boot under the table, placing it against the seat of the chair across from him, so if the man made a sudden move he could shove it into his legs.

The Kyamurai stopped and bowed, "Lord Tetsushiro humbly requests you honor his house with your presence."

Shasp curled the edge of one lip. He doubted the word 'humble' was in Tetsushiro's vocabulary. Sitting quietly, he considered the proposition, while adding to the man's discomfort.

"I would be honored," he said unconvincingly. "When?"

"As soon as possible. I will accompany you."

Shasp nodded and pushed his chair back. He considered getting his armor but decided it would seem inappropriate and might reveal his feelings of distrust for Tetsushiro, something he would just as soon keep secret.   Besides, his katana was still strapped across his shoulders and he wore leather armor beneath his cloak as a precautionary measure against assassins. He threw back his head, quaffing the last of the liquor, and headed for the door. Within a few minutes, the Evatan stallion was saddled and they were galloping through the driving rain toward the stronghold of house Ishaharo.

Shasp spent his time puzzling over the request, given the weather, and decided it must be urgent, perhaps another assassination attempt on the emperor. Water splashed beneath the thundering hooves, splattering the men with muddy water and staining his escort's expensive robe. By the time they drew reign and dismounted before the main house, both were drenched. Shasp looked about for guards or servants to come take the horses, but the Kyamurai simply took his reign and motioned toward the house with his dripping head.

As Tetsushiro's man took the horses and headed for the stables, Shasp jogged up the stairs and around the horseshoe porch toward the main doors. The cloying scent of incense filled the air as another Kyamurai let him in and took his saturated cloak. Shasp was becoming uneasy at the presence of warriors in the place of household servants. He ran his fingers through his short brown hair, removing as much water as possible, then dragged them down his face for the same effect before passing through the foyer and into the main hall. Reclining on a low couch, Tetsushiro sipped a cup of black tea. Capricious lantern light deepened the lines of the warlord's face, intensifying his already sinister appearance. He looked up and smiled when Shasp entered, "Welcome, please sit down. We have much to discuss."

Shasp dropped onto a chair across from him, kicking his legs out in a very Nomerikan repose. "It must be important to ask me here so late at night and in such rain."

"Very," replied Tetsushiro. "I understand you have been entertaining visitors at the inn."

Shasp felt his pulse skip but remained calm, "Who did you have in mind?"

The warlord sat up and for the first time, Shasp saw that his sword was leaning against the end of the couch, easily within reach. "Kumi, of course."

Ironwrought tensed at the sound of her name but did not alter his relaxed pose. "What is that to you, Tetsushiro? I understand that you have not graced her bed in years and now you are surprised to find her with another man. What is it you really want? Or are you just looking for an excuse to try to kill me?"

Tetsushiro laughed, "I am no fool, Masatsuo. I know of your

483

feelings for her. You killed Matashumi because of her . . . a woman," he finished with a snort of disgust. "Ten thousand women could never replace one of him, but I am willing to let the transgression pass."

Shasp cocked his head, eyes narrowing, "Neither am I a fool, Tetsushiro. I know how much you hate me. If not for the emperor, I imagine we would have settled this long ago."

Tetsushiro laughed again, "The emperor? His will means less to me than dirt. He is a dog . . . a dog which I must obey until my plans are complete."

"You intend to overthrow him. You are behind the assassination attempts," said Shasp.

"Really, Masatsuo. You suspected it all along, did you not?"

"Yes, but one must be extremely careful about pointing fingers at royalty. So, what do you want from me?"

Tetsushiro leaned back again, "You want Kumi . . . I want the throne."

Then it hit him. Kumi. Where was she? "What have you done with her, Tetsushiro?" said Shasp with a menacing edge to his voice.

"Oh, she is here, under heavy guard. Please, do not consider trying to free her, or I will have to order my men to kill her."

"You want me to be a part of your scheme, to betray Muhara."

"Of course; you have no loyalty to him. You have no country, no people. Do as I ask and Kumi will be yours. I will forgive my brother's death and her infidelity."

Shasp followed no man. Tetsushiro was right about that, but he was not a traitor either. He stood slowly and drew his katana, "I have a better idea. Instead, I'll just cleave your head in two, so your men won't need to listen to your orders. Then, I'll haul your corpse up to the palace and tell Muhara just what has been going on under his nose."

"Masatsuo, be reasonable. Do we really need to go through this? Must Kumi die for your pride and honor?"

"Not if I can help it," said Shasp as his katana flashed down, but Tetsushiro rolled off the couch leaving only gashed fabric where he had been. His sword was out so fast that Shasp had hardly seen him move.

Tetsushiro smiled, "This changes nothing. You will see

things my way soon enough." He lunged forward; the Kyamurai sword flashing over and over like lightning strikes against Shasp's ringing katana. So fast did the attack come, that Ironwrought had but an instant to turn the slashes and firm his stance. Back and forth they rained down blows and darted in with wicked thrusts, each hungry for the other's blood. Within seconds, sandaled feet were slapping the plank floors on their way to Tetsushiro's aid, but Shasp knew the warlord needed no help. At the first sight of his men bursting into the room, Tetsushiro yelled for them to stand down and continued the attack.

The warlord employed his weapon with perfect skill, yet Shasp's unorthodox mixture of styles was troubling. Shasp leapt onto a table then somersaulted off the other end to gain some space, but Tetsushiro had spun and leapt, meeting him before his boots hit the ground. Shasp was thankful for the thick leather armor which had already turned several debilitating cuts but it also impeded his movements slightly. Tetsushiro's defense was flawless and his speed was like nothing Shasp had ever seen before. Much to Shasp's chagrin, the warlord wore only a light silk robe, allowing him full freedom of movement. Shasp retreated just enough to allow him access to his knife and jerked it free, switching to a two-handed style. Normally, an astute warrior would have deployed his own knife to keep from a disadvantage, but Tetsushiro was confident in his skill and simply maintained the pressure of his attack. Faster and faster the Kyamurai sword darted and cut as Tetsushiro pivoted, ducked, spun and leapt, its keen edged grating against the katana with flying sparks. Desperately Shasp tried to find a weakness in Tetsushiro's defense, but instead found only a length of Kyamurai steel every time he attempted to draw blood. The warlord, however, was slowly wearing down his victim, opening gash after gash in the gaps of Shasp's armor, while his men looked on in astonishment. No one had ever lived under Tetsushiro's blade for more than a few moments. Bleeding badly, Shasp gritted his teeth against the sting of his cuts and stood his ground. The two Kyamurai ceased their movement about the room and stood toe to toe in a hurricane of flashing steel. Tetsushiro was using the additional length of his Kyamurai sword to full advantage and Shasp fought to get inside his guard so he could use the heavy knife, but the warlord would have none of it. Finally, Shasp took a strike to his bracer and stepped inside Tetsushiro's reach, attempting to thrust with the knife. Tetsushiro spun away at the last second, receiving a gash across his chest, but Shasp went off balance, lunging past him. That was all the warlord needed. In the split second that Shasp's back was exposed, his adversary thrust the Kyamurai blade through his shoulder. Pain shivered through him like a violent shock, causing his arm to lose feeling and the Somerikan knife to clang against the floor. Shasp barely regained control of his mind in time to stop another barrage of hungry steel. He struggled to keep his focus and stay in the battle, though he was bleeding profusely. If Tetsushiro had sliced an artery, he would have been dead before he even realized it, but he was glad he could still feel his fingers. The nerve at least was intact, but his situation was growing desperate. He could not stay on the defensive much longer before Tetsushiro would find an opening. He retreated under the onslaught until he came close to a toppled chair, hooked it with his foot and flung it. The flying chair forced Tetsushiro to duck and in that instant, Shasp threw the katana. Tetsushiro batted it out of the air, but before he could redirect his blade, Shasp had struck the warlords wrist, knocking the Kyamurai loose. Both were unarmed and Shasp kicked at Tetsushiro's head, hoping to knock him unconscious, but his kick was easily blocked. Tetsushiro slammed his fist into Shasp's ribs, knocking the air from his lungs and causing Ironwrought to gasp for breath. The warlord smiled and came full on. Shasp was an accomplished fighter in hand to hand but now he had but one arm and could only block a fraction of the blows which Tetsushiro rained down on him. Slowly, his strength leaked out along with his blood as he blocked a kick with the bottom of his foot but took another blow to his head. The copper taste of blood filled his mouth and Shasp spat. Tetsushiro paused and touched the weeping cut on his chest then smiled.

"It has been a long time since I have seen my own blood."

Shasp took in a ragged breath, "Don't worry, you'll soon see more of it."

Tetsushiro nodded with an almost satisfied expression then leapt in again, throwing up two high side kicks toward Shasp's head. Shasp dodged one and blocked another but before he could retaliate, Tetsushiro slipped in a straight punch to his abdomen. The blow took away what little air Ironwrought had left and he crumpled, breathless. Tetsushiro stood over him, gloating, "You are nothing!

486

You always were nothing, and to think you were fool enough to believe you had the right to draw royal blood!"

Shasp had heard enough. He lashed out with his foot, catching Tetsushiro at the ankle. The warlord toppled to the ground beside him, and Shasp wasted no time in flipping on top of his prone opponent. Using a wrestling technique he had learned in Kalyfar, he swept his legs around Tetsushiro's neck in a figure-four, locking one of his feet behind the knee of his opposite leg. Tetsushiro's confidence drained as his face began to turn blue and he beat futilely against Shasp calves and thighs. The warlord's men shook themselves from their awe when they saw the unhealthy hue of their master's face, and rushed to aid him. They piled on top of Shasp, beating him mercilessly, but the stubborn Ironwrought refused to release his hold. Only when he became unconscious did his legs relax enough for the angry Kyamurai to release Tetsushiro. He clawed his way to his feet, using the clothes of his closest henchman for handholds, then lurched about drunkenly, fighting for air. When he thought he would never breathe again, his lungs expanded and he drew in a ragged breath, barking it back out again in a horse cough. His fit continued for some time before he was able to scream at his men. "Take that scum to the prison at Hung Lai! Wrap his face so no one recognizes him! We will see how arrogant he is when he is under the torturer's flaying knife!"

With great attention, Tetsushiro's Kyamurai bound Shasp, hand and foot then lifted him between the two of them. Once they had stumbled out with their burden, Tetsushiro turned and carelessly splashed some rice liquor into a cup. He had just raised it to his lips when he heard a familiar voice behind him.

"The prisons of Hung Lai? Nasty place."

Tetsushiro spun toward the words to find the assassin standing near a window. "How long have you been there?"

"Long enough. Is that the man I fought on the roofs?"

Tetsushiro nodded, "Why are you here?"

"I believe I have an answer to our problem; a way to finally kill Muhara."

"A way better than the last five attempts?" scoffed Tetsushiro.

"Yes, better but more daring, risky. Are you game?"

"What is your plan?"

487

Chapter 16

Lexia tossed her sea bag over her shoulder and headed down the gangplank. Captain Belico watched her strong feline form as she descended toward the docks and sighed, then turned to look at what was left of his crew. They were but a shadow of the group he had left with. Lexia's first demonstration had not been enough to deter the men once they had a little rum in them. Two and three at a time they had stained the deck of the ship with their blood and yet the warrior woman scarcely came away with more than a few cuts. It was a good thing that they reached Aypon when they did; otherwise there may be no crew left to pilot the ship home again. As it was, he was going to have to find replacements for the dead in Aypon. Still, he was going to miss her.

The smell of the markets reached Lexia well before the chatter of bustling merchants, and her eyes darted from side to side, hoping to see Shasp among the shops of the waterfront. She mused at the architecture of the buildings, and of the roofs that looked like the bones of great whales, ribbed and spined. The almond-eyed people scuttled about to and from destinations unknown, some smiling and others never looking up from the ground. Despite their number, she found that a gentle calm pervaded the environment, unlike western cities which tended to be loud and unruly. Their language confounded and frustrated her as she moved from one storefront and inn to the next, repeating the name Sun Shi had given her, Masatsuo Tekkensei. It wasn't until she stumbled across one inn in particular that she had a response.

The young man nodded when she said the name and replied in broken Nomerikan, "Yes, he here."

Lexia's heart skipped, "Now? Where?"

"No now," he answered, "No today. No many days."

"He is staying here? Living here? Which room?"

The young man pointed toward the balcony at a door above, "Stay there, but no many days."

Lexia felt fear creep into her as she turned and started for the stairs. Shasp's door was locked and when she turned to call for the boy, she found him behind her. "You have a key?"

The boy gave her a suspicious look, "Masatsuo, he good to me. Pay well. You no go there."

She considered strong-arming the boy but decided on a different approach, "Masatsuo and I are good friends. I need to find him, he will not be angry. Please."

Again, the cynical look but it faded to a sheepish one as the boy brushed past her and unlocked the door with his master key, pushing it open. Lexia scanned the dumpy little room taking in the details. The rusty water basin, low bunk and Shasp's armor hanging on pegs near the door. His weapons were not among them. She threw her bag on the floor and handed the boy a gold coin. "I'll be staying here until he comes back."

The youth stared at the foreign currency, skeptical, but when he sank his strong white teeth into the soft metal, his smile was so big that it nearly caused his Azian eyes to close. "I Chung. You need food, things, you call Chung." Lexia nodded with a worried smile and, beaming, Chung walked away.

She closed the door and fell on the bed, staring at the wall, "Where the hell are you?"

Pok Cho paced before his desk until Shau Lan thought he would wear out the rug beneath his felt shoes. "Sir, please sit and have some tea."

Pok turned, "I think better when I am walking. Are you sure there is no word?"

Shau Lan looked down into his cup, "I am certain. None of our informants have seen or heard anything from or about Masatsuo. I fear the Shadow Foot have killed him, like the rest."

Pok sighed, "No one has come so close to finding the assassins as he. We must not give up Shau. Offer more money to our informants and threaten them with torture if need be, but motivate them. I want them combing this city and asking everyone if they have seen or heard from Masatsuo. Someone must know something."

Shau Lan picked up a delicate pastry from the tea tray and took a half-hearted bite. His chubby face was a reflection of Pok's sour mood, but unlike Pok, Shau found he thought best when he was eating.

The two were silently pondering the disappearance of their

friend when someone rapped on the door. Pok jerked his head toward the sound, "Enter."

The panel slid aside and a ragged looking man in a worn out robe stepped into the chamber. He smiled at Pok Cho. "Inspector," he bowed low, "You asked for information about a man named Masatsuo."

Pok took a step forward, "Yes, go on."

The informant scratched his head, "Ah, yes. Uh what was it? My poor old head doesn't work so well anymore. I forget things so easily."

Pok reached into his yellow robe and flipped a coin at the man, which he caught with lightning reflexes.

"Yes, I remember now. Pyang Hong's inn. A woman came in yesterday, looking for this Masatsuo. She paid the innkeeper's son, Chung, in gold and even now occupies Masatsuo's room."

Pok Cho and Shau Lan exchanged looks, then Pok took a step toward the informant. "What else?"

"That is all, sir."

Pok waved him out of the room, went to his desk and pulled open the top drawer. He took out a long sharp knife and slid it into his wide sleeve, then found his brimless black cap and placed it on his head. "Come on, Shau. We have someone to meet."

Lexia was just sitting down to a steaming bowl of fish stew when she saw the two men enter the inn. One was tall and lean with a wispy black mustache, the other shorter and chubby. The leaner man was dressed affluently in yellow silk robes with wide sleeves, typical of Ayponese dress. Shau stopped at the counter and began to speak with the youth, Chung, but Pok Cho grabbed his sleeve and pulled him away. In a sea of Azian faces it was not difficult for Pok to pick out the only one that was western and he winced at Shau's lack of observation. "How did you ever become an assistant inspector?" They pushed their way through the crowded tables and patrons toward the woman.

Lexia unhitched her sword and continued to eat while watching them out of the corner of her eye. The taller man stopped short and said something in Ayponese. Lexia looked up, "I don't speak your language."

The man pulled out the chair across from her while his friend

490

stood at his shoulder. "It is not a problem," said the man in acceptable Nomerikan, "I speak yours. I am Inspector Cho, agent of the emperor, Muhara of Aypon."

"What do you want, Inspector Cho," said Lexia, pausing between bites with a hint of annoyance.

Pok Cho took in her appearance, the scarred, blind eye and chestnut brown hair. Her light armor and weapons surprised him. "Word has reached me that you seek a mutual friend, Masatsuo Tekkensei . . . or you may know him by his Nomerikan name, Shasp Ironwrought."

Lexia dropped her spoon into her bowl and leaned back in her chair, "You said you were an Inspector. . . Yes, I'm looking for him. Do you know where I can find him?"

"No. I was hoping you would know. He disappeared several days ago. We have feared the worst."

Lexia tilted her head, eyes narrowing, "Just who the hell are you and what is happening here? The last time I saw Shasp, it was months ago in Oshintan. We were mixed up in a scrap and I nearly died. By the time I came around, days later, he was gone. I looked for him everywhere in Attle until I came across a woman in the Azian quarter, named Sun Shi." Pok Cho stiffened at the name but Lexia continued, "She told me someone had been looking for him, an inspector from the Ayponese city of Hung Lai and now here I sit with an Inspector of Hung Lai. Were you the one who was hunting him?"

Pok gave a nervous laugh, "Hunting is not the word I would use. I was simply looking for him. Unfortunately, the man I hired to find Masatsuo took his work a little too seriously. In fact, he was hoping to ransom him. If it is any consolation, I killed the bounty hunter, Morgit, for his treason. Masatsuo came back with me of his own free will. He was unconscious when we left Attle. He told me later during the voyage, about a woman who was killed in the brawl. I assume it was you . . . Lexia, is it?"

Lexia took a deep breath, "So, Shasp thought I was dead." A mild relief swept through her at the thought; she should never have doubted him. He would never have left her wounded. "You will excuse me if I remain suspicious, Inspector Cho. What else?"

Chung appeared at Cho's side and left a cup of tea. The inspector took a sip, "We were seeking assassins. He killed some of

491

them and they may have taken revenge. The last time he was seen was with one of Tetsushiro's men, but when I spoke to him, he assured me that he and Masatsuo had a brief discussion and then he left House Ishaharo. There has been no sign of him since."

Lexia leaned forward, "Maybe this Tetsushiro is lying. Maybe he had something to do with Shasp's disappearance."

"I have considered that and have not ruled that out. Tetsushiro may be involved, but he is the head of the highest house in Aypon. Accusations of nobility are not made lightly."

Lexia finished her stew and then sat back, "Well, I couldn't give a damn if he's royalty or not. We'll see how well his story holds at the point of my sword."

Pok laughed lightly, "I am sorry my dear, but Tetsushiro is the deadliest Kyamurai in Aypon, perhaps even in all Azia. Hundreds of men have fallen under his blade, so I would not recommend that course of action."

"What would you recommend, Inspector?"

Pok hesitated and stared down at his tea, "I do not know."

Lexia smirked, "Some inspector you are. Well, I don't intend to sit around here on my ass doing nothing. If he's alive, I intend to find him, wherever he his."

Chapter 17

Masatsuo had grown in size, stature and skill. His tormentors had become his peers and most respected him. He walked along a stream outside the compound and a beautiful young girl walked with him. They stopped at the edge of the trickling brook and reclined on the soft verdant grass. Kumi lay facing him, a smile playing on her face. "So, you want to wed me."

He met her gaze, "If your father, Kamira, will allow it, but my blood is not noble. I think he favors me but that does not mean he will want his daughter to marry a common soldier."

Kumi leaned closer, her face touching his, "Your blood may not be noble, but your heart is. Which do you think is more important to my father?"

Masatsuo looked past her, "Matashumi has been talking. Telling the others he will wed you when he is head of House Ishaharo."

"My heart is my own and I will give it to who I please." Her velvet lips pressed against his.

Shasp awoke to a throbbing pain deep within his skull. All was black. After a few moments he realized his head was wrapped in cloth, but when he tried to pull it away, he discovered his hands were chained above his head and he was in a sitting position. He rose up painfully, feeling the shooting pain of pummeled muscles, until he could bring his head to his hands, then tore at the cloth, pulling it free. Darkness still surrounded him. The air was dank and reeked of human sweat and waste. Shasp knew immediately where he was; the dungeons of Hung Lai, the caves. He prodded his swollen lips with his dry tongue and finally stood, the chains now bringing his arms to a lowered position. With a hoarse cry he yelled, "Jailer!"

A minute later, a weak yellow light crept along the walls as the keeper of the prison's depths ambled toward Shasp's cell. Hugasaro lumbered up to the bars and Shasp squinted against the light. "Let me out of here, torturer. I am the emperor's agent and I have news for him."

Hugasaro raised a wan smile, "I know who you are. Inspector Cho brought you down some time ago." He did not say the words as

493

if he just realized who Shasp was but, rather, as if he had known all along.

"Good, then unchain me."

"No, I think I'll keep you right there, where Tetsushiro wants you. How is your shoulder?"

Shasp glanced down at the stitches and poultice covering the wound where the blade had exited through the front. He remembered what Hugasaro had said the last time he was there. His victims needed to be well before they could be tortured.

"Hugasaro, release me and I will say nothing of your treason to the emperor, but if you don't, I'll see to it that you suffer under another just like you. I will search all Azia for the very best torturer."

Hugasaro laughed, "You aren't going anywhere, and no one but Tetsushiro and his men even know you are here. Not only does he pay very well, but it would be death to betray him. He will be arriving soon to speak with you."

Shasp noticed for the first time that Hugasaro had brought a long pole with him and he took it from where it leaned against the bars of his cell. A length of rope ran up and back its length, leaving a loop on the end. The torturer snapped it up, flipping the loop over Shasp's head as he struggled vainly then pulled the rope, tightening the loop around Shasp's neck. Shasp fought for air but quickly felt his knees buckle. Keeping the tension on the loop, Hugasaro reached out and unlocked the manacles, then quickly came back to the end of the pole, dragging Shasp behind him. It was all Shasp could do to stay on his feet and keep from being dragged by his neck. The torturer was so expert with the device that, when he sensed Shasp was gaining strength, he immediately strangled him again, keeping him just conscious enough to follow but nothing more. Once they were in the torture chamber, Hugasaro twisted his gnarled hand in the rope until Shasp went unconscious. By the time he came to, he was chained again, but this time he was hanging by his wrists. Hugasaro was hovering over a smoking brazier when Tetsushiro ducked through the door, dressed down in armor and weapons. He walked to where Shasp dangled, pain shooting through his arms, Tetsushiro's face only inches away. Shasp looked back through swollen eyes, saying nothing.

"I wonder, Masatsuo, if you are seeing the error of your ways now, too late. Before Hugasaro begins his work, I wanted to take care of a loose end." He looked at one of his men who left the room, returning with a struggling Kumi.

Her face was a mask of absolute terror when she saw Shasp beaten and hanging from the ceiling, his face nearly unrecognizable, and her heart broke within her. "No!" she screamed. "Please, Tetsushiro let him go! I'll do anything . . . anything!"

Tetsushiro nodded at his man and he released her. She flew to Shasp and threw her arms around his neck, sobbing, her tears running down his chest. He whispered to her, "Kumi, listen. Everything will be alright, I'll make this right."

Tetsushiro suddenly grabbed her by the hair, jerking her backward and holding her in front of Shasp. Shasp shook his chains, "Tetsushiro, she has nothing to do with any of this. It's between you and me. Release her and do your worst to me, just let her go."

Tetsushiro brought his face close to Kumi's, leering over her shoulder, "She has more to do with you and me than you think. You see, I want you to know anguish beyond imagination, and sometimes the worst pain has nothing to do with the flesh. Slowly, he drew the long tanto knife. Shasp screamed, "No! Don't do it Tetsushiro! No!" but the warlord lifted the keen edge to Kumi's throat and with a single, fluid motion, drew it across her fair skin. Kumi's eyes widened as blood poured down her white kimono. Tetsushiro released her and she staggered forward, throwing her arms around Shasp one last time. Shasp leaned his head toward her, "I have always loved you, Kumi," he said, his voice breaking with uncontrolled sorrow and rage. Kumi placed her lips against his face, her voice so faint only Shasp could here, "And I have always loved . . . ." Slowly she slid down Shasp's body, streaking him with her blood, and collapsed on the dirt floor. Shasp looked down at her in disbelief, then shook violently in his chains, screaming in wordless rage, his roar echoing from the walls and carrying into the darkened tunnels and caverns beyond. "I will kill you, Tetsushiro! Do you hear me! If it is the last thing I do in this world, I will kill you, you son of a whore!"

Tetsushiro snorted, "The last thing you will do in this world is beg for death." He spun on his heel and swept out of the chamber.

Shasp's guts twisted with anguish as he howled after the warlord, then clenched his eyes shut and wept.

495

Hugasaro raised a long whip, "Hold on to your strength, Masatsuo. You will need it."

Chapter 18

The Black Tiger's compound lay just beyond the palace, a teeming center of perpetual training full of low squat buildings but without the need for walls. Only a few sentries guarded the open perimeter, for what fool would enter a den of tigers, not being a tiger himself?

The Black Tigers were divided into cohesive units that fought, ate, slept and trained together, each unit having its own facilities

From one of these, a mess hall, a dark-clad assassin peered out from the door while his comrades worked frantically. Their victims looked on with staring dead eyes as the Shadow Foot quickly undressed the lifeless Black Tigers.

"The poison worked quickly, master, just as you said it would."

The leader, taller than the others, stood to the side supervising his men, "Hurry damn you and stop talking. If the Tigers find us here we'll all die like rats."

Quickly, they assisted one another, donning the red armor of the Black Tigers then dragging the bodies into the adjoining kitchen

"When do we go?" whispered a subordinate.

"If the information Tetsushiro gave me is correct, then a runner will come when the guard is ready to change. Be patient."

Suddenly, there came a rap on the door, and the assassins snapped the tiger masks down over their faces. The leader yanked the door open, revealing himself to a young man in a court robe who bowed, "It is time, sir." The imposters nodded and they followed the youth in single file across the compound, past the unsuspecting Black Tigers who trained all around them and through the palace gates. Countless courtesans, diplomats and other sycophants chattered unaware as the assassins passed by until at last the troop stopped before the portals of the emperor's great hall. The Black Tigers at the door stepped aside sharply and opened the doors. They marched through as the guard they were relieving marched out, then they took their places along the walls in front of Emperor Muhara. Petitioners still filled the hall, waiting for a turn to gain an audience with the reagent, but the evening wore on, until many hours later,

Muhara stood and waved the remnant away. Reclining on his throne, he called for his personal scribe to review a few dispatches which had arrived, and he seated himself before Muhara at a low table. He spread the dispatches out and began a long dissertation of distant state affairs.

When a Black Tiger stepped out of his place and stood before the emperor, the scribe stopped, perplexed and filled with wonder at this breech in protocol. Muhara raised an irritated brow, "Why have you left your post? What is it?"

Without answering the guard looked over his shoulder, and with a gesture, the rest of the Tigers also left their places, slowly surrounding the emperor.

Fear and rage rose up in Muhara, "You dare approach me without permission!"

The leader reached up, lifting the helmet and mask clear of his face, "Do you recognize me?"

Muhara shook his head as he stared at the man's grey hair and beard. He considered screaming for the other guards but knew he would be cut down before he could say a word. "I do not."

The Shadow Foot stepped closer, "Look again, harder."

Muhara's eyes widened as recognition flashed across his face. "You! I was told you were dead!"

"You were told wrong. Now you know who has been trying to kill you all these years . . . and why. Of course, it was much easier with Tetsushiro's gold."

Muhara raised his hands, "Wait! I can give you great wealth! Lands and power!"

The leader stepped up to Muhara, "Can you give me back my wife!" His blade flashed from the sheath and punched through Muhara's heart with such force that the hilt was against the emperor's chest. With a choked cry, the emperor jerked then sat rigid, his eyes bulging as the assassin leader gripped the hilt with both hands and, gritting his teeth in rage, held him there. Blood trickled from the corner of Muhara's mouth and his face slowly grew slack and pale. The assassin yanked the blade free with a scrape of steel against bone, allowing the corpse to fall over. Horrified, the scribe jumped to his feet and ran, but one of the other Shadow Foot ran him through before he made it three steps.

With fierce hatred twisting his face, the leader leaned over and spat on Muhara, then turned to his men. "Clean him up and put him back on his throne. We'll let him reign a little longer until the guard changes again."

In the early morning hours, the relief guard marched into the hall as the assassins marched out. The assassin leader paused and stopped one of the incoming Back Tigers, "The emperor is exhausted. He was up all night reading dispatches, so tell your men to post quietly." The Tiger nodded and joined his comrades.

Later that morning, the cook stood horrified by the pile of naked bodies in his kitchen; a horror which quickly spread to the palace and the discovery that the emperor was not sleeping at all. The Black Tiger compound erupted in fury as hundreds of men swarmed the compound and palace grounds for any signs of the assassins but all they found was a pile of Black Tiger armor in the woods beyond the gates.

Chapter 19

Beneath angry grey clouds, people poured through the streets, some weeping and others calling out, "The emperor has been slain!"

Shau Lan spit his noodles back into his bowl when he heard the proclamation, dropping his breakfast onto the street vendors counter, then hurrying away to find the Inspector as fast as his thick legs would take him. He pushed past the confused mob that seem to pour into the streets with ever increasing numbers, until he came to the government building and huffed up the stairs to Pok Cho's chambers. Unlike the rest of Hung Lai, Pok seemed lost in thought and simply stood at his window, staring down at the chaos. When Shau blustered through his door, Pok turned with an inhuman calm, his air of apathy ever present.

"Have you heard?" said Shau between breaths, hands on his knees.

"How could I not hear?"

Shau gathered himself and stood beside Pok, looking out the window with him. "What does this mean, Inspector?"

Pok shrugged, "It could mean any number of things, Shau, but one thing is certain. Tetsushiro will have the throne."

"Does this mean we will no longer look for the Shadow Foot?"

Pok almost smiled, "Indeed, does it mean we will be alive tomorrow? I have always been careful of Tetsushiro, knowing this day might come, but we have been working closely with someone the warlord truly hates. The question is . . . will his animosity extend to us?"

Shau shuddered at the thought, "I hope not, Inspector, but what do we do? Just wait here until the Black Tigers come for us?"

Cho moved away from the window, his hand on is chin in a thoughtful pose, "Hhhmm, I'm not sure, but I'll wager Masatsuo would know something about this if we could find him."

"You mean, if he is alive."

Pok Cho sat down, "I have an intuition, Shau. Something in my chi tells me Masatsuo is still alive. It is rarely wrong, so the question is still where?"

Well," said Shau, "if Tetsushiro has him, wouldn't he just kill him?"

"There are worse things than a quick death, and if I know Tetsushiro, he hates Masatsuo enough that he would only be content with a slow and painful death. Now who, in all Hung Lai, could cause such a death . . . the slowest and most painful kind?"

Shau thought a moment then whispered, "Hugasaro. Do you think the woman, Lexia, knows something?"

"No. I am used to looking into the faces of liars.   There is always something in their demeanor that will give them away. A twitch of the mouth, a nervous gesture, but I saw no such things in this Lexia. She is who she says she is, his woman."

Shau snickered a little in spite of his fear, "She never said that, Inspector."

Pok jerked his head around, "Didn't she? You really need to be more perceptive, Shau. It was written all over her face. She has no other connections in Hung Lai therefore, she is a reliable ally. All others are suspect."

Shau sat down on the window sill and sighed, "We are in a terrible position. If Tetsushiro does have Masatsuo, we would be committing treason if we helped him, now that Tetsushiro is emperor."

Pok Cho stared at the ceiling, "It will not be official for a while yet. I just wish I could be certain about his location. Getting into the prison is no small matter even on official business, not something I would want to risk on a whim."

"It is no whim, Inspector. He is there." The statement had come from a shadowy corner of the room and as soon as the words reached Pok's ears, the source emerged into the weak light of the window. A tall figure wrapped in darkest blue.

Pok shot back away from his desk, ripping the sharp knife from his sleeve. At first, words escaped him, not sure how to address a Shadow Foot assassin in his own chambers. But his calm, disconnected demeanor quickly returned, "A bold move to show yourself here. I could have a dozen city guards in this room in an instant."

"Perhaps, but I would be gone like a vapor before they arrived. I came to confirm what you seem to have already presumed. Your man, Masatsuo, is indeed in the caves and has been there for

501

several days. If you want to free him before he loses any skin, I suggest you hurry."

Pok's eyes became slits of suspicion, "Why would an assassin of the Shadow Foot take the risk of coming to an inspector's office; especially when it is to deliver information regarding the very man who nearly killed you? Of course, he told me of the encounter."

The assassin eased closer, "My reasons are my own, but take my word for what little it is worth, if you wait, he will die." Like a darting sparrow, the assassin suddenly dove past Pok and Lau, lunging through the open window. Startled by the man's speed, the inspectors hesitated in their surprise then ran to the opening, but there was no sign of the man. Lau looked up toward the roof and down into the tumultuous crowd but saw nothing. "Is he a spirit?" he asked with eyes wide from amazement.

"Humph," said Pok, "Very skilled. Come with me Shau. We need to find Masatsuo's woman."

Chapter 20

Shasp tried to keep from losing his mind as he sat in the dark on a pile of rotting straw with his hands chained overhead. Hatred burned in Shasp's mind like a smoldering coal as he contemplated his last two sessions with Hugasaro. The last had been worse than the first and his body ached from the bruises left by a steel rod. A multitude of schemes played out in his mind as he contrived a way to break out of his cell and kill his tormentor, but the torturer was so expert at maintaining control that he never allowed him an opportunity. After an indeterminable amount of time, for time had no meaning in the caves, Hugasaro came for him again. Once more, Shasp struggled against the strangling pole and lost, then awoke to find himself hanging by his chained wrists. Below his dangling feet he saw the blood and excrement left behind by Hugasaro's last victim, and Shasp would never forget the man's screams.

The slack-faced torturer dragged a smoking brazier beside Shasp, bristling with a variety of pokers and pliers, red hot from the glowing coals. He plucked one out and examined its smoking point, smiling with satisfaction. "So, Masatsuo, did you get some rest?"

"Go fuck yourself."

Hugasaro took a step forward, reached out with the hot poker and dragged it down Shasp's chest with the hissing sound of melting flesh. Shasp clenched his teeth against the pain, screaming behind his teeth as the point left a smoldering black streak in its wake. The torturer stopped when it reached his waist, "We will save the more sensitive parts for later, but today is a special day for you, something you will never forget. It's the day you will lose your sight." Mindful of Shasp's feet, he reached out again and aimed the red glowing point at the socket of Shasp's eye. Ironwrought jerked his head to the left causing the device to miss, but it slid across the bridge of his nose, hissing along the skin and leaving another charred line. As his mind threatened to shatter, Shasp used his Kyamurai training to control his pain and focused on the chuckling face of Hugasaro.

The torturer was excellent at his work but he lingered too long, savoring his victim's pain, and Shasp seized the moment. Lashing out with his foot, he struck Hugasaro's extended wrist, and the poker fell from his numb hand, clattering on the ground beneath Shasp's feet. Hugasaro cursed and punched him in the abdomen, a blow which normally would have incapacitated a weakened prisoner, then bent to retrieve his tool. In his confidence he forgot to make sure his victim was subdued before getting too close, but Shasp had tightened his hardened stomach muscles the moment before impact. When Hugasaro leaned over, Shasp snapped his legs around the man's neck in a scissor, ankles crossed and squeezing with all his strength. The torturer only managed a curt squeak before his air was cut off. Violently, Hugasaro jerked and lunged against Shasp's hold, trying to break free but discovered he was trapped like a rabbit in the teeth of a wolf. Shasp gripped the chains with his hands, his teeth clenched in hate. What little strength he had left was quickly waxing as he squeezed his bulging thighs all the tighter around Hugasaro's neck. Face purple, Hugasaro gave up on trying to pull himself free and began to claw at Shasp's thighs with his dirty fingernails until they were bloody with tiny shreds of flesh. In a final desperate act, he dropped his weight against Shasp's legs, reaching for the fallen poker. Shasp screamed with pain as the extra weight slammed down on his already swollen wrists and wounded shoulder, but he refused to release his hold. A few seconds later, the torturer ceased his thrashing, yet Shasp was reluctant to let go, afraid the man might still revive. For long minutes he kept the trapped head between his bleeding and bruised thighs until he could no longer hold on, then released the limp body. Hugasaro flopped onto the ground with the poker beneath him. The hissing of the torturer's flesh pervaded the silence and Shasp raised a tiny, grim smile, yet there was still a problem.

Shasp shook his head with resolution. Only Hugasaro and Tetsushiro knew he was in the caves and it could be days before someone discovered him. Giving his present condition, he would be dead long before that, but at least he wouldn't be tortured to death. Though he had reckoned some degree of revenge, he decided he would have to hunt Tetsushiro in the next life.

"Take this," Pok handed a folded canvas to Shau Lan where he sat beside Lexia on the wagon. It was getting late in the day and Shau's anxiousness was almost tangible. Lexia pulled her straw hat down over her eyes to hide their color and rubbed some more horse dung on her robes. Pok hoped that the stench of fresh dung on his actors would keep the guards from inspecting them too closely. That morning, Shau had rubbed Lexia's skin with wet tea leaves until it took on an Ayponese hue then painted a mustache on her face with charcoal.

Shau adjusted his ragged brown robe, "I still don't understand why you are not coming."

"I told you already. If I stay on the outside, I might be able to free you if you get caught. I still have some authority here . . . until Tetsushiro replaces me. Now go on, it will be dark soon."

Shau frowned and snapped the reins, causing the small cart to lurch forward behind the sad looking mule. They followed the cobbled road out of Hung Lai, but by the time they reached the prison, the road had turned to mud. They halted, waiting patiently in front of the prison's heavy outer gate until a guard peered down from the wall. "What's your business?"

Shau was sweating, "We have come for the dead."

"Where is the old man who usually gets them?"

"He's ill and asked me to come in his place."

"And who is that with you?"

"My nephew. I have a bad back."

With a grunt the guard disappeared. Shortly afterward, the gate squealed open, and Shau drove the rickety cart through the entrance.

Looming inside the walls was the main structure which capped the caves and tunnels beneath. Like a gigantic brick with a single door, it was illuminated by torches and surrounded by the churned muck of the grounds. Slowly, the swayback mule tugged the cart across the open area, the mud sucking at its hooves until they came to the prison doors. Lexia raised her head just enough to see the guards along the wall, counting over thirty, then grabbed up the canvas and dropped into the mud, but Shau hesitated.

She turned on him and hissed, "Get down, damn you. It's too late to let fear rob you of your senses. Would you like to live here?"

Shau rubbed his sweating palms on his robe, jumped down, waddled to the doors and slammed the iron knocker against its plate. There was the sound of metal sliding as someone inside opened the peep, and suspicious eyes regarded the ragged peasants through the slit.

"What do you want?"

"We come for the dead. The old man is sick and couldn't come."

The eyes roved over them for a time then the peep slammed shut and the doors groaned open. Inside, smoke clung to the low ceiling and torchlight revealed a group of armed men playing a game that Lexia thought looked like dice. When they came through the door, the guard stumbled back, his arm flung across his nose and mouth.

"Phaug! You stink!"

Shau bowed several times, "My apologies, but we work gathering dung for the fields during the day. If you could direct us, we will be about our business and need not offend you any longer."

The guard pointed to an archway, "Down there, stay to the right or you'll never find your way out. No doubt Hugasaro will have a fresh pile of corpses for you, now get out of here."

Their footsteps echoed in their ears as Lexia followed Shau

506

down the steep narrow decline. She had seen her fill of dungeons and jails, but they all paled in comparison to the horror of the caves, such a scene of hell it was. She wrinkled her nose at the stench, strong enough even to overpower the odor of their own clothes. Shau whispered prayers to his ancestors while continuously looking over his shoulder to make sure no guards were following. Deeper and deeper they descended into the bowels of the prison until they came to Hugasaro's torture chamber, and Shau stopped, motioning her to silence. Lexia slid her saber out from under her cloak and, together, they slipped inside, looking around, but the braziers had burned so low that it was difficult to see. Shau eased along the wall until he stumbled onto a pile of coal, scooped up a few handfuls and dumped them onto a nearby brazier, causing the fire to rise quickly, fully illuminating the room.

Lexia's eyes fell on the man hanging by his wrists, "Shasp!" she cried throwing down the straw hat and dashed over to him, "Shasp, I'm here." but there was no reply. "Shau! Take the pin out of the holding rings!" Lexia wrapped her arms around Shasp's waist to keep him from falling when the slack from the chains clattered through the rings. Carefully, she laid him on the dirt floor, appalled by the whip marks and bruises. Her eyes welled with tears as she caressed his face, "What have they done to you?" she whispered.

Deputy Inspector Lan eyed the crumpled figure of Hugasaro and leaned over him, examining his purple face. The torturer's blood red eyes were protruding and so was his swollen tongue. Shau lifted an arm stiff with rigor to examine Hugasaro's bloody fingernails then squatted next to Lexia, and touched the rake marks on Shasp's thighs. "I think Hugasaro underestimated Masatsuo."

Lexia leaned down, placing her ear to Shasp's chest and heard the weak thumping of his heart, "He's alive! Shau, help me." She spread out the canvas and with Shau's help, lifted the unconscious Shasp on top of it. Carefully, they wrapped the canvas around him, leaving room inside for him to breath but maintaining the appearance of a corpse ready for burial. Shau bent down to lift Shasp's feet, but Lexia had unfinished business. Even though Hugasaro was already dead, she felt the need to vent her rage on the man, and with a shriek only a woman warrior could evoke, she split the torturer's head all the way to its blubbery lips.

By the time they reached the exit, both were drenched in

sweat and Shau was near to feinting. After a few minutes rest, Lexia bent down and with some effort, lifted Shasp over her shoulder. "I'll take him the rest of the way." Shau nodded gratefully, unable to form words yet. Staggering under the burden, Lexia came out of the tunnel, the smoky air seeming fresh compared to what lay below. Shau wiped his forehead with a rag as they made their way toward the exit.

"Just one today?" asked the guard.

"Yes," replied Shau, "just one."

The guard snorted, "Old Hugasaro must be feeling his years. Normally there is at least three."

Shau returned with a nervous shrug, "I'm sure he is, but I don't know how the old undertaker carries three bodies at a time out of that pit."

The guard smiled, "He doesn't. We usually do it," and laughed.

Shau smiled at the jest as the guard let them out.

As the cart lumbered out through the gates and into the starlight; a feeling of relief washed over them. Lexia jumped into the back of the cart and pulled the canvas away from Shasp's bruised face, almost grateful for the lack of light so she didn't have to see his terrible injuries. "Who did this to him, Shau?" she asked with menace in her voice.

Shau glanced back over his shoulder with a sad expression, "Tetsushiro, I think; the new emperor of Aypon."

She ran her fingers gently through his matted hair as the cart bumped along the wounded road. They crested a hill and the lights of Hung Lai sparkled in the distance. Shau spurred the poor mule even harder toward town, and eventually the crowded stone walls and fishbone roofs loomed overhead once again. Shau breathed a sigh of relief as he approached his home, but Pok Cho stepped out from an alley, startling him

"Were you successful?"

Shau sucked in a deep breath and clutched at his chest," Sir, please. I can't take much more of this. Yes, we have him and he is alive, though barely, but we did not have to dispatch Hugasaro. Masatsuo had done it before we even arrived."

Pok raised an eyebrow, "Too bad. Hugasaro was an excellent torturer. Come, let's get Masatsuo inside."

508

"I wouldn't do that," came a deep voice, emanating from the shadows. The three of them spun toward the alley Pok had just left. A dark clad figure materialized from the enfolding darkness, "Tetsushiro's men have been watching the house since yesterday. It seems he does not trust you, Inspector Cho."

Shau and Pok remained frozen as they contemplated the sudden appearance of the assassin, while Lexia's hand eased toward the saber pommel. Pok bowed and resumed in his typically aloof, yet polite manner, "How kind of you to warn us, yet I must ask myself why an assassin should care. First you confirm our suspicions over the whereabouts of our friend then you warn us about Tetsushiro's spies. What do you stand to gain from helping us? Or perhaps you simply wish to torture Masatsuo yourself to avenge your fallen comrades."

The assassin folded his arms over his chest, "I have my reasons, and they don't include harming him. Come with me and I give you my word that none of you will be molested."

"The word of an assassin," scoffed Shau, "well, that makes all the difference."

"I may be an assassin," he said to Shau, "but I am not a liar. The alternative is to let Tetsushiro's men swarm your house and take all of you back to the dungeons of Hung Lai."

Pok thought for a moment then looked up toward Shau's house. "Would I be wrong to assume you have men surrounding us." he said in his matter-of-fact way.

"You would be correct."

"Then we have no choice, but still, a reassurance of some kind would be appreciated."

The assassin waved and two men emerged from the darkness behind him, one leading a black stallion and the other carrying a large bundle. "Masatsuo's horse and armor. I could not retrieve his weapons because I don't know where they are." The assassin with the bundle laid it in the cart then stood behind his leader. Pok was struggling to understand but simply could not put all the pieces together. "You realize that I have many questions."

The assassin nodded, "I do and I promise they will be answered in good time." He turned on his heel and walked back through the alley. Several Shadow Foot appeared behind the cart and one of them motioned to follow.

Lexia looked up at Shau, "What the hell is going on, Shau?"

He was nearly frozen with fear, "A change in plans. We have become the guests of the Shadow Foot. Never, before Masatsuo and Pok, have I ever heard of anyone surviving an encounter with these men." He saw Lexia's hand slip down to her sword, "No," he said, "don't even think of it."

The short procession lurked through the darkest parts of the city then left it behind as they moved silently north of the bay. All through the night they continued along snaking trails, leading them farther inland and higher in altitude until they came to the base of Aypon's sacred Suji Mountains. The lush grasslands gave way to sharp white rocks, and the small group halted at a small shelter with an attached horse stall.

When a stocky Azian man came out to greet them, the assassin leader looked at Lexia, "This is one of my men," he said in Nomerikan. "He tends the horses and warns us of intruders. Now step down and rid yourself of that foul garment.

Lexia, surprised that he spoke Nomerikan, jumped down and tossed the dirty robe away, revealing her armor and weapons. The assassin studied the form-fitted cuirass, finely crafted greaves and chain mail apron, "Bretcombian. It has been a long time since I saw one of your race." The Shadow Foot assassins began saddling their horses as the leader jumped into the cart. "He will have to ride from here," and he unwrapped the canvas from Shasp's body. He called quietly to one of his men who darted off and returned with a heavy fur.

Lexia felt anger ignite within her, "Are you blind? Can't you see that he can't ride? It could kill him!"

Without pausing the leader and his man eased Shasp out of the cart and lifted him onto Tempest's back. "He is stronger than you think. I'll tie him to the saddle then you and I can ride alongside to hold him up."

Lexia thought about sticking him with her dirk but knew it wouldn't help Shasp. Angry, but resigned, she leapt onto a stout pony and came alongside Tempest. An assassin threw the fur over Shasp's slumped back and the caravan began its long ascent into the Suji. The sharp rocky peaks surrounding them slowly turned from blue to lavender and eventually orange as their white surfaces reflected the changing light of the approaching dawn. As the air cooled, a harassing wind tugged at their cloaks and splotches of snow appeared among the sparsely forested slopes. By the time the sun had crested the horizon, their journey had ended. The trail wound upward toward a sheer cliff with structures hanging from its face, like a village plastered against the rock, hundreds of feet overhead. A variety of long, narrow buildings rested on platforms with heavy wood beams and stone arches making up the supports. Each terrace reached out to the next by rope bridges and ladders. All in all, Lexia thought it looked rickety and struggled with the idea of being so high up on such questionable engineering. The assassin leader chuckled under his swathing, "Don't worry, it has been here for several hundred years. It's not going anywhere."

"How do we get up there?" Shau asked.

As they approached the bare rock wall, the assassin leader pulled his horse around and veered left along the towering wall. At first it seemed that he was riding into a dead end, but then he turned his horse again and disappeared behind a mammoth boulder. Keeping one hand on Shasp's shoulder, Lexia followed, leading Tempest around the rock and discovered a hidden cave entrance. The natural tunnel beyond was large enough to ride two at a time and the roof arched a dozen feet overhead. Clomping hooves echoed off the walls as they rode in the dark and up the winding tunnel until it released them onto a high broad mesa. Small huts had been built on both sides of the natural table for the sentinels who watched the pass miles below. The assassins led them to a steep wooden ramp which zig-zagged back down and across the cliff face toward the hideout. Eventually, the descending ramp terminated at a spacious horse stall. As servants bustled out onto the landing, taking the reins and pulling off saddles, several horses huffed and snorted at the familiar sight of other mounts. The Shadow Foot leader helped Lexia ease Shasp from his saddle and carry him on a litter across a series of bridges. Lexia followed at his shoulder, occasionally peaking over the railing at the dizzying drop. They arrived at a small room with large windows and a balcony where a wizened old man led them inside. With great care, they laid Shasp on a bed beside an open window while others brought in a smoking brazier. The old man leaned over examining his face and lifting an eyelid then inspected his swollen hands and wrists. After a few minutes of tapping on his patient's chest, listening to his heart and looking over the myriad of wounds,

511

he motioned for everyone to leave. Lexia stood stubbornly beside the bed, "I'm not going anywhere."

The old healer cast a questioning glance at the leader who nodded his concession then left. The old man shrugged, spat a curt phase in Ayponese and put a kettle on the brazier.

Outside, the Shadow Foot leader turned to Pok and Shau where they gazed out over the vast sprawl of mountains. He motioned to three other assassins, "These men will be your escorts. If you require something, they will see to it. Inspector Cho, will you promise on the honor of your ancestors that you will not attempt to escape until you have heard my explanation. It may be some time."

Pok smiled politely, "Of course."

The leader bowed and left down the rope bridge.

Shau wrung his hands, "When do you think they will kill us?"

Pok was as calm as ever, "If they intended to kill us, we would be dead already."

Chapter 21

The eyes of Tetsushiro narrowed in anger as he studied Hugasaro's mangled head. "Who did you last let in?"

The guard blanched, "Just a couple of peasants who came to collect the dead, gracious Emperor."

Tetsushiro nudged the empty shackles with his toe, "Did you get their names or inspect the dead they brought out?"

Fear gripped the guard, his bladder emptying as he struggled to reply but could only stare dumbly.

"I see," said Tetsushiro, "So, you don't know who they are or where the prisoner who wore these manacles went." Slowly, he drew the Kyamurai sword from his sash. Eyes pinched with horror, the guard dropped to his knees, begging for forgiveness, but Tetsushiro was a man without mercy. His sword flashed down and the guard's head clunked to the floor. Tetsushiro looked up from the twitching corpse as blood gushed onto the dirt floor, "Kill them all, prisoners too, but leave the assassin Masatsuo caught. I have yet to learn where the Shadow Foot laid their heads." His men bowed then turned to their work. Quietly, he meditated on who all would know that Masatsuo was imprisoned in the caves but could only think of his men and the Shadow Foot. He shook his head to clear it; they had no reason to want him, but Inspector Cho may have unraveled his plans. He kicked at Hugasaro's body as anger flared up inside him. Vengeance had been in the palm of his hand, but someone had plucked Masatsuo out of his grasp.

He left the dankness of the prison and returned to the decadence of the palace. After Muhara's death, Tetsushiro did not waste time taking over the throne of Aypon. There would be other scheming royal houses vying for power and a quick grab was the surest way of solidifying his claim as emperor. His men teemed about the halls and chambers now, for he had reassigned the Black Tigers to General Hatsuro's command. After the death of Muhara, Tetsushiro no longer trusted the zealots with his security, even though he had been behind the assassination. At least now he could see the faces of the Kyamurai he recognized as loyal, and besides, he had trained each of his men, knowing them to be as equally skilled as the Tigers. Grave matters weighed heavy on his dark mind, for seizing the throne was one thing but keeping it was quite another. Only a few of his Kyamurai and the Shadow Foot knew of his takeover, but if the assassins should want more gold, they could easily blackmail him. The citizenry of Aypon were so endeared to the symbolism of the emperor that they would consider his treachery nothing short of sacrilegious. If he did not want rebellion, he would need to tie up some loose ends by finding the Shadow Foot and Masatsuo, then killing them all.

It was days before Shasp awoke. In the interim, he tossed in fitful slumber and Lexia felt the sharp arrow of jealousy when he murmured the name of Kumi. She stayed at his side, assisting the healer when she could and eating little, waiting anxiously for the moment when Shasp's eyes would flutter open and he would speak, if he didn't die.

It was late in the morning when he groaned and sat up, bewildered at his surroundings, until he saw Lexia's smiling face. Blinking, his eyes widened in disbelief, "Lexia? Am I dead? Have you come to greet me in the afterlife?"

She threw her arms around him, kissing the side of his face and then his mouth. "No, you're alive!" she laughed.

Shasp wrapped his arms around her, crushing her against him with what strength he could muster. His mind was still wrestling with the idea that Lexia was alive, "Am I dreaming? You were dead. I saw you fall with an arrow through your chest. How can you be alive?"

"I was as close to death as one can get, but before they could dump my body outside the city walls, an old woman found me and nursed me back to health."

"I didn't know . . . ."

"I know, Shasp," said Lexia as she buried her face in the pocket of his shoulder, "I know." They held each other for many long minutes before she sat back, wiping the moist tears that threatened to fall from her eyes, "You could have at least stuck around to give me a decent burial," she jested.

Shasp did not return her grin, disturbed by the thought that he had not been there when Lexia had needed him most. "Pok Cho hit me with a narcotic dart. I was asleep for days, and when I woke up, I was out to sea in a storm. The ship was blown off course, and by the

514

time we were headed in the right direction, I thought . . . there was no point."

"It's alright, Shasp, we're together now." She leaned back in her chair and cleared her throat as she prepared to ask the question that had been stinging her mind. "Who is Kumi?"

Shasp, surprised by the question, did not answer right away but turned and looked out the window, eyes gazing absently over the peaks. After a few seconds he turned back to her with an expression that was a mixture of sadness and shame. "She was the daughter of the man who trained me and wife to Tetsushiro. Many years ago, we were lovers, before I left Aypon and I consigned her to life with a sadist."

Lexia dropped her chin and stared down into her lap, "You called to her in your fevered dreams," her voice was small.

Shasp always had a knack for knowing what Lexia was thinking and easily read her demeanor. "She's dead, Lexia. Tetsushiro killed her as part of his revenge against me." He reached out and took her hand, "I'm sorry that I didn't come back for you."

"We are soldiers and soldiers die. We both know this. I don't blame you; I'm here with you and that's all that matters. All we ever have is today."

"I promise I'll never leave you again, Lexia, as long as I have breath." He looked around the room, "Where are we?"

"The Shadow Foot stronghold high up in the Suji Mountains."

He sat forward wincing and holding his wounded shoulder, "I love your sense of humor, but I would really like to know where I am."

Pok and Shau stepped into the room before Lexia could respond. "She is telling the truth," said Pok, "We are their guests, though I use that term loosely. I do not know why the leader of the Shadow Foot wants you alive, but thank your ancestors that he does."

Shasp's head was swimming with all of the staggering news, Lexia being alive and, now, prisoner of the assassin's guild. "I want to see him."

Lexia pushed him back down, "In a few days when you have regained your strength. In the meanwhile, you'll be *my* prisoner."

For the rest of the day, Pok Cho and Shau Lan told him about the emperor's death at the hands of the Shadow Foot, dressed as Black Tigers, and Tetsushiro's ascension to the throne. It stabbed at Shasp that he had failed the emperor, though he never really liked the man, and it kindled his anger to know the assassins had gotten the better of him. He didn't understand how the Shadow Foot could be in league with Tetsushiro and, yet, spirit away the same man who had fought against them from the warlord's wrath. Unless they intended to ransom him back. They were assassins, after all.

Days later, he dressed in a fresh tunic since his breeches and riding boots had disappeared along with his weapons. At least his armor and horse had been salvaged. Still stiff and sore, he walked with Lexia through the assassins' eyrie, exploring their surroundings. The Shadow Foot and their servants simply ignored them most of the time, only answering their questions with the briefest of responses. Shasp had seen a large structure near the upper tiers and his curiosity prodded him up ladders and across dizzying bridges until he came to its door. Shasp and Lexia slipped inside and his first thought was of how similar the gymnasium was to those he'd seen in distant Kalyfar. The roof was high and vaulted with only tiny windows near the floor for minimal lighting. As his eyes adjusted to the dark, Shasp made out the figures of dozens of assassins, climbing ropes and running along ledges. Some leapt across vertical poles while others climbed up the sheer walls with claw hooks strapped to their hands. The training was taking place in near silence and the quiet, yet intensive, activity reminded Shasp of a box full of spiders. They watched in silence until one of the men recognized them and quickly ushered them out.

The day waxed long and Shasp was feeling anxious toward the end of it. That evening, he and Lexia ate a late supper with Pok and Shau, sharing their thoughts on the perplexing circumstances until late into the night. Still baffled, the inspectors made their way to their own quarters, leaving Shasp and Lexia alone in their chamber.

Shasp had sensed Lexia's passion for him, a yearning that intensified daily, and it was clearly conveyed every time their eyes met. Yet, he also understood that she was reluctant to approach him because of his wounds. "I'm well enough, you know."

"For what," she answered coyly.

He took her hand and stood, lifting her from the chair and

enfolding her in his arms, "Don't play shy with me," he laughed.

She smiled at him and jerked an eyebrow up, "Then give me your strength. What little you have."

"I'll show you that I have more than a little." Taking her tunic by the hem, he pulled it gently over her head and tossed it aside. Her breath came in sharp sighs as his hands glided down her bare back, cupping her buttocks. The wine of their mouths mingled as Lexia finally unleashed her pent-up desire.

Chapter 22

In the early hours, long before sunrise, Shasp was awoken by an instinct long ingrained in him; someone in the room. He moved Lexia's arm off his chest and reached out to grasp the pommel of her saber, but before he could slide the blade free, the assassin leader stepped into the moonlight. He stood with his thumbs in his belt, a very relaxed pose, and whispered, "I hear the woman calling you Shasp, but the others call you Masatsuo. Which is it?"

Shasp sat up and swung his legs off the bed, being careful not to wake Lexia. "It depends on where you are from. The Nomerikans call me Shasp and the Ayponese call me Masatsuo . . . what do you want?"

"Follow me."

Shasp dressed in a pair of black silk trousers and a brown tunic then quickly laced his sandals and followed the assassin out onto the terrace. They moved silently across bridges and over arches until the Shadow Foot stopped at a door and opened it. "This is my quarters." The burning coals of a brazier radiated an even warmth and cast a weak orange glow over the meager belongings within. Plank walls; a simple bed; a table with chairs; a chest and some assorted clothing hanging on the wall.

Shasp sat down at the roughly-hewn table, "This is a humble chamber for the master of the Shadow Foot."

"Possessions will enslave a man," answered the assassin indifferently as he took a chair across from Shasp.

Silence hung for a moment before Shasp asked the question that had pricked at everyone's minds. "Why am I here?"

"I think the answer will come as a surprise to you."

Shasp leaned back in the chair and crossed his arms, "I'm listening."

When you and I fought on the roofs that night, I intended to kill you."

"Shasp's eyes narrowed with suspicion, "Yes, I've often wondered about that. Why didn't you?"

The answer did not come right away and the assassin paused a long while, "I saw your face in the moonlight."

Shasp inclined his head and the chair legs clunked down as

he leaned forward, "So?"

"It was a face I recognized from long ago, someone I knew, and if there had been any doubt in my mind, it was wiped away when I caught the glint of your grey eyes." The man began to unwrap the dark blue silk from his face and Shasp's eyes widened as he beheld a face that was clearly not Ayponese. Grey hair, streaked with strands of reddish brown, hung to the man's shoulders. His beard was the same except for a place on his neck where the twisted ropes of a puckered burn scar ran down under his shirt. The face was a testament of conflict, hardened and meshed in deep cracks, but these were not the characteristics which struck him. It was his crystal grey eyes.

"The face I saw," the assassin continued, "was the face of your mother. I am Lyan Morgenon and you are my son."

Shasp jumped to his feet, pacing silently as he clawed at his scalp with barely controlled emotion. Suddenly, he turned on his host, "Is this some kind of game? Lyan Morgenon is dead!"

"It is no game and I am not dead. When we met on the roofs over Hung Lai, I knew your face even though I had not laid eyes on you since you were five years old."

"Hatsuro told me you were killed in battle when you rushed the gates of a city under siege."

Lyan took a step forward with his hands raised slightly for an embrace, but the hard look of distrust in Shasp's eyes halted him. Lyan's arms dropped to his sides in defeat, "No doubt that was all he told you. Sit down and I'll tell you the rest. Your mother was Ayponese. Her name was . . ."

Shasp cut him off, "Ikuru Hashita; I know. What happened to her . . . to you?" Shasp sat down and scooted the chair in as Lyan poured him a cup of hot rice wine. He could feel the tension building in Lyan as he struggled to read his son's expressions, but even Shasp was uncertain of his emotions as they streamed through his mind.

"I married Ikuru when she came to Arrigin with her father. He was an ambassador from Aypon, and I was a captain in charge of the king's royal bodyguard. We fell in love the moment we met," he paused and smiled to himself, "but it wasn't easy to win her away from a traditional father. It was only with pressure from the king himself that I managed to convince him. Four years later, the emperor of Aypon and the king of Arrigin decided it would be helpful to exchange officers so they could share philosophies and views on war tactics. Ikuru's father called in the debt of allowing his daughter to marry a common captain and insisted that the king send me back with him so he could be with his daughter in Aypon. It turned out to be a pointless gesture because the poor old fool died from sickness on the way. When we arrived, we were introduced to the aristocracy and met the newly appointed Emperor, Muhara. He was a few years younger than I, and I sensed greed and evil within him. Unknown to me, he had become fixated on Ikuru, not surprisingly as her beauty was unmatched on either continent, and he was determined to have her. Of course, he couldn't just take her away from a high ranking ambassador of Arrigin, nor would his warlords allow such treachery."

Shasp's eyes widened, "Hatsuro!"

Lyan nodded, "Yes, Hatsuro. Muhara made a deal with him. Put the Arriginian captain in the forefront of the battle and Hatsuro would become a general, and he did, but I did not die as he supposed. The defenders of the city rained down flaming oil on our heads and all the while I was asking myself why Hatsuro had placed me in such a dangerous position. Most of my troops were killed, but I managed to escape the worst of it, receiving only a few burns," and he pointed at the scar on his neck, "because I hid beneath a shattered battering ram. As I looked around at the devastation, it became clear that Hatsuro intended for me to die . . . but why? Nonetheless, I wasn't going to stay around to give him a second chance. I exchanged my clothes for another who was burned beyond recognition and fled the battlefield. I knew that when Hatsuro found the soldier wearing my uniform he would think it was me. Then, I stole a horse and rode as hard as I could for Hung Lai, but when I arrived home, I found the old servant woman dead and my wife and son missing. It was months later when I heard of Muhara's decree of engagement . . . to Ikuru. I knew she would never have agreed to such a thing so close on the heels of my death and, suddenly, everything became clear. It wasn't until just after the marriage that I managed to get word to her that I was alive, but the palace is a fortress and Muhara kept her under heavy guard. As I racked my brain to think of a way to get inside and steal my wife and son back, Muhara was having his way with her. I was living in squalor, trying to keep my identity a secret and working on a way through the palace defenses, when I received word from my spy, a woman who worked in the kitchens. Ikuru was no longer able to withstand the dishonor and had committed suicide. I also discovered that my son had never been taken into the palace. He simply vanished, perhaps killed by Muhara. My mind shattered and I went into a rage, a rage that did not leave me until I rammed my steel through Muhara's guts. The day I lost her, I vowed revenge on him and joined the Shadow Foot. No small matter, I will remind you. Most of the assassins wanted to kill me, but the master overruled them. I learned their art, keeping my motivation close to my heart until I became the master of the Shadow Foot. Each time I almost killed Muhara, I reveled in his discomfort, and the thought of being funded by his own warlord just made everything all the more satisfying. I want you to know that I looked for you for years before I gave up, and I have always carried a hope in me that you still lived."

Shasp had listened quietly, "How did you know I was in the prison?"

"I overheard Tetsushiro the night he fought with you."

"Then why didn't you come for me when I was being tortured?" Shasp said with accusation in his voice.

Lyan shifted uncomfortably, "I couldn't get in so I told your friends."

"You mean you had more important things to attend to, like Muhara's death. You didn't tell Inspector Cho where I was until after you killed him."

"I was afraid you would get between us and I did not want to have to kill you."

Shasp was floored by the answer, "Your hate was even stronger than the love for your son? Why didn't you just tell me!"

"I thought about it but didn't know how you would respond. Would you join me or would your honor keep you between Muhara and me?"

"My honor would not have allowed me to protect the murdering scum who killed my mother and father and then sold me into slavery!"

Lyan hung his head, "I'm sorry, I didn't know."

Again silence reined as he fought over what to say next then Shasp sighed, "What is my real name?"

Lyan smiled at some old memory, "We called you Ariss."

"Not anymore. All my life, I wanted to know about my parents, but now . . . I wonder if it wouldn't have been better to be kept in ignorance."

Lyan looked up from his hands with watering eyes, "I want to make it up to you, just tell me what to do, anything."

Shasp stood up placing his knuckles on the table, "Teach me how to kill an emperor."

Lyan tilted his head, "Like father, like son."

Chapter 23

Shasp waited a few more weeks before attempting any rigorous training, bringing his muscles along slowly until they could take the punishment he would inflict on them. The Shadow Foot training came along in phases, most of which Shasp flew through because of his Kyamurai upbringing, but the later phases had proved more difficult.   For weeks he practiced, walking tight ropes, contortionist positions for small spaces and, most important, how to move through the shadows unseen and unheard. Most people never consider the light with the scrutiny of the Shadow Foot; its intensity, direction, height or tint, but each of the traits were critical to one who wished to move around its fringes unseen. A good assassin knew how to stand in a single strand of shadow, with light all around him and yet remain undetected. There were other aspects too, like distraction, concealment and misdirection. Moving silently did not just require soft footwear but was also an art which took into consideration the way a foot was placed on the ground and with what pressure, even the composition of the ground. The other assassins slowly warmed to him, adding their advice on different techniques for climbing and hanging under roofs. No wonder the Shadow Foot were so feared, he thought, they were consummate experts in the art of invisibility and killing.

Pok, Shau and Lexia had been just as stunned to hear the truth about Lyan as Shasp, and Cho became distant and thoughtful, leaving Shasp to wonder at what was transpiring inside the inspector's mind. Shasp was deep into his training when Pok Cho approached him, restless from being on the cliff for so long with so little to do but think. Shasp took a break, wiping his face as he leaned on a balcony railing and looked down at the trail hundreds of feet below. Pok stood beside him with his brimless black hat pulled low on his head and his hands hidden in his sleeves.

"You intend to kill Tetsushiro?"

Shasp clenched the rail with his hands, "I do."

"The nature of my office is to serve at the will of the emperor. Muhara was not a benevolent man and emperors rarely are, but Tetsushiro has taken the throne with treachery. It has always been my occupation to seek out the truth and illuminate the deeds of the guilty. My respect for Ayponese law comes from the fact that even the emperor must obey it. I wish for you to know that I understand your anger, Masatsuo, but still, I do not approve of your training with assassins.

Shasp nodded, "That does not mean I intend to become one. When I fight Tetsushiro again, it will be on my terms. I have no intentions of poisoning him or stabbing him in his sleep. No, I want to look him in the eye when I kill him and for him to know it was me who took his life."

"That will be difficult as it seems he defeated you soundly the last time."

"Hatred will give me the strength I need, Pok Cho."

"Very well," conceded Pok, "But I cannot stay away from Hung Lai much longer. Tetsushiro will become suspicious."

Shasp squinted at Pok, wondering if he could trust the man to leave the hideaway. "It will be difficult to convince Lyan with so much at stake."

"I was hoping he would listen to you," said Pok as he met Shasp's stare, "there is more at stake here than this place and these men. All of Aypon is at risk."

Silently, Shasp considered all that Pok had done for him and struggled to find the trust within that would allow Pok to leave. "I'll talk to him."

That evening Shasp discussed Pok's leaving with Lyan, but Morgenon was hard pressed to let the inspector ride back to Hung Lai.

"What if he brings down the armies of Aypon on our heads? My men trust me and I can't betray that trust."

Shasp stepped up face to face with Lyan, "Cho has saved my life where you did little. I trust him and I'll vouch for him. Things are brewing in Hung Lai and we need to know what they are. Inspector Cho is in an excellent position to gather information for us and give us an edge. I say, let him go."

Lyan turned away suddenly, shaking his head, "You ask too much from me."

"I have never asked anything from you and you were never there to give it. You said you wanted to make things right, well here is your chance. We need Cho to help us, because the warlord knows

I am alive and he knows I will stop at nothing to kill him. He will not make it easy. Hundreds of his own Kyamurai are guarding the palace, how else will we get him?"

Lyan's eyes softened as he faced his son once again, "Are you sure you trust him?"

"With my life."

Lyan gave a deep sigh, "Then find him a good horse."

Chapter 24

Pok Cho waited patiently outside the doors of the Golden Hall while the Kyamurai guarding it eyed him suspiciously. Not wanting to come before the new emperor looking like a commoner, Pok had exchanged his dusty robe for a dark blue one with woven designs and some black felt shoes. The doors swung wide and two more warriors swept through, motioning for Pok to lift his arms then checked him thoroughly for weapons before escorting him before the throne. Tetsushiro sat, legs stretched out and his head resting on his knuckles in what Pok believed was a very un-regal looking posture.

Pok knelt and bowed his head to the floor, waiting for Tetsushiro to give him permission to stand. After a few distressing seconds, the warlord spoke.

"Where have you been, Inspector Cho?"

"My lord, I have been searching for the lair of the Shadow Foot, of course, or is there no longer a need for that mission now that Emperor Muhara has gone to his ancestors?"

Tetsushiro regarded him with narrow eyes, suspicion clicking in his thoughts, "And Masatsuo? Have you found him?"

"The news I have is quite disconcerting, my lord."

"Stand and speak, Inspector Cho," Tetsushiro said with his usual condescending tone.

Pok did not hesitate to answer, "I have located Masatsuo and the lair of the Shadow Foot, your highness. It may come as a surprise to you, but Masatsuo is working with them. It will take a large force to surround and destroy the stronghold because their numbers are greater than I anticipated and the fortress will be difficult to siege."

Tetsushiro sat up at this. So it *was* the Shadow Foot who spirited Masatsuo out of the caves. "How did you come by this? We have yet to break the assassin in our custody."

Pok gave a humble smile, "It was difficult, your highness. I was captured by the Shadow Foot and taken to their fortress in the Suji Mountains. It seems my own deputy inspector, Shau Lan and Masatsuo have been in league with them for some time. He believes I am still loyal to the dead emperor Muhara and tried to convince me that you were responsible for his death. I led him and the others to believe that I was with them, but my allegiance is to the living emperor. I would be a fool to take the word of conspirators over the head of the House of Ishaharo. I told Masatsuo that I needed to return to Hung Lai to gather information for them but, instead, I came here to inform you and request to take a sizeable force under the command of General Hatsuro into the Suji."

Tetsushiro eyed Pok with suspicion, "What about the assassin Masatsuo wounded, and the other one he killed? Why would he do that if he was in league with the Shadow Foot?"

Pok Cho shrugged, "I have wondered that same thing and came to the conclusion that the man is probably not an assassin at all, but rather a decoy. Some poor fool who fell into their clutches, dressed up like one of their own so Muhara would believe he was loyal."

Tetsushiro listened to Pok's theories and realized the truth about his scheme hovered dangerously near the surface. He jumped to his feet, "I will lead the army myself and put an end to Masatsuo once and for all!"

Pok raised a hand, "If I may be so bold my lord, you are the soul of Aypon now and should not endanger yourself in combat. It is no secret that you are the most fearsome swordsman in all of Azia and, therefore, have nothing to prove, but to risk your life when others can do your bidding would seem undignified to the people. There is no need to cause unrest."

Tetsushiro gritted his teeth as if he was preparing to unleash his fury on Pok, but he relaxed and sat back on his throne. "Very well, Inspector Cho, but I warn you, if you fail me in this mission you had better die on the slopes of the Suji because I will make your punishment much worse than death." He turned to the scribe sitting at a low table on his left, "Write the order to General Hatsuro . . . Tell him, he will be under Inspector Cho's authority and to set no limit on men or resources."

The scribe finished the document, scurried off the dais toward Pok, and handed him the rolled up parchment. Pok bowed and began to leave when Tetsushiro called to him.

"Take no prisoners except for Masatsuo. He is the only one I want alive and make certain that General Hatsuro knows he will share your fate if he fails."

Pok Cho bowed again and hurried out of the great hall. He was an inspector of Hung Lai and his allegiance must be to the

527

emperor of Aypon, it was the first rule of his oath of office and he constantly reminded himself of that.

Pok waited until evening before riding to the military complex on the hill near the uppermost edge of Hung Lai. He approached the sentries at the gates and handed them the scroll, which they quickly read, then passed him through. While riding past trickling fountains and small courtyards of trimmed trees and bushes, he considered how the officers of Aypon's army lived in modest splendor. Inspector Cho did not find Hatsuro hovering over military documents as he had expected but, rather, sitting behind his desk with an arm curled affectionately around a half-empty bottle of sake.

"General, it is a little early in the evening to be drunk, is it not?"

Hatsuro squinted trying to focus on Pok's face, "Yes it is, Inspector Cho, but did you come here to chastise me for my bad habits or is there something else you want?"

Pok Cho handed him the orders, "There is."

Hatsuro sighed with exasperation and read the orders, blinking repeatedly to clear the haze before his eyes. When he finished, he dropped the papers onto the desk, "I will send my colonel with you. This is a simple raid, he can lead the men."

Pok sat down, "I was told to inform you that if it fails, you will share my fate, one worse than death, I imagine. Are you sure you want to trust this colonel with your life?"

Hatsuro poured another cup, "How many men will we need?"

"Maybe three-hundred, but there is more."

"More?"

Cho sat back, studied Hatsuro's face and weighed his words carefully, "I have always known you to be a man loyal to the emperor, are you not?"

Hatsuro became incensed by the idea that Cho should even ask such a question. "My family line has served the emperors of Aypon for more than ten generations, unswervingly. Do you doubt my loyalty?" He stood and began to clumsily draw his sword, but Pok stood and pushed him back down in his chair.

"Clearly, your loyalty is intact, General, but there is much more to this mission than a quick raid, as you are about to find out."

General Hatsuro spent most of the next morning picking out

his most seasoned troops. Pok Cho sat impatiently on his horse, having exchanged his robe for more appropriate riding gear, a gold tunic and dark bloused trousers. Slowly, the ranks filled with infantry and a small force of cavalry, their unit flags flapping in the wind over their heads. As the ranks formed, Hatsuro saw a figure riding toward him on a tan pony, the leaping silhouette of a black tiger on his red armor was clearly visible. The rider drew rein beside the general's horse and the Black Tiger peeled off his mask and helmet.

Captain Chi Wong saluted Hatsuro, "My men are eager for action, General, are you sure you won't reconsider?"

Hatsuro took in the man's cleanly shaven face and close cropped black hair. Chi Wong had led the Black Tigers for the last eight years and the general knew how devastating a blow it had been for them to be banned from the palace grounds. They all harbored a fierce loyalty to the emperor. This same loyalty was the very heart and essence of the Black Tigers. It motivated them to be elite and they looked for any opportunity to prove their worth and redeem their honor, but in the meantime, the trust was shattered and the heart of the Black Tigers was broken.

Hatsuro gave the captain a friendly grin, "My men will be capable enough for this mission, Captain, but I will need your men, soon. Keep them sharp until I return."

Chi Wong began to protest but choked down his pride. He knew it would do no good to argue with a man who had a reputation for being hard-headed, so Wong turned his pony around and galloped back toward his men.

Cho watched after him for a moment, feeling sadness for the Black Tigers he rarely felt for others.

By afternoon the force was assembled and marching through Hung Lai toward the north end of town. People flooded out of their shops and houses to see the procession of warriors as they tramped by and wondered at their destination. Everyone knew that the day would come when Tetsushiro would lead them to war, but none believed it would be so soon. Slowly, the troops moved through the anxious streets and out of the north gate, disappearing into the woodlands beyond.

Chapter 25

Grey clouds swept over the Suji Mountains, driven by a capricious north wind. As the sun set, it peeked under the canopy of vapor, its dying light painting the underbelly of the coming thunderheads a fiery red. The first rains had just begun to fall when Shasp and Lyan left the gymnasium, famished and ready for a meal, but their appetites shriveled when they heard the resounding echo of a sentinel's gong.

Lyan raced down a rope bridge, leapt across the gap of an adjoining balcony and continued toward the lower lookout with Shasp on his heels.

"What is it?" Shasp panted as he kept pace with Lyan.

"The watchers have spotted something." Even as he answered, assassins and servants were jostling past one another on their way to their posts.

By the time Shasp and Lyan reached the lower terraces of the fortress, Lexia had caught up to them, "What's going on?"

"We're about to find out," Shasp answered as he snapped open his spyglass and focused on the trail below. Suddenly, he stiffened as if shocked by what he saw then jerked the glass away, clenching his jaw in anger. He and Lyan exchanged a hard look before Shasp handed him the spyglass. Lyan scanned the lower trail, and then dropped the glass to his side as his expression went slack.

"What is it," said Lexia looking at Shasp.

"Pok Cho and General Hatsuro are leading a large force. He's betrayed us." He clamped his hand on Lyan's shoulder, "We have to get the men out of here, Lyan, before they hem us in."

Lyan shook his head, "There is no way out, only the tunnel. The back face of this peak is just as sheer as the front and just as high."

Shasp spun on his heel and started to move off, "Then we better fortify that entrance while we still have time."

Lyan and Lexia split off, grabbing men as they went and shoving them toward the ramp which led to the plateau above. Others prepared pots of oil and filled quivers, teeming back and forth across the bridges like the ants of a disturbed colony.

A few minutes later, Shasp hovered near the edge of the

mesa, his toes hanging over the edge as he watched the Ayponese troops fan out far below, a tactic that would minimize their losses. There was no doubt in his mind, it was going to get bloody, but at least the defenders had the upper hand. Hatsuro would lose most of his troops just fighting his way through the tunnel, but the assassins had no egress. The general could keep them penned in and send back for reinforcements at his leisure. Shasp cursed and paced across the plateau as dark clad assassins swarmed into the tunnel entrance. With a final look over his shoulder, he gazed at the fiery horizon with a longing that suggested it may be the last time he ever saw it, then drew his new katana and headed into the gaping maw of the mountain.

Pok Cho's horse sensed the electricity of war filling the air and reared back. Undisturbed by his mounts anxiety, Pok simply leaned forward until the beast returned its hooves to the ground. He twisted around in the saddle to face Hatsuro, "Keep the men at a distance General; we don't need to lose too many soldiers to archery fire just yet."

"I am no fool, Pok Cho," huffed the general, "I have more knowledge of warfare in one toe than you will ever know, and I have no intentions of needlessly throwing away soldiers."

"My apologies, General. I simply do not wish to fail the emperor."

Hatsuro was quiet for a moment, "You are certain it is Lyan Morgenon who leads these assassins?"

"I am, but that must not shake you. We must serve the Emperor of Aypon; it is the reason for our existence, to protect the spirit of our country. Without that, we cannot remain a nation. I know you are afraid, General, but you must remember your duty."

"Morgenon has much cause to see me dead; I just wonder why the Shadow Foot did not kill me long ago."

"Perhaps he believed you were already dead, for you seem a shell of man, let alone a general. You followed the emperor's orders, you believed you were doing your duty, yet it ate a hole in your spirit. Now it is time to awake and do your duty once again, for the emperor." Pok turned his horse and spurred it toward the cliff and, under a hailstorm of arrows, galloped toward the entrance of the assassin stronghold.

531

Chapter 26

Rain fell from the dark grey sky in torrents, hammering against the spiny roofs and cobbled streets of Hung Lai with the intensity of a thousand war drums. Pools of water collected in the depressions of the street and ran in rivers along the hillsides as the train of soldiers marched in a haggard line back through the north gate. Less than a hundred pairs of feet splashed in a chaotic tramp. Rain poured down their Kyamurai helmets onto their backs as they kept their tired eyes forward, trying to maintain order. The shuffling feet and clatter of armor brought the citizens to their windows and they stared in wonder at the men who marched by and the wagons which followed. Wagon after wagon filled with dead soldiers and limp dark clothed bodies. Their arms and legs lay askew over one another as if they had been unceremoniously tossed in like so much cord wood. Dirt and blood caked the clothing of the soldiers and the dead alike, though the living wore bloody bandages over their wounds. Only a single prisoner trailed behind the general's horse, with a long tether running from the saddle of the mount to the man's bound wrists, and he wore the same dark blue garments as the piled dead in the wagons.

The rain had washed most of the caked blood and dirt from Shasp's face, and plastered his hair against his forehead. Though he was tied and led, his intense grey eyes showed no sign of defeat, as if the thought had no place in the mind behind them. Slowly, the soldiers dragged by, through the torrent, unmindful of the pelting droplets that splattered against their faces. They wound through the streets and up the long hill, halting at the palace gates as Hatsuro raised his hand.

Hatsuro tilted his head back until the rain was falling into his eyes and called to the sentry on the wall, "Open the gates!"

The Kyamurai yelled down, "State your business."

"I have returned from doing the emperor's bidding and have brought him the bodies of the Shadow Foot and the man who conspired with them, Masatsuo Tekkensei.

The sentry disappeared and Pok gave Hatsuro a comforting smile, "You have done well, General."

Hatsuro kept his eyes on the gates, "We shall see."

The gates swung open ponderously on the massive hinges, groaning under the weight. The soldiers dragged their tired feet as they marched inside and the palace gates slammed together behind them.

A dispatch rider had already brought word to Tetsushiro about the triumphant defeat of the Shadow Foot stronghold and the emperor was eager to look into the eyes of the man he hated and remind him that there was no escape from his wrath. His face was a mask of evil satisfaction as he strode through the halls toward the courtyard and closer to the completion of his diabolical plans. His men gathered behind him as he swept through the palace corridors, leaving their posts to protect their master, and by the time he reached the main courtyard, a sizable contingent followed.

The inhabitants of the palace grounds had also gathered to gawk at the soldiers and their prisoner. Tetsushiro's Kyamurai watched intently from their posts as the emperor moved gracefully down the palace steps. Hatsuro and Cho dismounted as to not look down on their regent, a serious breach of protocol. They knelt and bowed their heads, yet Shasp stood defiantly glaring at the warlord with boiling hatred. Tetsushiro moved past them and with a smile playing on his lips, slowly circled Shasp, examining his torn wet clothes.

"So, Masatsuo, you thought you could escape me and even dared to assist the enemies of this nation."

"You are the only enemy of this nation, pig; you and that traitor Pok Cho who kneels before you."

Tetsushiro returned Shasp's glare with an equal dose of venom, "Your impertinence does not move me, Masatsuo, because you will return to the caves and remain there under the torturer's knife until you beg me for a merciful death, but it will not come to you. Every day you suffer will be a day of joy for me." Like an adder striking, Tetsushiro backhanded him, rocking Shasp's head back with the force. "Take him back to the caves."

Shasp raised his bound hands and wiped at the blood on his lips as Tetsushiro walked away toward the palace steps, "Tetsushiro! Who says I'm going anywhere?" The warlord turned just in time to see a soldier on Shasp's right step toward him and slash his bonds. Another soldier on his left bowed his head and held out a katana which Shasp lifted from his palms.

Tetsushiro's face twisted with rage and bewilderment, "What is this! General, hang those men!"

Hatsuro and Pok stood up and the general smiled, "Not today, Tetsushiro."

Suddenly, the column formations of Hatsuro's command broke apart and the dead in the wagons sprang to life. With the piercing Kyamurai war cry on their lips, the dead assassins and soldiers leapt from the wagons, grabbing the weapons that had been hidden beneath them. The courtyard erupted into pandemonium as the startled palace guards fumbled to clear their swords and screaming men clashed in a chaotic swirl of clattering steel.

Once Tetsushiro threw off the shock of what had just happened, he set his jaw and leapt into the fray. General Hatsuro was unfortunate to be the one closest to him and had scarcely managed to block the first slash, but his long nights of drinking had stolen his agility and the next thrust slipped past his guard and through his waist. The old general crumpled but Tetsushiro never paused, lunging toward his goal. The warlord's Kyamurai were trying to surround him and Shasp had already cut down two of them, but Tetsushiro was just as frustrated by the presence of his own men as they stymied his progress toward his nemesis. With cold vengeance in their eyes, Shasp and Tetsushiro hacked their way to one another until at last they came face to face.

Tetsushiro did not wait but lunged at his foe, the Kyamurai blade licking out like a serpent's tongue, and cut Shasp across his cheek. Blood streamed down his face from the superficial wound, but he knocked aside the rest of Tetsushiro's attacks. The warlord rained down a torrent of steel but Shasp focused on his defense, giving no mind to any returning blows.

Tetsushiro's men poured down from the battlements and swarmed out from the palace, surrounding the smaller force of soldiers and assassins, but the invaders stubbornly held the position around the wagons. Men locked together in deadly combat as steel crashed against steel in the driving rain, and footing became slippery. Water mixed with blood on the flagstones as it poured from the dead and wounded.

Tetsushiro's men were excellent warriors, having been trained by the best swordsman in all Azia, and their superiority was becoming evident as they easily cut down the inferior soldiers and assassins. Slowly, the knot around the wagons was shrinking and just when it seemed things could not get worse, a group of archers, still on the battlements, began firing into the massed men of Lyan's command. Men crumpled left and right as the stinging darts found their way into vital organs and the leader of the Shadow Foot knew instantly that there was no way they could continue to stand under the withering rain of broad heads. He cut his way through the warriors that stood between him and the closed gates, then dashed across the compound toward their only hope for survival. Arrows zipped through the air, hissing past his ears and slashing at his arms and legs. Suddenly, he felt the slam of steel between his shoulder blades as one missile found its mark. Lyan toppled to the ground, his momentum causing him to roll and snapping the arrow off above the point. He gasped for air as pain from the wound flooded his brain, but then clenched his jaw with determination, staggered up and stumbled onward. More arrows bit into his legs and arms, but Lyan threw himself at the gates, grasping the rope and pulley system of the massive bar which sat in the locks. With the last of his ebbing

535

strength, he heaved down on the rope and freed the ponderous beam.

Suddenly, the gates exploded from the unseen pressure beyond and men poured through the entrance like rushing water through a floodgate. The Black Tigers, hundreds of them, flooded through the gates and into the palace courtyards, rain streaming off their lacquered red armor and their war cries rising above the coming thunder. Tetsushiro's men recoiled from the impact of the Tigers as they crashed into them. As the Black Tigers swarmed forward, the weary assassins and soldiers fell back, finding cover from the relentless hail of arrows. A group of Tigers, armed with bows, broke off and began to return fire on the battlements. Archers fell from the catwalks, unable to find cover while others raced along the wall trying to escape the hissing death. With the danger of raining arrows driven from the field, the Black Tigers were able to press Tetsushiro's Kyamurai back against the palace. Aypon's best warriors fought against each other before the palace steps in a seething mass of brutal fighting. The battle cries of the living mixed with the screams of the dying until the roar carried over the walls and to the ears of a horrified Hung Lai.

Pok Cho and Shau Lan sat under a wagon, out of the rain. Pok's face was a mask of indifference but Shau's was taut with fear.

Shau looked out from under the wagon, "How is the battle going? Do you think we can win?"

Pok made a face as he examined the stained edge of his robe, "I have ruined more garments since this business began than ever in my life. Destiny is what it is Shau, it cannot be changed, only accepted."

Shau didn't care for the nebulous answer, "How come you are not fighting with the others?"

Pok looked annoyed, "Because it is not my occupation, now calm yourself and be patient."

Lexia ducked her head under the wagon. She was covered in shallow cuts and blood was streaming down her limbs in the rain. She had fallen back for a rest when the Black Tigers swarmed past them and was on her way back into the fray. "Are you two alright?"

Pok made a curt smile, "Other than my pants being wet from sitting in water, yes."

Lexia shook her head and charged back into the battle,

stepping up beside two Tigers and taking on an opponent of her own.

Shasp had told her a long time ago that warriors in Aypon were not like the ones in the west. They were perfectionist and if she gave them the smallest opening they would use it to kill her. She was learning that he had not exaggerated and was glad she listened to his advice when she faced her first. Nearly every warrior she had fought so far was her equal and luck had been on her side more than once. Her saber clanged off a Kyamurai sword, she blocked and returned a thrust, but the press of men made complete movements difficult. Nevertheless, this was to Lexia's advantage for she had been in many a fray where fighting was close and she was used to the idea of adjusting her techniques into more restricted movements, whereas the men she faced had not been so experienced, though well trained. She grabbed the wrist of her adversary's sword arm and slammed her pommel into his forehead, then thrust him through. One more.

Steel crashed together with a velocity the eye could scarcely follow as Shasp and Tetsushiro unleashed their rage against one another. The fierceness of their struggle was such that the Tigers and Kyamurai gave them a wide berth even in the crushing press. Rain flew from their blades with each slash and thrust. Tetsushiro's soaked black mane whipped back and forth as his arm and body changed direction with each new tactic, plastering against his face and neck as his lips curled back in the snarl of a wolf. Shasp returned each strike, hissing through his teeth every time he countered. Like a fierce storm on a wind-swept sea, the two raged one against the other but Tetsushiro's frustration over Shasp's defense only fired his resolve to press harder, forcing Ironwrought to slowly retreat against the perfect barrage of lightning fast attacks.

As the battle raged on, the sky darkened until shadows fell heavy over the palace grounds, for no torches had been lit, and men struggled on in the coming darkness of the blood filled courtyard. Slowly, the Black Tigers, fired by the prospect of regaining their honor, pushed Tetsushiro's men back into the palace. Now, part of the battle raged in the hall of the emperor, filled with milling men hungry for each other's blood. Ringing steel echoed off the vaulted ceiling as palace servants and courtesans fled in panic from the flood of battling men.

Shasp and the warlord had remained outside and it became clear to Tetsushiro that he was about to be cut off from his warriors.

Nevertheless, he continued to war against his enemy with
unrelenting ferocity and, with a movement too quick to follow, he
snaked his blade past Shasp's defense, gashing his left arm. Shasp
struggled to maintain his footing and keep his blade in front of him
as Tetsushiro continued to press, but the warlord smelled victory.
Another thrust slipped past Shasp's guard, driving the point of the
Kyamurai blade into his thigh, but Shasp knocked away another
slash then leapt sideways and sprinted into the gardens. An evil grin
split Tetsushiro's face as he ran after his prey, like a wolf incensed
by a bleeding rabbit, but when he thought he was about to close on
the wounded Shasp, his quarry ducked through a clump of bushes
and disappeared.   Tetsushiro forced his way through, believing he
was still on Shasp's heels, but when he came out onto the adjoining
path, he found he was alone. "Coward! Fight me or be dishonored by
the code of the Kyamurai under which you are sworn!" Lightning
cracked and flashed over the garden, illuminating Shasp briefly with
its flickering light, but as the warlord stepped forward he
disappeared again. Tetsushiro was about to scream another taunt
when he heard the hiss of steel and felt its stinging bite across his
back. He spun backward, raking his blade in the direction where his
attacker should have been, but it tasted only air. The warmth of his
own blood ran down his back but he only smiled, "So, it is a game
we are to play! So be it!" He hacked at a shrub that moved slightly
but had only just brought his sword out of the clutching branches
when he felt another slash across his legs. Pain shot through him and
he howled with indignation. It was clear that Masatsuo was not
going to fight him man to man without a little prodding. Tetsushiro
backed up to a broader place in the cobbled path and screamed into
the night, "You were a fool to love Kumi! She was a whore and I
treated her like a whore! When I am done killing you, I will kill your
other woman! Oh yes, I saw her in the fight, a Nomerikan!"
     Lightning flashed again and a burning voice answered
Tetsushiro's threat. "I'm here," but before Tetsushiro could turn
completely around another lick of the katana disabled his left arm.
     This time, Shasp did not vanish and, face to face, the
wounded lions circled under the crack and blaze of lightning, swords
tipped forward and dragging their hurt limbs. Like primordial beasts,
they lunged forward in a terrible exchange of hammering steel, teeth
bared and roaring the hatred that boiled in their blood. All thoughts

of defense evaporated as their blood lust overcame their humanity and like animals they attacked instinctively, hacking and slashing, as if their swords were but extensions of themselves, claws and fangs. Minds gone to madness they sliced into each other, raking and plunging but only Shasp was used to fighting hurt, and the pain of Tetsushiro's wounds played around the edges of his infuriated brain. More wounds sprang open on both men, rivers of blood gushing and splattering the ground, yet neither would relent, neither could find his way back to humanity and, like true beasts of the wild, they battled without regard to self-preservation. Tetsushiro whipped his Kyamurai back and forth in a vicious pattern of death, but Shasp drove into it, taking another terrible wound on his shoulder. Once inside Tetsushiro's guard he spun backwards raking his katana across the warlord's ear, severing the lobe and leaving a red gash across his face. Tetsushiro never missed a moment and flicked his sword up as Shasp spun away, slicing open his chin to the lower lip. Blood cascaded down Shasp's neck and he gave Tetsushiro a ghoulish smile in the pause that followed, then shot back in. The warlord was wounded in a dozen places and losing blood but Shasp was no better off. Shasp had used the Shadow Foot tactic of moving silently through the darkness and given the warlord some wounds to level the field, and so far it had worked. At least now, they were fighting on equal footing. Shasp could have continued to use the tactic to take his enemy apart, but his pride demanded that he end it face to face. Sparks flew into the night as the blades slammed and ground together beneath the raging force of the combatants. Both were exhausted from the tremendous taxation on their bodies and breathed in ragged gulps of air between the howling war cries. Shasp lunged, but in his fatigue, stumbled on a raised stone and tripped, twisting as he fell. Tetsushiro flashed a bloody smile at Shasp's misstep and slashed downward, but Shasp let go of his katana at the last instant and seized Tetsushiro's wrist pulling him to the ground with him. Twisting and grunting, their bodies churned the mud along the path as Shasp struggled to disarm his opponent. Tetsushiro kicked himself over until he was straddling Shasp, and tried to force his sword down across Ironwrought's neck, but Shasp held his wrists in a vice-like grip. Slowly, Tetsushiro bore his weight down, bringing the razor sharp edge ever closer to Shasp's throat until it hovered a hairs breadth from his pulsing jugular. In that moment, all

539

the indignation Shasp had suffered under the warlord, all the pain and anguish, came to a volcanic head and with a powerful roar, he surged up and threw Tetsushiro aside. He rolled his legs up and jumped back onto his feet, lunging for the fallen katana as Tetsushiro stumbled after him. The warlord raised his sword overhead, preparing to split open the back of Shasp's exposed head, but Shasp rolled the instant the blade came down and, in that fraction, caught up his katana and flung it at Tetsushiro. The katana hissed through the air and shot through Tetsushiro's neck at the same moment the warlord's Kyamurai sword clanged against the ground. Tetsushiro, shocked by the pain and finality of the wound, stood with his arms extended and blade resting against the flagstones then jerked upright, eyes wide with disbelief. He stumbled backwards and Shasp staggered after him. The Kyamurai sword clattered from Tetsushiro's fingers as he lurched away from the gardens, his mind reeling from loss of blood, but Shasp caught him by the shoulder and spun him about. Face to face, Shasp reached up and grasped the pommel of his katana and ripped it out of Tetsushiro's throat. The warlord collapsed onto his knees, gaping up at Shasp as he hovered over him.

"For Kumi," then the katana whipped sideways with a sickening sound, and Tetsushiro head clunked onto the paved path, and rolled against a tree with an expression of surprise still etched on the face.

Shasp turned his back on his fallen nemesis and staggered back toward the palace, leaving a trail of blood in his wake. He let the rain splatter on his face and in his eyes as he looked up into the sky, then with his sword hanging at his side he walked out into the courtyard. The Black Tigers were just mopping up the defending Kyamurai from House Ishaharo, but the battle had been costly. More than half the Tigers and nearly all the palace defenders lay dead. Intending to look for Lexia, Shasp stumbled up the palace steps, but his legs were being stubborn, only obeying his commands with forced effort. Bloodied and limping, Lexia appeared and, seeing Shasp cut to ribbons, cried out in despair at his appearance.

"I'll live," he said stepping toward her.

She took his bloodied hand, "Shasp, its Lyan. He's asking for you." They crossed the courtyard and walked to the gates with the remnant of warriors following.

Lyan lay with his back to the wall and some of the men lingered over him trying to keep him comfortable as he coughed up blood onto his lips. Shasp dropped to his knees beside him and gathered his hand.

Lyan's head lolled to the side, "Good . . . you're alive," he whispered hoarsely. "I just wanted to tell you . . . how sorry I am . . . and how proud."

Shasp shook his head, "It's not for you to be sorry. You redeemed your honor against all odds. A common captain brought justice to the head of an empire. It's me who is proud, now you just rest easy until we can find a surgeon."

Lyan's hand flopped as he waved off the idea, "No, boy. I have brought death to enough men to know . . . . when time is short. Besides, your mother is wait . . . ing." Lyan's chin fell onto his chest and his face tilted away. Shasp looked up at Lexia where she knelt on the other side, his pain reflected in her eyes. As he knelt on the ground, he laid his father's hand upon his chest and hung his head in grief, unaware of the men who slowly surrounded him. When he finally looked up again, he saw all the Black Tigers, assassin and soldiers who had survived the battle. Captain Chi Wong gave a victory cry that was immediately taken up by the rest of the survivors, and they thrust their red blades toward the thundering heavens. Slowly, through the cloud of pain and sadness, it occurred to Shasp that every warrior's eye was on him. One by one, they lowered their weapons and bowed their heads to the wet earth, and Shasp gazed at them in wonder, surprised and perplexed until Pok Cho came and stood over him.

"What is this Pok?"

The inspector smiled, "My loyalty and the loyalty of these men have always been to serve at the will of the Emperor of Aypon."

Shasp dropped his eyes back to his father's still form, "Yes, well there is no more emperor, so why are these men bowing to me?"

Pok tilted his head, "How do you think I convinced General Hatsuro and Captain Chi Wong to join us? Your mother, Ikuru was married to Emperor Muhara. He had no heirs to his throne except one. His stepson, Masatsuo Tekkensei, who he banished to slavery and forgot. Your claim supersedes Tetsushiro's. You are the rightful Emperor of Aypon and have been from the moment Muhara died."

Shasp was already dizzy from loss of blood and he laughed at the jest, but the inspector just knelt and bowed.

In awe, he stood and Lexia curled her arm around his waist, "Emperor Ironwrought," she smiled, "I like that."

Epilogue

It was months before Shasp's wounds were completely healed, though he doubted if his shoulder would ever be the same, and a new scar tugged at his lower lip. The Black Tigers had been reinstated to the position of palace guardians, and General Hatsuro and Lyan Morgenon were given an entombment that would be remembered for many years. Hung Lai's population seemed satisfied with the claim of Masatsuo Tekkensei, through Inspector Cho, and the palace advisors agreed it was valid. Peace had returned to Aypon, yet Shasp struggled to find it within himself. He thought often of Kumi and his past but could not yet relieve himself from blame.

Shasp walked beside Kamira Gami under the hanging blossoms of the crowded cherry trees. Neither said a word, only listened to the faint swish of their feet as they moved through the grass. The rains of spring had given way to an early summer and the afternoon rays of the sun scattered through the boughs, causing the swollen pink petals to glow. Occasionally, one would fall and spiral to the ground. In spite of the warm air and glimmering light, Shasp still felt troubled. From the time he had first returned to Aypon, he had wanted to see his old master, but with the death of Kumi, his stomach turned at the prospect. Shasp had ordered that the body of Kamira's daughter be exhumed and brought to her home in the country with great honors, but he could not bring himself to accompany her. It was several weeks before he graced the doorstep of Kamira Gami and was horrified when the old man began to bow to his new emperor. Shasp had caught him half way to the ground and made an official decree that Kamira was to bow to no man, unless he wanted to.

They stopped at a large, crystal clear pool and Shasp knelt to pick up a fallen petal. "I can't tell you enough, how sorry I am, Master Gami. I failed her . . . and you."

Kamira ran his hand over his thin white beard, "Do not blame yourself for the evil deeds committed by others. It is Tetsushiro whom I blame for Kumi's death, not you. It was you who avenged her, and I am grateful. I have shed my tears for Kumi and there will be many more, but my faith is strong and I am old. I will see her

543

again, soon enough."

Shasp nodded solemnly, stood up and tossed a blossom into the water where a shining coy surfaced and nibbled at its edges. "Still, it will haunt me forever."

"I understand and I will pray for you to have peace." Kamira eased himself down on a stump with a tired groan, "So now, tell me about this nonsense I hear of our emperor leaving Aypon."

Shasp grimaced and leaned against a tree, "A man told me once that if a man has too many possessions, they will eventually possess the man."

"All the more reason for you to stay if material things mean so little to you."

"Not just that, I've been languishing in luxury for months now and, instead of feeling content, I feel like a caged animal. I need my freedom; it's all I've ever really had and all I really wanted. Besides, Pok Cho will make an excellent steward. The man is a consummate perfectionist with a calculating mind, and his loyalty to the throne is unquestionable. It would have been much easier for him to side with Tetsushiro rather than me."

Kamira nodded and smiled, "I hear the ravens are still picking the flesh from the dead warlord's bones. It is bad karma to leave him so. His spirit will be restless until his body is entombed and it is not good that such a spirit should wander."

"That was the sentiment of many, so I ordered Pok to release his remains to House Ishaharo after the birds have had their fill." A long silence fell over them as they quietly watched the shimmering sunlight on the pond.

Shasp turned to Kamira, "Before I go, I just wanted to tell you how grateful I am, that you let me become more than what I was. I respect you more than anyone."

Kamira chuckled, "You are what you are, and you were what you were. That is why I continued to instruct you. I recognized that you had the heart of a Kyamurai, not of a slave."

Shasp laughed and pushed himself off the tree, "I will miss you." Kamira struggled to his feet and began to bow but Shasp reached out to stop him again.

Kamira looked him in the eye, "Your decree stated I could bow to whomever I wanted."

They stepped apart and bowed respectfully to one another.

Shasp walked Kamira back to the school then jogged up the hillside to where Lexia waited on a sturdy Ayponese pony. Tempest neighed and shook his mane as Shasp gracefully leapt into the saddle.

He turned the Evatan stallion toward the trail, "Did you find us a ship?"

"Yes," she replied, "but we might have to pay a little more for the voyage."

"Why is that?"

"Well, the captain . . . a man named Belico, did not care for the way I disciplined his crew on the way over from Oshintan."

Shasp lifted an accusing eyebrow, "Why not just take a junket from the royal navy?"

Lexia gave him a mischievous smile, "Now, how interesting would that be?"

He shook his head, "Lexia, you are going to be the death of me."

They rode for a few miles in quiet and Lexia began to sense a conflict within her lover. "Are you going to miss Aypon?" she asked.

Shasp shrugged, "Why should I?"

"It was your home once."

He stopped his horse, "Can anyone ever go home, truly?"

She gave him a sad stare, "What about your past Shasp? Doesn't it mean anything to you?"

He sighed, "My past wasn't good to me. No, all we ever really have is now, today, and I'm happy with that."

"So where to now?" she asked.

"Wherever the wind takes us."

She eased her pony against Tempest's shoulder and leaned toward him seductively. "That will be fine with me," she purred and received his kiss.